THE
TYRION & TECLIS
OMNIBUS

More great fiction from the Warhammer worlds

WARHAMMER®
CHRONICLES

• THE LEGEND OF SIGMAR •
Graham McNeill
BOOK ONE: *Heldenhammer*
BOOK TWO: *Empire*
BOOK THREE: *God King*

• THE RISE OF NAGASH •
Mike Lee
BOOK ONE: *Nagash the Sorcerer*
BOOK TWO: *Nagash the Unbroken*
BOOK THREE: *Nagash Immortal*

• VAMPIRE WARS: THE VON CARSTEIN TRILOGY •
Steven Savile
BOOK ONE: *Inheritance*
BOOK TWO: *Dominion*
BOOK THREE: *Retribution*

• THE SUNDERING •
Gav Thorpe
BOOK ONE: *Malekith*
BOOK TWO: *Shadow King*
BOOK THREE: *Caledor*

• CHAMPIONS OF CHAOS •
Darius Hinks, S P Cawkwell & Ben Counter
BOOK ONE: *Sigvald*
BOOK TWO: *Valkia the Bloody*
BOOK THREE: *Van Horstmann*

• THE WAR OF VENGEANCE •
Nick Kyme, Chris Wraight & C L Werner
BOOK ONE: *The Great Betrayal*
BOOK TWO: *Master of Dragons*
BOOK THREE: *The Curse of the Phoenix Crown*

• MATHIAS THULMANN: WITCH HUNTER •
C L Werner
BOOK ONE: *Witch Hunter*
BOOK TWO: *Witch Finder*
BOOK THREE: *Witch Killer*

• ULRIKA THE VAMPIRE •
Nathan Long
BOOK ONE: *Bloodborn*
BOOK TWO: *Bloodforged*
BOOK THREE: *Bloodsworn*

• MASTERS OF STONE AND STEEL •
Nick Kyme and Gav Thorpe
BOOK ONE: *The Doom of Dragonback*
BOOK TWO: *Grudge Bearer*
BOOK THREE: *Oathbreaker*
BOOK FOUR: *Honourkeeper*

• THE TYRION & TECLIS OMNIBUS •
William King
BOOK ONE: *Blood of Aenarion*
BOOK TWO: *Sword of Caledor*
BOOK THREE: *Bane of Malekith*

WARHAMMER®
AGE OF SIGMAR

• HALLOWED KNIGHTS •
BOOK ONE: Plague Garden
BOOK TWO: Black Pyramid

Eight Lamentations: Spear of Shadows
Josh Reynolds

Overlords of the Iron Dragon
C L Werner

Nagash: The Undying King
Josh Reynolds

Neferata: Mortarch of Blood
David Annandale

Soul Wars
Josh Reynolds

Callis & Toll: The Silver Shard
Nick Horth

The Tainted Heart
C L Werner

Shadespire: The Mirrored City
Josh Reynolds

Blacktalon: First Mark
Andy Clark

WARHAMMER®
CHRONICLES

THE
TYRION & TECLIS
OMNIBUS

WILLIAM KING

BLACK LIBRARY

A BLACK LIBRARY PUBLICATION

Blood of Aenarion first published in 2011.
Sword of Caledor first published in 2012.
Bane of Malekith first published in 2013.
This edition published in Great Britain in 2018 by
Black Library,
Games Workshop Ltd.,
Willow Road,
Nottingham, NG7 2WS, UK.

10 9 8 7 6 5 4 3 2 1

Produced by Games Workshop in Nottingham.
Cover illustration by Alexandre Mokhov.
Icon by Nuala Kinrade.

A CIP record for this book is available from the British Library.

ISBN 13: 978 1 78496 835 9

See Black Library on the internet at

blacklibrary.com

Find out more about Games Workshop
and the worlds of Warhammer at

games-workshop.com

Printed and bound by CPI Group (UK) Ltd, Croydon, CR0 4YY

This is a dark age, a bloody age, an age of daemons and of sorcery. It is an age of battle and death, and of the world's ending. Amidst all of the fire, flame and fury it is a time, too, of mighty heroes, of bold deeds and great courage.

These are bleak times. Across the length and breadth of the Old World, from the heartlands of the human Empire and the knightly palaces of Bretonnia to ice-bound Kislev in the far north, come rumblings of war. In the towering Worlds Edge Mountains, the orc tribes are gathering for another assault. Bandits and renegades harry the wild southern lands of the Border Princes. There are rumours of rat-things, the skaven, emerging from the sewers and swamps across the land. And from the northern wildernesses there is the ever-present threat of Chaos, of daemons and beastmen corrupted by the foul powers of the Dark Gods.

An ancient and proud race, the high elves hail from Ulthuan, a mystical island of rolling plains, rugged mountains and glittering cities. Ruled over by the noble Phoenix King, Finubar, and the Everqueen, Alarielle, Ulthuan is a land steeped in magic, renowned for its mages and fraught with blighted history. Great seafarers, artisans and warriors, the high elves protect their ancestral homeland from enemies near and far. None more so than from their wicked kin, the dark elves, against whom they are locked in a bitter war that has lasted for centuries.

CONTENTS

BLOOD OF
AENARION

 PROLOGUE

79th Year of the Reign of Aenarion,
the Cliffs of Skalderak, Ulthuan

From high atop the cliffs of Skalderak, Aenarion looked down on the camp of his enemies. The Chaos worshippers' fires blazed in the darkness, more numerous than the stars. There were hundreds of thousands of his monstrous foes down there and even if he killed every last one of them, more would come.

He was going to die. The whole world was going to die. There was nothing anyone could do to stop it. He had tried, with all his enormous strength, with all his deadly cunning, with power greater than any mortal had ever possessed, wielding a weapon so evil it was forbidden by the gods, and still he had failed to stop the forces of Chaos.

Their armies surged across Ulthuan, crushing the last resistance of the elves. Howling hordes of blood-mad beastmen smashed through the final defences. Armies of mutants overwhelmed the last guardians of the island-continent. Legions of daemons revelled in the ruins of ancient cities.

After decades of warfare, Chaos was mightier than ever, and his people were at the end of their strength. Victory was impossible. He had been mad to think it could be otherwise.

He cast his gaze back to his own camp. Once, he would have deemed his own army mighty. Hundreds of dragons slumbered amid the silk pavilions spread out across the mountaintop. Tens of thousands of heavily armoured elf warriors awaited his command. They would throw themselves into the attack once more if he gave the order, even though they were outnumbered more than twenty to one. With him to lead them they might even win, but it would be a fruitless victory. The Chaos army at the foot of the cliffs was only one of many. There were other armies, equally great and many greater, scattered across Ulthuan and, for all he knew, the rest of the world. They could not all be beaten by the forces at his disposal.

He turned and strode back inside his pavilion. It was futile to contemplate the size of the enemy force.

He unsheathed the Sword of Khaine. It glowed an infernal black, casting out hungry shadows that dimmed the hanging lanterns within the great silk tent. Red runes burned along a blade forged from alien metal. The Sword whispered obscenely to him in a thousand voices, and every voice, whether commanding, entreating or seductive, demanded death. It was the most powerful weapon ever forged and still it was not enough. It was heavy in his hand with the full weight of his failure. For all the good it had done him, he might as well have kept using Sunfang, the blade Caledor had made for him back when they were still friends.

The Sword was killing him by inches, bleeding away his life a droplet at a time. Every hour aged him like a day would age another elf. Only the unnatural vitality he had acquired when he passed through the Flame of Asuryan had enabled him to survive this long and even that would not last forever.

If the Sword was not fed lives it feasted on him instead. It was part of the devil's bargain he had made when he had still thought it was possible to save the world, when he had still thought that he was a hero.

Morathi stirred in her sleep, one arm thrown out, casting off the silken coverlet, leaving one perfect breast revealed, a strand of her long curly black hair caught between her lips as she writhed in some erotic dream. The potions still worked for her. She could still find sleep, no matter how troubled. The drugs had long ago ceased to work for him even when taken in dosages that would have killed anyone else.

Wine had no savour. Food had no taste. He lived in a world of moving shadows, far less vivid than the one he had known as a mortal. He had given up much to save his people – his ideals, his family, his very soul.

Kill her. Kill them all.

The Sword's ancient, evil voices kept whispering in his head. In the quiet of the night he could still ignore them. There had been times when the mad bloodlust was upon him when he could not, and he had committed acts that made him burn with shame and wish that the wine still worked so that he could find forgetfulness in it.

Had there been time enough left, the day would come when he would no longer be able to resist the Godslayer's urging, and nothing within his reach would be safe. If the daemons did not end the world, he would do it himself.

He laughed softly. Phoenix King they called him now. He had passed through the sacred flames and come out the other side, not burned but stronger, faster, more alive than any mortal should be. He had offered himself as a sacrifice to save his people when the gods had rejected all others, and they had taken his flesh and his agony as their offering and sent him back, transformed, to do their work.

He had died and been reborn the day he passed through the Flame of Asuryan, and he had caught glimpses of things that had blasted his sanity. He had seen the vast damaged clockwork of the ordered universe and that which lay beneath it and beyond.

He had looked upon the Chaos that bubbled around everything for all eternity. He had seen the smile on the face of the daemon god who waited to devour the souls of his people. He had witnessed that god's kin use worlds for their playthings and populations for their slaves. He had glimpsed the great holes in the fabric of reality through which their power and their servants poured in to conquer his world.

He had seen eternities of horror and he had come back reshaped, remade, reborn to fight. He had tried then with all his new-found might to save his people from the tide of daemonic filth engulfing the world.

At first he thought he could win. The gods had gifted him with power beyond that of any mortal. He had used it to lead the elves to victory after victory but every triumph had cost them irreplaceable lives and for every foe that fell two more came to take their place.

He had not realised then that it was all a black cosmic joke. He was only slowing down the destruction of his people, making it more painful by drawing out the agony.

He had taken the Everqueen as his wife and she had borne him two perfect children, a promise of a brighter tomorrow, or at least a pledge that there still would be a tomorrow. He had believed that then, but his family been taken from him by the daemons and slaughtered. In the end he had not even been able to protect his own kin, and their loss had ripped the heart from him.

It was then that he had sought out the Blighted Isle and the Godslayer. It was a weapon never meant to be drawn from the Altar of

Khaine, but he had drawn it. If the gods had given him strength, the Sword had made him all but invincible. Where he walked daemons died. Where he led, victory was inevitable. But he could not be everywhere and with every day the forces opposed to him grew stronger and those who followed him grew fewer and fewer.

The evil of the Sword had seeped into him and changed him, making him angrier and less sane as the odds against him mounted. His closest friends had shunned him and the people he was pledged to save had drifted away, leaving only hardened embittered remnants, elves as angry and deadly as himself, a legion of warriors almost as mad and twisted as the foes they faced. They too had been changed by the baleful influence of his unholy weapon. He had taught his people too well how to make war.

A mood of black despair had come upon him, and at that darkest period of his life he had found Morathi. He glanced at her beautiful sleeping form, loathing her and wanting her at the same time. What he had with her he could not call love. He doubted he was capable of any tender emotion any more, even with a woman less twisted than his current wife. This was a mad, sick passion. In Morathi's caresses he had found some respite from his troubles and in their wild love-making he had found distraction from his cares.

She had brewed potions that, for a time, had let him sleep and made him almost calm. And she had borne him a son, Malekith, and taught him that there was still some spark of feeling within him yet. He had found something to fight for once more and returned to the fray, if not with hope, at least with determination. But now, at long last, he could see that it was over, that his enemies would win, and that his people were doomed to death and an eternity of damnation.

A glow in the air warned him. Long, sharp-edged shadows danced away from him. He turned, sword raised ready to strike, and only at the last heartbeat did he stay his hand.

'Aenarion, can you hear me?' asked a voice of eerie quietness that seemed to be carried on some dismal breeze from the desolate margins of the world.

Caledor stood there, or at least his image did, a glowing translucent ghost, cast across long leagues by the force of the mage's magic. Aenarion studied his former friend. The mightiest mage in the world looked half-dead. His body was wasted, his cheeks were sunken, his face looked like a skull. His features were schooled to impassiveness by the power of his will but terror glittered in his eyes. It was never far from the eyes of any of the elves now.

'Aenarion, are you there?' The image flickered and Aenarion knew that all he had to do was wait and the image would vanish as the spell collapsed. He did not want to talk to the one who had turned his back on him, who had walked away from the doom he felt that Aenarion was leading their people towards.

He bit back words of anger and reined in the rage burning in his breast. In his more lucid moments he knew that Caledor had done the right thing, taking some remnant of the people out from under the shadow of the Sword and the doom that Aenarion carried within him.

'I am here, Caledor,' Aenarion said. 'What do you wish of me?'

'I need your aid. We are besieged by land and sea.'

Aenarion's laugh was bitter. 'Now you need my help! You turned your back on me but you do not scruple to seek my aid when you need it.'

Caledor shook his head slowly and Aenarion could see the weariness eating away at him. The mage was at the end of his tether. His last resources of strength were dwindling. Only willpower was keeping him going. 'I never turned my back on you, my friend, only on that cursed thing you carry and the path you set your feet upon.'

'It comes to the same thing. I saw the way that would save our people. You, in your arrogance, refused to follow.'

'There are some roads it is better not to travel even if they are the only way to escape death. Your way would make us worse than the things we face. It would merely be a different kind of defeat. Our enemies would win in the end either way.'

In his heart of hearts Aenarion agreed, but he was too proud to admit his folly. Instead he gave vent to his bitterness and anger. 'Accursed you have called me, accursed till the end of time, and all of my seed to be accursed. And yet you dare ask for my aid?'

'I did not curse you, Aenarion. You cursed yourself when you drew that blade. Perhaps you were accursed before that. I know you were always chosen by destiny and that in itself is a sort of curse.'

'Now that you need my help, you seek to twist your words and give them a honeyed meaning.'

Anger passed across Caledor's features. His lips twisted into a sneer. 'The world ends and yet your pride must be salved. It is more important to you than life, the life of our people. You will not aid me because of harsh truths I once spoke. You are like a child, Aenarion.'

Aenarion laughed. 'I have not said I will not aid you. What is it you seek?'

'There is only one way to save our world. We both know it.'

'You intend to put your plan into effect then, to sing your spells and try and banish magic from the world.'

'That is not what I seek and you know it.'

'Morathi says that will be the effect of what you do.'

'I doubt your wife knows more of the ways of magic than I do.'

'Now who is mad with pride, Caledor?'

'The gates of the Old Ones are open. The winds of magic blow through them like a hurricane. They carry the energy that causes the humans to mutate and lets the daemons dwell here. Without that energy they must leave our world or die. This is truth. We have constructed a mighty network of spells to channel that energy, to drain it away, to use it for our own purposes. All we need do now is activate it.'

'We have been over this a hundred times. Too much could go wrong.'

'We are dying, Aenarion. Soon there will be none of us left to oppose Chaos. We have tried your way. It has not worked. The forces of Chaos are stronger now than they were the day you passed through the Flame.'

'That is not my fault, wizard.'

'No, but it is the truth.'

'So you seek my permission to try your plan?'

'No.'

'No?'

'We have begun.'

'You dare to do this when I have forbidden it?'

'You are our leader, Aenarion. We are not your slaves. The time has come for a last throw of the dice.'

'*I* will decide when that is to be.'

'It is too late for anything else, Phoenix King. If it is not done now, it will not be done at all. The forces against us will be too strong. Perhaps they already are.'

'If you have decided to defy my will, why bother telling me?'

'Because the daemons sense our purpose and try to stop us, and we do not have the strength to prevent them.'

'So you want me and mine to protect you, in spite of your defiance.'

'We are all one people. This will be the last stand of the elves. If you do not wish to be there, that is your choice.'

'There will be other battles.'

'No. This will be the last. If our spell goes wrong the fault lines beneath Ulthuan will be torn apart, the continent will sink, drowning our enemies. Perhaps the whole world will end.'

'And yet you will still proceed.'

'There is no other choice, Aenarion. You told me once that mine was the counsel of despair and that you would find another way to win this war. Have you done so?'

He wanted to cast the mage's words back into his teeth but he was too proud and too honest to do so. He shook his head.

'Will you come to the Isle of the Dead? We need you.'

'I will consider it.'

'Do not consider too long, Phoenix King.'

Caledor put his hands together and bowed and vanished. Morathi's eyes snapped open and she screamed.

He turned to look at his wife. She stared at him as if looking at a ghost.

'You are not dead, thank all the gods,' she said.

'Apparently not,' he said.

'Do not joke about such things, Aenarion. You know I see the future and tonight in my dreams I had a vision. A battle is coming. If you take part in it you will die.'

'So?'

'If you leave my side, you will die.'

He stared at her hard, wanting to ask her how she knew and not daring to because he feared the answer and what he would have to do if she gave it.

Morathi had studied the ways of their enemies for a very long time, and, he suspected, far too closely. There were times when he was not sure where her true loyalties lay. He only knew that she looked at him, as he looked at her, with a mixture of lust, respect, hatred and anger. It was a potent, heady brew that had fuelled many memorable days and more memorable nights.

'Everyone dies,' he told her.

'I will not,' she said with certainty. 'And your son Malekith will not. And if you listen to me, you will not either. If you go today you forfeit immortality. Stay with me and live forever.' She stretched out her hand in entreaty. It seemed for a moment as if she were actually going to beg. She would not ever do that. And yet...

'That is not possible,' he said quickly, to break the spell of the moment.

'You are the Phoenix King. Anything is possible for you.'

'Whatever else I am, I am a warrior, and today may be the last battle the elves ever fight.'

'You are going to help that fool Caledor with his insane plan.' She was angry now. Rage did not make her ugly. It made her more beautiful and more dangerous. He stared at her, unintimidated. She had never frightened him. He suspected that intrigued her. He was probably the only one her rage had never daunted. 'It is the only way we can win this war. I know that now,' he said calmly, because he knew that would goad her more.

'And I say to you, if you go, you will die.'

He shrugged and began donning his armour. As he fastened the clasps, he spoke the words that activated its dormant power. Titanic fields of protective magic shimmered into place around him. Potent spells amplified his already enormous strength. It was a barrier between himself and her that he wanted at that moment though.

She walked towards him, arms outstretched in entreaty. 'Please stay with me. I do not want to lose you forever.'

As ever he was astonished by her beauty. He doubted there had ever been a woman as lovely as Morathi. At the same time, he was untouched by her loveliness. It had no hold over him. It never had. And he knew that in some way that was the secret of the power he held over her. Other elves might be driven mad with longing and lust for her. He was not. There was a coldness in him that she could not touch but nothing could stop her trying.

He pulled on his gauntlets and reached out and touched her cheek with his armoured hand. He could not feel the softness of her skin but that was not so different from the normal way of things. He felt neither pleasure nor pain as much as normal mortals did after he passed through the Flame.

'I will return,' he said.

She shook her head with absolute finality. 'No. You will not. You are a fool, Aenarion, but I love you.'

The words hung in the air. It was the first time she had ever said them.

She stood there waiting for him to say something, obvious entreaty in her eyes. He knew how much it cost her to say such words. Not to hear any response must be humiliating to one of her enormous pride.

There was nothing he could say or wanted to. He had only ever loved one woman and she was dead, along with the children she had borne him. Nothing could change that fact. Nothing ever would.

Morathi was merely wicked and she had drawn him into her wickedness. Even now she was trying to prevent him from going forth to face his foes. At that moment he felt certain that she was numbered among his enemies and the enemies of his people, and she would be forever.

Kill her, whispered the Sword.

He would be doing the elves a service if he struck her down. He stared at her for a moment, certain that she knew what he was thinking, and just as certain that at that moment she did not really care what he did.

She moved closer as if daring him to strike. He reached out with one hand, jerked her to him and crushed her lips against his, putting all his lust and rage and hatred into one long and brutal kiss. She responded in kind, writhing against his metal-encased form until he thrust her away, her naked body bleeding in a dozen places from pushing against the edges of his armour.

He smiled at her savagely, turned on his heel and left the pavilion without another word. He thought he heard her crying as he left. He told himself he did not care.

Indraugnir stood before him like a living mountain. The span of the dragon's wings blocked out the sky. His head arched downwards on the titanic column of his neck. Aenarion looked into his strange glittering eyes and saw a ferocity and anger there that matched his own. The dragon sensed his fey mood and responded with a bellow. The other dragons took up his war cry until the mountains around them echoed as if to the sound of thunder.

Horns rang out summoning the elves to war. Dragon riders rushed forth to greet the dawn, clutching their long spears, strapping on their glittering armour, making the air shimmer with the enchantments on their gear. Grooms attached saddles and harnesses to the dragons' necks. The air stank of sulphur and leather and the deadly gaseous breath of the great beasts.

All eyes were upon him now. His whole army watched him. All of them were grim, scarred elves with hard eyes and a cruel set to their mouths. All of them had suffered in this long war. All of them were consumed with a mad hatred of their enemy that Aenarion understood only too well. All of them knew they had been summoned forth for some mighty effort. Enormous ranks of ground troops formed up beyond them. They would be useless in the coming battle. They would not be able to travel to the Isle of the Dead fast enough to take part. They expected him to speak. The magic of the dragon armour carried his calm measured tones to the furthest units of the assembled army.

'You have followed me far. Some of you must follow me a little further. We must ride far and fast and only those mounted on dragons will be swift enough to follow me. The rest of you must remain here and guard my queen.'

He saw anger and pride war in the faces of the infantry and cavalry. They knew he had already lost one wife and they would not let him lose another. These troops had followed him through hell and they loved him in their cold, cruel way. 'Those of you who stay must guard this place and endure. After today you may be the last elves in the world. You will need to follow my queen and my son and rebuild our kingdom come what may.'

They heard the knowledge of his own death in his voice at the same moment as he heard it himself. He had given them implicit instructions for the succession. These veterans would see they were carried out. He turned his attention to the dragon riders, the elite of the elite, the greatest warriors of the elves. He paused for a moment and let his gaze sweep over them all, meeting the eyes of every soldier. As he did so Indraugnir roared again, and the other dragons took up the chorus till the mountains echoed.

'Today will be our last battle. Today, for better or worse, this war ends,' he shouted, and his voice carried even over the bellowing of the dragons. 'Today we go forth from this place to victory or to death. Gird on your armour. Make ready your lances. We ride!'

Aenarion leapt into the saddle and tugged the reins. Indraugnir threw himself into the sky, his enormous leathery pinions beating the air with a crack like a storm hitting the sails of an ocean-going ship.

The roar of the wind was loud in his ears as they gained altitude, the great line of dragon-borne elf warriors taking their place in formation until a huge arrowhead filled the sky behind him. For the first time in a long time, wild joy filled him. This might be the last dawn he ever saw but there were still wonders in this world that could stir his heart and make it beat faster.

'To the Isle of the Dead,' he shouted and the wind carried away his words so that only Indraugnir could hear him.

He did not need to know the direction in which they should fly. In the distance an eerie glow filled the sky, rivalling the dawn. His elven senses told him that there a great confluence of magical energies gathered. Caledor had lit a beacon that would attract the attention of anything with the slightest sensitivity to magic and there were things out there that could sense the casting of the faintest spell at a distance of a thousand leagues.

Their journey carried the dragons over mountains and forests, plains and seas. He had time to take in the wild beauty of the land he had sworn to protect for one last time. Even marred by the monstrous hordes of Chaos, it was lovely. As the leagues and hours rushed by, the land beneath him came alive with monsters and mutants and daemons all racing towards the place where the most powerful spell ever woven was being cast.

As they approached the Isle of the Dead, horror and wonder filled his mind in equal measure. Thousands of crude ships filled the sea, delivering legions of monsters to the shores of the island.

Hundreds of thousands of twisted beings filled the beaches beneath him, some the size of elves, some the size of dragons and every size and shape in between. Here and there things raised hands or claws or a staff to the sky and a futile bolt of magical energy blasted skyward to strike a dragon impotently. At this range and height there was nothing their foes could do to harm them. Those flying Chaos creatures that dared to rise and challenge them were blasted from the sky by the power of dragon-breath or elven magic.

Ahead of him now, he could see the great open-roofed temple where Caledor had chosen to work his ritual magic. The air above it shimmered with power. Already the sky was changing colour, clouds becoming yellow and gold and crimson and sapphire as they swirled like a great whirlpool in the air. Multi-coloured lightning flickered. The winds became stronger, slowing the flight of even a dragon as mighty as Indraugnir.

Aenarion swooped lower. He saw lines of apprentice wizards standing in geomantic formation around the centre of the temple, chanting words of power, feeding their strength to the archmages who stood at the point of each column, all adding a tiny morsel to the overall pool of energy.

At the centre of it all stood Caledor and his circle of the greatest of all elven magi. Each was limned with an aura of awesome power. From their outstretched hands, writhing bands of energy fed the ever-more complex enchantment growing in their midst. The force of magic at the centre of that web was already so great that nothing unprotected could survive there for long. He sensed that the spell was spinning on the edge of being out of control. Something mighty enough to shatter the world was being shaped down there. Nothing like this had ever been attempted before and Aenarion doubted anything like it would ever be attempted again.

The daemons were drawn to it like sharks to blood. The clever ones must know that what was being done here was not for their benefit. The less clever ones just wanted to reach this great trove of power.

A seemingly endless horde of Chaos worshippers surrounded the place, brandishing the banners of the four great Powers they worshipped: Khorne, Slaanesh, Tzeentch and Nurgle.

Each of the armies was led by a Greater Daemon sworn to those powers, chosen representatives of the daemon gods. They were mighty beyond the understanding of mortals. They had led their forces to countless victories in countless places. The fact that they were all gathered here argued that the daemonic leaders understood quite as well as he did exactly how important this place was, that the fate of the world would be decided by what happened here today.

He took in the battleground at a glance, understanding the play of forces on it instinctively. The elves were doomed. Their foes were too numerous and too powerful. Nothing could stop the forces of Chaos triumphing today. The best that might be achieved was that they be delayed long enough for Caledor to finish working his spell.

So be it, Aenarion thought. If the only road to victory is by way of death, we will take it.

Kill, whispered the Sword.

Aenarion raised his blade and the first wing of dragons peeled off and descended on the advancing Chaos hordes. They swept over the teeming multitude, breath of fire cleansing the tainted earth. The Chaos worshippers were packed so closely together there was no way to avoid the flames raining down from the sky. They died in their thousands, like a column of warrior ants marching into a pool of burning oil.

Wave after wave of dragons descended. Legion after legion of Chaos worshippers died. The smell of scorched flesh rose to reach even Aenarion's nostrils as he circled high above the battlefield.

The winds grew stronger. The columns of fire above the temple grew brighter. In the distance the earth erupted as towers of magic sprang into being in answer to the spells of Caledor and his fellow mages. As far as the eye could see fingers of swirling magical light stabbed into the sky, illuminating the darkening land and revealing the great crowds of Chaos monsters racing towards the site of battle. All over Ulthuan the same thing was happening as Caledor's vortex came to life.

Clouds obscured all of the sky now. Below him it was dark as night save where the hellish illumination of the glowing columns lit their surroundings or the dazzling flash of some mighty polychromatic lightning bolt split the sky. The geomantic pattern the elf mages had been arranged in was plain now, a great rune made of flesh and light visible from the sky through which Aenarion flew. The terror and the wonder of it filled his heart.

This was a sight worth seeing even if it cost the life of the world.

In the distance the sea boiled with ships and huge monsters. All sensed that the hour of final battle was at hand. The screaming, chanting horde surged up the stairways of the shrine. The Isle of the Dead was never meant to be a fortress but a holy place. The makeshift defences of the elves were smashed by the rampaging daemon worshippers.

Chaos sorcerers on glowing disks of light rode the skies, howling incantations as they tried to breach the spell walls protecting the shrine. One by one, the barriers fell, for there were not enough elven mages left to maintain them. Too many were committed to the creation of the vortex.

As he passed over, Aenarion saw mighty banners fluttering over enormous moving towers. Each bore the sign of the greater daemons who were the generals and champions of the besieging force. Even in the shadow of the gigantic spell Caledor was weaving, Aenarion sensed the power of these deadly creatures. They were the mightiest of their kind, hardened by millennia of constant warfare in the hells they came from. Normally they would have been the deadliest of enemies, but on this day, in this place, they seemed to have managed a truce in order to crush the one threat remaining to their domination of this world.

The dragons swooped and slew like great birds of prey. Hills of smouldering corpses rose on the way to the temple but it did not matter. No matter how many they killed more came on, rushing forwards to inevitable death as to the embrace of a lover. Now the dragonfire began to weaken as the dragons reached the end of their resources. Flocks of winged daemons surrounded individual dragons and smashed them from the skies.

They could not prevent the great horde reaching the outer defences of the temple and engaging the thin lines of desperate elf soldiers waiting there.

A terrible wave of agony and terror rippled out from the temple. For a moment, the huge spell at the centre of it trembled and threatened to collapse. Aenarion swooped lower and saw that one of the archmages had fallen along with all the apprentices who had been linked to him. The power of the spell had burned the life out of him. The whole mighty edifice Caledor was creating threatened to collapse like a palace hit by an earthquake.

Somehow the mage at the centre of it all managed to stave off the disaster and continue. The structure of the spell stabilised and the ritual went on. Aenarion was not sure how much longer it could endure.

How many of the archmages could die before Caledor was unable to constrain the forces he had unleashed and destruction rained down on them all? For better or worse, Aenarion thought, it would all be over soon.

Four gigantic forms made their way to the temple, each surrounded by a bodyguard of potent worshippers. The Greater Daemons who led the Chaos horde were vying to see which would be the first to reach Caledor and end the threat he posed. The greatest enemies of all wanted to be in at the kill.

Ahead of them the first wave to reach the walls of the temple looked as if they were about to break through and interrupt the ritual. If they were not stopped, they would succeed.

He dropped Indraugnir into the middle of the melee. They landed on top of a massive self-moving siege engine within which the living essence of a dozen daemons was bound. The dragon took the great battering ram in his claws and beat skyward, lifting it and sending it toppling backwards to crush a hundred foes beneath its weight. It lay there broken, like a beetle turned on its back. Indraugnir smashed into the press of bodies, tearing foes asunder with his claws, searing them with his fiery breath, snapping twisted Chaos monsters in half with his jaws.

A group of elf soldiers tried to fight their way towards the embattled Phoenix King but died before they could reach him, overwhelmed by the sheer number of their foes. Aenarion leapt from Indraugnir's back, like a swimmer diving into a sea of monstrous flesh. His blade flickered faster than mortal eyes could follow, smashing through the bodies of his enemies as if they were made from matchwood.

A beastman leapt at him, jaws snapping; he caught it in the air one handed, and sent it flying a hundred yards with a flick of his arm. It cartwheeled through the air to splatter against the walls of the shrine.

Aenarion cleaved through his opponents, killing everything within reach, his blade sending pulses of black light over the battlefield, the red runes glowing ever stronger as it drank life. His enemies died in their hundreds and then their thousands. Nothing could stand against him, and seeing his unleashed wrath his foes turned to flee.

For a moment, Aenarion thought he had turned the battle but then the air in front of him shimmered and a hole appeared in the fabric of reality. A figure of horror emerged, towering twice as high as any beastman, monstrous wings snapping on its back. A huge vulture-like head, gazed down with eyes that held more than elven wisdom. The appearance of this Greater Daemon, this mighty Lord of Change, halted the rout.

'Long have I wanted to meet you, Phoenix King. Now the hour of your death is at hand.' The daemon's voice was high-pitched and shrieking and it would have broken the nerve of a less bold warrior than Aenarion just to listen to it.

'What is your name, daemon,' Aenarion said, 'so I can have it etched on my victory stella that all may know who I conquered?'

The daemon laughed. There was madness in its mirth that would have blasted the sanity of most mortals. 'I am Kairos Fateweaver and I will send your soul to Tzeentch so he may use it as a bauble for his pleasure.'

It stretched out its taloned hands and ravening streamers of multi-coloured light flashed towards Aenarion. Whatever they touched, living or unliving, warped and changed. Beastmen devolved into protoplasm, hardened stone ran like water. Aenarion raised his blade in front of him and the ribbons of light parted on either side of him. He pushed forward, like a swimmer against a strong tide.

The Lord of Change bellowed its rage and fury and invoked another spell, but by the time it was complete Aenarion was upon it, and the black blade bit home into its flesh. Where the weapon struck, chunks were hacked away and ectoplasm swirled forth in a choking cloud. The daemon screamed, unable to believe that anything could cause it so much pain. Its mighty taloned hands reached out to grip Aenarion.

Such a feast, whispered the voices in his head. *More.*

Sparks flickered where the daemon's grip bit into Aenarion's breastplate. The Lord of Change was a being of awful magical energies and not even the potent spells woven into the elf's armour could completely resist it. The talons bit flesh and drew blood as they sought out the Phoenix King's heart.

Aenarion stifled his own cry of pain, and, knowing he had only one chance to live, struck a blow with the black blade, piercing the daemon's head and striking its jewelled brain. It exploded into a thousand pieces. The force of the blast hurled him through the air to land sprawling on the steps of the temple. He felt ribs break on impact.

Behind him the Vortex surged, and a high-pitched keening roar filled his ears. The air stank of ozone. A thousand voices screamed in unison as death overtook them. Another archmage had fallen. Who could it be, Aenarion wondered? Rhianos Silverfawn? Dorian Starbright? Undoubtedly it was someone he had known and now did not have the time to mourn.

He glanced around him dazedly and caught sight of another gigantic figure slaying the last guardians of the doorway beyond which Caledor and his mages still struggled to maintain their spell. The warding spells could not stop it. The guardians were not even trying to. They were throwing themselves willingly onto the monster's claws, and greeting death as they would a newfound lover. There was something obscene about the way they went to meet their doom.

Aenarion's heart sank. He knew this four-armed creature. It had taken all his strength to kill it once and now here it was again. This was N'Kari, the Keeper of Secrets, one of the deadliest of all the servants of the Gods of Chaos, the leader of the forces of Slaanesh, Lord of Pleasure.

'I see I must slay you again,' Aenarion shouted to get the daemon's attention. 'Or will you escape your just doom by some new trick as you appear to have done in the ruins of Ellyrion?'

N'Kari laughed its beautiful woman's laugh, and the wind bore its pungent erotic aroma to Aenarion's nostrils. Normal mortals would have been bemused, but Aenarion was hardened against any temptation it might have borne.

'Arrogant mortal, I let you live once so I might experience the sensation of defeat. Now I am gorged on ten thousand souls and I am invincible. Be honoured! Your soul will learn agony and ecstasy under the lash of the Dark Prince of Pleasure once I send it to meet him.'

N'Kari sprang, and its huge crab-like claw snapped together where Aenarion had been standing a moment before. It was a feint, and it caught Aenarion with its other hand. Aphrodisiac poisons poured from its nails. Its cloying perfumed breath filled Aenarion's nostrils. For a moment, he was dizzy and his legs threatened to give way beneath him.

'Now is the moment of ultimate pleasure,' said the Keeper of Secrets. 'You will fall to your knees and adore me before you die, Phoenix King.'

Aenarion lashed out with his blade, slashing the creature's chest. Such was the daemon's power that the flesh tried to knit behind the blade as it passed, but nothing could resist the fatal power of the Sword, and after a moment, N'Kari's flesh smoked and burned.

'I do not fear you or that blade you carry,' said N'Kari, but there was an odd strain in its voice.

'I will teach you to do so before this day is much older,' said Aenarion. Rage filled the daemon's eyes at his mockery. The massive claw swung round and gripped Aenarion's chest. It closed. Aenarion felt the weakened armour buckle and his ribs snap.

'You will not defeat me again, mortal.'

Aenarion reached out with his hand into the cavity the black blade had made. He pulled forth the daemon's still pulsing heart and raised it before him.

'No,' bellowed N'Kari. Aenarion closed his fist, crushing the heart. The daemon spasmed as if the organ being pulped were still within its chest. Poisonous blood dripped over Aenarion's mailed fist, burning through the armour and threatening to make his hand useless. Aenarion forced its own blood into the daemon's eyes, blinding it, then he raised the blade once more and drove it into N'Kari's shattered chest.

Ectoplasm poured forth as the daemon sought to evade the killing power of the sword. Tiny fragments of its essence flickered through the air towards the Vortex and vanished. As they did so, some of the chanting sorcerers moaned in ecstasy and died.

Aenarion reeled. His left hand was burned and useless now. His chest was a fiery cauldron of agony. The pain mingled with an odd pleasure caused by the effects of the daemon's blood.

More. More. More. The voices in his head were crazed with demented passion now. The Sword was feasting on essences stronger than any it had known in a long time and it was enjoying its meal.

A monstrous giggling form loomed over him. The smell of excrement and rotting flesh overcame the scent of everything else. He looked up to see the towering figure of a Great Unclean One, mightiest of the servants of the plague lord, Nurgle. It was the largest of the daemon princes by far. It loomed over him like a living mountain of filth, its vast flabby belly rippling in time to its idiot laughter.

'Two of my peers have fallen to you, Phoenix King, and I would not have thought that possible.' The daemon's voice was deep and rich and humorous. Its tone was conversational. The cruelty of its gaze belied the warmth of its manner. 'Still I, the Most Amiable Throttle Gurglespew, shall do my humble best to claim the victory.'

The Great Unclean One vomited forth a mass of maggots and bile onto him. The creatures began to burrow their way into Aenarion's flesh through the gaps in his armour, and force themselves into his eyes and mouth through the open visor of his helmet. He tried to keep his mouth closed but they wriggled up his nostrils and into his ears. They found gaps in his armour and squirmed across his flesh.

Each of the maggots had a tiny face that was a perfect copy of the features of the massive daemon that had belched it forth. All of them tittered with an insane mirth that was a high-pitched echo of the greater daemon's. They bit and gnawed at him and every bite was infected. He felt even the fires of the Phoenix within him gutter as his life force was drained away.

A wave of fire passed over him, hotter than the heart of a volcano, brighter than the sun. The tiny daemons vaporised under the incandescent barrage. Aenarion, who had passed through the Flame of Asuryan, remained standing. Through the blaze he saw Indraugnir blast the greater daemon of Nurgle with flames and then rend its putrid flesh asunder with its mighty talons.

Aenarion cheered his companion on as it tore its foe to pieces, reducing the greater daemon to a foul-smelling stinking pool of sewage on the ground. Indraugnir raised its head to the sky and let out a long bellow of triumph.

An explosion of dragon flesh and dragon blood smashed into Aenarion's face. An enormous gash appeared in the dragon's side and a burning axe emerged from it. Indraugnir toppled backwards, a huge hole carved in its flank. Its triumphant cry died in its throat.

Aenarion's heart sank. Before him was a Bloodthirster, a greater daemon of Khorne, perhaps the deadliest creature in all creation save for the Blood God himself. It was a massive thing with mighty wings and a monstrous animal head. Its eyes blazed like falling meteors. Its huge form was encased in runic armour of bronze and black iron. It radiated an aura of power greater than that possessed by any living creature Aenarion had ever faced.

The Bloodthirster struck again, with the force of a thousand thunderbolts, and Indraugnir bellowed and was still. Only its tail gave one last reflexive twitch and all life seemed to go out of it. Aenarion's awareness narrowed until it contained only himself and the daemon. They were like the last two living things moving in the ruins of a dead world.

Kill it. Kill it. The voices chorused in his head. They sounded even more demented than ever as they advised him to use his waning strength against this all but invincible opponent.

Limping painfully Aenarion forced himself to confront the last and mightiest of his foes.

It tossed back its head and laughed at the sight of him. He understood its mirth. His body was broken, his armour shattered, his flesh seared by the dragon's cleansing flame. Poisons and disease spores raced through his bloodstream. It was a race between them and loss of blood to see which killed him first. That was if the final greater daemon did not do their work for them.

He staggered towards it, holding his blade at the ready with both hands. The daemon sprang forward in a cloud of fire and brimstone. Its weapons lashed out and Aenarion twisted to avoid the blow. It caught Aenarion in his already wounded arm, breaking armour, shattering bone, sending the Phoenix King flying through the doorway of the temple to land amid the last few surviving wizards who still chanted the spell.

Aenarion looked around, appalled. So few mages were left. They had given up their lives to create the Vortex. At the centre of the chamber, near that towering whirlwind of unleashed magical power, only a few of the archmages remained, with Caledor standing on the central rune frantically trying to complete his spell even as the effort killed him.

The greater daemon roared with triumph. 'I am victorious,' it said in a voice like the blast of a thousand brazen trumpets. 'Only I remain and soon this world will be mine to do with as I will. I will take this power you have so conveniently collected and use it to reshape the face of this creation.'

Aenarion forced his broken body to move and staggered between the Bloodthirster and its prey. It stared at him with burning eyes. 'You cannot live through this, Phoenix King.'

'I do not need to live,' Aenarion said quietly. 'I only need to kill you.'

'That is not possible, mortal. I am Hargrim Dreadaxe and I am invincible. Never have I known defeat.' The Bloodthirster pounced like a tiger leaping on a deer. Its speed was almost too fast for mortal eyes to follow. Its power was all but irresistible.

Aenarion unleashed the last of his carefully husbanded strength. A mighty blow arced downwards. The Sword howled in triumph as it smashed through eldritch armour, bit into unearthly flesh, shattered bone and ribs and cleft the daemon from head to groin. It fell to earth chopped almost in two, leaving Aenarion standing over its swiftly evaporating form.

'There is a first time for everything,' Aenarion said.

The Phoenix King turned to stare at the wizards. He was near the end of his strength and he remembered Morathi's prophesy. Once again his wife's predictions had proven to be correct. He would die soon.

Only Caledor stood now, his form incandescent with power.

Thunder boomed. Lightning jumped from peak to peak. The great towers of light blazed brighter than the sun. Caledor's flesh shrivelled and turned black until only something like a mummified corpse stood there, still chanting. Then even that desiccated husk blew apart, turning to ashes on the howling wind, leaving only the afterglow of the mage's spirit, standing there, imprinted on Aenarion's retina like the image of the sun seen through closed eyes.

Aenarion leaned on his sword, unable to move his broken body. Pain burned every nerve ending. His ragged breathing rasped through broken lips. Something gurgled deep within his chest as his lungs filled with blood. He had taken more punishment than even his mighty frame could endure. He had been smashed, poisoned, blasted with fire and magic. He had defeated four of the mightiest daemons ever to blight creation. His army was all but dead. His friends were dead. And still the spell was not complete.

They had rolled the dice and they had lost. The last gamble of the elves was over and all that remained was to pay the price of failure. He threw back his head and laughed.

They had tried and there would be none left to witness their failure. He considered throwing himself into the still half-formed Vortex and offering himself up as a sacrifice as he had once done before the Flame of Asuryan but he knew that this time it would not work.

There was nothing left to be done, except to return to the fray and slay what he could until he was pulled down into death.

Yes, whispered the voices. *Go! Kill until the world itself ends.*

A moment of awful silence came. The Vortex spun and danced before him, about to fall like a child's top that had run out of energy. Aenarion watched fascinated and horrified as it began to collapse. Then the fading image of Caledor stabilised. The ghost turned to the Vortex and continued its spell. Shimmering figures appeared around him as if summoned by his will. Aenarion recognised them as the ghosts of the dead archmages. Somehow, something of them still survived in this place. Even in death something now bound them to it.

The spirits of the other archmages joined in the ritual, walking one by one into the Vortex and vanishing. Aenarion peered at them through fast dimming eyes. He could see them becoming frozen, trapped in the awful centre of the spell as they continued the ritual. Something within him told him what was happening, that the ghosts were giving themselves up for all eternity to hold together the spell they had woven.

No! The voices in his head shrieked. He felt the chorus of mad hatred build up in his head, threatening to overpower his will. *Destroy it! Destroy them all! Destroy the world!*

The chant was seductive. He wanted to obey it. Why should anyone else live when he was dying? What did he care whether the world went on, if he could not be in it, ruling it?

He walked slowly towards the centre of the Vortex. The ghost of Caledor stood before him and made a gesture for him to stop. The archmage shook his head, and pointed at the blade. It howled within Aenarion's grasp, urging him to cut down Caledor and then leap into the Vortex, slashing all around him. By doing so, he would undo everything, slay the entire world by unleashing all the pent up magic the mages had struggled so long and so hard to control.

He was tempted. He could end everything, kill everyone, and the blade could feast upon the death of an entire planet. Part of him wanted to do it, to end all life even as his own life ended. If he was to die, why not take everything else with him?

He stood there, gazing at the ghost of the elf who had once been his friend. Caledor's spirit sensed the struggle within him but there was nothing it could do to either aid or hinder. The decision was Aenarion's own, or it was the Sword's.

That thought at last made Aenarion stir. He was his own master.

He had always gone his own way. He had not bowed to his people, to Chaos, to the gods of the elves. In the end he would not bow to the Sword. It howled in frustration as if it sensed his decision and fought against it.

Caledor smiled and waved farewell, and turned and walked into the place where he would be trapped for all that remained of eternity.

Slowly, Aenarion turned his back on Caledor and the Vortex and walked away. The Sword fought him every step of the way.

Outside, all was howling madness. Lightning lashed down from the sky. Time flowed strangely within the range of the Vortex's influence. The daemons were vanishing, turning back into the stuff of Chaos that had formed them. Their worshippers aged before his eyes, years passing in seconds, putrefying flesh falling away from corpses even as they fell. Piles of bones formed everywhere.

Aenarion stood and watched. Even the elves caught within the range of the newborn Vortex were ageing. He gestured for the survivors to flee and they obeyed.

Aenarion knew he was dying from the wounds and the poisons burning in his veins. He knew he had to leave, to return the Sword to the place from whence it came. He could not risk it falling into the hands of anyone else. Not so near the heart of the Vortex. Not with the possibility of some daemon or creature of evil finding it. He knew now why the gods had not wanted any to wield it.

He looked upon the corpse of Indraugnir. 'It is a pity you cannot help me now, old friend,' he said.

One great eye opened, and the dragon tried to bellow. Instead of its usual proud roar, its voice was a mere hiss, but it forced itself upright on weakened legs, and stood there tottering as its heart's blood pumped forth.

'One last flight then,' said Aenarion and the dragon nodded as if in agreement. 'We take the blade back to the Blighted Isle and drive it so deeply into the altar that no one will ever be able to take it out again.'

Aenarion forced himself into the saddle on the dying dragon's back and strapped himself in. He took one last look about him at this place of destruction. Strange magic flowed all around him. The shadowy outlines of ghosts were visible in the ruins of the temple working on some great mystical pattern, performing the rites of some vast incomprehensible ritual. He tugged on the reins and the dragon leapt into the sky, soaring through the swirling clouds, climbing towards the sun.

The winds of magic howled beneath Indraugnir's wings as he and his dying rider flew into legend.

N'Kari the Keeper of Secrets looked out from within the newly born Vortex and watched Aenarion depart. He was lucky to be alive and he knew it. The weapon the Phoenix King had carried was potent even beyond the imagining of daemons.

Never in all his aeons-long existence had N'Kari experienced anything like this. He was reduced to the barest nub of sentience, a thing little greater than a maggot or a human, barely aware of its own existence. He had only just managed to escape from Aenarion by casting himself within the roaring magical energies summoned by the elven archmages and hiding there. And he was barely a shadow of what he had been. The Sword had weakened him greatly, in some way he still did not quite understand.

Still, all he had to do was escape and his power would regrow as it always did.

He willed himself elsewhere, trying to plunge into the great Realm of Chaos to bathe in its eternally renewing energies. Nothing happened. He could not escape.

Rage and something else he did not quite recognise filled his mind. Perhaps it was fear. He was trapped within the huge spell the elves had cast. It was preventing him from departing this world for his own.

Even now, some vague sense of self-preservation warned him to keep still, to do nothing, to gather his strength. Around him were beings of awful power, the ghosts of the archmages who had given their lives to weave this spell. They were weaving it still.

His encounter with Aenarion had left him so weakened that he would have no chance if one of those terrible ghosts were to turn its attention on him and the small flaw in the vast matrix of spells he occupied. They could squash him from existence with the barest effort of their will.

It was painful and humiliating for N'Kari to admit his plight to himself, but it had been a long time since he had enjoyed these sensations and he determined to make the best of it.

Now he needed a plan, a way to escape from this enormous trap of a spell without the ghosts noticing him. He needed to wait and husband his power and let his strength regrow until he was himself again.

He did not doubt that it was possible, that he would get out of this place. He was a daemon. Time had little meaning for him, even the strangely altered flow of time within the Vortex. As long as he was careful and did not draw attention to himself he would survive, and he would work out a way to be free.

Then he would enjoy another sensation – vengeance on Aenarion and all of his blood.

◄ CHAPTER ONE ►

There are those who express wonder that Aenarion was never told that Morelion and Yvraine, his children by the Everqueen, survived. It might have changed the whole course of elven history if he had known. Perhaps he would never have visited the Blighted Isle and drawn the Sword of Khaine. He might never have met Morathi. Malekith might never have been born.

Such speculation is fruitless. What happened, happened. The Sword was drawn. The elves of Nagarythe followed Aenarion into its shadow and into damnation. And the world was saved.

Perhaps because Aenarion was never told that his children were alive.

Many scholars think that once the Sword was drawn, Oakheart and those princes in his confidence were right to keep the knowledge of the children's survival from Aenarion. They point out what happened to those elves who followed the Phoenix King, and what happened to Malekith who was to become known as the Witch King. By keeping the children apart from their father, they kept them safe from the Sword's baleful influence.

And thus, from Yvraine, the elves of Ulthuan still have an Everqueen unsullied in her purity, for which we should all give thanks.

Perhaps those who kept the secret from Aenarion had other reasons. Scholars point out that given the ambitions that Morathi had for her son, Malekith, it is unlikely the children would have survived long in Nagarythe where they would easily have been within her grasp. Aenarion's second wife has become famous for her knowledge of poisons, potions and malefic sorcery. Who knows how long

Morelion and Yvraine would have lived had she known of their existence?

Whatever their reasons, by their actions, Oakheart and the princes ensured the survival of Aenarion's line in two main branches – one line has given us all the succeeding Everqueens unto the present generation. The other line has blessed and cursed Ulthuan with many heirs of Aenarion's brilliant, tainted blood. In part, they, like their great ancestor, have given the elves as much cause to curse them as to be grateful.

– Prince Iltharis, A History of the Blood of Aenarion.

10th Year of the Reign of Finubar, Arathion's Villa, Cothique

Tyrion sat on the edge of the wall of his father's villa, legs dangling, enjoying the sense of danger. Behind him lay a twenty-foot drop and the one in front of him was even steeper, for the ground sloped away downhill. If he fell from here he might break a limb on the rock-strewn ground below.

The late winter sun burned bright in the clear blue sky. It was cold this high in the mountains of Cothique. His breath came out frosted and he felt the chill through the thin cloth of his tattered tunic and his patched woollen cloak. In the distance, he could see a troop of mounted figures riding up-slope towards the hilltop villa.

Strangers were rare in this part of Ulthuan. Very few people ever came to visit them. Most were passing hunters dropping off part of their kill as a tithe for hunting on his father's lands. One or two were highland villagers who came to consult his father about a sickness in their family or on some minor matter of magic or scholarship.

Things had been different when his mother was alive, or so Thornberry claimed. The house had been busy then, when his parents had arrived to occupy it for a summer season or two, escaping from the heat of the lowlands. Sorcerers and scholars from all over Ulthuan had come to visit it along with his mother's rich relatives. People had liked his mother and were prepared to travel to even this remote place to visit her.

Tyrion was in no position to know. She had died during the difficult birth of himself and his brother and he had never known a world with her in it. There was one thing of which he was sure – none of the locals except his father could afford a horse, let alone a warhorse.

Tyrion's eyes were keen as an eagle's and he could see that the strangers were mounted on steeds even larger than his father's, caparisoned in a way he had only seen illustrated in books. Most of them were carrying lances. He could not imagine what else that long pole with its fluttering pennon might be.

The truth was he did not want it to be anything else. He wanted them to be knights, glamorous warriors such as he and his brother were always reading about in their father's old books. He wondered if this were somehow connected with his birthday, which was tomorrow, although his father appeared to have forgotten yet again. He felt somehow that it was. It seemed right.

He sprang up, balanced on the thin lip of the wall, then walked along it to the roof of the stables, arms held out from his sides to maintain balance. He let himself in through the large hole in the slates and dropped down onto the support beam. The dusty, musty smell of the old building filled his nostrils along with the warm animal scent of his father's horse. He ran along the beam, grabbed the rope he had left knotted round the edge and jumped.

This was always the best part, the long swing to the ground, the dizzying sense of speed as he careened downward and let go, landing rolling in the bales of hay. It always made him smile.

He raced out of the stable, past the startled Thornberry. The wrinkled old elf woman watched him with a look almost of embarrassment on her face, as if young Tyrion's energy somehow baffled and upset her.

'Strangers are coming,' Tyrion yelled. 'I am going to tell father.'

'Hush, young Tyrion,' said Thornberry. 'Your brother is sick again. You will wake him.'

'My brother is already awake.'

Thornberry raised an eyebrow. She did not ask how Tyrion could know that. Tyrion could not have answered her anyway. He had no idea how it was possible that when he was in close proximity to his brother he could sometimes tell whether he was asleep or awake, happy or sad or in great pain. To tell the truth it always seemed strange to him that others could not. Maybe it was something to do with them being twins.

'He is now – with you making all that noise,' said Thornberry. Her tone was grumpy and she was trying to make her face stern but her gaze, as always, was kind. Nonetheless, as always, she managed to make him feel guilty.

He raced upstairs, and ran into his father's chambers.

His father held up a hand for silence. He was standing over his workbench, peering at something through the eyepiece of a magnascope. 'Hush, Tyrion, I will be with you in a moment.'

Tyrion stood there almost bursting from his desire to give the news but he knew his father was not to be hurried when he was about his studies. To occupy himself he gazed round the room, taking in his father's huge library of books and scrolls, so beloved of Teclis, the jars full of pickled monster heads, and odd chemicals and weird plants from the jungles of Lustria and the rainforests east of Far Cathay.

His gaze was drawn as ever, and no matter how much he tried to avoid it, to the gigantic, terrifying suit of armour that stood on its wire frame in the corner. It looked for all the world like some monstrous golem waiting to be animated. His father claimed that this armour had been forged in the magical furnaces of Vaul's Anvil for their legendary ancestor Aenarion and that it was broken and dead now, needing magic to bring it back to life and grant it power and make it once again fit to be worn by a hero. Tyrion was not entirely sure of the truth of this but he hoped it was the case.

It was discoloured around the chest and arms where his father had repaired the ancient damaged metalwork with his own hands. In those places the armour did not have the patina of age it had elsewhere.

It was his father's life work to make the armour whole again. He had dedicated a lifetime of scholarship to it, ever since he had inherited it from his father, who had inherited it from his father before him and so on back into the mists of time. Family lore had it that the armour had been presented to their ancestor Amarion, by Tethlis himself, as a reward for saving the life of his son. It was their family's most precious heirloom.

As far as Tyrion knew his father was the first of his line who had tried to remake the armour. So far his efforts had proved fruitless. There was always just one more thing needed, one more piece of rare metal, one more fabulous rune to be re-discovered and re-inscribed, one more spell to be re-woven. Many times Tyrion had heard his father claim that this time, he would do it, and always he had been disappointed. It had cost his father his not-inconsiderable fortune and his life's energy and it was still not complete.

Tyrion studied his father now and realised how frail he was. His hair was fine as spun silver and white as the snow on the peak of Mount Starbrow. A mesh of wrinkles spun out from his eyes to cover most of his face. The purple veins stood out thinly on his hands. Tyrion looked at the smooth skin of his own hands and saw the difference at once. A life of failure had aged his father prematurely. Prince Arathion was only a few centuries old.

'Tell me what you came to say, my son,' said his father. His voice was calm and gentle and remote but not without a certain mocking humour. 'What brought you into my workroom without even knocking?'

'Riders are coming,' Tyrion said. 'Warriors mounted on warhorses.'

'You are certain of that?' his father asked.

Tyrion nodded.

'How?' His father believed that observations had to be tested and justified. It was part of his method of scholarship. 'Not just book learning' were his watchwords.

'The horses were too large to be normal mounts and the riders carried lances with pennons on them.'

'Whose pennon?'

'I do not know, father. It was too far away.'

'Might it not have been more useful, my son, to wait until you could see it? Then you might have been able to tell me more about who the strangers were and what their purposes might be.'

As always Tyrion could not help but feel that he was somehow a disappointment to his gentle, scholarly father. He was too loud, too boisterous, too active. He was not brilliant like Teclis.

His father smiled at him.

'Next time, Tyrion. You will do better next time.'

'Yes, father.'

'And fortunately I have a spyglass here in my study that will allow me to find out the information you missed, despite the fact these aged eyes are not as keen as yours. Run along now and tell your brother. I know you are dying to give him the news.'

Teclis lay in the great four poster bed, covered in piles of threadbare, patched blankets. The room was so shadowy that it was impossible to see how moth-eaten the bed's canopy was and how old and rickety the room's furnishings were.

Teclis coughed loudly. It sounded as if a bone had come loose inside him and was rattling round in his chest. He twisted in the tangle of covers and looked up at his brother with bright feverish eyes. Tyrion wondered if this time Teclis was really going to die, if this illness would be the one that would finally claim him. His brother was so weak now, so feeble and so full of pain and despair.

And selfishly Tyrion wondered what would happen to him then. He felt the echoes of his brother's pain and his weakness. What would happen when Teclis went on the dark journey? Would Tyrion too die?

'What brings you here, brother? It is still light out. It is not yet reading time.'

Tyrion looked guiltily at the copy of Maderion's *Tales of the Caledorian Epoch* that lay on the chipped table beside the bed. He walked over to the windows. The drapes were fusty and smelled of mould. Cold air whistled in through gaps in the shutters, despite the torn shreds of sacking he had stuffed into the gaps. There was no place in the old villa where Teclis could escape the cold that seemed to leech all vitality from him.

'We have visitors,' said Tyrion. Interest flickered in Teclis's eyes and for a moment he seemed a little less listless.

'Who are they?' The tone was a dry echo of their father's, as was the question itself. Tyrion wondered at the resemblance. For all his weakness Teclis was very much their father's son, in a way that Tyrion never felt himself to be.

'I don't know,' he was forced to admit. 'I did not wait to check their heraldic banners. I merely ran in with the news.' He could not keep the sullenness from his voice even though he knew his brother did not deserve it.

'Father has been subjecting you to inquisition again, I see,' said Teclis and was wracked by another long, horrible paroxysm of coughing. Laughing was sometimes a mistake in his case.

'He makes me feel stupid,' Tyrion confessed. '*You* make me feel stupid.'

'You are not stupid, brother. You are just not like him. Your mind runs in different channels. You are interested in different things.' Teclis was trying to be kind, but he could not keep a certain satisfaction from his voice. His twin was eternally conscious of his physical inferiority. His sense of intellectual superiority helped balance that. Normally it did not trouble Tyrion but today he felt unsettled and insecure. It did not take much to put him off-balance. 'Battles and weapons and such are what interest you.'

The tone of his brother's voice let him know exactly how unimportant he considered such things in the great scheme of things.

'One of the riders at very least is a warrior. He carried a lance, and his armour shone brightly in the sun.'

At first Tyrion thought he was making up the latter detail but even as he said it he realised it was the truth. He had observed more than he thought. It was a pity his father had not questioned him about that detail.

'And what of the other riders?' Teclis asked. 'How many were there?'

'Ten with lances. One of them without.'

'Who would that be?'

'I don't know, a squire perhaps or a servant.'

'Or a mage?'

'Why would a mage come here?'

'Our father is a wizard and a scholar. Perhaps he has come to consult him and the warriors are his bodyguard.'

Tyrion saw that Teclis was twisting events to suit his own views and fantasies. He wanted one of those riders to be a scholar and the others, the warriors, to be in the inferior position. It stung. He felt like he should say something but he could not think what, then Teclis laughed.

'We really are country mice, aren't we? We sit in our rooms discussing strangers who may or may not be coming to visit us. We read of the great battles of the Caledorian Age but some horsemen in search of a night's shelter are a source of great commotion to us.'

Tyrion laughed, glad that he was not going to have to argue with his brother. 'I suppose I could go and ask them what they want,' he said.

'And rob us of a delightful mystery and the anticipation of its solution?' Teclis asked. 'We shall have those soon enough.'

Even as he said the words, the great gate bell rang. There was something ominous in its tolling, and Tyrion could not help but feel that it heralded some massive change, that for some as yet unknown reason, their lives would never be the same after today.

The great bell tolled again, as Tyrion raced down into the courtyard. He got to the gate at the same time as Thornberry. They stood facing each other for a moment, each waiting to see what the other would do.

'Who goes there?' Tyrion shouted.

'Korhien Ironglaive and Lady Malene of the House of Emeraldsea and her retinue. We have business with Prince Arathion.'

'And what would that business be?' Tyrion asked. He was overwhelmed by the glamour of those names. His father had talked of Korhien. House Emeraldsea were kinfolk of his mother's, merchant princes of the great city state of Lothern, where the twins had lived when they were small children. What could they possibly want here?

'That is for me to discuss with Prince Arathion, not his doorkeeper.' The elf's voice sounded impatient. There was definitely something martial about it. It had the clarity of a great bronze horn intended to ring out over a battlefield.

'I am not his doorkeeper, I am his son,' Tyrion replied to show he was undaunted, even though he was a little.

'Tyrion, open the gate,' said a gentle voice from behind him. Tyrion turned, surprised to see his father there. He was wearing his finest over-cloak as well, and a torque of intricately worked gold on which were set certain blazing mystical gems. 'It would not do to keep our guests waiting. It is uncouth.'

Tyrion shrugged and put his shoulder against the bar of the gate. It raised easily for he was very strong for his age. He stepped back as the gates swung open and found himself looking up at the mounted strangers. One of them was the tallest elf male Tyrion had ever seen, as tall and broad as he was, with a great axe over his back and a sword strapped to his side. In his hand he did indeed hold a long lance. Over his shoulders was a cloak made from the hide of a white lion. Tyrion was thrilled. He had never met a member of the Phoenix King's legendary bodyguard before. What could such a one want here?

Beside the White Lion was a female elf in a beautifully woven and cowled travel gown. Her expression was haughty, her amber-eyed stare piercingly direct. She wore a number of glowing amulets that marked her out as a mage. A lock of long raven-black hair emerged from beneath the cowl of her cloak.

Behind them a group of riders sat, mounted on caparisoned horses. All of them wore the same tabard and had the same emblem on the pennons of their lances; a white ship on a green background. A line of spare mounts and pack mules straggled out behind them. It looked like quite an impressive expedition.

Before Tyrion could say anything the White Lion had planted the lance in the earth of the gateway, vaulted down from the saddle, strode across the courtyard and swept his father off his feet in a massive hug. Much to Tyrion's surprise his father did not object, he was laughing merrily. It was the first time Tyrion had ever seen such a thing.

He glanced at the woman to see if she was as wonderstruck as he, and noticed that her expression was sour and disapproving. She looked around the courtyard as if she were inspecting a pigsty. Her horse was smaller than the warriors' but even more beautifully accoutred. She caught him watching her and frowned. He met her gaze though and held it till she looked away.

'Korhien, you old warhound, it is good to see you,' said Father.

'And you, Arathion,' said the warrior, slapping his father's back with a force that Tyrion feared would do him injury. His father winced under the impact but made no protest. It suddenly occurred to Tyrion that Korhien and his father were friends. It was a novel concept. In all the years of his childhood, Tyrion could not recall his father showing affection to anyone or anything, even his sons. 'How long has it been?'

'Not since you retired here, after Alysia...' Korhien said, and the way his expression changed showed he knew he had made a mistake even as he spoke. He closed his mouth. A wave of sadness flashed across his father's face and he looked away into the distance.

'Lady Malene,' said his father at last. 'Welcome to my home.'

'So this is where my sister died,' said the woman. 'It is not a very... prepossessing place.'

Another faint shock rippled through Tyrion's chest. This woman was his aunt. He studied her even more carefully now, wondering just how much she resembled his mother. Now that he looked closely he saw that some of her features bore a resemblance to Teclis's and even to those he saw in the mirror. She was staring at him just as hard. There was hostility in that gaze and something else he could not make out, curiosity perhaps.

She held out her hand and looked at him again. It occurred to him that she was a lady who was not used to mounting or dismounting a steed without aid. He felt tempted to go and help her, but something in him rebelled against it and after a moment, he realised why.

It would be servants who would aid this woman, and he was most definitely not her servant. She saw the knowledge strike him, and she smiled coldly, dismounted gracefully and strode over to where he stood. She walked all around him inspecting him the way a mountain housewife might inspect a calf she was thinking of buying. Tyrion did not like the way she did it.

'Do you like what you see?' he asked.

'Tyrion,' his father said, his tone disapproving. The warrior laughed. The elf woman's response surprised him.

'Yes, very much,' she said. 'Although its manners could be improved.'

Korhien laughed at that too. Tyrion felt his face redden. He clenched his fists defiantly, not used to being mocked by any but his father or Teclis. Then he saw the funny side and laughed himself.

'You look like her when you laugh,' Malene said, and there was a sadness in her voice that reminded him of his father sometimes. 'Alysia was always a merry soul.'

Alysia had been his mother's name, and it was obvious from

Malene's tone that she missed her. It occurred to him that perhaps this proud, cold woman might be something like he would become if Teclis died, and he found he had a certain sympathy for her then.

'Are we going to stand out here in the dust all day?' asked Korhien, 'Or are you going to ask us in and ply us with some of the fine old wines in that cellar of yours you always boasted about.'

'Of course, of course,' said his father. 'Come in, come in.'

It was the first time Tyrion had ever heard about fine old wines in their cellar. It was certainly turning out to be an interesting day. The riders still sat on their horses, impassive, as if waiting to charge. There was a sort of menace in their stillness.

'Perhaps your retainers would care to join us,' his father added. 'It seems like a very large party for a social visit.'

Tyrion did not miss the quick look of warning that flashed between Father and Korhien.

'The roads grow dangerous again,' Korhien said. Tyrion sensed that he would like to have said something else but was constrained by the presence of the others.

What was going on here?

——◄ CHAPTER TWO ►——

The sitting room was damp and fusty and cold, and Tyrion could tell that the Lady Malene was less than impressed. For the first time he felt ashamed of his father and his home.

Looking at her raiment, woven from silks and magical cloths he could not even name, Tyrion saw for the first time how very shabbily he and his father were dressed. For so long he'd had nothing to compare his family to other than the local villagers who were, he now realised, simple mountain folk.

It was obvious that Korhien and Malene belonged to a very different order of people, and one to which he felt he and his father did not. Perhaps his father once had, but, if so, no longer.

Lady Malene sniffed the air and looked at the chipped wooden armchairs. They were not padded or cushioned and he guessed that was something else she was not used to. Korhien laughed. 'I have been in army camps that were more prepossessing, Arathion. Not much chance of you going soft out here.'

'Be seated, I will soon have the fire lit,' said Father, and he was good as his word. He exited the chamber and returned with some of their precious supply of winter logs. He tossed them into the fireplace any old way and lit them with a word of power.

Each log erupted simultaneously into blue mystical flame when he spoke. Sparks flickered and faint popping sounds filled the air as the sap within ignited. Tyrion looked at his father in amazement. It was the most, and the most obvious, magic he had seen him use in years. He wanted to run and tell Teclis but was kept frozen to the spot by curiosity, a desire to see what extraordinary thing might happen next.

Thornberry brought in a clay bottle of wine and three goblets on an ancient-looking bronze tray. She seemed uncomfortable but tried not to show it, keeping her face stone-like in its lack of

47

expression. She placed the wine on the low table and retreated from the room as quickly as she could.

His father gestured for the guests to be seated. 'There will be food soon.'

Tyrion wondered at this as well. His father must have given instructions for the food to be prepared which was something of a wonder in and of itself. Often he forgot to eat for days at a time, and, when Thornberry was not there, Tyrion had to cook for himself and Teclis.

Korhien and Malene sat while his father poured the wine. Tyrion went over to the fire and stood with his back to it, luxuriating in the unaccustomed heat.

'To what do we owe the honour of this visit?' his father asked eventually.

'It is time,' said Korhien. 'The twins are almost of the age to be presented at the court of the Phoenix King.'

'It is their right,' said Lady Malene. 'And their duty. They are of the Blood of Aenarion.'

'Yes, they are,' said his father. He sounded oddly sharp and looked more combative than Tyrion had ever seen him. His father was never aggressive to anyone. 'I am wondering why House Emeraldsea has chosen to send its fairest daughter and its greatest ally at court to collect them.'

Tyrion felt another shock. Collect them. What did his father mean? He could tell from Malene's expression she had not expected this response either. She had the look of a woman who people did not talk to in that tone. Korhien too was looking at Tyrion's father oddly but not without admiration.

'What do you mean?' Malene asked eventually.

'I mean for the past fifteen years or so, House Emeraldsea has shown little enough interest in my sons. And yet today, here you are, reminding me of my paternal duty to have them presented before the Phoenix Throne in the company of a troop of armoured warriors. I am curious as to why.'

'They must be presented,' said Korhien. 'You know the law as well as I do, Arathion. They are of the Blood.'

'And if they are to be presented at court, I must see that they do not disgrace our family,' said Malene.

His father let out a soft laugh. 'I thought it must be that.'

'Why must we be presented at court, father?' Tyrion burst out, unable to contain his curiosity.

His father looked at him, as if noticing for the first time that he was there. 'Leave us, Tyrion, your aunt and I have much to discuss. I will tell you what you need to be told later.'

His father sounded stern, and what he was saying was unfair, but there was such a look of pain in his eyes when he spoke that Tyrion did not have the heart to argue with him or question him. He stalked to the door and closed it behind him, resisting the urge to slam it although the temptation was very great.

'Think,' said Teclis. His voice sounded even more husky and rasping than usual. His cough was worse, but there was a feverish interest in his eyes now. He sat upright in his bed, a blanket draped round his shoulders like a cloak. 'Try and remember, what else did they say?'

Tyrion shook his head. 'I have told you all of it.'

He drew his cloak tighter around him. After the warmth of the sitting room downstairs, Teclis's room seemed colder than ever. Perhaps he should carry Teclis down and let him sit by the fire for a while. He knew better than to suggest it though. His brother would never agree. He did not like his weakness to be exposed before strangers.

'You are sure she said we are to be presented to the Phoenix King?'

'Yes.'

'I suppose it makes sense. We are potential inheritors of the Curse, after all.'

Tyrion laughed. 'The Curse? The Curse of Aenarion? Be serious!'

'The Archmage Caledor claimed that all of those of the Blood of Aenarion could inherit his curse and be touched by Khaine, god of murder.'

'Surely that only applies to those like Malekith, born after Aenarion picked up the Godslayer and was tainted by its power.'

'You would think, wouldn't you? But such were not Caledor's words. And if you think about it, it would make no sense. Malekith has been sterile since he passed through the Flame. He has never had any children.'

'Why? I do not believe you are cursed by Khaine nor I, for that matter.'

Teclis gestured at his wasted form and raised one eyebrow. 'I think it is possible.'

'I don't think you are cursed.'

'How many elves ever get sick, Tyrion? How many are as feeble as I am?'

Tyrion tried to laugh the matter off. 'I hardly think that qualifies you as a threat to the Realm.'

'It does not matter what we think, Tyrion. It matters what the Phoenix King and his court think.'

'We are being presented there so they can inspect us for the taint of Khaine?'

'I believe so.'

'That does not seem fair.'

'They may be right.'

'You cannot mean that, brother!'

'Aenarion was unique. He did things no elf ever did before and very few even attempted afterwards. He passed through the Flame of Asuryan unaided and unprotected. He drew the Godslayer from the Altar of Khaine. There was something different about him, something that allowed him to wield the power of the gods, and for them to act through him. Who is to say that difference is not passed on through his blood. Caledor Dragontamer certainly thought so, and he was the greatest mage this world has ever known.'

'How do you know all this?' Tyrion asked. He knew the answer already but as usual the full extent of his brother's learning astonished him.

'Because while you roam abroad, I have nothing better to do than read, when I have the energy.'

'Yes, but what you read, you always remember. I wish I could do that. With me it always slips in one ear and slides out the other.'

'Unless it's to do with war or heroes,' said Teclis. 'Anyway, don't you think it unusual that Lady Malene and Lord Korhien came to visit us this way?'

'What do you mean?' Teclis gave him a warning look.

A draft of air hitting his back told him that someone had just opened the door to Teclis's room. Tyrion turned and saw the Lady Malene standing there. She did not look embarrassed to be intruding. She matched their stares and then marched right into the chamber without waiting to be invited.

'You would be Teclis,' she said. 'The cripple.'

'And you would be Malene, the rude.' Teclis replied.

She laughed. 'Well said, boy.'

'You may address me as Prince. It is my title.'

'That has yet to be determined. I will know what to call you after you have stood before the Phoenix Throne.'

'Why don't you start practising now?' Teclis said. 'We can pretend that we are all well-bred elven nobles together.'

Malene stared at him for a long moment, obviously taking in the difference between his haughty manner and his wasted form and being forced to reassess the situation. 'Indeed, Prince Teclis, why don't we do that,' she said at last.

'Very good, *Lady* Malene. And further let us make an agreement that I won't enter your chamber without knocking if you don't enter mine.'

Tyrion thought his brother might be pushing things a little too far but Malene laughed and nodded in agreement. For some reason she seemed pleased with Teclis's insouciance. 'I am pleased to make your acquaintance and will bid you good day then, Prince Tyrion, Prince Teclis.'

As the door closed behind her, Teclis gestured for Tyrion to lean closer.

'She has come here to kill us,' he whispered.

'Kill us?' Tyrion asked.

'Or have us killed, by the redoubtable Korhien.'

'No.' Tyrion was quite certain this was not the case.

'Be assured of it. If she thinks we may prove to be tainted by Khaine, we will have an accident on the road to Lothern. Why else did they come?'

'You are being over-dramatic,' said Tyrion. He simply did not want to believe what Teclis was saying. 'Why would they want to do that?'

'Perhaps because House Emeraldsea has ambitions to seat its own candidate on the Phoenix Throne and it does not want the embarrassment of being associated with two tainted princes.'

'We are not princes yet,' said Tyrion. 'You heard what Lady Malene said.'

Teclis laughed sourly till his mirth ended in a fit of coughing that brought tears to his eyes. 'I must sleep now,' he said. 'Good night to you, brother.'

'Isha smile on you, Teclis,' said Tyrion hating the irony of the words even as he gave the traditional farewell. His brother was one of those that the goddess had most definitely not smiled upon. 'May you live a thousand years.'

Disturbed by Teclis's suspicions, Tyrion padded through the house. He reached the head of the stairs. From his vantage point he saw his father and Korhien sitting by the fire, a chessboard between them.

Looking at the big warrior, Tyrion found it impossible to imagine him being involved in stealthy murder, in anything dishonourable at all. Such would not be Korhien's way, Tyrion felt certain. If there was killing to be done, he would do it face to face, weapon to weapon.

Korhien leaned forward and moved a silver Gryphon. His father stroked his chin and contemplated his response. Tyrion padded down the stairs, luxuriating in the unaccustomed warmth of the sitting room, and moved quietly over to the board so as not to disturb the concentration of the players. He took in the position at a glance.

His father was playing gold with his usual cautious, reasoned approach. He was already on the defensive, despite having the advantage of the first move. Playing silver, Korhien had a formation of Archers massed on the right flank, and was mounting a strong attack on Father's Everqueen with his Everqueen's Dragon supported by his Gryphon riders and a Loremaster attacking down the long diagonal. His father's hand hovered over his King's Gryphon which would be a mistake.

'Your doorkeeper disapproves of your strategy,' said Korhien with a booming laugh when he noticed Tyrion's expression.

'Then I had better pay attention,' said Father. 'Tyrion is the best player in this house.'

Korhien raised an eyebrow. 'Is that so? Better than you? Better than this brilliant but sickly brother I have yet to meet?'

'Better than you,' Tyrion said, nettled by the way Korhien's words seemed to disparage Teclis.

'Are you challenging me, doorkeeper?' Korhien asked.

'I could beat you from my father's position.'

'Oh ho, you are a cocky one. I would say I have your father well beaten.'

'It looks that way now perhaps, but there are some glaring weaknesses in your tactics.'

'I don't see them,' said Korhien.

'Tyrion, if you please.' Father rose from his seat and gestured for Tyrion to sit down. 'If you are going to make such outrageous claims, you should be able to provide us with proof.' His father was smiling though. Tyrion guessed he was not enjoying being beaten even by his friend. Few elves enjoyed defeat in anything.

Tyrion sat down and confidently moved an Archer two squares forwards, on his Phoenix King's flank.

'What?' said Korhien obviously amused. He picked up his Gryphon and skipped it over Tyrion's Archer into a position where it threatened a Loremaster. Tyrion contemplated the board. As always, he played quickly, by instinct, seeming to feel the strengths and weaknesses of the pieces and the complex web of forces woven by their placement and interaction.

He moved another Archer forwards, clearing space to bring his own Loremaster and Phoenix King into play, building a flanking position of his own. The exchange of pieces Korhien planned occurred and by the end of it he had gained an Archer, but was looking at the board thoughtfully. He clearly sensed that the balance of power was changing. He was a good enough player to understand what Tyrion was doing but he had not quite grasped the young prince's plan yet.

He maintained his own attack, but Tyrion blocked it, with a cunning combination of Loremaster and Archers used to block the long diagonal that was Korhien's main line of attack. A few moves later, Tyrion began his own attack. By the end of it, Korhien was laying his Everqueen on her side to show that he had resigned. He laughed loudly, seemingly delighted.

'Are you always this good, doorkeeper?'

'Yes, he is,' said Father, with a pride which surprised Tyrion. 'Better actually, since he would not have made the mistakes I did in the opening.'

'I must see if this was a fluke,' said Korhien. He picked up one gold Archer and one silver Archer in his huge hands, placed them behind his back and asked Tyrion to choose one. Tyrion chose silver this time and the game began. He won this game in forty-two moves and a third, in which he started as gold, in thirty. He could see that Korhien was impressed.

'Your father is an excellent chess player and I am considered one of the best at court, and yet you have bested us without much trouble. You are not at all what I expected, doorkeeper.'

'What did you expect?'

'Not you,' said Korhien clearly not wanting to say any more.

'Another game,' Tyrion suggested.

'No, I have had quite enough defeats for one day.' He said it with a smile though. There was no sourness in this Korhien. Tyrion liked him.

Tyrion shrugged and, well pleased, made his way outside. He was surprised to find that there was still some daylight left. It was the first time he could ever recall there being a fire in the grate before nightfall, no matter how cold it got in the mountains. He drew his cloak around him and thought about his chess games against the older warrior. Korhien was a better player than both his father and Teclis, which was not what he would have expected at all.

He felt flushed with his small victory and filled with restless energy, so he went out through the small postern in the main gate and began to run, slowly at first, just to warm himself up, and then faster and faster, vaulting over the rocks and bounding down the treacherous trail with careless disregard for life and limb.

It was dark by the time he returned, and he still was not tired, not even breathing heavily. The huge greater moon was in the sky. The lesser moon was a small green spark in a different quadrant. It seemed like a good omen. He was even more surprised to find Teclis warming himself in front of the fire in the sitting room, talking with Korhien. The chessboard was in front of them. Tyrion took in the board at a glance. Korhien was winning. Teclis saw him noticing this and gave a sour grimace. He did not like being beaten, which was why he did not often get the chance to play with his brother.

Teclis looked up sardonically as Tyrion entered. 'Where is father?' Tyrion asked.

'He is closeted with the Lady Malene,' said Teclis. 'Apparently they have much to discuss.'

There was a warning note to his voice. Teclis suspected that something was going on and he wanted Tyrion to know this too.

'I hear you have been winning again at chess, brother,' Teclis said, changing the subject. He, at least, did not sound at all surprised when he said it. 'It is not something I seem to be able to manage against Lord Korhien here. How do you do it? Win, I mean.'

Tyrion studied the board. 'You could win from this position.'

'Pray explain to me how?'

Tyrion looked at Korhien. 'May I?'

The warrior laughed. 'I am not sure I am going to enjoy this, but go ahead.'

'Get used to being beaten by my brother; he does not like to lose,' Teclis said.

'That is a useful trait in a warrior,' said Korhien. Tyrion proceeded to demonstrate how Teclis could win.

'How do you do that?' Teclis asked again.

'How can you not? It just seems very obvious to me.' It was true too. Tyrion really could not understand why his cleverer brother could not see what was so clear to him.

'In what way?' Korhien asked. There was a sharpness to his tone that Tyrion could not quite understand. He gave more thought to his response than he normally would.

'Certain squares are more important than others, most of the time. Certain combinations of moves fit together. There are always weaknesses in every position and always strengths. You play to minimise the weaknesses and maximise the strengths.'

'Those are sound general principles,' said Korhien, 'but they do not really explain anything.'

Tyrion felt frustrated. He understood how Teclis must feel when his twin tried to explain the principles of working magic to him. 'It's like I can see the way the patterns will work out. I see the ways all of the pieces potentially interlock. It's like when I look at the maps of battlefields in old books...'

'What?' Korhien asked even more sharply.

'There are certain obvious lines of attack on every battlefield. Places where troops should be placed. Places where they should not be. Hills with clear fields of fire for archers out over the rest of the field. Flat areas where cavalry can advance quickly. Woods and swamps that can guard flanks. You can see these things when you look at the maps.'

'*You* can,' said Teclis, stifling a yawn.

'Blood of Aenarion,' muttered Korhien. It was Tyrion's turn to stare hard at him.

'What do you mean by that?' he asked.

'They say Aenarion could do the same thing. See the patterns on a battlefield.'

'Anybody can, if they take the trouble to think about these things,' Tyrion said.

Teclis laughed again.

'It is not often I hear my brother laud the virtues of thinking,' he said, by way of explanation. 'You should be applauding.'

'Anyone can look at a map and say something. The trick is to be correct,' said Korhien. Tyrion shrugged. He went over to the book shelf and picked up a copy of *The Campaigns of Caledor the Conqueror*. He opened it to a well-thumbed page and then walked over to where the warrior sat.

'Look,' he said. 'Here is an example of what I mean. Here are Caledor's dispositions against the druchii General Izodar. See the way he has placed his war machines to cover the approaches to Drakon Hill. Notice also the way the main strength of his cavalry is placed out of sight here behind this range of hills but with easy access to the defile that will allow them to emerge onto the field of battle at his signal.'

'Yes, everyone knows about this, though. It was a fine trap, one of Caledor's greatest victories.'

'Yes,' said Tyrion. 'But he made mistakes.'

'Oh ho, you do not lack for confidence, do you doorkeeper? The Conqueror was the greatest general of his age. His record is one of more or less unbroken victories. You look at a map of one of his greatest triumphs and claim he got it wrong.'

'No. I do not. He won. No one can fault that. I said he made mistakes.'

'An important distinction,' admitted Korhien. 'So, by all means, explain to me the mistakes he made, doorkeeper.'

'Look where he placed the bulk of his cavalry. In full view, close to the enemy, and when the battle started, they closed too quickly with the druchii right flank. It could easily have spoiled the trap.'

Korhien smiled. 'Your analysis is flawless, but you have failed to consider one thing.'

Tyrion was not offended to hear his theory so casually dismissed. He sensed that here was a chance to learn something about a subject that intrigued him from one who possessed some expertise in it.

'What have I missed?' he asked.

'I doubt Caledor wanted to place his cavalry there, or that he gave the order for that early charge.'

'Then why did it happen?'

'Because Prince Moradrim and Prince Lelik were rivals, and they both wanted the glory of breaking the enemy. They insisted on being where they were. Then one of them charged and the other, not being able to endure the possibility of his rival grabbing all the glory, followed suit.'

'Why did Caledor allow that? He was the Phoenix King, he was in charge. Why would they disobey him?'

Korhien's mighty laugh gusted around the sitting room.

'Once you have spent some time around our glorious aristocracy, you will not have to ask me that, doorkeeper.'

'Indulge my curiosity and answer me now.'

'Because our princes are a law unto themselves and their warriors swear service to those princes, not direct to the Phoenix King. They follow the leaders from their homeland, not some distant king.'

'That is not what our laws say,' said Teclis.

'I am sure you have read enough, Prince Teclis, to know that what the laws say should happen and what actually does are not always the same. In the heat of battle, when sword rings on sword, and the battle-shout echoes over the field, warriors follow their usual loyalties and instincts, not the law. And princes often crave glory more than the common good. It is not unknown for them to think they know better than their commanding general. Sometimes it is even the case, for the warrior on the spot often sees things invisible to the general on the hill.'

Tyrion nodded. He could see the sense in what Korhien was saying. It was something he had suspected himself when reading the descriptions of these old battles. It was nice to have it confirmed by one who knew what he was talking about.

'Why don't our historians mention this?' Teclis asked.

'Because they dwell at the courts of princes, and their pens and paper are paid for by the treasuries of those princes. Have you ever read a chronicle in which one historian blames one ruler for defeat and praises another for almost snatching victory from the jaws of defeat? Then gone to another scroll and had a different historian say exactly the opposite? It happened to me so often when I was young my head hurt.'

'I've had that experience,' said Tyrion.

'My brother's head often hurts when he tries to read,' said Teclis.

'I meant I have read two conflicting views,' said Tyrion. This was serious and he was in no mood for Teclis's flippancy.

'I suggest that when it happens next, you check where the historians were living when they wrote their tomes, or who their patron was. A bronze bracer will get you a golden torque that they have some connection with the court of the prince they are praising and there is some enmity between them and the ruler they are disparaging.'

'You are a very cynical elf, Lord Korhien,' said Teclis. He sounded more admiring than condemnatory. He was a very cynical elf himself.

'There are honest historians,' said Tyrion.

'Yes,' said Korhien. 'And those who believe themselves to be honest, and those who are in the pay of no prince because they are sponsored by the White Tower or dwell at the court of the Ever-queen, and those who have their own estates. But it's odd how often those who dwell in Avelorn praise the wisdom of the Ever-queen, and those who live at Hoeth dwell on the excellence of the

Loremasters – except the ones they have a personal feud with, of course. And those who are independently wealthy tend to find previously unsuspected virtues among their ancestors and relatives.'

'I see you are corrupting my sons with your cynicism, Korhien, and undermining their simple faith in scholarship.' The twins' father had entered the chamber unnoticed while the brothers listened to the White Lion.

'I am simply pointing out that all scholars bring their own biases to their work. It is inevitable, part of elven nature. You know this better than I do, my friend.'

'To my cost,' said their father with some bitterness.

'How goes the great work anyway?' Korhien asked.

'Slowly as always, but I am making progress.'

'May I see it?'

'You may.' Father gestured for Korhien to follow him. Tyrion helped Teclis up and supporting his brother on his shoulder, they made their way to their father's chambers. By the time they made it up the stairs, Teclis was breathing heavier than Tyrion had after running for hours. Tactfully Korhien pretended to ignore his eel-like walk, the way his body twisted first one way and then the other as he moved.

'Where is Lady Malene?' Korhien asked.

'She has retired to her chamber for the moment. She has many letters to write.'

'Have you finished the business she came to discuss with you?'

'I have told her I will consider it,' Father responded. There was an undercurrent of tension to the words that Tyrion caught but did not understand.

'I suggest that you do,' said Korhien. Again, there was that note of warning in his voice.

—◄ CHAPTER THREE ►—

'I see you have made progress,' said Korhien. He walked around the suit of armour, inspecting it but not touching it. The metal suit somehow dwarfed him while simultaneously giving the impression of having been made for someone about his size.

'Not as much as I would have liked,' said Father. He eyed the armour the way he would have gazed upon a personal enemy with whom he was about to fight a duel. Tyrion had never seen him look at it this way before. Maybe the presence of Korhien reminded him of something.

As usual Teclis was gazing at it in awe. His magesight was far better than Tyrion's and he had often helped their father trace the runes on the armour and the flows of magic they were intended to contain. He even claimed to have sometimes seen the faintest flickers of power within it, a thing which had at first intrigued Father but which he had never witnessed himself.

Looking at the three of them now, Tyrion felt excluded, a blind man listening to three artists discussing painting, or a deaf man reading about musical composition.

Korhien looked at the suit once more. 'When do you think you will be done with it?'

'Who knows?' Father responded. 'I have given up trying to predict that. There have been so many false dawns and broken promises with this.'

'It is a pity. It looks fine, and would put fear into the heart of Ulthuan's foes whether Aenarion wore it or not.'

Father glared at his friend. 'Aenarion wore it. I am certain.'

Korhien nodded soothingly, obviously aware he had touched a nerve with his quiet musing, even if he had not intended to.

'The spells woven around this armour are old indeed,' said Teclis. Korhien shot him an amused glance.

'I am sure the Council of Loremasters will take your word for that, Prince Teclis.'

'They ought to, if they are not fools,' said Teclis.

Korhien laughed outright.

'One son criticises the battle-plans of the greatest of our generals, the other is prepared to dismiss our most learned sorcerers as fools if they do not agree with his assessment of an artefact. Your children do not lack for confidence, Arathion.'

There was no malice in his tone, and yet there was a warning there that Tyrion did not quite know how to interpret.

'They have been brought up to speak their minds,' said Father.

'You have made them in your own image then, which is only to be expected, I suppose. I am not sure it will serve them well in Lothern.'

Tyrion caught his breath. Father had said nothing yet about them being sent to the great seaport. Had Father already agreed to their going? Tyrion supposed he did not have much choice in the matter. If the law required them to be presented because they were of the Blood of Aenarion, presented they would be.

'When?' Tyrion asked. His father shot another venomous glance at Korhien and then at Tyrion.

'Very soon,' said Father. 'If I choose to permit it. There are still details to be worked out.'

Tyrion looked at Teclis and smiled. He could sense his brother was as excited as he was by the prospect of seeing one of the greatest of all high elf cities once more, a place where they had not been since they were both small children.

There would be libraries there to consult and they would look upon wonders. They would see the Sea Gates, and the Lighthouse and the Courts. There would be soldiers and ships and tournaments. There would be the palaces of their mother's family and their own old house. A whole vast dizzying prospect danced before his eyes. Korhien sensed their excitement too and laughed with them, rather than at them.

'There are many things to be discussed,' said Father. 'Before you go. If you go.'

He sounded saddened by the words even as he said them. 'Before *we* go,' said Tyrion. 'You are not coming with us?'

'I have been presented at court,' said Father. 'I do not feel any great need to meet a Phoenix King and his courtiers again. And I have work to do here. You will be back soon enough.'

He did not look at them as he said this but there was a faint catch to his voice. He turned towards the armour and began to tinker with the scales on the left upper arm.

'If you will excuse me,' he said. 'I will need to get on with it.'

'Of course,' said Korhien quietly. 'Come, lads, let us leave your father in peace.'

Teclis pushed himself painfully up from his chair and limped over to Father, his body writhing as he moved. He laid a hand on Father's shoulder and whispered something in his ear. Tyrion wished that he could bring himself to do the same, but he felt sure that Father would not have accepted it from him. Instead he waited for Teclis and then helped him along the corridor to his room.

Tyrion lay in bed, staring at the ceiling, tired and excited. All around him he sensed the presence of the strangers in the house. Some of them were still awake, talking in low voices so as not to disturb the others. Tyrion, who knew every night noise of their very quiet house, was disturbed by the sound. He had read of ship's masters who knew there was something wrong with their vessels because of a faint, unfamiliar creaking. He suddenly understood how that could be.

He made himself relax. His breathing became deeper and slower and he closed his eyes. He became aware that a vast weight pressed down on him. He felt as if all of the breath was being crushed from his lungs. He had to force air into them. He tried to sit up but his body was weak and would not obey him. He burned as with a dreadful fever and ached all over as human victims of plagues were said to. He opened his eyes but the room was unfamiliar to him. There was a bell on the table for summoning assistance and a flask of the cordial his father had prepared to ease his sickness.

He reached for it, but his limbs felt wasted and numb. They refused to obey him with their customary alacrity. He forced more air into his lungs but it was a struggle. He opened his mouth to call for help but he could not force the words out. He knew he was dying and there was nothing he could do about it.

Suddenly his eyes snapped open and he was back in his own room, his own body. It had been a dream, but not just any dream. He got up from the bed and raced through the house to where Teclis lay, burning with fever, struggling to breathe, desperately reaching for his medicine. Tyrion moved over to the bed, poured some of the cordial and helped his brother to drink.

Teclis swallowed the medicine like a drowning man, a look of strange revulsion on his face that Tyrion understood. What must it be like to feel like you are drowning and have to force yourself to drink?

'Thank you,' said Teclis at last. His breathing had become more regular. The rasping sound coming from his chest had died away. His eyes were no longer bright with panic.

'Shall I call father?' Tyrion asked.

'No need. I am all right now. I think I shall sleep.'

Tyrion nodded. His brother looked terribly frail and wasted in the beams of moonlight coming in through the gap in the shutters.

'I shall sit a while,' he said. Teclis nodded and closed his eyes. Tyrion watched silently and wondered whether his twin was dreaming about being him. He hoped so.

It would be the only experience of good health Teclis was ever likely to have.

Tyrion moved silently through the house, unable to get back to sleep now that he was awake. Night noises seemed determined to keep him up. Downstairs he could hear his father and Korhien talking quietly of old times as they sat beside the dying fire. Lady Malene was locked in her chamber. Teclis had finally drifted into fitful slumber.

Tyrion found himself inevitably drawn to his father's work room, filled with curiosity as he sometimes was, and half-lost in a waking dream of adventure and glory and things that might yet come. Visions of grim knights and silken princesses and mighty kings filled his mind along with great ships, huge dragons and proud warhorses. He saw himself in palaces and on battlefields. He pictured jousts and sword fights and all manner of adventures with himself as hero. Sometimes Teclis was with him, a proud mage from the storybooks.

Beams of moonlight came in through the crystalline window, illuminating the huge armoured suit that was his father's life's work. Not for the first time, Tyrion thought how strange it was that this room should have windows of precious crystal when Teclis's did not. When he was younger such thoughts had never troubled him. The world was the way it was and he had neither required nor expected any explanations from it. Now he found himself questioning things more and more.

In the moonlight the armour looked like a living warrior, tall and lithe and deadly. He approached it as he would a great cat he was hunting, padding in on silent feet till he stood before it, looking up at the massive helmet, measuring himself against the titanic figure of the elf who had once occupied it and finding himself insignificant and all his dreams of glory were tiny, meaningless, insect things.

At this moment Tyrion had no trouble believing his father's theories. It seemed perfectly possible that Aenarion had once worn this damaged armour. Even without the magic that would give it life, there was a power about the thing. Its simple presence spoke of an earlier, more primitive age when mortal gods strode the earth and made war with foes the likes of which no longer existed in the modern world.

The metalwork was beautiful but it lacked the sophistication and loveliness of much later elven armour. It had been forged by masters in an age of war. The elves who had made it had other things on their mind than the creation of an object of beauty. They had been making a weapon for the solitary being who stood between their world and utter destruction.

'What were you like?' he asked himself, trying to picture Aenarion, to imagine what it must have been like to walk the world in that ancient time of blood and darkness. It was impossible to imagine a being of flesh encased in this suit of armour. It was easier to picture a creature of living metal such as some claimed the Witch King now was. Yet Aenarion had lived and breathed and fathered children, from one of whom Tyrion was descended. There was a link of blood and bone and flesh between himself and the one who had once worn this armour.

He reached out and touched it as if by doing so he could reach across the ages and touch his distant ancestor. The metal was cold beneath his hand and there was no life in it, no sense of presence other than that the armour itself possessed.

He felt obscurely disappointed. There was no echo down the ages from the avatar of the godhead who had saved his people. And he felt obscurely relieved that he had disturbed no ancient ghost, felt no ancient power. Perhaps it was true as some scholars now claimed that the great magics had departed from the world and that the high elves were but pale shadows of what they had once been.

He stood there for a long moment, enjoying the cold and the odd sense of being linked with ancient glories and terrors that could not touch his life. It was thrilling to imagine the time of Aenarion but he was happy too that he would not have to confront the horrors the first Phoenix King had been called upon to face. He was safe within the walls of his father's house and nothing could touch him.

Somewhere off in the night something screamed, a hunting cat that had found prey perhaps or maybe one of the monsters that sometimes made their way down from the Annulii. A trick of the moonlight made it seem as if a mocking smile twisted the armour's helmet-face and for a moment Tyrion thought of ghosts and deadly destinies.

Then he shook his head and dismissed his fears and padded softly to his own bed.

N'Kari dreamed. He relived the ancient days of glory when he had led the horde of Chaos that had come so close to conquering Ulthuan. He saw himself lolling on a throne made of the fused bodies of still-living elf-women and giving orders for the sacrifice of a thousand elf-children. He saw himself storming ancient cities of carved wood and putting them to the torch. He relived inhaling the scent of the burning forests as if it were incense as he devoured the souls of the dying. He saw again his first battle with Aenarion in the burned-out ruins of that ancient city and found himself once again facing that terrible blade. Something about that image brought him, shuddering, back into the present.

All around him the fabric of the Vortex flowed in a way that would have been incomprehensible to anyone but a daemon, a mage or a ghost. It was like being trapped in an infinite labyrinth of light.

He needed to escape. He needed to break out of this place.

He forced himself to think, to concentrate on his plans. It was too easy to lose track of time in this place, to lose himself in his far too vivid dreams. He had slowly become himself again. Over the long millennia he had gathered power. He had found holes in the fabric of the Vortex. He knew where it was deteriorating. He knew where he could break out when the time came.

The time was almost right. The stars were in the correct position. The power was within his grasp. Soon he would escape from this sterile, dull, haunted place and write his name in blood on the pages of history.

He would take vengeance on all of the line of Aenarion.

CHAPTER FOUR

'What do you know of the Art?' Lady Malene asked.

She had knocked this time before entering Teclis's chamber. She still looked around distastefully though, then went over to the windows and threw the shutters open, letting in fresh air and the unaccustomed sunlight.

It was morning then, Teclis thought. He had lived through another night.

'Just what I have read in my father's books of theory and what I have picked up from talking to him. He will not let me read his spellbooks yet.' Teclis coughed and could not stop coughing. His lungs felt full of something and made a horrible wheezing sound.

Malene looked at him with distaste. She was not used to being around the infirm. Few elves were. It made him want to limp away and hide.

'One of the things your father and I have been talking about is your education,' she said at last. 'He feels that you would be better apprenticed to one such as I than to him. He says your gifts are more suited to an active school of magic. You are sixteen today. You are of an age to begin proper study of the Art. If you wish to be taught.'

Teclis looked at her with wonder. He tried to push himself upright. The effort made his shoulder ache and left him feeling exhausted. Even that could not dim his excitement. Was it possible that Malene really would teach him to work magic? He forced himself to look her in the eye and say, 'I want to learn all you can teach me.'

'That may take a very long time,' she said.

'We are elves. We have time.'

'I am not sure you do.'

'You do not want to waste your time teaching one who might not live to be grateful for it, is that it?' Teclis could not keep his bitterness from showing. He felt as if someone had shown him a treasure he had desired all his life and then snatched it away.

Lady Malene shook her head. 'No. I will teach you what I can, in whatever time you have to learn it, once the Seers have pronounced you fit to be taught.'

'So I must await their permission?' He could not keep the sourness out of his voice. Another barrier between himself and his heart's desire. 'That is not fair.'

He wanted so hard to be a mage. He knew he could never be like Tyrion, swift and strong and certain, but he felt he had it in himself to be a mage like his father. He could see the winds of magic perfectly when they blew and felt the tug of power whenever his father used the slightest of cantrips.

'There are certain secret societies and cults who believe that one of the Blood will draw the Sword of Khaine and bring about the end of the world,' she said this as if she was imparting a great secret.

'It won't be me. I want to be a mage. What use have I for a sword?'

She smiled at that and her face was lovely for a moment but then it became serious again. 'The Art can be a terrible weapon and a mage under the Curse of Aenarion can be a terrible foe.'

Teclis cocked his head to one side. 'There have been such then?'

'Of course.'

'How is it that I never read of them?'

Lady Malene's smile showed her amusement at his arrogance. 'So in your sixteen years, you have become acquainted with everything written in seven millennia of asur history? You are quite the scholar.'

Teclis felt his face flush and he started to cough again. The spasm wracked his body painfully. He realised how foolish and arrogant he must sound to Lady Malene, when really he was just frustrated. 'I have not. But I want to. Where can I find these books?'

She reached out and ruffled his lank hair. It was a gesture of affection that surprised and touched him as well as embarrassed him. He was not used to such things. He looked away. 'You will not find them here, or in any library outside of the Tower of Hoeth. It's the sort of knowledge that the Loremasters keep to themselves.'

'You have been to Hoeth?'

She nodded.

'You have seen the library?'

'I have seen the parts of it I was allowed to see.'

'Allowed?'

'The library is a vast, strange place, like the Tower itself. There are sections that some people never see and yet others can visit every day. Sometimes, a mage will find a chamber full of books just once in his life and never be able to find the way back. The library is part of the Tower and the Tower has a mind, of sorts, of its own.'

'It sounds wonderful and terrible at the same time,' said Teclis.

'I do not think the mages who built the Tower entirely understood what it was they were creating. I think the spells they cast had unforeseen consequences. It is often the way with magic.' She sounded a little sad when she said that, as if she had direct personal experience of such a thing. 'A thousand years in the building, a millennium of work by hundreds of the greatest mages of the elf people. Webs of geomantic power spun within webs of geomantic power, monstrously powerful spells layered upon monstrously powerful spells, built in a place that was already sacred to the God of Wisdom and a font of awesome power. It is the greatest work of the elves, I think it will most likely endure after we have gone. I sometimes think that it will endure the wreck of the world and that it was intended to do so.'

'What do you mean?'

'I believe the Tower is a vault as well as a repository of knowledge. When the elves are gone, it will still be there, preserving our knowledge, all that we are, all that we were, all that we will be. There was never a place like it built before and there never will be again. Bel-Korhadris, its architect, was the greatest geomancer since Caledor Dragontamer and I doubt there are any living now who can fully encompass his design or his intention.'

Her words started a great blaze burning in Teclis's heart. A desire to look upon this place and to walk through its library and penetrate its secrets, insofar as he might, filled him. He had never heard of anywhere so attractive. He wondered if they might take him there, even in the meanest capacity, as a sweeper or scribe or a warden. He felt like he would do anything required to look upon this place and be part of it.

'My father never talked of the Tower as you do,' he said. He had never heard anyone talk of any place with such passion. She sounded like his father when he talked about the dragon armour of Aenarion or Tyrion when he talked about warfare.

'All elves who see it, see it slightly differently. All elves who go there experience it slightly differently. I am not so sure your father's experience was as pleasant as mine. Or it may be that he does not like to talk about it the way I do. Some people are secretive that way. In general I do not speak of my time there much. It is odd that I feel compelled to discuss such a thing with you, Prince Teclis. I wonder why that is?'

Teclis could not answer because he did not know. He did feel that in Lady Malene he had found a kindred spirit. Perhaps she felt the same. 'Why did you ask me what I know of the Art?'

'Because there is a very great power within you. I can sense it, your father has sensed it, any mage with the Sight can sense it. If you live and are not accursed you may become a very great wizard one day.'

'Will I get to see the Tower of Hoeth?'

'Most assuredly.'

'That would make me very happy,' said Teclis and once more he fell into a long fit of coughing until he felt like he was almost unable to breathe.

'Poor child,' said Lady Malene. 'Not much has given you happiness, has it?'

'I do not want your sympathy,' Teclis said at last. 'Only your knowledge.'

'I may be able to give you more than that.'

'Really?'

'I may be able to help you with what ails you.' Teclis looked at her disbelievingly.

'That would be a gift beyond price,' he said.

'Well, it is your birthday after all.'

'Yes, it is,' he said, surprised. He had not expected to live to reach sixteen years of age.

'I make no promises,' she said. 'I will see what I can do.'

She left the room. For the first time in a very long time, Teclis felt like crying. It was odd. He had thought there were no tears left in him.

'I have a birthday gift for you, doorkeeper,' said Korhien. Tyrion looked at the giant warrior, not sure whether he was being mocked. He glanced around the courtyard but all of the soldiers who had come with Lady Malene were busy about their own business. If this was a joke no one could see him being the butt of it.

Korhien loosed the belt and scabbard at his waist, folded the leather strap neatly and handed the equipage over to Tyrion.

'What do you want me to do with this?' Tyrion asked.

'It is yours,' said Korhien. 'Unsheathe the blade.'

Tyrion's heart leapt as he obeyed the White Lion. He drew the longsword from its scabbard. It was a true elven blade, long and straight and keen edged and it glittered in the mountain sunlight. Runes were etched in the metal. A blue sunstone inscribed with a dragon glinted from the pommel. He held it easily in his hand although it was heavier than he had imagined such a thing would be.

'I cannot take this,' said Tyrion, although he very much wanted to keep it. He was too proud to accept such an expensive and beautiful thing from a stranger. It was a charity he did not require. He might be poor but he was of a most ancient lineage. His father had taken the time to instil that knowledge in him.

He slid the blade back into the scabbard and presented it, hilt first, scabbard held over his left forearm back to Korhien. Tyrion felt the wrongness of his words even as he said them. He knew that in some way he was insulting Korhien but at the same time he did not want to be beholden to any elf for something as important as his first sword.

Korhien seemed to understand.

'Keep it for a season and if you do not want it, return it to me in Lothern. You are going to need it now, for how else I am going to give you a lesson with it? That will be my birthday gift to you if your pride will not allow you to accept more than a loan of the sword.'

Tyrion smiled back. It was a compromise his pride was prepared to accept and his father would too. And he really, really wanted the sword. It fitted in perfectly with his image of himself and his unspoken dreams of glory. 'Very well. I thank you for your loan.'

'Don't be so quick to thank me, doorkeeper. I mean to repay you for your lessons in chess-play,' Korhien added. 'Your father has told me you have not been schooled with a sword.'

Tyrion shrugged. He did not want to say there were no swords in the house. It seemed shameful to admit that his father had sold them for the money needed to continue his research. 'I know how to use a bow and a spear well enough,' Tyrion said.

'I am sure you do,' said Korhien seriously. 'But the sword is the weapon you will be called on to use in Lothern, if you have any cause to use a weapon there at all.'

Tyrion did not need to ask why. Duels were not fought between asur nobles with spear or bow, not unless the situations were very unusual.

'So when do we begin?' Tyrion asked.

'No time like the present.'

Tyrion shrugged and unsheathed the sword and fell into the stance he had always imagined wielding it. Korhien looked at him puzzled.

'I thought you told me you had no training with a sword.'

'My father has never given me any. Swords were not his weapon when he was in the levies. He says he is more likely to cut himself with one than any enemy.'

Korhien walked around him, inspecting his stance. 'That is nothing less than the truth. Your father was the worst sword-bearer I have ever seen. Better to have no training at all than be taught incorrectly. That said, who has been teaching you?'

'No one,' Tyrion said.

'Why did you choose that stance, that grip?'

'It just seemed right.'

'It most assuredly is, perfect for fighting one-handed with that blade, and without a shield.' The big warrior looked at him thoughtfully. 'A moment if you please.'

He walked away and returned. He returned with his enormous axe. 'I would not normally allow another to bear this weapon, but show me how you would hold this axe.'

Tyrion shrugged and took the weapon, holding it two-handed across his body, feet apart, left in front of right.

'Like you had been training with it for years,' Korhien muttered. He seemed perplexed.

'You say you can use a bow. Show me!'

'I thought you were going to teach me how to use a sword,' Tyrion said.

'Time enough yet for your first lesson,' said Korhien. 'For the moment, indulge me.'

Tyrion brought his bow and strung it, strapped on his quiver and aimed at the target he had set up on the western wall of the villa. He breathed easily and loosed three arrows one after the other, placing them easily in the central ring he had made. They were not difficult shots and yet Korhien seemed impressed. A small crowd of warriors had begun to gather around them. They had begun to talk quietly among themselves.

'Technique with a bow... perfect,' he said, as if he had a list in his head and he was checking something off against it. 'Spear now.' He handed Tyrion one from the rack. 'Cast it at the target.'

Tyrion smiled and turned, throwing the spear as part of the same motion he had taken the weapon. He was showing off now and he knew it. The spear landed in the central ring of the target and buried itself there, among the arrows. Korhien's eyes narrowed.

'I think I have seen enough,' he said.

'Enough for what?' The warrior considered his answer for a long moment, as if undecided as to what he should actually say.

'Enough for me to see that you will not be as difficult to teach as your father.'

'I am glad to hear that. Shall we begin?'

'Are you so anxious to learn how to kill?' Korhien asked.

It was a serious question, and Tyrion sensed that more depended on his response than at first appeared. He decided, as he inevitably did, that honesty was the best policy.

'I already know how to kill,' he said. 'I am anxious to learn to use a sword.'

'Who have you killed?'

'I have killed deer,' said Tyrion, a little embarrassed now.

'Killing another elf, or even an orc or a human, is not the same thing,' said Korhien.

'In what way?' Tyrion asked, genuinely curious. He did not doubt for a moment that Korhien possessed personal knowledge of this subject.

'For one thing they are intelligent beings who know how to fight. They will try to kill you in turn.'

'I have killed mountain lions and monsters come down from the Annulii.'

'Monsters?'

'Mutated creatures with the forms of animals all mixed together, or so the other huntsmen assured me.'

'You take me aback, doorkeeper. I came here expecting sheltered and scholarly princes, like their father once was, not someone who speaks quite so casually of killing.'

'Is it a bad thing?' Tyrion asked, well aware that his father found him coarse, violent and unruly, and was often embarrassed by his behaviour.

'Not in the world we live in,' said Korhien.

Tyrion was relieved. He had already discovered that Korhien's good opinion was important to him, and he felt the big warrior was capable of teaching him about those things that were important to him, not just to Father and Teclis. He had long ago outstripped the local hunters in his ability with bow and spear.

'You said you were going to teach me how to use a sword.'

'And I am an elf of my word,' said Korhien. 'I thought I would need to begin by telling your father's son which end of a sword was which, and which parts were used for doing what, but I suspect that in your case this might prove redundant. So let us move on to the practice swords.'

'Wooden swords,' said Tyrion, disappointed.

'Everyone has to start somewhere, even you, doorkeeper. Do you have some around here?'

'In the stables, on the rack.'

'Typical... of your father I mean... to keep them there.'

Tyrion laughed at the obvious truth of what Korhien was saying and went to fetch them. The wooden swords were much more like clubs than real blades. They had handles and cross-hilts but where the blades would have been on a real sword were circular wooden poles.

Korhien weighed them in his hands critically and said, 'These will do, to begin with, anyway.'

He handed one to Tyrion and then saluted; unconsciously Tyrion mimicked the moment. It was Korhien's turn to laugh.

'Did I do something wrong?' he asked, face flushing.

'No, doorkeeper, you did not.'

'Then why did you laugh?'

'Because like everything you do connected with fighting you do it so well.'

He took up a guard stance, and Tyrion mimicked it too.

'Try and hit me,' Korhien said.

Without any further prompting, Tyrion sprang forward. Korhien parried his blow, but did not riposte. Tyrion kept attacking, lunging and swinging. At first he was not trying too hard, not wanting to take a chance of accidentally hurting Korhien as he had done with Teclis and local hunters when he had tried using the wooden swords on his own. Soon he realised that Korhien was having no difficulty parrying him and he speeded up his attack, striking with greater force and precision.

'Surely you can do better than this, doorkeeper,' Korhien taunted.

'Indeed,' Tyrion murmured but did not allow himself to be provoked. He kept on attacking, looking for weak spots in Korhien's defence, areas where his guard came up too slowly, where his responses were a beat behind. To his surprise, he did not find any. He kept on attacking, and Korhien kept on parrying, and then suddenly the sword was knocked from his hands. When he replayed the action in his mind, he saw the trick that Korhien had used, and was surprised that he had not thought of it himself.

'That was embarrassing,' said Tyrion.

'In what way?' Korhien said.

'In that you disarmed me so easily after I could not lay a blow on you.'

'Trust me, doorkeeper, you did not do so badly. There are elves with a century of practice who have done worse than your first efforts here.'

'My father, for one,' said Tyrion sourly.

'No. Elves who would kill your father in the first passage of blades.'

Tyrion found this talk of anyone killing his father disturbing. It made him uncomfortable, and it must have showed on his face.

'It's something you need to know, doorkeeper. Anyone you fight will be someone's father or mother, someone's son or daughter or brother. That's what makes it difficult. That's why some elves, like your father, to his credit, never really learn.'

'Why do you say to his credit?' Tyrion asked.

'Because the loss of any elf life is something to be mourned.'

'Even dark elves?'

Korhien nodded even if he could not bring himself to say the words. 'There are not so many elves left in the world, doorkeeper. The loss of any one of us is a grievous loss to our people.'

'It's a pity Malekith's subjects do not feel the same way.'

'Who is to say they do not?' said Korhien. 'We are all still kin after all, even after all these centuries of Sundering.'

'Perhaps someone should tell them that,' said Tyrion.

'Perhaps you are right,' said Korhien. 'Or perhaps they already know.'

'It has not stopped them from raiding us.'

'Nor us them, doorkeeper. It's worth remembering that it takes two sides to make a war.'

'You do not sound much like I expected a warrior to sound,' said Tyrion.

Korhien laughed. 'I am sorry to disappoint.'

'That is not what I meant.'

'What did you mean?'

'You talk less of glory and more of reasons.'

'I have heard too many people talk about glory, doorkeeper, and usually they meant their own. Normally when you hear an elf talking about glory and the spilling of blood, they mean their glory and your blood.'

'You are doing it again.'

'I am telling you this, doorkeeper, because I suspect you will turn out like me,' Korhien's voice was softer now and sadder. 'I suspect you will end up spilling a lot of your blood and other people's for causes not your own, in places you would rather not be.'

'Why?' interrupted Tyrion, now genuinely curious and quite excited. He did not think turning out like Korhien would be such a terrible thing.

'Because you are already very good with weapons and you will become very much better unless I am greatly mistaken. And our rulers have need of warriors, our world being the sort of place it is.'

Again, Tyrion suspected he was missing something. He did not find the idea that there was a place where an elf like him might be needed as saddening as Korhien appeared to. He found it hopeful. It meant that there might yet prove to be something he could do with his life, and there would be people who were not disappointed with him.

'Do you really think I could be a White Lion like you?' Tyrion asked. He had promoted himself in his own imagination, he realised, and he felt as if he were overstepping the mark.

'You will be whatever you choose to be, doorkeeper. You have that in you. I suspect it is your destiny to be something more than me. You are of the Blood of Aenarion, after all.'

'Is that why you are really here?' Korhien considered his answer very carefully and seemed to come to a decision.

'Yes,' he said. He threw his arm around Tyrion's shoulder and took him to one side, out of earshot of the other soldiers. It looked like a casual thoughtless act, but Tyrion knew that it was not.

'My brother thinks they will kill us if we turn out to be cursed.' Tyrion felt as if he had truly overstepped the mark this time, particularly given what Teclis suspected. Korhien's eyes widened. Tyrion guessed he had never expected to hear this.

'He might well be right. Or you may find yourself in some isolated tower or dungeon.'

'Would you kill us?' Tyrion asked, feeling the sword heavy in his hand, not sure of what he planned to do if he got the wrong answer. He knew that if he wanted to Korhien could kill him quite easily for all that they were of the same size and strength. Korhien was silent for a very long time.

'No,' he said eventually.

Tyrion was uneasily aware that Korhien had taken the question very seriously and was giving a truthful answer. 'I would not. But they would find others who would try.'

'Why do you say that?'

'Because I am sure you would not prove so easy to kill, doorkeeper.'

'They might be right to kill us if we are truly accursed, as Malekith was.'

'They might be. If you were. I do not think you are.' Korhien smiled again and there was genuine humour in it. 'This is a very morbid conversation and I am sure your aunt would be very disturbed to know we have had it.'

'She shall not hear of it from me,' said Tyrion.

'Nor from me,' said Korhien. It felt as if they were partners in a conspiracy, and Tyrion knew in that moment he had found another person in the world he could trust.

'We should return to our lessons. You have a long way to go yet before you are a blade master,' said Korhien. He never seemed to doubt for a moment that Tyrion would become one. Nor at that moment, did Tyrion. He picked up the wooden sword with the sudden seriousness of a boy who had just found his vocation.

◀ CHAPTER FIVE ▶

Lady Malene entered the room. She carried a glass beaker of a clear sapphire liquid in her hands. She walked carefully as if unwilling to take the risk of spilling a drop. Teclis struggled upright. The effort made him dizzy. The room seemed to tilt sideways for a moment before righting itself.

When she reached the bedside Malene handed the container to Teclis.

'Drink,' she said.

'What is it?' Although he was starting to trust her, Teclis was still unwilling to drink anything she had prepared without question.

'It is a mix of aqua vitae and sunroot. I have woven several spells into it.'

Teclis looked at it dubiously. 'What will it do?'

'Help your body resist the infection currently raging through it.'

'My father's potion already does that.'

'Your father's potion does not. It soothes your nervous system and boosts some of your body's resistance to disease. It lets you breathe easier and, by taking the strain off your lungs, it makes it easier for your body to fight the disease in it. It does not do anything else to help you.'

'You are claiming you know more about these things than my father?' Teclis knew he was simply putting off the moment when he had to drink the potion. He realised it was not because he feared it might poison him, but simply because he was afraid of disappointment. What if it did not work as well as he hoped it would?

'I hate to puncture your childish illusions but your father is an artificer, not an alchemist. He knows a lot about making and repairing weapons and armour but comparatively little about medicinal herbs.'

'And you do know, of course,' said Teclis with as much sarcasm as he could muster.

'Actually, yes. Better than your father at least and very much better than you. I did not notice any volumes on herb lore or advanced
alchemy in your library.'

'I will have to take your word for that.'

'I would advise you to do so, if you wish to recover your health.'

Teclis grimaced. He did not like being told he had to do anything.
He was naturally contrary that way.

'What is the matter, Prince Teclis? Are you afraid I am going to
poison you?'

Teclis stared at her. 'Do I need to be?'

'What exactly do you mean by that?'

'What exactly are you doing here with your soldiers and your
over-muscled lover?'

Lady Malene cocked her head to one side and stared at him. He
met her gaze and for a long time neither of them looked away. A
slow smile, almost of understanding, crossed her face. 'Are you
jealous?'

Teclis was annoyed because he had not realised that he was, in
part, until she had asked him. He knew how ludicrous that must look
to her and beyond all things he disliked being made to look ludicrous.

'Answer my question, please.' It sounded more imploring than he
would have liked. Normally he was better at controlling his expression than this.

'I have come to take you to Lothern.'

'Why?'

'So that you may be presented to the Phoenix King and then, most
likely, to the Priests of Asuryan.'

'Why?'

'So that you may be judged and found untainted by the Curse
of Aenarion.'

'What if I am not so judged?'

'You are worried that you might be found to be cursed?' She sat
down on the bed beside him, still holding her flask of medicine.

'Would you not be, if you were me?'

'I suspect I would, Prince Teclis, but I am in no position to know.
I am not a descendant of Aenarion.'

'There are times when I wish I were not. There are times when
I think I am accursed, that I must be, to have turned out the way
I have.'

'If your illness is your only manifestation of the Curse, you have
nothing to fear.'

'I fear my illness,' he said.

'I meant from us, from the Council of Mages, from the Phoenix King's personal magi, from the Priests.'

'What if you do see a reason to be worried, some echo of the doom of Aenarion down all the long centuries? What will happen then?'

'I do not know, for certain.'

'Feel free to speculate.'

'You are a very odd youth, Prince Teclis.'

'I would not know. I do not have much to compare myself to. Only my brother, Tyrion, and comparisons with him are invidious.'

'Why? Because you lack his health, his charm, his beauty?'

It was all rather too close to the truth for his liking.

'Please do not hold yourself back to spare my feelings,' said Teclis.

Malene laughed.

'You have your own charm, and you have wit and more to the point you have very great potential in the Art. You are also much cleverer.'

'Do not make the mistake of underestimating my brother.'

'I do not. The fact that you are brilliant does not make him a fool.'

'I think you will find he is quite brilliant in his own way.'

'And what way is that?'

'Show him anything to do with warfare and he understands it at once, instinctively. Play him at any game, any, and you will be beaten.'

'Korhien says that he is... gifted beyond any young warrior he has ever met. I suspect you will prove to be the same when it comes to magic. I am not sure that is such a good thing.'

'Why?'

'Because the ones who are exceptional are the ones who are feared. Aenarion was exceptional. Malekith was too. There have been others. Prince Saralion, the Plaguebearer, the Daemonologist Erasophania. They are the ones who bring doom.'

'There are others of the line of Aenarion who were exceptional too and they did great good,' said Teclis, aware of how desperate he sounded. 'The healer Xenophea. Lord Abrasis of Cothique who found a way to stabilise broken waystones. I could name a dozen more.'

'Then let us hope you are one of those.' She smiled again and it came to Teclis that Lady Malene, whatever else she might be, was not his enemy. She did not mean him any harm, simply because of who he was, or who she was.

That did not mean she would not turn on him if he turned out to be cursed, of course.

'Do you think I could be?'

'Yes. Now will you drink this medicine? Or should I pour it out?'

'You would not poison me, would you?'

'If I was going to, would I tell you?'

'I bow to the logic of your argument.' Teclis drank the medicine and grimaced.

'It tastes foul,' he said.

'Next time I will add some peppermint.'

'I doubt that would improve the flavour.'

'No, but it would really give you something to complain about.'

'How long before I feel the effects?'

'Give it an hour to start working and then a couple of hours after that to take effect. By that time you should be dead.'

Teclis shot her a black look.

'You are not the only one with a dark sense of humour, Prince Teclis,' she said.

Teclis laughed. He was already starting to feel better.

The sitting room was quiet and the fire was still on. Tyrion was amazed. It had burned the whole time the visitors had been here. Such extravagance was unheard of in his experience. Father stood as far away from it as possible, in a corner of the room, as if he felt too guilty to enjoy the heat. Tyrion felt pleasantly tired. His muscles ached. He had spent all day sparring with the wooden swords, first with Korhien and then with the warriors of Lady Malene's retinue. He had loved it. He felt like he was finally getting to do what he wanted to do.

Teclis sat near the fire, wrapped in a blanket. He looked more alert than he had in quite some time. It looked like he was passed the crisis of his latest illness and would live. The medicine Lady Malene had prepared for him seemed to have done its work.

Tyrion was glad. He went and stood beside his brother, hands outstretched towards the heat. The embers burned orange amid the ashes, and small blue flames danced over them. Here and there they took on an alchemical green tinge as something strange within them, some trapped magic perhaps, caught fire.

'You are going to Lothern with your aunt,' Father said.

'Both of us?' Tyrion asked.

'Both of you.'

'Why?' Teclis asked. He always wanted to know why.

'Because you must present yourself before the Phoenix King. It is an honour that those of our line have long had to endure.'

'Did you?' Teclis asked.

'Most assuredly.'

'What will happen?' Tyrion asked.

'You will see his Exalted Highness, and he will be very gracious to you and tell you how much Ulthuan owes to those of our blood. Then, most likely, you will be taken aside and sent to be examined by a cabal of sorcerers and priests and seers to determine whether your lives have been bent by the Curse. For this you will be sent to the Shrine of Asuryan.'

'They did this to you?' Tyrion asked.

'Yes. They do it to every descendant of Great Aenarion. There are all sorts of prophesies concerning those of our blood, some of them good, some of them bad. Sometimes, the seers present have visions concerning the future of those before them and speak as the compulsion of prophesy comes upon them.'

Tyrion did not much like the sound of this. He pictured something vaguely shameful and sinister here, and he did not like the idea of being singled out in such a way because of who he was, and from whom he was descended. Teclis, on the other hand, was fascinated. He had known a little about the process from his reading, of course, but his father had never spoken of it.

'Do they cast spells?' he asked.

'Divinations of all sorts,' said father. 'From the simplest to the most complex. I did not recognise them at the time but I came to know what they were latterly.'

'Was there any prophecy made about you?' Tyrion asked.

'They said I was marked for greatness by fate,' said their father sourly. He gestured around the barren sitting room in the cold and tumbledown mansion. His expression was ironic. 'They said my children would cause me great pain.'

Tyrion's face fell. Teclis took on the blank expression he always thought masked his feelings. Their father laughed.

'You did. Your mother died the night you were born and that was the greatest pain of my life. But you have never caused me any other pain, either of you, only sleepless nights. You have both been good boys as far as you are capable.'

It was not exactly a resounding declaration of pride or love. Their father could not bring himself to look at them while he talked.

Instead he kept staring at the portrait of their mother above the fireplace.

'I am not sorry,' he said very quietly and almost apologetically, and it took Tyrion a long moment to realise that he was talking to her about them being born. The curious idea struck him that Prince Arathion could have avoided a great deal of pain simply by never having fathered them. He was a wizard. He knew ways of preventing conception if he wanted to.

Or perhaps fate would have taken a hand and seen they were born anyway. After all, what was the point of a prophecy if it was not going to come true?

Perhaps it was simply that their father had not known what form the pain they were going to cause was going to take. He wondered if Prince Arathion would have made the same decision if he had known it was going to cost him his wife. He wondered what it would be like to live with that notion, and only at the end did it strike him that his parents had conceived the pair of them anyway, even knowing it would have terrible consequences.

How little he knew of this quiet, unworldly elf with whom he had shared a house for all of his life.

Father shook his head and looked from Teclis to Tyrion and back again. 'The two of you are going away and there is little I can give you save my blessing. I wish that there were more.'

'You have given us enough,' said Tyrion.

'I do not think so, my son. And you cannot know that, for you have never seen Lothern as it truly is, only through the eyes of a very small child. It is a wonderful place but it can also be a terrible one for such as you. It is a place of jealousy and malice as well as wonders and greatness. The Lady Malene has promised me she will look after you but I am not sure how far she will be capable of that.'

'What will happen to us if they decide we are accursed?' Teclis asked. He had always been better at divining the current of their father's thoughts than Tyrion.

'You are not accursed,' said Father.

'What will happen if they find us so?'

Their father smiled, thin-lipped. 'You have always been very quick of understanding, Teclis. It has gratified me.'

Tyrion felt a stab of jealousy. 'Of course, there is the possibility that they might find you so, even if it were not true. Politics can be a nasty business among the elves. I am glad you understand this.'

'And you still have not answered my question,' said Teclis gently.

'I do not know the answer, my son. I would like to believe the best.'

'But...'

'But I fear that something terrible might be done.'

'We are not cursed,' said Tyrion. He believed that as well and he did not like the way this conversation was developing. This might be the last night they spent with their father in a long time and he would prefer it to be a happier memory than this.

'Of course you are not, and I am sure you will both make me very proud.'

'We will do our best,' said Tyrion.

'We will pass their tests,' said Teclis.

'Once you do, Teclis, Lady Malene will begin your instruction in the ways of magic. I would do it myself but I have the great work to continue.'

Tyrion looked at his unworldly father and wondered how unworldly he really was. He had certainly chosen the best way to deflect Teclis from his line of questioning. His twin's face glowed with pleasure. He had for a very long time wanted to begin his studies in the Art and now it seemed like they were to begin.

'And Tyrion, Korhien Ironglaive has offered to see that you learn the ways of the warrior. He says you have a great gift for it and few elves know as much about these matters as he does. Pay attention to what he tells you. I have heard it said that he is quite possibly the greatest warrior in Ulthuan. I am no expert on these things but I have heard it from the lips of those whose business it is to know.'

Tyrion's heart leapt. He could think of nothing he would like more than to learn how to be a warrior under Korhien's tutelage. Prince Arathion smiled, seeing the happiness written on his sons' faces.

'I shall miss you both,' he said. 'Having you both here has been the light of my life.'

The twins were both too excited to notice the sadness in his voice although Tyrion was to remember it well in years to come.

'We shall miss you too,' he said with all the sincerity of a youth of sixteen who sees only excitement and good fortune ahead of him.

'I bid you both good night,' said their father and returned to his workroom. The light burned there long into the night.

'Lothern,' said Teclis as if he could not quite believe the word. 'It's not Hoeth, but it's a start. It has one of the greatest libraries in all Eataine. And Inglorion Starweaver and Khaladris have mansions there.'

'The Sea Guard are there,' said Tyrion. 'Perhaps I will be able to find a place in one of the regiments. Who knows some day I might even become one of the White Lions, if the opportunity to win glory presents itself.'

Teclis looked as happy as Tyrion could ever remember him being. 'At last, I will have my chance to see a bit of the world before...'

He did not finish his sentence. He did not have to. Tyrion knew he was thinking about his illnesses and the possibility of death. That always lay over his brother like a shadow even when he was in his brightest moods.

'Maybe we will be able to get on a ship,' said Tyrion, playing to his brother's fantasies, 'and go to the Old World and the Kingdoms of Men.'

'Cathay and the Towers of Dawn,' said Teclis naming a place they both knew he would never see. Teclis laughed. He was happy and that was infectious. Tyrion could not remember the last time he had heard honest mirth from his brother. The laughter stopped as suddenly as it came.

'In truth, I will be happy just to see Lothern again,' he said. 'Just to see... there have been times when that seemed a wish beyond all fulfilling.'

'What do you think will become of us?' Tyrion asked, just as suddenly serious. He felt as if their lives had just come to some vast shadowy crossroads. It was like being a traveller lost in the dark in the mountains, who realises suddenly he is standing on the edge of a precipice with no idea how deep it is. Soon they would be leaving the only home they had ever known and voyaging to a land of strangers.

'I don't know,' said Teclis. 'But we will face it together.'

It came to him then that his brother was not as confident as he sounded, that he was seeking reassurance, as much as making a statement.

'Yes, we will,' Tyrion said, smiling. With the confidence of youth he could not imagine anything that could tear them apart. 'You will be a great wizard.'

'And you will be a great warrior.' Teclis sounded as sure as if he could see it with his own eyes.

Tyrion hoped he would live to do so.

It was almost time, N'Kari could feel it. The ancient spells were weakening. The terrible ghosts were weary. Something was happening. Somewhere far off at the very edges of this great net of magic, something was beginning to unravel. The world was changing once more. In recent centuries the flows of dark power had become ever stronger. Something was happening out there in the worlds beyond worlds, something that was drawing the forces of Chaos to this mudball planet once more.

Perhaps the ancient dormant gates in the Uttermost North were awakening. Perhaps it was merely the whim of the Powers that they would return to this place and amuse themselves for a time. It did not matter to N'Kari what it was. It was the results that counted for him.

He sniffed with nostrils that were not nostrils and drew tainted magic into lungs that were not lungs. He had waited in the centre of this web of power for thousands of years, keeping still, drawing no attention to himself, accumulating tiny amounts of magic whenever he could, when he knew that it would not draw attention to his presence.

He had become familiar with the strange lines of the spell, and the even stranger paths left by an ancient race that lay underneath them. It was obvious that the master wizards among the elves had known about the presence of the ancient ways beneath the fabric of time and space made by this world's original masters. They had incorporated elements of them into their grand design. It was both a strength and a weakness.

The strength lay in the fact that they could tap into the energy wells of the Old Ones, use their ancient grids to strengthen their own magic.

The weakness lay in the fact that the Paths of the Old Ones were corrupt and slowly unravelling and letting elements of the Realms of Chaos, the Daemon Realms in which N'Kari had been spawned, seep into them.

N'Kari had fed on that corrupted energy and regained a small fraction of his original strength. In a sense he had done the elves a favour he had never intended. He had helped maintain their construct by consuming a great deal of the Chaotic magical energy seeping into it. He had helped lessen the corruption of the ancient spell although he was sure that the ghostly wizards would not see things that way.

He had projected his consciousness to various points along the interstices of the Vortex where the waystones stood. He had mapped the whole huge system. He knew it as well or perhaps better than any of the elf wizards did. He knew where it was strong and where the protective spells held good. He knew where it was weak and the ancient defences were crumbling.

He moved a part of his mind now to the area he had selected. It was a waystone that looked out from a mountain top down into a hidden valley. It was a long way from anywhere inhabited on Ulthuan and no one had come to it for many centuries to perform the rites that would strengthen it.

The waystone itself was crumbling. Lichen had grown in the channels of the carved runes, despite the spells that should have prevented its growth and burned it away. The very pattern of the stone was eroded by wind and weather and that was important, for the shape of the stone was as much a part of the spell as the flows of magical energy around it, or the runes chiselled into it. Every aspect had been part of its design, every element contributed something to what it did.

Now it was like a rusty nail from which a heavy picture hung. It was slowly bending and slipping from its original position and it would not hold for much longer. All it would take would be for something to give it a nudge, to apply a little bit of extra pressure and that part of the spell would collapse. The barriers that contained the vast energies of the Vortex would be punctured. Things could get into it, and, more importantly from N'Kari's point of view, things could get out of it.

He knew he would have to be careful. The ghosts still watched over their handiwork and would repair it where they could. They would notice the collapse of any small part of it and if they thought any sentient entity was behind it, particularly any entity trapped within their realm, they would destroy it.

The Greater Daemon knew there would be only one chance to do what needed to be done. At best if it failed it would mean spending many more centuries acquiring the energy for another attempt at escape.

At worst it would mean complete and utter destruction. N'Kari knew that if the patterns of energy that made up his consciousness within the Vortex were destroyed, he would be destroyed forever. He had no physical form to anchor him and his connection to the Realms of Chaos was still blocked by the intricate wards of the Vortex.

He was only going to get one chance. He had better do it right. He shifted the focus of his consciousness to the furthest extent that he could, somewhere out in the deep ocean of the lands that had once been part of Ulthuan but had now sank beneath the waves.

Overhead he sensed a storm being born. He measured the vast swirls of air, the huge pattern of wind and moisture and energy that was waiting to be unleashed, and he reached out as subtly as he could from within the Vortex, feeding it dark energies, setting up currents and systems that would drive it in a certain direction.

The storm began to move inland, gaining energy as it went, driven from within by elementals of dark magic that steered it towards the distant mountain top.

Soon, thought N'Kari. Soon.

CHAPTER SIX

Eastern Ulthuan, 10th Year of the Reign of Finubar

Tyrion could smell the sea. The air tasted different; saltier, fresher. The wind was cooler and damper. Gulls drifted overhead. Just the sound of it and the sight of the white birds made him smile. He felt as happy as he ever had in his life.

He was mounted on a horse. He was riding down from the mountains and, within hours, he would catch a ship to the greatest city in Elvendom. He felt in some ways as if his life had finally begun.

As soon as the thought struck him, he felt guilty about his father and about his brother. He rode back along the small column to where Teclis lay stretched out on a bolster in the back of a wagon. The tented canvas cover of the wagon was drawn back and his twin lay looking up at the sky. They had hired it from one of the villagers who dwelled near his father's villa and used it for taking his produce into town to market. The elf would come into town in a few days and collect it.

'Isn't this wonderful?' Tyrion said, unable to contain his enthusiasm.

'If you can call having your bones jarred on this wooden instrument of torture wonderful then I suppose it is,' Teclis said. He was smiling though and he looked better than he had in months. Tyrion had worried that the hardships of travel might finish off his brother but the potions Lady Malene had brewed really seemed to have improved his health. More than that, the prospect of travel and of learning magic seemed to have eased his troubled spirit and made life more endurable for him. Tyrion suspected it had given Teclis a reason to live. He felt grateful to Lady Malene for that at least.

He glanced ahead. The sorceress was riding side by side with Korhien Ironglaive. The two of them exchanged secret smiles but there was nothing sinister in them. They looked like the lovers which Tyrion supposed they were. It was hard to imagine what the open-handed and hearted warrior and the stony-faced mage-woman saw in each other, but they obviously saw something.

Tyrion wondered how Father was getting on. He was not concerned for his welfare. Prince Arathion was quite capable of looking after himself without any help from his sons and his work would keep him from being lonely. It was just strange to think of him wandering about the empty villa with only Thornberry for company.

It made Tyrion uneasy. Sometimes monsters came down out of the mountains. Maybe one of them could get over the wall. He told himself not to be foolish. His father was a mage. He was capable of handling any monster that might find its way down to their home.

Teclis had raised himself up on one elbow and was looking over the side of the wagon into the distance. 'I think I see the sea,' he said. Tyrion followed his pointing finger. They had just crested the brow of a hill and below them there was indeed a wide slice of shimmering blue starting where the green land ended.

The land was starting to change around them. It looked much more heavily cultivated and they had passed the fields worked by yeomen and many glasshouses where enchanted fruits were grown in magically controlled environments.

It was the richest and most fertile place Tyrion knew although he would have been the first to admit that his experience of such places was limited. Here and there on the higher grounds were mansions of such a scale that their father's house could be easily fitted into one wing. Indeed, it seemed little better than some of the yeomen's cottages they had passed. Tyrion was used to his father being the richest property owner in the area where he had grown up. Once again, he realised now that compared to the elves of even this small town, his father was very poor indeed. It was odd to realise how small his life had been and how large the world was. Exciting too.

On many of the buildings green paper-lanterns hung outside windows or on verandas. People were beginning to prepare for the Feast of Deliverance, the great festival that celebrated the return of spring and the saving of Aenarion's children from the forces of Chaos by the Treeman Oakheart. Alongside the streets stood little carved models of the Treeman, a creature that looked like a friendly cross between an elf and a massive oak. All elves had reason to be grateful to him. Without his intervention, there would be no Everqueen. Every spiritual leader of the elves since that time had been descended from Aenarion's daughter, Yvraine. Tyrion had a more personal reason to be grateful. He was descended from Aenarion's son, Morelion.

He rode back to where Teclis lay. His brother grimaced. He was tired and the strain of the long day's ride showed in his face. 'We will be in town soon and aboard ship after that.'

'I look forward to it,' said Teclis. 'I can't imagine anything could be worse than this.'

A few fishing boats rode at anchor in the harbour along with a vessel that dwarfed them like a whale alongside dolphins. It was an elven clipper, part trading vessel, part warship, long and sleek and three-masted. It had a huge eagle head carved on the prow. There was a massive ballista on the aft deck and near the prow. Sailors swarmed through the rigging and moved across the deck with purpose. A set of planks had been laid from the midships to the pier, wide enough for horses to be led up.

The messenger bird Lady Malene had sent must have got through for they were expected. The ship's mistress waited at the docks to greet them. Much to Tyrion's surprise she reported to Lady Malene and not to Korhien; she seemed to find the enchantress a much more important figure than the White Lion. The flags fluttering from the ship's masts bore the same device as the bodyguard wore on their tabards. House Emeraldsea owned this ship and the lady was the highest ranking representative of the House present.

'Are we ready to depart, Captain Joyelle?' Malene asked. She cocked her head to one side and sniffed the air. 'I smell a storm coming in and there is magic on its winds.'

The ship's mistress nodded. She was even taller than Lady Malene and if anything looked sterner. Tyrion was starting to wonder if all the women of Lothern were so hard-faced when he noticed some of the female sailors were staring at him. They were younger and much prettier. As was his habit, he smiled back. Some of them met his gaze boldly. Others looked away shyly. It seemed that sailor women were not so different from the hunter-girls of the hills with whom he had experience.

'The *Eagle of Lothern* is ready to sail, Lady Malene. We can catch the tide if Captain Korhien and his men can get their horses aboard quickly.'

The horses looked restive. They had obviously been aboard ship before and had not much enjoyed the experience but they were elven steeds and they obeyed their riders. One by one they allowed themselves to be led up the gangplanks and lowered by a small winch into the hold. It seemed that all had been made ready for them, for the mangers were full of fodder and the act of eating seemed to settle the beasts.

Tyrion noticed that the captain too was staring at him as he helped Teclis up the ramp. At first he thought he had committed some sort of faux pas by not asking permission to board. No one else had, but presumably they were already known to the ship's mistress. Then the thought crossed his mind that perhaps she was unsettled by the sight of Teclis. His brother's infirmity often had that effect on his fellow elves. They were not used to the sight of illness. When he glanced back the captain had stopped staring and said something to Lady Malene in a low voice.

The mage nodded agreement and then walked over to them.

'The captain has had cabins assigned to you.'

'What else was she saying?'

'Nothing of any great importance,' said Lady Malene, a little too casually. Tyrion remembered Teclis's suspicions about her. He thought about the upcoming voyage. How many people would notice anything or say anything if they were to vanish over the side during the voyage south to Lothern? He told himself not to be so suspicious. There was almost certainly an innocent explanation for the mage's attitude.

Nonetheless, he resolved that he would keep his eyes open and the door barred. Despite his fears he could not keep his heart from soaring when the ship raised anchor and headed out of port a couple of hours later. The sun was sinking behind the mountains, and he could not help but think about his father once more.

He wondered if any of those tiny lights on the mountainside belonged to their home and he wondered how long it would be before he saw it again.

'This is cosy,' said Teclis. He looked around the cabin thoughtfully. It was tiny, like all such chambers on ships. There was just room enough for a couple of narrow bunk beds and a couple of sea chests. Between them the twins did not have enough to fill even one. There was a tiny porthole that let in some moonlight.

'Two of the junior officers gave this up so we would have a place to sleep, or so Korhien told me,' Tyrion said. 'It seems we are honoured guests. The rightful owners are sleeping on the deck.'

'I am not sure that I would rather not be there myself,' said Teclis. He did not sound too good.

'Are you all right?' Tyrion asked looking closer. His brother looked sick again. He had gone a nasty shade of green.

'I have not felt right since I got aboard this accursed vessel. There's something about the way it sways that makes me feel very uncomfortable.'

'Seasickness,' said Tyrion. 'I've heard some people get it.'

'And I am one of them, and you are not. What a surprise! Normally I am so healthy and you are so feeble!'

'If you don't like it here, I can ask for us to be allowed to sleep on deck. This is more sheltered if rough weather comes though.'

'Isha's blessing – don't talk to me about rough weather. This is bad enough.'

'It should only be for a few days, if we get decent winds, and there's no reason we should not. Apparently they blow southerly at this time of year.'

'You are becoming quite the sailor, brother.'

'I've been listening to the sailors. I intend to learn what I can on this voyage. You never know when it might come in useful.'

'My plan involves lying on my back here and hoping my stomach settles and the room stops spinning.'

'I think they call this a cabin.'

'They can call it what they like as long as it stops moving!'

Tyrion sprang into the upper bunk. The ceiling seemed very close above his head. It felt odd just to be lying there, with the boat gently rocking up and down as it moved. Aside from his nights camping with the hunters, he had never spent the night away from their father's villa before. This was the first time he had ever slept in an actual bed that was not his own. The strangest thought of all was that even as he lay there, he was getting further and further away from home and closer and closer to Lothern, a city they had not seen since they were very small children.

It occurred to him then that this was what made ships such a swift way to travel. A boat did not move any faster than a horse, really. It could just keep on moving through the night if it needed to as long as there was someone on watch. Ships never got tired and they kept steadily moving towards their goal.

He was thinking that there was a lesson to be learned from this somewhere, when he drifted off to sleep.

Tyrion was woken by the rays of the sun beaming in through the cabin window and the sound of Teclis being noisily sick into the bucket beside his bunk. The smell was overpowering in this tiny cabin.

He lowered himself from the top bunk, being careful to avoid landing with his foot in the bucket. He waited for Teclis to finish and then tossed the contents out through the porthole. It took him a fair bit of time to unscrew the handles that held it in place, and he decided to leave it open to let the stink escape.

'I was thinking that perhaps I should try flying next,' said Teclis. 'My head will probably fall off. Every mode of transportation I have tried so far has been worse than the last.'

'You will get used to this. It might take a few days but your body will get over it.'

'I sincerely hope so.'

'You want to take a turn on deck and see if perhaps we can find some breakfast?'

'A walk on deck, yes. Breakfast? What daemon possessed you to suggest such an infernal torture?'

'Well I am hungry.'

'And doubtless, as always, you will eat enough for the both of us.'

'I will try, if I can find some food.'

He helped Teclis up onto the deck. Many of the crew were already up and about. They worked away, scrubbing and sanding the planking and coiling ropes. They clambered over the rigging, making adjustments to the sails on the orders of the ship's officers. One of them sat in the crow's nest, another stood watch by the great figurehead on the prow. It seemed like the seas around a ship took a great deal of watching.

As they came up out of the stairwell, Tyrion was aware that they were being stared at again. It was not just Teclis who was attracting the looks either, it was him. It made him feel uncomfortable even though he made a point of smiling at everyone when he caught their eye. He was used to being looked at by women but the males were giving him odd looks too.

He looked around for Korhien or Malene but neither were visible. One or two of the soldiers were on deck, sharpening their weapons and chatting casually and trying hard not to look completely idle amid this bustling hive of activity.

'Where can we get something to eat?' Tyrion asked. One of the soldiers jerked his thumb in the direction of a small chamber behind him. Tyrion saw a firepit and a cauldron bubbling away within.

'I might have known you would be close to where the food was,' said Tyrion.

'Spoken like an old campaigner,' said the elf. 'We will make a soldier out of you yet.'

'I hope so,' said Tyrion.

Tyrion entered the ship's cookhouse. 'Could we have something to eat?' he asked. 'Please.'

The cook smiled and tossed him two bowls and a package of ship's biscuits wrapped in a large leaf. Tyrion held out the bowls and the cook ladled out some form of spicy fish stew into them. Tyrion handed one bowl to Teclis and took the other for himself and they made their way back onto the deck.

Tyrion was surprised to find the stew was good, and that the biscuit was nutritious and filling.

'There is some sort of enchantment in it,' said Teclis. 'Like with waybread.'

'I suppose they need to keep the crew fit,' said Tyrion. 'You want yours?'

'I don't feel like eating.'

'Take the soup, at least. I would not want you dying of starvation before we get to Lothern.'

'It would be a mercy,' said Teclis.

'Don't even joke about it.'

One of the sailor girls was watching them closely. Tyrion smiled at her. She smiled back and then looked away shyly. She was the prettiest girl on the ship for sure.

'I see you are going to be breaking hearts again,' said Teclis. Tyrion had shared some of the details of his experiences with the hunter-girls with his brother.

'Such is never my intention,' Tyrion replied.

'The gap between intention and consequence is as large as that between heaven and hell,' said Teclis.

'Who are you quoting now?'

'No one. I just made that up.'

'Are you contemplating a career as a philosopher then?'

'It would be useful to have something to fall back on if I fail as a mage.'

'I doubt that is going to happen.'

'You never know. My life has not been conspicuous for its successes so far.'

The twins stood on the deck for a long time, watching the life of the ship around them. Tyrion found it all infinitely fascinating. Teclis seemed to find it just tiring.

CHAPTER SEVEN

Tyrion stood on the prow of the great ship, staring out over the bird of prey's head carved there. A school of flying fish erupted from the water nearby. The sight of them flickering silver in the sunlight before they vanished once more beneath the waves made him smile.

The wind filled the sails and the vessel seemed almost to skim over the sea. Green flags with the insignia of House Emeraldsea fluttered in the wind.

Sailors leapt from mast to mast and clambered over the rigging in response to commands given by the ship's mistress. To Tyrion, it was all incomprehensible and all very exciting. So far he had loved every moment of it. He liked the feel of the hard wooden deck beneath his bare feet. He liked the salt smell of the sea.

Laughing, he leapt up and caught a cable, and pulled himself up to a crossbar. When he had first started doing this the ship's officers had been worried that he might fall and break his neck but it had swiftly become obvious that he was far more at home in the rigging than most sailors and far more agile than any of them.

None of the sailors objected as long as he did not get in their way. He clambered all the way to the crow's nest high atop the second mast. The figures on deck looked tiny beneath him. It felt far more exposed than being atop a hill of similar height. For one thing, hills did not sway with the movement of a ship.

The wind tugged at his linen shirt. Gulls perched just out of reach. He swung himself out onto the spar and then ran out along it to where the gulls sat. Seeing him coming, they fluttered away, circling over the ship, cawing mockingly at him. He wished that he could fly so that he could follow them.

He shaded his eyes with his hand and glanced off into the distance. Huge shapes moved beneath the clear water, perhaps whales, perhaps some of the legendary monsters that were said to haunt this part of the sea. So far none of them had paid any attention to the ship, for which he was grateful.

Some leagues away he sometimes thought he could see islands. Sometimes they were there. Sometimes not. A faint shimmering covered the waves, as far as he could see. It resembled a heat haze but it was not. To his eyes it looked tinged with magic, more than that he could not say.

Far below him, Teclis waved. Tyrion leapt out into space, grabbed a dangling rope and slid down it with dizzying speed, laughing aloud until his feet hit the deck. He sprang forward exuberantly, performed a handspring and landed upright beside his brother.

'What were you looking for?' Teclis asked. He lounged on a wicker deckchair, looking even sicker than usual. Despite all the good Lady Malene's potions had done him, the voyage did not agree with him. He still suffered from seasickness worse than any dwarf.

'I don't know,' Tyrion replied. 'But whatever it is I think I will have trouble finding it. There is some enchantment on these waters, stronger than the glamour that covers the Annulii.'

Teclis laughed at him. 'Perceptive as ever, brother. You are looking on the effects of one of the most potent and far-reaching spells ever cast. Bel-Hathor and his mages wove magic here to hide Ulthuan from the humans. Believe me, any confusion you are feeling would be increased a thousand-fold if you were one of them. When they enter the weave of this spell they get lost and turned around by a labyrinth of spells and eventually, if they do not starve, or run aground, they find themselves back out on the open ocean.'

'I believe you.'

'Good. You ought to.' He made a face and for a moment looked as if he was going to be sick again. Somehow he controlled the impulse. 'By all the gods, I hate this.'

'You are not enjoying this voyage?' They had been at sea two days now, and Tyrion was growing concerned about his twin's health. His seasickness had not improved over the long days of their sailing. The smell of stale vomit hung constantly over their cabin. They spent a good deal of time on deck, as they were doing now.

'Let us say I cannot wait to begin my magical studies so that I can learn a charm against seasickness,' Teclis responded.

'I am astounded by your towering ambition. It is nice to know I have a brother who aims so high in life. Seven thousand years of elf magic to learn from and the biggest thing driving you to master this ancient and terrible lore is your desire to avoid seasickness.'

'If you had been as sick for as long as I have you would understand why I feel that way. Lady Malene's potions had only just helped me get over my last illness.'

Tyrion immediately felt guilty about his joking manner. He had never endured a moment's illness in his life. Seasickness did not affect him in the slightest nor had he expected it to.

For Teclis things were different. Perhaps they always would be. He himself had spent most of the voyage learning the ways of the sea from sailors who looked at him as if he were a young god when they were not giving him superstitious looks. Teclis had spent his daytime sleeping on deck, trying to keep from vomiting and being looked down on by everyone who passed him, save the few among Korhien's riders who also suffered from the same malady.

'You always wanted to go on a ship,' he said eventually.

'I still do,' Teclis responded. 'But only once I have achieved immunity to this vile plague. In the few brief instants I have not been heaving what I have eaten over the sides I have greatly enjoyed this voyage.'

'Do you think we will see pirates?'

'I was just starting to feel better. Why did you have to say that?'

'Because I have heard stories that these are dangerous waters, full of Norse raiders and human pirates and dark elf sea marauders despite all the spells that are supposed to keep them out. We might meet some that have gotten lost.'

'This might seem like an adventure to you, Tyrion, but what I am I supposed to do if we are attacked by pirates – be sick all over them?'

'That might prove to be a very effective defensive strategy.'

'There are times when I doubt that you understand military matters quite as well as you pretend you do.'

'Don't worry. If we are attacked, I will protect you.'

'And who is going to protect you?'

'I think I can manage to protect myself, brother. Never doubt it.'

'Look over there.' Tyrion followed his brother's gesture. Korhien and Lady Malene strolled hand in hand across the deck towards them. It seemed Tyrion was not the only one enjoying this sea voyage.

'Greetings, young princes,' said Korhien, sounding more than usually amiable.

'Good afternoon to you both,' said Teclis.

'It is,' said Lady Malene. 'There is something to be said for the fresh sea air, I always find.' She looked at Korhien as if sharing some secret joke. Korhien smiled.

'It is invigorating,' he said.

'I find it so,' said Tyrion, wondering why the two of them looked as if they wanted to laugh at him. They had just spent a long time in their cabin below. They had not been enjoying a lot of the fresh sea air. Suddenly he realised what they had been up to and looked away.

'This is a wonderful ship,' said Teclis. 'Very fast.'

'It is one of many House Emeraldsea owns,' said Lady Malene.

'How many?' Teclis asked. He always liked to pin things down exactly.

'Thirty or so. They sail and they trade and explore. Sometimes we use them to raid the coast of Naggaroth.'

'Thirty ships, is that a lot?' Tyrion asked.

'It is,' said Korhien. 'A significant contribution to our fleets in wartime. There are very few Houses in Lothern who can match that number and only Finubar's House exceeds it.'

'Well, he is the Phoenix King,' said Teclis.

'We were just talking about pirates,' said Tyrion. 'Do you think we shall see any?' 'My brother is keen to try his hand at fighting them,' said Teclis sardonically.

'There is no need to worry my young friend,' said Korhien. 'If we are attacked, Lady Malene will protect us.'

'She will?' said Tyrion.

'Oh yes, like many a mage of Lothern she started her career of wizardry aboard ship.'

'Is that true?' asked Teclis. As ever, mention of any aspect of magic got his attention instantly.

Lady Malene nodded. 'Most mages of Lothern spend half their lives aboard ship.'

'Why?' Teclis asked.

'Summoning winds, protecting them from monsters, blasting enemy ships with spells when the need arises and preventing enemy wizards doing the same to our vessels.'

To Tyrion that sounded like just about the most exciting use of wizardry he had ever heard. It almost made him want to study it himself, despite his total lack of any gift for the Art. 'You can summon winds?' he asked.

'Yes.'

'Why not do it now?'

'Because there is no need,' Malene replied. 'We have a fair wind driving us as fast as we can sail naturally, and I see no need to tire myself out to make us go faster. If any pirates do show up, I will need my strength for then.'

Tyrion saw it at once, 'Of course,' he said.

'Of course, what?' Teclis asked.

'Better to bind the winds then than for travel. With a mage aboard capable of doing so we could sail against the wind, or increase our manoeuvre speed.'

Korhien beamed like a teacher proud of a prize pupil. 'I told you he was quick on the uptake,' he said to Lady Malene.

'Show my brother the military possibilities of anything and he grasps it instantly,' said Teclis. 'Unfortunately he is not so quick on the uptake for anything else.'

'He is quick about all he will need to be quick for,' said Korhien. 'Nothing more need be asked of him.'

'I would not be so quick to make such statements if I were you,' said Lady Malene. 'Who knows what Prince Tyrion's destiny will require of him?'

Tyrion laughed. 'I doubt it will be anything too exalted.'

The others looked at him as if they did not believe that. He noticed the pretty young sailor girl had been listening to all of this from nearby. She looked away when she saw him notice her. He wondered if she was really as shy as she pretended or whether this was simply a way of getting his attention.

He resolved that before the day was much older, he would find out.

'What is this called?' Tyrion asked, pointing to the large sail above them.

The sailor girl smiled. They stood alone high on the central mast of the ship, perfectly balanced as was the way of elves. They swayed slightly with the motion of the ship, but both of them were perfectly at ease, as if they were standing on dry ground, not above a drop that would shatter their bodies if they were to accidentally fall to the deck sixty feet below.

'This is the topsail,' she said.

'And what are you called?'

'Karaya.'

'I am Tyrion.'

'You are Prince Tyrion,' she said. 'You are the nephew of Lady

Malene. We were sent all this way to pick you up. You must be a personage of some importance.'

'Really?'

'A trading Eagle is not normally dispatched to a small fishing port in Cothique for matters of no consequence. We should be sailing to the Old World or Cathay. Instead, we are off the coast of Ulth-uan carrying a cargo of warriors and horses.'

'I had not realised I was so valuable,' said Tyrion.

The girl smiled at him. 'House Emeraldsea thinks so.'

'You have a pretty smile,' he said.

'And you have strange and lovely eyes,' she said. He found the intensity of her look somewhat disturbing. It reminded him of a question he had been wanting to ask for a while.

'Why does everyone look at me so oddly?' he asked. The girl looked startled. It was obviously not what she had been expecting him to say. The mood of the moment was broken.

'You really don't know?'

Tyrion shook his head.

'I hate to strike such a blow to your vanity but it is not just because they are overwhelmed by your sheer physical beauty.'

'I do find that hard to believe,' said Tyrion.

Karaya smiled.

'It's because you look like a statue.'

'Are we talking about my chiselled good looks?'

'No. We are talking about the fact that you look like the statue of Aenarion in Lothern harbour. That's why the whole crew spend so much time staring at you.'

'No!'

'Yes. The resemblance is uncanny.'

'You mean aside from the fact that the statue is six hundred feet tall and I am not.'

'You will have a chance to judge for yourself soon. We will arrive in Lothern in the next few days if the winds are fair.'

Tyrion noticed dark clouds gathering in the distance. He won-dered if a storm was coming in.

From below an officer bellowed an order and Karaya jumped to obey.

'Perhaps we can continue this discussion later,' said Tyrion.

'Perhaps,' the sailor girl replied. 'There are other things I would like to discuss too.'

* * *

N'Kari felt his storm being birthed. He felt like howling with glee. The first part of his plan was under way. The weather was shaped to his will. Now he needed to make sure the other elements were in place.

Carefully, with infinite patience, he extruded tiny filaments of himself through the waystones. He was not yet powerful enough to break out physically but he could send out a message to every elf with even the slightest sensitivity to such things and blend their dreams with his own. He would prepare the world for his coming and make sure the first recruits were ready for his army.

Mages across the face of the world would sense something, for their gift would make them sensitive to his magic. That would not be such a bad thing. Some of them would provide him with excellent recruits.

He invoked the name of Slaanesh and sent thistledown splinters of dream out from the waystones into the night. Borne by the winds of magic, they floated over Ulthuan and touched the dreams of those they were drawn to.

In southern Cothique, a group of orgiastic cultists were touched by magic. As they lay naked and spent from their ritual lovemaking, they felt an odd desire enter their minds, to go to a certain place at a certain time and make themselves ready for the rise of a new prophet who was about to enter their world.

In the Shadowlands, a group of dark elf infiltrators learned that if they headed eastwards, they would find something of great use to their master. It seemed to them that Morathi herself had appeared naked in their dreams with the instructions and promised them the ultimate reward of her person if they obeyed.

In Saphery, an archmage who had long dabbled in the ways of the Dark Prince of Pleasure dreamed that he would learn a great secret if he ventured to the western waystone of the realm.

In Lothern, the greatest assassin in the world dreamed of rebellion against his master and a life of luxury among the enemies he had been raised to hate. He woke beside the sleeping wife of a friend and covered his stolen eyes with a hand covered in the flayed skin of elves.

All across Ulthuan, the dreams of wizards and the sensitive were troubled, and visions entered their mind that carried the promise and the threat of the power of Slaanesh's greatest follower.

Teclis hauled his painful way up onto the deck, one shoulder rising, the other falling with every step. It was dark. The night sky was full of stars and the beams of the moon fell on his face. The sound of the waves lapping against the sides of the ship was oddly relaxing. The wind was cool on his skin. At night, he felt stronger, and he suffered the seasickness less. He felt more able to limp around and less self-conscious about his infirmity with most of the crew save for the nightwatch and the officer in charge asleep.

His dreams had been dark, troubled things, full of images of walls closing in and four-armed daemons stalking innocent elves and flaying them alive while they screamed in what might have been agony or ecstasy or some combination of both. In any case, the image was disturbing enough to make him want to leave the little cabin and come up into the fresh air.

There was a splash and a plopping sound and he saw something silver wriggling on the deck in front of him. At first, he was startled and a little scared but he saw it was a flying fish. It had leapt from the water and was now spasming on the deck as if drowning in air. He felt a stab of sympathy. He knew what that felt like. He lifted the fish, ignoring the slimy wriggling between his fingers, limped to the edge of the deck and dropped it back over the side into the ocean.

He looked out onto the black waters and saw the moon reflected in them. He saw his own reflection as a shadowy, broken outline in the rippling waves. It made him look even more ill-made than usual.

He heard someone moving behind him and turned to see the girl who was always following Tyrion about. He smiled at her. She looked at him oddly for a moment, and he thought she was going to speak but she walked away, unwilling to meet his gaze, receding into the night.

He turned away himself so as not to show his hurt. He schooled his features to cold composure and told himself he did not care anyway. It was a hard thing to be ugly and a cripple among the elves. They did not like to look upon things less beautiful and less perfect than themselves. In his father's villa, with only his family and Thornberry, he had been shielded from that, but he was starting to realise how isolated his life was going to be among what were supposedly his own people. He wondered for a moment whether that was why his father had retreated there.

Tyrion was going to have it easier now. He was good-looking even among elves and he was good-natured, easy going and charming. His sunny disposition would always win him friends and admirers.

What is going to become of us, he asked the Moon Goddess. What is going to become of me? There was no answer. The waves rolled on. The sea was empty, a vast dark mirror to the sky.

It was a long time before he slept and, once again, his dreams were dark.

The wind grew stronger, ruffling Tyrion's hair with invisible fingers and making the sails crack as they fluttered. The sea was choppier, white caps of foam appearing atop waves that grew larger and larger. The ship rose and fell more as it cut into them. From the east, purple clouds streamed across the sky, covering the sun and overhauling the ship with surprising swiftness.

Tyrion watched with interest. The sailors reacted with practised discipline, tying things down, making sure everything was in place. In the hold, one of the horses whinnied in fear, catching something in the air. The rest of the steeds became uneasy. Tyrion could hear them moving restlessly. One by one the soldiers went down into the hold and began to whisper softly to their animals, calming them.

Slowly it dawned on Tyrion that there really might be something to be uneasy about. The wind was blowing ever more strongly. The gulls perched on the masts were taking to the air. The *Eagle of Lothern* turned slightly, setting a new course towards the coast. Tyrion was no sailor but he wondered at the wisdom of this. A storm might drive them onto the rocks, run them aground, break the ship up.

'What is going on?' he asked Korhien. The White Lion stood near him on the prow of the ship watching the onrushing clouds. He turned to face Tyrion, stretched ostentatiously as an elf without a care in the world. He looked as if he was contemplating simulating a yawn.

'Big storm coming in. The captain is looking for a safe harbourage although I doubt she will find one on this stretch of coast.'

'Is that wise? Might we not run aground?'

'Your guess is as good as mine. I am just going with what Lady Malene told me. I think it's because you are here. Normally they would run before the storm but they don't want to take any chances with the Blood of Aenarion being onboard.'

Tyrion was not sure whether Korhien meant they were not tak-ing any chances because they valued the lives of himself and Teclis or whether they feared the curse. Perhaps it was a little of both.

'What should we do?' Tyrion asked. Korhien laughed.

'Not a lot we can do, doorkeeper. Neither of us are sailors. We can offer up a prayer to the sea gods and trust in the fact that the cap-tain knows what she is doing.'

Tyrion smiled.

'You don't look too worried, doorkeeper.'

'I wanted to find adventure. It looks like adventure has found me.'

'You have a good attitude. Let's hope that your first adventure is not your last.'

'I am going below to check on my brother,' Tyrion said.

'I think I had better close the window,' said Tyrion. Huge waves were already splattering against the side of the vessel and water was sopping onto the floor. He was very conscious of the *swoosh* of the sea against the hull.

'I think you will find that sailors call it a porthole,' said Teclis. 'They can get very sniffy if you call it a window.' He mimicked the tone with which Tyrion had earlier explained the ways of sailors to him with uncanny accuracy. It was a gift he had.

'Window, porthole, big round thing with bullseye glass panes – whatever it's called I had better close it.' Tyrion wrestled with the handles. The wetness was making them slippery and the increased motion of the ship was making it difficult to force the porthole into place. Eventually he managed to. Turning, he noticed Karaya stand-ing in the door.

'I was just sent down below to make sure the porthole was closed,' she said. 'Glad to see it is.'

Tyrion nodded and she ran off up the stairs again. Teclis lay on his bed. His face looked strained and Tyrion could tell he was doing his best not to moan.

'Spit it out,' he said. 'You know you want to.'

'I suspect the gods have found a new way to torture me. This is worse than normal seasickness – which is quite a feat.'

'You are not in the least green. And you are not throwing up.'

'That is because I am too frightened to.'

'Really?'

'Not everyone is so stupid that they feel no fear.'

'You are afraid?'

'Terrified.' Tyrion wondered why he almost never sensed his brother's emotions when he was close enough to see him. Was it because he did not need to know them then?

'What are you afraid of, brother? Getting wet?'

'Where do I start? Sinking? Being struck by lightning? Running aground? Being attacked by a maddened sea monster?'

'Why not all of them at once?'

'Why do I feel that you are not taking my distress entirely seriously?'

'We are safe, brother. The crew have been through these storms a thousand times. This ship was built to endure these things.'

'Ships still sink, brother, despite the best intentions of their builders. Crews make mistakes. Monsters get hungry.'

Tyrion shrugged. 'There is nothing I can do about any of these things.'

'You know how to swim.' Tyrion felt like telling him that under the circumstances that would not make too much difference. He doubted anything could live in a sea like this if the ship went down. Saying that would not improve his brother's mood though.

'Don't worry if the ship goes down, I will save you.'

'How? We will both be stuck in this cabin. The ship will be a coffin for both of us.' Now Tyrion sensed Teclis's fear. It was becoming so intense his own heart was starting to pound. He was feeling a little uncomfortable. Normally nothing much frightened him. It was not part of his nature to let fear rule him. He had never really experienced anything like the terrors he had read about in books save as an echo of Teclis's fears.

'Would you be happier on deck?'

'I think I would.'

'It might be easier to be swept overboard.'

'We can rope ourselves to the railings, the way real sailors are supposed to.'

'You sure?'

'I would rather be above than trapped down here.' Tyrion understood. Spending your last few moments watching a small cabin fill with water would not be a good way to leave the world.

Tyrion helped his brother up the stairwell. He was not sure this was a very clever idea. He was confident he was sure-footed enough not to be swept away. He was not so sure about his twin. Teclis could barely walk at the best of times.

Nonetheless it appeared the decision had been made.

* * *

The rain splattered onto the deck, huge droplets hitting the wood and bouncing with a flicker that reminded Tyrion of miniature lightning bolts. White foam surged over the prow of the *Eagle of Lothern* and added to the slick wetness underfoot.

He left Teclis near the afterdeck and went to find some ropes. The sailors looked tense and ready for action, like soldiers getting ready before a battle. Their enemies were the sea and the storm. The officers bellowed last minute instructions. Down below the horses whinnied in panic and it struck Tyrion what a cruel trial this must be for them. How unnatural for creatures reared to race across an endless plain to be imprisoned within a bobbing wooden box as it was battered from all sides by mighty waves.

The ship rose and fell through the long swells. He swayed to keep his balance as he moved. He was surprised to see Lady Malene come on deck and ask permission to join the captain on the afterdeck. He was even more surprised when the officer beckoned for him and Teclis to come up and join them. Malene nodded to emphasise this and the twins went to join the officers. The wind had risen to a dull roar now. The waves smashed against the ship. The decks creaked. The sails boomed and cracked.

'If you are going to remain on deck, lash yourself to something,' said Lady Malene. He could see that she was already lashed to the railings. 'Particularly Teclis. We do not want to lose you overboard.'

He cinched his brother to a banister, making sure the knots were tight and in the style he had observed the sailors using, then he stalked across the deck, sure-footed as a big cat.

No one seemed to want to question them about why they had not stayed below. No one minded that they were on the aft-deck, the sacred space reserved for officers and mages. It seemed that on this ship at least they were regarded as personages of some importance.

Lightning flickered in the distance, and the sullen boom of thunder rippled in its wake. Somewhere down below a horse whinnied in terror and tried to kick its way out of a stall. A rider shouted words meant to be reassuring but which just sounded panicked.

Suddenly the rain intensified. Within heartbeats Tyrion was soaked to the skin and looking at everything as though through a thick, grey mist. The ship heeled to the right as it struck a wave at the wrong angle. The roll was disturbing, as if some great monster had risen from the sea beneath the ship and was trying to push it over. That was not an image he wanted in his head.

The captain yelled something to the steersman, who twisted the great wheel that guided the ship. In response to bellowed instructions, sailors overhead did something to the sails, Tyrion was not sure what. The vessel righted itself. The prow rose like a bucking horse. Tyrion felt himself begin to slide back down the deck. He looked around to make sure that Teclis was still held fast. His twin stood by the rail, clutching it as if it were the only thing that stood between him and watery death, and yet despite this, his gaze was riveted to Lady Malene.

Tyrion followed his look and understood why. An aura of power played around the sorceress, its nimbus visible even to Tyrion's sight. Tyrion was not sure what she could do against the unleashed fury of the storm, but he sensed enormous power pooling within her.

The rain lashed his face, and his eyes stung with salty tears. It was difficult to tell where the rain ended and the sea spray started. It was hard to remember that only a few minutes ago the waters had seemed relatively calm and he could see all the way to the horizon.

The ship's timbers creaked and groaned now and he realised that something, somewhere was putting the hull under enormous stress. The wind and the waves roared like angry daemons.

The worst of it was that he had no idea of how likely things were to go wrong. It seemed entirely possible to him that the whole ship could break in two at any instant, or that the power of the waves could swamp the vessel, filling the hold with water and sending them to the bottom like a stone.

He glanced at the captain and at Lady Malene and then at the rest of the officers. They looked tense but not worried and he decided that it would be best to take his cue from them.

Part of him realised that they were in the same position as him. Even if they knew the vessel was about to break up, it would do them no good to panic. It helped that they remained calm. The sense of authority radiating from them affected the crew, who went about their duties with a will. If the officers had seemed frightened, the crew might panic as well, and in that panic the whole ship could be lost.

There was a lesson in the duties of command here that was not lost on Tyrion. He filed it away in his memory for future reference, swearing that he would remember the demeanour of the captain and the mage if and when he was ever in a similar situation.

Lightning erupted in the sea in front of them, so brilliant that it was blinding. Someone, somewhere, screamed and Tyrion wondered whether the bolt had hit the ship. An instant later thunder bellowed like an angry god overhead. A huge gust of wind and a giant wave hit the ship simultaneously. Water crashed over the deck and surged towards Tyrion like a moving wall.

Despite the raging seas, despite the swaying deck, despite the lightning flare and the thunder roar, only one thing held Teclis's attention – Lady Malene. She had begun working magic almost as soon as the storm started, a slow, subtle weaving that most elves would never have spotted but which was obvious to Teclis with his peculiar sensitivity to the flows of power.

He watched, fascinated. He had never seen anyone work magic like this before. His father was a wizard, for sure, but his craft was the slow, subtle assembly of runes and flows of power that went into making and moulding things. It was rare he had ever seen his father do anything that was not directly connected with the armour of Aenarion, and even that was usually small, trivial stuff like the making of light or fire.

This was something of an entirely different order. He was not sure what Lady Malene was going to do but he was sure it was going to be something much greater than anything he had ever seen Prince Arathion cast.

Malene summoned more and more of the winds of magic to her. She pulled power from the very air surrounding her and moulded it with gentle, small motions of her hands and body.

Teclis watched, understanding instinctively what was happening. He was tempted to copy it the way a child copies the action of a parent but he was sufficiently conscious of what was happening to know that any interference on his part might prove disastrous. Instead he made himself watch and memorise, hoping that at some point in the future he might be able to recreate what she was doing.

As the storm intensified, Lady Malene wove her spells. Teclis moved as close as the ropes binding him to the ship's railings would allow so he could hear what she was saying over the howling of the wind. There was magic in the words and in her voice. They were laced with power and his magic-attuned senses caught what she was saying in a way his hearing alone never could have if she was merely speaking words.

He saw the relation between her words, her gestures and the flow of the winds of magic. She was the still centre and she was doing something that manipulated the forces around her. Something about her mind and her spirit anchored the whole structure of spellwork she was creating.

Even as he watched, she made a gesture like a fisherwoman casting a net, and a lattice of power, complex and tight, flew forth from her hands.

It enmeshed the *Eagle of Lothern*, bolstering its timbers and strengthening them against the storm, aiding it to cut through the water. The ship, which had been heeling before the wind, righted itself. The timbers creaked but held. He sensed that in some way Lady Malene was communing with the vessel. It was bound to her as she was bound to it.

An enormous wall of water smashed over the prow and raced towards them. Teclis saw Tyrion brace himself for impact. Lady Malene gestured and the waters parted in front of her, sloughing off over the afterdeck, leaving Tyrion standing a little bemused at being hit only by spray.

No sooner had she completed weaving that spell than she began another, summoning sentient vortices, forming the wind into air elementals, calming their anger and directing them about the ship as if they were a second crew. The sails billowed outwards but did not rip or tear or drive the ship down. Some of the elementals ran before the ship, shielding it from the worst buffeting of the storm; others gathered the fury of the wind and harnessed it, sending the vessel scudding along like a cloud over the angry sea.

Teclis was no longer frightened. He no longer worried that the ship would go down. He understood that Lady Malene was completely the mistress of the situation and as long as she remained so, the *Eagle of Lothern* was safe.

Here was something he understood, something he could do. This woman was capable of teaching him it. Chance or fate, whatever anyone might choose to call it, had placed her in his path and he was determined to make the most of the opportunity. For long hours he watched fascinated, as she as much as the captain and crew brought the ship through the worst of the storm.

As suddenly as it had come upon them, the storm passed, leaving the sea calming in its wake as it raced off inland towards the mountains where it could continue to wreak havoc. The ship continued to sail its course, moving on steadily towards its goal, the only sign it had ever been captured in the storm's embrace the pools of water left puddling on the deck.

Lady Malene looked a little tired but also triumphant. Perhaps the oddest thing and certainly the one that impressed itself most on Teclis in that moment was that, though everyone around her was soaked to the skin, she was absolutely dry. Neither the sea nor the storm seemed to have touched her.

'That was the worst storm I have seen in a long, long time,' said Captain Joyelle.

'Yes,' Malene said. 'And there was dark magic in it. I fear that it may serve some fell purpose before it is done.'

The captain nodded and was silent, unwilling to discuss the matter further.

Lady Malene turned and looked at Teclis knowingly. 'You saw all of that, didn't you?'

He nodded. 'It was very impressive.' The words were an understatement but they were all he could think to say. 'I have read about such things but I never thought to witness them.'

'You will witness far more impressive things before you are done, unless I miss my guess,' she said. 'Work them too.'

'I hope so,' he said. She smiled at him again and walked off the deck and down the stairs below. The looks of the captain told him that now she was gone, he and Tyrion were no longer welcome on the command deck either. He did not really care. He went below himself and for the first time in a long time, he did not feel sick.

The storm blew in from the east. It toppled trees and blew off roofs and hurled the seas around Ulthuan forwards in great churning waves. Enormous winds drove brutal, black thunderclouds before it. Savage rains poured down as if intending to drown the world.

The storm roared through the mountains of Ulthuan, passing over a carved stone so ancient it was crumbling. The runes on its face, despite their magical protections, were all but obscured by the millennia-long erosion of the elements.

As if tossed by the hand of a wicked god, a bolt of lightning surged down and struck the ancient waystone. Sparks flew and the stench of ozone and something else filled the air. Thunder roared and then died away and for a moment there was eerie silence. Then it seemed as if the thunder's growl was answered from deep within the earth.

The tip of the mountain shook. The ancient stone danced and then toppled. As it fell ancient spells became undone and things erupted outwards onto the mountain top, winged things that beat up into the stormy night, laughing and cackling.

A moment later a massive claw emerged, and then an arm, then a deformed bestial head and finally a monstrous androgynous body. Two additional arms pushed it from the ground.

N'Kari looked down from the mountain top for a long moment. He breathed air as he had not breathed it in six thousand years. He looked down the slopes of a great mountain illuminated by the hellish flicker of lightning. Overhead winged things soared and cackled on the storm winds. He raised one clenched fist in a gesture of triumph and defiance.

With his escape from the Vortex full cognisance of what he was and who he had been came crashing in on him. In the Vortex, he had been a pallid ghostly thing, his mind and memories dull, his passions shadowy, his desires weak and suppressed. Now that he had regained physical form once more, his emotions were stronger, as if they needed glands and hearts and blood and bone and organs to give them their full strength.

He remembered a great deal he had forgotten and felt once again the titanic towering passions that were his birthright.

He smiled, showing his fangs, and then with an impulse of his will changed his shape to something more resembling an elf, albeit one horned and fanged whose long nails were talons and whose eyes glowed like bloody fire.

In this world his will was constrained by foolish rules and the magic he worked would have to be done in accordance with them. So be it. The knowledge of what was necessary was instinctive to him. He could feel the constraints that hemmed him in in the way a man would feel walls surrounding him or the tug of gravity on his body. It took him mere moments to work out what was needed and then he inscribed a circle in the ground with his claw.

Now, he thought, I will take vengeance. It was time to locate his prey. He reached out with his mind and formed a vision of Aenarion as he had been at the height of his power.

He could recall the slightest detail of his foe and recollect him on a scale that was unimaginable to the weak minds of mortals. He remembered the exact pattern of Aenarion's spirit and the genetic markers that had flowed in his blood and which would flow in the blood of all of those descended from him.

As the lightning blasted the ground about him, he pricked the flesh of his hand with one of his talons. A drop of his magical blood flowed forth. He flipped it into the air and ignited it with a word. It became a mote of energy, a pulse of magic that he could shape to his will.

He imprinted the genetic rune that he remembered upon it and then summoned more magical energy. As he did so the original mote divided and replicated like an amoeba, again and again and again as more power flowed into it. Soon N'Kari was surrounded by clouds of tiny motes of light, swarming around him like fireflies. With another gesture he sent them racing away from him to seek out the ones he was looking for.

The motes flew across Ulthuan fast as sunbeams, seeking the few remaining possessors of the marks that N'Kari sought. They flashed around them invisibly and then hurtled back across the vast distances to their master.

As they returned, they swirled around him once more, each of them bearing an image of the being they had found. Visions of faces and places danced in his mind. He saw young women waiting to be married, wizards in their laboratories, princes in their palaces, a pair of twins little more than children riding aboard a ship. All of them bore the unmistakeable imprint of Aenarion's blood.

Now, N'Kari knew the locations of his prey and his tiny pets, following an invisible magical scent, would always be able to find them again.

He smiled to himself revealing very sharp fangs. One of those he was looking for dwelled not too far from here. It would not take him long to begin his revenge. Within the passing of a moon, he swore he would have wiped all of the line of Aenarion from the face of Ulthuan. He would make this world pay for all of the long millennia of his incarceration. He roared with the ecstasy of it.

He began work on another spell, one that would reach out to all those whose dreams he had touched and who were vulnerable to his influence. It would draw those he needed to him and it would let him sense their presence.

He would need followers, an army of them if he was to achieve his goal and he would need other things, daemons to follow him and slay his enemies on his command. He would need worship to nourish him and souls on which to feed.

His great bellow echoed for scores of leagues and those who heard his voice above the crack of thunder shuddered.

◄ CHAPTER NINE ►

Lothern, 10th Year of the Reign of Finubar

At first it was a day like any other. They followed the coastline of Ulthuan as it grew steadily more rugged. The breeze was strong, the weather warmer than Tyrion was used to. It had been getting steadily hotter as they made their way south.

In the mountains of Cothique, winter was still present but here in the south it felt like spring. Tyrion sat on the highest cross-spar on the ship and watched the sun spring over the horizon and the day grow ever warmer. The sea and the sky were of almost matching blue. In the distance, he could see more and more ships, converging from every point on the horizon, all of them heading towards the same goal.

There were mighty elven warships and larger, slower but still sleek cargo clippers. There were ungainly looking vessels that he guessed must belong to humans. There were small fishing boats and huge galleons and every size of sea-going craft in between. He felt as if the *Eagle of Lothern* was becoming part of a great crowd of pilgrims all heading towards the same holy spot. He had been keeping his eyes open for pirates but this interested him just as much. He would not have guessed there were so many ships in the world. Just the vessels he could see and count probably held as many people between them as the population of a city in Cothique.

It was not long before he caught sight of what he was waiting for. On the horizon, rising like the masts of a ship heaving into view, he caught sight of first one huge tower and then another. They were tall and slender, tipped by elongated minarets and swirling spires. Flags fluttered on their tips. He looked over at the sailor occupying the crow's nest. It was Karaya, the pretty one who he had seen many times before. He had not had a chance to talk to her since the storm.

'Lothern?' he asked.

'Your eyes are very good,' Karaya said, once she lowered her spy-glass. 'Yes, those are the towers of Lothern. We shall pass through the sea gate this evening – wind, weather and the favour of the gods permitting.'

Tyrion grinned at her. 'The last time I was here, I was a small child. I don't remember much about the place.'

'I am surprised you could forget,' she said with a teasing smile. 'Lothern is the greatest seaport in the world, the greatest city of the elves as well. And I am not just saying that because it's my home. I have seen many cities here and in what the humans call the Old World and in Naggaroth too, although I went there only to burn them.'

'You have seen the land of the Witch King?' Tyrion asked, envying all of her experiences. He got up and walked along the cross-spar until he reached the crow's nest then dropped in beside her. Their bodies were very close. She did not object. 'What was it like?'

'Cold and bleak and harsh and full of people who did not like us very much. Their hospitality was execrable and we did not stay for long.'

Tyrion laughed. 'I have heard that said.'

'It is nothing but the truth. We would give Malekith and his people a warmer welcome if they chose to come visiting us.'

'I do not think that is very likely.'

'Nor do I. Their land was empty. There were few dark elves to see. I think the druchii are dying out more quickly even than our people.'

'I had heard that Lothern was a lively place.'

'That it is,' she said. There was sadness in her voice. 'But even Lothern is not as populous as it used to be, and it is by far the most populous city in Elvendom.'

'I look forward to seeing it.'

'You will be made welcome there.' She reached out and touched his arm. It was as if a sudden electric shock passed between them. 'Whatever your business is.'

'I am to be presented to the Phoenix King.' He leaned forward, moving his head closer to hers. Their breaths seemed to mingle in the air before them.

'Then you have nothing to fear. There was never a fairer nor more open-handed ruler than Finubar. He is from Lothern you know. The first Phoenix King ever to come from our city and our land. It is a sign of the times.'

'How so?' He looked directly into her eyes.

'You have the strangest eyes,' she said. 'There are gold flecks in them, the colour of the sun.'

'You have very lovely eyes,' he said. 'Like the sea.'

She pulled back a little as if suddenly aware of their closeness. 'You asked me about the times.'

'I did,' he said, knowing that delay before gratification was part of this game.

'Our land grows in power and wealth and influence in proportion to the growth of our trade with the humans. I do not doubt it is the richest city in Ulthuan.'

'Surely wealth isn't everything,' Tyrion said. It was what his father would have said and it seemed right to him.

'No,' the sailor agreed. 'But it counts for a lot. It takes a heap of money to pay for our fleets and build our ships and equip our armies. It is not something to be despised.'

She sounded almost defensive and Tyrion could guess why. The elves of Lothern were often looked down on by the inhabitants of the other elven lands. They were seen as money-grubbing merchants, not proud warriors or noble wizards. Now did not seem like a good time to mention this though.

'It takes a mountain of gold to fight a war,' said Tyrion. 'Caledor the Conqueror said that, and he was one of the greatest generals who ever lived.'

'And he was right. Although it takes swords and spells also.'

'I am going to be a warrior,' said Tyrion.

'I do not doubt it. You have the look of one,' she said. 'You will be made a White Lion at least, if Master Korhien has his way. He is very proud of you.'

Tyrion laughed. He was pleased and flattered to be told this. 'That would be a great honour.'

'It would be, but if it's battle you want you should join the Sea Guard of Lothern. My brother is one and he has fought in many frays.'

'I will be happy to join any company of warriors,' said Tyrion. 'It is what I have always wanted to do.'

'Isha rewards those who follow their dreams, or so I have heard.'

'I sincerely hope so,' said Tyrion. He stared into the distance intently. He could hardly wait to reach the city. At that moment, it felt as if he only needed to stretch out his hand and whatever he wanted would fall into it.

He reached out for her and pulled her to him. Their lips touched.

They shed their clothes swiftly. Soon their naked bodies moved in time to the motion of the ship and the gulls were not the only things who cried out.

'Look at that,' said Tyrion barely able to keep the wonder from his voice. To their left, the titanic tower of Lothern lighthouse loomed out of the sea. Its lights already blazed even as the sun started to slide below the horizon.

Ahead of them were the vast sea gates of the city, open at this moment to let ships pass through into the harbour beyond them. They were enormous things, cut out of the huge sea walls of the city, large enough for a tall-masted ship to sail through with room to spare.

'You sound happy,' said Teclis. 'And have sounded so since you climbed down from the crow's nest.'

'I am always happy,' said Tyrion.

'Then you sound even happier than usual.'

Tyrion did not doubt that Teclis knew what had happened between him and the sailor girl. He could sometimes sense such things.

'I am happy to see Lothern,' said Tyrion.

'Of course,' said Teclis sourly. 'That must be it.'

All around them ships moved in stately order towards the gate. There were human vessels with elf pilots aboard to guide them through the correct channels and to give the signals that would prevent the mighty siege engines on the walls from opening fire.

There were elven trading vessels returning from every part of Ulthuan and beyond. Fresh painted, gleaming clippers that traded along the coast moved alongside battered-looking vessels that had made the long haul from the Old World, Araby, Cathay and beyond. Ships from Lothern traded with every part of the planet. There was no sea into which they did not venture, no land they were afraid to visit.

When they emerged from the maze of channels that lay beyond the gate, Tyrion could see the vast harbour. It was large enough to shelter all the fleets of every nation. Even without the sea walls it would have provided a safe haven and deep water anchorage for visiting vessels. The walls sheltered it from the worst of weather as well as all incoming marauders. In the centre of the harbour, upon a plinth as large as a small island, the gigantic statue of Aenarion glowed in the last light of the sunset.

Tyrion looked at it, seeing it as if for the first time. It was a titanic figure, a hundred times the height of a normal elf and carved so brilliantly as to appear almost alive. It was a very disturbing thing for him to gaze upon.

He heard Teclis gasp as he looked at it.

Looking up at the statue of the first Phoenix King, Teclis felt only wonder. It was an astonishing work of art. It captured in full the grandeur of Aenarion and his nobility and his tragic loneliness. The huge stone warrior leaned on a great sword around which flames seemed to writhe. He gazed outwards, the line of his vision passing far over the heads of the viewers as if he was looking into the distance and seeing things further and higher than any mere mortal might view.

'Do you think he really looked like that?' Tyrion asked. He sounded genuinely curious.

'They say this statue was made from drawings and paintings saved from before his fall. Those who knew him say it was accurate. Even Morathi remarked it was a likeness to the life, or so the historian Aergeon claims.'

'I don't see the supposed resemblance,' said Tyrion. He sounded piqued. It took Teclis a moment to realise what his brother was talking about. He glanced from the statue to Tyrion and then back to the statue.

'You do look like him,' Teclis said eventually. 'A lot like him.'

'I don't see it.' Tyrion shook his head for emphasis.

'Then you are the only one.'

'His chin is nothing like mine and his ears are a different shape.'

Teclis laughed. 'Those are very small differences.'

'Not to me. They are as clear as day.'

'You have the great privilege of staring at yourself in the mirror for hours every day – such being your vanity, of course – you can spot the small differences that might be invisible to the eye of lesser and less beautiful mortals like myself.'

'They are not small differences,' said Tyrion. He sounded genuinely troubled now. Teclis wondered what was really disturbing him.

Surely it could not be something so simple as the fact that there was a physical resemblance between himself and the first Phoenix King? That was something that would please most elves; it should, in fact, please him. He was the one who had always dreamed of being a legendary hero like Aenarion.

Perhaps that was it. Perhaps he was being confronted by the

reality of what that really meant carved in stone, a hundred times life size.

Aenarion did not look like the common idea of a hero. His brow was furrowed in thought, and there was a haunted look about his eyes that the sculptors had somehow caught. He did not look merely bold or complacently self-confident or simply brave. He looked lonely and a little lost and burdened by the weight of an awesome responsibility.

Looking on that proud handsome face brought things into focus for Teclis. Here was an elf who had carried a burden too great for any mortal to bear for longer than anyone could be expected to carry it, who had faced daemons within himself as well as outside, who had carried on when all seemed lost and who had, in the end, given his life to save the world and his people. Perhaps Tyrion was coming face to face for the first time with the reality of what it meant to be a hero, and he was finding it not quite what he had expected.

'Is that the Sword of Khaine?' Tyrion asked.

Or perhaps Tyrion felt no such thing, Teclis thought wryly. He now seemed merely curious about a sword. A glance at his brother showed he was still in a thoughtful mood and had changed the subject to try and distract himself.

'No. That blade is never represented anywhere.' said Teclis. 'This sword is Sunfang.'

'The first blade? The one Caledor forged for him in the fires of Vaul's Anvil? The one that blazed with fire and could shoot jets of flame like a dragon?'

'The very same.'

'Do you think it is an accurate representation?'

'Again the historians say yes. The elves took care about these things in those days.'

'Whatever happened to it?'

'No one knows. They say Aenarion gave it to Furion, one of his favoured commanders. It remained in his family for generations. They say Malekith coveted it and schemed to get it on many occasions. They say it was carried off by Nathanis, the last of Furion's line on his great ship, *Farwind*, and was never seen again, for the ship never returned. They think it was lost somewhere on the coasts of the Old World, but no trace of it was ever found.'

'You think the blade still exists?'

'It might.'

'It was made by Caledor. Surely the spells he wove would endure for as long as the Vortex does, at very least.'

'It might be at the bottom of the sea. Or in some dragon's hoard. Or in Malekith's treasure vaults for all we know.'

'It would be something to find it though, would it not?' Tyrion sounded excited and the grim mood that had fallen on him when he looked at the statue of Aenarion was lifting.

'It would indeed. If it still exists it would be one of the few fully functioning artefacts created by Caledor in the world. It would be a thing well worth studying.'

'I was thinking more of using it as a weapon.'

'Naturally! Of what possible use could it be to study the hand-iwork of the greatest mage that ever lived? Better to bang people over the head with it instead.'

'It is the purpose it was made for.'

'The sheer literal-mindedness of your response is irrefutable.'

'Anyway, I was thinking more of blasting them with its flames. That would be a useful power on the battlefield.'

'There might be something about it that would allow our father to complete his work. If the spells on the sword still function, they might give some clue as to how to remake the armour. They were both made by the same elf. They would both carry the same type of magic.'

Teclis could see that idea really caught Tyrion's imagination. With that thoughtful look on his face he resembled Aenarion more than ever, although a bright, merry Aenarion, not nearly so grim. Perhaps Teclis thought, that was what Aenarion had looked like when he was young.

They continued to look at the statue in silence and in wonder, as they passed into the waters beyond. At some point, the sailor girl Karaya came down and joined them. She did not seem compelled to say anything either.

Around the edges of the harbour were many more giant statues all on the same scale as that of Aenarion and all of them sharing something of his statue's power and pride and dignity.

On the western edge of the docks, a massive new statue was rising. Scaffolding still surrounded it. Masons laboured away unremit-tingly. At the moment it was faceless and somewhat shapeless, but Tyrion knew that within the next few decades it would take on the aspect of Finubar. The statue had only just begun to rise at the start of his reign, a mere ten years ago. It would be some time until it was completed. But what did that matter, Tyrion thought? If there was one thing that elves did not lack it was time.

Vessels lying at anchor crowded the harbour. Many were tied up at the long piers belonging to the great mercantile houses. The flags of their owners flew over ship and warehouse alike. Off to the west, on a walled complex of islands shut off from the rest of the city and accessible only through a series of bridges, walls and small forts was the Foreigners' Quarter, the only part of the city where the humans were allowed to dwell and to wander freely without special permission from the Phoenix King or his representatives.

'I can remember when that place was only the size of a fishing village,' said Karaya. 'Now they say there are almost as many humans living there as there are elves in the city. It will not be long before we are outnumbered in our own land.'

'The humans breed quickly.'

'It is not just that. More and more of them come here every year, seeking to trade. They bring us their goods. They buy our wares and the goods our ships bring in from the far corners of the world.'

'What could they sell us that we could possibly want?' Tyrion asked.

'They bring dwarf-made clockworks from the Worlds Edge Mountains. The dwarfs still refuse to trade with us directly. They bring gold and silver and gems that cannot be found here on Ulthuan. They bring ores and wool and tobacco. They bring preserved meats and grains and books of lore.' She seemed to be working her way through a long list.

Tyrion laughed. 'I believe you. I had not thought there were so many things they had that we could want.'

'I can tell you come from the old kingdoms of Ulthuan, Prince Tyrion. No one from Lothern could possibly think that way.'

In the early dusk, the ship glided towards an enormous warehouse over which the Emeraldsea flag fluttered, propelled by a gentle magical breeze Lady Malene had conjured. The crew dropped anchor. Guards in house colours waved to the arriving sailors.

Gangplanks were run down from the side and longshoremen with hooked staves and hooked knives ran aboard when given permission. The ship's captain bowed to Lady Malene. The horses of Korhien's guard were raised from the hold using levered cranes and dropped kicking onto the pier. Their riders stood nearby waiting to gentle them with words and softly spoken charms. Korhien observed the whole operation with satisfaction. Tyrion noticed that others watched from nearby, and ran off when they saw him watching.

'What was that about?' he asked.

'All of the houses spy on each other. The watchers saw Lady Malene and you and ran off to report to their masters.'

'What possible consequence could our appearance here have?' Tyrion asked.

'Twins of the Blood of Aenarion? It could have incalculable consequences. Who knows what gifts you might possess or what importance you may have in the future?' He seemed to be talking as much to himself as Tyrion and he looked very thoughtful. 'Also Lady Malene and myself are both personages of some consequence in the city, believe it or not.'

Tyrion smiled at the big warrior. 'That I can believe.'

He turned around looking for Karaya to say goodbye, but she was already gone, without taking leave, after the manner of elf maids and strangers they met a-journeying.

They took the road from the docks, joining the evening traffic making its way into the great city. They rode alongside wagons full of silk bales, and fish on ice, and piled high with fruit. They passed vendors selling everything from snacks to bits of jewellery.

The escort bantered with passing traders, purchasing bits of fruit to eat. A fresh-faced elf maid offered Tyrion a peach, causing the warriors to whistle knowingly. Tyrion accepted with all the good grace he could muster and fumbled for his purse.

'A gift,' said the girl, touching his hand gently. Tyrion was glad, for he had no money to offer her anyway.

The inner gates of the city lay ahead. Soldiers in the tabards of the Sea Guard of Lothern watched them enter. It was obvious from their manner that they knew most of the elves coming in, and were known by them in turn. Their easy manner altered perceptibly as the group rode up and Korhien's white lionskin cloak became visible. They stood taller, looked sterner, and saluted smartly. The White Lion responded in kind.

It occurred to Tyrion then that there was being known and being known. The guards knew who Korhien was in a different way from the friendly manner in which they acknowledged the local traders.

The White Lion was obviously an elf of some consequence. It was only natural, he supposed; Korhien was one of the Phoenix King's elite guard. It was more than that though – people looked at him with awe and his name was whispered among strangers as they passed along. It had never occurred to him that Korhien was famous.

He wondered if Malene or any of the others were too but got no hint of it from the demeanour of the people around them. He noticed that he was coming in for a lot of attention as well, then he realised it was his resemblance to that statue in the harbour that was the cause of the attention. He wondered if ever he would be judged here for himself.

They rode beyond the inner walls. Immediately there was a sense of age and beauty. Lampposts lit by incandescent magic kept the night at bay. Long streets wound up tree-clad hills. Many flights of stairs ran up the steeper slopes. There were palaces with towers and spiked minarets. There were fountains everywhere. It seemed like a legion of sculptors had been kept busy for many ages of the world beautifying the city. There were statues of mages and warriors and kings, as well as people he did not recognise but guessed were lawmakers and orators and poets. He pointed out these wonders to his brother; stone worked to look life-like, auras of glamour and ancient warding sorceries protecting the work from the ravages of time and weather.

'It's amazing,' he told Teclis, as they passed a row of towering warriors garbed like Korhien. 'Just think of the work that went into this.'

'Think of the ego and the pride,' said his twin.

'What do you mean?'

'You don't think these were put up just to beautify the streets, do you?'

'What other purpose could they have?'

'Your brother is right, doorkeeper,' said Korhien riding up beside them. 'These statues and fountains were all put up for political reasons. They represent the power and the wealth of the people who paid to have them created. They praise the ancestors of those people, or in many cases the living elves themselves.'

Tyrion laughed.

'I am serious, doorkeeper. Politics is a serious business in Lothern, although you are right to laugh at it. Every one of the statues on the pedestals on the roof of that palace represents a glorious ancestor of the occupants. It reminds the mass of the citizens of the power and greatness of the family, just in case its members have not performed any worthy deeds lately.'

Teclis squinted at Korhien with something like respect. He obviously had never expected to hear such words coming from the White Lion's mouth.

'Not everyone who wields a blade is brainless, Prince Teclis,' said

Korhien with the elaborate courtesy with which he always treated Teclis and which Tyrion suspected concealed a genial contempt. 'You will soon find that out in this place. You will need to, if you are to live and prosper here.'

'I would settle just for living at the moment,' said Teclis. 'This odious beast has half-killed me on the ride.'

'Not much further, prince,' said Korhien. 'Soon you will have a bed for the night. In the bosom of your loving family.'

There was a subtle irony in his tone that Tyrion could see Teclis appreciated.

'Where do you come from, Lord Korhien?' Teclis asked. There was an edge to his voice but he was curious too.

'I was born in a barn in the mountains. My father was a freeholder. My mother was the local archery champion. No ancient high blood there, I am afraid. Well, no more than any other elf.'

'You are allied to Emeraldsea though, aren't you?'

'I am allied to Lady Malene,' said Korhien with a wink. 'She is my only entanglement with House Emeraldsea. My loyalty is to the Phoenix King. As is only right for an elf of my position.'

Why was there tension between the two of them, Tyrion wondered? Perhaps his twin sensed a rival for his loyalty. Tyrion had never looked at the matter in that light before. Perhaps Teclis feared being abandoned in this vast city with its palm trees and roof gardens and endless streets full of echoing, half-empty palaces.

Now they were away from the gates, the crowd had thinned out and the streets seemed much emptier. Some of the houses, not too far from the main thoroughfare, had patched and crumbling roofs. Some of the people who gazed at them out of half-shuttered windows had a lean and hungry look to them, although as far as Tyrion knew there was no hunger or famine in Ulthuan.

What then could they be? Were they diseased? Was it true that some of the human plagues could jump to elves? He had heard some of the mountain villagers claim such things, that humans should never have been allowed into Lothern, and should be sent packing back to their homelands.

For himself, Tyrion was curious to see one of the semi-legendary savages. He knew he would find the opportunity soon. They were mostly associated with the dark elves who kept them as slaves and occasionally allied with their daemon-worshipping medicine men. As he had seen, many of them lurked down by the harbour, living in the area of land set aside for them and quarantined from the rest of the city. He found himself unwholesomely curious about them.

They turned a corner and entered a massive plaza. On one side of the square was a huge mansion, made from green-tinged stone, topped with emerald towers. Flags with the emblem of a mighty elf warship on them fluttered above the entrance. Gigantic lanterns set atop corner towers lit the entire street with a green-tinted light.

'You're home,' said Korhien. 'This is the Emeraldsea Palace.'

Tyrion felt overwhelmed by awe. The building was on the scale that he had imagined a city would be built. It looked large enough to house the population of an elven town, and unlike many of the surrounding buildings it did not seem deserted. Small armies of people seemed to come and go from it. Korhien caught his look.

He rubbed thumb and forefinger together. 'Lothern is built on the wealth of its merchants. House Emeraldsea is one of the wealthiest of the merchant houses.'

He rode closer and spoke so quietly that Tyrion was not sure he caught the actual words, 'And the most hated.'

Tyrion knew better than to ask about that now. He resolved that he would have some questions for Korhien later.

When they passed through the great gates of the House they entered a different world. Green paper-lanterns hung everywhere, illuminating a courtyard that contained a pool the size of a small lake. In that pool were fountains carved in the shape of dolphins and sea-drakes and other legendary creatures of the ocean. Around the courtyard, the mansion rose a full five storeys high.

Retainers in the livery of the House went about their business. Richly dressed elves strolled around discussing tonnages and rates of interest and market prices. Even though the hour was getting late, they conducted business with the intensity of farmers haggling over sheep at a morning market.

Tyrion had no idea what was meant. For all he knew these serious-looking elves could be discussing magic spells. Some of them paid attention to him, particularly the women. They stared quite openly. He smiled and was smiled at in response. The male elves noticing this sometimes glared, sometimes smiled knowingly.

'I see you are going to be popular,' said Lady Malene, riding close to him.

'What makes you think that?' he asked, although he already knew the answer.

'I think you'll find out for yourself soon enough,' she said. 'For the moment, let me enjoy your country-born innocence. I am sure the ladies here will.'

He was conscious of the fact that elf girls in Cothique considered him good-looking, but there was very little to compare himself to: his father, Teclis and the uncouth villagers. But he lacked the sophistication and polish of these city-bred elves. He was not nearly so well-dressed or so well-groomed. It had never occurred to him that the mere fact that he looked different might be considered a point of attraction, not a strike against him. It was something to bear in mind.

Live and learn he told himself. If he was going to survive and thrive here, he was going to have to, and he saw no reason not to enjoy himself at the same time.

Retainers helped the riders dismount, and led away their horses to the stables. The warriors who had escorted them noticed acquaintances around them and shouted greetings and went their separate ways. Soon, only Tyrion and Teclis, and Lady Malene and Korhien were left, standing together in a small group near one of the fountains.

Korhien looked around at them. He smiled broadly. 'I must go soon and present myself to Finubar. He will want to know I have returned.' He leaned forward and kissed Malene. He stretched out his hand and clasped Tyrion's arm just below the elbow. Tyrion returned the gesture. He was surprised. It was the grip that warriors used for comrades and for friends. He bowed to Teclis and then turned and strode away.

Tyrion paused for a moment and considered what had just been said. He had known Korhien was a White Lion, but it was one thing knowing that and another hearing him speak so casually of reporting to Finubar. Tyrion wondered what he was going to tell the Phoenix King about himself and Teclis.

From under the arched walkway at the west end of the palace, Tyrion noticed a small group of extremely well-dressed young elves were studying him. They wore the long loose robes favoured by the upper class at leisure, all trimmed with silk and gold.

They were attempting to look nonchalant but he sensed that they were more interested in him and his brother than they would have cared to admit. He smiled easily and waved at them. They did not wave back. He laughed, honestly not caring, and noticed that Lady Malene was watching him from the corner of her eye. A young elf girl in the tunic of a retainer approached. The girl looked at Tyrion as if seeing a god.

'Yes, indeed,' Malene said. 'You will get on very well here.'

The girl whispered something to her. She looked suddenly a lot more serious. 'Your grandfather will see you now,' she said. 'You would do well to watch your manners around him. He is not as tolerant as I am.'

'Welcome to my home,' said Lord Emeraldsea. He did not look very welcoming, Tyrion thought. He looked as if he were inspecting a couple of very dubious cargoes he was considering investing in.

'Thank you for having us here,' said Tyrion, with all the politeness he could manage. Teclis murmured something inaudible.

Lord Emeraldsea sat at a huge desk piled high with documents awaiting his inspection and signature. His study was on the topmost floor of the house. Out of his window, he had a fine view of the harbour below. His balcony held a bronze telescope on a metal tripod. Tyrion guessed he took a proprietorial interest in the ships arriving in the harbour.

Lord Emeraldsea was tall and thin and quite the oldest elf that Tyrion could ever remember seeing. Blue veins were visible in the ancient hands that toyed with a small set of scales. His hair was the colour of spun silver, his eyes cold and grey as the northern sea before a storm.

It took Tyrion a moment to accept the fact that this was his grandfather. In the elf's manner there was no real suggestion of any familial relationship. There was distance, the implication of hostility, perhaps a suggestion of contempt or dislike.

Lord Emeraldsea rose from his hard wooden chair, walked round the desk and stood before them. He walked with a very straight back and the same air of command Tyrion had noticed in Captain Joyelle. There was something in Lord Emeraldsea's manner suggestive of the sea. He was very tall, taller even than Tyrion. For the first time in a very long time, Tyrion experienced the sensation of being looked down upon. Cold eyes measured him, calculated his worth and placed it on the scales at the back of his grandfather's mind.

'You do look like him,' he said, and Tyrion had no doubt as to who *he* was. 'You look a little like my poor daughter too. I am pleased to see that you have grown up into such a fine figure of an elf.'

He strode over to Teclis and loomed over him. 'I wish I could say the same for you.'

'Why don't you try, out of politeness,' said Teclis with poisonous sweetness.

Lord Emeraldsea looked taken aback. Tyrion could tell he was not used to being mocked. His smile was wintery and not without humour. Like many people before him he was being forced to reassess his opinion of the sickly young elf standing before him. The two of them locked gazes and the air fairly crackled between them. Here were two elves of very different ages and enormously strong wills.

'You look like my daughter,' Lord Emeraldsea said. 'And like your father. But you seem somewhat... firmer of character.'

Tyrion wondered what his grandfather meant by that. In any case,

Lord Emeraldsea did not seem displeased to discover that Teclis was not some sort of feeble half-wit. 'I like that, lad, but don't push my goodwill too far.'

'I am a prince,' said Teclis.

Lord Emeraldsea's stare was cold, a captain looking at a disrespectful cabin boy. 'That remains to be determined. We will know soon enough if you are blessed or cursed by the Blood of Aenarion.'

There was a strong emotion in his voice when he said that that Tyrion did not recognise at all. He followed the old elf's gaze to the wall behind him and saw that he was looking at a portrait of their mother. He looked back at Lord Emeraldsea's lined face and he knew then the emotion was grief. Lord Emeraldsea caught Tyrion's glance and for a moment there was flicker of genuine emotion between them.

'It's an ill thing for a parent to outlive a child,' Lord Emeraldsea said. Tyrion could see that took Teclis off guard. His mouth shut just as he was about to say something sardonic again. Perhaps he understood that their appearance here must be difficult for their grandfather.

'My other daughter tells me that you have a gift for sorcery. Let us hope you live long enough to enjoy the use of it.'

Tyrion wondered if there was threat implicit in his grandfather's words. Perhaps it was only a warning. They were in a place now inhabited by elves that would kill you if you provoked them. Tyrion was grateful for one thing. No one would ever call his brother out to duel because of rudeness. There would be no honour in it. Perhaps the old elf was merely making a reference to Teclis's sickliness.

Lord Emeraldsea returned to his desk and sat down. He lifted a quill, sharpened the end with a small knife, dipped it in his inkwell and made an inscription on one of his scrolls, as if acknowledging the delivery of a cargo with a receipt.

'Rooms have been prepared for you,' he said. 'Go to them.'

It was clear they had been dismissed. A servant appeared from somewhere to show them out. Tyrion had no idea how she had been summoned.

'This is very nice,' said Tyrion, looking around the chamber.

Very nice was something of an understatement; the apartment they had been installed in seemed as large as their father's villa and considerably more luxurious. It had windows of polished crystal.

Murals depicting sea-scenes covered the walls of the reception chamber and numerous busts of proud-looking elves stood on columns in the alcoves.

There was a small library of books, mostly about the sea and ancient lands. The furnishings were lovely and lovingly crafted. A small table of Sapherian dragonwood sat in the middle of the reception room. A number of carved chairs were placed around it. They were well-upholstered and comfortable in a way that nothing had been back home.

Tyrion had taken the bedroom that overlooked the street outside. It contained a large bed, and more books, a mirror and paintings of ships and sea battles executed by a painter with a gift for detail. The bed was massive and draped with a gauze curtain for keeping out night-biting insects. There was a balcony with a fine view of the street two storeys below. When he stood on it he had wondered if this was how the Phoenix King felt when he looked down on his subjects.

Teclis was installed in the bedroom that faced the inner courtyard. It was quieter and cooler and smaller. There was a painting of a sea-wizard summoning a wind to propel a ship across the ocean. It was the presence of this painting more than anything that had influenced his brother's choice. Teclis lay on the bed exhausted, but his gaze was bright, and Tyrion could tell he had absorbed everything about their surroundings, and would remember it.

'What do you think?' Tyrion asked. He was excited. There were chambers in the apartment he had no more than glanced at. Teclis even had his own sitting room which Tyrion had not seen yet. Apparently it had a mirror in it. This was luxury indeed.

'I think our relatives are very rich,' Teclis replied.

'As ever, brother, your powers of observation astonish me.'

'I wonder why they feel so compelled to show interest in us now. They paid no attention whatsoever for nearly sixteen years.'

'I am guessing the fact that we are summoned to the court of the Phoenix King may have something to do with it.'

'Of course, Tyrion, but why did Lord Emeraldsea send Lady Malene and her riders and a White Lion? Why draw attention to our presence this way?' He appeared to have been giving the matter some thought since their ride through the city.

'Why not?' said a girl's voice from the door.

Both twins looked around. A young elf maiden stood there, garbed in a simple but expensive gown of greenish silk trimmed with cloth of gold. Her hair was elaborately coiffed. Her features were extraordinarily beautiful. 'Everyone knows about you anyway, or will do soon. You are our kin. Whatever we do and however we treat you, it will be talked about.'

'Hello,' said Tyrion, smiling.

'I thought it was polite to knock,' said Teclis.

'I thought it was impolite to be ungrateful to your hosts,' said the girl seemingly unabashed by his tone.

'So we are supposed to be grateful to you?' said Teclis, caustic as ever.

'My name is Tyrion,' said Tyrion. 'The rude, ungrateful one is my twin, Teclis. And you, our impolite host, would be...?'

He said it without malice and both Teclis and the girl laughed.

'I am Liselle. I am your cousin. I came up to welcome you but the door was open and I overheard you speaking. I was wondering what you were like, so I listened.'

'We don't have a lot of experience with great houses, I am afraid,' said Tyrion. He did not feel at any disadvantage because of this. He would learn his way around. But he felt the need to explain the situation so there were no misunderstandings.

'So I gathered,' said Liselle. She walked over and looked up at him. Her eyes were a very beautiful shade of green. Her skin was very pale, her beauty willowy. Tyrion reached out and moved a strand of her hair that had come loose as if it was the most natural thing in the world. She did not object. Teclis stared.

'Has your curiosity been satisfied?' he asked.

'Not yet. I have never met twins before. You are not what I expected. I thought you were supposed to be identical.'

'Not all twins are identical. Those are quite rare.'

'There have been only twenty-five recorded pairs of identical twins in elven history,' said Teclis. 'Out of three hundred and fifteen recorded births of twins.'

It was the sort of thing he would know. His knowledge of the obscure facts of genealogy was incredible and he forgot nothing. Liselle looked less than impressed. She kept looking up into Tyrion's eyes.

A handclap announced another visitor. Tyrion saw Lady Malene standing in the doorway. 'Liselle, pray give our guests some time to settle in before disturbing them with your curiosity.'

'She was not disturbing us,' said Tyrion.

'Ah, but she will,' said Lady Malene. 'Liselle, if you would be so kind as to leave us alone for a moment. There are things I need to talk about with your cousins.'

'Yes, mother,' said Liselle, departing with good grace.

'What is your wish, mistress?' the chief cultist asked. He was a tall, stately elf of considerable dignity. He had emerged from the group of twenty or so naked elves gathered in the grove of pleasure.

N'Kari wore the form of a beautiful elf maiden with hooves instead of feet and small curling horns emerging from her head. Her appearance and sensuous aura caused lust and a desire to obey in dedicated followers of the Lord of Pleasure.

And these were certainly all elves who followed the Way of All Pleasures. She had sensed their corruption from afar, smelled their decadence like the odour of a rich and corrupt night-blooming orchid. She had surprised them and filled them with wonder and terror by materialising at their orgiastic rites to celebrate their devotion to Slaanesh.

These were some of those who had been summoned by N'Kari's original dream-spell who had made their way into the mountains seeking to answer its call. N'Kari smelled her spell on them like the last lingering remnants of some old perfume. Their rite had already provided a morsel of sustenance, and before this night was over they would provide a great deal more.

N'Kari studied their leader closely in the light of the moons. 'I require your obedience,' she said.

She sensed their confusion. These elves had been playing a dangerous game, performing rites of pleasure for their own gratification, thinking that there was no price to be paid, that nothing would come in answer to their summons. They had discovered they were wrong and they were at once exalted and terrified by what they had done.

'We are your slaves, mistress. We live only to abase ourselves at your feet and give our lives for your slightest pleasure.' At the moment, the elf believed this. He had no choice under the impact of N'Kari's presence. The nodding of heads, licking of lips and shining bright eyes of the rest of the cultists told of their agreement.

N'Kari looked upon them and found everything to her liking. She needed an army to work her vengeance, and here she had the core of one. It was a small start to be sure but it was a beginning on which she could build, and she would make the elves of Ulthuan tremble when they heard her name before it was over.

'What is your name?' N'Kari asked.

'Elrion, great mistress.'

'And your purpose?'

'I exist only to obey you, great mistress,' said Elrion.

'I know,' replied N'Kari. 'Come now. We have matters to attend to nearby. There are those I have ancient business with.'

'You are in a different world now,' said Malene. She glanced around to make sure the door was shut and spoke a Word. Tyrion felt as if the lightest of breezes had passed over him. Teclis cocked his head to one side, suddenly intensely curious. 'There are some things you need to know and some words that need to be spoken plainly.'

'And you are going to speak them,' said Teclis.

'I am, and I will thank you not to use your haughty tone with me, Prince Teclis. I like you but I expect you to treat me with the same respect I extend to you. We are not on the ship any more, not on a journey. Things are more formal here.' She sounded almost as if she regretted that fact.

Teclis looked surprised, not so much at her manner but by the admission she liked him. He was not used to that. He smiled, suddenly looking very young and intensely vulnerable.

'You are guests in this house. I would ask you, Tyrion, to remember that. Some of your cousins are at a dangerous age and you are a very handsome youth. I am sure you will find plenty of opportunities for amorous adventure outwith the confines of your immediate kinswomen.'

'I'll try and remember that,' he said.

'You would do well to do so. Your grandfather does not like the harmony of his household disturbed.'

'We did not ask to be here,' said Teclis. He was back to his usual sullen self now.

'No, but the Phoenix King requested the pleasure of your company and here you are. We must now see to it that you are suitably prepared for entering the royal presence.'

'What do you mean?'

'We must see that you do not disgrace us in his presence.'

'You mean to teach us manners?' There was an edge to Teclis's voice. He sounded as if he was getting ready to unleash his temper again.

'I intend that you should learn protocol.'

'I am already familiar with how one addresses the Phoenix King,' Teclis said with superlative arrogance.

'There is a difference between knowing what to say and knowing when and how to say it.'

'On formal occasions he is addressed as Blessed of Asuryan. Under some circumstances, most notably when haste might be required, he is to be called Chosen One, or simply Chosen. On high holy days, he is known as Fireborn. The last sentence of any address on such days is always: Watch over us, Vessel of the Sacred Fire. Normally a simple sire will do if you are addressed in conversation.'

Lady Malene looked impressed. 'How many different forms of address are there?'

'Twenty-one. Shall I recite them?'

'No. I am sure you will astonish me with that phenomenal memory of yours. Tyrion, can you match your brother's scholarship?'

Tyrion was sure Malene already knew the answer to that, but she was making a point.

'I am afraid not. I have never had much of a gift for it,' he said.

'You will need to learn them. You will need to know the titles of all the officials at court. You will need to know how to respectfully address his Sacred Majesty under every circumstance that might arise. You will need to learn the same things concerning the Everqueen for that matter.'

Tyrion groaned. 'When am I ever likely to meet the Everqueen?'

'Don't worry, brother, I will help you,' said Teclis.

'That's what I am worried about,' said Tyrion. 'It will be as much fun for the both of us as me teaching you how to use a sword.'

'There are times when the right words and the right manner are as useful as being able to use a blade,' said Lady Malene. 'And they can be as deadly under the right circumstances.'

She sounded very serious. Tyrion looked abashed. She laughed.

'Be grateful you did not grow up surrounded by this protocol, Prince Tyrion. You at least have had some time in which to be free of it.' She sounded as if she envied him, which surprised Tyrion.

After a moment, she said, 'There are some clothes in the wardrobes. They will be a poor fit but wear them for the moment. In a few minutes, the house tailors will visit you and see you are more suitably accoutred. Your grandfather wishes you to be dressed as is fitting for your station. So do I, for that matter.'

After she had gone Tyrion looked in the wardrobe. The most beautiful clothes he had ever seen hung there. He felt almost embarrassed when he put them on. Looking at himself in the mirror was like looking at a stranger.

There was another knock on the door. The tailors had arrived.

The woman stared at Tyrion and then walked around him, studying him with intense, more-than-professional interest. She walked over to where Teclis sat and gestured for him to stand. She nodded to herself twice, made some notes in a wax tablet with her stylus and then produced a cord of silk in which regular knots had been set. She used this to measure Tyrion's chest size, his waist and the length of his leg. She nodded approvingly then went over to Teclis and did the same thing although she seemed less pleased with the results. All of this having been done, she left the room.

A male elf entered this time, placed a piece of parchment under each of Tyrion's feet, and drew a line around them in charcoal. He too measured Tyrion's thigh and ankle girth, did the same for Teclis and then left.

A jeweller arrived and used small copper rings to take the measure of their fingers, and copper torques to take the measure of their necks, and copper bracers to take the measure of their wrists. He too made notes in a wax tablet and departed.

A girl arrived, sat them down, and then began to cut their hair with a long razor and some scissors. When she had finished Tyrion studied himself in the mirror. His hair was no longer long and unkempt. It was combed out and thick and looked much better.

Teclis's dark hair was cut close in a way that revealed his fine pointed ears and enhanced his gaunt, sallow features. He looked almost handsome, or would have if there had been more weight on him. The moon shone in through the window and in its light there was something skeletal about him, something sinister. Its gleam caught in his eyes and they seemed for a moment to burn with internal fire. Just for an instant his brother looked like a stranger. It was the haircut and the unfamiliar clothes and setting, Tyrion told himself, but could not quite believe it.

Teclis was different now. The journey, the city, the meetings with strangers, the promise of being taught magic had all changed him incrementally. Tyrion found it easy to imagine that some day the sum total of all these tiny changes would make his brother into a complete stranger. It also occurred to him that the same thing might be happening to him, in Teclis's eyes, although he himself felt no different.

'You have an odd expression on your face, brother,' said Teclis.

'I was just thinking the same about you,' said Tyrion, making a joke of it.

'I was thinking that one day all of the small changes we undergo might make us into total strangers.'

Tyrion did not need to tell him that he had been having exactly the same thought. He knew then that his twin already understood that. Teclis had always been more perceptive about these things than he.

'It will take more than a change of clothes and a change of hair-style to do that,' said Tyrion.

'Those are just the start,' said Teclis. 'They have already started trying to teach us manners, how to behave, what we must do. They want to remake us for their own purposes.'

'The trick is going to be finding out what those purposes really are,' said Tyrion.

'I am sure they will tell us in their own good time.'

Tyrion was not at all sure of that. Still, at least they were safe for the moment. It did not look like their lives were in any immediate danger.

Looking out of the window, Lady Fayelle thought it was a lovely night. The moon was bright. The stars were shining. Unable to keep still she paced across her room. She was excited. Soon she was to be married. Soon she would be leaving her father's home forever. She was saddened by the prospect of leaving her aged parent alone in his gloomy old palace.

She had asked him to come and live with her new husband in Lothern. He had refused, saying he was too old and too set in his ways to move now. And he really loved this old place. She understood that. He had spent most of his long life here, had raised his children and buried his wife within its grounds. And it was all that was left to him, that and his pride in his ancient lineage.

Sometimes she thought he was a little too proud. He thought her new husband beneath her. His kin were merchants from Lothern and his family had been mere freeholders while her ancestors had ruled a kingdom and married into the Blood of Aenarion himself.

Her father was proud but you could not eat pride, nor repair ancient buildings with it nor pay the required number of retainers unless they too were like you, old and with nowhere else to go.

Her father understood these things, she knew, but he was too set in his ways to change. It had fallen on her to improve the fortunes of her house by marrying well, and to tell the truth, she had found it no hardship. She took out her locket and opened it and stared at his picture. Moralis, her husband-to-be, was as good and kind an elf as one could hope to meet, and he was handsome too.

More than that he brought a dash of the swashbuckling adventurer with him, for he was a sea captain and had travelled to many far places while helping make his family's fortune. She liked him, and he liked her, and there was love there, which was not something she had ever thought to find, growing up as she had in this remote place far from the centres of civilisation.

She counted it a blessing of Isha that he had bought the land beside their estate. It had proven even more of a blessing that he had taken to her when he had first seen her.

She thought she heard a noise somewhere in the gloom. She went to the window and looked out into the night once more. She could not see anything.

She was not frightened. There was nothing really threatening in this part of Ulthuan. No wolves prowled here. No monsters strayed down from the mountains. No marauders had made it this far inland in a couple of centuries. The worst things she had ever heard about were some rumours of the spread of the old cults of luxury in the area, and those were most likely just Elrion and his friends playing at being decadent, and frightening themselves with the thought of the old dark magics.

She heard a stone bang against the shutter of her window. She knew who it was without having to look. Only one elf had ever done that. She opened the shutter. As if summoned by the thought of him, Elrion emerged from the gloom. There was something wild in his appearance. He looked different although she could not quite put her finger on how and she had known him since childhood.

'What is it, Elrion? What is wrong?' she asked. She thought she heard some large animal growling in the dark behind him. Perhaps some wild thing had strayed into the area after all, and he had fled before it. That might explain the wildness of his appearance.

'In the name of Isha run down and open the door, it's following me,' he said, but he said it quietly, as if he did not want anyone to hear. Perhaps he was afraid of attracting the creature's attention.

She thought about ringing the bell to summon the servants but realised it would be faster just to go down herself and open the gate as she had done when they were younger. She raced down the stairs, threw the bolts on the gate and opened it.

'Quickly, come in,' she said, peering past his shoulder to see if whatever it was was still out there. She thought she caught sight of glowing eyes glittering in the gloom. There was something terrifying about them. He stepped passed her into the courtyard. As he did so, old Peteor emerged from inside the mansion. He carried a bow in his blue-veined old hand and he had an arrow knocked and ready.

'I thought I heard the bolts being thrown,' he said. 'What is it? Who would come calling at this time of night?'

'It is only Elrion,' Fayelle said. 'Some night-stalking beast followed him here.'

'It's an odd time of the night to come calling,' said Peteor. He had never liked Elrion, and his liking had grown less as tales of Elrion's debauched lifestyle and wild parties had become common knowledge in the neighbourhood.

'I have urgent news for Prince Faldor,' said Elrion. He strode over to Peteor with his hands outstretched. 'It concerns the wedding. It's not going to happen.'

'Has there been an accident? Has something happened to Moralis?' Fayelle asked.

'What else could bring him at such a time of the night,' said Peteor. 'News brought after dark is usually bad news.'

'I am afraid Peteor is right,' said Elrion. He seemed to slap Peteor on the back. The old elf coughed and lurched forwards. Red stuff emerged from his nose and lips, and something bubbled in his chest, causing him to have trouble breathing.

'Are you sick, Peteor?' Fayelle asked. Peteor struggled to say something. He reached up and tried to grab Elrion who leaned against him and moved his arm again. Peteor bent double and more red erupted from his chest. Fayelle ran over to him 'What is wrong?' she asked, reaching out to touch him. She was shocked at how wet he was and how red her hand came away, then suddenly in a rush, she realised what was happening. 'You are bleeding,' she said. Frothy red bubbles erupted from Peteor's mouth as he tried to speak. His eyes opened wide and he slumped forward.

'He's dead,' said Elrion.

Fayelle felt sick and panicky and she did not quite understand what was going on even when she saw the red knife in Elrion's hand.

'And I am afraid everyone else here soon will be. Come now, there is someone I must introduce you to.' He twisted her arm painfully up her back and pushed her towards the gateway, seemingly not caring any more that her screams were rousing the house. Lights were coming on everywhere and she could hear retainers moving within.

From out of the shadows, a massive and sinisterly beautiful humanoid figure emerged. It was the most handsome-looking elf she had ever seen, except for the fact that its feet ended in hooves, one arm ended in a crab-like pincer and small curling goat horns emerged from its forehead. She opened her mouth to scream and took in a lungful of oddly calming, musky perfume. She was suddenly filled with the urge to reach out and stroke the goat-horned elf's naked flesh. He seemed to understand this and smiled back. It was a most winning smile.

'Greetings, Blood of Aenarion,' he said in the most thrilling voice imaginable. 'You should be pleased. You will be the first to know my vengeance. And you will be the first whose soul I offer screaming to my god.'

The next morning, when he awoke, Tyrion found a pile of new clothes on the table in his room. Under the table was a complete set of new footwear. In a sandalwood box was a necklace, a torque and a pair of sunstone rings. He donned all the apparel including a very fine green cloak trimmed with cloth of gold and studied himself in the mirror. He looked every inch the asur prince, he thought, but he did not look like himself.

As he studied himself, a servant entered, without knocking. 'Korhien Ironglaive requests your presence in the courtyard, Prince Tyrion. It appears he would like to give you a lesson in swordplay.'

'Please tell Korhien I will be right down.' He began to change out of his new clothes into the old ones he had used on the journey. He did not want such beautiful things ruined in weapons practice. The servant watched him uncomprehendingly for a few moments, lifted a shirt and a pair of britches and said, 'I think you will find these were intended for you to wear at practice. I was told to take away all of your old clothes and burn them.'

Tyrion laughed. 'I shall wear what you suggest but don't burn my old clothes. Have them washed and mended and brought back to me. I may have some use for them yet.'

'As you wish, sir.' The servant looked confused. He could not imagine what Tyrion wanted these rags for. Tyrion decided it was better that way. He had an idea of doing something for which they might be useful. He was not sure he wanted his relatives to find that out yet.

⤚❮ CHAPTER TWELVE ❯⤙

'Good of you to join us,' said Korhien Ironglaive. The big elf was stripped to his tunic and looked as if he had just finished some hard sparring with wooden swords. A group of younger-looking elves stood nearby with their weapons in the guard positions.

Korhien tossed him a wooden practice blade. Tyrion caught it easily by the hilt as it tumbled through the air. 'If you would be so kind as to demonstrate your technique in the practice circle.'

Tyrion saw that a chalk circle had been marked in the centre of the courtyard. He strode into it, sword held ready. Korhien coughed. The other students laughed. Tyrion looked at Korhien.

'You don't lack for heart, lad,' Korhien said. 'I am not so sure about your wisdom but your courage is impressive.'

He indicated a stand which contained a suit of padded armour just like the others were wearing. Tyrion smiled at his mistake, strode over and laced it up. He did not need to be shown how. It was as if he was born knowing how to tie the stays in the correct way. When this was complete he returned to the circle.

Korhien said, 'Atharis! You shall spar with Prince Tyrion.'

'As you wish, sir,' said a blond haired, good looking elf, stepping forward into the practice circle. He was not as tall as Tyrion, but he was well-muscled and lithe. His nose had been broken and not badly set, and his mouth had a cruel twist to it. He looked as if he took this whole thing very seriously.

'I shall try not to hurt you,' he said in a very low voice. His tone implied that he meant to do exactly the opposite of what he said.

'That's very kind of you,' said Tyrion. He moved more slowly and clumsily than he normally would. He saw Atharis sneer, as Tyrion deliberately held the practice blade incorrectly. 'I shall endeavour to do the same.'

'Begin,' said Korhien.

Within three strokes, Tyrion had put Atharis on his back. The other student seemed very slow to Tyrion and his moves very predictable. Korhien looked at him from the corner of his eye.

'As you can see, Prince Tyrion is not quite as simple as he chooses to appear,' he said.

Korhien strode forward into the circle and spoke to the watching group of students. 'In case you are in any doubt, Prince Tyrion has exceptional gifts. You would do well not to underestimate him as Atharis did. There is a lesson here about combat in general. Don't judge your foe by what you are told about him. Don't judge him by his appearance. Don't judge him by what he says about himself. Judge him by how he fights against you. You might live longer if you do.'

He gestured for Tyrion to leave the circle and join the other students. Tyrion did so, helping Atharis up as he went. The other elf grinned at him ruefully.

'You are all here to learn to fight,' said Korhien. 'I am taking time to teach you. There are not so many elves that we can afford to lose any. Bear that in mind. Every asur life lost is a terrible blow to our people and we can ill afford such losses. It is your duty to see that you live. It is your duty to see that you are fit and that you are capable. It is your duty to learn from your mistakes and master your weapons. All of you, and I include the gifted Prince Tyrion in this statement, have a good deal to learn, but you have the time to learn it, and learn it you shall. I intend to see to that.'

'Still giving that same old speech, Korhien,' said a mocking voice from under the colonnaded arches.

'Why not, Prince Iltharis? It is a good one and there is truth in it.' Korhien did not seem to mind the mockery.

Tyrion studied Prince Iltharis as he came into view. He was a tall, slender elf, dark-haired and fair-skinned with piercing grey eyes and a languid manner. He was garbed in a very elaborate, scholarly fashion. He carried a bunch of scrolls negligently under one arm.

He sauntered over to inspect the students, smiled and bowed to Korhien. 'Indeed it is, and who can disagree with the sentiment?'

'I sense that you do.'

'Not in the slightest, my dear fellow – I just wish you would express them less pompously and with slightly more originality.'

'I see you are determined to undermine my authority with my students, Iltharis.'

'You were doing that quite well enough without my help, Korhien. I am surprised that they could keep from laughing at you.'

Tyrion was surprised that an elf as fierce as Korhien would put up with this banter, but he saw that the White Lion was not put out by it in the least, in fact appeared to enjoy it.

'Perhaps you would care to instruct them instead.'

'I am not in the least suited to being a teacher of weapons,' said Iltharis. 'Poetry or history are more my forte. When it comes to teaching, anyway.'

'That is something we can both agree upon, my friend. Perhaps you would care to leave me to giving the lessons then?'

'Indeed. Perhaps I shall remain and watch. I might pick up a few pointers.'

Korhien laughed.

'I somehow doubt that, Prince Iltharis, but you are welcome to remain.'

'Well, I am interested in your latest pupil anyway. I am writing another monograph on the Blood of Aenarion.'

Tyrion spend the next few hours sparring, losing himself in physical activity, learning everything Korhien had to say. He was aware all the time that Prince Iltharis was studying him with a watchful eye. He found that he was getting a little bit tired of being inspected so closely all the time.

Prince Iltharis eventually said, 'Your new pupil is quite exceptional, Korhien.'

'Indeed,' said the White Lion. Tyrion was annoyed at this fop passing judgement on him.

'Perhaps you would care to try a turn with the blades,' Tyrion said. Iltharis looked at him and smiled mockingly.

'It is not something I would usually do, but in your case I shall make an exception.'

He sauntered over to the sword rack, examined the wooden blades like a connoisseur selecting a bottle of wine and picked up the one that he liked the most. A moment later he was strapping on the practice armour.

Tyrion could not help but notice that for all his languid manner there was muscle there. Iltharis stretched like a big cat to get the kinks out of his muscles, saluted Korhien and then turned to face Tyrion. 'When you are ready, young prince,' he said. The rest of the students watched with interest. Some of them smiled. One or two laughed. Tyrion wondered what he had gotten himself into.

He approached Prince Iltharis, sword held ready. They exchanged two blows and his sword was out of his hand. Tyrion replayed what had happened in his mind. Iltharis had used a similar trick to the one Korhien had played when first they duelled, but had done it much faster. His speed of reflex was uncanny. Tyrion suspected that for the first time in his life he had encountered someone even quicker than himself.

'That was a pretty trick with which you disarmed me. I will wager you could not do it again.'

Iltharis raised an eyebrow. 'What will you wager?'

Tyrion felt his embarrassment deepen. He owned nothing, not even the clothes he was wearing. 'It was a figure of speech,' he said lamely.

'Prince Iltharis is also very wealthy,' said Korhien. 'Or his family is, which comes to the same thing.'

'Your plebeian roots are showing, Korhien. One would think you almost jealous.'

'The only thing I envy of you, prince, is your skill with a blade.'

'Well, it's always nice to be envied for something. But I was talking to your young friend here about the terms of a wager.'

'I have nothing to offer,' said Tyrion, thinking as always that honesty was for the best. 'As I said, it was a figure of speech.'

'I will lend him a gold piece,' said Korhien.

'Are you sure, my friend? I know it is a large sum of money for you.'

'I do not want it,' said Tyrion.

'You may not have the wealth of Aenarion, but you have some of his pride,' said Iltharis. 'I can set a term for the wager that I believe will be acceptable.'

'Go on,' said Tyrion.

'If I win, you will do me one favour when I request it. If you win, I will do the same.'

'Fair enough,' said Tyrion.

'I would not be so quick to accept, doorkeeper,' said Korhien. 'You do not know what the favour might prove to be.'

'Nothing dishonourable or hurtful to your ancient pride,' said Iltharis. 'Be sure of it.'

'Very well,' said Tyrion.

They fell into fighting stances again. This time Tyrion's attack was less reckless and he watched for Iltharis to try the same disarming technique. When it came, he was ready for it. His response was swift and sure and almost successful. Instead of being disarmed himself, he almost disarmed Iltharis.

Only the other's cat-like quickness of reflex saved him. He sprang backwards, aimed a blow at Tyrion's knee, paralysing it and then knocked him off his feet with a powerful blow to the chest.

Ruefully, Tyrion picked himself up. His leg felt numb from the nerve-strike. 'I guess I lost the bet,' he said.

Iltharis shook his head. 'No. You won it. I could not disarm you with the same technique again. You were quite right.' He raised the wooden blade in an intricate salute and then returned it to the rack. 'I congratulate you, Korhien. Your pupil is everything you claimed and more.'

Tyrion glanced at the White Lion. It seemed that he and Iltharis had been talking about him in private and Iltharis's appearance was not mere happenstance.

'It is good of you to say so.'

'No, Korhien, it is honest of me to say so. Now I must thank you for an interesting morning's entertainment and bid you adieu.' With that Prince Iltharis bowed and strolled away across the courtyard.

The other pupils were looking at Tyrion now with something like awe. It appeared that Prince Iltharis was well-known and respected among the young warriors of the Emeraldsea Palace.

'Who was he?' Tyrion asked Atharis, after Iltharis was out of sight.

'Prince Iltharis is one of the deadliest swords in all Ulthuan. He has killed more elves in duels than anyone in living memory. Some whisper that he is an assassin for his House.'

'An assassin?'

'Sometimes duels are fought over more than points of honour. Sometimes they are fought to remove political inconveniences or as part of political manoeuvres.'

Tyrion stared at him for a long moment then smiled. 'I start to understand why you all take this practice so seriously.'

'It is, as Korhien said, a matter of life and death. Sometimes it has larger consequences for our House and our families. I doubt you have very much to worry about though.'

'I do if Prince Iltharis comes after me. Or anyone nearly as good.'

'There are very few that good in Ulthuan and his House is allied to our own.'

'Alliances can always be broken,' said Tyrion.

'I see you have a swift grasp of politics as well as how to use a blade,' said Atharis. 'We could be useful friends to each other.'

Tyrion extended his hand and clasped the others'. 'I can always use a friend,' he said.

* * *

Teclis woke to find Malene sitting by his bed. She looked a little worried.

'What happened?' he asked. The last thing he could remember was watching Tyrion leave for his fencing lesson. He had walked over to the table and bent over to pick something up. Then he had felt dizzy...

His heart sank. It seemed like his illness had returned.

'You were taken ill,' she said. She looked rueful. 'I think you have been over-exerting yourself recently. You have not recovered as much as you appeared to have. It seems I am not quite as good an alchemist as I thought.'

'Yes, you are. I have never felt better in my life than the past few days,' Teclis said.

'Nonetheless you must be careful not to push yourself too hard. You are still far from healthy.'

'I believe I am in a position to understand that,' said Teclis, gesturing at his recumbent form. Malene smiled. There was a knock on the door, an odd double tap that sounded unlike any knock Teclis had heard before. Malene seemed to recognise it. She made a face.

'Come in,' she said.

A tall, lithe looking elf entered. His hair was dark and his eyes a piercing grey. His skin was pale compared to the elves of Lothern. His manner was quite exquisite. His clothing had the elegance of the dandy. A faint lingering perfume billowed in advance.

'Ah, the delightful Lady Malene. I was told I would find you here,' he said. 'And this will be your new pupil. Let us hope that he is as good a student of magic as his brother is of the blade.'

'Prince Iltharis,' said Lady Malene smoothly. 'It is a pleasure to see you as always.' She did not sound as if it was a pleasure. Her expression was reserved as it normally was.

'I am Prince Iltharis,' said the elf, bowing formally and smiling. It was a very charming smile, open and friendly. 'Since Lady Malene has not seen fit to introduce us, perhaps you would do me the favour of telling me your name.'

'I am Prince Teclis.'

'Excellent. As I suspected, you are the brother of that splendid specimen down in the courtyard.'

'I heard you were teaching him a lesson with the sword,' said Lady Malene.

'News travels fast around here. He does not need too many lessons from me, or anyone else for that matter. He is a natural with the blade.'

Prince Iltharis brought a chair over to beside the bed. He carried it one-handed although it was made from heavy carved wood. He was stronger than he looked, Teclis thought.

'That is quite a compliment, coming from you,' said Malene. She did not sound convinced. She turned to Teclis. 'Korhien says Prince Iltharis is the best elf with a blade in Lothern, possibly Ulthuan.'

Teclis filed away that information. Iltharis did not look like a warrior. He looked like a scholar. There was a great deal that was deceptive about this elf, he decided.

'Korhien does me too much honour,' said Iltharis.

'You are in an unusually modest mood this afternoon,' said Lady Malene.

'Perhaps I am daunted by the grandeur of my surroundings,' said Iltharis mockingly. 'The Emeraldsea Palace is looking particularly imposing. You are spending a lot of money to celebrate this Feast of Deliverance. Is there any particular reason why?'

He looked pointedly at Teclis.

Of course, Teclis thought, if House Emeraldsea wanted to stress its ties with the Blood of Aenarion then this was exactly the time of year to remind people of them.

'It has been a good trading season,' said Malene. 'All of our vessels have returned home laden with precious cargoes. Some of the gold is being used for the entertainment of the Families.'

'So, it's not true then; you are not making a statement.'

'What statement would that be, Prince Iltharis?'

'The usual one that the elves of Lothern always feel compelled to make. That they are wealthier than the rest of us and that they have the support of the Phoenix King. And, of course, they are directly related to the most famous elf of all.'

'I doubt we are any wealthier than your family, Prince Iltharis. The House of Silvermount is fabulously rich.'

'And prodigiously ancient as well,' said Teclis. 'Its members have won renown in the service of many Phoenix Kings and the line has produced many great sorcerers.'

Iltharis tilted his head to one side and smiled again. 'I see you are quite the scholar Prince Teclis. You number genealogy among your interests?'

Malene smiled but did not say anything. Teclis was beginning to recognise Iltharis's style now. He enjoyed provoking people, getting them to say more than they intended, to reveal themselves. And he did not fear being challenged either. For all his languid manner, he seemed to have perfect poise and self-confidence. Teclis found himself torn between admiration and dislike.

'I have many interests,' said Teclis blandly.

'Rumour has it that one of them is magic, and that Lady Malene is teaching you.'

'Why are you here, Prince Iltharis?' Malene asked. She sounded almost rude. 'Prince Teclis is sick.'

'I had heard he was a scholar so I brought him some reading material.' He took the scrolls out from beneath his arm and handed them to Teclis. Despite his unease, Teclis took them and studied them becoming more and more excited as he read.

'This is an original of the *History of the Mages of Saphery*,' he said, unable to keep his enthusiasm from his voice. 'Written by Bel-Hathor himself.'

Iltharis nodded. 'It is from my library,' he said. 'You can return it when you are finished.'

'Thank you,' said Teclis, genuinely pleased and not a little troubled. 'But why are you lending it to me? You do not know me.'

'I knew your father, and your mother. They were both special friends of mine. I thought it might be pleasant to make the acquaintance of their sons. And I confess a personal interest. I am writing a monograph on the Blood of Aenarion, and it seemed like a good idea to make the acquaintance of the latest members of that line to be presented to the Phoenix King. Who knows what great deeds you and your brother will eventually perform?'

Malene was studying the prince closely now. Her face was colder than ever.

'I am sure Prince Teclis is grateful for your gifts, prince. But it might be better if we left now. He needs his rest if he is to regain his strength.'

'I am not as strong as my brother,' said Teclis, coughing uneasily. The fit grew stronger until he was almost bent double.

Lady Malene produced a small bottle of a coloured cordial which she handed to him. He drank it and the fit passed, leaving him red-eyed and wheezing. Teclis was used to elves moving away from him during such bouts, but Iltharis did not. Teclis was surprised to see something like sympathy in his eyes.

He seemed to be about to say something but at that moment Korhien Ironglaive entered through the nearby archway. He smiled at Lady Malene and kissed her hand, then bowed to Prince Iltharis in his usual exuberant way. He nodded to Teclis. 'I see you are all enjoying yourselves,' he said.

'I suspect Prince Teclis is enjoying himself less than the rest of us,' said Iltharis. 'Perhaps we should take ourselves elsewhere.'

'Perhaps we should,' said Lady Malene.

Prince Iltharis bowed to Teclis as he departed. 'I look forward to discussing those scrolls with you at some future date. It will be nice to have someone civilised to talk to around here.'

Teclis opened the scrolls. Weak as he was, he could not stop himself from reading them.

CHAPTER THIRTEEN

On his arrival home, Prince Iltharis went to his chambers. They were in the old part of the Silvermount Palace, on the ground floor. The building was extremely ancient and this part looked as if it has not undergone very much reconstruction in the past few centuries.

Two thousand-year old tapestries hung on the wall, preserved by the magic woven into them. Busts depicting the faces of elves dead millennia ago but still remembered and honoured by their descendants lined the corridors.

Iltharis looked around, smiling fondly, then locked the door. He pulled the drapes to stop any light finding its way in and then retreated deeper into his chambers, locking the doors behind him as he went.

When he reached the room deepest in his apartments, he unlocked a glass cabinet case, and produced a hookah and some incense sticks. He took a somewhat disreputable, not to mention very expensive, narcotic from a pouch and placed it in the hookah, setting it alight so that the scent would be faintly noticeable throughout his chambers and so give a suitable explanation for anyone who wondered why he had locked so many doors.

He turned the key on the final lock. It was very strong as was the door it was set in. It had been built in more troubled times and was intended to protect the occupant from assassins. It would take a group of strong elves a long time to break that door down.

Having completed his preparations, he pulled aside the wall hangings and, with the ease of long practice, pushed a pressure pad set in the wall. A section of the wall rotated to reveal a secret passage beyond. It had been intended by the builders as an escape route for the occupants of the chamber protected by that very strong door. Iltharis closed the secret panel behind him and followed a ramp that went a very long way below the city.

The air grew more stagnant and musty. The way grew darker. Prince Iltharis moved along the passage with remarkable ease considering the absence of light. Eventually his steps took him to a dead end. Here, he reached up and found another pressure plate in a place that would have been too high for anyone to find by accident. Another secret door opened. Iltharis went through it and closed it behind him, and then reached out and found a lantern hanging there and lit it. Here, deep below the earth, shielded by many spells and many tons of solid rock above him, he looked upon a potent magical artefact.

In the centre of the chamber stood a huge, silver mirror. He studied his reflection in it for a moment, smiled, swallowed his nervousness. He pricked his thumb, smeared blood on the surface of the mirror and invoked a spell.

It grew colder as he chanted. At first it looked cloudy as if some giant's breath were misting the glass, then, within its depths, a cold blue light became visible and the view in the mirror grew clearer although it no longer reflected Prince Iltharis's surroundings.

He looked now into a vast hall, dominated by a mighty iron throne on which reclined a huge armoured figure. The figure seemed out of proportion to its surroundings, an adult sitting in a child's playhouse. The armour of the figure glowed with dreadful runes but the glow of that fatal magic was no more terrifying than the glow in its eyes. Iltharis looked into them and, as ever, was shocked by the force of their owner's will.

Iltharis fought down a shudder and made himself meet the gaze of his master, Malekith, Witch King of Naggaroth.

'Well, Urian, what have you to report?' The voice was cold and stark and beautiful in its strange fashion, the same way as the frozen landscapes of icebound northern Naggaroth were beautiful.

'Greetings, majesty, I have seen the latest of the Blood to report to the court of the False King.'

'And?'

'They are... unusual.'

'In what way?'

'They are twins. One of them very much a warrior, one of them will be a mage of some considerable power, unless I miss my guess.'

'Do they show any signs of the Curse?'

'Teclis, the one who will be a mage, is physically very weak. I do not know if he will live for much longer.'

'Then he can hardly be of much concern to us, for good or ill, can he? What of the other one?'

'Tyrion does indeed seem to be of the line of Aenarion, sire. He is tall and well-formed and very fast and strong. If he lives he will become a most formidable warrior.'

'As good as you, Urian?'

'I doubt he will live that long, sire. Word has it that the Cult of the Forbidden Blade already plans his death.' The Cult plotted the death of any they felt might be able to draw the Sword of Khaine and thus end the world. They were idiots, but they were dangerous idiots, and they numbered some very deadly duellists as part of their ancient conspiracy.

'But if he does live, Urian?'

'Then, yes, sire. It is possible he would be my match.'

'He must be formidable indeed.'

'He is, sire. And by all accounts he is quick of mind and gifted at tactics.'

'Does he bear any signs of the Curse, Urian? The Curse?'

'Not as yet, sire, but he is very young. What would you have me do about him?'

'Keep a close eye on him, Urian. If he shows any signs of the Curse, we shall let him live. If not...'

'As you wish, sire. And the other, the sickly one?'

'It does not sound like he will be a problem, does it?'

'No, sire. It does not.'

'You like them, don't you, Urian?'

As always Iltharis was surprised by the perceptiveness of his master. He did not know why that should be. It was impossible to rule a kingdom like Naggaroth for long ages without great insight into the elven heart.

'I do, sire,' Iltharis said. He always felt that honesty, insofar as he was able to manage it, was the best policy when dealing with his master. He had known too many elves suffer terrible fates through lying to Malekith.

'I do hope you are not becoming soft over there among our degenerate kinfolk, Urian.'

'I will do whatever is needed, sire. As I always do.'

'I know Urian. That is why you are my most trusted servant.'

He made a gesture and the great mirror went dark. Iltharis once again found himself facing his own reflection. He laughed out loud at his master's final words. Malekith trusted no one. Iltharis began to suspect that he himself might be marked for death.

'No one lives forever,' he muttered to himself. Not even you,

Malekith, he thought but he kept that part to himself. Even down here, you never knew who might be listening. The Witch King had eyes and ears everywhere.

Urian looked at himself in the now dormant mirror. He was not sure he recognised himself any more. He touched the long dark hair that ran down to his shoulders. Back in the beginning, before he had been singled out to become what he was today, his hair had been white. He was fairly sure of that. His skin had been pale and he had a few freckles. His eyes had been a simple green. His nose had been snub for an elf. Or perhaps his hair had been the colour of copper. He truly could not remember. His memories were twisted and there had been times when he had been less than sane. He was certain of that.

So many times now, his skin had been peeled from him and replaced with the flayed flesh of others. The bones in his face had been restructured. His eyes had been replaced by orbs stolen from someone else's sockets and kept preserved in jars of alchemical brine. He touched his eyelids now, wondering who these eyes had once belonged to; an elf, of course, but whether a high elf or a dark elf he could not tell. There was no real difference between the two, after all. Who knew that better than him?

How many hours had he spent chained to the altars in Naggarond while sorcerer-surgeons worked on him with blood-stained scalpels, peeling off his skin, magically grafting on new flesh? How many days had he spent with his brain magically altered to perceive pleasure as pain and pain as pleasure, except for those moments when the surgeons for their own amusement had chosen to let the spells lapse? How many weeks would he one day spend claiming his vengeance on those same magi?

He raised his glass and toasted himself. The wine was pallid and tasteless but he kept it here to give him something to steady his nerves after his little chats with his master. He missed the hallucinogenic vintages of Naggaroth, just as he missed the gladiatorial games and the easy availability of slave girls. He had kept a harem of them in his palace in Naggarond. They had been his, to do with whatever he wanted, to dispose of however he willed when he had done with them. That had been in another lifetime, one that seemed like a dream now. Perhaps it had been. Perhaps he had always been Prince Iltharis and he was mad, and the life of Urian Poisonblade, champion of Malekith, was some sort of deranged fantasy. Or perhaps he just wished it so.

He smiled mockingly and his reflection smiled back. He had worn so many other faces, lived so many other lives, he sometimes lost track of these things. There were times when he really believed himself to be Prince Iltharis and a loyal friend to the Phoenix King and Korhien Ironglaive. Those were not bad things to be, he thought, and then scoffed at his own weakness.

He was getting soft. He had spent too much time amid these spineless creatures that called themselves high elves and too long away from the harsh certainties of Naggaroth. He had grown accustomed to not having to carry a dozen concealed weapons and look for treachery in the faces of those who called themselves his closest friends. Now the only face he looked upon that hid treachery was his own. It winked back at him from the mirror and then it smiled sourly.

This was not what he had expected, not at all. He found he quite enjoyed living this life. He enjoyed being respected and not simply feared for his talent with a blade. He enjoyed living among people who thought of things other than their own interests occasionally.

Once, like all the other druchii, he had scoffed at the asur and their hypocrisy, the way they felt they were better, more moral. He had come to realise that in some ways they were. Even if they were hypocrites, their very hypocrisy made them better than the dark elves. The fact that they wanted to appear good, even for the wrong reasons, made them behave in a way that was better.

It did not matter that they aided each other because they wanted to be seen to live up to some ancient ideal. The fact was, that for whatever the reasons, they did. And some of them really did believe in their ideals, Korhien and young Prince Tyrion for example, unless he was much mistaken. They were fools, of course, but it was a folly that it was possible to respect. Nor were they weak – their folly gave them strength and courage.

He took another sip of wine and wished that it were laced with the ecstatic poisons made from powdered lotus. At times like these he missed them. Before he came to Ulthuan, to assume the role of Prince Iltharis that had been long prepared for him among Malekith's secret followers in Ulthuan, he had been forced to abstain for months. It had been a hard time. He had sweated through withdrawal symptoms that would have killed other druchii. He had lost the bright, mad clarity that never, ever having his bloodstream free of the drugs had given him. In some ways, he realised he really had made himself into a high elf. He had been forced to live as they did.

It was not entirely unpleasant. He was no longer given to mad rages or picking quarrels with strangers for reasons he could never quite remember the next day. He lived in a place now where that would not be acceptable. Here, elves needed good reasons to kill each other, they did not do it simply to gratify a momentary whim. Of course, he missed being able to do that sometimes. Who would not? But he found these days that he had fewer regrets.

He admitted it. He sometimes wished that he could simply forget who he was and become Prince Iltharis. He would put aside his divided loyalties and fragmented personality and become wholly one thing. For a moment, and a moment only, he allowed himself to imagine what that would really feel like.

Then he dismissed the fantasy.

There were those who knew who he was, who would not allow him to do that. And even if he killed them, there would be others, secret watchers whom he never suspected. They would bring word of his treachery to the Witch King. And Malekith was not a forgiving master to those who betrayed him. He would stretch out his cold metal hand, and a suitable vengeance would be wreaked. There was nothing more certain in this life.

No, even if he wanted to give up this life, he could not. There was no escape. There was nothing to do but make the best of it.

◄ CHAPTER FOURTEEN ►

Prince Sardriane looked up. The face he saw was beautiful and reassuring. It was that of a lovely elf woman, his mother. He was surprised but he could not quite remember why. He felt as if he were awakening from a deep, languorous sleep and had not quite woken fully yet. He tried sitting up, but he could not. He tried moving his arms, but he could not. Something seemed to be restraining his hands and his legs and when he tried to lift his head something bit into his throat.

'What is going on?' he asked.

'Hush,' said his mother. 'There is nothing to worry about.'

Why was she naked? Why did she caress him so lasciviously?

There was something odd about her voice. It sounded like mother, or rather it sounded as she would have if she were in great pain while she spoke. There appeared to be something wrong with her head. Two small curling horns grew out of the side of her brow. Her mouth looked a little distorted too, as did her face.

Sardriane sniffed. There was a hideous stench in the air of burned meat, mingled with charred wood. He turned his head to one side, as far as whatever was restraining him allowed, and he saw that he was in his home, or what was left of it.

The roof had crashed in, and the walls looked burned through. A few of the more intricate carvings, of which his dead father had been so proud, were still intact, but they were soot-blackened in some places and the colour of ash in others. There was something else in the air, a strange sickly perfume that was cloying and yet thrilling at the same time. It smelled of musk and rot and hinted at other things that he did not want to think about.

'I remember,' he said, for he suddenly did. He remembered the fall of Tor Annan, the way the howling daemonic horde had come racing towards the walls, some falling to elf shafts, the daemons ignoring arrows that had not been enchanted by a mage.

The winged things had flapped down from the sky and attacked first the siege machines and then the archers. Death had come so very close to him in the opening moments of the battle. The winged furies had struck down the elves on either side of him. Daemons had smashed through the gates and clambered onto the walls, killing everybody they encountered. One had loomed over him, been about to strike and then at the last second, at the shouted command of what might have been a leader, had struck down Alfrik instead. Mad cultists had come swarming through the broken gateway, howling and chanting ecstatically as they slew.

At first the elves of Tor Annan had fought bravely. Archers had died where they stood, still unleashing their arrows at targets that ignored them. Warriors had tried to halt the monstrous red-skinned daemons. But as the fight went on it became obvious they could not overcome their foes. Some had fled. Some had tried to surrender. And some, seeing the daemonic leader of their enemies, had been overcome by a strange madness and had started throwing themselves at its feet and grovelling in ecstatic communion.

Sardriane had been one of the ones who had fled. He had raced through the streets to the ancestral home he shared with his mother and a few ageing retainers. He had told them to bar the door and to make ready to withstand a siege. Some of them, feeling that death was preferable to falling into the hands of their enemy, had taken their own lives using poisons preserved for that purpose. Sardriane had urged his mother to do so, for he feared what might happen if she were to fall into the taloned claws of the besiegers. She had refused, saying that while he lived, she would. She had as much pride as he. After all, she too was of the Blood of Aenarion.

For a while they had huddled in their chambers while the town burned around them and screams echoed down the streets. It sounded as if some hideous carnival of torture and wickedness were taking place outside. He prayed that if they waited long enough, they would be unnoticed by their enemies and escape with their lives. He hated himself for his cowardice. He hated himself for running. It seemed unworthy of his proud ancestry. The only defence he could offer up was that he was young and he did not want to die.

At last the screaming had stopped and he had dared to peek out through a gap in the shuttered windows. He had seen lines and lines of silent faces watching the building. Some of them belonged to brazen horned, crimson-skinned daemons. Some of them belonged to cultists. Some of them belonged to people who had once been his neighbours and who now gazed at his house with features dazed and numbed and subtly altered.

As if his looking upon them had broken some evil spell, they all shouted and rushed forwards, smashing in through the doors and revelling through the halls of Sardriane's home, smashing the ancient furnishings, burning the ancient tapestries, maiming and killing the retainers, howling with insatiable blood lust and something else, a primitive deep-throated pleasure that was even more disgusting than their desire to do harm.

They had overpowered Sardriane and his mother and carried them to their leader, a strange creature whose outline shimmered and shifted constantly sometimes suggesting a crab-clawed hulking daemonic thing, sometimes the most beautiful woman he had ever imagined, sometimes the most noble king. He had thrown himself towards the monster, trying to strike at it with a dagger he seized from the scabbard of one of his tormentors, and had been struck unconscious by a blow to the head.

That was the last thing he remembered until this moment of bleak consciousness, when he had come to and been confronted with this evil parody of his mother. He wished that he was not awake now. He wished that he was not seeing anything. He wished that it was all a horrible dream. He knew it was not. He had seen more elves die in the last few hours than he had ever expected to see die in his life. He had witnessed a whole small town wiped out and he was not even sure why. The sheer malevolence of it was virtually incomprehensible. He closed his eyes again and wished the whole thing away.

'You are awake, little elfling. Do not pretend otherwise.' The voice was impossibly sweet and impossibly malevolent and still it bore an odd resemblance to his mother's.

'Go to hell,' he said. His mouth felt dry and it took a huge effort to force the words out, but he felt the need to make up for his earlier cowardice by a show of defiance now, even if it would do him no good whatsoever.

'I will eventually,' said the thing that looked like his mother. 'Most gratefully too shall I leave this tedious place. But there are a few things I need to put right before I go. You shall help me.'

'Never.'

'Oh, but you will. You will help me by dying. Eventually.'

Sardriane swallowed. He did not like the sound of this at all. He had heard tales of what Chaos cultists were capable of, and this thing was mistress of such a cult. Judging by the earlier slaughter, the stories of their cruelty were not exaggerated.

'You are going to kill me... so do it.'

'I will at the end, but first you will beg me not to, and then you will beg me to do so, and then when I have broken your will and your sanity and made you worship me and love me, I shall kill you. I might even tell you why.'

'I do not care.'

'That is simply perverse, which I admire. Don't tell me you are not in the slightest bit curious why I have slaughtered your tiny little town and killed all of your family and yet let you live.'

'I have had other things on my mind.'

The daemon's laughter was gentle and mocking. It reached out with one soft hand and caressed his cheek. A thrill of depraved pleasure came from the contact, a magical spark jumping from one to the other.

A moment later the tip of a thumb claw flipped out his eye. He did not feel much pain, only an odd ripping sensation and then a wetness as the empty socket filled with blood. The daemon muttered something and raised its hand and twisted. Sardriane's brain lurched as it tried to cope with the impact of what was happening. One eye floated in the air above him. He was looking up at it with the eye still in its socket. A thin taut rope of nerve fibre seemed to connect it to his head. With the other eye he was looking down on himself as he wept tears of blood. The daemon reached out and put out his good eye, so that now he seemed only to be looking down on his body. His vision settled and he saw that he was lying on a pile of skinned corpses, held in place by ropes of entrails.

'Yes,' said the voice, simply malicious now. 'That is what awaits you in the end, although I confess I am tempted to animate the corpses and re-enact the Masque of the Fleshless. Perhaps later...'

It reached forward and touched Sardriane's forehead. As the elf watched he saw his own skin split and begin to part and the daemon peeled his body like a grape. He tried to swallow his own tongue but this was expected and the daemon prevented it.

'No, Blood of Aenarion,' it said. 'This game has a while to run yet.'

Sardriane was a long time dying. Everything the daemon promised came true.

This evening N'Kari wore the form of a mighty, muscular human warrior with the head of bull and the lower body of a horse. It allowed him to move quickly and he enjoyed the sensation of being a quadruped. There was something about that he had always found stimulating.

It was easier to hold the shape for longer now. He was growing accustomed to this reality and its restrictions. He was learning to use the flows of its magic almost at will.

Behind him his army awaited their instructions.

It was not as impressive a force as he would have liked but it was growing. It now consisted of a few dozen bound daemons, and several hundred cultists. Some of them had been recruited from farmers and smallholders encountered en route to Tor Annan. Many more had joined him after the destruction of their town.

The souls of those who refused to submit to the ecstatic disciplines of the Cult of Pleasure were swiftly dispatched to the netherworld, bait and sustenance for the daemons N'Kari had used them to summon. In general that had not proved necessary in more than half the cases. There was a strong pleasure-loving streak in most elves, and given the choice between death and a life of drug-fuelled, esoteric pleasure a significant number made the right choice.

The rest had provided an interesting distraction.

Sometimes the allegiance of families had been split and N'Kari had required the new recruits to prove their loyalty by sacrificing those who refused to join. Sometimes this had engendered second thoughts in the recruits, sometimes in the recalcitrant converts. In any case, it had provided a few moments of relief from ennui. He delighted in the savour of any strong emotion, and these elves were good for that, at least.

'You have orders for us, Great Master?' Elrion asked. He was beginning to look haggard as the toll of nights of pleasure and days of horror overtook him. He twitched and frothed and broke into tears at odd times. Sometimes he would rant at the other cultists, delivering terrifying if somewhat unimaginative sermons on the nature of Chaos and the goals of their master.

N'Kari enjoyed the storytelling and the embroidery of the facts and so far had seen no reason to contradict him. If anything, some of Elrion's more visionary passages had made the rest of his cultists even more devout. The elf had acquired his own small harem among the impressionable worshippers but did not seem to take much pleasure in it.

Typical mortal really. So hard to please. Give them what they claimed they wanted and they would inevitably discover it was not what they expected or desired. Even to a devotee of the Lord of Perversity this sometimes seemed a little too perverse.

He thought about those he had killed back in Tor Annan.

N'Kari felt the desire for vengeance swell within him. His desire for it grew with every death. Feeding on the souls of the Blood of Aenarion made him hunger for more. There was something about the spirits that gave him more nutriment and more power than any others he had ever consumed. He was going to need it, for his plan was approaching its most difficult stage.

It had taken longer than he would have liked to find this place due to the restrictions this reality placed on his abilities to travel. Even the strange paths of the Vortex had allowed him to move more swiftly when he had been entrapped within them, and he had become used to the freedom they offered. It was this fact that had provided the germ of his original plan, and the reason why he had chosen the place for his escape to which he had now returned.

Nearby there was a waystone and an entrance into the odd underworld that the first so-called rulers of this world had created to allow themselves swift travel from point to point. He could call upon its power and make it serve his own purposes.

'Tell my best beloved to prepare themselves. They are going to witness a miracle,' the daemon said.

Elrion's face lit up with curiosity. He knew that his master did not make such promises lightly and that something ominous and awesome was to be expected. N'Kari smiled, revealing his enormous fangs. He reached out and stroked Elrion's cheek with his taloned hand. 'Yes, little mortal, you're going to witness a mighty sorcery.'

N'Kari approached the waystone.

To his daemonic eyesight it glowed, revealing the faint seepage of energy from within the Vortex. His smile grew wider, his fangs glittered in the moonlight. He knew all about this sort of magical power and how to wield it and shape it to his purposes. He was going to perform a feat of magic here that the elves would remember for as long as they existed – which, Slaanesh willing, would not be very long even as mortals measured time.

He was going to do something here that had never been attempted before in this world and probably would never be attempted again because there was no one who could match his knowledge, magical power or skill when it came to this. There was no one else who had paid the price of being imprisoned within the Vortex for five millennia either. It had allowed him to maintain his form here in a way that few other daemons could manage without the winds of magic blowing strongly. It was going to allow him to do something else as well.

He decided that he would need to make a few sacrifices before he began. It was not that the magic required them – it was simply that he liked to begin a new venture with an offering to his patron daemon god in order to curry favour and bring good fortune. It could not do any harm, it might do some good, and at very least it would give him some pleasure, which was the main thing.

He used a waystone as an altar and offered up six choice souls to Slaanesh. If through force of habit he stole most of their essence for himself, it was only fitting because he was going to need some of the power they provided to work the spell he intended.

He drew a six-pointed star using the blood of his victims and placed a severed head at each point. Once that was done he began to chant, as much to focus his mind as to impress his followers. As he chanted, he drew more lines in a mightily convoluted hiero- glyphic that represented a path between this waystone and another one, within a day's march of where his next victim dwelled.

In his mind he visualised the tunnel of light between the two points and, as he tapped the powers of magic, he forced his view of the world onto the world itself. The thing that he was creating in his mind through the power of his magic was also coming into being in the malleable substrata of reality that the waystone tapped into.

By the time he had finished his ritual, a glimmering archway hov- ered in the air before him, its surface shimmering like oily water reflecting firelight. With a gesture of his claw, he indicated that his followers should pass through it. Not without some reluctance the first of them did so, disappearing through the iridescent arch, as if they had dived into strangely coloured water.

Only when he had witnessed the last of them pass through did the daemon join them and do the same, plunging into a gap in reality and venturing through the strange tunnel in which kaleidoscopic sensations assaulted his senses.

Takalen the Ranger sniffed the air. There was something odd about it, a smell of rotting flesh that should not have been there. The lord who owned this mansion was old but the place should not have looked so deserted and that ominous scent should not have been hanging in the air. A feeling of foreboding passed through Takalen's mind and she shivered. Overhead her companion shrieked and she knew that the great eagle was also disturbed. It was hanging in the air far above and its eyes were much keener than hers so perhaps it had already seen what was causing the smell.

Takalen moved cautiously towards the door of the old mansion. She did not like the look of it at all. She had occasionally visited Prince Faldor and his daughter Fayelle when she had passed this way previously and she had never known them to be careless. Just because this area was comparatively safe compared to the rest of Ulthuan did not mean the old noble had relaxed his guard. In the past the door had always been shut, which was only sensible, for in these dark times who knew what strange things might emerge to threaten the peace of the locality.

The door was open now, and even as Takalen watched, a fox emerged through it, carrying something in its mouth which on closer observation proved to be the remains of an elf hand. Takalen drew her sword, and passed through the doorway. She did not expect anything dangerous – the fox would not have been there had attackers still been within. It was just that there was something about the atmosphere that set her teeth on edge and made her wary.

Inside the walls of the villa was a courtyard. She saw the first of the corpses and, although she was no weak-gutted town-dweller, it made her want to heave. The bodies had been flayed and mutilated and the dismembered parts laid out in some odd pattern. The outline had been disturbed by scavenging animals but the fact that someone had intentionally laid the parts out in an ordered way was obvious. Splashes of blood and dried out strips of intestine made that absolutely clear.

There was a strong stink of magic in the air. Takalen was no mage but like all elves she was sensitive to the flows of magic. She could tell that something dark and awful had been done here. She pushed on into the main building, knowing already that what she would find would be terrible.

The air was close and foetid. Flies buzzed everywhere, brushing against her face, getting in her long ash-blonde hair, skittering across her exposed skin. There were too many of them for this to be entirely natural. The stink of dark magic was stronger here.

The old furniture was broken. It was as if a crowd of maniacs had rushed through this place, breaking everything precious they could find. Discarded clothing, blood-soaked, lay everywhere. There were odd outlines of elven shapes imprinted on the walls. It took the trained tracker long minutes to work out what had happened simply because her mind did not want to accept it. It looked like lust-maddened elves, and other things, had rolled in blood and had wild sex against the walls.

What in the name of Isha had happened here?

Takalen had heard rumours that some of the locals had been dabbling in the old rites of the Cult of Luxury. It looked like they had gone beyond dabbling here. It looked like they had taken to summoning things using the old dark magic.

Slaanesh! She deciphered another of the words crudely written on the walls, smeared in blood and excrement. Her lips curled. Her nose wrinkled. Slaanesh. The word was repeated again, mixed with other names, and curses and imprecations.

N'Kari was one of those names, an appellation almost as dreadful as that of the daemon lord of forbidden pleasures. It belonged to the Keeper of Secrets responsible for the Rape of Ulthuan in the dawn ages, a creature twice destroyed by the mighty Aenarion and thought gone forever.

N'Kari has returned.

The sentence was sometimes spelled out in crude block characters and sometimes in the graceful looping script of modern Elvish. It was repeated over and over again like the monotonous repetitions of a lunatic.

N'Kari will have vengeance.

In the great hall she found the remains of what might have been a daemonic orgy or a cannibal feast or some dreadful combination of both. Staked out in the middle of a curious ritual circle was the naked body of Fayelle, or at least something that might have looked like her, if her corpse had been desiccated and aged a thousand years.

It was a long time before Takalen could think clearly and do what had to be done.

Tyrion put on his old clothes. He stepped out onto the balcony and looked down into the street. It was late but there were people moving around down there still. Along this street he could see that the villas and mansions were all well lit but whole huge areas of the city were in darkness. Buildings loomed large in the moonlight. There was just no one in them as far as he could tell.

He felt excitement build up in him. He was really going to do this. He was going to slip out into the night and explore the city. He felt as if he were planning a prison break. It was not as if he was really a prisoner in the Emeraldsea Palace. He was sure they would let him go out if he asked. It was just that they would hem him around with guards and chaperones of other sorts and this was not what he wanted. He wanted to be on his own, to look at things at his own pace, to explore. He remembered some things about the city of his birth. He wanted to see how well it matched his childhood memories.

He considered waking Teclis to tell him what he was doing, but pushed the thought to one side. His brother would most likely want to come and that would make the logistics of the expedition so much more difficult. He would tell him about it tomorrow, when he returned. Tonight would just be a reconnaissance. There would be other nights or even days.

Plus, he wanted this for himself. He wanted to do it alone.

He lowered himself off the balcony. There was plenty of climbing ivy on the wall beneath but he doubted it would take his weight. Instead he used the gaps between the blocks of stone that made up the wall for foot and finger holds and made his way down, dropping the last ten feet to the ground. As soon as he hit, he picked himself up, dusted himself off and strolled away, whistling nonchalantly, walking with confidence as if what he was doing was perfectly normal.

As he walked he paused for a moment to study his surroundings and get his bearings. He felt certain he could find this place again. Things looked different at night but the Emeraldsea Palace was distinctive, so massive and with its towers greenly lit. He stared up at the hills above the harbour. A few lights glittered up there but not many. He knew what he was seeking was there though and he headed off, selecting a path that would take him up hill.

It was not long before the streets became much quieter, and he was alone in them. He moved more cautiously now prompted by instincts that told him in lonely places there was danger. He had his sword with him, strapped to his back for the climb. He adjusted the position of the scabbard to his waist so that it would be easier to draw, and practised unsheathing it a few times so that he could bring it forth, if needed, with eye-blurring speed. He enjoyed that. It made him feel like the hero in a story.

The buildings around him were old and gave off a fusty smell. No lights showed in any of them; they were empty. The windows of some had been boarded up. Others seemed completely abandoned. No one had lived in these places for many years. If he wanted to, he could simply pick one of these buildings and go and live in it.

For a moment he entertained the fantasy of dwelling like a castaway in the shell of one of these forgotten mansions. It made him smile to think about but then it struck him that all of these houses had once been lived in by his own people, by whole families and their retainers and cousins and distant kin. Now all of those people were gone. For the first time ever it really struck him that the elves were a dying people, were vanishing from the face of the world, never to return. Every one of these empty houses represented a great noble family that was now extinct.

How had they died? Had they been killed in war? Had they simply faded away with fewer children born every century and the old dying off? Had they died in accidents, one after the other, year after year, century after century, assassinated by chance and unlucky fate?

He supposed it did not really matter. The simple, melancholy truth was that they were gone. He suddenly understood in his gut, as he had never really understood it before, what it was that Korhien had meant when he said every elf life was precious. There were so few of them left now that each death was another small defeat for the entire people, the putting out of another candle in a vast echoing chamber that would soon be dark and empty.

It was not exactly that the thought frightened him. It made him uneasy and sad. Briefly he considered abandoning his whole expedition and returning to the palace. Doing so would be to admit a defeat though, or at very least a failure of courage, so he pushed on up the hill, following the promptings of half-remembered memories from when he was very small, until at last he found it, or at least what he was fairly certain was it; the house where he had lived when he and Teclis had been very young children.

It sat high on the hill in a row of other houses just like it. In some of these lights still shone. They had not been entirely abandoned. Their old house stood tall and old and proud. It was older by far than the Emeraldsea Palace, built in ancient days when his father's ancestors had looked down on the merchants literally beneath them. It was tall and narrow and five storeys high and each window facing outward on this side had a balcony. He could remember standing on one of these balconies as a child and looking down into the harbour. He had been too young and too small then to really understand anything that was going on around him. He felt much older than that now.

He walked to the door. It was chained. Someone had taken the trouble to lock the place up and it looked like someone visited every so often to see that it was maintained. He suspected it must be people in the employ of his mother's relatives. They seemed like the sort who would be careful about property. He supposed that he could pry open the locks or the rings of the chain if he really wanted to but it seemed a bit like sacrilege. So he clambered up the front of the building and onto the first balcony.

Memories came flooding back. He had been here before when the barrier had been so high he had to stand on tiptoes to look over it and his father and his father's friends had seemed like giants.

He knew there would be an even better view from above so he clambered up until he had reached the highest balcony and the ground was a dizzying drop beneath him. All of those hours spent clambering around in the rigging of the *Eagle of Lothern* proved their worth then. He was neither nervous nor afraid. He enjoyed the physical activity of the climb, almost as much as he enjoyed the view that was his reward.

He was very high above the city of Lothern now, and he could see all the way down into the harbour. The waves glittered silver in the moonlight. The thousands of ships looked like shadows. Their masts were like a forest floating on water.

Large patches of the city were lit up, a blaze of lights and life. Even larger parts were dead, all darkness and shadow and silence. It was as if a cancer was eating out the heart of Lothern. He was sure it had not been quite this bad when he was young, but it must have been. In the timescale of elves, a decade was an eye-blink. He had simply been young and unaware.

He saw the Foreigners' Quarter was ablaze with light. Down there, naked flames burned and torch bearers walked through darkened alleys and thousands of people went about their business in the flickering shadows. It was fascinating and attractive and he knew that at some point he was going to have to visit it. But tonight he had other things on his mind.

He went to the shuttered windows. There were no chains on the outside, and there was a bar that was easily lifted by slipping the blade of his sword through the gap in the wood. The air inside smelled musty and stale but it still had the smell of the place he remembered – waxed floors, incense, the metallic tang of something connected with his father's researches. It was dark within but he did not feel at all uneasy. He felt, in truth, as if he was coming home.

He went within and more memories came flooding back. The house was much larger than it looked from the street. It was tall and narrow but it ran a long way back from the road and it had many, many chambers. There was lots of furniture all covered in sheets and tarpaulins and there were mirrors in wooden cases that opened to reveal the glass within. He found a glow-globe and rubbed it to life. Its faint illumination was enough for him to see by. There were odd noises, bumping and creaking sounds as the wooden floors settled. There were probably rats moving around as well, although what they found to eat here he could not guess.

He strolled through the house until he came to the room he was looking for, and he found the thing he sought. A full length portrait of his mother looked down on him. She looked very lovely and very frail and there was something of Teclis in her features and appearance. Perhaps that was why Father has always preferred his twin. Not that it mattered much. He studied the portrait as he had done as a child, wondering what this woman had been like, and what she would say to him if she could talk to him now.

But she could not speak and there were no answers. He was walking through a city of ghosts, he thought. This was a place where the dead outnumbered the living and there were more mementoes of the past than people to remember events.

Sadness settled on him as he contemplated this beautiful frail stranger he had never met. After a while he got up and left, walking away from the dead and back towards the bright life of the Emeraldsea Palace. He doubted anyone would challenge him if he came in through the front door, but he went back to his room the way he had left, clambering up the walls and sliding easily over the balcony.

'Where have you been?' Teclis asked. He was sitting there, a book open on his knee, the moonlight bright enough to read by for someone with elven vision.

'I went to see the old house.'

'I always hated that place.'

'It's not so bad. I always liked it.'

'Did you see her?' There was no need to ask who was meant.

'Yes. She looked the same.'

'I would be very surprised if she looked any different,' said Teclis, rising from the chair and limping painfully to the door. 'She's been dead for a long time.'

Tyrion wanted to tell his brother that it was not so long in the elven scheme of things but he kept his silence and watched his brother go.

CHAPTER SIXTEEN

Urian strode confidently into the audience chamber. He glanced around. Many of the Phoenix King's advisors were already present. Lady Malene was there along with half a dozen other powerful wizards he recognised. A lovely woman, Urian thought, but very severe. She caught him looking at her and gave him a sour smile. He smiled back as if unaware of her dislike.

Five minutes in my harem, woman, and you would learn to smile properly, he thought.

Urian loved these midnight councils. They reminded him of being home. He had lost count of the number of times he had spent plotting late into the night with his confederates back in Naggaroth.

Of course, this was not exactly the same. The chances were that no one would be murdered because of tonight's events. There would not even be a significant change of power in the realm of Ulthuan unless something went very wrong.

No, it was the atmosphere he loved, the idea of being part of a cabal of people, meeting in secrecy under the shroud of darkness, whose decisions might affect the whole kingdom. There was an energy to such meetings that he fed on, that made his heart beat faster and pandered to his elven love of intrigue. He felt as if he really was someone, set apart from the common herd.

And, he thought sourly, in this he was like every other elf who had ever lived.

More wizards and scholars were arriving by the minute. All of them wore the worried looks of powerful people summoned in the dead of night to a secret council. Korhien Ironglaive entered, went over to his paramour and started talking in hushed tones with her.

Urian wondered what was going on here. It was not every night he was summoned to the Palace. Something big was happening. He would need to report it to Malekith.

A huge table dominated the room. On it were plates of cold meat, loaves of bread, jugs of wine, pitchers of water. There were books and scrolls and maps. It looked like someone was anticipating a long session.

'What is wrong?' Urian asked. Everyone looked shocked. No one was eating. The silence deepened and glancing around, Urian realised that Finubar had appeared. He was wearing his robes of state which made him look taller and more slender. The Phoenix King's gaze was distant but his voice was as resonant and powerful as ever.

'Do not mind me,' said the Phoenix King. 'Carry on with your discussions as if I were not here. I need to hear what you all have to say.'

'There has been another attack, sire,' Archmage Eltharik said, stroking his white goatee beard, a thing unusual in an elf male. He looked old. His skin was nearly translucent. His hair was white as bleached parchment. He was a specialist in all sorts of mystical lore, particularly that to do with summonings. 'The daemons have struck again. They completely destroyed a small town in Ellyrion.'

Malene let out a long breath. 'How did the word come in?'

'A mage survived. He performed a Sending.'

So that was what had caused Korhien to rush off earlier from their drinking party. The summons had been most urgent.

'How bad?' Malene asked.

A certain morbid curiosity filled Urian. It was obvious that many of those here knew more than he did. It looked as if some of the rumours he had picked up on were correct. There was some new threat to the realm and one the present Phoenix King was trying very hard to keep secret, at least for the moment.

'The town was burned down. All of the inhabitants had been subjected to the most hideous torture. Their flayed bodies had been laid out in a pattern that spelled the name N'Kari in the ashes. Along with other things. Threats, warnings, promises.'

'That's the name of the daemon who led the forces of the Lord of Pleasure during the reign of Aenarion,' Finubar said. He looked at Urian, who suddenly understood why he was here. His scholarship in all matters concerning the line of the first Phoenix King was famous.

'A greater daemon, a Keeper of Secrets no less,' said Urian. This was indeed news, Urian thought. If such a creature had emerged out of legend, it was epochal. There were few more deadly creatures on the face of creation. 'A being unseen since the time of Aenarion. Is someone trying to invoke him?'

'We don't know,' said Eltharik. 'All we know is reports are coming in from all across Ulthuan about attacks by daemons and their worshippers. There have been at least a dozen so far from locations as far north as Cothique, and as far west as Tiranoc. All of them involve Slaanesh worshippers and evil magic and powerful daemons. In most of them the name of N'Kari has come up either from survivors or from inscriptions on the site.'

A White Lion appeared. He carried a map of Ulthuan. When it was unrolled on the table, Urian could see the location of all the attacks had been marked on the map in red elven runes. They were widely scattered. Too widely spaced for it to be the work of one group, he thought. The distances were too great for any one army, even one mounted on eagles, to cover in the time available.

'Why now?' Archmage Belthania asked. She was a tall dark-haired elf woman who did not look her five centuries of age. It was rumoured she kept a stable of younger lovers tired out in her bedchambers. She was known to have a penchant for all manner of hallucinogenic mushrooms as well. It did not prevent her from being one of the sharpest scholars of the Vortex alive, although it kept all manner of strange rumours swirling around her.

'We don't know,' Eltharik said. 'We are trying to find out. The Council has called a meeting of all the seers and mages in Lothern. Archmages and Loremasters are being summoned from Saphery and the White Tower.'

'What do you think is happening?' Malene asked.

'I have no idea,' Eltharik replied. 'There are a few signs that the winds of magic are growing stronger and the power of Chaos is increasing but nothing that would suggest a manifestation by dozens of such powerful daemons across Ulthuan.'

'Do any of the places attacked have anything in common?' Belthania asked.

'We are looking into that. At a guess I would say they are all close to waystones,' said Eltharik.

'The pins that hold the Vortex together?' Belthania looked thoughtful and not a little worried. 'That could be very dangerous.'

'The Keepers of the Stones have not reported any tampering with the Great Pattern. There have been no attempts to unmake it, only some strange surges of energy within it and those happen from time to time.'

'Do they?' Urian asked.

'The winds of magic blow softer or stronger. Sometimes there are storms of magic, sometimes absolute calms. The Vortex and the Pattern are intended to channel the energy of the winds so sometimes there must be fluctuations as the levels of ambient magic change.'

Urian considered this. 'The daemons are not attacking the Vortex though?'

'As far as we know, no. There has only been one broken waystone found and it seems to have been the result of a lightning strike. There were traces of dark magic visible nearby though and an aura of great evil such as you might find near where daemons have manifested.'

'Was there an attack near that waystone?' Korhien asked.

'Yes,' said Eltharik. 'There was.'

'And it was probably among the first, wasn't it?'

'Too early to say yet, Korhien, but it is possible.'

'But it is definite the daemons are not attacking the waystones.' Belthania said. 'They are attacking towns and killing elves.'

'It is strange,' said Malene. 'But who can fathom the thinking of daemons?'

'I thought someone had to summon them,' said Urian 'That's what all the chronicles say. Some mighty sorcerer raises them for his own purposes.'

'They can enter the world through the Chaos Wastes when the winds of magic blow at their strongest and most corrupt,' Eltharik said.

'But they are not doing so now. You said that yourself.'

Eltharik nodded.

Malene said, 'Who would do this? Who would summon them? The druchii? The Witch King?'

Urian considered the possibility. He had heard nothing of any such plan. Of course, his master rarely saw fit to keep him informed about such things.

'If any wizard living has the power to do so, he has,' said Eltharik. 'No dark elf armies or fleets are attacking us though, and surely there would be if this was part of one of his plans?'

'It does not sound like Malekith,' said Urian. 'It is not his way. Too random. Too messy.' He saw a number of those present including Korhien nod their heads at that.

'A renegade wizard then? A Chaos cultist?' Lady Malene asked.

'Perhaps. But the attacks are too wildly spaced to be the work of one mage summoning. The reports are coming in from all across the continent.'

'Could an army of Chaos worshippers have gathered in secret and unleashed their attacks all at once?' Finubar asked.

'The attacks did begin just after the full moon,' said Eltharik. 'That is a time of great mystical significance.'

'Yes,' said Lady Malene. 'I was at sea about that time and there was a strange storm. I thought it was tainted with dark magical energy.'

'Was that before or after the attacks began?' Belthania asked. She looked even more troubled.

'It would have been just before, I suspect.'

'Where were you?' Belthania toyed with her long black hair. It was still very dark. Urian wondered if the rumours were true about her dyeing it.

'Off the coast of Yvresse,' said Malene. 'Near where the waystone was smashed.'

'It might well have been in the storm's path.'

'It is possible these things were connected. The storm broke the waystone. The daemons attacked there or manifested there.' Malene knew it sounded weak even as she said it. Urian could tell from her expression. 'Perhaps they came out of the Vortex. It was weakened at that point.'

'Daemons in the Vortex? That seems unlikely as well.' Belthania was emphatic. She did not seem to even want to consider the possibility that it might be so. Urian could sympathise – it was a most unsettling prospect. Still, it was one that they might need to face up to.

'Perhaps the place was picked by cultists for a ritual? Perhaps the storm was merely a coincidence? Perhaps it provided them with the power they needed to summon the daemons?' Malene said.

Belthania pursed her lips. 'That is a lot of perhapses. We need to find out concrete facts. We need to know who is behind these attacks. We need to know how strong our foes are and what their goals are. It is the only way we are going to be able to stop them.'

'Let us hope we can.'

'Do you have any recommendations?' Finubar asked. 'Is there anything we can do?'

He clearly wanted to know if there was some place where he could order his troops or fleets to go. He was a warrior and he saw things like a warrior.

'We need to know what the daemon wants, sire, before we can prevent it from achieving its goals.' Belthania said.

'Then we had better work that out, hadn't we,' said the Phoenix King. 'And quickly before more lives are lost.'

Urian helped himself to some wine. It was going to be a long night, and he had better make sure he missed nothing. Malekith would want a full report on this.

'It seems my rebellious subjects are in something of a panic, Urian,' said Malekith. His gaze burned coldly out of the great mirror beneath the Silvermount Palace. There was a certain chill satisfaction in his voice. He had listened intently to Urian's report without interrupting once, which was unusual for him.

'Indeed, sire. They are. Apparently Ulthuan is under attack by a legion of greater daemons. They have returned from the time of legends and are hellbent on destroying the entire island and sending us all beneath the sea.'

'I sense that you are not in agreement with this, Urian.'

'As ever, sire, you are correct.'

'Your simple faith in me is touching, Urian,' said Malekith, with a trace of his acid humour. 'What has been the response from the False King's court?'

'They are mustering their armies and fleets. They have sorcerers working on divinations. Scholars such as my humble self are scouring through ancient texts. They seek to ascertain the daemons' purpose.'

'Do you think they will do so?'

'Not yet, master, but it is merely a matter of time before they do. They are not without competent wizards here in Ulthuan.'

Malekith nodded. 'I do not think it is an uprising or a group of invading armies. My spies would have informed me of such a thing and I am sure that in this matter at least the False King is at least as well informed as I.'

'You think it is the daemon, sire? This N'Kari of legend?'

'It is possible, Urian. Such creatures do not age any more than I do. If it is N'Kari he will be terrible.' Urian needed to exert all his self-control to keep from shuddering. He gazed on his ruler with a feeling of something like awe. Malekith had been alive when Aenarion had defeated and banished the Keeper of Secrets. He had walked the world in that time of legend. And if he saw fit to remark that its return would be a terrible event, Urian had every reason to believe it would be so.

'This daemon, if daemon it be, is moving very quickly around Ulthuan with a very large force. Much faster than it should be able to by ship or road.' The Witch King sounded even more coldly thoughtful than usual. What was he thinking?

'Magic, sire?'

'Magic indeed, Urian and of no usual kind. If a Keeper of Secrets were simply moving itself we could assume it was being summoned by worshippers although this would speak of a level of Slaanesh worship in Ulthuan far greater than any we were aware of.'

Urian was of the opinion that Morathi was fully aware of the extent of the Lord of Pleasure's worship in Ulthuan, but whether she would share this knowledge with her son was a different matter entirely. 'You think this contingency unlikely, sire?'

'We do, Urian. Even if he were being summoned, there is no way he could bring a large force of mortals with him. There is some other form of magic at work here, one that interests me greatly.'

Urian could understand why. Anything that might allow the movement of large bodies of troops around Ulthuan so swiftly would be of great interest to the Witch King. His eventual goal was nothing less than the unification of the two elven realms under his own legitimate rule.

'You wish me to investigate this matter, sire?' Urian said, risking much. It was always dangerous to assume you knew what Malekith wanted and always dangerous to speak to him when he had not asked you a direct question.

'Precisely so, Urian. I want you to keep your ears open for even the tiniest scraps of information about this thing. Nothing is too unimportant to report as far as the daemon N'Kari is concerned.'

'I will pay scrupulous attention to all I hear concerning this. I will gather all the information currently available and hunt down every shred of rumour.'

'Diligence will be rewarded in this matter, Urian. Failure...' Malekith let the word hang in the air. There was no need whatsoever for him to spell out the penalties of failure in his service. 'Concerning the matter of the twins, do nothing at the moment. This takes precedence.'

'As you command, sire,' said Urian.

Malekith placed his hands together and the mirror went dark. The audience was clearly over. Urian was glad. He wiped cold sweat from his brow and helped himself to some wine. He had his work cut out for him.

'It looks like they are preparing for a feast here,' said Tyrion to Liselle. The morning sun shone down on the courtyard, illuminating the bustling activity all around them.

His cousin was dressed in another expensive gown of green Cathayan silk and watching the retainers hang more lanterns on the trees in the courtyard. Twigs of oak and wreaths of oak leaves were being placed over doorways. Trestle tables were being placed in the courtyard. Carved wooden statues of treemen guarded every entrance.

'It will be the Feast of Deliverance soon. My grandfather is giving a ball to celebrate it, and the fact that you and your brother are among us.'

'You are certainly doing it in style,' he said. 'Making a statement, I suppose.'

'Yes and yes,' said Liselle smiling.

The Feast was a celebration of the return of Aenarion's children, Morelion and Yvraine from the heart of the Forest. They had been believed dead even by their father when in fact they had been under the protection of the Treeman Oakheart. He had saved them from the forces of Chaos and hidden them in the depths of the forest, thus preserving the life of the future Everqueen and her brother. Tyrion was descended from Morelion as was every other surviving child of the Blood of Aenarion save Malekith, the Witch King of Naggaroth. He could see that House Emeraldsea was reminding everyone of their connection with the Blood by ostentatiously giving this feast. If it turned out that he and Teclis were judged accursed it was a potentially very risky move.

'It looks like it is going to be a very big party,' said Tyrion. 'When exactly will it be?'

'In less than a week, on the night of the Rejoicing.' That was the traditional night when balls and parties were given and offerings made in temples. 'Although there may not be much to rejoice over this year.'

'What do you mean?'

'Word is that Ulthuan is under attack. Outlying mansions have been ravaged by worshippers of the Dark Prince of Pleasure. A whole town was sacked by an army headed by a daemon.' She sounded a little worried as she said it, but not as if she was taking it entirely seriously.

'How do you know this?'

'A messenger brought word to my mother last night. She was summoned to the palace. A ranger found bodies at a mansion in the mountains. It seems a mage survived the attack on Tor Annan and managed a Sending. Other places have been attacked. The Phoenix King called a council to discuss what happened and decide what to do about it.'

'A town sacked by daemons – that sounds very serious. Perhaps he will have no time to attend parties.'

'You obviously have not had much experience of life in Lothern, Prince Tyrion. The social round would go on if the world was ending. It is the life blood of this city. Anyway, I doubt Finubar is about to strap on a sword and go hunting daemons himself. That's what he has people like Korhien for.'

Tyrion paused to think about what she had said. Cultists attacking outlying mansions. Towns destroyed by daemon-led armies. It all sounded very unlikely standing here in this bustling courtyard in the bright light of day. And yet he supposed that was how these things must always seem to those not directly involved in them. This was nothing to do with him. Of that he felt sure.

'I hear you have been slipping out at nights,' said Liselle. She smiled. 'It did not take you long to find a secret lover.'

Tyrion smiled back. He should have known that his comings and goings would not be unobserved. There were other observers than guards watching over the mansion.

'There is no secret lover,' said Tyrion. 'I merely wanted to see the city without an entourage of retainers.'

'Use the front door,' she said. 'It's the easiest way.'

'I have the elven passion for secrecy and intrigue,' he said.

'Good,' she said. 'That always makes things more interesting.'

Before he could ask her what she meant by that, she strode away, pausing in the doorway to turn and smile at him. It looked posed but she was still lovely.

Life in Lothern was certainly interesting. There was no mistaking that.

Tyrion had never seen a place quite so crowded, dirty, smelly and wonderful as the Foreigners' Quarter. He was glad he had put on his old clothes and snuck out of the Emeraldsea Palace again.

He was free and just for this evening, he felt like his old self again. It was not just wearing his old clothes. It was not being hemmed in by endless formalities and the rituals of life in the palace.

He was already starting to be bored. Weapons practice was fun, but the endless lessons in protocol were not. He had enjoyed the dancing lessons and flirting with his pretty relatives but he had not enjoyed being told how to behave. He felt like he was somehow on probation, less than a guest, something of a prisoner.

Servants watched his every move. Bodyguards followed him everywhere, supposedly for his own protection. Tonight he had climbed down from the balcony of his chambers into the street and slipped off where no one would dream of looking for him. He knew he was being childish, that he should simply have taken Liselle's advice and used the front door, but he liked doing this.

This was the sort of adventure he had dreamed of ever since he was young.

For the first time ever Tyrion was seeing beings of a different race, and lots of them. They bustled through the Foreigners' Quarter as if they owned the place, and they paid less attention to him than he did to them. He supposed they must be used to seeing elves. He was not at all used to seeing humans.

They were smaller than he was, shorter than almost all elves, and yet heavier, bloated with fat and muscle. They looked clumsy and graceless and their voices sounded like the squawking and bellowing of beasts in a jungle. There were so many different types of them: tall, pale elaborately dressed men from Marienburg and the Empire; dusky hawk-featured, scimitar-bearing Arabyans from the lands of the south; Cathayans clad in silk robes.

He understood why some elves affected to despise them. There was a coarseness about them, a brutal directness of speech and gesture combined with a grubbiness and stench that was off-putting. And yet he was not put off – he found the differing accents and voices and clothes and body language exhilarating, as entertaining as any book or poem he had read.

Their clothes were coarsely made and their foods smelled of fat and salt and spices. Sausages of some indescribable meat sizzled on spits. Fish blackened on braziers. Sellers stomped everywhere with trays of savouries strapped to their chest, small but vicious-looking dogs snapping at their heels.

These humans were a long way from their homes but somehow they had made themselves at home here. The architecture of the quarter had taken on a humanish look. Brick buildings leaned at crazy angles against the remnants of much older elven structures. Ancient palaces had been turned into vast warrens and mazes of dwellings and shops and merchants offices.

There was none of the courtliness or formality of elvish culture. Men bumped into each other in the street and either backed away swiftly, hands reaching for swords, or grinned and nodded and passed on their way.

Merchants argued prices. Harlots led drunken sailors into side alleys and in pairs they humped and groaned against the walls. In quiet corners, men played chess on odd-looking boards with carved wooden pieces of strange design. He stopped to watch a game and just from a few moves he could tell the rules were not so different from those he was used to.

When the humans noticed him, they stopped and looked at him as if they anticipated him saying something. He gestured for them to continue but they just stared until even he felt a little uncomfortable and a little rude for distracting them from their game, so he sketched a bow and moved on deeper into the great bazaar.

Carpets hung overhead, draped over wooden racks intended to display them to best advantage. Perhaps it would have worked as intended if the skylights had not been blackened with soot and grime and the shadowy interiors of the corridors lit only by lanterns and flambeaux.

From the gloom he saw smaller, bearded figures peering and he was astonished to see dwarfs. Despite their long beards and squat builds these dwarfs were garbed more like humans than the heavily armoured warriors he expected. Had the race really changed so much since the times of Caledor the Second or were these some strange new hybrid of dwarf and human? He remembered Teclis telling him once that several clans of dwarfs had gone to live among the humans of the Empire. Perhaps these were such.

He passed pawnbrokers and factors' offices and doorways where lurked small groups of armed men who appeared to have no business there. These looked at him with a real sense of menace. At first he thought they were simply as curious about him as he was about them, but after a while he realised that there was a different quality in the glances they gave him.

One of them, more elaborately dressed than the others, with a peacock feather in a slouched hat, strutted up to him and walked around him, inspecting him and all the time glaring at him.

'What you want, elfie boy?' he asked, mangling the elvish language with his teeth and tongue. His pronunciation was poor and his grasp of the subtleties of grammar non-existent, but it was still astonishing in its way, like listening to a dog that had learned to talk. It made Tyrion smile.

'What you grinnin' at, cat-eyes?' the human asked and his companions laughed. For the first time Tyrion realised there was a note of disrespect in the man's voice. He was more astonished than angered. It was like being mocked by a monkey.

He kept quiet because he could not think of anything to say and his silence seemed to encourage the human. His companions egged him on. As he came closer, the stench of coarse strong alcohol from his breath hit Tyrion with the force of a blow.

The man was drunk, Tyrion realised, and looking for a fight. Tyrion had never had any great need to learn the human speech and he greatly regretted that deficiency now. Perhaps if he had been able to speak to the man in his own tongue he might have been able to defuse the situation.

At the same time as the thought crossed his mind, another realisation hit him. He did not really care. If this monkey-man wanted a fight, he would get it. Tyrion had never backed down from one in his life and he did not intend to do so now.

It occurred to him that perhaps this was not the most sensible attitude – he was alone in the Foreigners' Quarter and there were none of his own kind to help him. This human had a whole gang of friends and it was perfectly possible all the other humans within earshot would aid him out of solidarity with their kind. Still, Tyrion decided, even taking all of these factors into account, he was not about to back down.

'What you lookin' at?' the human demanded in his pidgin gibberish.

'I don't know but it's looking back,' Tyrion responded. He did not know whether the man understood his words, but he certainly understood the tone of contempt. The man went for his sword. Before he could draw it, Tyrion struck him, the force of the blow smashing him to the ground. His friends rose swiftly, reaching for knives and blades.

'That was a good punch,' said a voice from behind him. From its tone and timbre, Tyrion could tell it belonged to a human but the words were not mangled or slurred. They could almost have been spoken by an elf. 'So fast I did not see anything but a blur.'

The owner of the voice said something in their own tongue to the gang of warriors. They sat down again as quickly as they had risen.

The speaker came into view. He loomed over the fallen bruiser and berated him. Tyrion's victim lay on the ground, abashed, a stream of blood running from his nose, and a dazed expression on his face. He seemed to grow smaller and smaller and less and less confident as the newcomer's tirade went on. Eventually he pulled himself up and slunk back to his friends, and they vanished through the archway they had at first appeared to be guarding.

'What did you say to him?' Tyrion asked. The newcomer turned to look at him. He was tall for a human and broad, running to fat. His face was ruddy but it had an open, honest quality that even Tyrion could read on a human face.

'I told him he was an idiot.'

'You seemed to tell him a lot more than that, or is idiot such a long word in your language?'

The stranger laughed. 'I was explaining to him exactly why he was an idiot, like his father and his father's father before him.'

'And why would that be?'

The stranger cocked his head to one side and inspected Tyrion for a long moment. There was nothing sullen or aggressive about that stare and Tyrion felt no resentment of it.

'You really don't know, do you?'

'I really don't,' Tyrion agreed.

'And you are much younger than you look.'

'How old do I look?'

'It's hard to say. All elves look the same and they could be a thousand years old.'

'Most do not live that long.'

'Yes but mostly you die through misadventure or violence. You don't age the same as we do.'

Tyrion thought about all of the humans he had seen in his wanderings through the Foreigners' Quarter. Some of them were more decrepit than any elf could ever be. 'We age more slowly and perhaps differently. I do not know enough about your kind to say.'

'Nor I about yours.'

'You seemed to have avoided my question, sir,' said Tyrion. 'Why was that man an idiot?'

'Because he was drunk and because by attacking you he could have gotten all of us banned from Ulthuan and that would be true idiocy, for there is a power of gold to be made in trading with elves, too much to be risked by the drunken stupidity of one ignorant fool with a chip on his shoulder.'

'That makes sense,' said Tyrion.

'Most assuredly it does, sir,' said the newcomer. 'Most assuredly. I try to make sense whenever I speak, I would like to think I am a sensible man, sir elf.'

'You seem so to me.'

'Thank you, sir. It is a compliment indeed that you should say so.' Tyrion noticed that the man had been almost imperceptibly guiding him out of the labyrinth of the bazaar as they walked. He found it amusing to have been so neatly manoeuvred and to his own advantage. Clearly the man did not want to say there was the possibility of Tyrion's presence creating another disturbance deeper in the bazaar, and just as clearly he was trying to avoid the possibility arising. It was handled most adroitly. Tyrion realised that he would have to reassess his opinion of the humans. They were clearly cleverer and capable of greater grace than most elves gave them credit for.

He could not wait to share this information with Teclis. He knew it would amuse his brother.

'And then with the greatest of ease, he led me out of the market-place, and to the gates. He was saying farewell in such a natural and easy manner that it seemed only natural that I should pass through them and come back into Lothern proper.'

Teclis laughed but there was something else written alongside the amusement on his thin face, a wistfulness that made Tyrion realise just how much his twin envied him this little adventure.

'Who would ever have thought you could have a sitting room like this?' Tyrion said, to change the subject. The chamber was impressively furnished. The table was massive, worked from rich aromatic wood from Cathay and inscribed with intertwined nymphs and godlings. Over two walls hung heavy tapestries of the richest sort. There was crystal in the windows and they had no shutters, only a thick pair of curtains capable of cutting out any draft.

On the wall opposite was a picture depicting merchant ships at sea, the source of their relatives' great wealth. Near the table was a freestanding mirror in which Tyrion could see his own reflection and that of Teclis. He stood in the light of the lantern, Teclis was partially concealed in shadow.

'I think the servants have chambers as good as ours,' Teclis said, his tone caustic.

'I do not care,' said Tyrion. 'I have never seen a room as sumptuously appointed as my own.'

'That's because you have so little to compare it to. There are other houses in Lothern as rich as this one and with rooms ten times as well furnished.'

'How do you know so much about this place already?'

'Because I read, brother, and because I quiz the maid who comes to make up my room and see to my needs.'

Tyrion could imagine his brother's questioning and felt a little sorry for the maid. Teclis was blunt to the point of being almost human, and he had a most un-elven way about him.

'I do not care if anyone is much richer than us. I, for one, intend to be happy here.'

'You would be happy anywhere. It is your disposition to be so, disgracefully, bright, optimistic, sunny.'

How could I not be, when I have this great city to run around? Tyrion was about to say, but he realised that would only make Teclis more bitter and envious. It came to him then, and he was astonished at his own slowness of mind, that the reason why his twin was being critical of their cousins was because he was angry at Tyrion for having his adventures but could not bring himself to say so.

Teclis was making his anger felt in other ways, unfair to their kindred and unworthy of him. Tyrion felt almost guilty for a moment, but pushed the feeling aside. He was who he was through no fault of his own, he was not going to apologise for it to his brother.

'And it is yours to be bitter, brother,' said Tyrion. 'Although I can understand why...'

'I honestly doubt that, Tyrion. You have no idea what it is like to be stuck here, knowing that out there life is going on and a great city is going about its business while you are trapped and can do nothing... nothing.'

'I can try,' said Tyrion weakly. And behind all the other bitterness he sensed a deeper one. Teclis had briefly enjoyed a few weeks of good health before his relapse. It was a cruel blow to him. No wonder he was angry.

'Yes, and you do.' Teclis said.

'What is that book on the bedside table?' said Tyrion to change the subject again.

'It is a book of conjurations. Lady Malene has a whole library of such things here.'

'You've visited this library then?'

'Mara, the maid, told me of it so I had to see it.'

Tyrion could imagine his brother limping along the corridor to reach such a prize. He had gone through all of the books in their father's house except the ones their father kept locked in his magically sealed cabinet because they were too dangerous for any but a skilled sorcerer. Tyrion could well remember his brother's obsession with that cabinet. It looked like nothing was locked here. He supposed the spells must be harmless, otherwise they would be kept under lock and key.

'And you... ah... borrowed this one?'

'Yes.'

'Does Lady Malene know?'

'Take a look at this,' said Teclis, going from bitter and caustic to excited in a flash. He opened the book and Tyrion saw lines of words separated by multiple straight lines marked with what looked like musical notes.

'It looks like music with words,' said Tyrion. 'Is it a song?'

'No, it's a spell. The words are the incantation, the first line of symbols below shows right-hand gestures, the line below that left-hand gestures, the last line shows inflexion.'

'Inflexion?'

'It's a sort of twist of mind that you must perform to touch the power of the spell in the right way – violent, sad, passive and so on.'

'Like a mood?'

Teclis made a face which showed what he thought of his brother's suggestion.

'In a way, I suppose,'

'They are just squiggles on a page to me.'

'Trust me they are more than just that. Lady Malene has told me enough of the theory for me to know.'

'I'll take your word for it.'

An urgency came into Teclis's voice. 'It all just fits together. There is a unity to it and when you understand that you can do almost anything. You change your own internal state, you touch the winds of magic, you tap their power, you change your state again, and shape the forces with your mind, your words, your gestures and all the time what you are really doing is altering the world.'

'In all honesty, I can't say I follow you.'

'I will show you, look. Put a chair in front of the mirror and help me to it.'

Tyrion was not sure he liked the way this was going but he did as his twin asked. It was good to see him so animated and for once not touched with bitterness. Teclis sat with the book in his hand, and then made some odd gestures, fingers rippling, hands twisting as he crooned words in an archaic version of the elvish tongue.

A chill touched Tyrion's spine. He felt uncanny forces flow around him. He looked into the mirror and saw concern on his face. Teclis's features had become a mask, and his gaze was fixed and staring. Even as Tyrion watched, the mirror misted as if someone had breathed on it, although no one had. Their outlines became shadow and blurred and then vanished altogether. The surface of the mirror rippled and settled and became normal again.

'It looks just the same,' said Tyrion. 'I don't know what you were trying but it did not work.'

Teclis smile was a ghastly rictus. He made a gesture with his left hand as if he were spinning a top. The image in the mirror turned. At first Tyrion wondered if Teclis had made him dizzy with his magic but then he realised that he was perfectly stable and so was the room. It was the point of view in the mirror that was changing.

Teclis made another gesture and he was looking at the two of them from behind. It was as if the mirror had become the eye of some great roving beast and they were looking out from behind that eye. Tyrion laughed at the wonder of it and Teclis joined in, obviously enjoying the feeling of power, and the use of magic.

The view in the mirror shifted again, moving through the door and out into the corridor. It flew along now as fast as Tyrion could run, and Tyrion guessed his brother was enjoying the vicarious experience of running at a speed he would never achieve in life. Tyrion wondered if the point of view could fly. That would be truly a wonderful thing.

Even as that thought struck him, he saw Lady Malene running along the corridor towards them. She reached a point just in front of the eye and gestured. The mirror went suddenly dark. Teclis gasped as if stabbed. A few moments later, the door in the room opened and she entered.

'What is going on?' she demanded, in a tone of utmost urgency.

She gazed around the room as if seeking some threat, a faint nimbus of light played around her hands. Tyrion realised she was prepared to work magic at a moment's notice, and he guessed from her expression that it would be a spell of a potent and deadly sort. 'Did something try to break in here?'

He could hear the sound of many running feet now. Armed warriors poured into the room as if in answer to some unheard summons. They gazed around the room too, obviously as baffled as Lady Malene. They looked like soldiers who having nerved themselves up for combat were disappointed to find no foe awaiting them.

'It was me, lady,' said Teclis.

'What was you?' she said.

'I worked a spell.'

'You are not a mage yet, boy. I sensed the presence of an awful power. I thought we were attacked, that you were attacked because the focus of the power was here.'

'I worked a spell,' said Teclis stubbornly. He indicated the open book on his knee.

Lady Malene came over and snatched it up. 'You cast this?' There was naked disbelief in her voice. 'Impossible.'

'My brother does not lie,' said Tyrion rankled by the tone their aunt was taking. He would have been more annoyed at her tone had he not sensed that she was angry as much from concern about their well-being as annoyance at what Teclis had done.

She looked at the spell again, and then at the mirror. Her hand moved through a small circular gesture. She spoke a few words in the archaic version of Elvish that Teclis had used to invoke the spell. The surface of the mirror shimmered brilliantly and then faded. She turned her gaze back upon them.

'Look at me,' she said. 'This is no joke so don't smile. Answer me and answer me true. Did anything enter this chamber? Did anything breach the wards on this palace?'

'No,' said Teclis with utter assurance.

'Did you cast the Spell of the Invisible Eye?'

'Yes.'

'Who taught you how to do that?'

'No one.'

'Don't lie, boy. What did your father teach you?'

'Nothing, witch,' said Teclis just as annoyed, and seemingly completely oblivious to the way armed elves reached for weapons when they heard his tone. 'My father taught me nothing. The basic procedures were all in this book. I worked out the rest for myself from what you have already taught me.'

'You worked out the rest for yourself? Do you seriously expect me to believe an untrained lad could derive from first principles the knowledge to cast a third order spell of transvisualisation?'

'I don't care whether you believe me,' said Teclis with superb arrogance. 'I did it. I could do it again.'

Lady Malene stared at him for a very long time. 'You are either a wonderful liar or the greatest natural mage who has ever lived.'

Later Tyrion was to remember that her words had the force of a prophecy.

CHAPTER EIGHTEEN

'What am I to do with you?' Lady Malene asked. She sounded as if she did not really know. She looked as if she had not slept since last night. Teclis had, the most peaceful and natural sleep he had enjoyed in many days.

'I am not yours to do anything with,' he said. Her manner made him nervous. He was glad Tyrion was not here in his room to witness this. He was not in her power exactly but she had something he wanted, knowledge, mastery of technique. It would be possible for him to teach himself magic based on what he had seen in the grimoires but she might well forbid him access to any more books. If that happened he would find a way to get them if he could, but they might stop him. In any case it would be a much longer and slower route to learning, and he wanted to learn magic the way an elf lost in a desert craves water.

'Your life is,' she said with some certainty. 'At this moment.'

'Is that a threat?'

'No. I mean your path in life. I can teach you or I can report you to the Phoenix King's palace and you will be restrained until after you have been tested.'

'That is not fair.'

'Life is not fair, Prince Teclis. I regret that you should have been introduced to this concept so young, but you are wise beyond your years so I am sure you will have no difficulty grasping it.

'I do not require platitudes or irony.'

'No. You require teaching – that much is obvious. You will experiment on your own if you do not get it or are not actively restrained. And to one of your power that could be very dangerous.'

'I am not unaware of the dangers of magic.'

'Fire will not hurt me, says the child who has never yet put his hand in the grate.'

'I am not a child.'

'Then do not behave like one and do not sound so petulant. You know nothing of the dangers of magic... Nothing! One of your power can so easily do so many things and do them wrong.'

'Like what?' He was more curious than angry now.

'You could overdraw your power and burn it out forever. Believe me that is not a fate that anyone born to the Art would want. Death would be preferable.'

Teclis could see how that would be true, but he sensed a hesitation in her manner. There was something she was not telling him and did not want to. Of course, he had to know.

'And?'

'And what?'

'What else could go wrong?'

'Is that not enough?'

'There are other dangers you are not mentioning.'

'And should not, not until your studies are far more advanced than they are now.'

'How can I avoid a danger when I do not know what it is? You say you fear what I might do. Help me avoid that.'

She looked at him warily and with something more like respect. To her, until that moment, he had been nothing but a gifted adolescent. She had never considered the possibility of treating him like an equal although she must have known she was going to have to one day. She seemed to come to a decision.

'Very well. For your own good I will tell you. Heed my words and heed them well – for not just your life but your soul might depend on them.'

He felt a thrill then, and not the one she expected him to feel. He was on the verge of dark and secret knowledge and he felt its unrelenting tug. It was something he knew had power over him and likely always would. Perhaps he thought this was how the Curse of Aenarion worked on him.

'Speak,' he said.

'There is something about working the Art that draws the attention of daemons. There is something about the souls of those who can use magic that attracts them, something daemons desire the way an epicure craves larks' tongues in honey. If your soul is not properly warded, if you cast a spell unthinkingly and without protecting yourself, you can draw their evil to you.'

'That is the sort of superstition that humans believe,' Teclis said.

'It is nothing less than the truth. When you work the great high magics you will know it. You will sense the presence of Chaos and its minions around you. You will sometimes sense their hunger and their rage even when you work the slightest of spells. It is the way of things.'

'You are saying this to frighten me.'

'Yes, I am. And you should be frightened! For there are magics you will never work without placing your soul and the lives of everyone around you in peril. That is why what you did today was foolish and wrong. You risked not just your own being but that of your brother. You put me at risk and the guards who came to investigate. If something had reached out from the great abyss and taken possession of you, it could use your body and your talent to wreak great evil. The more natural power a mage has, and you have more of that than anyone I have ever encountered, the greater the prize they are going to be for the powers of Chaos.'

She spoke calmly and with authority and with utter conviction, and much to his surprise Teclis began to feel ashamed of himself. 'I will not do it again,' he said at last.

'That would be wise. There will be many temptations placed in your path, Prince Teclis, some of them very subtle. It is best to be wary when you are a student of the Art. Always remember that. Always!'

'I shall.'

'Do so. There is something very strange happening in the world today. Daemons have come to Ulthuan once more and I would not like you to draw them to you.'

N'Kari felt strong. For the first time since he had escaped the cursed Vortex he was starting to feel like himself. He had fed well on blood and souls and agony and ecstasy. He had bathed in the blood of the Blood of Aenarion and feasted on their hearts and eyeballs then used their corpses for his pleasure.

His followers had grown to be quite an army. Cultists from all over Ulthuan had come to join them as word of what they were doing spread, a company of renegade dark elves had come to do homage, and a crew of shipwrecked Norsemen had been seduced and broken to his will. He had summoned more daemons and drawn more monsters to him. His legions could face an army in the field, but he was not quite sure that was necessary yet.

Of course, there had been the problem of food. The perennial problem of supplying an army on the move had arisen. N'Kari had solved it in the traditional way. Some of the captives had been used as pleasure slaves, some had been taken as recruits, others had become cattle to be devoured by his soldiers.

He had taught his followers the exquisite epicurean pleasures of the Dark Feast and he suspected that now they would have trouble going back to lesser foods, even if he let them. He had imbued the spiced elf-meat with some of his own dark magical power and was well-pleased that some of the mortals were starting to show the stigmata of mutation. They were well gone down the path of Chaos and would go much further before their adventures were over.

'There are magicians within,' said Elrion. The chief of his followers looked demented. His sanity had not been improved by the fact that his skin had started to harden on his arms and chest, providing him with some natural armour at the cost of some diminishment of his personal beauty. N'Kari rather liked the effect of his wild, staring eyes, and the crack that came into his voice whenever he tried to pronounce certain words. His teeth were becoming fangs and something was happening to his tongue and throat. N'Kari could hardly wait to see what.

'Yes,' said N'Kari. So much was obvious from even a cursory examination of the tower on the hilltop before them. It was wrapped in powerful protective spells and had a number of sophisticated wards in place. A few of those who waited on the walls surrounding it were mages. He could tell easily enough from the way they wrapped themselves in shimmering spells of illusion and battle. Their weapons too had enchantments placed upon them, as did the weapons and armour of the warriors. 'And their flesh will taste all the sweeter for being spiced with power. Trust me there is nothing quite like the savour of a wizard's soul when you devour it.'

'I think the master of the tower is expecting us,' said Elrion.

Of course, he would be expecting them, for he was a mage. He had probably seen their approach at leagues of distance through his scrying crystal. It was a pity the tower was not closer to the entrance to the elder paths; then they could have taken him completely by surprise. Then again that would have deprived N'Kari of much of the pleasure of battle and slaughter. One always had to take a balanced view of these things.

N'Kari doubted being forewarned would do the defenders much good in the end. His forces were too numerous now and there was no chance of reinforcements reaching the elves unless they used the same means as N'Kari did to transport their forces, and they had not the knowledge or the courage needed to do that.

Some of his troops possessed the wit and the skill to begin to construct crude siege machines – catapults and covered battering rams. They had cut down the trees from sacred groves to make them, and one or two of the cultists had even managed to imbue them with magic to improve their utility. It would only be a matter of time before the gates or the walls surrounding the tower were breached and his followers were within. All he had to do was give the order and the battle would begin.

N'Kari paused for a second to savour the moment. As he did so a tall figure appeared on the battlements and began incanting a spell. It was an order of magnitude more potent than anything being woven by the apprentices. The master of the tower had decided to take a hand. A ball of pure magical energy arced towards the nearest siege machine, blasting it to blazing fragments, searing the flesh from its crew and leaving only vitrified bones standing there for a heartbeat before they collapsed.

N'Kari was not amused. He had been about to give a rousing speech to his followers, to act the part of the great leader. It would seem their opponent for the day did not intend to give him time to play that role. So be it. He would find his amusement in other ways, by tormenting the soul of the one who had robbed him of that fleeting pleasure.

'Attack,' N'Kari shouted, shifting his form to something like his natural and most beloved one. He was rewarded by screams of terror from the walls. You could usually rely on magicians to recognise a daemon when they saw one. It seemed like some of those on the walls had some idea of N'Kari's capabilities. Perhaps he would spare a few of the most abject of them, if they grovelled enough.

Then again, perhaps not.

'You're very good, doorkeeper, and you're getting better all the time,' said Korhien. He was actually breathing heavily from the workout. He leaned on the practice sword and he stared at Tyrion. 'You have made a lot of progress in the past weeks.'

'I'm pleased to hear you say it,' said Tyrion. He glanced away. More and more porters were arriving, bringing decorations and food for the upcoming ball. 'I feel like I am getting better but I have nothing to judge my progress against.'

'I have,' said Korhien. 'And you can take my word for it – there have been very few warriors who have learned how to use a sword as quickly or as well as you have. You have an uncanny ability with weapons. It's as if you were born to use them.'

'Maybe I was,' said Tyrion. 'But I think that is true of most elves who live in these times. We are all born to use weapons whether we like it or not. It is an age of war.'

'That it is, doorkeeper. Although I doubt that you have much of an idea of what that really means just yet.'

'I'm sure that I will have before much longer,' said Tyrion.

'I hope not,' said Korhien. 'You're a bit young yet to be going to war.'

'It is what I have dreamed of since I was a child.'

'You will find that the experience does not bear much relation to what you have dreamed about. These things never do. It is one thing to read about them in stories or to hear warriors tell tall tales around a campfire. It is another thing entirely to chop an elf into pieces or stick a sword through his body.'

'You have done these things,' said Tyrion. 'And you do not seem to be any the worse for it.'

'I have done these things and there are times when I wish I had not.'

'And there are times when you're glad that you have,' said Tyrion. 'I can tell.'

'It is a complicated thing, doorkeeper.'

'In what way?' Tyrion asked.

'Killing someone in combat is a complicated thing. It is not how you imagine it to be. It is wonderful and it is terrible and it is not at all what you expect.'

Tyrion looked at the older warrior. Korhien's face was thoughtful and Tyrion could tell that he was choosing his words with care. He stared off into the middle distance as if remembering something that was important to him and which he wanted to communicate exactly.

'It is like this,' Korhien said. 'When you kill someone in battle you have proven your own superiority over them. You are alive and they are dead and there is no more definitive proof than that. It is thrilling in a dreadful way. It is horrible and it is terrible but it is also thrilling. You feel more alive than you ever have before or quite possibly ever will again. You are very aware of the presence of death and how close it has come to you and that lets you know that you are alive in a way that nothing else ever will. Do you follow me?'

'I think so,' Tyrion said. 'But what is so terrible about it?'

'At that moment, nothing. But later you will find yourself thinking about what happened and about how you felt and about how the other person feels now.'

'They won't be feeling anything,' Tyrion said.

'Exactly,' Korhien said. 'They won't be feeling anything at all and you will have ensured that. You will have made that happen. And after a while you'll start to wonder about what you have done – was it justified? What right did you have to kill that person? Would it perhaps have been better if they had killed you?'

Tyrion could see that Korhien was not just talking in the abstract here. He had someone specifically in mind. He was thinking about things that had affected him deeply in his time. It was not so much what the older elf was saying that affected Tyrion. It was the way he said it.

Tyrion could not imagine ever regretting killing someone who had been trying to kill him. In a case of his own life or that other person's, he would feel entirely justified in his victory. And yet something in Korhien's tone gave him pause for thought. If the older warrior had found something in all of this that had affected him so deeply, at very least Tyrion felt it deserved his deepest consideration.

'Do you wonder about such things?' Tyrion asked.

'All of the time,' Korhien replied.

'Why?'

'I wish I knew. When I was younger they troubled me not at all but I have found that over the centuries I have thought more about them and I have found the easy answers harder to find.'

'You are a warrior,' Tyrion said. 'It is your duty to kill the enemies of the Phoenix King.'

Korhien smiled. 'I wish I was young again and everything seemed so simple to me.'

Tyrion resented that. 'Have you heard any more about these attacks everyone is talking about? The servant girls seem to think Lothern itself will be besieged by an army of daemons any day now.'

Korhien shook his head. 'It will not come to that. Not yet anyway.'

'Then there have been more attacks.'

'Yes. And many of them. Not a day passes without reports coming in by messenger bird, sending spell or word of mouth. The whole island-continent seems to be under attack by an army of daemons. And yet when our troops investigate, they find nothing. It is as if the attackers have vanished into thin air.'

'The daemons are using magic,' said Tyrion.

'I see your genius for understanding military matters was not understated, doorkeeper,' said Korhien sardonically. 'Of course, the daemons are using magic.'

'Why are they attacking the places they do? What do they want?'

'No one knows and no one can see any pattern to it. Not even the cleverest of mages. The daemons appear out of nowhere, they attack, they slaughter like maddened wolverines and then they depart, taking nothing. It is a kind of madness, or so it seems.'

'It is what you would expect from daemons,' said Tyrion. 'Who knows why they do what they do?'

'Not I, that is for sure,' said Korhien. 'Nor anyone else at the moment. Nothing like this has happened for centuries. Panic is spreading everywhere.'

'Perhaps that is the intention,' said Tyrion. It seemed absurd to be thinking this way, watching tradesmen bring flowers and lanterns for the ball, and chandlers bringing in provisions for a great feast.

'You are not the first to suggest that, doorkeeper.'

'At least we are safe here,' said Tyrion. 'Lothern is the best defended city in Elvendom.'

Korhien nodded. 'It galls my heart to remain here doing nothing while our land is ravaged,' he said.

'I am sure the time will come when you will be called upon to fight,' said Tyrion. He rather envied Korhien that chance.

Korhien smiled.

'I will see you tomorrow night at the ball,' he said. 'I understand it is going to be a special one.'

'No training tomorrow?' Tyrion asked. He was disappointed.

'The Phoenix King has called another council to discuss these attacks. I must be there. Some things take precedence even over your training, doorkeeper.'

'Apparently balls are exceptions.'

'Believe me, after one of these councils, we will all need a party to cheer us up.'

◄ CHAPTER NINETEEN ►

Floating spheres of spell-woven light illuminated the great hall of the Emeraldsea Palace. An orchestra of the finest musicians played on a raised dais at one end of the room. Huge fans swirled in the high ceiling propelled by unseen magic. Hundreds of beautifully garbed and noble-looking elves crowded the room. They stood at the edge of the chamber in the shadow of alcoves housing enormous statues or round the tables on which a buffet of the finest elven viands lay. They chatted in dark corners or drank wine from carved crystal goblets or danced in the centre of the floor, performing the steps of the vast intricate ritual quadrilles demanded of this sort of social gathering.

Teclis had never seen anything like this. It was his first ever ball in one of the palaces of Lothern and it was, to say the least, impressive.

Tyrion stood on the balcony, watching everything and smiling easily and amiably at all who passed. He looked perfectly at ease in his beautiful clothes. His natural charm and good looks made up for any lack of formal courtesy in his manner. Teclis envied him all of these things. His own clothes felt too loose for his tall, spare frame and no matter how often the retainers adjusted the cut and flow of them, they could never seem to make him look like anything but a gangling scarecrow.

Back home, Teclis had been the one favoured by their father and Tyrion had been the outsider. Here it was obvious their roles were always going to be reversed. Tyrion was the one who was the centre of attention and Teclis knew beyond a shadow of a doubt that it was going to be that way from now on.

He felt a touch on his elbow. Lady Malene stood there in a sparkling blue dress of some mage-woven cloth that shimmered with cosmetic glamour-spells. Her hair was piled high on her head and held in place by jewelled pins. Long diamond rings depended from her pointed ears.

'You are not enjoying this, are you, Prince Teclis?' she murmured.

'How can you tell?' he asked sardonically.

'You hang back from the gathering. You have not talked to anyone or asked anyone to dance. Your brother does not seem to suffer from any such restraint.'

'Tyrion is the soul of charm. People like him. He knows how to put them at ease.'

'It's unsurprising. He is good looking, poised, confident – he is not shy.'

'You think I am, lady?'

'You are not easy with yourself or with other people. Perhaps you never will be.'

'If you are trying to bolster my self-confidence with this little chat, you are failing.'

'These are not uncommon failings among practitioners of the Art. We have a reputation for eccentricity, reclusiveness and a lack of social skills.'

'I have not noticed that you possess any of these qualities.' He said it because it was true. She was a very lovely woman and capable of being quite charming despite her severe manner.

'I have had several centuries to gain some polish. Hopefully you will get the same opportunity.'

'Do you think what people say about mages is true then?' Teclis was curious.

'In some ways, yes. It's hardly surprising that mages should be reclusive. Ours is a life that requires study and a great deal of time spent alone with books. We need a lot of specialised knowledge that can be of no possible interest to the layman. It also requires that we be strong-willed and self-centred.'

'I follow you. Where does the eccentricity come from?'

'A lot of time spent isolated will make even the most balanced seem eccentric and give them a chance to develop strange notions and habits. And I think there is something about exposure to the winds of magic and the practice of the Art itself that lends itself to mental instability.'

'So I can look forward to even more isolation in the future,' he tried to make it sound like a joke, but he was feeling somewhat sorry for himself. Tyrion had enthusiastically thrown himself into a quadrille and was dancing with a group of smiling young elves. He said something that made them all laugh.

'No – you will find comradeship with other mages, if you do not alienate too many of them. They are the ones you will have most in common with – shared interests, shared knowledge and shared needs.'

'Well that is something to look forward to at least,' he said.

'There is no need to mock, Prince Teclis.'

'As if I would ever do that to you, Lady Malene.'

Tyrion was dancing with their cousin now, the lovely Liselle. He said something. Liselle smiled. She said something. He smiled. How effortless he made it look, and yet when Teclis tried such things, it never worked. People did not respond to him the way they did to his brother.

At moments like this, Teclis thought he would be willing to give up the Art to be able to make a girl smile the way Tyrion could. The feeling never lasted more than a moment though. The Art would make him master of his world eventually. He felt sure of that.

Tyrion drew Liselle away from the dance floor. Her bare arm was warm beneath his fingers and he felt the erotic spark pass between them. She smiled at him, glanced at the direction of Lady Malene and Teclis and said, 'Your brother is watching us most intently.'

'He is watching you most intently,' said Tyrion. 'He is captivated by your beauty. As what elf would not be?'

'He is very odd.'

'In what way?'

'The way he stares so. He is intense and cold and calculating. You feel as if he is measuring you and finding you wanting.'

'I have never found him to be like that.'

'He thinks he is cleverer than us.'

'He *is* cleverer than us. Take my word for it.'

'You always stand up for him, don't you?'

'He is my brother.'

'And that is reason enough to take his part? Against anyone?'

'If I do not take his part, who will?'

'My mother will. She likes him, I can tell.'

'Then I like her,' Tyrion said, hoping Liselle would take the hint.

'Your brother is a cripple. Has he always been so?'

Tyrion did not like the direction this conversation was taking at all. 'Would you care to dance once more?'

'They say that among the dark elves cripples are exposed upon the mountainside as babies, to prevent them being a burden on the rest of the community.'

Tyrion stared at her. 'And you think that is a good idea?'

'Our ancestors used to do the same, before the Sundering.'

'Those were crueller times. They had just fought a war against the forces of Darkness. In many places they still were doing so.'

'I have heard people say that we are becoming weak and decadent.'

'You think that becoming more like the dark elves will make us less decadent?' He smiled, hoping she would see the joke. 'Perhaps we should try being more like dwarfs to make ourselves less stubborn.'

'There are some who say we became decadent during the reign of the last Phoenix King. They hope that Finubar will bring back elven boldness and elven strength. He is a seafarer and an explorer, not a decadent conjurer.' She spoke with obvious pride. Finubar was of Lothern. He exemplified the virtues of her people.

'It is not necessary to denigrate one person in order to praise another.'

She laughed at his serious words as she had not laughed at his joke. 'There are times when I think you cannot be an elf, dear cousin, but some sort of changeling. There does not seem to be much malice in you.'

'I don't think you need to be malicious to be an elf either.'

'Then you have a lot to learn, my dear Tyrion. You are in Lothern now. It's a nasty, vicious place.'

He glanced around at all the rich people, in all their fine clothes, eating their fine food and drinking their fine wine. 'Yes, I can see that. It's really cut-throat.'

'Do not be deceived,' she said. 'Many of these people would stick a knife in your back if they thought it would get them ahead in the world. And in some cases, I am not just speaking metaphorically.'

'Are you always this cynical?'

'I am a realist,' she said. 'I grew up here. I know what they are like.'

'I have always heard it said that the high elves are the noblest people in the world.'

'And I am sure you have always heard it said by high elves. We are not ashamed to praise ourselves, are we?'

'Should we be?'

'It would not matter if we should. It would not stop us. Oh dear, it looks like Lord Larien has noticed us.' She made a small grimace but he thought she was not really so displeased.

'Why is that a bad thing?'

'He has been paying court to me for some time. He can be quite jealous.'

Tyrion had noticed the tall, athletic-looking elf earlier. He had not appeared to be so jealous. He had been surrounded by a coterie of admiring beauties to each of whom he seemed to be giving a portion of his attention. All of them appeared to be flattered to receive it too. He strode closer, straight backed, head held high. He smiled at Liselle, nodded curtly to Tyrion.

'Ah, the delightful Liselle,' he drawled. 'And this would be your cousin from the mountains we have heard so much about.'

Tyrion smiled at him. 'I only see one of you. Is that the royal we you are using?'

Lord Larien looked at him a little more closely, as if he had not been expecting any rejoinder from Tyrion.

'I am Prince Tyrion,' said Tyrion, to make the point that he did have royal blood. He bowed. 'I am pleased to make your acquaintance.'

Liselle laughed. This did not please Larien. 'Larien. Delighted,' he said, his expression making it very clear he was anything but. 'It has been a pleasure. Lady Liselle. I hope we can expect a dance later if your cousin does not insist on monopolising your time.' His tone made it clear how boorish he considered this.

Gracefully, Larien bowed to them in a way that made it clear he was only really bowing to her, and then he backed away to his coterie of admirers. Liselle laughed and smiled at Tyrion admiringly.

'There is more to you than meets the eye,' she said. He smiled back but he was not happy. He sensed she was playing a game here and he was a counter in it. Her real interest was in Larien and he was being set up as a potential rival to generate a little jealousy and interest.

Larien said something to his female admirers. They all looked at Tyrion and laughed. He waved at them gracefully as if delighted to be the centre of attention although he knew he was somehow in trouble.

A very pretty young elf maid detached herself from the laughing group orbiting Lord Larien. She glided closer, a picture of grace in her long ball gown. 'Lady Liselle,' she said. 'Why do you not introduce your beautiful companion to the rest of us? We are all ab-so-lute-ly dying to make his acquaintance.'

'Prince Tyrion, Lady Melissa,' said Liselle. He bowed. She curtsied. Lady Melissa looked up at Tyrion through very long lashes. Her eyes were a very pale grey.

'You do not look much like your brother,' she said. 'It is hard to believe you are related. One so fair, the other so... interesting.'

'We are twins,' said Tyrion. 'I am the older by a few minutes.'

'Twins. That is so unusual. Twins are very rarely born to high elves,' said Melissa.

'They are very rarely born to any sort of elves,' said Liselle.

'Indeed. That is what I meant. It's very, very unusual. Perhaps your parents used certain occult fertility rituals.' She placed a strange emphasis on the last two words, and Tyrion could not help but feel that he was being insulted although he had no idea how.

'I don't think so,' he said. 'My father was a mage, of course...'

Melissa sniggered. Liselle looked torn between embarrassment, anger and a desire to laugh herself. He did not see how what he said was funny. He kept smiling smoothly though, unwilling to let them make him uncomfortable. If they wanted to play games, that was fine. He knew that once he had worked out the rules, he would win. He always did.

'I have said something amusing,' he said. 'Perhaps you would care to explain to me what it was.'

They were discomfited by his response. It was not what either of them had expected. He smiled easily and stepped forwards, invading Melissa's personal space. He was aware of exactly the effect his physical presence had on women. He leaned forwards, intimately and whispered in her ear, 'Tell me what was so funny.'

She stepped away a little flustered. He smiled at her friends as if they had been sharing a confidence. He saw that they were all looking in this direction now. Melissa looked down over her left shoulder and then back up at him, and he was suddenly aware that he had changed the dynamic between the three of them completely.

'I meant nothing at all,' she murmured and retreated to her circle of friends.

Tyrion looked at Liselle and raised an eyebrow. 'I think Melissa was hinting, rather indelicately, that your parents might have used certain forbidden magics,' said Liselle. 'Or been involved with certain forbidden cults. Just as she was at first hinting that twins might be rare among high elves but not among dark elves. She likes to think she has a subtle wit.'

'Why would she say that?' Tyrion asked, genuinely puzzled. 'About my parents.'

'There are certain rumours,' said Liselle. 'There always are. It's that kind of city.'

Tyrion decided he would need to take this matter up with his brother. Teclis always knew more about this kind of thing than his brother. 'If you will excuse me for a few moments, I will be right back.'

He walked over to Teclis, passing Melissa and Lord Larien and their little clique. He smiled as he passed, as if there was nothing more delightful than their attention.

'An animal,' he heard one of the women say, as he walked by.

'But a rather beautiful one,' said somebody else. He thought it was Lady Melissa.

'She said what?' Teclis sounded annoyed. Tyrion smiled as if his brother had just made a joke. He glanced around. Lady Malene was involved in a discussion about seafaring with Iltharis and Korhien. No one was paying them any attention.

'Hush, brother,' said Tyrion. 'Do not let them upset you. I suspect that it is what they want. They seem to take pleasure in that sort of thing around here. In this game it appears to be the way you score points.'

'They are talking about our parents, Tyrion. They are hinting that they were members of the Cult of Luxury, a forbidden cult, associated with the worship of daemon gods. With the Lord of Pleasure, the One Who is not Named.' Teclis had lowered his voice now. This was not a subject anyone wanted to be overheard talking about. This was a thing mentioned only in whispers, talked about obliquely, never confronted directly.

'I cannot picture our father being involved in such a thing,' said Teclis. 'Can you?'

Tyrion tried to imagine his father anywhere else but in his workroom or reading a musty tome of magic. It was impossible. There was no way to picture him being involved in forbidden rites. It was as easy to imagine him captaining a slaving ship from Naggaroth. 'No.'

Teclis became thoughtful. 'And yet we are here, twins. And twins are indeed rare among elves.'

Tyrion remained quiet. He could see his brother was giving serious thought to the matter. He had always been one to try and see all sides of an issue.

'I do not think it is possible,' he said eventually.

'I am glad we are in agreement then,' said Tyrion. 'Why would anyone spread such rumours?'

'Malice,' said Teclis. 'You know what elves are like.'

'Surely there are better targets for such malice,' said Tyrion. 'Our father is an old, poor elf living in seclusion in the mountains. No one gains anything by saying such things about him.'

'Everybody always has to have a reason with you, don't they, brother? Has it ever occurred to you they might do it for the simple pleasure of the thing.'

Tyrion could not see what that pleasure might be, but he was starting to realise that he might be unusual in that last respect.

'You have a good heart,' Teclis said eventually. He said it as if it was an accusation of weakness. Tyrion did not take it personally.

'Be that as it may, I think it is safest to assume someone somewhere has a motive for spreading this rumour now. If it is not aimed at our father, it is most likely aimed at our dear, rich relatives.'

Teclis nodded. 'Possible. Or it may just be that we are the topic of discussion of the moment and people are throwing mud in the delightful elven fashion.'

Tyrion laughed. 'You are probably right. I may be taking this too seriously.'

'Frankly I am surprised that you think about these things at all, brother. If it's not to do with war or battle, you are usually not interested.'

Tyrion inclined his head in the direction of Liselle and Melissa and the small faction of extremely lovely young elf maids around them. 'I am starting to realise there are all sorts of battlefields and all sorts of ways to compete for glory.'

'Are you sure it's glory you are interested in?'

'The span of my interests is wider than you believe.'

'I should add girls to war and battle, should I?'

'Girls were always included. I am starting to think about politics.'

'The reason why wars are fought – according to one of our more ancient philosophers.'

'When diplomacy fails, wars begin,' quoted Tyrion.

'So you have taken to reading other things than histories of battles and legends of heroes.'

'No. Korhien told me that.'

'Perhaps you should emulate your mentor and start reading more widely.'

'Lady Malene told him that. Or so he said.'

'At least he listened.'

Tyrion did not tell him he suspected Korhien was lying about that. The White Lion read much more widely than he wanted anyone to know. It suited him to be seen as the bluff and not-too-intelligent soldier but he was actually something more.

It was not surprising when he considered it. Korhien was a companion and a bodyguard to the Phoenix King. He went on diplomatic missions for him. He acted as a go-between between Finubar and the great houses and the princes. Of course, he was more than a simple soldier.

Tyrion could also see the advantage he gained by having people underestimate him. It was not too difficult to understand the advantages Korhien gained from the role he played. Perhaps he should consider doing the same.

'You are thinking too hard about something again,' said Teclis. 'There is a nasty smell of burning wood.'

'You know me too well, brother,' Tyrion said. 'Now if you excuse me I must return to the ladies.'

'They look as if they are getting lonely without you.'

'I will see what I can do to change that,' Tyrion said. He walked back over to Lady Liselle smiling pleasantly, the very picture of a simple, true-hearted, lusty young elf with only one thing on his mind.

◄ CHAPTER TWENTY ►

Tyrion walked back into the lion's den. He smiled amiably at anyone who looked at him, giving no indication that he felt embarrassed or flustered by the gossip circulating about his parents, his brother or himself. There was no reason to. He had no quarrel with any of those present, unless they chose to make one. In that case, he would not back away from a fight.

The Lady Melissa glanced at him and smiled again. Larien stared rudely. It seemed like a deliberate attempt at intimidation. Tyrion shrugged and walked over.

'I trust running to your crippled brother and your frosty aunt has put your mind at rest,' said Larien. His face was a little flushed although whether with wine or anger or something else Tyrion could not tell.

'About what?'

'About your dubious parentage.'

There was a moment of silence. This was not the sort of thing said in polite elf circles. Even those nearby were quiet now, waiting to hear Tyrion's response.

'There is nothing dubious about my parentage,' said Tyrion calmly.

'I am sorry, perhaps I should have said your dubious parents,' said Larien.

Definitely drunk, Tyrion decided. The goblet in his hand was empty, and Tyrion could recall seeing it refilled more than once.

'Hush,' said Lady Melissa. 'This is not the time or place for this. You are a guest of House Emeraldsea.'

She shot Tyrion what looked like an apologetic look, but he could not miss the glitter in her eyes and the faint twist of her lips. She was enjoying this.

'Yes, hush, Larien,' said one of her friends. 'You are embarrassing yourself.'

Nothing could have been better calculated to goad Larien than pointing this out, Tyrion thought. Perhaps that was the intention.

'I am not the one who should be embarrassed. I am not the one who was conceived at some Slaaneshi orgy.'

'Nobody here was,' said Tyrion.

Larien gave a cruel laugh that was all the more shocking because of the note of pity in it. 'You really don't know, do you?'

'Larien,' said Lady Melissa. The warning in her voice was obvious. Larien paid it no more attention than a drunken dockman would pay an ant.

'Know what?' Tyrion asked. He knew that he really should not, but he was curious.

'You and your brother were conceived in the Temple of Dark Pleasures. That is why your brother turned out the way he did...'

'How would you know?' Tyrion asked pleasantly. 'Were you there?'

'Are you implying that I am a member of the Cult of Luxury?' Larien asked. He looked a lot more sober all of a sudden. His words were said very loudly, as if he wanted everyone to hear them.

All around was silence. All eyes in the room were on them now. Tyrion understood what was going on but there was no way he could stop it. It had all happened so quickly.

Out of the corner of his eye, he saw Korhien moving across the room towards the disturbance. He would not get here in time to intervene.

'Well, are you?' Larien was almost shouting now. He cocked his head to one side as if Tyrion had already replied. 'How dare you imply such a thing?'

Tyrion decided he might as well make the best of a bad situation. He smiled mockingly at Melissa and her friend and then at Larien. 'I was merely astounded that anyone could claim such familiarity with Slaaneshi ritual as you did. If anyone implied such a thing, it was you.'

Larien's hand shot out towards Tyrion's cheek. He obviously intended to strike the blow that marked the formal challenge to a duel. Tyrion had been expecting it. He stepped to one side and struck Larien hard in the stomach. The goblet fell from his hand.

When he had regained his wind, Larien said, with some satisfaction. 'You struck me.'

'It seemed better than allowing you to strike me,' said Tyrion.

'There can be only one redress,' said Larien. 'The Circle of Blades.'

'As you wish,' said Tyrion, ignoring the way Korhien was shaking his head.

Larien pulled himself upright and glared around.

'Leave now,' said Korhien. 'You've got what you came here for.'

Larien smirked at him.

'And I would not smile like that if I were you,' Korhien said. 'If this young elf does not kill you, I most assuredly will.'

That took the smile off his face, Tyrion thought. He grinned and then the thought struck him that the only circumstances that Korhien would be taking vengeance for him, was if he himself was dead.

'You cannot do that Ironglaive, duelling is forbidden to White Lions,' said Larien. His smirk had returned. Surrounded by his clique of adoring ladies he made his departure.

The air seemed suddenly very chilly.

'That was very foolish, doorkeeper,' said Korhien. He had led Tyrion into a side room. Outside, the hall was in an uproar.

'Listen to the commotion,' Tyrion said. 'Apparently challenges to duels are not as common at Lothern parties as this evening's experience has led me to believe.'

'This is not a joking matter. That elf intends to kill you and he is quite capable of doing it. Sober he is one of the best blades in this city.'

Korhien's seriousness communicated itself to Tyrion. 'I wish you had told me that before I hit him.'

'Go ahead! Joke your way into an early grave, doorkeeper.'

'I did not start it.' It was the sort of thing a child might say and Tyrion was conscious of it as soon as the words left his mouth.

'I am sure you did not.' Korhien expression was bitter. 'I should have seen this coming.'

'Who would have expected anyone to be so boorish as to start a brawl at a Lantern party,' said Lady Malene. She had just entered the chamber. Teclis was beside her, his face pale.

'The question is who put him up to it and why?' said Korhien. 'We need to know who it is so we can put pressure on them to make him withdraw.'

'What?' Tyrion asked. He had never heard of such a thing. Or read about it. 'No one withdraws challenges.'

'It happens all the time,' said Lady Malene. 'Larien will lose face and have to leave the city for a few years.'

'If we can make whoever set this hound on Tyrion call him off,' said Korhien.

'We are going to have to,' said Malene. 'I do not think he is ready to kill his first elf just yet.'

She was wrong. After what Larien had said about his parents Tyrion was more than willing to kill Larien. In fact he would enjoy it. It was the first time he had ever realised such a thing about himself. It was not a pleasant thought.

He was disturbed to discover that Liselle had been wrong earlier. There was malice in him. It was just more deeply hidden than it was in most elves. And there was a terrible anger too although most times he hid it from everyone, even himself.

Tyrion heard a knock at the door. Cautiously he padded over on his bare feet and answered it. He could hear someone just outside. He was not too worried but he slid the bolt back cautiously and pulled the door open. He was surprised to see Liselle standing there. She was dressed in a night robe which clearly had nothing underneath it.

'What do you want?' he asked.

'I'm sure you already know,' she replied.

'Then I suppose you had better come inside,' he said. He pulled the door fully open and gestured for her to enter. She strode inside and looked around.

'My room is just down the corridor,' she said. He reached out and pulled a strand of hair from behind her ear. He leaned forward as he had done earlier, and whispered into that ear, 'That is very fortunate.'

She leaned forward and kissed him on the lips. It was a long kiss and it started experimentally, tentatively but it ended up being very passionate.

'Yes,' she said, 'it is. Let us both make the most of that fortunate accident of geography.'

She led him by the hand towards the bed.

N'Kari roared as he raced through the streets of Tor Yvresse, killing as he went. He was strong now. He had eaten many souls and supped on many pleasures, his own and others. He felt almost as mighty as he had been on the day he had faced Aenarion millennia ago.

His army was an army now, no longer a mere raider band or an ill-organised group of cultists. It was a force strong enough to take even an ancient walled city like this one.

Hundreds of partially altered warriors had joined him. He had found more humans, shipwrecked mariners from the Old World. Groups of beastmen who had somehow survived in the high mountains and kept to the old ways had been drawn to him. Decadent elves had responded to the summons of his magic. Souls offered up in sacrifice had multiplied the number of daemons bound to his will. All of them rampaged through the streets of the city now, maiming, killing, raping, torturing, pillaging.

Terror and pleasure and hatred and fear pulsed through the air around N'Kari. It was like a banquet to him. He drank it all in.

A company of elf soldiers formed up in the square ahead, moving in a disciplined phalanx to repulse a company of his beastmen. The brutes threw themselves against that steady line with simple-minded ferocity that might have worked if they had been facing tribesmen as primitive as themselves but which had no chance of success against these foes.

Briefly N'Kari considered aiding his followers, of using his own power to break the bodies and spirits of the enemy but he sensed the opposition to his presence was growing and he still had a task to perform here. Somewhere out there a cabal of wizards was using its power to strengthen the ancient wards against his kind that had been built in ancient times. These were spells that could hurt him. They were already making him uncomfortable and they had the potential to banish him from this place if he was not careful. He was not going to take the risk of that happening, not until he had completed his vengeance on the Blood of Aenarion.

He could sense the nearness of the prey he sought. His nostrils flared in response to what his spiritual senses detected. Saliva filled his mouth and dripped onto the ground. Elrion leapt forward and grovelled in the dirt, licking it up, moaning in ecstatic pleasure that contact with N'Kari's secretions always gave to mortal things. N'Kari trampled on his back, leaving great talon marks on the writhing acolyte's flesh, forcing Elrion face down in the puddle of drool as he strode forwards.

Ahead of him was a small tenement house, inside of which a few warm bodies huddled. The ones he sought, two elves half-garbed in their militia gear who had obviously been trapped here en route to joining their unit, were being menaced by a group of beastmen. They bore the spiritual scent of the Blood of Aenarion.

N'Kari shifted his form, becoming an elf of spectacular beauty, goddess-like. He blasted his own beastmen in the back with a bolt of purple lightning and raced up to the elves. They stood there bemused by his loveliness and the narcotic cloud surrounding him.

'Quickly, follow me,' said N'Kari in a voice at once seductive and commanding. 'I will see you to safety.'

The elves looked at him, grateful for being saved, bemused at the appearance of a powerful sorceress they did not recognise. N'Kari reached out and stroked the cheek of the nearest one. He quivered with pleasure. 'We do not have any time to waste. Follow me. I will weave a spell that will get us out of here.'

He opened a portal and without giving the elves time to think, shepherded them through it before following him themselves. The elf he had touched was already looking at the other with insane jealousy. N'Kari chuckled, thinking of the sport he would have with this pair.

Behind him his army battled on. It would take them some time to realise they had been abandoned by their leader and begin a fighting retreat. N'Kari did not care. He had found what he had come for. Soon there would be two fewer of the line of Aenarion left.

There were not many more now. Soon his vengeance would be complete.

Lord Emeraldsea looked up from his telescope. He had obviously been studying the ships in the harbour. He gestured for Tyrion to join him on the balcony. Tyrion walked over, curious why he had been summoned into the august presence this fine morning.

'It took us a thousand years to put Finubar on the throne,' said Lord Emeraldsea. His words took Tyrion off guard. He had expected to be lectured about the events of the previous evening, about challenging other elves to duels at family parties.

'A thousand years?' Tyrion said, just to see where this was going. He was exaggerating. Finubar was not that old.

The old elf obviously sensed the current of his thoughts. 'He was the first Phoenix King ever to come from Lothern. You have no idea how difficult it was to make him that. The work began long before Finubar was born.'

Tyrion wondered why his grandfather was telling him this. Perhaps the old elf was lonely and just wanted someone to talk with, to go over old triumphs with, but somehow he doubted it. Lord Emeraldsea did not strike him as someone who did anything without a purpose.

'Why was it difficult?' Tyrion asked, because he felt he was expected to.

'The princes of the Old Kingdoms objected to it, of course. They have had a monopoly on the throne since before the time of Caledor the Conqueror. Aenarion was the only one they never had a say in the choosing of.' He glanced at the huge statue of the first Phoenix King in the harbour with something like admiration. From up here all they could see was his back. 'It's always been one of their own they made ruler.'

'Why did they object to Finubar?'

'Because he was from Lothern.'

'Because he was not of ancient blood?'

Lord Emeraldsea laughed bitterly. 'Finubar's house is as ancient as that of Caledor. So is mine for that matter. We have been here since the Kingdoms were founded.'

'But you are not of princely blood,' said Tyrion. He did not really care about that himself, he was just trying to understand the argument. Lord Emeraldsea looked hard at him, as if attempting to discern any trace of mockery or pride in his own ancient lineage. Apparently he was satisfied with what he saw.

'No, we are not. But nowhere is it written, nowhere did the gods dictate, that our rulers must be of that blood. In the past, some of them were not, some were simple scholars or warriors.'

'But they were chosen by the princes.'

'Indeed. They were chosen by councils of princes, selected from candidates put forward by them, usually because the princes felt they could control them, or because they were in the debt of one prince or another.'

Lord Emeraldsea was tampering with his faith. Tyrion had always liked to believe that Phoenix Kings were chosen from the best elves available with the best interests of Ulthuan at heart. This all sounded rather sordid. He said as much.

'All the workings of the machinery of power look sordid when you see them from close up,' his grandfather said. 'And they are. But that does not mean they are a bad thing. At least we do not have Malekith as our ruler like the dark elves. And that is the point. It is why he is not our king and we still fight wars with the druchii.'

Tyrion understood at once. 'You mean because he wanted to be the single absolute ruler like Aenarion, and because the princes would not let him be. They chose one of their own to make that point.'

His grandfather seemed gratified by the quickness of his understanding, which pleased Tyrion. He was not used to being appreciated for that. 'In a way, Malekith wanted more power than Aenarion ever really had. Aenarion was a war leader, accepted as such because in times of danger it is necessary to have a clear line of command. Any ship's captain can tell you that. Malekith wanted the same power as Aenarion held in war in peacetime, or rather his mother wanted that for him, or so it seemed at first. Our system is as much about preventing that sort of tyranny as it is about the exercise of power. The dark elves have a different system. You can see what it has brought them to.'

'Surely they have a bad system because they have a bad ruler,' Tyrion said. 'What has happened there merely reflects the personality of Malekith.'

'Or perhaps they have a bad ruler because they have a bad system,' his grandfather countered. 'There are no checks on the power of the Witch King. He does what he wants. He rules by fear and terror with a fist of literal iron. He does not need to consult with anybody, or take the interests of anyone except himself into account. I think that sort of power would make anybody mad, and believe me I have had some experience of wielding power in my life.'

'I do not doubt it,' said Tyrion.

'It's a very seductive thing,' said Lord Emeraldsea softly. 'To stand on the command deck and issue orders. To know everyone has to listen to you and obey and that their lives depend on it. Even when you are not on the command deck, it distorts life around you.'

'What do you mean?'

'Sit at a captain's table on a ship. Watch his officers and his crew as they eat. They laugh at his jokes, acknowledge his wisdom, burnish his pride. They have to because their own assignment of duties and their own prospects of promotion depend on his assessment of them. Power exercises its own magnetic field. Never doubt that, Prince Tyrion, and remember it if you exercise power yourself.'

'I will,' said Tyrion, and he meant it. He was glad of the circumstances that had forced him from his father's house at times like this. He felt he had a lot to learn from elves like his grandfather and Korhien and Prince Iltharis. He could never have learned it if he had stayed at home.

'I know you will, which is why I am telling you it.'

'You were telling me about the election of Finubar,' Tyrion said. 'Of how difficult it was and how much it cost.'

'It was and it did. We needed to convince a large number of the old princes that we were serious. We extended loans to some, bought up the debts of others. Gifts were given to those who could not be pressured. In the end, we still could not have done it, if it had not been Finubar's time.'

'What do you mean?'

'The princes recognised that the world had changed and we needed a new style of leadership, one that engaged us with the younger races and the world beyond Ulthuan. They saw that we needed allies and those allies would need to be made by someone with an understanding of those far lands. That's one advantage that

Finubar had and one advantage that we have. We tend to get the leadership we need when we need it because in the end all of our interests are conjoined. Your idealistic view of the world is not so far from the truth as it may sometimes sound, lad.'

'Why are you telling me this?' Tyrion asked.

'Because I was thinking that the day will come when we might need a leader like you could become, a warrior who thinks.'

'Who also happens to be a member of your family?'

'That would be a bonus. You have everything needed, lad. An ancient line, the look of Aenarion, connections. You could go very far.'

Lord Emeraldsea paused to let his words sink in. They did, far and fast. Tyrion understood what his grandfather was offering and why. Right now, he was very far from being a Phoenix King but he had the potential. Once his grandfather was certain Tyrion understood he spoke relentlessly on.

'Of course, you have put any chance of that at risk by allowing yourself to be provoked into this foolish duel.'

'Larien insulted my father and my mother.'

'He insulted all of us, and he would have been dealt with in time, trust me on that.'

Tyrion did. He realised that he would not like to be subject to any desire for vengeance on his grandfather's part. 'Revenge, Tyrion, is a wine which improves with age. It's one of the things you will need to learn, if you live. If you are to end up where you deserve to be.'

'I cannot stand by and let my father be insulted.'

'You will need to learn how to deal with such provocations better. Even if you live, this will not be the last such you will face.'

'I will do my best.'

'See that you do, lad, and one last thing...'

'Yes, grandfather.'

'Rest assured that if Larien does kill you, my vengeance will be one of which elves will talk for a thousand years.'

'That would almost make it worth being killed,' said Tyrion sardonically.

'No, it would not. Go now and rest and practise. I want you to live. You have a lot to live for.'

Tyrion departed, feeling as if he had just been offered the world, and did not quite know what to do with it.

'Are you proud of yourself for having provoked this brawl?' Tyrion looked at his brother, then sprawled in the chair of their shared sitting room. Tyrion could see that he was worried, and that was what was behind his brittle sarcasm.

'No,' said Tyrion. 'I am not. I would have avoided it if I could. I should have avoided it. I can see that now. But I lack your quick wits.'

'That is not true,' said Teclis. 'You are sharp enough when you want to be. I think perhaps you wanted this fight. I think you want the glory of being a famous duellist. I think you are making an early start on a career of violence.'

Tyrion laughed, not least because his brother was right. He could see that now. He did want this fight. He was looking forward to it.

'It might be a very short career,' Teclis said. 'Larien is, by all accounts, something of an expert with the blade. He has killed almost as many elves as Prince Iltharis.'

'You have been asking around, have you?'

'Lady Malene told me.'

'It seems I have become almost as much of a topic of conversation as these daemonic attacks.'

'Don't let it go to your head. It most likely will though. There is nothing in that vast empty cavern to stop it.'

'I am touched by your concern,' said Tyrion, stifling a yawn.

'Do not let cousin Liselle keep you awake too long. You are going to need your rest, if you are to survive this thing.'

'I will survive it, brother, never doubt that.' It seemed to Tyrion that he was the only one who thought that way.

Tyrion lay beside Liselle on the bed. He stroked her naked back with a feather that had come loose from the pillow during their love-making.

'That tickles,' she said, turning to face him and looking long and hard into his face.

'You are going to have to fight Larien tomorrow, you know,' she said. Tyrion looked at her. She had obviously heard something he had not.

'I already knew that,' he said. 'I knew it when I struck him.'

'He cannot be bought off. He cannot be intimidated. He seems to want to go through with this fight almost as much as you do.' She sounded thoughtful. Tyrion tickled her once again. She squirmed away.

'You should take this very seriously,' she said giggling. 'My grandfather has brought a lot of pressure to bear and it has not worked. That is not usual at all. Usually what he wants, he gets.'

Tyrion did not wonder that his grandfather had not tried to dissuade him. If Tyrion withdrew it would besmirch his reputation and that of his family. He would no longer be a potential candidate for the Phoenix Throne and would become useless as far as his grandfather's plans were concerned.

'You do not sound unhappy that this is not the case.'

'It will not do the old megalomaniac any harm to discover he is not a god. My concern is that you will have to pay the price for his self-knowledge. I do not want anything bad to happen to you.'

Tyrion smiled at her, sensing the insincerity of her words. She was saying them because she felt she had to, because the role she was playing in this drama demanded them. There was no real concern there. She was as self-obsessed as most elves. He could not blame her for this. They had only really known each other for a few weeks. It saddened him. He began to have some idea how lonely a place a city like Lothern was going to be.

'Rumour has it that Larien belongs to the Cult of the Forbidden Blade,' she said. 'They are sworn to kill the Blood of Aenarion to prevent one of them from drawing the Sword of Khaine and ending the world.'

'Maybe they should start with Malekith. He is a more likely candidate for that than me. I find this world quite appealing.'

'I don't want anything bad to happen to you,' she said. Again, she sounded like an actress playing a role.

'Nothing bad is going to happen to me.'

'Death might,' she said.

'Well we are alive now and if I am soon to die I want to sample some more of life's pleasures.'

He reached out for her once again.

CHAPTER TWENTY-TWO

It was an odd sensation, rising on what might be his last day of life. Tyrion dressed with care, inspecting himself in the mirror as he did so. He was not pale. He did not sweat. His hands were steady. His heart did not race or pound in his ears. The only thrill he felt was excitement. He considered his response, observing himself dispassionately as an outsider would. He was definitely not afraid. He doubted that whatever happened he would disgrace his family or his famous ancestor. That, at least, was good.

He was aware of the possibility of death, perhaps even its likelihood, but he suffered none of the symptoms of fear or nerves he had heard or read about. He was merely curious as to his own reaction or lack of it.

If he was honest with himself, he was looking forward to the Circle of Blades. It would be his first real test as a warrior. He felt as if he was finally getting to do something he had always wanted to. His curiosity extended to what it would be like to have a life or death combat and how he would perform.

Perhaps this excessive calmness was a reaction to the situation. Maybe his mind was trying to deal with the danger by minimising it. He had read that such things happened. He did not think it was the case for him. Something told him that he would always be this way on the morning before a battle. If it was abnormal then he was abnormal. He was of the Blood of Aenarion, a descendant of the first true elf warrior.

When he came downstairs to breakfast, he could see that others were not taking it quite as well. Teclis looked pale and afraid. His eyes looked huge. Tyrion could tell that he had not slept at all. Lady Malene did not look any better. Her expression was filled with foreboding. Liselle looked wan and pallid.

Tyrion grinned at them as he sat down at the table. He helped himself to water and a slice of bread and butter. He did not want to eat heavily for it would slow him down but he wanted to make sure he had some energy.

His grandfather merely smiled his chilly smile, apparently pleased by the way he was going to meet his fate.

The servants moved quietly around him as if afraid to say anything, as if he were an invalid or a ghost. It was as if some vast formal ritual were taking place, as if they wanted to show support or say farewell. Most of them looked at him curiously as if he were a rare specimen the like of which they might never see again. Many were sympathetic. Some looked jealous or disbelieving, as if they were watching a poor performance by an actor.

Why would that be, he wondered? Did they resent him being the centre of attention? Were they envious of his supposed bravery? Did they secretly dislike him and wish him ill? He felt sure that some did. It did not matter to him. He smiled at them all alike.

Korhien and Iltharis entered. They were formally garbed. Korhien wore his lionskin cloak. Iltharis was garbed in sombre black.

'Ready?' Korhien asked.

'Ready,' Tyrion said. His voice sounded calm and normal. He wanted to tell everyone not to worry, that it would all be all right, but that did not seem like appropriate behaviour. Instead as he passed Teclis he squeezed his shoulder. Then he was out of the dining room and into the courtyard where the horses were waiting for them. Thirty armed retainers were there as well. They would be needed to make up the circle.

It occurred to him that he might just have seen his brother for the last time. As a thought it was troubling but he felt no emotional response. It came to him then that he really was behaving differently. This calmness and clarity of thought were unnatural. So was the retreat from emotion. They were his body and mind's response to the danger of the situation.

He was absolutely aware of everything around him, the faint sheen of the sunlight on the horse's skin, the animal smell, the bulk of it. When he vaulted into the saddle he felt his body's movements and the interplay of his muscles with the horse's as he had never done before.

This intensity of perception continued as they rode through the city. He saw the cracks in the pavements and the plasterwork of the buildings, the feathers on the gulls that perched on pillars. The streets were busy as merchants set up shop and farmers drove their flocks into the city for market. Workers were already making their way down to the docks. Other riders moved through the streets on their own errands. Tyrion drank it all in, noticed everything, smiled at everyone who looked at him.

They rode through the north gate of the city and along the Sea Road, pushing through the late arriving drovers and early arriving travellers as they moved towards Lothern. Korhien took the left-hand path up the Watch Hill. It was traditional that the other protagonist would arrive by the right-hand one. Idly Tyrion wondered who would be first to arrive. Some people made a lot of that. Some chose to arrive early to show they were not afraid, some to come late to unsettle their opponent. For him, it did not matter. The fight was the thing. He was looking forward to it.

They rode to the hilltop and he could see his opponent and his two seconds were already there along with the thirty warriors of his part of the circle. They stood ready, looking at Tyrion with contempt graven on their faces. Tyrion smiled at them with the same friendliness he had shown everyone else this morning. The two seconds looked away. Larien shook his head as if Tyrion had committed some kind of faux pas.

Tyrion turned to look down from Watch Hill. He had a fine view of the Inner Sea approach and the Northern Walls of Lothern. It was not as impressive as the view of the Great Harbour coming in from the ocean but it was still striking. From the hill, you could see over the walls and he noticed the slate roofs of the buildings, the layout of the streets, the size of the largest statues. The waters of the Inner Sea were a calm mirror.

The sun had fully risen now and the morning was already warm. The sky was a very clear blue overhead. Gulls cawed. In the distance tiny figures made their way along the road. It was curious that they still had everyday business. Down there in the city, merchants bought and sold, lovers held hands, families were sitting down to breakfast. Up here two elves prepared to settle a matter of life and death.

It was the way the world worked. Always somewhere someone would be going about their daily routine while elsewhere mortals fought for their lives.

He rolled his shoulders and stretched his muscles and became aware that the others were looking at him curiously, as if they could not quite understand how he could be so calm. He knew they thought he was young and inexperienced and he supposed they expected him to show nerves. He did not feel any. He was enjoying himself. In a way he even took pleasure in being the centre of attention here. He would have smiled again, but this was a serious business now and deserving of a serious response.

He focused his attention on Larien. His opponent did not look so relaxed. He looked tense but not in a way that would be bad for a fighter. His movements crackled with nervous energy. His pupils seemed very large. All of his attention was focused on Tyrion. When their gazes met, he turned his head and spat, sending a gob of spittle to land at Tyrion's feet. It was a very grave insult.

Tyrion merely shrugged. This was all posturing, an attempt at intimidation, to unsettle Tyrion and put him in a frame of mind where he would make a mistake. Tyrion looked at Korhien who nodded, and Iltharis who was studying him closely in the way a gambler might study a horse before a race. Tyrion wondered if Iltharis had made a bet with someone and whether it would be for or against him.

It would have to be a bet for me, Tyrion decided. The odds against me would not make risking gold worthwhile. You could get good odds on me winning. That was the decision he himself would have made at least.

'For or against?' he asked. Iltharis seemed to understand at once what he meant. He smiled ruefully.

'For,' he responded.

'How much?'

'Ten gold dragons.'

Tyrion whistled. It was a hefty sum.

'Your confidence is inspiring,' Tyrion said.

'I got excellent odds.'

'I thought you would. What were they?'

'You sure you want to know?' Tyrion understood the question. It might damage his confidence if he knew how little was expected of him.

'Absolutely.'

'Fifty to one.'

'I wish I had known. I would have asked you to put something on for me. It would be a good bet. If I win, I get to spend the winnings. If I lose, I don't care.'

'You will not lose,' said Korhien. He did not sound entirely confident of that, but it was heartening that he cared.

'You are right,' Tyrion said, with sudden absolute confidence. 'I will not.'

Iltharis said, 'Larien has a tricky feint. He will mount a strong attack high and right and then will stab for the stomach. He will try to get you into the rhythm of defending against the flurry and then switch when you think you see an opening yourself.'

'I will bear that in mind,' Tyrion said. He would too, but he would not put too much faith in it. He preferred to study his opponent for himself and work on his own observations.

'He will use the early parts of the fight to feel you out,' said Korhien. 'He will pretend to be slower than he is, so he can take you off guard with the killing strike.'

Tyrion smiled at them both. 'I thank you for your advice.'

'But you have had enough of it,' Iltharis said. 'I recognise that tone.'

'I will win this for myself.'

'Never refuse any advantage you might get in a fight,' Korhien said. 'It can make the difference between life and death.'

'Even if it's dishonourable?' Tyrion asked.

'Especially if it's dishonourable,' Iltharis said with a grin. Korhien shot him a warning look. The other seconds were coming forward now. The duel was about to begin. All sixty warriors were forming in a circle, presenting their blades, points towards the centre. The duel would take place within a ring of sharp steel. The warriors would strike down any contestant who tried to flee from the battle.

The formalities were already gone through. Larien was not willing to retract the insult. Tyrion felt that honour must be satisfied. The seconds had done their best to make sure the quarrel had been settled amicably. Duty was done. The fight could begin. Both participants stripped to the waist and took up their weapons.

'I shall kill you slowly and painfully,' said Larien, as they walked down into the depression and took their places in the flat space below.

'The way you think,' said Tyrion and smiled brightly.

Larien looked hard at him.

'Slowly and painfully,' Tyrion said, to make sure Larien got the point.

Things were obviously not going the way he expected. Tyrion's nonchalance had evidently surprised him. He had come expecting to kill a nervous boy. He had found someone more self-possessed than he was. Tyrion decided that in part this fight was to be won in the mind. He suspected that most individual combats were. It was as much about the attitude of the fighters as it was about skill.

'I am of the Blood of Aenarion,' said Tyrion, simply, as if he were explaining something to someone slow of mind. It was an attack designed to increase Larien's unease and make him less sure of himself.

'I will soon see what that looks like,' said Larien. 'I am guessing it is the same colour as anyone else's.'

It was a good response and Tyrion smiled at it as if hearing a joke he enjoyed particularly.

'Shall we begin?' he asked, looking from Korhien to Larien's chief second. The two of them nodded. They stepped back to take their places on the edge of the ring. They too presented their blades. There was no way out of the circle now. All of the gaps were closed. Anyone trying to get out would be impaled upon a blade.

Larien sprang forward as lithe as a tiger. Tyrion parried easily enough and stepped forward. Blade strokes blurred between the two of them for the moment. Tyrion kept his guard up and made a few ripostes. He was content simply to ride out the fury of the initial attack and take the measure of his opponent.

Larien was quick and he was strong and his technique was excellent. Tyrion did not need Korhien's training to know this. Something in his mind was aware of it, in the same way as he was aware of the strength and weakness of a chess position. He doubted Larien had the same quickness of reflex as he himself possessed but he decided not to act on that assumption until he had more proof of it. Larien could, after all, easily be faking it, hoping to make him overconfident.

A few more passes of the blades told him this was not so. The elf's personality was reflected in his blade work. His swordplay was intricate and deceptive but the deception was in the technique. Larien relied on that and his natural strength to overcome his opponents. He was much better with a sword than most elves ever would be. He smiled at Tyrion, teeth gritted.

'I see what you mean about killing me slowly,' said Tyrion as they stepped apart. 'Are you trying to lull me to sleep?'

'No,' said Larien, springing forward. His blade was aimed high. An elf less quick than Tyrion might have had his head split. As it was Tyrion merely stepped backwards, parrying as he went, noticing that the rain of blows Larien had unleashed did indeed have a rhythm, and one most likely intended to lull the opponent into parrying the pattern of it.

He found himself falling into the pattern almost automatically, as an elf might sometimes find himself tapping his fingers in time to a drumbeat. He could see the danger of what Iltharis had predicted happening. It came as no surprise when suddenly the blade was not where it should have been according to the pattern of strokes. Tyrion had already predicted where it would be and parried it. He brought his left fist crashing into Larien's face.

Cartilage broke under the impact. Larien went reeling back, blinded by pain and tears. Tyrion leaned forward to full extension, ramming his sword into Larien's stomach. He felt the impact all the way up his arm. There was a scraping sensation as his sword hit bone. Larien screamed like an animal being pole-axed. Blood gouted forth, covering Tyrion's sword and hands, spraying onto his naked chest. Some of it got in his mouth. He caught the coppery taste.

Part of his mind was aware that this should be horrific. It was certainly not beautiful or glorious. There was a stink of blood and entrails, of things that should normally be inside an elf's body but now were not.

He did not mind it, just as he did not mind the screaming, or the sight of the light dying in another elf's eyes. The main thing was that, at some point, the sword had left Larien's hand and was now lying on the ground. His own life was no longer in danger. He had wiped out an insult to his family's honour and he had forestalled an attack on his clan by their enemies.

He felt a twinge of sympathy for Larien's pain. Korhien had been right in one way. It was hard to watch another elf die, but that too was a problem easily solved. He struck again, aiming for the heart, and silenced Larien's screams forever. He looked around at the other elves present. They stared at him in wonder and something else; it might have been horror.

'Unorthodox and inelegant,' said Iltharis. 'But effective.'

Korhien nodded. 'The main thing is that you are alive.'

He stepped forward and hoisted Tyrion into the air, laughing. He seemed more relieved than Tyrion felt and suddenly it struck him why. Korhien had not been looking forward to explaining to Prince Arathion how he had led his son to his death. Tyrion looked down at the corpse of Larien. Already it looked different. The face looked stark and all animating spirit had left it. The eyes were glazed.

Larien's two seconds were covering his corpse with a cloak. Tyrion contemplated the shrouded form for a moment, only too aware that it might so easily have been his own. He felt no rush of reaction,

no urge to scream or shout or sing with joy. He was keenly aware
of his triumph, that he was alive and he had proven the victor and
that was enough for him. He had a sense of satisfaction and pleasure though.

'By all the gods,' Iltharis said. 'You are a cool one.'

Tyrion was barely aware of his surroundings as they rode back towards
Lothern. He kept going over the fight in his mind, replaying every
move, reliving every blow, remembering every small detail lovingly.
He was excited, not disturbed. He had never felt better or more alive.

Larien had tried to kill him, for reasons that Tyrion was still not
very clear about. He had never done anything to hurt Larien and,
as far as he knew, he hadn't given the elf any reason to pick a quarrel with him. Larien was dead through his own choice. Tyrion had
merely been his chosen means of execution.

He was sure that Larien would not have looked at things this way.
He was quite certain that Larien had expected to be riding away
on his own horse while Tyrion lay cold on the ground. He imagined that no one ever thought that they were going to be the ones
who died when they picked these quarrels but it was inevitable that
somebody was and Tyrion was glad it was not him.

He was more than glad – he was pleased and proud. He had
demonstrated his skill against one of the most famous duellists in
Lothern. He had beaten Larien fair and square and he knew that
in some ways he was going to inherit the elf's reputation. Now he
was going to be famous. Now he was going to be the one that people studied when he walked down the street and he was going to
be the one that they whispered about in taverns and salons.

He glanced around him and saw the way that his companions
were looking at him. Korhien looked troubled. Iltharis looked
pleased. The rest of his companions looked at him admiringly and
enviously. He could tell that some of them wished they were him
and that was a heady feeling. They were all basking in the reflected
glow of his victory.

Tyrion glanced around at the road and his surroundings. He had
not been really aware of it before. He had been too lost in his own
thoughts. Now he could see everything with an almost perfect clarity. He was aware of the greenness of the grass and the brightness
of the sun and the caress of the wind against his flesh. He knew
that food would taste better and that kissing a girl would be much
more pleasant.

Korhien rode up beside him. 'How are you feeling?'

'Never better.'

'You are taking it very well. I have seen some warriors be sick after their first kill, some of them after many kills.'

'I don't feel sick,' said Tyrion. 'I feel great.'

'That is because you are a natural,' Prince Iltharis said. He had ridden up on the other side and Tyrion found himself sandwiched between the two. 'A natural killer.'

Korhien grimaced. He did not like the sound of those words at all. Tyrion was not sure he liked the sound of it himself. It made him sound like a murderer. Iltharis could tell that he had given offence. He smiled coldly. 'I did not mean that as an insult. It is a compliment in its way. You are like me, Prince Tyrion, you do not feel any remorse when you kill someone who deserves it.'

'You're always very certain that the people you kill deserved death,' said Korhien. Iltharis's smile widened and he looked even more sardonic than usual.

'If they had not deserved death, I would not have killed them,' he said. He laughed and there was a genuine humour in his laughter that chilled Tyrion a little.

This was not a subject he felt that one joked about. It was a serious matter, a matter of life and death. On the other hand, he did feel closer in his attitude to Iltharis than to Korhien. He did not really see why he should regret killing Larien. After all, Larien would have had no regrets about killing him.

'I don't think everyone I killed deserved death,' said Korhien. He seemed to be taking the matter seriously too and Tyrion liked him for that even more than usual. He felt like he had something in common with both of these elves and that was not a bad thing. They were equally great warriors in their way and he could learn something from both of them. He was going to have to if he was going to become the fighter he wanted to be.

'You think too much, my friend,' said Iltharis.

'I don't think you can ever do that,' said Korhien. 'Too many people kill without thinking in this world.'

'You and I are in agreement about that, at least,' said Iltharis. 'But come. Let us celebrate the fact our young friend is alive. We can all agree that is a good thing and raise a glass to it.'

'Let us not get too drunk. There will be another council this afternoon. You would not want to embarrass yourself in front of the Phoenix King.'

CHAPTER TWENTY-THREE

Urian took another sip of the very fine wine the Phoenix King had provided for his advisors. There was some subtle narcotic in it, something that sharpened the wits and blunted the edge of fatigue. Of course, it was not nearly as potent as the equivalent vintage would have been in Naggaroth, but that was not necessarily a bad thing. If these elves had been drinking that wine they would most likely have been at each other's throats by now. He set the goblet back down on the highly polished table and listened to the equally polished debate.

By this stage of the proceedings, it was not so much about deciding what was to be done or what the problem really was. It was more about who would get to make the decisions, who would make his rivals look foolish or weak or lacking in knowledge, who would get the credit if there was any credit to be had and who would be apportioned blame in the event of anything going wrong.

It did not matter where elves came from, Naggaroth or Ulthuan, in this their councils were always alike. Of course, in Ulthuan the stakes were not as high as they were in Naggaroth. Here, the worst that was likely to happen to anyone coming out on the losing side in a debate was that they might lose face or some fractional increment of prestige. In Naggaroth, where the stakes were in favour of Malekith, there was always the stimulating possibility that death might await the loser. The Witch King did not tolerate failure and he did not love bad advice.

Listening to some of these windbags, Urian thought they might benefit from the lash of Malekith's iron discipline. It would certainly stop them from rambling on and on and on. One thing he could safely say about the wizards of Ulthuan was that they loved the sound of their own voices.

It made him almost nostalgic for those councils where the Witch

King would execute those who bored him. Like all tyrants, Malekith loved only the sound of his own voice and was intolerant of those who would steal away some small fraction of the attention that he craved. That was his rightful entitlement, Urian corrected himself ironically.

At the moment the archmage Eltharik was laying markers on the maps of Ulthuan spread out on the great table of the council chamber. He was making the point yet again that all of the attacks had taken place near waystones. He was also placing the names of those who dwelled in areas that had been attacked and were known to have been killed.

As he listened to the long list of casualties, Urian almost sat bolt upright. For a moment he thought he perceived the pattern and he listened carefully to what was being said. As the evening wore on and Eltharik continued to bore with a list of names that he had so lovingly compiled for this purpose, Urian again and again heard names that were familiar to him from his studies.

He wondered if anybody else had seen the pattern, and decided that they had not because they did not share his fascination with the heritage of his master Malekith and his very potent father.

He wondered whether he was really correct. Perhaps it was simply seeing something random. It was the nature of the mind to try and make order out of chaos, to try and see patterns in everything. That was a danger that he was well aware of. And yet, the more he thought about it, the more what he saw made sense.

He cast his mind back over the research he had been doing for his monograph on the descendants of Aenarion. Every single one of the places that had been attacked was a place where one of the Blood had dwelled and would most likely have been dwelling still had not the daemon attacked. And it seemed very likely that a creature as malicious as N'Kari would seek revenge upon the descendants of the Phoenix King who had caused him so much inconvenience as to slay him twice.

Yes, he thought, I have it. The Keeper of Secrets is killing the descendants of Aenarion one by one. He intends to wipe out the line. Urian smiled a secret smile, knowing that for once he really was ahead of every other elf in the room.

The question was, what was he going to do with this knowledge? It would be a very dangerous thing to keep this from his master. If N'Kari was killing all of the descendants of Aenarion, the Witch King himself must surely head the list of potential victims. It would be interesting to see what happened when an ancient and powerful daemon clashed with the mighty ruler of Naggaroth.

For Urian the question became whether the reward his master would give him for finding out this information would be of greater value to him than the amusement to be gained from letting the struggle happen.

Lady Malene noticed him smiling. She looked at him sourly and said, 'Prince Iltharis, perhaps you would care to share the joke with us. I do not really see anything to smile about in this long list of the dead.'

'Forgive me, Lady Malene, my mind is full of butterflies tonight. I was merely pleased by the taste of this fine vintage. There is indeed nothing to smile about in this catalogue of horrors. Now if you could excuse me, something has just occurred to me and I must beg leave to return to my mansion and consult with my books.'

'Your hypothesis is an interesting one, Urian,' said Malekith. Even over all the long leagues between the two communicating mirrors, Urian could hear the anger in his master's voice. 'And it concurs with some information my mother has seen fit to pass on to me.'

'She has had one of her visions, sire?' Urian was suddenly glad he had chosen to pass on his information to Malekith. Not to have done so and then to have the Witch King even suspect he had behaved in this fashion would be inevitably fatal.

'Precisely so, Urian, or so she would have me believe. It is also true that my mother has her own sources within the Cults of Luxury in Ulthuan, some of them hidden even from me.'

It was typical of Malekith to speak that way, Urian thought. It implied that he knew a very great deal even as he admitted he did not know everything. Knowing his master it was most likely an accurate summation as well. Malekith was only imprecise when he wanted to be.

'What would you have me do, sire?' Urian asked. This was the nub of the matter.

Malekith was silent for a long moment. Urian could almost feel the force of his thoughts, the titanic brooding immensity of his calculations. He was looking at the matter from all sides, weighing advantages and disadvantages closely.

'I think it would be useful if you were to share your theory at the next council. It would redound to your credit. And if perchance our misguided kinsfolk should teach this arrogant daemon a lesson then so much the better.'

'As you wish, sire,' said Urian, feeling certain as always that his master had kept his real purposes hidden and his real reasons obscure. It certainly could not be that Malekith was frightened by the possibility of the daemon coming for him.

Nothing frightened the Witch King. Urian was very certain of that. Still if anything might, the possibility of a Greater Daemon of Chaos coming to seek vengeance would surely head the list.

Urian looked around the chamber. His expression was grave but inwardly he was enjoying the commotion he had caused. He was also feeling secretly smug. It was he, after all, who had divined the daemon's intentions, not these clever wizards, or proud scholars or even the Witch King himself.

'I do not believe this, Prince Iltharis' said Eltharik.

Urian smiled at him. 'Perhaps that is because you did not think of it yourself.'

The wizard's mouth fell open. He was obviously not used to being talked to this way, except perhaps by other archmagi.

'It fits the facts as we know them,' said Lady Malene. 'And so far it is the only theory we have that does.'

'That does not mean it is correct,' said Belthania.

'But if it is correct,' said Finubar, 'then every surviving descendant of Aenarion is in danger.'

'Perhaps that is why Eltharik quibbles with my theory,' said Urian. He kept his voice reasonable. 'Perhaps he sees a way to end the problem of the Curse for all time.'

It was a possibility that had almost certainly occurred to most of the elves in the room, even if none of them had dared mention it. He thought it best to get it out into the open, and if by doing so he could cast a slur on this haughty archmage, so much the better.

'That was not my intention at all. I merely think we should not accept an untested hypothesis without proof.'

'How do you intend it should be tested?' Lady Malene asked. 'Shall we wait until every descendant of Aenarion is dead and every place where they dwell is ravaged?'

There was anger in her voice. She was obviously concerned for her nephews.

'I can assure you that the facts are testable. I have access to all of our genealogies and I have talked with many of the people killed,' said Urian. 'If you check the records you will find their names and places of abode are all stored by the Priests of Asuryan and the Loremasters of Hoeth.'

Urian looked around the room. This was indisputably his area of expertise and no one was prepared to challenge him on it. He could see that many of those present were coming around to his point of view. It would indeed be too bad, he thought, if Eltharik was correct and all he was doing was projecting an imaginary pattern onto the course of events.

He looked at Finubar. The Phoenix King's face was bland but there was something about his manner at that moment that reminded Urian of Malekith. The Phoenix King too was making his calculations, and they were not all about preserving the lives of the Blood of Aenarion. They were to do with enhancing his prestige and strengthening his position.

Finubar's eyes snapped open and Urian found himself meeting the Phoenix King's gaze. For a moment he felt that something else was looking out at him, something that could see into his very soul and plumb all of his secrets. He told himself that could not be so, for if Finubar really could do that, he would be ordering his White Lions to cut Urian down where he sat.

'I think Prince Iltharis has spoken to the heart of the matter,' Finubar said. 'We cannot allow any of our subjects to be terrorised by this daemon, nor can we take the risk of the descendants of Aenarion being wiped out. After all, the Everqueen herself is counted among their number.'

Urian could see that got everyone's attention. None of the elves of Ulthuan wanted to risk of anything bad happening to their beloved spiritual leader. None of them wanted to be the one who spoke out in favour of doing anything that would cause it to happen either. Urian knew his point was carried.

'What shall we do, sire?' Lady Malene asked.

'The descendants of Aenarion must be protected. There is only one place we can be certain they will be beyond this daemon's reach. The Shrine of Asuryan itself. Not even N'Kari would dare attack that place.'

Urian shot Finubar an admiring glance. He was a deep one, like Malekith. There was more going on here than met the eye, Urian felt sure of that. Finubar was using the crisis to strengthen his political position using both politics and religion. An attack on the shrine was the only thing more likely than an attack on the Everqueen to unite the whole nation behind him.

'What about the Everqueen?' Urian asked.

'We cannot command her, nor will she leave Avelorn. But she must be warned so that she can take steps to protect herself.'

'What about my nephews, sire?' Lady Malene asked.

'They must be summoned to our presence without further delay. I must decide whether they are in need of protection too.'

Urian already knew the answer to that.

'You have been summoned to the Palace,' said Lady Malene. 'An escort awaits you.'

'To see that we do not run away,' said Teclis.

'Do not even joke about that,' said Malene. 'I suggest you treat this interview with the utmost seriousness and the utmost circumspection. Your lives may depend on it.'

'Surely our lives depend on whether Finubar believes we are under the influence of the Curse of Aenarion?' said Teclis. 'I doubt our behaviour has anything to do with it.'

Tyrion wondered at the obtuseness of his twin. Could he not see that Malene was worried about them, and that she was trying to say something, anything, that might let her believe they had some control over their fate. Not that it mattered. Teclis was a realist in this.

'Run along and put on your court clothes. Do not do anything to disgrace us,' said Malene.

Teclis smiled. 'So that is what you are really worried about.'

Tyrion wondered how anybody so clever could also be so stupid.

'Yes,' said Lady Malene. 'That is all I am worried about.'

Her tone gave the lie to her words and even Teclis saw it then.

'I would do nothing to disgrace you, lady,' he said with a courtliness that compensated for his earlier tactlessness. Tyrion smiled. His brother was still sometimes capable of surprising him.

As they approached the throne room, Korhien came towards them. He was all seriousness, and very impressive in his court uniform and his lionskin cloak. He stood before them, barring their way with his axe. He looked grim. Tyrion suddenly had a sense of what it would be like to face him on the battlefield. He would be a terrifying opponent.

'I must ask you to remove your weapons, princes, and place them in my keeping. On this day of all days, you may not enter the royal presence armed.'

It was what they were expecting. Teclis had even been given a sword for the occasion; otherwise he would have nothing to surrender. They placed their weapons in the racks that Korhien indicated as he stood watching them.

'You will enter the presence one at a time, in order of age. Prince Tyrion you will go first. Prince Teclis I must ask you to be seated in the attendance chamber over there.' Korhien opened the door to attendance chamber first, and Teclis went within.

Then he opened the door to the audience chamber and Tyrion was ushered into the presence of the Phoenix King.

Tyrion found himself facing a tall, powerful-looking elf, narrow of face and keen of eye. He was dressed in what at first appeared to be a simple robe of Cathayan silk but which when studied revealed itself to be woven in patterns of subtle complexity.

The elf smiled in a friendly fashion. His manner was open and relaxed but there was something different about him. He seemed somehow distanced from the elves around him, much more remote. And he seemed larger, although not in any physical sense. It was as if he was somehow more real.

Tyrion stood there caught in a web of complex emotions and reactions. He was face to face with the Phoenix King, in the presence of someone who was more than merely an elf, who was not quite mortal.

Something looked out from behind Finubar's eyes. It was not unfriendly, bore him no malice, was even concerned for his welfare in a very distant fashion, but it was not something like him. It was an entity of an entirely different species.

Finubar smiled and the spell broke. Whatever had looked at Tyrion was gone, swift as the flickering dance of a flame. Now he was facing a friendly-seeming, young-looking elf who studied him with an unfeigned interest.

'You would be Prince Tyrion,' he said. The voice was rough and much deeper than Tyrion had expected. It had odd accents in it, a twang picked up in distant places and an air of authority of the sort you picked up on the command deck of ships.

'Yes, sire,' said Tyrion. 'I am. I am here to be tested for the Curse of Aenarion.'

Finubar laughed. 'I do not do the testing myself, Prince Tyrion.

The priests and the mages do it. My part of the process is simply to look at you and recommend a course of action. It is one of the gifts of the Phoenix King. I can see when certain elves are of... consequence. I can tell for example that you are very strongly of the Blood of Aenarion and I will need to send you to the seers. I suspect the same will prove true of your twin.'

Tyrion felt some unease, facing the tranquil gaze of the Phoenix King. Once more he got that sense of remoteness, but it was of a different type. Finubar seemed unaware of the fact that he might well be condemning Tyrion and his brother to death. Or perhaps he simply did not care.

Was it passing through the flame that had done this, Tyrion wondered, or was it simply the responsibility of kingship?

'May I ask how you can tell, sire?'

'You may ask – but I am damned if I can tell you.' Finubar laughed and the simple sea captain was back. 'I just know, or rather the part of me that was touched by the flame knows and it deigns to communicate its knowledge to me. I can see that there is something about you that is different from others. I could tell you were of the Blood. It was the same in the old days when I was a captain on my father's ships. I could tell when a storm would be a bad one or whether the wind was about to change suddenly.'

'I can see patterns on a chessboard that tell me how the game will play out, most of the time.' Tyrion did not know what it was that made him say that just then. He just felt the urge to communicate with this remote but not unsympathetic figure. He sensed they had something in common and it was something to do with his gift.

Or perhaps he was simply trying to let Finubar know that in him the Curse had come in a harmless form.

'That must be a very useful gift. I wish I had it. I would not lose nearly so much gold playing against my White Lions.'

'You lose gold playing against your bodyguards?' Tyrion was so astonished by the confession that he forgot to use the honorific. The Phoenix King did not appear to notice or to care.

'Oh yes. I bet on their play sometimes too. Korhien tells me you can beat him. That is quite unusual. You and I must try a game or two sometime. I am curious about this gift of yours. I understand it is not the only one you possess. Korhien tells me you are a natural with weapons, and by this he does not mean merely gifted.'

'He is very kind, sire,'

'No, he is not, Prince Tyrion. He is a warrior and a killer and that is not something you should ever lose sight of.'

'I meant it as a figure of speech, sire.'

'I know you did. I chose to misunderstand it to make a point.' Finubar smiled as he said it, but Tyrion was suddenly on guard. He sensed that there was more going on here than he understood, that he was in deeper waters even than he had thought.

'Good, Prince Tyrion. You have a brain as well as a gift for the blade. That is a useful combination of talents in a warrior. I can always use elves who possess them in my service.'

Tyrion wondered if he was being offered future employ as a White Lion or whether Finubar had something else in mind. Perhaps Tyrion was merely misunderstanding him.

'Assuming I pass the tests your priests put me through, sire.'

'They are not my priests, prince. They serve Asuryan.'

'You are his chosen representative, sire.'

'I fear you have a lot to learn about politics and elven priestcraft, Prince Tyrion.'

'I am sure you are correct, sire.'

'I wish more of my subjects shared your belief,' said the Phoenix King. Again he smiled, but Tyrion sensed that he was not entirely joking. Of course, there were those who opposed him. There always were. It was the nature of asur politics.

'What do you think of the rumours of this new terror besetting our land?'

The sudden change of subject threw Tyrion. He considered for a moment.

'You mean that the daemon N'Kari, Aenarion's enemy, has returned to take vengeance on the elves?'

'Precisely so.'

'I thought the daemon slain by Aenarion, sire.'

'You think it unlikely to be it then?'

'I do not know enough about these matters to venture an opinion, sire.'

'And you are unsure why I have asked you for one and are too polite to say.'

'Something like that, sire.'

'You must never be slow to voice your opinion to me, prince. A Phoenix King needs those around him who speak the truth as they see it. It is the only way he keeps any grip on reality at all.'

'I will bear that in mind, sire.'

'Well, bearing that in mind, what do you really think in answer to my original question?'

'I think it unlikely that anyone would call himself by the name of Keeper of Secrets as a jest, sire, although there are some who would take the name of one of our ancient enemies merely to frighten us.'

'And yet...'

'And yet my heart tells me that it is not the case. I believe it quite possible the daemon has returned to take vengeance on the elves, sire.'

'I am afraid my advisors agree with you, prince. N'Kari has returned to slay all of the Blood of Aenarion. He has already made a very good beginning.'

A thrill of horror and concern passed through Tyrion. 'What about my father, sire?'

'A messenger will be dispatched to warn him. One he will trust and hopefully listen to.'

'Korhien Ironglaive, sire?'

Finubar nodded. 'They have been friends for a very long time.'

'And what of myself and my brother, sire? What is there we can do?'

'Stay alive, Prince Tyrion. And to that end you will be dispatched to the safest place in Elvendom. The Shrine of Asuryan. If there is any place that we can put you beyond the reach of the daemon, it is there.'

'It is the holiest spot in Ulthuan. Do you really need to send us so far, sire?'

'You were going to have to go there anyway, Prince Tyrion. You are of the Blood of Aenarion and that is where you will be tested for the Curse. We are killing two birds with one stone, you see.'

'I understand.' A courtier approached the Phoenix King and murmured something in his ear.

'If you will excuse me, Prince Tyrion,' Finubar murmured.

Tyrion understood that he had been dismissed.

Teclis studied Finubar with just as much interest as the Phoenix King studied him. He might never get another chance of doing it so he might as well make the most of the opportunity.

He saw a tall, athletic elf with an air that reminded him of every other Lothern merchant or captain he had so far encountered. Finubar had that air of command they all had and that air of brisk informality. His garb was much richer, of course. His robes were luxurious and formal, subtly understated but the finest in the lands. They were in keeping with this chamber.

Finubar was armed, even though Teclis was not. There were other White Lions in the room, at a discreet distance, just out of earshot of a murmured conversation, close enough to spring to Finubar's rescue in the unlikely event of Teclis attempting an assassination. They were taking no chances. He understood why. There had been numerous attempts on the lives of Phoenix Kings in the course of asur history, all of them blamed on Malekith and the Cults of Luxury. Teclis was inclined to wonder whether that was a convenient fiction that covered up other conspiracies.

It was not just the external appearance of Finubar that interested Teclis though. It was the fact that he had been touched by a Power. Teclis could sense that about him. It was well concealed, hidden deeply in fact, but it was there. Finubar's whole body was saturated with magical energy of a very particular kind. Teclis did not doubt for a moment that if he entered the chambers of the Sacred Flame at the Shrine of Asuryan he would sense the same power there.

He was not entirely sure what the magic of the Flame did for Finubar. It was, of course, a measure of the god's blessing, but it seemed unlikely that so much energy could have been imprinted on him for only that effect. He warned himself to be careful and not make assumptions.

Who knew why the gods did anything?

'You are very quiet, Prince Teclis,' said Finubar. His voice was friendly, his manner open, and yet Teclis sensed something strange here. It was as if Finubar were acting a part of someone attempting to put somebody else at ease without really having a connection with them at all.

'I am sorry, Chosen One,' said Teclis.

'I trust you are not going to tell me you were overwhelmed by my presence,' said Finubar. There seemed to be genuine warmth in the smile now.

'No, Chosen One, I am not.'

'You see the Flame, don't you? And please spare me the title. I do not often have private conversations these days. Call me Finubar at least while we are in this chamber or sire if you must.'

'Yes, I see the Flame,' Teclis said, wondering how Finubar knew. 'It glows through your flesh.'

'Loremasters and archmages and those very sensitive to magic see that. You are not yet one of the first two so I must assume that you are the latter.'

'I always have been.'

'So I have been told. I have also been told you are extraordinarily gifted at magic. Perhaps after you return from the shrine you will have the chance to study it.'

'I am going to the shrine then, to be tested for the Curse?'

'You and your brother both.'

'You think we may be cursed then?'

'The Flame thinks you need to be tested. I merely relay the message.'

'What is it like?' Teclis asked. Another elf might not have dared ask, but he was curious.

'It is not at all what I expected before I passed through the Flame,' said Finubar. 'It is not entirely a comfortable thing to spend your life in the presence of a living god. More I am not allowed to say.'

Teclis did not ask who did not allow him that. Finubar had already answered.

'When do I go the shrine, sire?'

'At once. Your relatives have been notified. A ship waits for you at the docks. It will take you to the shrine at once.'

'Is it so urgent we be tested?'

'You are being sent there for your own protection. We have reason to believe a daemon is hunting you, for all the Blood of Aenarion.'

'Is that why N'Kari has returned?'

'My advisors think it likely. I see no reason to doubt them. It is unlikely even a Keeper of Secrets will seek you out within the reach of the Flame. It will find its fires very hot if it does. Believe me I have had some experience of the process.'

'I thank you for your kindness, sire,' said Teclis.

'You have my blessing and my leave to depart,' the Phoenix King replied.

'Oh no, another ship,' said Teclis. The twins stood on the dock at Lothern's northern harbour. It was neither as busy nor impressive as the Great Harbour. It lacked the variety too – the only ships in view were asur vessels. No others were allowed on the waters of the Inner Sea.

'I sometimes doubt you are my sister's son,' said Lady Malene. 'She was a true daughter of Lothern, as at home on the water as on land.'

Teclis looked oddly at her. He did not seem to know quite what to say or quite how to take this parting. Tyrion suspected that he had become accustomed to her company and that, unusually for his twin, Teclis trusted her. 'I take after my father. He always preferred the mountains.'

'I know,' said Malene. There was a world of wistfulness in her voice. Tyrion suspected she was thinking of the distant place in which her sister had died.

Tyrion was surprised when his twin walked forward and with great awkwardness hugged her. She hugged him back.

'We will come back,' Teclis said.

'Be sure that you do,' said Lady Malene. 'You still have a great deal to learn.'

'When you come back we shall see about making a warrior out of you, not a duellist, doorkeeper.' Korhien said. His manner was joking and jovial, a soldier who had said many goodbyes. Tyrion could see he was champing at the bit to get away as well though. He needed to bring a warning to their father.

'What do you mean?'

'There will be armies in the field this season. This business with the Cult of Pleasure has got everything stirred up. We will be sweeping the mountains of vermin. There will be raids on Naggaroth too.'

'The world must be shown the might of Ulthuan,' said Tyrion.

'Your quickness of understanding is gratifying, doorkeeper,' said Korhien.

'That's the first time anyone has ever told my brother that,' said Teclis. Korhien looked at him and smiled. He understood Teclis's joking manner.

'Be grateful he is your brother, otherwise he might call you out for insulting him.' There was an edge to the White Lion's words. Korhien was unhappy about the duel with Larien or something it had revealed about Tyrion. It was a matter he would have to take up with Korhien on his return.

If he returned.

'You had better get aboard,' said Lady Malene. 'You sail with the tide and the captain will want to get under way. Best not keep him waiting.'

'Blessings of Isha upon you,' said Korhien.

'May you live a thousand years,' the twins responded in unison.

Tyrion stood on the bowsprit of the ship, balancing there, watching the dolphins surge through the water alongside. They were keeping pace with the vessel, leaping high and landing in the water, frolicsome as children at play. The coast of the Inner Sea was visible in the distance, a soft-looking land in this light, rising away to the distant mountains.

'Stop showing off,' said Teclis. He sounded a little peevish. Perhaps he was more affected by their departure than he wanted to let on. Realising his harshness of tone, he made a joke, 'I could do that if I wanted to.'

Tyrion performed an elaborate courtly bow to him, still balancing on the bowsprit, ignoring the rise and fall of the ship.

'If you were not so seasick, of course,' he said. He too felt odd. He missed the bustle of the Emeraldsea Palace, the feeling that he was standing at the centre of the world. He even missed Liselle a little.

It felt like he was alone with his brother now, among strangers. There was a time that would not have bothered him. He had been changed by his time in Lothern. Of course they both had other things on their mind – the upcoming test, being hunted by a daemon.

'I don't feel quite so bad,' said Teclis. 'Perhaps it's the medicine Lady Malene gave me. Perhaps it's the sea itself. It feels somehow different from the wild outer ocean.'

'They say the storms are not so bad here, and there are not the same ocean currents,' said Tyrion. 'Maybe that makes a difference.'

They were talking around something. His brother would get to it sooner or later given time. 'Would you like to take my place here?'

'No. You make a better figurehead for a ship,' Teclis said. 'After all, your head is made of wood.'

A dolphin erupted from the water. It came almost level with Tyrion. He could have reached out and touched it if he wanted to. Its skin was slick with sloughing water. Its eyes looked oddly merry.

'The audience appreciates your jokes,' said Tyrion. He bounced on the bowsprit a couple of times to build up momentum then used its springiness to propel him into the air. He backflipped onto the deck, landing beside Teclis.

'It's sad you've been reduced to competing with dolphins,' said Teclis, but the pain in his eyes showed that he understood who Tyrion was really competing with. No amount of magic would ever allow him to do what Tyrion had just done, or enjoy the ease his brother had. As soon as he did it, Tyrion felt guilt mingle with a natural elven malignant satisfaction.

'Would you like to tell me what is really bothering you?' Tyrion asked.

'I am worried about our father. What if the daemon has already found him?'

It was a disquieting thought, imagining their old home besieged by an army of daemons. Even more disquieting was the idea that it might already have happened and they would not know about it. 'Me too,' said Tyrion.

'You have another idea in that thick skull of yours, I can tell. Spit it out!'

'I think we are being used as bait.'

'You think that we are being sent to one of the safest places in Ulthuan to tempt N'Kari to attack us.'

'No, I think we are being sent there to tempt N'Kari to attack it.'

'Go on.'

'What would happen if N'Kari attacked the Shrine of Asuryan?'

'He would be destroyed.'

'What if he was not? What if he escaped to try again?'

'He would be hunted down and destroyed.'

'And how would that affect the population?'

'I see where you are going with this – they would unite behind Finubar. They would be outraged and they would demand action.

They already are. Congratulations brother, you have been using your head for something else other than to block blows.'

'The princes will have to unite around Finubar. His position will become stronger. Theirs will be weaker. For a time.'

'Lothern has made you cynical, brother.'

'No. It has merely showed me how our rulers think. Now why don't you tell me what is really bothering you?'

Teclis looked at him for a long time. It seemed like he was not going to answer then, eventually, he gulped and said, 'We will be tested soon. What if I am cursed? What then?'

Tyrion could see that his brother was afraid and he could understand why. He wanted so badly to be a mage, to have a life, and that might well be denied him by the decision of the priests at the Shrine of Asuryan. They would not even have to put him to death. Interring him would be just as bad.

'You are not cursed,' Tyrion said.

'Look at me. Who would believe that?'

'Being the way you are means you were unlucky, not cursed.'

'Let me tell you something, brother,' Teclis's voice dropped so that only Tyrion could hear. 'I knew I was doing wrong when I took that spellbook from Malene's library. I did it anyway. I would do it again. I want the power and I am drawn to it, no matter what the cost. If that is not a sign of the Curse, what is?'

Tyrion smiled coldly. 'Then let me tell you something, brother. I was not horrified when I killed Larien. I enjoyed it. I enjoyed killing another elf. What does that say about me?'

They stared at each other in silence for a long time. Eventually Teclis said, 'I would have enjoyed killing him too. If I was able.'

'I am, brother, that is the difference. And I very much doubt Larien will be the last elf I kill.'

'Being a killer is not such a bad thing. In the world we live in it counts as a useful talent.'

'I think I enjoy it too much.'

The words hung in the air for a long time.

After three days and nights of sailing, a small island rose out of the Inner Sea ahead of the ship. It looked volcanic. Palm trees covered some of the slopes. Caves and terraces dotted its sides. On the highest point of the island was a large stepped pyramid. It must have been massive indeed, Tyrion thought, to be visible at such a distance.

In spite of everything, his worries and his fear for his father's safety, Tyrion was glad that he had come here, and seen this. It was one of the most sacred sites in all elvendom.

This was the place where Aenarion had first passed through the Flame of Asuryan and became Phoenix King. This was the place where, ever since, every Phoenix King from Bel Shanaar to Finubar had made his own ascension to the throne. It was the place where Malekith had made his doomed attempt to wrest the power of the gods from its rightful wielder.

It could be said that elven history began in this place. Before Aenarion had shaped them into a warrior people, the elves had been peaceful farmers and herders. They had lived in harmony with their land in the eternal springtime of their devotion to the Everqueen.

After Aenarion had passed through the Flame everything was different.

Aenarion had taught the elves how to make war, to follow kings, to fight and to conquer. They had become a different people after that day. He had remade the elves in his own image, into what they needed to become in order to survive. Peaceful farmers could no longer survive in a world from which the old gods had fled and through which the evil powers of Chaos marched. Aenarion had made them into something that could.

The ship moved ever closer and the island loomed ever more massive until they entered a small harbour. Statues of the Phoenix Kings lined the entrance. Images of the gods looked down from the cliffs overhead. The crew brought the ship in and moored it and soon Tyrion found himself on dry land again.

An escort of Phoenix Guard, proud in their distinctive uniforms waited to greet them. The ship's captain exchanged silent greetings with their leader in hand sign and soon the twins were walking up a long pathway on the side of the island towards the shrine, surrounded by twenty of its proud guardians.

Tyrion found his thoughts drawn inevitably back to one of the reasons why they were here.

N'Kari was looking for Teclis and himself. In a way it was like being told Aenarion himself had summoned them to an audience. A creature had stepped directly out of ancient myths and into the modern world and it was seeking to kill them. Tyrion had often dreamed of taking part in stories like the ones he and his twin had read as children. It seemed as if his dreams had come true.

He was not frightened exactly. It all seemed too strange. Walking here on the slopes of this ancient island, passing vineyards and flower gardens as the sun beamed down, the very idea that a daemon was looking for the two of them seemed a mad fantasy. Birds sang, huge butterflies almost as big as the songbirds moved from hedgerow to hedgerow and flower to flower. This was not a world in which things like daemons could possibly exist.

And yet his brain told him otherwise. Why else was he here? Why else were these heavily armed elves marching in regular pace beside him? Was not this island itself a place of legends and dreams? Was this not a place where the gods reached into the world and spoke to their chosen people? Even an elf as insensitive to most forms of magic as Tyrion could tell that this was a mystical place. Power charged the atmosphere all around them. He could feel it as he could feel the presence of a fine cool mist on his skin on a winter morning.

The Phoenix King himself had ordered them placed under guard here, which argued that he at least took the threat of the daemon seriously. And if Finubar did so, could he and his brother do anything less? No. The daemon was out there and soon it would come looking for them, and when it did he had better be ready, although he was not entirely sure how that was possible.

And tomorrow they would be tested. The Keeper of Secrets was not the only thing they had to worry about. It seemed that very suddenly his short life had become very dangerous.

The Temple of Asuryan rose above them. The stones were ancient and weathered, covered in an ochre moss. It was difficult to tell the real scale of the place. It seemed as if it was part of the cliffs, a mountain that had been partially sculpted by the ancient builders. It was as if the gods themselves had placed it there.

Even he could tell that there was a power contained within this place. He could sense the energy pulsing out through the very stone and he was sure that his brother, who was far more sensitive to these things than he was, was even more aware of it. Teclis stared as if he were looking at some natural marvel: a mountain landscape, a perfect beach, a glorious sunset. His face was transformed as if he were looking upon a wonder.

'A god dwells in this place,' he said.

'What gave you the first clue?' Tyrion asked. 'Was it the fact that it is the Temple of Asuryan? Or was it something more subtle like the religious symbols carved into the cliffs? Perhaps it was the smoke rising from the Sacred Flame at the top of the temple.'

'I can see the Flame burning through the cliff.'

'You can see it through the rock?'

'Perhaps see is the wrong word. I can perceive its energy. This is a place where a power from Outside touches our world. Something vast and slow and terribly ancient.'

There was a mixture of awe and something else in his brother's voice. Tyrion could not tell what it was. He looked at the temple again.

'It does not look like it was built by elves, does it?' he said.

'It is not in a typically elven architectural style, that's true,' said Teclis. 'The ziggurat echoes the patterns of ancient cities of the slann. Some think it was they who first contacted Asuryan and taught his worship to the elves.'

'Aenarion was in this place,' said Tyrion. It was a strange thought – the first Phoenix King had not yet been touched by the power of Asuryan when he first looked upon the spot. He could have walked away and the whole course of history would have been different. There would never have been any Phoenix Kings. Perhaps the forces of Chaos would have engulfed the world and there would be no Tyrion standing here to look up at the temple with wonder and unease in his heart.

He noticed the Phoenix Guard seemed to be paying attention to them now. He was tempted to ask them what they thought but he knew he would get no answer. These warriors were sworn to silence and he did not know the hand signs they used to communicate. They guarded sacred mysteries and it was said they knew their own dooms.

'Malekith was here too,' said Teclis. 'He tried to emulate his father. He tried to walk through the flame. He failed and was damned.'

How like his brother to concentrate on the dark side of things, Tyrion thought. But Teclis was correct. The Witch King of Naggaroth had once walked here too. He had gone forth from the spot, a wretched, scorched cripple, twisted by the experience. And yet, for all that, he had left. He had survived for far longer than his mighty father.

'Every Phoenix King who was ever crowned has stood near where we are standing now. From this small island, a great deal of our history was shaped.'

'Well, brother, now our history will be shaped. The course of our lives will be decided here,' said Teclis.

A priest of Asuryan awaited them at the entrance to the walled temple complex. The Eye of Asuryan worked into the surplice of his robes mirrored the symbols set in the wall. It gave Tyrion the feeling that he was in the gaze of the god.

They passed through a small postern gate and into the grounds around the great ziggurat. Within the cool shadow of the massive stone walls a host of smaller stone structures waited attendance on the mighty stepped pyramid of the temple proper.

The priest led them through courtyard after courtyard.

Ominously, the temple was full of elf soldiers, warriors of the levies hastily dispatched to increase the garrison camped in every courtyard and open space. There were hundreds of them, and Tyrion gathered that more were due to arrive soon. It seemed the Phoenix King was taking this threat very seriously.

Tall, grim elves in the uniforms of the Phoenix Guard moved everywhere. They said nothing, merely glancing warily at the twins, assessing them for any threat and then moving on.

They came to a small refectory and were offered food then showed to monastic cells. After the luxury of the Emeraldsea Palace, the size of the chambers and the sparseness of the furnishings came as a shock to Tyrion. Somehow small cabins had been easier to accept on a ship.

'Spit it out,' Teclis said. 'I can see you have something on your mind.'

'This place is a fortress,' said Tyrion. 'But there are not enough warriors here to defend it against a really powerful enemy. It is too big and the guards are still too few.'

'It is a temple not a fortress,' said Teclis, 'which might explain that. Also it is defended in other ways, my magic-blind brother.'

'How so?'

'There are extremely ancient and powerful wards woven into the walls. And there is a mighty presence here. It is not exactly chained, but it is constrained in some way. I can feel it.'

'Asuryan?'

'The same thing as touched Finubar, so yes.'

Tyrion smiled. 'We are here. In the same place as Aenarion once walked. Who would have thought this a season ago?'

'I wish it were under happier circumstances,' said Teclis. 'I wish we were at home with Father.'

'What could we do for him if the daemon comes?' said Tyrion. 'He is a wizard. He can look after himself.'

'The daemon has killed other wizards. Some of them vastly more powerful than our father.'

'There is nothing either you or I can do about that now, Teclis. I wish there was but it is not so.'

'I do not like being hunted,' said Teclis. 'One day I intend to be powerful enough to destroy a daemon like N'Kari if he troubles me or mine.'

'You do not lack for ambition, brother. I will settle for a good sword, nothing too ambitious, say Sunfang or the Sword of Khaine, then I will be able to do the same thing.'

'Hush, brother, that is not something to be joked about in this place, at this time.'

'Then I shall bid you goodnight and retire to my cell. Tomorrow a lot of things will be decided.'

Looking out through the window, Tyrion saw clouds scudding across the face of the moon. It looked like there was a storm coming. He wondered whether it was an omen.

N'Kari stood among the rubble of another destroyed town drinking in the emotions of fear, misery and disgust along with the adoration of his worshippers. He laughed as the buildings around the central square finally collapsed into a charred heap. In the distance he could hear the sound of his followers destroying the last few standing structures and rounding up the last of the terrified survivors.

It was time for the next phase of his plan. He was strong enough now to bargain from a position of power with those he needed. He had gathered enough sacrifices to begin the ritual. So far, his triumphs had been almost too easy but he was going to attack the Shrine of Asuryan and for that he would need allies of enormous power.

He looked at the assembled captives milling around like sheep in a pen. They had the eyes of those who had known defeat and enslavement and who knew that their fates were only going to get worse. N'Kari ensured they knew this by wearing his true battle form. He was not doing this just for their benefit. There were others he was going to have to impress more.

With the claw that tipped one of his four arms, N'Kari drew the symbol of Tzeentch in the ground, digging out channels with the talons of his fingers. By the time he had finished the sacrifice the channels were filled with blood. With a word he set the blood alight and with another twist of his magic he sent the scent drifting through the hole his ritual had punched in the fabric of reality and downwards into the uppermost Hells.

He let his spirit drift along behind it, following strange paths into the realms of Chaos that were his natural home. For a moment he was almost overcome with nostalgia. He considered giving up his quest for vengeance and returning to this malleable reality that would respond to his every perverse whim. It was a temptation, and as a servant of Slaanesh he felt almost obligated to give in to it, but he resisted, not least because this was a place where he needed all his wits about him.

The dark miracle of the burning blood had attracted the attention of something and in this place, it was massive and powerful. N'Kari recognised it for what it was immediately, an old enemy and an old ally, a potent servant of the Changer of Ways, the daemon god Tzeentch. It sensed his presence and approached warily, as if it suspected a trap. Under the circumstances N'Kari could hardly blame it for this. He made the signs and ritual gestures that among their kind showed that he wished a truce and that he had come with offerings. The Lord of Change responded in kind and soon they were in discussions.

By the end of the negotiations, N'Kari was well pleased with the outcome. He had gained a potent ally and in return he had given up very little that meant anything to him. All he had to do was provide the Lord of Change with a way into this world and the souls of several scores of elves to devour. He did not care about that. They were not his souls.

He sent his spirit hurtling back to mortal reality. He had other rituals to perform, other mighty allies to gather. By the time he was finished he would have a force the likes of which had not been seen since the time of Aenarion. They would respond to his summons.

They would come to this world. They would kill and maim and destroy if not exactly in obedience to his commands then at least in accordance with his plans.

'There is no need to be nervous,' said Teclis. 'They are not going to find anything wrong with you.'

'I am not nervous,' said Tyrion. In truth his brother looked more nervous than he felt. Tyrion had come to terms with the fact that he was going to be tested. Whatever the results were, he would deal with them.

An acolyte entered the cell and gestured for Tyrion to follow him. He bowed to the priest and clasped Teclis by the arm after the fashion of a comrade.

'Good luck!' Teclis said. He looked very young and very vulnerable and Tyrion could see that he was scared.

'And to you,' he replied.

The priest led him deeper into the temple. They came to an archway guarded by warriors of the Phoenix Guard, who gestured that the acolyte should come no further. Tyrion nodded and walked through the archway. Another priest led him to a robing chamber. His clothes were taken from him. The priest indicated a pool that was obviously fed from a bubbling hot spring.

'Purify yourself,' he said. Tyrion walked down into the water. It was hot, almost unpleasantly so, and had a faint sulphurous stink. He washed himself and emerged from the pool.

The priest waited, arms outstretched holding a simple robe with a belt of cloth. Tyrion took it and put it on. It smelled faintly of incense. He noticed that a small corner of the cuff had been patched.

The priest led him deeper into the temple. Slowly the downward sloping corridors of the building gave way to the walls of a cavern. He was deep beneath the earth. Lanterns lit the way. He passed walls carved with glorious scenes from the life of Aenarion. Here he was passing through the Sacred Flame. There he defeated hordes of Chaos monsters.

As he strode deeper into the caves it came to Tyrion that all of this had happened not far from here. He had a sense of passing backwards into history as he walked. This was a holy place and the power of the gods was strong here.

The priest brought him at last into a large cave far beneath the ziggurat, lit by flickering flames that surged and roared from a great pit. Enormous statues inhabited shadowy alcoves. A great altar flanked each side of the volcanic maw. It looked like a bridge that had been broken. It came to Tyrion that during the ritual in which the Phoenix King ascended he would pass from one of those altars to the other. This was the deepest and most sacred shrine on the island. He was closer to the presence of a god than he had ever been.

A group of masked elves waited there. They indicated that he should disrobe. They walked around him and inspected him minutely.

'No blemishes,' said one.

'No stigmata of Chaos,' said another.

'No visible taint,' said the third.

They chanted together and a glow gathered around each of them and then to Tyrion as the spell took effect. He felt tendrils of magical power pass through him, aware of it in the elven way even if he was not aware of what they were doing.

'There is no taint in this one,' said the first masked figure.

'There is no taint,' said the second.

'There is no taint,' said the third. The flames suddenly surged and roared and it seemed to Tyrion that they twisted for a moment into a gigantic robed figure. The eyes of the priests suddenly glowed, mirroring the dancing flames. Their voices became clearer, more distinct and far less elven. They seemed filled with a transcendent presence that even Tyrion could sense. He wondered if they were about to make the sort of prophesy that his father had talked about.

'This one will bear the weapons of a Phoenix King,' said first.

'This one will wear the armour of a Phoenix King,' said the second.

'Weapons and armour both,' said the third.

'Pass from this place and walk free, Blood of Aenarion,' they said in unison. The flaring flames died down. The sense of god-like presence vanished.

'I am not cursed,' said Tyrion. His voice sounded loud and awkward.

'All of the Blood bear Aenarion's curse, even if only to pass it on to their children. You do not bear the taint of evil and Chaos,' said the second priest. He felt sure from her voice that she was female. She sounded tired now and certainly nothing more than mortal.

'Yet,' said the third.

'You are pure in the gaze of Asuryan. Pass on into the Light of his Flame,' said the first. Tyrion walked out through the exit and took a flight of stairs upwards. He emerged onto a ledge that looked out onto the sea. The sunlight seemed blinding after the gloom of the caves. Gulls fluttered away from him and came to rest on a great stone banister.

He smiled. He had passed the test. He would have a life among the elves. And he would bear the weapons and armour of a Phoenix King, if they were correct.

What did they mean by that? Was he to be Phoenix King? Or did they simply mean he would wear gear given to him by a Phoenix King and be a White Lion like Korhien? In any case, it did not seem like a bad destiny.

He stood a little taller and it came to him that he had not even felt the weight of the knowledge of doom pressing down on his soul until it was removed. He laughed out loud and performed a cart-wheel on the ledge. He felt fairly certain it had never been used for that purpose before.

He looked up at the sun, and then he wondered what was happening to his brother back down there in the gloom.

The old, patched robe was scratchy and uncomfortable on Teclis's skin. The air was close, humid and warm. There was a sulphur stink in the air, doubtless from the volcanic springs deep below this place. The carvings on the walls were ominous, disturbing scenes from the life of Aenarion, battle and warfare and bloodshed.

Teclis felt like a prisoner forced to walk a path of doom to his own execution. He did not like this place. He did not like the reason he was here. He did not like being this deep underground.

He felt like he had to force air into his weak lungs. He was having difficulty breathing. The walls pressed down on him. The weight of old earth was heavy. At the same time he was uncomfortably aware that all it would take would be for the ancient volcanoes below this place to stir into life and those walls could easily fall in on him. Or hot lava could come gushing up from the depths and flood these corridors, burning him alive. If the ancient philosophers were right though, he told himself, that would not happen. The poison breath of the volcano would kill him first. It was not a reassuring thought.

He was aware of the enormous flows of magical energy around him. This entire site was a nexus of enormous power, of a very specific, sacred kind. This temple was not just located on a fault line in the earth's crust but on a fault line on the surface of the universe. The god or extra-dimensional entity or whatever Asuryan was could reach into the world of mortals here.

Aenarion had made his ascension here for a reason. This was the only place in the world where he could be invested with Asuryan's blessing. There must be other places in the world like this, he thought, where other Powers could reach in.

Vaul's Anvil would be one, which would explain why so many artefacts had been made there. It was a certainty that the Chaos Wastes must be like this for the daemon gods. There must be other shrines where elf, human and dwarf gods could touch the world. There must also be ways in which that magical energy could be tapped, if only a wizard could find a way.

The sudden insight lifted Teclis out of himself for a moment, and took away his fear and uncertainty. If he could only find a way to do that... It was a blasphemous thought but one that came naturally to him.

The fear returned, redoubled as the priest led him into a dimly lit cave where three masked and shadowy figures waited. He knew he had reached the shrine itself. Titanic statues of all the old elf gods were suddenly visible as flames leapt from the great central pit. They vanished back into shadow as the fire died down.

A glance told him that the three were all wizards of great power but the most potent presence by far dwelled within that pit flanked by twin altars. He walked towards the priests. Their hands moved in what might have been a blessing but which instinct told him was the beginning of a divinatory spell.

'Disrobe,' the first told him. He did so slowly and uncomfortably, aware of how weak and unfit his body must look to them. He coughed, in spite of all his efforts not to. He did not want to show weakness here of all places. He felt sure that they would hold it against him. They were elves and elves were like that.

The three circled around him, inspecting him minutely. He thought he sensed their contempt and their mockery. It took all his strength of will to avoid covering his private parts with his hands.

'No blemishes,' said one. 'But he is very infirm. His muscles are wasted.'

Teclis felt ashamed of himself. He knew he had been judged and found wanting.

'No stigmata of Chaos,' said another. 'He may not live. His lungs are weak.'

That comment made him angry. He was well aware of how precarious his grasp on life was. He did not need these three to rub his face in it. Who were they to pass judgement on him?

Presumably very well qualified indeed, the calmer and more

sardonic part of his mind observed. Otherwise they would not be here.

'No visible taint,' said the third. 'It is not Chaos that has made him this way. If he is cursed it is with ill-health.'

The three stopped and looked at each other and began to commune as if he were not present. 'It is too early to pass judgment on that,' said the first.

'I concur. With such a one as this the taint will not be visible. It will be spiritual and connected with power,' said the second.

'I stand corrected,' said the third. 'Let us proceed.'

The three of them began to work a ritual magic of great power and sophistication. Teclis watched fascinated as they wove the spell. It was divinatory magic of awesome complexity. He followed every part of the weave even if he did not understand all of its functions.

If he had possessed any doubts about the skill of these wizards, their ability to work this spell would have removed them. It was part ward, to contain any inimical magic that might be unleashed, and part revelatory spell designed to inspect his body and soul for the effects of the curse and the taint of Chaos.

The number of wizards present had been carefully calculated. No single mage could stand against three wizards of such skill. Even if he was tainted, and had been fully trained, there was nothing he could do here against the three of them. And he was not a fully trained wizard, merely a sixteen year-old elf with some stolen scraps of knowledge.

He felt the spell invade his form, passing along nerves and blood vessels, touching chakras and soul lines. He felt tiny flares of energy within his body respond, blazing up like a stoked furnace.

'He has the Art,' said the first.

'He has worked magic,' said the second.

'Interesting,' said the third.

'If he lives this one will be mighty indeed,' said the second.

'The seeds of greatness are in him.' Suddenly a huge jet of flame erupted from the pit. Gigantic plumes of molten magma formed themselves into the image of a huge, robed figure. Flames flickered in the eyes of the priests. Teclis saw the lines of force connecting them to the thing in the pit.

Teclis realised that the spell had joined not just the mages and himself. It had joined the mages at least in part to the power this shrine was sacred to. They were receiving wisdom from somewhere outside of normal space and time.

'He sees us. He senses the presence of the god,' said the third.

'Mighty indeed,' said the first. 'And perhaps wise.'

'This one will commune with ghosts,' said the second.

'This one will bear a crown,' said the second. Her voice was altered. It seemed as if something else was speaking through her. 'And a staff.'

'And confront the greatest daemons,' said the first. His voice sounded exactly the same as his comrades now.

'And stand at the centre of creation.'

'And face the Ender of Worlds.'

'And fight against his own blood,' said the third.

'Against his own blood,' all three of them said in one terrible voice. Then all of them slumped, like puppets whose strings had been cut, and the spell ended abruptly. The power went suddenly out of them, and they seemed less like threatening and mighty wizards and more like soul-weary ancient elves.

All of them looked at each other as if shocked, and Teclis wondered what they had seen, what visions of his future had passed through their mind. Fight against his own blood? Did they mean that he was to fight Tyrion? Surely that was not possible. It was something he would not do. He wanted to demand answers from them, but the part of him that was a wizard already knew that they would not answer and he could not compel them.

'There is no taint in this one,' said the first masked figure.

'There is no taint,' said the second.

'There is no taint,' said the third.

'Pass from this place and walk free, Blood of Aenarion.' All three of them spoke in unison. Weak, and sick at heart, Teclis limped up the stairs. It took him a very long time to reach the light of day emerging out onto a stone ledge. The smell of the sea assaulted his nostrils and made him feel sick.

Tyrion waited there for him. His heart started to pound. His head started to spin.

'I passed,' said Teclis and collapsed.

By the light of the two moons, through the curtain of pouring rain, N'Kari looked upon the Shrine of Asuryan and gloated. The portal shimmered closed behind him as the last of his followers emerged from its glowing surface. Ahead of him, the misty outlines of a huge ziggurat were visible through the gloom.

N'Kari studied the walls with eyes that saw more than light. He inspected the great patterns of magic swirling around the shrine. Potent spells woven by great mages in the days of high magic were there, but they were old. There were areas where Time's endless entropy had frayed them. There were places where the physical foci had gone and the spells were worn so thin that they were vulnerable.

He looked at them, seeing the patterns of magic superimposed on his vision of the world. He saw the souls of his own army, purple and sickly green cultists, bright blood-red Khornate daemons, lilac and lime for the Slaanesh daemons. He saw the sun-gold souls of the elven defenders.

His current force numbered in thousands with scores of daemons. They would have troubles of their own on the sacred soil within the shrine. Its very purity would make it difficult for them to maintain their present forms in the material world. Still, what was that to him. They would serve his purposes anyway. He knew he could maintain his own form even down there. He was still imbued with the energy he had stolen in the Vortex.

He gestured with his great claw. His followers responded. Sticks of bone thrashed drums skinned with elf flesh. Flutes carved from the thighbones of still-living maidens wailed dire tunes. Brazen war-horns sounded cacophonously. The stormy weather did not trouble his force. They revelled in it.

He was going to need all of his magic and all his followers to achieve his goal. The Shrine of Asuryan was a place where something akin to his kind and yet opposed to them made contact with this world, communicating with its followers, feeding off their worship, touching this plane with its magic. It was a mighty enemy.

It would oppose him every step of the way once he stepped on its sacred ground. More to the point it had the strength to oppose him, could cause him great pain, banish his daemon followers, twist the minds and destroy the bodies of his mortal worshippers. The core of this place was protected by spell walls that would make it difficult to work magic until he was within them.

But the shrine was not without weaknesses. Spell walls would be useless without warriors to protect them. The stones in which their magic was embedded could be battered down, swarmed over, destroyed in a dozen physical ways. Destruction of their physical housing would disrupt the spells themselves.

There had been a time when there had been enough elves to hold a place like this, but their numbers were fewer now than in Aenarion's time. There were weak points where he would concentrate his attacks, forcing the elves to defend them and throw away life after life, giving the elves the choice of guarding their outer defences or retreating within the Inner Shrine.

Either suited N'Kari's purposes. If they stayed he could use magic more easily against them. If they withdrew, they surrendered access to their inner defences without a fight.

Elrion looked up at him with mad, adoring eyes, his rain-soaked clothes clinging to his skin. He was like a hound now; he lived only for N'Kari's approval. It would be amusing to teach him hatred, so that he adored and resented at the same time. N'Kari resolved to do it when he had the time.

'Once I give the signal, order all the forces forwards. Attack the point where the walls are weakest. Draw the elves into combat at every point.'

'Yes beloved master.'

'We shall devour these elves.'

'The Dark Feast will be celebrated.'

Saliva dripped from the corner of Elrion's mouth and vanished amid the raindrops running down his face.

Thunder boomed overhead.

Teclis woke from a nightmare with the sense that something was terribly wrong. He looked around at the rough stone walls of his small cell. They seemed to be closing in on him. Tyrion looked up from the book he was reading. He sat cross-legged near the door. The last thing Teclis could remember was talking to him before he collapsed. His brother must have carried him back here.

'You are awake then,' Tyrion said. 'That's good. I thought you would sleep forever.'

'There is something wrong. Can't you feel it?' Teclis said.

Tyrion looked serious. 'Feel what?'

'There is something very powerful and very evil very close.'

'The daemon?' Tyrion asked.

Bells began to sound, stridently.

'He's here,' said Teclis.

'Then let us go and take a look,' said Tyrion. 'You can get a fine view from the top of the temple.'

Teclis shook his head. 'I do not have the energy. I will remain here.'

Tyrion shrugged and departed.

Banners bearing the rune of Slaanesh and the symbol of N'Kari unfurled. Beneath them demented cultists cavorted deliriously. Lust-maddened elves paused to steal a kiss from dancing, lascivious daemonettes. Gargoyles took wing through the buffeting winds. Mutated berserkers raced towards the walls bearing ropes and grapnels and makeshift ladders made from magically fused bones.

Arrows darkened the sky in response, descending on the oncoming horde in a shower of death. Deadly spells woven into their tips allowed them to pierce the magical flesh of daemons almost as easily as they parted the armour of cultist and skin of mutant. It seemed that there were more elves left alive within than he had thought and their mages had somehow managed to shield their essence even from N'Kari's magical vision.

Good, N'Kari thought. It would be more stimulating this way. It would lend a little piquancy to the conflict. Opposition would provide a little relish.

Things were going well. Vengeance would soon be his.

The elves were proving troublesome. A storm of arrows had descended on N'Kari's troops, along with a hail of spells. His warriors had been thrown back again and again. The greater daemons in his retinue, loath to be the first forward in case it was a trap, were holding off from the attack. The lesser ones were not powerful eough to clear the walls on their own. It was time for another tactic. He called his army back and ordered them to cease attacking, to give their foes an hour to rest, to snatch sleep, to dream...

He breathed deeply and exhaled, emptying his lungs in a cloud of narcotic perfume that all but stunned Elrion and the other cultists who watched him with bright, mad eyes. He extended one of his claws and inscribed runes in the dirt. He indicated to a cultist that she should bow her head, and took it off with one clean sweep. He breathed in again as the huge jet of blood spouted into the air. All of the crimson fluid was sucked into his chest, bringing with it the faint taste of its supplier's tainted soul.

Swiftly N'Kari worked his spell, changing the blood within him, adding some of his own eternal essence, drawing corrupt phantasms from the Chaotic netherworlds. He added visions of sin from his extensive memories and lustful dreams taken over the centuries from the souls he had devoured.

He breathed in again through his nostrils, drawing on the winds of magic and adding power to the witch's brew he exhaled through his mouth. An army of phantoms emerged in his breath, beautiful elf maidens and boys, translucent, dancing seductively.

His worshippers reached out and tried to embrace them but N'Kari shooed them away. These things were not for them. These wraiths were half-formed, malleable, responsive to dreams and whims. He did not want them shaped by the demented drives of his worshippers. These were meant for other beings. They would offer temptation to the guardians of the wall.

N'Kari aimed a coruscating bolt of energy at the weakest point in the spell walls. Even weakened the defences were still powerful. It took effort to blast even the smallest chink in them, but that small gap was all he needed to create. The wraiths flowed through the gap like water seeping in through a small hole in a ship's hull, carrying within them a freight of dreams, desire and demented horror.

The sky was dark with thunderclouds. Rain poured down. The heavens themselves seemed angry. Lightning split the night.

From the top of the temple, a soaked Tyrion looked down on the onrushing horde illuminated by the sudden stark light of the thunderbolt. This looked bad. The attacking force was far larger than anyone had ever imagined it would be, and it had arrived far sooner than anyone had expected.

Tyrion was not frightened. He was rationally aware that there was a very strong possibility that he was going to be dead before this day ended but that did not scare him. He was fascinated. Below him were creatures out of legend – daemons the likes of which had not been seen since the time of Aenarion.

If the stories were true, the howling horde of attackers throwing themselves at the walls were led by N'Kari, a being who had commanded the attack on Ulthuan in the dawn ages of the world and who had twice faced Aenarion himself. He thought he could make out a monstrous four-armed figure that might be the Keeper of Secrets ordering his troops forward.

He had certainly seen with his own eyes a Lord of Change's fire blasts of multi-hewed Chaotic energy directed at the archers on the walls. Its magic carving through the protective enchantments and then the flesh of the defenders. Its raptor-screams of triumph echoed across the battlefield, their very sound freezing the weaker-willed in fear.

He wished Teclis were here to see this. He felt sure his brother would be at least as fascinated by the sight as he was. Tyrion did not need his brother's gift to see that there was powerful magic at work here on behalf of the elves as well as the daemons. Elven weapons harmed hell-things that ought, according to the legends, to have been invulnerable to them. Something shielded the defenders from many of the daemon's spells. He felt sure that the greater daemons were holding back because of the presence of something they feared although he was not sure for how much longer they would do so.

All night the daemon worshippers had attacked in waves, and then at last, as the defenders had tried to snatch some rest, that horrific cloud of sorcery had come. Tyrion had no idea what had happened within it, but screams of agony and delight had echoed over the battlements and when the cloud had finally dispersed the ground around the exterior walls had been littered with the half-naked bodies of fallen elven troops. The Chaos worshippers had come surging over.

There simply were not enough elves to hold the shrine against the force assaulting it. The speed with which such a huge attack had come had thrown the elves off guard. They had never imagined such a force could set foot on the sacred soil of the holy island so quickly.

What had been intended to be a safe refuge for himself and his brother had turned out to be a death trap. There was no way off the island without passing through that daemonic horde. Perhaps reinforcements would arrive soon but if they did not come in force, they would be destroyed piecemeal as they tried to leave the harbour.

In the distance brazen horns sounded. Winged furies descended from the sky, falling on the defenders with terrible rending claws. Down there people were dying to protect him and the sacred soil of this most holy place. Part of him wanted to leap into the fray and aid them but that would not be wise. Needlessly exposing himself would make the defenders' task harder and perhaps even make a mockery of their efforts if he were to be killed.

The most sensible thing he could do was to retreat into the deepest and best protected parts of the shrine and pray that the battle turned out well. He already knew that it would not. He could see what would happen quite clearly. The daemons would clear the last few defenders from the outer walls, and force them to fall back.

Tyrion heard feet on the stairs behind him. The rain-soaked cowl of a priest of Asuryan rose into view. He was breathing hard, his face was pale and he was obviously frightened.

'There you are, Prince Tyrion,' he said. 'We have been looking all over for you. The abbot has ordered me to take you the inner shrine. You will be safe there along with your brother... if you are safe anywhere. The god will protect you.'

He did not seem at all sure of that.

* * *

Teclis knew the battle was going badly. He did not even have to look at the faces of the messengers bringing reports to the captain of the warriors guarding the innermost shrine to know it. The news had been bad ever since the priest had come to lead him to this sacred sanctum deep within the shrine. There were a few wounded warriors here in the shadows cast by the great fire pit and twenty Phoenix Guards. The warriors looked worried. The Phoenix Guards stood as impassive as the massive statues surrounding them.

Teclis could sense there were many daemons, some of enormous power, outside the shrine and drawing ever closer. He felt their presence like an evil shadow lying on his heart. It made him want to howl with terror. Only by an enormous effort of will could he keep himself from doing so. When mortals faced daemons the evil ones usually had the advantage in power and magic and morale. They need not fear for their infinite lives. Mortals did. The mere presence of daemons was enough to ensure terror.

The daemons were not the only supernatural entities making their presence felt in this hour. He looked up at the great flame burning in the centre of the chamber. It roared like a city on fire. Its heat was enormous. At any other time he would have felt privileged to witness this manifestation in the most sacred heart of elvendom, the chamber of the Flame of Asuryan.

He was more aware of the flows of power around him within the shrine than he ever had been in any other place and at any other time. He sensed the presence of the god as it leaked out of whatever realm Asuryan dwelled in and into this world. It was visible to his magesight all around. The air seemed full of glittering sparks. His skin tingled where they touched and the hairs on the back of his neck rose.

If he reached out with his own senses, somewhere infinitely remote and yet so close he could almost touch it was the presence of Asuryan. Being here and being a mage was like swimming in murky water as a leviathan rose from the depths beneath. He sensed the imminence of the god as a massive displacement of energy from one world to another.

If only there was some way to tap into the power of the Sacred Flames and use it as a weapon, he felt sure that the daemons could be defeated. The mighty mages of old could perhaps have managed such a feat. Others had mastered the art of bending the Flame to their will too. The priests who protected the Phoenix King as he passed through it must know some way. That showed it could be done by mortals in this age of the world.

Of course they were shaping the energy in a completely different way, or perhaps they were merely shielding someone else from it, but the thought gave him hope. There might be a way to use the power of the Flame to save himself and Tyrion and the warriors who were trying so valiantly but fruitlessly to protect them. All he needed to do was work out how that could be done.

He offered up a prayer to Asuryan for guidance. Somewhere far off he thought he felt an answering call. Something out there would aid him, if only he could find a way to contact it and make his prayers clear to it.

Tyrion entered the chamber, his clothing soaking wet. His brother looked torn between wonder and unease, but he did not look afraid. His unbounded bravery astonished Teclis.

'How is it going?' Teclis asked.

'Not well,' said Tyrion. 'The priests don't think they will be able to hold off our attackers much longer. I expect we shall be seeing the famous N'Kari soon.'

His idiot brother did not even sound troubled by the prospect.

Teclis took his brother to one side. None of the soldiers were paying any attention to them. They had their own worries.

'The guards will not be able to stop N'Kari,' he said.

Tyrion nodded. He had already made his own assessment of the situation, and doubtless, as in all matters military, it would be an accurate one.

'There is nothing we can do about it,' Tyrion said. 'The Phoenix King's advisors miscalculated. We are not safe here. The reinforcements will not get here in time. Perhaps we would not have been safe anywhere. Who would have thought our foe could become so strong in so short a time?'

'The soldiers cannot stop the daemon, but perhaps I can.'

Tyrion's eyes widened in surprise at Teclis's words. He tilted his head to one side. At least he was not showing outright disbelief in the fact that one barely trained sixteen-year old was claiming to be able to do what an asur army and its contingent of wizards could not.

'How?'

'I may be able to tap into the power of the shrine here.'

'That sounds sacrilegious. Dangerous too.'

'Believe me, I don't like the idea any more than you do but it may be our only chance. I am of the Blood of Aenarion. I may be able to touch the power of the Flame and live where others could not.'

'You are not planning on walking through it?' Tyrion did show some alarm now. The last person who had tried that unprotected was Malekith and his fate had been awful. He had been a mighty warrior too, not a sickly child.

'No. I am planning on begging for aid. Perhaps the power behind the Flame will respond. Perhaps not. If it does not we have lost nothing but our lives, which are already forfeit.'

'What can I do to help?' This was the part Teclis did not like at all. He was going to have to ask his twin to risk his life, perhaps even sacrifice himself so that his plan might work.

'If I have not completed my spell by the time the daemon gets here, you must distract it for as long as possible. Keep it away from me at all costs.'

'I would do that anyway,' said Tyrion immediately.

Teclis looked at his twin with wonder and admiration. He had always known Tyrion was brave but never realised exactly how brave. He asked no questions, made no excuses, did not prevaricate. He was ready, instantly, to go into battle, to give up his life if necessary. He did not even seem to realise how courageous he really was. Teclis wanted to say something to his twin at that moment, but he knew he was wasting time.

'Just be ready,' he said, knowing that Tyrion would understand how he felt. He always did.

Teclis picked a place behind the altar, by the flame pit, that would hide him from view from the doorway. He took a deep breath and concentrated as hard as he could. He was not simply praying. He was working magic as best he could. He pulled power purified by the sacred flame from the air around him and wove it into a structure that would suit his purpose. He created a thin filament of light that he could extend down the well that connected the Flame in this world with the being known as Asuryan in the other. In some ways it was a spell very similar to the one he had used on the mirror in the Emeraldsea Palace only instead of the mirror, he was using the Flame as a focus.

With invisible fingers of magic, he probed the rent in the fabric of reality until he could find the place where it was holed. Once he had done so, he pushed the line of energy through and extended it as far as he could.

He was like a fisherman dropping a line into deep, still waters. He was not sure what response he would get to his efforts but he knew

Asuryan could not be pleased to have his sacred space invaded by his ancestral enemies. Over all the millennia the elves had known of him, Asuryan had hated Chaos and warred against it. Teclis held this thought firmly in his mind. There was aid to be had here, if only he could reach it.

He kept extending the line of energy and still he did not make contact. The strain mounted. Mortals were not meant to reach too deeply into this place. He could feel that. There was a power here that only the most rugged could wield, and he was very far from that.

His head spun and his stomach heaved. He felt himself getting weaker and weaker as he extended himself more. It was possible that all life would be drained from him by his efforts. Or something else even more terrible might happen – his soul might be drawn from his body and flee into the depths of the well, never to return.

He felt as if he were drowning. He could not breathe. His chest felt as if it was being crushed. He remembered the flying fish on the deck of the *Eagle of Lothern*, drowning in air.

At this moment, he knew that was him.

He was going to die.

Inside the cool depths of the shrine everything seemed calm. No screams had so far penetrated the rock walls. No tainted footsteps were heard echoing within. Tyrion knew it was only a matter of time. His blade felt heavy and useless in his hand. He longed to be outside, in the fighting, doing his part to beat back the attackers. Inaction did not suit him. He was a fighter.

Be calm, he told himself. The time for blades will come soon enough. You will have your chance at combat and you will most likely die of it, in a place where no one will see you fall and no one will remember your fate.

One of the Phoenix Guards came over. His face was as impassive as if it had been hewn from stone. He looked at Tyrion and then at the door and nodded his head. His expression was peculiar, as if he recognised something. He squared his shoulders and let out a long breath. His face was calm, as if reconciled to something.

Teclis suddenly shrieked and spasmed, as if he was having a fit. Over and over again, he repeated the name of Asuryan. It looked as if something had gone terribly wrong. Tyrion rushed over to his brother, feeling helpless, for once not knowing what to do.

* * *

N'Kari strode into the shrine. Behind him the gate was broken and corpses lay strewn everywhere. He was alone. The other daemons would come no further and the mortals were distracted by pillage and rapine. The air crackled with inimical energy. The light of Asuryan was strong here but not strong enough to keep him from his goal, not saturated as he was by power stolen from the Vortex. He was enjoying using the full power of his battle form. It had been a long time since he had given full and free rein to his lust for combat. His only regret was that even with the backing of their god, these elves were barely worthy of death under his claws.

He raised his great sword in one hand and swept it down, cutting two of the Phoenix Guard in two with one blow. He snipped off the head of the first bisected corpse with his claw just to enjoy the expression on its face. The brain still lived and thought for seconds even after it was cut off from the body.

Ahead of him were a set of stairs leading down into the depths of the temple. He sensed the presence of his prey down there where Asuryan's power beat most strongly. The presence of that old god was all around here. The Flame blazed strongly as if trying to hide those N'Kari sought within the shadows its light created.

Given time, Asuryan himself might even manifest himself and deal with the interlopers. That would be a sight worth seeing. Unlikely though. It took long ritual magics to get the god's attention. Beings like Asuryan moved and thought in different timescales from their little elf puppets. An eye-blink to a god could be the lifetime of an elf. N'Kari reckoned that he could easily be finished his work here before Asuryan even realised there was a threat to respond to. Unless very powerful magic was used of a type that was beyond the high elves now.

The elves had thought that placing them here would put his prey beyond his reach. He would enjoy showing how useless all of their efforts were. Once he had done that, he thought he would consider finishing the work he had begun five millennia ago and turn Ulthuan into his personal fiefdom.

Laughing with joy, basking in the adoration of those elves who looked at him longingly, even as he killed them, N'Kari made his way down the stairs towards the innermost Sanctum of the Shrine of Asuryan.

The contact was sudden and shocking. Teclis felt something ancient, ageless and terrifyingly powerful. It inspected Teclis as Teclis might inspect an insect. The mind was not mortal. It bore no resemblance to elven consciousness. It operated on a different level entirely, one that Teclis knew he had no chance whatsoever of comprehending.

He sensed the presence was waiting for something but he had no idea what. He concentrated with all his mind, asking for help, for power, for aid against their mutual enemy. Something vast and slow responded but he was not sure it was responding in the way he wanted it to. It was too alien and immense.

There was something, a sense of recognition that might have been an image, a rune, a name. *Aenarion*. Whatever it was, it knew Teclis was connected with the Phoenix King. It must be his blood. Or perhaps it remembered him from his trial. Now he had to make the being understand that he needed help and the nature of the help he needed.

He pictured the daemons. He pictured the shrine. He pictured what was going on around him. Nothing happened. Perhaps the being the elves knew as Asuryan worked on such a timescale that it would take hours for it to respond. All of the rituals concerned with contacting him had taken time and had been performed by elves who were his priests and presumably thus already had established some link with the entity. Teclis had never done so. Perhaps all of his efforts would be in vain. He felt the contact slipping and tried desperately to re-establish it.

A spark of enormous power passed into him so painfully strong that Teclis almost passed out. He knew that if this kept up the force of the magic would kill him. Asuryan was trying to help but seemed unaware that his colossal strength might be too much for the one he sought to aid. He thought again of himself picking up the flying fish. He had never even thought to wonder what had happened to it. Had he crushed its gills with his fingers, killing it even as he tried to save it?

Would that happen to him now?

The screams of the dying and the dreadful roars of their killer were audible now even through the thick walls of the shrine. They echoed through the corridors like notes within the cone of a trumpet. Tyrion waited, loosening his muscles, breathing deeply and letting the tension seep out of him. He looked over to the shadow of the great altar.

Teclis's face was pale and Tyrion could sense his twin's fear and agony. Its distant echo made his stomach churn and his muscles tense. Teclis's brow was knotted in intense concentration. His eyes stared off into the far distance as if he was looking out on things others could not see. His thrashings had stopped and he seemed to have regained some control over himself.

Images of what might be happening outside intruded themselves into Tyrion's mind. He pictured elves being torn apart by ravening daemons, and the hordes of Chaos rampaging through the most sacred shrine of the elves.

He realised that he was not afraid. He was angry. He was angry about the desecration of this holy place, of the threat to his brother's life, about the strange twists of fate that had brought him to this place to die.

Anger and fear are two sides of the same coin, he told himself. Both can get you killed. He forced himself to breathe deeply, to remain calm. Now was not a time when he could afford any emotion-driven mistakes. He saw one of the wounded soldiers looking over at him with something like admiration.

'I wonder that you can remain so calm, Prince Tyrion,' he said. The effort of keeping his voice steady showed in his speech. His voice seemed about to crack when he mentioned Tyrion's name.

'We are in the keeping of Asuryan,' Tyrion said, gesturing to one of the massive statues. He was remembering the way Lady Malene and Captain Joyelle and the officers of the *Eagle of Lothern* had stood on the deck in the storm and given their confidence to the crew.

'Your faith is inspiring,' said the soldier, with only the faintest hint of irony. What he obviously wanted to say but did not dare do in this holy place and in earshot of his comrades was that he did not share Tyrion's faith.

Tyrion smiled at him and the soldier squared his shoulders and gripped his weapon tighter. As Tyrion had suspected he was not about to show himself less brave than an untried sixteen-year old. Tyrion looked away. He had been glad to deal with the soldier's doubts, they had distracted him from his own dark thoughts. Deep in his breast he felt a titanic rage building once more, an anger that could consume him if he let it, the sort of rage his ancestor Aenarion might have felt when he confronted the hosts of Chaos.

Is this how the Curse manifests itself in me, he thought? Am I a child of rage, like those elves who followed Aenarion in the dark days after he lost his wife and children? Is that why I can kill without conscience? Am I chosen by Khaine in that way?

He knew he might not live to find out. The leader of the remaining

Phoenix Guards gestured to the warriors present. The Guards and the wounded alike moved to place themselves between the twins and anything that sought to get at them. Tyrion knew they had no chance of doing it, but he was touched by their bravery anyway.

Something enormous bellowed outside the door.

'Whatever you're going to do, do it soon,' Tyrion told his twin.

Teclis stared sightlessly at the ceiling.

The great wooden doorway of the sanctum crashed open. A four-armed form stood there, brandishing an enormous greatsword in one oddly delicate arm. A huge claw clicked at the end of another. With its remaining two arms it wove potent spells. The last twenty of the Phoenix Guard faced it.

Tyrion wondered if there would be any of the order left after this battle. It was said that each of the Phoenix Guard was granted knowledge of his own death during the intricate rituals performed when they were raised to the status of member. He wondered if the proud warriors around him had always known that this moment would come.

He studied their faces. All of them were grim. None of them showed fear, even in the face of the horror confronting them. Tyrion looked back at N'Kari. He had always known the daemon was going to be massive, what he had not conceived of was how oddly beautiful it would be. It was not that the creature's form was lovely, rather it was that it moved with the lithe grace of a dancer and the beckoning, seductive movements of a high-class courtesan. It should and did look obscene, but it was also fascinating.

Magic, he told himself. The daemon's aura was working on him. He shook his head and was surprised how easy it was to throw off the spell that had even the steel-willed Phoenix Guard standing quietly before the monster like rabbits before a serpent.

For a moment that seemed as long as eternity, the spell held, and all stood, seemingly frozen. Then the first of the Phoenix Guard sprang forward to strike at the monster. N'Kari parried and cut the elf in two with his return stroke. Silent as stalking cats, the remaining elf warriors threw themselves into the fray.

I am going to die.

The knowledge beat against Tyrion's brain with utter certainty as he watched N'Kari rip one of the Phoenix Guard asunder with his great claw. There was no way he was going to survive this. He simply was not a match for the daemon, even weakened as it was by the magical radiance of Asuryan's flame.

I am going to die.

N'Kari beckoned with his hand and some of the wounded soldiers abased themselves before him. N'Kari sprang forward walking on the backs of his newfound worshippers, the great claws on his feet tearing flesh and shattering bone with every stride.

Tyrion was not afraid. He was not angry. He was simply struck by the futility of any action he might perform. He knew in part this was a reaction to the languid vapours the daemon emitted and in part it was his own mind responding to the hopelessness of the situation.

I am going to die.

The remaining Phoenix Guard threw themselves forward to meet the daemon. Its blade reaped their lives like wheat. It laughed with soul-flaying mockery. Blood and brains splattered everywhere, hitting Tyrion on the face. Calmly he wiped them away to clear his sight.

It was all just information. His death was one of the rules of this game. Accepting the truth of it, he could still win. The goal was to distract the daemon until Teclis cast his spell. It was now simply a problem of tactics.

I am going to die.

The daemon gestured again. Polychromatic lightning surged from its extended claw. It hit one of the defenders and consumed his flesh even as he groaned in what might have been agony or ecstasy. The flare of the bolt cast the huge statues of the old god into stark, blasphemous illumination.

WILLIAM KING

N'Kari was huge and very fast and enormously strong. Its claw was capable of shearing a fully armoured elf warrior in half with as little effort as a seamstress cutting thread. It could fire bolts of magic at its targets. It was all but invulnerable to mortal weapons.

I am going to die.

Blades shattered on N'Kari's flanks or passed through flesh that knitted behind them. Whatever protected the daemon seemed random but it was effective.

The invulnerability did not matter. It was not his goal to kill the daemon. Only to waste its time. To draw its attention. His task was to keep himself alive as long as possible. To hold its attention. To save the life of Teclis until he could cast his spell. If he could cast his spell.

I am going to die.

The pitifully few remaining defenders threw themselves forward. The daemon pounced to meet them and rend them asunder.

Time was passing. Every second he did not do something was a second that brought N'Kari closer to victory and Tyrion closer to defeat. He needed to act soon if he was going to act at all. He raised his sword. His hand was steady. He considered wasting an instant to turn to Teclis and wave goodbye but that would merely draw N'Kari's attention to the one he was trying to keep it from.

I am going to die.

He smiled. He had never expected to live forever. His life was going to prove a lot shorter than he would have wished.

Why was he hesitating?

There were things he still wanted to do and would never get the chance to and once he started he never would. No matter. It was too late for that now anyway.

'Face me, daemon, and meet your master,' Tyrion shouted. His voice was as steady as his hand.

Teclis felt the electric thrill of contact with the presence of the god. Knowledge surged into his mind, showing him where to put his hands, how to move his fingers, which words to say. He did what he was told, binding the power and shaping it into a weapon that he knew would prove inimical to the daemon.

He moved in the patterns shown, spoke the words he was told, adapted his mind to the sorcerous inflections demonstrated. The power flowed into him like wine poured into a cup. It thrilled him and it pained him. His life and soul were in danger, for mortal forms were not intended to act as conduits for god-like power. He was filled with so much magical energy that any elf who was not a sorcerer would already have been fried to a crisp. He wondered at how much he could bear. He knew it was going to have to be a lot more if he was to have any chance of harming the daemon.

The voice was the same, N'Kari thought. He paused for a moment in something that was almost shock. The face was the same. It might have belonged to Aenarion himself although a younger, less stern, less time-ravaged Aenarion. The scent was the same, flesh for flesh. The spirit was almost the same. It did not blaze so bright. It did not burn with the Flame of Asuryan. It was not corrupted by the Sword of Khaine. It was not dimmed by the shadow of that all-devouring blade.

Astonishingly, it was not afraid. It had not yet learned the meaning of fear as Aenarion had, even when he had his fears most under control.

This was indeed a bright tender morsel to offer up to Slaanesh. The spirit burned bright but it was not the only one of the Blood that N'Kari detected. There was another nearby. No matter. This one would do. It would give N'Kari the greatest of pleasure to teach this foolish mortal the meaning of terror before he killed it.

He would torment it as a cat torments a mouse.

He sprang forward, aiming just in front of it. The elf was quick indeed. N'Kari had intended to do no more than scratch it but the elf was already gone. A pinprick in his left side, near where the heart would have been in an elf told him his opponent even had the temerity to strike back.

N'Kari smiled. This might prove even more amusing than he had hoped.

'I will start with your fingers and toes,' he said. 'I will snip them off so delicately you will not even miss them at first.'

The blade flicked at his eye. It stung. It did not really hurt. It merely interfered with vision for a moment until it healed.

N'Kari struck again, faster this time, certain that this time he would connect. The elf was no longer where he had aimed. Once again it eluded with a speed much greater than N'Kari had anticipated.

'I thought daemons were to be feared,' said the elf with the sword. 'You cannot even hit me.'

It was already backing away though, as if it sensed that on the third attempt N'Kari would unleash his full fury. Tempting as it was, N'Kari resisted. He struck again and thought at first he had connected but then realised his claw had only hit the elf's blade. It was not exactly a parry. There was no way the elf had the strength to either hold or deflect N'Kari's blow. He had simply managed to evade.

It was only a matter of time, the daemon thought. Nothing mortal could defeat him.

Tyrion moved away as fast as he could. N'Kari was fast, faster than anything Tyrion had ever faced and he sensed that the daemon was not even exerting itself. It was over-confident. It knew it was going to win and that it had time.

Up close the creature was fearsome. It bulked much larger than him. Its hide was armoured. Its massive claw looked too heavy even for its mightily muscled arm but somehow was not. The scent of the thing was odd, musky and spicy, and oddly disturbing. Aromatic sweat or some other secretion glistened on its armour.

That was wrong. Flesh sweats. Armour does not.

He pushed aside the thought as a distraction and aimed a blow at where the skin and armour joined, at a point which on any living thing would have been vulnerable. He ducked a blindingly fast claw sweep and lashed out with his blade. It pinked the daemon where he had aimed but the flesh knit behind the blade almost as soon as it was pierced.

N'Kari struck again, aiming low, trying to hamstring Tyrion. He leapt forward, feeling the wind of the displaced air below him, careering off the daemon's side. He hit the ground rolling, let his momentum carry him to his feet and turned to face his foe again. N'Kari was already reaching for him.

Tyrion was glad that he had entered this fight with no illusions as to his chance of survival. It would have been very discouraging otherwise to discover just how fast and strong and powerful the daemon really was. He was outclassed completely. He began to have some inkling of just how mighty Aenarion had been. He had triumphed over this creature and others just as powerful.

Discouraging, he thought again. There was an understatement. Somehow the thought made him laugh.

This offended the daemon. It bellowed in incoherent rage then its surprisingly beautiful voice said, 'Chortle all you like Blood of Aenarion. The last laugh will be mine.'

Tyrion did not doubt it. He kept fighting. He might not have any hope of victory but he did have a goal and it appeared he was achieving it.

He aimed a blow at the daemon's eyes once again. It expected it this time and its riposte was so swift it took Tyrion by surprise. He ducked just in time. Its claw snapped shut just where his head had been. At first he thought it was trying to behead him but then he realised it was trying to grab him. If that happened, he knew things would go very badly for him.

Teclis burned. He felt sure his flesh was crisping and turning to ash but when he looked it was still intact. His hand glowed with a strange white light. The aura radiated out from his body. His vision had changed. He saw everything wrapped in shimmering auras.

Tyrion stood out golden and bright as the sun, fearless, unafraid, fighting calmly and methodically against an opponent he could not hope to beat, simply to give Teclis a chance.

N'Kari glowed lascivious purple and sickly green and radiated colours there were no mortal words to describe. There was a strangeness about the daemon's aura. In a way he resembled a mobile version of the great well of power here in the shrine. His form somehow extended out of this world and was yet connected to it. It was as if the thing that was N'Kari was merely a finger-puppet on the end of a claw that had been poked through the walls of reality by some much greater being.

That was what daemons were, he realised. The mighty things we think we see and against which we were vain enough to imagine we fight were not the daemons themselves but the merest fraction of vast cosmic entities, constructs made from a tiny portion of their power and sent into this world to work their will.

He had no idea why it should be so – he was like an insect trying to imagine the motivations of an elf. These things operated on a different order of intelligence in a different scale of reality. It was a humbling thought but not, at that moment, a useful one.

Mighty as the thing was, he needed to sever its contact with this reality, break its link with its extra-dimensional creator. If that could be achieved the mortal shell that remained could be cracked and broken and killed.

He focused the energy that was flooding into every cell of his body, shaping it into a weapon. As he did so, every nerve burned with agony. His weak heart raced. The air filling his lungs burned. He unleashed a bolt of energy at his foe.

* * *

N'Kari decided that this little battle had gone on long enough. He had enjoyed toying with his foe but it was time to get on to the real meat of the experience. He had a mighty soul here to offer up to Slaanesh, one which he would have taken great pleasure corrupting into the ways of pain and pleasure, making it love and adore him before he offered its screaming spirit to his patron daemon god.

It was a pity he simply did not have time for this. The presence of the accursed Asuryan was making it more and more difficult for him to maintain his form here and somehow that presence was increasing.

There was another descendant of Aenarion present here and he was going to have to kill it before the pain became too great for him to endure. Of such little trials is life made up, he thought, and laughed.

He lunged forward with all his strength, catching the elf even as he tried to dance away from the blow. A moment later, N'Kari's claws were on either side of the elf's neck. The warrior looked up at him with a defiance that was amusing, and then spat in N'Kari's eye.

'Great and loving Slaanesh, I offer up this soul to thee,' said N'Kari, twisting the currents of magic around him with his mind. The power thrilled through him. He felt an immense sense of satisfaction. His vengeance was almost complete.

All he had to was close his claw and twist and another descendant of accursed Aenarion would be gone. He paused for a moment to enjoy the sweet sensation of victory. After all there was going to be only one more opportunity to enjoy such a delicious sensation today.

He would make his last offering to his patron special he decided, something so depraved and unspeakable that the elves would remember it for the few paltry centuries their race would continue to exist. Yes, he thought, vengeance would be ecstatic indeed.

A wave of fire crashed into him and he screamed in agony. His claw spasmed open. The elf dropped from his grasp.

The power of Asuryan blazed through Teclis. It crackled like lightning, burned like volcanic flame. It struck N'Kari like a tidal wave. The daemon's anguished howl was deafening. Its carapace blackened and cracked, greenish-purple pus leaked out and was consumed.

N'Kari turned his jewelled gaze on Teclis and beckoned lasciviously, using some sort of spell of compulsion and seduction. Filled as he was with the power of Asuryan it barely touched him.

Twin blazes of power emerged from his hands. The daemon howled and burned but it still lived. It moved towards Teclis, pushing against the blasts like a man pushing upstream against a strong river current. His great claw clicked together menacingly. Clearly, it intended to do with physical force what its magic had been unable to achieve – end Teclis's life and cut off the source of the god-like destructive power aimed against it.

Teclis concentrated as hard as he could on burning it down, but he knew that he was too slow, and that he did not have time to achieve his goal.

Death came closer, step by step.

One moment, Tyrion knew he was doomed. The daemon was through playing cat and mouse with him. It was going to kill him.

The next moment the daemon was surrounded by a blaze of incandescent energy, screaming orgasmically in agony. It turned away from him towards Teclis. Its flesh was crisping, its carapace cracking like that of a crab baked too long in an oven too hot.

Tyrion took a moment to recover himself and assess the situation. Teclis had somehow conjured enough power to harm the daemon, if not to kill it, if such a thing was even possible. But something had not gone quite according to his twin's plan. Perhaps he needed more time, which meant Tyrion was not done trying to get the daemon's attention.

He sprang towards its back, aiming his sword at one of the cracks that had appeared in the carapace. This time the blade plunged home. He felt as if he were carving through flesh. The daemon was vulnerable.

N'Kari felt the sword blade slam into the gap in his armour. It hurt, but not as much as the magical flame did. He concentrated his mighty will on keeping himself moving forwards. The mage was the main threat. He could see that now. He had been duped into thinking only of one of the Blood of Aenarion while the other sought a way to destroy him.

This mage was another of the accursed descendants of the Phoenix King. Only one of them could channel so much of the god's power unscathed. No other mortals could have endured such a divine contact for so long.

Perhaps this one would not survive it either. Mortals were so fragile. N'Kari could not risk the wait.

There would be no time to slay this one elegantly. Asuryan was using the mage as a vessel for his wrath, outraged as he was by N'Kari's desecration of his shrine. The god would not care whether the mortal lived or died, only that his vengeance was fulfilled.

Five more steps, he told himself, and he would destroy the wizard and then take special pleasure in destroying the warrior to make up for the loss.

The daemon loomed over Teclis. Its great claw was wide open. Within moments it would lunge forward and snap him in two.

He would not survive that but it did not matter. He saw a way to save Tyrion. Swiftly he wove a knot of power and sent it arcing over the daemon to wrap itself around Tyrion's blade, turning it temporarily into a new focus for Asuryan's power so that even if he died, the god would be able to use it.

Tyrion's sword glowed as if it had just emerged from the forge. For a moment, Teclis feared the surge of power would prove too much for it, that the metal would melt, that the blade would prove useless, but it was a good blade, of ancient elven make, and it endured.

The thing was done.

Tyrion's sword blazed like a weapon of legend, like Aenarion's Sunfang in the tales. He did not know how it had happened and he did not care.

He drove it down between the daemon's shoulder blades. It burned through N'Kari's flesh, scorching it. A sickly sweet stench of corruption and narcotic incense filled the air. Tyrion drove it home again with all his might, aiming towards where the heart would be in an elf.

He had no idea whether even this blade could kill a daemon, but he was going to find out.

Searing agony burned between N'Kari's shoulder blades. He had thought the pain could not get any worse. He was wrong. The mage had done something new and terrible.

Even as the power of his onslaught decreased, he had transferred some of the god's force to the warrior. N'Kari could kill the mage now but if he did so all the god's power would flow into the sword. It already held more than enough to destroy this physical form. If he turned to defend himself, he might be able to slay the warrior but only at the cost of giving the mage a chance to escape.

It was a hard choice, to forgo part of his vengeance and wait for the time to recreate his form. The one good thing about the situation was that his victims were elves. If one of them survived it would most likely live through the hundred years it would take N'Kari to return to this world. He could take his vengeance then.

N'Kari decided to kill the mage. It was better to be certain under the circumstances.

The daemon did not turn. Tyrion knew why. It was going to slay his brother. It was determined to kill one of the Blood of Aenarion and that was the option most likely to succeed.

He leapt over the daemon, using its shattered shoulder carapace as a springboard, twisting in the air to bring himself down in front of the daemon, between it and Teclis. With his free hand he pushed his brother away even as he turned to strike.

He felt fast, faster than he ever had. The blade seemed to move of its own will in his hand. He drove the blazing sword forward, striking the daemon with the power of a thunderbolt. He struck it again and again. The daemon reeled back, howling and cursing, great chunks torn from its flesh by the power of the blade, wounds cauterised by the cleansing flame.

The twins drove N'Kari from the chamber of the sacred flame, through the long corridors until they emerged on a ledge in the side of the ziggurat, looking down upon the sea. Tyrion recognised it as the place he had come to after passing the test of the priests of Asuryan. It seemed appropriate. He felt as if he had passed another test.

The daemon seemed to be fading in the sunlight, mist emerging from its charred skin. Perhaps it sought to escape.

Tyrion kept pushing forward, smiting as he went. Teclis sent more bolts of magic crashing into the daemon. N'Kari staggered away, making for the great balcony overlooking the sea.

Tyrion struck again and again. N'Kari turned at bay, claw held high, bellowing defiance. He seemed to have given up on thoughts of escape. He was going to make his last stand and now he would be at his most dangerous.

Tyrion brought his blade down in a thunderous arc. The force of the blow, combined with the daemon's enormous weight, drove it through the banister. It tumbled headlong towards the sea below, disintegrating like a meteor hitting air, burning up like a falling star and disappearing even before it had hit the waters far, far below.

Tyrion let out a long sigh of relief. Teclis limped into place beside him. He looked exhausted and his hair and clothing were scorched.

'I think it's over,' said Tyrion.

'It's not over, you know,' said Teclis. The two of them stood at the very top of the temple. The clouds had blown away and the sky was a clear, brilliant blue. Below them, the elves had begun to clear away the debris of the battle. With the demise of N'Kari, the will that had bound the remaining daemons to this world was lost, and they had vanished, unable to bear any longer the holy air of the shrine. Without their daemonic patrons the remaining cultists had proven no match for the elves. The battle was won.

'You think the daemon will return?' Tyrion asked.

'Aenarion himself could not kill it. I don't think we did. It will be summoned into this world again before too many years pass; and gain a new body, and it will return to finish its vengeance on us.'

Tyrion nodded. 'He certainly seemed a very persistent fellow.'

Teclis laughed. 'You are in remarkably good spirits for an elf who has just been told that he will have to spend the rest of his life being the object of a Keeper of Secret's desire for revenge.'

'I am happy enough just to be able to watch this sunset. I did not expect to see it.'

Tyrion laughed with the pure pleasure of being alive. Teclis leaned against the broken banister and wondered how long it would be before N'Kari returned.

SWORD OF
CALEDOR

◄ PROLOGUE ►

Morathi, queen of the elves of Naggaroth, watched the tidal wave of flesh thunder towards her. Hundreds of thousands of feral warriors emerged out of the grim, grey wasteland, mounted on horses, drawn on chariots, carried by monsters, borne by their own booted feet. Enormous plumes of contaminated dust rose in their wake. Savage, sinister chants boomed out, audible even over the thunder of hooves and the turning of iron-bound wheels.

The onrushing horde bore the marks of Chaos on their skin: the stigmata of mutation, the tattooed runes of evil magic. The banners of the Dark Gods fluttered in the chill wind that blew out from the uttermost north.

Morathi moistened her lips with her tongue. Her spell of far-seeing allowed her to make out the smallest details if she focused on them: the rings that pierced warped flesh, the blood that caked the spikes of black armour, the unholy fanaticism that glittered in every eye.

How many times had she seen their like before, she wondered? How often had she encountered the followers of the Dark Gods since that first time more than six thousand years before? Her own legion trembled. They feared for their lives and rightly so. Compared to these deadly newcomers they were a flock of lambs in the path of a pack of wolves.

She strode to the front of her force and stood beneath her unfurled banner. She raised one delicate and lovely fist in the air. Her musicians struck up. Trumpets sounded. Braziers were lit. Narcotic incense drifted on the wind.

Her followers slowly deployed in the cold desert, a carnival procession in the midst of a slag-strewn wasteland. There were thousands of them, selected for their beauty, their erotic skills and their ability to endure the caresses of even the most repellent with a smile. Hers was not an army that could conquer anyone in battle nor was it expected to. Her son had legions of warriors who could kill and slaughter. This army would triumph in another way.

It was just as well she was not expecting these pampered pets to fight, she thought. Most of these beautiful girls and boys could not hold a blade properly. Their talents ran in other directions, just as hers did. The difference between her and them was that she could do battle if she needed to and would if the necessity arose.

She had fought beside Aenarion in the days of her youth, killing daemons, slaughtering the enemies of her people with wild abandon. She had cast spells and brewed poisons and worked out battle strategies for his armies. She had used her gift of visions to grant the elves victories innumerable.

The so-called high elves had forgotten that now, preferring to cast her as the villain in the simple-minded morality plays they so enjoyed since her son had sundered the realm. They had no idea what it had cost to win those battles back when all thought the world was ending, or the price she had paid for victory.

Still, she felt no need to crow about those millennia-gone triumphs. She preferred to live in the moment. All across the world, she was known, feared and desired. Her reach was long, longer even than her son's and quite as strong in its way.

Malekith would learn to appreciate her again. He always did. At the moment, he was going through one of his independent phases, but he would learn soon enough that his followers were unreliable. At the end of the day, they were elven nobles and one of the things that made them so was the secret belief that they owed allegiance to none but themselves, and that no one was better or cleverer or stronger than they.

It was ironic. Out of the whole self-satisfied race, only one really had been so unique, and Aenarion had not needed to prove it or boast about it. He had been respected, loved and feared as their son tried so hard to be and never would.

Poor Aenarion. He would have been more than seven thousand years old today if he had lived, but he had turned down the immortality she had offered him to walk his own fatal path. It was one of those things that had made her hate him as well as love him.

She glanced at the dreary land around her once again and the huge army of deformed barbarians moving towards her. She would need to act soon but she felt a strange lassitude. She let her thoughts drift back to her first husband. She could still picture him all too easily, tall and mighty, with his strange, sad eyes and that terrible blade glowing on his hip.

Better to be ashes than dust he always said, and yet in the end there had been no hero's pyre for him. He had walked into the fire and it had rejected him. Now his bones were dust that mingled with that of the millions his sword had killed. No one even knew where he had fallen in the end. She had looked many times and she had never found him.

They said that Tethlis the Slayer had found his broken armour but there had been nothing in it. She could not believe that he had rotted away. She did not like to think about it either. She preferred to remember him as he had been, brutal and beautiful and burning like the sun. There had never been another elf like him and she did not know whether that made her sad or grateful.

Poor Malekith, she thought. Her son had tried so hard to be like his lost father but he had never managed it. Malekith had his own cold genius, and he could make himself feared but never loved. He was stronger in some ways than Aenarion and certainly cleverer, but he lacked the fire that had made Aenarion what he was. He built empires as monuments to his desire to impress his absent father, a goal that defeated him even when he succeeded.

Aenarion was not there to be impressed and his achievements could not be matched. Malekith did not even understand why. Aenarion was safely dead. The elves could project onto him their own idealised image of themselves and there was no awkward living being to contradict them with his inconvenient goals and desires.

She sometimes wondered whether that was his appeal to her too. Their love, if love it had been, had not had time to grow stale, for her to learn to hate and despise him. She pushed that thought aside, not wanting to consider it.

No, Aenarion was the one the elves would always remember, their first Phoenix King, the warrior demigod who had saved them from certain doom.

Except, of course, that he had not.

He had won every battle and yet he would still have lost that ancient war had it not been for his so-called friend, the Archmage Caledor Dragontamer. Caledor had been the architect of the spell that had finally driven the daemons away and stabilised Ulthuan, keeping its quake-ravaged lands from sinking below the sea.

The elves choose to remember only the great battle and the heroism of Aenarion as he fought to protect you during those final hours, but it was you who saved the world, wasn't it, Caledor? You built the spell that drained magic from the world and sent the daemons back to hell.

The Chaos army had noticed her now, as she had intended that they do. Even at this range, she could hear the bellowed threats and promises. They were so lacking in originality that she could not even muster any contempt. The worshippers of the Dark Gods were ultimately so banal that she struggled to keep her attention focused.

It seemed to be a day to remember ancient times so she gave in to the desire. She thought about Caledor. With his gaunt features, his high balding forehead so unusual in an elf, his eyes cold and blue as a glacier in the Mountains of Frost, the master wizard had been as memorable as Aenarion. Perhaps he would have been a better tool than Aenarion. But no – he was too cold to be manipulated and far too clever, and she could not have loved him as she had loved Aenarion. Caledor was no hero.

And yet in his calm, calculating way he had been as terrifyingly brave as her husband. In the end, he and his fellow archmages had laid down their lives to make their great spell work, knowing that it would bring them only death and worse. Their ghosts were trapped to this day, frozen in the eternal amber of the moment they had died by the power of the spell they had woven.

Are you out there now, old ghost? Can you see me? Do you understand what I do and do you shiver at the thought? For millennia you have woven and re-woven your ancient fraying spell, and for millennia I have tried to unravel it. The day is fast approaching when I will succeed and this world will change forever.

She felt her age sometimes. She had lived long enough to see the shape of continents change, to watch the great rivers of ice advance and retreat, grinding mountains down as they went. She had watched nations rise and fall. There had been times when she had given them a push. It kept her amused.

She was perhaps the oldest living being in the world. Only the gods were older and they did not dwell in this place as she did and were not bound to it as she was.

All of those around her were moving shadows, alive for a few flickering moments and then gone. How many were there now who remembered the days of ancient glory? Herself, her son, a few daemons and the mad ghosts who guarded creation from destruction and rebirth.

It was a shadow-play but it afforded her some entertainment as she waited for the end of the world. She still pursued her pleasures as relentlessly as her son pursued his dreams of empire.

It had all seemed so different when she was young. Then the

world had been bright. The shadow of Chaos had not yet fallen on the land. The elves had been at peace. It had been disgustingly boring but she was too stupid and naive to know it.

Or at least she had been until the visions came.

They had been her gift from her eleventh year, tormenting her with glimpses of the apocalypse to come. She had seen the dark, daemon-haunted future and no one had believed her. She was a prophetess whose gift it was to see and yet not be heard. Or so it had seemed back then.

The elves had not believed her visions of destruction because they could not believe her. Their lives had been so sheltered during the long golden reign of the first Everqueen that they had no idea of just how dreadful the world could be.

She had told them and they had not listened, simply because they were incapable of understanding. They were cattle grazing in summer fields, unwilling to believe in slaughterhouses because they had not yet been inside one. The sun was shining, the grass was tender, and their alien masters looked after them and fed them well.

Long before the other elves had learned what the world was really like, she had known. She had seen the coming bloodbath and she had tried to warn them.

And no one had believed her.

Sometimes that thought could still outrage her. Mostly now it just amused her.

She had tried everything to get their attention. She had prophesied, she had seduced, she had used her great beauty to get the attention of princes, of the Everqueen herself. No one had taken her warnings seriously, because they had not wanted to. Their world was golden and it was ending and they had wilfully blinded themselves to its coming destruction. They had been taken by surprise when the daemons of Chaos came and the Old Ones had fled or been destroyed.

None of the people who had refused to believe her were alive now and she was. She would live forever and she would remake this world in her own image. The day would soon be here when she was a goddess and these barbarians would help her bring that dawn.

The huge metallic arm of a daemon-forged siege engine sent an enormous boulder arcing towards her. The rock hit the ground a hundred strides ahead of where she stood, bounced forward and came to rest not too far from her feet. It was close enough so that she could see the cursed runes scratched on it. Behind her, her legion moaned with anticipatory terror. She knew they only stood their ground because she did.

They were among those who worshipped her and adored her as something divine. But that was not what she wanted. She did not wish merely for the empty gratification of her ego, although she enjoyed it. She desired the real, actual power of a god and she knew how to get it. All she had to do was destroy Caledor's masterwork, the Vortex.

Her visions had shown her that too. In the beginning, the knowledge had horrified her. She had thought that daemons sent them. She thought what she saw was evil beyond imagining, but over the long lonely years she had come to see the power of the daemons as well as their horror. She had realised that they too could be manipulated and used and bound to her will.

Knowing the end was coming, she had prepared for it. She had sought out all manner of forbidden knowledge. She had made pacts with the enemies of her people while the sun still shone and the invasion was merely the tiniest cloud on the horizon. If her folk would not help themselves, the best she could do was ensure her own survival.

It was strange how in all of those tormenting visions she had never seen Aenarion. Perhaps if she had, things might have been different. *She* might have been different. But she had already walked a long way down a dark road when she met him and it was far too late to turn back, even if she had really wanted to.

He was famous then and mighty beyond all others, a grim, mortal god with haunted eyes. He had believed in her visions too. It was easy, for they had all come true. And oddest of all, he had not wanted her. He did not abase himself before her beauty. He looked at her and saw just another elf woman.

His indifference had been a gauntlet thrown in her face, a challenge she could not back away from. She had set herself to win him, to woo him from his grief, to bring him over to her cause. And the oddest alchemy of all had been the trick fate had played on her. In pretending love, she had discovered the real thing. In trying to snare him, she had snared only herself.

She laughed at the irony of it. The sweet malice of her voice attracted the attention of her followers. She smiled at them, enjoying the fact that they did not understand, taking pleasure in their pleasure at the sight of her. They thought she was laughing at the oncoming horde, and it heartened them.

She had won Aenarion over in the end, but he had never loved her as she loved him. He was not capable of it. His dead Everqueen and his lost children filled his heart with gall. He was too lost in his own black grief and his dark desire for revenge. It had consumed him in the end. It had threatened to consume the world.

The barbarians laughed now too at the sight of the force they thought opposed them. Their laughter was bright, mad and cruel and it sounded so like the mirth that echoed through the towers of Naggarond that it was chilling. These humans had much in common with the elves of Naggaroth. Their Dark Gods had taught them well.

Briefly Morathi considered the fact that she might die here, that her visions might be wrong, that the lords of Chaos might for their own reasons have decided to stamp on her face and end her immortal existence.

Part of her would honestly have welcomed it. She was sometimes weary unto death of the ways of this world, and longed to see what might wait on the other side of death's dark doorway. Unfortunately, she had a good idea of what waited for her and those like her. In the endless night of the Realm of Chaos, the daemon lords lusted to devour the souls of her people. She would make a particularly tasty morsel for them, a soul fattened on millennia of sin. No, she was not keen to undergo that ultimate experience just yet.

She called for her mount. It was led to her by nervous grooms, a coal-black, burning-eyed hell-steed with enormous folded wings. Mist emerged from its nostrils, suggestive of the poisonous gas vented by the chasms of this unwelcoming place. It greeted her, eyes blazing with lust and hatred and a curious, twisted love. She stroked its cheek and it whinnied with pleasure from the spells woven into her hands. She vaulted onto its back and rode towards the Chaos horde, her mount becoming airborne after a dozen strides.

She heard her own followers gasp in wonder and fear. Perhaps they thought she was abandoning them to their fate and, for a moment, her malicious elven mind considered it, but she was too wise to do so merely to gratify a whim of the moment. Instead she soared above the oncoming tide of warriors, allowing them to view her half-naked form and luxuriate in the aura of unbridled, wanton lust that she projected. Ancient spells amplified the effects of her matchless beauty. All who looked on her groaned with desire.

She landed her steed defiantly in front of the chieftains of the horde, touching her heels to its flanks so that it reared and whinnied.

A dozen brutal faces inspected her, a dozen muscular, mutated bodies stiffened with lust.

She paused for a moment to let them examine her as she examined them. They were powerful but primitive and they were already responding, although they did not know it, to the ancient sorceries surrounding her. She smiled at them and they smiled back and licked their lips. She knew that in that moment she had them in the palm of her hand.

She dismounted, showing no fear, and strode towards them, and they waited expectantly to hear what she had to say, as they would have if a messenger from their own Dark Gods had descended in their midst. It was a role she was perfectly suited to play. She carried herself with the imperiousness of one who had ruled for nearly seven millennia and who expected homage as her right.

She had much to offer them, and they to offer her, and she was sure that a pact could be made with them. She would divert them from their drift southward into the lands of men and offer them a much more tempting prize, the island-continent of Ulthuan. Her son saw it as part of a plan to put him back on his rightful throne, which it was, but she had reasons of her own as well.

The end of time was coming. She would begin the unmaking of the world soon, as a necessary prelude to its reshaping. The time of her ascension was close. Soon the daemons would return and the time of mortals would be at an end. New gods would be born. She intended to make sure that she was one of them.

In a cold cavern chamber beneath his freezing winter citadel, hidden even from the eyes of his mother's sorcerous spies, Malekith the Great, Witch King of Naggaroth, prepared to perform the ritual that would make him master of first a continent and then the world. Frozen spikes of ice sheathed the stalactites surrounding him. Their cold gave him some relief from the divine fires that burned eternally and agonisingly within his flesh.

The whimpering of terrified virgin slaves did not disturb him any more than the icy chill. He had long ago ceased to let trivial things interfere with his concentration. He was about to seize control of the destiny of millions and he would not allow himself to be distracted by the mewling of the worthless. By casting one monstrous spell and binding one dreadful being to his will, he would alter the fate of kingdoms.

A girl looked at him. Tears ran down her face. She was frightened and alone. Malekith knew that the appearance of his gigantic metal-sheathed figure terrified her. He spoke a spell of calming and the fear disappeared to be replaced by a numb smile.

Malekith felt no sympathy but he had no desire to be needlessly cruel either. He was not like his mother or those of his drugged, deranged, self-indulgent subjects who feasted on the pain of others. He was merely doing what was needed to ensure that right prevailed. He would take the throne of Ulthuan in accordance with his father's command and his own desires.

He raised one huge armoured hand before his face and studied it through the visor of his helmet. Hotek, that renegade priest of Vaul, had done his blasphemous work well. The ancient runes inscribed millennia ago in the aftermath of his greatest failure glowed with power. Caledor Dragontamer's jealous disciple had forged this armour in the wake of Malekith's attempt to pass through the Flame of Asuryan. Malekith had ordered him to wield the hammer despite the agony that had almost crippled him with every blow. It had kept him alive ever since.

He told himself he barely felt the pain any more. It was merely the reality in which he lived, as water was to a shark. There had been a time when his scorched flesh had both pained and humiliated him, a badge of the rejection of the gods who had refused to acknowledge him as great as his father, a symbol of his failure and weakness. Over the centuries the fire in his flesh had burned down and his own control had grown greater.

Even during the worst of times he had not let it stop him. He had learned from his mistakes. He had emerged from the period of agony and despair stronger than ever. The armour had hidden his scorched flesh from the view of his enemies and made him more potent than any living being before or since.

Before you can rule others, you must first rule yourself. That was the maxim he lived by.

He had lived for millennia and every passing year had added to his power and to his knowledge. He had studied his mother's secret grimoires until he was more proficient in sorcery than she. He had outlived the generals who had defeated him in the long gone ages of the world.

As ruthless with himself as with his subjects, he had learned from his errors and drawn strength from his mistakes. No one would ever or had ever beaten him the same way twice. He was still here when his ancient opponents were in their graves. Despite the pain, despite the losses, despite a black despair that would have driven lesser beings to seek eternal oblivion, he endured.

He had toppled kingdoms and reshaped the world. He had lived longer and done more than his father, Aenarion, ever had. He would yet re-unify the kingdom that the treachery of his enemies had denied him. One day soon, all elves would bend the knee before him and acknowledge the righteousness of his rule. Then he would lead them into a new age of glory. They would subjugate the kingdoms of men and throw back the powers of Chaos and a new golden age would begin. All of them would see that they had been wrong.

And it started now.

Glory would be purchased by the suffering of these few slaves. They ought to be grateful to him. Without him they would have lived out their meaningless, insect lives. At the cost of a few of the years that would have swiftly passed anyway, they were being allowed to participate in the creation of a new world order. He pushed the thoughts away. They smacked of needless self-justification, of moral weakness. He was who he was. What he did was right. He need justify himself to no one.

He studied his handiwork with some satisfaction. He had carved the altar to the ritual specifications with his own hands. For six years he had sanctified it with blood and souls. He had forged the black iron sacrificial knife, tempering the blade by passing it through the body of a still living hero six times. He had inscribed the symbols of Slaanesh and his six favoured princes over the period of six moons.

He had prepared the chains from an alloy of truesilver and black iron and inscribed them with runes older than the world. At their centre was a gem so potently ensorcelled that it could entrap the soul of a daemon prince. The finding of that gem and the binding spells it contained was an epic in itself which would one day be recounted across his empire.

Everything was ready. It was time to begin.

He spoke the words he had memorised from the great grimoire and gestured for the first of the slaves to advance to the altar. She tried to refuse but his will bound her to obey. Slowly, one step at a time, as if pulled by overwhelming magnetic force, she advanced up the basalt steps and bowed her head before the altar.

A slash of the knife opened her jugular. Blood spurted into the font. He threw the flopping carcass to one side and summoned the next with a gesture of his armoured hands. The whimpering went on but his will was strong. He would allow himself no weakness.

One by one he sent their souls out into the void through the gap in reality his spell had created. They were his messengers to the dreadful being he intended to summon. Their very presence was part of the message.

As the ritual built to its climax, his words took on a strange sibilant resonance, as if they echoed through unseen chasms in the unhallowed places beyond. Somewhere far off, in a darkness so deep it could swallow worlds, something responded.

In a place that was not a place, in a time that lay outside time, N'Kari, Keeper of Secrets, great among daemons, felt the faint irritating tug of a summoning spell.

At first he ignored it. That a being should be foolish enough to draw his attention piqued his curiosity, but not very much. The realms of mortals were full of those who sought to barter their puny souls for the benefits they thought daemons could provide. Sometimes, when he was bored, N'Kari allowed himself to be called and then destroyed those who sought to bend him to their will. Sometimes he granted their wishes and allowed them to destroy themselves, just so he could have the amusement of watching.

There was something about the being making this summons though – something that nagged at N'Kari's vast store of memories and set them swirling, the way a scent of some half-remembered perfume makes an old rake remember the fleshpots of his youth.

Yes, something familiar indeed.

In this place that was not a place, in this time that was not a time, N'Kari's mind worked in a different way than it would have had he been bound to the chronal flow of mortal reality. He remembered many things simultaneously, sometimes as vividly as if he were actually experiencing them, sometimes as if they were as remote as the birth of the universe. This summons triggered a fugue of memories and images.

It reminded him of the mortal god Aenarion, and his descendants whom N'Kari had once tried so hard to kill. And there was about it a faint, frightening taint of the Flame of Asuryan, the god-thing that was numbered among N'Kari's greatest enemies.

N'Kari was curious now as he suspected he was intended to be.

More virgin souls were offered up to him, slain in exactly the correct ritual manner to please him. It was nice that the proprieties were being observed. Languidly, he extended a tentacle of thought towards the gap in reality from which the summons had come. He forced a small portion of his mighty essence through the portal, and allowed it to take shape according to the whims and expectations of the summoner.

In that moment, mortal reality crashed in on him. He found himself trapped within a sorcerer's circle in the dank underground depths beneath some cold northern castle. An armoured figure as monstrous as any daemon loomed before him.

He was pleased. This was going to prove more interesting than he had anticipated.

Slowly a shape arose out of the pool of blood in the font of the altar. It was a beautiful woman made of congealed red plasma, snakes of hair swirling from her impossibly lovely head. She beckoned at Malekith in a lascivious, enticing fashion. Her hips swayed sinuously in a way that promised great pleasure.

The Witch King was not even tempted. The wards on his armour neutralised the potent spells of intoxication. His destroyed olfactory nerves were insensitive to the narcotic musk. Seeing that this strategy was not working, the daemon changed tactics and shape, becoming something monstrous and four-armed and clawed. The blood congealed and hardened into a glistening carapace. The hands extended into talons and claws. The skull became horse-like, the teeth great tusks and fangs.

This was more like its true shape, Malekith thought, if a greater daemon could be said to have any such thing.

'N'Kari, I name you and bind you,' Malekith said. He spoke the ancient words of the ritual. The daemon resisted them. It was enormously strong, far more powerful than anything he had ever bound before. For a moment, and a moment only, the possibility that he might have encountered something too powerful for even his mighty will to dominate entered Malekith's mind.

'It is not so simple, little mortal,' said the daemon in a voice at once beautiful and terrifying. 'I am no mere daemonling to be bound by a passing sorcerer.'

'And I am no mere mage, hell-spawn. I am Aenarion's heir and Witch King. And you will do my bidding.' The air between them crackled with the force of their conflict.

'Aenarion. That is a name you should not have mentioned,' N'Kari said. 'You shall pay for your presumption.'

'I know you hate him and all his descendants, but I have summoned you to offer you a chance of vengeance.'

The daemon paused for a moment. 'Revenge I shall have. Starting with you.'

'That is not possible,' said Malekith, not letting any of the strain that he felt show in his voice. 'But I will let you drink the blood of those who humiliated you a century ago. I will let you have all of the others who claim descent from Aenarion.'

'I can take my own vengeance,' said N'Kari.

'No, you cannot,' said Malekith. 'I have wound you round with spells that prevent you from returning whence you came. And while this avatar is trapped here, you cannot bring another into this world. I can keep you here until the end of time if I so desire and vengeance will never be yours.'

The daemon raged against the ever-tightening web of spells constraining it but they held. N'Kari was trapped. His appearance changed again, becoming that of a seductive female elf. Its voice was the very essence of reason.

'State your terms,' it said.

N'Kari considered the Witch King. As mortals went, he was impressive. His massive armoured figure radiated power and not unjustified confidence. The spells he had woven were well-constructed, a trap that it might take N'Kari millennia to escape from.

He had already spent too much time in this pathetic place bound into the Vortex. In mortal form, ennui would press as heavily on him as any other resident of this time and space. He felt sure that he could free himself eventually, but it might be easier to appear to give the mortal what he wanted. He was also sure that, in the long run, he would find a way to turn the tables on the arrogant fool. He always did.

'State your terms,' N'Kari said.

The Witch King laughed triumphantly.

Laugh away little mortal, N'Kari thought. *I will have the last laugh.*

'Extend your arm,' said the Witch King.

N'Kari complied. Perhaps his foe would be foolish enough to break the magic circle binding him... Bracelets and chains snapped into place. The most powerful binding spell N'Kari had ever experienced snapped into place with them.

'Now you truly are my servant,' said Malekith, unable to keep the satisfaction from his voice.

N'Kari wanted to howl with rage, but the spells binding him would not even allow him that.

* * *

The dark elf assassin known as Urian Poisonblade and Prince Iltharis and dozens of other names looked across the carved table at the beautiful woman he was going to kill and smiled. She smiled back. Her glance moved from the table to the sleeping silks that filled the remainder of this small intimate tent. Outside throngs moved through the tent city that was the capital of the Everqueen. Inside spells kept all noise at bay. They could have been alone in the wild woods of Avelorn and not surrounded by her subjects.

It was a pity, he thought. She really was lovely and he liked her, and none of that emotion was caused by the aura of compulsive magic that surrounded her. It could not be. Centuries ago the Witch King of Naggaroth had wound him round with spells that made him immune to such sorceries.

Like Morathi, the Everqueen had great natural beauty and great natural charm and these were only amplified and enhanced by her magic, not a product of them. She was every bit as good-natured as she seemed and she looked genuinely interested in him as a person. Unlike some mighty personages he had encountered, she was not just acting the part.

If it had been up to him she could have lived out her natural span of days in peace. But, as always, it was not his decision, it was the Witch King's. He felt sure that he was only one small link in a very long chain of plans and conspiracies his master had woven.

Urian was only Malekith's tool in this matter as he was in so many others. Malekith had made him, had raised him up and could knock him down again. And if the woman sitting opposite him had been aware of his true history she would be calling for her guards right now.

Briefly he wondered why the Witch King was having the Everqueen killed now. She would simply be replaced by her daughter who was kept in a secure place far distant from the court, like all of an Everqueen's daughters. The elves had learned long ago from the loss of Aenarion's children by the first Everqueen. Never again would their royal family be assembled all in one place, able to be killed in one fell swoop, or saved only by an accident so unlikely it smacked of divine intervention.

Doubtless timing had something to do with it. Or perhaps Malekith had found the Everqueen's daughter and other assassins were even now at work...

'You look very thoughtful, Prince Iltharis,' the Everqueen said, reaching out to touch his hand in a most intimate manner. 'Are you contemplating some deep matter of ancient history once again?'

Urian smiled. She thought of him only as a scholar and a formidable duellist, one of the many glittering talents who visited her court. He had made his reputation as a student of the history of the line of Aenarion, to which she was not the least ornament. It was a cover story that he had actually enjoyed living and which he was going to miss once he had shucked it off. That was assuming he was still alive after this evening, which was not exactly a certainty.

'As a matter of fact, I was, your serenity,' he said. It was true in a way too. The grudge Malekith bore against the Everqueen was a very ancient one. They were of the same family, and she had what Malekith had always desired, the love and respect of the elves of Ulthuan. It was as much for this as for political and strategic reasons she had to die. The envy and malice of his master were boundless when aroused, as Urian had more cause than almost anyone to understand.

'It is ever the problem with true scholars that they are so easily distracted. You were telling me of the time when you worked out the plans of the daemon N'Kari, who planned to exterminate all the line of Aenarion, including myself, a century ago.'

'Mine was only a minor contribution. I saw the pattern in the apparently random destruction it had wrought, but it was mostly luck. I had talked with many of those who it killed, as part of my researches.'

'You are too modest, Prince Iltharis.'

'Alas, that is not something I have ever been much accused of, your serenity. I doubt even my worst enemy would say that of me.'

She laughed, a silvery sound. He enjoyed it, as he always had. His pleasure was given a certain piquancy by the fact that he knew he would never hear the sound again after this evening.

'And how is your new work coming?' she asked.

'Slowly, as these things always do. I have a great deal of research to go through before I even commit pen to vellum. That is why I am here. To consult the scholars of your court.' He stroked her hand in return. 'As well as to enjoy the boon of your company, of course.'

Urian lived his cover to the fullest, even though he knew he would not have any use for it much longer. Several centuries of deception were coming to an end. He was almost sorry. Soon he would be leaving Ulthuan forever and returning in secret triumph to Naggaroth to claim the rewards of his long covert service to Male-kith's interests.

It was strange – he was more at home now in the land of his ene-mies than he was in his ancestral home. He wondered what it would be like to go back to his estates finally and forever, never to have to look upon this place again.

He knew he should be filled with nothing but contempt for the high elves, but he was not. He had found a great deal to respect in Ulthuan and, over the long years, a great deal he would miss. Still his life was not his own. It never really had been since he had entered Malekith's service. The Witch King had taken a pit fighter from an impoverished ancient line and made him into the dead-liest assassin in the world. He really ought to be grateful for that, but he wasn't any more.

He leaned forward to pour more wine. As he did so, he allowed the powder he had palmed to drop from his hand. It was dragon-spike, a poison inevitably fatal to mages, its effects stronger the more magical power they possessed, and the Everqueen had a very great deal indeed. He would soon find out if the poison were potent enough to kill an avatar of godhead. According to legend it was, but legends were notoriously unreliable.

It would slow her breathing and destroy her nerves and stop her heart. It could be found only in the forbidden jungles of the lost continent of Lustria, and it had no effect whatsoever on those not possessed of magical power. Urian sipped his own wine. The taste was not in the slightest impaired.

The Everqueen's hand hovered over her own goblet. He wondered for a moment whether she had seen him, whether she suspected what was happening. Part of him rather hoped that she did. He was surprised by that. He was not usually sympathetic to his vic-tims. He kept the smile pinned to his face and waited to see what she would do.

She raised her glass to him, and then put it to her lips. 'Your health, Prince Iltharis. May you live a thousand years.'

'And you, your serenity.'

The queen drank. Her eyes widened. The glass dropped from her hands.

Urian rose from the cushions on which he rested and shouted out with genuine concern. 'Come quickly. Her serenity has been taken ill!'

Urian was possessed by a sudden sense that a war that would

shatter the world had just begun and that he had played a vital part in starting it.

CHAPTER ONE

Tyrion sprang to one side as the stegadon erupted from the undergrowth. It was reptilian, far bigger than an elephant, with a parrot-like beak large enough to snap an elf in two. Horns long as lances protruded from the huge shield-like crest protecting its head. The thing was massive, even by the overgrown standards of wildlife in the sweltering Lustrian jungles.

It felt like facing an angry dragon. He heard bones snap and flesh pulp as one of the human porters was crushed under the stegadon's foreleg. The rest of the expedition scattered in panic, hoping to find safety in flight.

Tyrion knew he was very close to death. The hot, humid air carried the acrid, lizard stench of the beast. The ground vibrated beneath its monstrous tread. It bellowed deafeningly and it felt as if the wave of sound alone might knock him off his feet.

He drew his sword, feeling faintly ridiculous. Trying to tackle this huge creature with such a weapon was like trying to fight a bull with a pin. He could not win this battle on his own. He needed help.

'Hold your ground, men!' Tyrion shouted to the humans. 'Stand steady! Don't flee! If you get lost in the jungle, you will die!'

There was something about his voice that commanded obedience even in the most fearful. There always had been. Over the past century he had bestrode hundreds of battlefields and always inspired courage and respect in those around him. It was no different now.

Most of the warriors, the majority of them Norsemen from Skeggi, paused in their flight and drew their weapons. They considered cowardice a great shame. All it had taken was Tyrion standing his ground to remind them of their own honour. The huge blond warriors would not flee when a lone elf refused to.

The porters were less brave, being only thralls to the Norse. They were not looking for a heroic death. Even they wavered though.

Only Leiber, their guide, a shipwrecked sailor from the Old World, looked calm, and he was seeking cover in the trees above. Sensible man, Tyrion thought.

Tyrion's shout drew the attention of the beast. Its head swivelled to inspect the small creature that had the temerity to defy it. Its beady eyes glared at him with ferocious hatred. Its huge razor-edged beak snapped open and it lunged towards him with a speed that was utterly unexpected in a creature so huge.

Tyrion threw himself forward, rolling under the creature's front legs, passing through their mighty arch and coming out on the creature's side.

As soon as he did it he knew that he had made a mistake. His twin brother Teclis had been standing behind him. He now became the focus of the creature's attention, the target of its attack.

Although he was no longer a sickly cripple, Teclis did not share Tyrion's speed and strength. He could not get himself out of the way of the charging beast before it closed the distance between them. Instead he spread his arms wide, chanting ancient words and making mystical gestures. He was trying to cast a spell, but there would not be enough time for him to work his magic before the creature was upon him. Tyrion needed to get the stegadon's attention now if his brother was going to live.

He lashed out with his sword, aiming for the weak point where the leg joined the torso. The skin there was soft, not covered in armoured scales like the rest of the beast's body. Flesh parted and muscle gave way slightly. The beast let out a deafening pain-filled roar. Tyrion barely managed to get himself out of the way as the columnar leg swung his way.

The Norsemen had taken up their spears and axes and joined the fray. Hagar, a large maniac with a bristling red beard, threw himself at the monster, chanting the names of the old gods of the Norse. His axe smashed into the creature's beak, chipping part of it and drawing blood.

The stegadon turned on Hagar, jaws snapping shut around his torso, beak cleaving through his flesh. His shield buckled under the pressure. Bones cracked as Hagar's ribcage gave way. The man gave a final defiant roar that was transformed into an agonised death scream as his body was snapped in two.

Watching their friend die gave the rest of the Norsemen pause. The beast raced towards them, a loud hiss escaping from its nostrils. Its beak was painted red with Hagar's blood but its lust for death was not slaked. In an instant, many more of the Norsemen died beneath its clawed feet. Tyrion winced. They had lost more men and they were no closer to their goal. It seemed like this expedition was doomed.

A sweep of the stegadon's gigantic head tossed another Norseman high into the air. He crashed through the branches above him and returned to earth, falling face-down in the mulch of the jungle floor. His body writhed for a few seconds, his bones broken by the impact, and then turned to jelly as the beast trampled him.

It was too much for the thralls. They raced off into the surrounding forest. At least one of them encountered some other terror, for an agonised scream rang out. Tyrion had no idea what might have killed him – the jungle was so full of perils that it could have been almost anything: some giant man-eating plant, a huge vampire bat, a sabretooth jaguar as large as a horse. He had seen all of these things on his recent travels.

One or two of the humans had taken refuge in the branches of the trees. This gave Tyrion an idea. He clambered into the bole of one monstrous plant, reached up and grabbed a vine, then swung himself out over the monster, dropping onto its back. So enraged was the giant brute that it barely noticed this presence. He ran along its spine, thinking that he would cut the vertebrae in the neck.

As he reached the bone shield, he caught sight of Teclis out of the corner of his eye. An aura of flame surrounded his brother. He made a gesture and a jet of fire blasted towards the creature. The pyrotechnic wave expanded to fill Tyrion's field of vision.

The stegadon let out a screech of fear and pain. Tyrion ducked down behind the bone shield to get out of the way of the fiery blast. Even so he felt its scorching heat. The vines dangling from the trees above withered and died. The monstrous brute reared on its hind legs. The bone shield swung backwards and it seemed like it might come down and crush him against the flesh of the monster's back.

Tyrion let go, dropping to the ground. He tried to scramble clear but his booted foot slipped in the bloody mess of one of the human corpses. He fell sprawling as the maddened dinosaur reared and roared and whirled around, threatening to trample him underfoot.

Tyrion half-crawled, half-sprang out of harm's way. The beast crashed into a nearby tree, sending some of the hiding humans tumbling to the ground and to death beneath its paws. The tree broke in the middle and fell into the inferno that Teclis had conjured. Sap bubbled and burst into flames as its moist interior was exposed to the fire. The explosive firecracker sounds panicked the giant reptile even more.

The monster turned and glared at Tyrion. He was directly in the path of the creature's escape. For a moment he met its gaze and he saw the fury there. The creature pawed the ground like an angry bull preparing to charge. There was no way he could get out of its path in time. He had seen how fast the creature moved. The stegadon lowered its head and raced straight at him, an enormous engine of living death.

Tyrion smiled and stood unmoving, making himself the easiest target possible. The creature came straight at him, covering the ground with appalling speed. At the last possible moment Tyrion sprang, vaulting onto its long snout, stabbing it in the left eye with his sword, before leaping over the great bone shield that protected its neck, landing on its back, slashing the vertebrae and then rolling clear.

It did not fall to the ground as he had expected. It kept moving as if unaware that the connection between its brain and its body had been severed. He recalled something that Teclis had once told him – that according to natural philosophers these monstrous creatures had several brains, and they did not die easily.

This creature certainly seemed to be living proof of that. It kept moving, and he thought that for one horrible moment all he had succeeded in doing was attracting its attention and providing a focus for its anger. But this was not the case. Bleeding heavily from its wounds, its flesh scorched by Teclis's magic, the great beast blundered off into the woods, trying to escape the flames and the source of its agony, bellowing its rage and pain to the heavens.

Tyrion stood up, half expecting the creature to return. Teclis moved over to where he stood. 'Are you all right?' his brother asked.

'Never better,' Tyrion responded. 'But I don't think some of the people with us feel quite so good.'

Tyrion looked around: a score of the humans lay dead on the ground, some of them reduced to a bloody pulp, many of them whimpering in agony as they died. He was not sure it was a good idea to shout out to draw the attention of any of the survivors because it might also draw the attention of the great beast back to them.

On the other hand, he could not see what else to do; if he waited too long then all of the people with them would get lost in the woods and separated forever. They still had need of their porters and guides if they were to achieve the goal they had set out with when they started this expedition into the green hell of the Lustrian jungle.

In the end they only managed to find a few humans alive and capable of following them. Fortunately one of those was their guide, Leiber, the one man who claimed to know where the lost city of Zultec lay. They divided the remains of their supplies between them and then wearily trudged on, deeper into the deadly jungle.

Giant plants blocked out the light. The air stank of perfume and rot. Brightly coloured birds shrieked amid the boles of the huge trees. Small scuttling things moved through the carpet of mulched plant life on the forest floor. The heat was sweltering. In the distance something huge and reptilian crashed through the undergrowth. Tyrion thought of the stegadon and slowed his pace accordingly. Reduced in numbers as their party was, it would be better to go around than encounter another of those great bad-tempered beasts.

He pushed an enormous cloying leaf to one side. It stuck to his skin. When he pulled his hand away from its sticky surface faint drops of red clung to his fingers. They were already disappearing from the surface of the leaf. He knew then that if he took his blade to the plant, blood would mingle with the gushing sap. Even the plants here were vampiric. Everything seemed to live to eat anything else that came within its grasp.

He glanced enviously at his twin. A faint aura of silvery light surrounded Teclis. He looked as cool as if he were out for a stroll along a windswept beach in Cothique during a day in early spring. His spells protected him from the heat and the jungle's claws.

Despite all the hardships they had encountered, Teclis looked confident and at ease. Over the past century, magic had filled out his scrawny form and removed the worst effects of the wasting ailments that had crippled him in childhood. The potions he mixed for himself kept him healthy and active. He would never be as tall or as muscular as Tyrion, but now he could go for leagues through the tropical heat and endure hardships that would have killed him only a century ago. The only sign of his many debilitating childhood illnesses was the faint limp with which he now walked and which no amount of alchemy seemed able to get rid of.

At this moment Tyrion very much envied his brother's mage-craft. He was sweating heavily even though he had stripped off everything except the undergarments he needed to keep his light mail armour from chafing. His face and clothes were dirty and torn although not as much so as their human guide's.

Leiber looked like a lunatic: tall, emaciated, with madness glittering in his bright blue eyes. His long hair was thinning on top and drawn back in a dirty blond ponytail at the back. A moustache that reminded Tyrion of a rat's whiskers drooped down past his chin and gave his whole face a mournful air of defeat.

Leiber was originally from the Old World, a shipwrecked sailor from the human city of Marienburg, but he had spent much of his life looking for gold and treasure amid the ruins of the slann cities of the Lustrian continent. He claimed to know these jungles better than any man alive, although Tyrion was starting to think that perhaps this was not so great a feat as Leiber made out.

Very few humans lived long in Lustrian jungles. They came here seeking fortunes but what they mostly found was death. Already most of the company of men the twins had hired as porters or guards had died or vanished, some from mysterious fevers that not even Teclis's medicines could cure, some from the attacks of the giant jaguars common in this part of the jungle. This had only been the latest of the misfortunes to bedevil their expedition.

One man had died screaming when the larvae of a bloodwasp emerged from where he had been stung a few days before. The foul little maggots had eaten their way out through his entrails. Two thralls had been devoured when a skittering cloud of piranha lizards dropped from the branches above them. The flesh had been stripped from their bones in the seconds it had taken Teclis to cast the fiery spell that had turned their killers into shrivelled exploding corpses.

Others had simply deserted, vanishing in the night, never to return. Tyrion did not blame them under the circumstances.

Leiber had not vanished. He was just as obsessed with finding the city of Zultec as the twins were. Of course, he had his own reasons. For Tyrion and his brother, Zultec was the last known possible resting place of Sunfang, the mystical blade forged for their ancestor Aenarion by the archmage Caledor Dragontamer during the wars at the dawn ages of the world.

For Leiber, it represented a trove of gold and mystical secrets that he hoped would let him reclaim the ancestral lands he had lost back across the wide ocean. He claimed to have penetrated to the very heart of the city once and to have spent the past few years trying to find a way back.

Tyrion was not sure how much he trusted the man or the remainder of his companions. They were desperate rogues even by the standards of the rough crew you met in the makeshift human camps of the Lustrian coast. They had the look of casual killers. Most of them were descended from the same Norse folk that had raided the coasts of Ulthuan for centuries: big, wild-looking, blond men with braided hair and beards. Their eyes were the blue of painted Cathayan ceramics. Their manner was bluff and fierce. They swore by the names of strange Kurgan and Hung gods. These ominous deities reminded Tyrion of the Ruinous Powers of Chaos, and he would not have been surprised to find out that they were related.

All of the humans except Leiber glanced at the two elves as if considering murdering them for their gold and scampering back to the old, decaying port of Skeggi, the only real permanent settlement along the whole coast. No one there would ask them how they came by the money, or what had happened to those who had gone off into the jungle with them. Skeggi was a city of pirates and robbers and mad dreamers.

Tyrion was not troubled. There were only five of the humans now and he could handle them himself even without the aid of Teclis's magic. Providing, of course, they did not cut his throat while he was sleeping. He smiled nonchalantly.

'You find something funny, sir elf?' said Leiber. His voice was a harsh croak well suited to his guttural native speech, so unlike the liquid tongue of the elves.

'No, Leiber, I am merely happy,' said Tyrion in Reikspiel, the common language the humans used. It was true too. There was something about this desperate venture that gladdened his heart. He was rarely happier than when off on some quest in the company of his wizard twin.

'You find all of these deaths cause for happiness? I had heard elves were cruel, my friend, but I had not thought to find you to be an example of that.'

'You are confusing us with our kinfolk, the druchii, whom you call dark elves. The deaths give me no happiness. It is the adventure I enjoy.'

He did not know if he could explain himself to Leiber or whether he should. At times like these, he felt as if he was living out one of the hero tales he and Teclis had loved when they were boys.

It seemed to him that their lives had turned out exactly the way they would have wished them too. He was a warrior who had fought in the service of the Phoenix King and made himself wealthy trading and raiding the coasts of Naggaroth. Teclis had served his apprenticeship in magic under Lady Malene in Lothern and was now a student at the White Tower of Hoeth in Saphery. He was the youngest Loremaster in generations. His twin was widely acknowledged as possibly the most brilliant wizard Ulthuan had produced since the time of Bel Hathor.

He was going to need to be. Both of them knew it was only a matter of time before the daemon N'Kari, the most ancient enemy of their family, returned and attempted to claim their souls. The Keeper of Secrets had very nearly succeeded in wiping out the entire blood line of Aenarion during his attack on Ulthuan a century ago. Only Teclis's invocation of the power of the Phoenix God Asuryan had defeated him and saved the twins' lives.

According to Teclis, at least a century would need to have passed before N'Kari could be summoned again, or could reform a body of his own will and emerge from the Chaos Wastes. That time had come and gone. If he wanted to, the Keeper of Secrets could return to this world.

Tyrion felt sure the daemon would not make the mistakes he had made during his last incursion either. Even for an entity as powerful as N'Kari, a direct attack on the shrine of Asuryan, mightiest of the elven gods, had been an act of self-destructive hubris.

The certainty of the daemon's return was one reason they were seeking Sunfang. A mighty weapon borne by the first Phoenix King, it should be capable of harming even a greater daemon and it would give Tyrion some chance of surviving an attack.

He smiled again somewhat ruefully. By some chance, he meant an infinitesimal chance. He had fought the daemon once and was a good enough warrior to know exactly how little hope he had of beating something like N'Kari, even with a magical weapon. Still, it was better than no chance at all.

'I wish he would stop smiling like that,' one of the humans muttered. 'It makes me nervous.'

Tyrion felt certain that most of the humans had no idea how well he understood their tongue, having learned it in the rougher quarters of Lothern during his long residence in the city. It was a small advantage but any advantage was to be cherished here.

'How much further?' he asked Leiber.

Leiber scratched his chin to make himself look more thoughtful. 'A few more leagues at most.'

'You've been saying that for some time now,' said Teclis. His ironic tone was understandable even to Leiber.

'Finding your way through this cursed jungle is not like sailing a ship, your honour,' said Leiber. 'I can't simply navigate by the stars. Things grow here. Landmarks get hidden. Rain washes away trails. It's guesswork at best.'

To be fair to Leiber, he had never lied about any of this, or made any bones about the difficulty of finding Zultec. He had been perfectly open about how hard it would be. He had merely claimed that given time they would find it, and he still seemed perfectly confident that it would prove to be the case.

'So your plan involves wandering randomly through the jungle until we stumble upon Zultec,' said Teclis. Tyrion gestured for him to stop provoking the human, but self-restraint did not suit his twin's temperament.

'No, your highness. We will continue to march westwards until we hit this stream here.' Leiber produced his grubby tattered map from within his shirt and stabbed his finger at the blue line that marked the position of the watercourse. 'Then we will turn north until we stumble on the outskirts of the city.'

'Your confidence is awe-inspiring,' said Teclis.

'Look, your honour, you hired me because I had been to the city and could find my way back. You paid for the gear and the guards and the porters and I am grateful. If you want to turn back, I can't say as I would blame you. It's been a hard road and no mistake. But we are so close now I can smell it. And I would advise you to stick with me for just a bit longer and we will reach our goal.'

It was an impressive speech, made more impressive by its delivery. There was a mad conviction in Leiber's eyes and his voice compelled belief. Tyrion believed him, as he had all along. He was sure his twin did too, but Teclis simply could not resist provoking the man.

'I am not sure I believe you have ever seen the city,' he said.

'I've seen it, your honour, and I almost died there when those scaly-skinned lizardmen attacked with their poison darts and their stone axes. I saw Argentes go into the central pyramid and never come out too. I was the only one of our party as did, and I only managed it by fleeing into the jungle and throwing away all my gear. It took me months to find my way back to Skeggi.'

'I am surprised your map is so accurate then,' said Teclis.

Leiber spat on the ground but he spoke with the air of a man who did not wish to provoke an argument. 'I am too, your honour. I did my best to remember landmarks and that stream stayed in my mind. I followed it all the way to the coast from that fork, and we can follow it back if you will stick with me.'

'We've stuck with you through the swamps and the pygmy attacks and the giant bats and the fevers. I see no reason to stop doing so now, when you say success is so near,' said Teclis.

'I am very grateful for that, your highness. Now, perhaps we can stop yakking and start walking. We need to get moving if we are ever going to find that treasure and Herr Argentes's sword that you have spent so long looking for.'

Somewhere far off, something roared. Tyrion wondered if it was coming their way. This did not sound as large as the stegadon, but there was something about the sound that suggested words or at least some form of communication. The roar was answered from across the jungle. He wondered if it had anything to do with their presence. He supposed he would find out soon enough.

—◀ CHAPTER TWO ▶—

The rain pattered down lightly on the canopy of leaves, dripping down to turn the track to mud. The birds were subdued and the light was dim. In some ways it felt like they were walking under the greenish surface of the sea. Tyrion's legs were spattered with runny earth and it was work just to lift them from the sucking, squelching path.

Teclis pushed on through the jungle following Leiber. He had no trouble with the path. His feet seemed to float above it and he left only the faintest imprint in its surface. Such were the benefits of magic, Tyrion thought sourly. He walked beside his brother, ready to intervene if there was an attack. Teclis might be a powerful magician but his reflexes were nowhere near as quick as his own. *A dagger in the back kills the mightiest mage* was a proverb in which Tyrion had implicit faith.

He fought to contain his own excitement. After decades of searching it seemed like the end of their quest was in sight. They had finally tracked down Sunfang. Or rather his brother had.

Teclis had spent years in the library at Hoeth searching through collections of obscure manuscripts for some clues as to the whereabouts of Aenarion's lost blade, the legendary weapon forged for him by the Archmage Caledor amid the volcanic fires of Vaul's Anvil, a companion piece to the armour the mage had made for the first Phoenix King.

Aenarion had put the blade aside once he had taken up the Sword of Khaine and its burden of damnation and ultimate power. He had given it to Furion, one of his most trusted lieutenants who had in turn passed it on to his descendants.

The Witch King of Naggaroth, with his customary hunger for all the possessions of his father, had coveted the weapon. Furion's family had refused him it. Over the course of time, agents of the

Witch King had made many attempts to acquire the blade, and always failed.

In the end, Nathanis, the last descendant of Furion, had sailed for the Old World on a trading trip. He had arrived there but never returned with his ship. There were tales of an elven adventurer fighting in the lands of the Empire armed with a magical sword that shot bolts of flame. He had visited the fabled forest of the wood elves and fought alongside wardancers and backwoods archers, eventually making his way down to Tilea and the Border Princes and on to Estonia. The elf had died there but his sword had been taken up by a human, or so the tales told. It had passed from father to son down the fast, fleeting generations that humans experienced.

The power of the blade had made its possessors heroes and mighty champions among humans. It had not brought them luck though. Johan Argentes, the last bearer, had become a landless wandering mercenary.

Tyrion and his brother had spent years following this long trail across the Old World, retracing Argentes's steps, following up all rumours of his whereabouts. The trail had been lost when Argentes had set sail from Estalia aboard an explorer's ship bound for the uttermost west. Leiber had been the ship's captain. It had never returned to its home port and it seemed the trail was lost.

Pure chance had brought word of a shipwrecked captain called Leiber washed up in Skeggi. He had been spotted by a trading captain from House Emeraldsea who knew something of the twins' quest and remembered the name of the lost ship's master. It was a very long shot, but the twins had followed it up, taking passage on a trading clipper to the coast of Lustria. They had heard another rumour about a human with a fiery sword who had vanished into the interior, searching for the gold of the lost slann cities.

Eventually they had found Leiber who had witnessed Argentes's disappearance and been the only survivor, and who brought word of Argentes's loss, staggering out of the jungle half-mad with hunger, thirst and fever.

He had spent months making a map to Zultec and seeking to tempt accomplices with tales of a hoard of treasure big enough to fire the imagination of a hundred pirate kings.

Leiber had agreed to guide the two elves to Zultec in return for gold and their protection. The three of them had organised this expedition and followed the long trail that had led them to this accursed place.

So far, Leiber had proved to be a bold and reliable companion, but Tyrion was not sure of his friends.

Not that it mattered much at the moment; they were all in the same boat, outnumbered and far from home, seeking a ruined metropolis haunted by the last degenerate remains of the once mighty race of lizardmen who had built the place when the world was young.

Tyrion could not keep from grinning. He was hacking his way through the overgrown jungle in search of a lost alien city, where he hoped to find a legendary artefact from the dawn ages of his people.

'Why do you have that inane smirk on your face?' his twin asked.

'I was just thinking that this was exactly the sort of thing we used to talk about doing back in father's villa when we were boys.'

Teclis smiled back. It was a slow secret smile, a mere sliver like a quarter moon seen through cloud, but coming from him it was like a belly laugh from any other elf. 'We've come a long way from the mountains of Cothique, brother.'

'That is something of an understatement.'

'I like to keep in practice at that. A talent unused rusts.'

'Of course, I did not imagine the mosquitoes. I thought it would be vampires that tried to drink my blood and dragons that tried to bite me to death.'

'An old swamp witch back in Skeggi told me that the mosquitoes there once drained a baby of blood while it slept. She swore to me it was true. She had seen it with her own eyes. Of course, she also swore to me that the charms she was selling would make me irresistible to women and a mighty warrior.'

'Stranger things have happened.'

Teclis shrugged. 'There was no magic in them, brother. Even you could have seen that with your vision.'

'I have heard it said humans practise a different type of magic.'

'There is only one type of magic. There are different ways of using it, true enough, but all magic draws its power from the same place and all magical objects radiate a similar aura.'

'I'll take your word for it.'

'That would be an excellent idea. If you keep giving me advice about magic, I will have to start giving you my views on warfare and blade work.'

'Let's not stoop to absurdities,' said Tyrion.

Leiber gave the sign that it was time to halt for food.

* * *

Tyrion slapped the mosquito that had landed on the back of his hand. It exploded in a small burst of blood and flesh, leaving a faint blotch on his tanned skin.

'How do you do that?' Leiber asked. It continued to rain, not quite the usual monsoonal downpour that could turn tracks into streams, but a light drizzle that collected on the leaves and overflowed in a million tiny random waterfalls.

They had paused to eat and their lack of motion seemed to be drawing the insects to them. The few remaining humans lay sprawled against the trunk of a huge tree chewing on strips of dried beef. Teclis prepared his drugs, mingling the contents of two silver flasks in an alembic he had produced from inside his pack.

'Do what?' Tyrion replied. He looked beyond Leiber into the shadow avenues made by the great trees. He was becoming uneasy and he was not sure why, although he knew enough to trust his instincts in this matter. They had kept him alive in many places where other elves had died.

'You always hit the buzzing little bastards. It does not matter how bad the light is, whenever one of them bites you, you kill it.'

'So?'

'You *always* kill them. Always. I have never seen you miss. I have never seen you even come close to missing or look like you are making any effort. Sometimes I never even notice the bloodsuckers until the bites swell and when I do try and hit them, the little swine are too fast for me. But they are never too fast for you.'

'That is because I am an elf and you are a human.' Even as he said it, Tyrion realised he was making a mistake. It was the sort of failure of diplomacy he would not normally have let happen. His only excuse was that he was tired and his mind had been on other things.

'And you think elves are better than humans?' There was an edge to Leiber's words that Tyrion could not miss. There had been a lot of deaths and a lot of fear lately and they still had not found what they were looking for. Such situations had a way of becoming slowly explosive. He knew this from bitter experience with his own kind. It seemed things were no different with humans. He tried to defuse the situation with a joke.

'Apparently we are when it comes to swatting mosquitoes.'

Leiber made a rueful grimace and took a pipe from out of the pouch on his waistband and then a flint. He walked over to Teclis's magically created fire and lit the tobacco that he had stuffed into the bowl of the pipe with a wooden spill. He continued to look into the distance for a long moment, puffing away and then letting the smoke billow out in two streams from his nostrils. Once he had done that he turned to look Tyrion in the eye and said, 'That is not what I meant and you know it.'

Tyrion felt his own temper rise in a way it would not normally have done. It was the heat and the humidity, he told himself, but there were other things involved as well. He was not used to being talked to this way by humans.

Did this man seriously think that there was any comparison between an elf and a human? Both races had a head and two arms and two legs. In some ways they looked quite similar. But elves lived longer, knew more, did not fall sick, and were not prey to the numerous superstitions that humans held. They were faster, more agile, more intelligent, more beautiful; superior in every possible way.

Leiber was less than a third of Tyrion's age but already he was starting to look decrepit. His skin was lined. Some of his teeth were missing. The way he squinted told Tyrion that his eyesight was not what it had once been. He looked like an elf might look after half a millennium had passed, and only if the elf were very unlucky.

Of course Tyrion thought he was better – he was just too polite to rub it in. Leiber seemed to be questioning his right to think that way, which was, to say the least, impertinent of him.

For a moment Tyrion saw the relationship between all of his people and all of the humans reflected in the way that he thought about Leiber and Leiber thought about him. He wondered if it was worthwhile trying to put his own thoughts into words and explain them to the man, but he realised that it could do no good, could cause only friction. Leiber would simply take it as an insult. Perhaps he would be right to.

After all, the elves were a dying race and it looked like humans would inherit the world. Their civilisation was becoming more powerful by the year, spreading across the globe in an irresistible wave. Already there were probably more humans in the city of Lothern than there were elves, and Lothern was by far the most populous city in elvendom.

He told himself that the ability to breed quickly and irresponsibly was not exactly a sign that humans were the equals of the elves. They could not create art the way the elves could. They did not know magic the way the elves did. They were not the intellectual equals of the people of Ulthuan.

But did that really matter in the eyes of the gods?

The elves were becoming extinct. The humans were not. Did that mean they were simply better adapted to living in this new and dreadful world? Did it mean that their gods were more powerful than the elven gods? Did it mean anything at all or was he simply speculating uselessly?

This was not really any of his business. He was a warrior not a philosopher. It was his duty to guard his people and he would do that to the best of his ability until the day that he died. He did not have any answers. He would need to leave that to people like his brother. And he was not sure that Teclis could get any better answers than he could himself.

'Do you think that we are better than you?' Tyrion asked, because he could not think of anything else to say.

'You are certainly better than we are at killing mosquitoes, your honour, that's for sure and I suspect that *you* are much better at killing almost anything. You have that look about you. And you're a damn sight prettier than I am, that's for sure. But I am not sure that you're a better man than me.'

'I am not a man at all,' said Tyrion.

'That's not what I meant. Are you braver than me? Are you morally superior? Or were you just born luckier? I sometimes think that the noble in the big castle on the hill is not a better man than the peasant he looks down on. He was just born into better circumstances – ones that ensured that he got better food, a better education and better training with weapons, as well as the weapons themselves.'

Tyrion could see that Leiber was talking about something he had given a lot of thought to. This was a matter that had deeply troubled the human for a long time. He was not really talking about the relationship between men and elves any more – he was talking about the way humans lived, the way he himself had lived.

'Why do you ask me this?' Tyrion asked.

'Can you see what I'm saying, Prince Tyrion? Can you see what I'm getting at? In my life I have met a lot of noblemen and a lot of them have looked down on me. Argentes for one. And the truth of the matter is that he was not any cleverer than I was, nor any braver nor any better. In the end, he is dead and I am still here. Who is to say who the better man is now?'

Tyrion understood the point being made only too well. And perhaps Leiber was right to make it. Perhaps it was simply the fact that Tyrion had been born in a different place to a different people that made him feel superior.

'I am still an elf, and you're still human. It does not matter what either of us think about that, the world remains the same.'

'Does it though, Prince Tyrion? The world is changing. Who knows what the coming centuries will bring?'

'Most likely I will still be here to see. Will you?'

Leiber did not have an answer for that. Tyrion had not expected him to. The human took another puff on his pipe and regarded Tyrion balefully for a moment, then he smiled and laughed out loud.

'I should have known I could not get the better of an elf in an argument.'

Teclis took a moment away from concentrating on mixing his potions to listen to what his brother was talking about with Leiber. He needed to concentrate. Like his sight, his hearing was not good at the best of times, and the spell he used to keep the insects and the jungle heat and humidity at bay made it even worse. It flattened out all sound as if he had placed a layer of beeswax in his ears.

He could see that Tyrion was troubled by the human's words and was giving serious thought to the matter, but his brother was not capable of looking beyond the common prejudice against humans.

Tyrion really did believe himself to be superior to the human and had ample empirical evidence to back this up. By almost any measure, he could prove himself to be better than the man. He was even prepared to admit it to the human when pushed. What he did not see was the simple fact that he was judging the matter by standards set by himself and other elves.

Teclis added a pinch of saltpetre and powdered gryphon bone to the mix and smiled sourly. The potion smelled infernal but it was necessary for keeping his strength up and not just his strength. Without these medicines his sight and hearing would be even worse than they were now. He would be more or less blind and deaf as well as decrepit.

Of course, elves were better looking than humans by any standards. Of course, they were more knowledgeable about lore. Of course, elves were better at all the things that elves were good at than humans were. It was a competition in which all of the rules were made by the elves and all of them reflected to their own advantage.

No elf bothered to think that there might be things that humans knew that elves did not. No elf ever was prepared to admit that humans already occupied and controlled a greater portion of the globe than the elves ever had and that this process was only likely to continue.

All of the elves imagined that just because they lived longer they enjoyed more favour in the eyes of the gods. Teclis felt sure that humans could judge this contest by their own standards and feel superior to elves if they really wanted to; it was just that so far they had not done so. They were still used to thinking of elves as the Elder Race. They were still dazzled by beauty and culture and magic. But that would not last.

One day, and that day could not be far off, the humans would see beyond the glamour and begin to judge the elves as they deserved to be judged. They would see that the elves were not really so much better than they were, after all.

They would see that the elves were split into two warring factions. They were, in their own way, just as divided as the human realms – perhaps more so. He could not think of any human kingdoms that were involved in so bitter a fratricidal struggle as Ulthuan and Naggaroth. Or which had been fought for so long.

And the humans did not seem to suffer from the madness that plagued the elves: the strange obsessions, the lust for power, the furious desire to acquire knowledge and magical lore that the elves suffered from.

Of course, these things did affect humans, but not with the same intensity as they affected elves. Some of his own kindred would see that as proof of superiority. The elves felt things more keenly, appreciated things more and moved through the world with much more intensity than humans could.

Teclis was not at all sure that this did make them superior. It merely made them different. In fact, there were times when he believed that the excessive nature of their temperament was a definite disadvantage. They were capable of focusing on one thing exclusively to the point where they would miss other more important things.

He finished swirling his medicine and drank it down. It was bitter and the aftertaste tingled on his tongue. He braced himself for the dizziness he was going to feel as it first took effect.

He thought with some bitterness about his own father, lost in his obsessive pursuit of the secrets of the dragon armour of Aenarion. Prince Arathion had neglected his own children and his estates and allowed the fortunes of his ancient family to fall into decline as he worked on his own personal obsessions. If Tyrion had not rescued the family finances with his ventures into piracy and trading, they would most likely be living in the gutter now or on the charity of their wealthy Emeraldsea relatives.

There had been times in his childhood when Teclis suspected he had almost died because his father was more interested in the secrets of ancient sorcery than he was in the well-being of his children. And yet, Teclis could not find it in himself to blame his father. He understood only too well the burning hunger that consumed him. He felt the same way about his own pursuit of magical knowledge.

Look at him now – he had followed the trail of an ancient artefact halfway round the world simply because it promised to reveal to him some secrets of how it had been created. He'd undergone a great deal of personal discomfort and boredom, and not a little danger, in pursuit of that knowledge and he'd done it without a second thought.

Of course, he had other reasons. He wanted to help his brother find a weapon that might help him survive when the daemon that pursued them caught up with them, as Teclis feared it inevitably would.

And he also thought that if he could locate the blade and penetrate its mysteries he might find something that would help his father with his magical research. He should be the last one to blame elves for their obsession; he knew that only too well. But he could not help but feel that elves judged themselves too favourably and humans not favourably enough.

And even knowing this he could not help but look at Leiber and his brother and judge his own kin as the better of the two. He was not immune to the normal prejudices but, at least, he was aware of the fact that he suffered from them.

And he knew the dangers of concentrating too much on one thing, while ignoring his surroundings. Out there innumerable dangers lurked. They might not be as lucky as they had been this time when the next attack came.

Was it the effects of the medicine or was something disturbing those nearby bushes? Even as the thought occurred to him, a long-snouted, tooth-filled monstrous head emerged from the undergrowth.

'Watch out!' Leiber shouted. 'We've got company.'

They were under attack.

◄ CHAPTER THREE ►

Wet leaves slapped Tyrion in the face, obscuring his vision. Something heavy and scaly and rain-slick crashed into him. Its momentum bowled him over.

Instinctively, he let himself go with the flow of the motion. Landing on his back in the soggy mulch, he kept rolling and kicked out with his feet, pushing the thing off.

Fang-filled jaws snapped shut in front of his face. Something slammed into his leg with bruising force. He caught sight of something green and vaguely humanoid. He continued his roll and somersaulted upright.

On his feet now, blade in hand, Tyrion sought enemies.

His attacker disappeared into the undergrowth. It looked like a big humanoid lizard, running upright, balancing itself with its long tail. The head was something like that of a dragon, with enormous powerful jaws and massive teeth that looked easily capable of tearing flesh right to the bone.

It was one of the legendary servants of the slann. A warrior of some sort, although very primitively armed. In one scaly hand it clutched a stone axe tipped with coloured feathers. Only luck had stopped the thing from braining him. As he watched, the thing's skin changed colour, scaly patterns altering so that it blended in with its surroundings. That chameleon-like camouflage was what had allowed it to get so close.

Tyrion's heart beat faster. His breathing deepened. He had a sense that he was lucky to be alive. Judging from the crunching noises nearby some of his own people had not been so lucky.

He looked around to see how Teclis was doing.

The glow of a protective spell surrounded his brother. A group of the lizardmen circled him, snapping at him with their massive jaws and striking at him with their axes. His alchemical gear lay discarded at his feet. His fire was scattered. So far, Teclis's spells had warded off their blows but it was only a matter of time before they managed to do him some harm.

Tyrion sprang forward, lashing out with his sword. His first blow separated the head from one lizardman's body. His blade caught another in the chest. Greenish blood flowed and the air took on an odd coppery tang.

The lizardman shrieked, the sound of its voice like the hissing of a boiling kettle until the note went too high to be audible. Tyrion twisted his blade, turning it until it grated against a rib. He leaned forward, hoping to hit the heart but not sure of the layout of the internal organs that a lizardman might possess.

Of one thing he was certain – he was causing his victim a great deal of pain, judging by the way it screeched. Its tail curled around, threatening to hit him with the force of a bludgeon. He leapt over the blow, even as two of the lizardman's companions closed in from either side.

Tyrion caught one in the throat with his sword, where the windpipe ought to be. Something crunched under the blow and the lizardman fell backwards, mouth open in a silent scream, no sound being emitted from its broken voice box, then the pommel of his blade connected with the snout of the other lizardman with sickening force. It too halted momentarily, stunned.

Tyrion split its skull with his sword and then wheeled to stab the other as it clutched at its slashed throat.

With the force of a striking thunderbolt he smashed into the melee, dancing through the swirl of combat with impossible grace. Every time he struck, a lizardman fell. Within heartbeats he had turned the course of the battle and slaughtered half a dozen more of the cold-blooded ones. The rest of them fled off into the undergrowth, shrieking and bellowing like beasts.

Something flickered in the corner of his vision. A dart erupted from the bushes heading straight at him with eye-blurring velocity. He plucked it from the air, careful to avoid its sharpened obsidian point. He had no doubt that the black goo smeared on the blade was a deadly poison. He hurled the thing point first into the bushes from which it had come, but whatever had fired it was gone. The dart stuck quivering in the bole of a great tree.

Around him, the humans went around finishing off the wounded lizardmen, smashing their skulls or stabbing them through the eye or heart. They were brutal, driven by fear.

A lot of their cruelty came from that fear. Tyrion disliked this. He enjoyed violence but he had never understood this need to abuse defeated foes that many people had. He supposed one thing bred the other. Fear was parent to cruelty.

He looked over to make sure that Teclis was unharmed. The wizard stood there, glaring around him, looking for a target for his spells. The battle had been fought so quickly that he had had no chance to unleash his power.

Tyrion could tell he was frustrated by that and he could understand why. His brother did not like to feel powerless in any situation – he had experienced too much of that in their youths.

'They are gone,' Tyrion said. 'For the moment.'

'How can you be certain?' Teclis asked.

'I can't,' said Tyrion. 'But normally when you kill things to the point where they run away, they don't come back quickly. Of course, with these slann creatures you can never be sure. They are too alien.'

'Those were skinks,' said Teclis. 'That's what they were called. According to the *Chronicles of Beltharius*, they are servants of the slann, not the slann themselves.'

'I'll take your word for that,' said Tyrion.

'You would do well to do so,' said Teclis. His brother sounded keen to assert himself, even if only by displaying superior knowledge. 'Beltharius is the only elf to have left any records of visiting an actual lizardman city, and he barely survived that.'

Beltharius was the captain of the explorers who had visited the Golden Pyramid of Pahuax back in the reign of Bel Shanaar. He had been one of the few to fight his way out of the city when the great toad-god that ruled it had turned nasty.

The tale was well known, but his brother had spent a great deal of time in the library at Hoeth, studying the actual journals Beltharius had kept. Before they had made this trip he had studied every scrap of information the elves had ever compiled about the jungles of Lustria and its inhabitants. With his usual thoroughness he had turned himself into an expert on the matter.

Tyrion glanced around to see how the humans were doing. One of them was on the ground, dead, his skull crushed by one of those stone axes. It had been left buried in his forehead.

'Bastards!' Leiber said. 'Those scaly bastards killed him. They killed Fritz.'

'These lands are sacred to them,' said Teclis.

Tyrion shook his head. This was not the sort of thing that Teclis

ought to be saying to the humans right now. They were upset by
the loss of their comrade and they were on edge, ready for violence.
It would not take much to turn them against the elves, or cause a
violent argument and Tyrion had no great wish to kill the humans
and still less of a desire to be killed by them.

'We need to move on,' said Tyrion.

'We need to bury Fritz,' said Leiber.

'We could all die if we don't get out of this place,' said Tyrion.
'Those skinks will be back with friends soon, and there will be a
lot more of them than us.'

Leiber looked as if he wanted to argue but he could see the sense
of Tyrion's words. His companions looked torn between their anger
and their fear. The way Fritz's dead eyes stared at the sky was a compelling argument for Tyrion's case. None of them wanted to end up
that way. Heads nodded.

'Dead men spend no gold,' said Teclis sardonically. Tyrion could
have cursed him. Now was not the time for his gallows humour, but
that argument too held considerable force.

'All right, let's go get us some treasure,' said Leiber. There was a
note of aggression in his voice that Tyrion did not like at all. It was
possible that before too long it would not just be the skinks that
would be numbered among their enemies.

The rain poured down, turning the track to flowing mud. It splattered off the leaves and splashed down from the giant trees in little
waterfalls and the noise of it covered the normal small sounds of
the surrounding woods.

Tyrion envied his brother's magic even more. His tunic was
soaked. His hair was plastered against his skull. The insides of his
boots squelched. The rain did not touch Teclis. It stopped a finger's
breadth from his form, leaving him looking dry and calm.

Leiber spluttered and coughed as he led them along the track.
Red mud stuck to his bare feet and made it look as if he was wearing a glistening set of magical stockings. The other humans tramped
along with slumped shoulders and miserable expressions in their
eyes. They looked as if they wanted to be anywhere but here.

The ruins emerged slowly from the jungle. At first Tyrion was
not sure that they were not simply large outcroppings or hills. It
took some effort to discern the shapes of the tumbled down buildings in the undergrowth, but if he looked closely, he could see
lichen-blotched, time-eroded statues and the chipped remains of

monstrous stone blocks partially buried in moss and peaty earth. Great trees had grown around them and sometimes through them, the power of their long slow growth tumbling even the heavy stonework.

'There must have been an earthquake here,' Tyrion said in elvish to Teclis. His twin looked thoughtful.

'Or monstrously powerful sorcery. They say the forces of Chaos struck these cities with mighty magics during the first incursion. For a long time, the slann and their lizardmen slaves bore the brunt of the Dark Gods' attacks.'

The ground squelched underfoot. It was as if they were moving through the limits of a great swamp.

'Flooded?' Tyrion asked.

Teclis nodded. 'Seems most likely.'

'Let's hope the whole city is not under water then.'

'It would not be the first slann city to be so.'

'You do not reassure me, brother.'

'We still have to find what we came here for,' said Teclis. 'We need to find the sword.'

Tyrion sprang upwards and grabbed a vine. It was wet and slippery, but he was agile even by the standards of elves and he had soon pulled himself up into the lower branches of the trees. From there he used his dagger as a piton and climbed as high as he could go.

He was hoping for a good view of his surroundings, and even through the downpour he managed one. Although these trees were not as tall as some of the millennia old giants of the deep forest, they were still far taller than the mast of an ocean-going ship. What he saw was as awesome as it was disheartening.

They had found Zultec.

The old slann city stretched to the horizon. Less than a league away were a number of ziggurats, partially overgrown but the size of small hills. They had been hidden by the jungle until he climbed above it. He counted at least a score and gave up. He knew that there would most likely be smaller ruins hidden among the wreckage. They had found the city but it might take years to search it for what they sought, assuming it was even there. He scrambled back down the tree and told Teclis what he had seen. His brother smiled. He did not look at all put out by Tyrion's discovery.

'Zultec is not all that huge by the standards of slann temple cities,' he said. 'This was a mere satellite town of Pahuax according to Beltharius.'

'If this was a small town, their cities must be gigantic indeed,' said Tyrion.

'They are.'

'What now, brother?'

'You have shown what brawn and eyes can do here. I will show you the uses magic can be put to.'

'I would be grateful if you could,' Tyrion said. 'I do not fancy spending the rest of my life searching this place for Sunfang. There is a woman in Lothern I am anxious to get back to.'

'I am not so sure her husband will be that keen,' said Teclis.

Tyrion shrugged. One of the reasons they had set out on this quest was to let that particular scandal die down. Lady Valeria's husband was a powerful ally of House Emeraldsea and he doted on her the way she doted on Tyrion. A duel would not have done anyone any good. It would have damaged a powerful faction in politics.

The humans were looking at them again, wondering what they were saying. Tyrion turned to them and said, 'It is Zultec, no doubt about it. Unless there is another huge slann city we have not heard of hereabouts.'

He turned to Teclis and said in elvish, 'Sorry, I meant to say small slann village.'

'I told you we would find it, didn't I?' Despite the wet misery of the rain, and the sunken look of their surroundings, Leiber could not keep the triumph from his voice. He sounded like a man who had come close to realising a lifelong dream. Tyrion could not deny the human his moment of triumph.

'You were right, Leiber,' he said.

Leiber smiled again, showing his missing teeth and blackened stumps. 'We are all rich, lads,' he said. 'The slann gold is almost ours.'

There was nothing like the prospect of wealth for cheering humans up, Tyrion thought. Even soaked to the skin and swatting at mosquitoes, they looked happy at Leiber's announcement and ready to run off into the nearest ruins to seek for treasure. Tyrion could not really blame them. For the most part their lives were short and miserable and gold helped humans find comfort in their hovels.

'The really big pyramids start about half a league away,' Tyrion told them, to add to the good cheer.

'What about the monsters that attacked you the last time you were here?' Teclis asked, always ready to spread a little gloom when things started to get too light-hearted.

Leiber nodded. 'We should move slowly and cautiously and try not to raise any ruckus. Once we find the gold we'll make a grab for it and do a runner.'

'You are supposed to help us find what we are looking for. That's what you are getting paid for,' said Teclis.

'That's what I meant,' said Leiber. 'We're all looking for treasure.'

'We're looking for a very specific treasure,' said Tyrion. 'And we won't be leaving until we find it.'

'Argentes died here. His burning sword will be here still. You'll find it.'

'Let us hope so,' said Tyrion. 'And let us hope no lizardman has made off with it. That will make finding it a lot harder.'

That did not lighten the mood any either, Tyrion thought. Maybe he was acquiring some of Teclis's talent for depressing people. The humans looked at him as if he had just announced a plan to start cutting off their noses one at a time.

'You might never leave if the lizards find you,' said Leiber. It was a good point.

'We'll all do better if we stick together,' Teclis said.

'No lie there,' said Leiber. 'We could all leave our bones bleaching in this jungle if we are not careful.'

'Can you remember where Argentes fell?' Teclis asked. There was an urgency in his voice too now. He was excited by the fact they were close to their goal.

'It was a lot closer to the centre, I think, in a pyramid much bigger than these ones,' Leiber said.

'Then we'd better get moving.'

They made their way through the streets of Zultec, pushing through the undergrowth and hacking their way through the bushes when they became too dense. All of them were nervous now as well as excited. All of them feared that death might spring upon them from the shadows at any time, and all of them held themselves ready to meet that threat. It would be a terrible thing to be slain so close to their goal.

Tyrion studied their surroundings. It would be an excellent setting for an ambush. The jungle and the ruins of ancient buildings provided so much cover. The sound of the rain would drown out any stealthy approach made by aggressors, aided and abetted by the natural noises of the jungle itself – the chattering of the monkeys, the screaming of the birds, the distant roar of the big predatory carnosaurs as they sought prey.

He did not like this place.

It had an atmosphere to it that made him uneasy and there were very few places in this world that had that effect on him. He was an elf; he was used to living in places that had an aura of antiquity. But they had been built by his own people.

This was more ancient than any place in Ulthuan and it had not been built by anything remotely like the elves. Minds, alien almost beyond his comprehension, had conceived the strange geometry of the architecture. He could look at structures created by humans and dwarfs and he could see that they were the product of a sensibility at least close to his own. Such was not the case here.

These buildings had been created by beings that thought in a very different way, according to a very different system. There was a pattern here but he could just not tell what it was. He doubted that he ever would be able to.

It had something to do with numbers. The builders had obviously been obsessed by them. If he counted the number of statues on the sides of each building, as he found himself unconsciously doing, he got the sense that they fitted into some numerical pattern, although he could not tell what that pattern was. He suspected it had something to do with basic mathematical formulae, but he could not tell what that formula was.

Perhaps Teclis could; he had a gift for solving such puzzles. His mind was more flexible. Perhaps he could gain some insight into the minds of the alien creatures who had built this place.

Looking at his brother, he was sure that Teclis was gnawing away at the problem. He had a look on his face that Tyrion recognised; he was confronted with something that he did not understand but he was determined to do so. If anyone could get to the bottom of this mystery, Teclis could. All it would take was time, and, being elves, they had plenty of that.

The humans' expressions were very revealing too. Leiber resembled a man on the verge of religious conversion. He was very close to achieving some long-held dream. He looked excited and intense. His gaze darted around their surroundings, seeming to take everything in, as if he wanted to memorise every single detail of every single building and every single object that they encountered.

The other men simply looked scared and greedy and torn between those two emotions. They too were excited to be here, but would have preferred to be somewhere else. They were dwarfed by the sheer scale of their surroundings, by these monumental, crumbling ruins emerging from the sticky humid jungle.

If he felt out of place here, Tyrion thought, what must these humans be thinking? Their civilisation was much younger than that of the elves and they believed the ancient slann to be daemons, in the same way that they believed almost every race but themselves to be daemons or descended from them. They thought that this was a place in which they could lose their souls if they died here. Maybe they were right. Who knew what was possible with the magic of the ancients?

Tyrion was astonished by their bravery. He never usually gave much thought to courage. He never really felt much fear himself, merely some prodding instinct which told him that his survival was in question and that he had better do something about it.

What must it be like to live with an emotion that could leave you paralysed at the moment of maximum danger?

He knew he was unusual even among elves for his inability to feel fear. Teclis certainly knew what it was and his friends back home in Ulthuan did too. He sometimes felt that there must be something missing in him, when he could not share in so common an emotion.

Perhaps it was all part of the curse of being descended from Aenarion. Perhaps this was the legacy that his great ancestor had passed on to him, like the killing rages that sometimes overwhelmed him in the heat of battle. It was said that Aenarion had felt no fear, that he had been willing to risk his life without a second thought on behalf of his people and his friends.

Tyrion pushed that thought to one side; he did not like to compare himself to Aenarion in any way. Too many other people were already doing that.

Everyone told him how much he looked like the great statue of Aenarion in Lothern harbour although he had never been able to see the resemblance himself. And back home in the city of Lothern and in other parts of the kingdoms, there were already those who compared him to the legendary Phoenix King.

That he and Teclis had defeated the Keeper of Secrets N'Kari had made him something of a celebrity among the elves. And certainly their deeds since they had overcome that potent daemon had won them a great deal of fame.

They had travelled to the four corners of the world while still very young, searching for Sunfang and ancient magical knowledge. Tyrion had already taken a distinguished part in several famous battles. He had raided the coasts of Naggaroth and sailed as far as the Citadel of the Dawn. He had been victorious in scores of duels and survived numerous attempts on his life. He was talked about in every corner of Ulthuan and many places beyond wherever elves gathered.

He had already heard himself mentioned as a potential candidate for the next Phoenix King even though Finubar's reign had only just begun less than two centuries ago. It was a truism of politics that the election of the next Phoenix King began with the coronation of the current one but while it was one thing to listen to those platitudes, it was another thing entirely to find yourself the subject of one of them.

He smiled. Perhaps he was deceiving even himself. Perhaps he had believed them all along. Perhaps this was the reason why he was seeking Aenarion's sword. It would be another link in the chain that connected him with his ancestor in the public mind, and in politics that could be a very important thing indeed.

He admitted it. It was certainly possible that one of the reasons he was here was to advance his political career.

What young male elf did not dream of becoming Phoenix King?

In most of the cases it was an empty dream but Tyrion knew that this was not so for himself. He had the potential to be a candidate backed by one of the great merchant houses of Lothern. If he acquired sufficient acclaim from his adventures, that would count for a great deal with many others who had some say in the process of selection. After all, had not Finubar himself built his reputation on his deeds in the Old World?

He shook his head; it was funny how these ideas intruded into your mind in the strangest of places. Here he was in the ruins of an ancient city that had been destroyed while Lothern had been a collection of small wooden huts around an empty bay and he was thinking about the consequences of his actions here when he got back home.

He forced himself to concentrate on his surroundings. None of these speculations would matter if he was cut down by some monster's blade here in Zultec.

They passed on through the shadows of the titanic stone buildings, under the glare of massive stylised heads that looked as if they were modelled on some bizarre combination of human, daemon and toad. They moved along immense causeways which ran through gigantic ponds, in whose murky waters strange and frightening shapes swam.

A shadow fell upon them. Looking up Tyrion saw a monstrous bat-winged flying lizard pass overhead. It screeched once as if in warning and then soared off, rising on the thermals until it was merely a distant point that vanished into the clouds. Tyrion wondered why it had not attacked them. Perhaps it was not hungry. Or perhaps it was spying on them for the benefit of some unseen master.

'I see an opening here,' said Teclis, pointing to an entrance that had appeared in the side of a crumbling step pyramid they had just passed. 'Let us get out of the rain and I will try a divination.'

The humans looked worried, as if he had just announced he was going to summon a daemon. Tyrion hoped there was not going to be any trouble.

◄ CHAPTER FOUR ►

Warm water tumbled down the sides of the ziggurat and poured over the lip of the entranceway. It ran down the back of Tyrion's neck and beneath his jerkin as he passed through. He cursed inwardly. It was difficult enough to maintain his gear in these tropical conditions; getting it wet was only going to make that harder.

Inside the gloomy chamber it smelled of mould and rotting leaves and ancient dampness. A snake slithered out of the light of Teclis's illumination spell. Tyrion reached up and touched the ceiling. It was low enough for him to do so easily.

The stone was chill and wet and blotched in places with some sort of fungal growth. This place had been built for a race shorter than humans or elves. He would have suspected dwarfs had something to do with its building if he had not known better. The stonework had some of the monumental quality he associated with the sons of Grungni. Massive blocks had been placed together with great cunning to make this structure.

It was the carvings in the stone that told a different tale. One look at them and anyone could see that this place had not been built by the dwarfs.

Pictograms had been chiselled into each stone block, depicting oddly square-looking humanoid lizards going about their incomprehensible business. They were of all different sizes. Some were apparently rulers, carried around on palanquins by ones who were obviously slaves.

'Fascinating,' Teclis said. For once there was no irony in his tone. He was genuinely interested in this alien artwork.

'I am just glad to be out of the rain,' Tyrion said. He spoke in the human tongue. Given their unease, he saw no reason for making the humans any more uncomfortable than they already were.

'Be grateful you are not in the Old World, your honours,' said

Leiber. 'It would be cold there as well and you would most likely take fever.' He paused for a moment and made a face at his own foolishness. 'Of course you would not. You are elves. You are immortal.'

'Not immortal,' said Teclis. His tone was sour. 'And some elves suffer from diseases.'

'I believe you, your honour, but let's get on with finding this treasure of yours. None of us is getting any younger.'

Teclis nodded and gestured for the humans to stand back. All of them did so as quickly as they could and all of them wore the worried expressions of humans who knew they were about to be in the presence of sorcery.

Tyrion wondered whether his brother was making a mistake exposing the humans to his magic in this way. They were uneasy enough as it was from the constant expectation of attack. This might push them past the breaking point. He stared hard at Teclis but his brother was already in a world of his own, preparing. He had that inward look that he always wore when getting ready to cast a spell.

Tyrion came to a decision and shepherded the humans out of the chamber and deeper into the pyramid. They looked at him with something between resentment and gratitude and then found their way into another cavernous chamber within the slann structure.

He told them to stay there before returning to where his brother was performing his magic so that he could stand guard. As always, he felt the need to do so. This time in particular, he had a sense of impending danger.

It was just this evil place, he told himself. That was all it was.

Teclis barely noticed that Tyrion had entered the room. His mind had sunk into a trance and he was reaching out with his soul to touch the strange, alien realm from which magic flowed.

He would have liked to have inscribed a pentagram and a mystic circle and all of their associated runes on the floor, but it was too wet and damp for that. And, of course, he had already passed beyond the stage of needing such props in order to work magic. They would have made casting a spell easier but that was all.

He could achieve what was needed simply by uttering the proper incantations and making the correct gestures to bind the winds of magic to his will. Eventually, if he worked at it long enough and practised hard enough, he would be able to work the spell without even needing chants or hand movements.

He spoke the words of power and trailed his fingers through the moist air, flexing them in the way he had been taught by the Lore-masters at Hoeth. As he did so sparks flared from his fingertips and his hands left trails of light behind them as they moved.

With those trails of light he sketched out the pentagram and the circle so that they shimmered around him. The mystical structure he had created sculpted the winds of magic around him, adding new layers to the spell, channelling the potent ambient energy. He shaped it with his hands and his voice like a potter shaping clay back in Lothern. He built something that was like the eye of a daemon.

Once his tool was formed he closed his eyes. He could still see although he now saw from the point of view of the magical eye that he had created and he looked out upon a different world. It was no longer a place of light and darkness illuminated by the blaze of the sun or the cold glimmer of the moon. It was not a place where walls blocked vision. It was a place where he saw the flows and patterns of magic, and the souls of living things. Stone did not block his sight but other things did – the remains of ancient spells of protection and warding, the static snowflakes created by the winds of magic themselves.

Looking around him he saw the golden glow of Tyrion's spirit. A little way beyond that he saw the flickering greed and hunger of the humans. All around him small pulses of light represented lizards and birds and stalking jaguars in search of prey.

Somewhere far off in the distance he felt the gigantic, terrifying presence of a monstrous alien intelligence, a thing half-asleep but still vaguely aware of what was going on around it. This would be one of the great slann lords of Hexoatl, slothfully vigilant, watching over its ancient ancestral lands even as it dreamed. He knew he had best do nothing to attract its attention and rouse it to full wakefulness. There was a power in the thing that was close to that of a god.

With an effort of will, he moved his magical eye and his point of view shifted, passing through walls as if they were not there and rising into the sky above the city. He could not move the eye too far from where he was without breaking the connection and ending the spell that he hoped would have leeway enough to get what he needed done. He raised the eye as far into the air as he could and looked down upon the city like a bird would have if it could see the flows of magic.

The city itself channelled magic in the same way as the spell he had created. He saw pulsing lines of light laid out beneath him. He was not sure what the purpose of this vast magical structure had been but he could see that, though it had been intended to fulfil some function, it was no longer capable of doing so.

Parts were dead. The pattern was incomplete. Something had gone wrong. He guessed that the whole city was like one huge rune and parts of that rune had been defaced by the destruction of buildings and the way the city had become overgrown by the jungle.

Whatever it had once been intended to do, the city was no longer capable of it. All that functioned now were the remnants of that vast spell. It still trapped power in pools and he dreaded to think what the effect of that could be. Perhaps it was what was responsible for the riot of growth here. Perhaps it had changed and altered the living things around it, making them angry mutants.

Fascinating as it all was, it was not part of his purpose here to study the magic of the Old Ones. He was looking for a specific object, one not made by the builders of the city but by an elf. It would have a very different magical signature, one that would stand out against this background like a gem on black velvet.

He made his point of view circle until he saw something that made him hopeful, a glittering pattern of light somewhere in the distance. He moved his magical eye as far in that direction as the tether of the spell would allow.

His heart began to race. He was looking at something that definitely had an aura. It could be only one thing. All they had to do was march in that direction until they found it and one of the greatest works of one of the greatest mages in history would be within their reach.

It was then that he noticed they were not alone in the city, that other sentient beings were present and that those beings bore no resemblance to either elf or human, but were something monstrous, alien and savage. The servants of the slann were out there, and they were most likely looking for him and his brother.

And there was something else that worried him. All around the place where the elven magic flared there was the glow of other, darker, more sinister sorcery. One of the pools where the magic channelled by the city had collected, had curdled and congealed into something inexpressibly loathsome that made him want to shudder.

He summoned the spell back to himself, and opened his eyes. Tyrion raised an eyebrow.

'I know where we must go,' said Teclis. 'Although there may be some slann in our way. And worse – Dark Magic too.'

'Oh good,' said Tyrion. 'We wouldn't want things to be too easy now, would we?'

Ahead of them, a monstrous ziggurat erupted out of the jungle. It was the largest they had so far seen and it was in somewhat better condition than the rest. It loomed over them like a mountain: gigantic, eternal, indestructible.

The rain had stopped, but water still dripped from the leaves as they pushed them aside. The moisture ran down the face of the humans like tears. Tyrion was soaked with rain as well as with sweat.

'This is the place. I remember it,' said Leiber. 'This is where Argentes vanished and where we were attacked as we waited for him.'

For once Teclis did not mock him. The other humans looked reluctant to continue. There was something about the sheer scale of the place that intimidated them. Leiber sounded angry when he spoke, as much with himself as with them. 'We've not got all day. There's treasure in there. Don't you want it?'

Up ahead, Tyrion could see that there had been hundreds of statues on every step of the ziggurat. Most of them were toppled over although he was not sure what had done it. It might have been an earthquake or a war or something else entirely, some magical disaster perhaps.

The main bulk of the structure was completely intact and that was hardly surprising. It was built of blocks of stone, each of which must have weighed tens of tons. The creation of this pyramid must have involved magic or the labour of tens of thousands of slaves.

He tried to imagine putting together this gigantic building in the sweltering heat of the tropical jungle. He tried to imagine it being built by the savage lizardmen who had attacked them earlier. It was difficult to believe that such creatures could have been capable of architecture on such a scale but he knew that such thoughts were deceptive. Once the slann had been the greatest of races, the master magicians of the world, the mightiest scholars, the chosen servants of the Old Ones, or so the most ancient legends claimed.

Look at them now, he thought – degenerate troglodytes barely capable of making stone tools. And yet this same people had once been masters of the world. It was alarming to consider that something similar might happen to his own people one day. Perhaps it had already started, this process of degeneration.

He thought about Lothern, with its empty palaces and its streets deserted by night. It was not so hard to imagine that one day it too would be overgrown and tumbled down, and that strangers might wander through the ruins overcome by a sense of melancholy and loss.

Perhaps one day, all that would be left would be the humans and their enemies, the beastmen of Chaos. Perhaps they would fight wars over the crumbled ruins of metropolises built by people who were by far their superiors. Perhaps all of this was merely a foretaste of the way the world would end.

They began to make their way up a massive staircase in the side of the ziggurat. There were both steps and ramps and it was easier to walk on the ramps because the steps had been placed at distances that were awkward for the human or elf stride.

Eventually they came to an extensive arched opening and Teclis stopped, considering. After a moment he nodded and pointed through the archway.

'We go down here,' he said. All of them paused. The humans were plainly reluctant to go down into the darkness within the pyramid and Tyrion could not exactly blame them.

A strange smell of rot and decay, stronger even than that which brooded over the jungle, emerged from the entrance like the stinking breath of some undead giant. It felt like entering the mouth of a huge monster, a thing that might devour them. The ziggurat had an unearthly, evil, inhuman presence. It seemed to be waiting like some gigantic beast of prey.

'We have no light,' one of the men said. It should have sounded pathetic but it did not. They were all afraid and none of them wanted to admit it. They were close to their goal and Tyrion sensed that this in part was what caused their reluctance to proceed. They were as afraid of what they might find as they were of any guardians. They were afraid that they might be disappointed and that their golden dreams might turn out empty. It would be a brutal blow after all the hardships of getting here.

Teclis gestured. A ball of light sprang into being around his clenched hand. He flexed his fingers and the ball of light drifted away, floating around like a will-o'-the-wisp, illuminating the shadowy interior with a dim yet adequate light. He repeated the process until each of them had his own personal floating lantern. This display of magic made the humans even more uneasy. Tyrion could not see what else there was to be done under the circumstances though. It would take some time to collect the right sort of wood to make torches and it would be so wet that getting them lit would involve magic anyway.

'Ready?' Teclis asked.

'I am, brother,' said Tyrion. The humans nodded reluctantly but still did not move. They needed someone to give them a lead and it looked like he was elected for that duty. He shrugged and moved through the archway.

'These lights are going to make a stealthy approach impossible,' he said with a smile, hoping to lighten the situation.

'I think anything down there would know that we were here anyway. They could probably smell us. It is said that some of the skinks can track like dogs. They use their tongues instead of their noses but the results are the same,' said Teclis.

'One of the joys of travelling with you, brother,' said Tyrion, 'is that you're always so full of interesting facts.'

That got a feeble laugh from the humans. Warily the party entered the pyramid and descended downwards into the darkness.

The ceilings in the corridors were so low that in some places Tyrion had to stoop. They were wider than he would have expected but lower. He suspected it had something to do with the way that the lizardmen walked. They kept their heads much lower, even if their bodies would have been longer than those of a human or an elf lying stretched out on the ground.

'Which way?' Tyrion asked.

'Follow me,' said Teclis.

Tyrion would have preferred to take the lead, but this seemed like a wise time to defer to his brother and his magic. He prepared himself to spring forward at the first sign of danger.

He sensed it would not be long before it showed itself.

◄ CHAPTER FIVE ►

'We need to be careful,' said Teclis in Reikspiel. 'This ziggurat was the central temple of Zultec. This means we are moving into the heart of the most sacred area in the city.'

'Why is that important?' Leiber asked.

'Because they did not want infidels to come here into the most holy shrines. Before this city was abandoned I believe the slann laid spells here to prevent that from happening and there may well be physical traps too. And there is something else present, something I don't like at all.'

Tyrion could see that, if anything, the morale of the humans had dropped still lower. They had thought they merely had to fight the degenerate remains of an elder race. Now they were being told that they would have to face dangerous magic and deadly traps too.

'What are we talking about here?' Tyrion asked. He switched language to keep the humans from understanding the nature of the discussion that he was having with his brother. 'Daemons? Fireballs? Strange runes that summon deadly clouds of poison?'

'It could be any of those,' Teclis said. 'There's something odd here. I think this whole city was built to be a sort of giant collector of magic and that this temple was its focal point.'

'And?'

'And I think something has tainted the power, made it corrupt. It may be why this place was abandoned.'

'I still don't see what kind of threat that might imply,' said Tyrion.

'Where magic flows strangely and is tainted by Chaos, there is the chance of all sorts of strange manifestations. Think of what happens in the Annulii, of all the monsters and mutations that emerge from those glittering mountains.'

'You are saying we might encounter something like that?'

'I am saying we might encounter things that are much worse.'

The humans were becoming restless because the two elves were spending so much time talking in their own tongue. They looked suspicious.

Teclis switched back to their language. 'I want you all to move very slowly and pay very close attention to what I say. If there is any inimical magic here I will see it and I will tell you what to do. I don't want anybody running ahead and setting off any traps. Is that clear?'

Tyrion did not think there was much chance of that. He was fairly sure that his brother's words were aimed at him. Teclis did not want him heroically striding into hidden dangers.

That was fine with him. He knew his brother's magesight was much better than his own and that Teclis was far more likely to discover any subtle spells in operation in the area.

'Shall we go?' Tyrion asked. 'I am keen to see Sunfang.'

'Just make sure your enthusiasm is not the death of you,' Teclis said. 'I only have one brother and I am not keen to lose him.'

'I am not any keener to be lost,' said Tyrion. 'Let's go.'

The inside of the ziggurat was a huge maze, obviously designed, or so Tyrion thought, to confuse any intruder. Teclis did not seem troubled by the way the corridors fitted together though. He clearly saw a pattern to it and Tyrion asked what that was.

'It was built according to slann geomantic principles,' Teclis said. 'Most of the central chambers of slann temple cities are laid out according to the same pattern. I've seen the maps in the library at the great Tower of Hoeth.'

'So you're following the layout of a map that you can remember seeing once upon a time. You don't actually know whether this city is laid out according to the same principles?' Tyrion was speaking in elvish again. Just the fact that he was doing so was a cue to make the humans uneasy, but he could not help it. He thought they would be even more disturbed if they knew what he was actually talking about.

'I have not gone wrong yet, have I?'

'There is a first time for everything, brother.'

'I'm sure it will give you some satisfaction when it happens.' There was a brittle nervous edge to his brother's words that told Tyrion that his twin was not quite as confident as he liked to appear.

'It would give me no satisfaction whatsoever for you to be wrong. I very dearly want to find that sword. And I would like to have it soon.'

'Don't worry, we are very close indeed. I sense a powerful aura of magic just ahead of us. Be ready! If there are going to be any traps, they will be here.'

The corridor ended in a massive stone wall. It was etched with the strange pictoglyphs of the slann and even Tyrion could sense the magic in it. It was too heavy to be lifted by mere strength and too thick to be broken through even with a battering ram. It looked like they had come to a dead end.

'Whatever it is, it's beyond this wall,' Teclis said.

'I knew you were going to say that,' Tyrion said.

'You seem to be developing a gift for prophecy. Perhaps you would care to use your powers of divination to reveal how we are going to get through this. No? Then pray have the good grace to remain silent while I work out a way of doing so.'

Teclis paused in front of the wall. The mass of the thing, the sheer thickness of it, did not trouble him. What bothered him was the magic woven into it. Powerful spells converged here. Magic flowed all around him. It had a strange taint to it. Some kind of energy that he did not fully understand was part of it, along with the unmistakable spiritual taint of Chaos.

Something was being done to the winds of magic here. Some alien element was being added. He was not sure to what purpose but he was certain that it was happening.

He concentrated on seeing the whole thing with his magesight. His vision of what most elves would call reality receded. Now he was looking at the world painted in the bright, vivid colours of the winds of magic. He could see currents of power pulsing through the walls and knotting together like nests of writhing snakes. It seemed clear to him that one purpose of the spells here was to control this great doorway, for that was what the wall was. It was a doorway blocking the entrance to whatever chamber held Sunfang.

Argentes had somehow managed to penetrate into the heart of this pyramid. He had got past this barrier. Teclis doubted that he had done it by magic although he could not be sure. None of the information they had collected pointed to Argentes's party having a mage with them, but that did not mean it was not so. Leiber did not know everything and there were many reasons why a mage might have kept his gift to himself among humans, not the least being a wish to avoid a knife in the back.

He was speculating too much. There was most likely a much more simple explanation. Perhaps the sword bearer had entered the secret chamber by a different route and if they circled round this maze they would find a different method of entry. Or perhaps there was some secret passage through the walls that the sword bearer had known about but they did not. It was said that the temple cities of the slann were riddled with such things. Or maybe the doorway had closed as part of an elaborate trap.

He was wasting time. If the tunnels were there, he did not know how to access them. If there was another route in, it would take him a long time to find it. This door in front of him would provide a means of access and it was controlled by magic which was something he did understand. All he had to do was work out the spell that would control it.

Magic was as much his gift as warfare was Tyrion's. Now was his time to shine. He still felt embarrassed and insecure about the way his brother had saved him during the attack by the skinks. He could have handled it if he had been given time. He could have blasted the lizardmen with his spells. But by the time his magic was ready, the skinks were already dead, killed by his brother's deadly blade.

Now they were confronted by a problem that could not be solved with a sword. He would find a way through this door using only his knowledge and his talents. And he'd better make a start soon or they would be here forever.

Once again he gave his full attention to the slann magic. He could see that untangling one knot of power would move the door. All he had to do was utter the words of an opening charm. What gave him pause was the web of magical energy that flowed out of that turnkey spell.

He was not sure what would happen if he did not neutralise those connections first. It might be that the whole complex of spells was completely harmless. Perhaps they fulfilled some ritual function. He doubted that was correct and he was not willing to take any chances with magic he understood so little.

He inspected the web of spells once again, concentrating not so much on their function as simply their place in the pattern. He wondered what would happen if he cut the connections.

Would it trigger something? Would some protective process react? Would guardians spring to life?

He did not know and he could not. The minds that had created this magic were too alien for him to understand. He was simply going to have to do what was necessary.

He hesitated for only a moment longer, knowing that he would gain nothing by waiting, but still reluctant to commit himself to an action that might have fatal consequences. Once again he found himself envying Tyrion. In moments like this he lacked his brother's decisiveness.

He cast his spell almost savagely. The door shook as if caught in an earthquake. The humans looked around in panic, ready to bolt. Another miscalculation, Teclis thought sourly. He should have warned them. Too late now anyway.

The doorway slid sideways, disappearing into a recess in the wall. It was an awesome feat by the builders, combining magic with engineering on a huge scale. What was revealed in the chamber beyond immediately stopped the humans from taking flight. Teclis heard Tyrion catch his breath and saw him begin to take a step forward.

In the distance lay bodies. Some magic had prevented them from decomposing although they did look desiccated. The corpses were human. In the hands of one was a naked blade which glowed with its own internal fire to Teclis's magesight.

They had found Sunfang and the last resting place of its bearer. Still he sensed something wrong. All he needed to do was identify it...

'Stop!' Teclis said. He said it loudly and with as much force as he could. But it was too late. The humans had seen the piles of gold objects strewn about the chamber. They had found the treasure they had searched for for so long; nothing was going to stop them taking it. As a group they plunged forward into the room, ignoring Teclis's desperate shout. 'No! Wait! Don't!'

It was already too late. The air within the room shimmered and ghostly, ghastly shapes began to take form. At first they were merely dancing sparkles of light but then the tiny shimmering motes raced together. They became outlines of creatures that looked like skinks. They hovered in the air above the corpses and then flowed into them, vanishing like poison gas breathed into the lungs of a victim.

The corpses shook as if the ground they lay upon was in the grip of an earthquake. One by one, the dead bodies pulled themselves upright. They lurched into motion like puppets on strings. More and more ghostly outlines shimmered in the air. They flowed towards alcoves in the walls and Teclis saw the mummified remains of other lizardmen lying in the darkness there. Once again, the motes of light vanished inside the bodies of the dead. Once again, the corpses began to move.

What had happened here? The slann were not famous for their

knowledge of necromancy. They were said to have shunned it. Was this spell the product of some later degenerate cult? Or was it a product of the curdled magic he had sensed?

Teclis cursed. This was his fault. He should have given them more warning before he opened the door. He should have stressed the fact that no one was to enter much more strongly than he had.

It was too late for regrets now. The trap was sprung. All he could do was pray to the old gods and hope they were listening.

There were dozens of dead bodies within the tomb now, all animated. Their flesh had an odd dry quality and as they moved they made a strange wheezing sound as if the air being forced from whatever remained of their lungs was whistling out through gaps in their flesh. There was a stink of herbs and embalming fluid and the faintest hint of the sickly sweet odour of corruption.

The animated human corpses moved strangely, as if whatever was wearing them was confused as to how to make them walk. The first of the reanimated had reached Leiber's men now. They were just standing there, slack-jawed, paralysed by the sight of one horror too many.

Tyrion was already in motion, blade held ready to strike. He was obviously torn between obeying Teclis's injunction against entering the room and leaping into the fray. Teclis did not know what to tell him. The best plan might be to retreat in the face of this undead horde.

One of the humans went down. The walking corpses simply tore him limb from limb, painting themselves in his blood then using his torn-off arms as bludgeons with which to attack Teclis's companions. That forced the still living humans to react. They responded violently, hacking with their swords, lunging blades deep into unbeating hearts, slashing the throats of things that no longer needed to breathe. The living humans could not kill their foes with normal weapons. Teclis tried a spell, but it fizzled out as it passed into the air of the chamber. Powerful wards were still active in there, dampening and negating his magic.

Another of Leiber's men went down, screaming and struggling, as the wave of moving corpses passed over him. 'Tyrion!' Teclis shouted. 'Help him.'

Tyrion sprang to the doomed man's aid, blade lashing out with the force of a thunderbolt. The impact sent the animated corpses reeling backward. The blade took large chunks out of their dry flesh. They did not bleed. They felt no pain. It looked like the only way to stop them would be to chop them to pieces. Fire might work, but without being able to use his magic there was no way to make it.

Or was there?

'Tyrion! Get Sunfang. That will hurt them.' Teclis wished he was sure of that, but it seemed like their best chance of getting out of this hellish place alive.

Tyrion seemed to have worked this out for himself. He was already in motion towards Aenarion's time-lost blade.

CHAPTER SIX

Tyrion leapt at the walking dead man with the burning sword. He knocked aside the clumsy stroke of Sunfang and struck Argentes's corpse in the face with the pommel of his blade.

Argentes clutched Aenarion's sword in the unbreakable grip of his dead fingers. Tyrion grappled with him, determined to get his hands on the weapon he had sought for so long.

But the animated corpse was incredibly strong and his many companions surged towards Tyrion, keen to rend his flesh. The elf prince grasped Argentes's hand and broke his wrist with a twist. White bone jabbed out through dry flesh. Still Argentes would not let go of the sword. He grabbed Tyrion's throat with his good hand and squeezed. Tyrion made his neck muscles rigid to resist being choked but iron-hard nails bit into his flesh, drawing blood.

Tyrion twisted Argentes's sword hand, smashing the last of the bone and tearing the strip of flesh and the tendons that still attached it to the arm. Sunfang dropped free and he caught it.

It felt like a living thing in his hand. The blade burst into tiny flames. Tyrion could feel the blazing heat coming from the sword but the flames did not seem to do the metal any damage. It did not soften or become malleable.

He lashed out at Argentes with the sword he had carried for so long.

The smell of seared flesh filled Tyrion's nostrils when the blade bit home. A hideous shriek emerged from dry lips. A grey tongue flickered forth as if imitating the action of a serpent. In a moment the bone-dry corpse was in flames. It reeled away from Tyrion, tumbling backwards into the ranks of its own undead companions, setting the clothing of some of them alight as well.

'For Emeraldsea and the Phoenix King!' Tyrion shouted his battle cry and leapt among the attackers, striking right and left, setting fire to animated corpses, searing their flesh, burning their bones black as they fell. The magic of the blade made it much more deadly to these creatures than it would be to the living.

Teclis saw the effectiveness of Tyrion's blade against the undead. He could work similar fiery magic, just not within the protected confines of the inner sanctum. He needed to lure the monsters outside their circle of protection before he could destroy them.

Inside the sanctum the humans had panicked and were fighting desperately, simply trying to stay alive. No one was paying very much attention to him. It was going to cost them their lives.

Why should he care? He could save himself and Tyrion. The others were only humans. He had no reason to care whether they lived or died.

By elven standards they were going to die soon anyway, so what difference would a few more years make? Chances were they would be carried off by disease or disaster within months if they made it back to their homelands anyway.

And yet he did care. He felt responsible for them. He had brought them here. They had followed him into this danger. And though their lives were short, they were the only lives they had, and if he did not do something they would be lost.

Most elves would not have given him a chance of living a few years when he had been but a sickly child. He found that he had a certain sympathy for humans that most other elves lacked. He could share their perspective. He could see himself in them. They were poorly made and despised by his kindred as well.

'Everybody out of the chamber,' Teclis shouted. 'Now!'

'They'll just follow us,' Tyrion responded.

'That's what I want!'

Tyrion shrugged. 'Come on, men,' he bellowed in his best battleground voice. 'Get out of there. My brother has a plan.'

His voice carried effortlessly above the din of battle. More importantly it had that note in it that commanded obedience.

Leiber and the other humans almost jumped to obey. They raced and scrambled for the doorway, tearing themselves from the grip of the ravening undead, twisting and writhing and scrambling over and through the moving corpses until they reached the exit.

Tyrion was behind them, pushing them on, encouraging them, helping them get free of their attackers, somehow never getting pinned down himself. The blade had given him the power to dominate this situation.

He pushed Leiber through the doorway and sent him sprawling. Another human ended up beside Teclis, terror and hope at war on his face. Teclis tried to smile reassuringly but it did not work. He lacked his brother's charisma. Tyrion was already fighting his way back across the chamber to get the rest of the men out.

Teclis breathed deeply, willing his heartbeat to stop racing and his mind to become calm. He reached out, twisting the winds of magic to his will, feeling them flow through him and around him, responding to his gestures and his voice and his attitude of mind. He thought of flame and tiny fires flickered into being around him, sending shadows skittering away into the gloom. He intensified his command and the fires grew hotter and brighter, blazing forth from his hands in sudden hellish eruptions.

The humans scrambled away from him, moving back down the corridor away from the combat as fast as they could. Forces flowed around Teclis in great spiralling serpents of fiery energy. Now all he had to do was trigger them. He waited for Tyrion to get out of the chamber.

His brother slashed his way through more walking corpses over to where the human had fallen. With a sudden flurry of blows he cleared the area, lifted the man over his shoulders, and made for the door again.

Burdened by the additional weight, unable to use his weapon, all he could do was run. Teclis wanted to shout for him to drop the human and get himself clear. His feelings of responsibility towards the man were as nothing to what he felt for his brother. Something made him keep his mouth shut though. Perhaps the belief that Tyrion could win free.

The undead clustered around his brother now, seeking to pull him down, clawing at his armour, scratching his face and exposed flesh. Tyrion kicked and butted and used his body weight to push assailants aside, but even he could not do anything against the enormous tide of desiccated flesh through which he was attempting to swim.

'Drop him!' Teclis shouted. 'Get yourself out. Don't be a bloody hero.'

Tyrion grinned and kept moving. Leiber surprised Teclis by springing back into the room to aid Tyrion. He said something that Teclis could not hear. Tyrion dropped his burden and started fighting again with the sword. Leiber dragged his companion through the archway and out into the corridor. Tyrion followed a moment later.

'Back!' Teclis bellowed. 'Get clear and don't come back!'

They took him at his word, rushing down the corridor. Teclis found himself facing the regiment of animated corpses. For a moment the sight of them almost froze his heart. He took a step backwards and they followed, leaving the chamber and its protections behind. Teclis kept back-pedalling. They kept following until the corridor was full of them.

Teclis spoke the final words of his spell.

A gigantic wall of flame sprang into being in front of him, hot as hell, with all the incandescent force of a blast furnace. Corpses shrivelled. Eyeballs popped. Skulls exploded as the brains within superheated. Blackened bones kept moving forward through the flames until even they were consumed.

Within moments it was all over. Tyrion looked at him with something like awe.

'That was impressive,' he said.

'If we are going to get the treasure we need to do so now,' said Teclis. 'We may not get another chance.'

Tyrion held up the blade. 'I've got what I came for,' he said.

Teclis gestured at the surviving humans. 'They haven't.'

'Go ahead,' said Tyrion to Leiber and the others. 'You have earned it.'

Teclis strode back into the death chamber and studied the inscriptions on the walls. He knew enough about the ancient slann writings to know that he had stumbled across something important. There was something about the runic language that he recognised, something that niggled at his subconscious, and told him that he really needed to pay attention to what he was seeing.

He recognised one of the runes in particular. It could mean either the end of the world, or the end of an age or both. Another rune concerned the elves. A third concerned the coming of Chaos. A fourth represented a Keeper of Secrets. The way they were laid out hinted at a conjunction of all these things. They were all inter-related although he did not know how.

He understood only a few of the words, or rather the pictoglyphs, but those that he did understand filled him with dread. He knew that the ancient slann had been master diviners and that they had left writings predicting the future that had often come true.

He was not entirely sure that he believed in the efficacy of these visions as exact prophecies. He sometimes suspected that the slann had the means to predict the ebb and flow of magic. If you could do that, you could predict the coming of a new dark age simply because you would know when it was possible for daemons to enter the world.

This was something for the scholars back at the White Tower to unravel. Teclis began to copy out what he had seen, sketching the runes as best he could upon parchment, doing his best to memorise everything that he could not copy down.

Leiber and his fellows filled their backpacks with golden objects and Tyrion watched them all bemused. The humans had gone from being terrified to being ecstatic in the space of a few minutes. They picked up glittering strands of slann jewellery and inspected them and then stuffed them into their backpacks, only to take them out moments later when they had found a yet more attractive and possibly valuable example of the gold worker's art. They were laughing out loud and whooping with joy.

Leiber looked around like a man who has achieved a long-held dream and no longer has any idea of what he wants to do with his life. In that moment Teclis felt sorry for him. Finding the treasure chambers of Zultec had been more than simply a means of getting rich to him. It had been something that had given his life meaning.

Teclis thought about his father and the dragon armour of Aenarion. He wondered what would happen to Prince Arathion if he ever worked out how to remake that ancient, potent artefact. Would his life suddenly be without meaning and purpose? How would he motivate himself to go on?

Teclis looked at Leiber with some curiosity. The man was not diving into the ancient piles of gold and jewellery. He was watching his followers do that but was not helping himself to anything. One of the men came running up to him and offered him a necklace. He was shouting about the value of it, about how much it was worth and how they could use the money to buy a farm, a ship, an estate, if that was what they wanted. He was laughing and crying at the same time and telling Leiber that never again would they want for women, wine or food.

Leiber just stood there, uncomprehending. After a moment, he reached out and inspected the necklace, letting the links drip through his fingers, holding it up before his eyes as if he did not quite believe what he was seeing. He turned to Tyrion like a child wanting to show a parent a new toy and then he let the necklace fall to the ground as if it was worth nothing to him.

One of the humans came up to him and tried to stuff a small gold statue into his backpack.

'Take it! Take it!' he said. Teclis smiled at him and gently shook his head. He did not need the gold. He needed space in his backpack for the notes he was making. The human understood him at last and walked away pointing at his forehead and circling his finger to tell his companions that he thought that Teclis was mad. Teclis did not care. He knew that he operated on a different scale of values to the humans. It mattered to him not at all how they judged him.

'I wish I had some wine,' said Leiber. 'I could use a drink. That's for sure.'

He had walked over to Teclis, curious as to what the elf was doing. He looked at the runes Teclis was copying and nodded his head.

'It's some mighty spell, isn't it?'

Teclis shook his head. 'Some lore of the slann.'

'I don't know what it is, but I think it could be very important.'

'I envy you your knowledge.'

'It is not knowledge yet, it's just a feeling I have that something here could be of the utmost significance.'

'I know what you mean,' said Leiber. 'I used to feel that way too.' He sounded almost melancholy.

⫷ CHAPTER SEVEN ⫸

General Dorian Silverblade, master of the army of the north, Lord of Halustur, by grace of Malekith, keeper of the iron key and lord high marshal of the realm of Naggaroth, waited nervously in the antechamber of the Witch King's throne room.

Frantically he reviewed all of his words and deeds for the past few months to see if there was anything that could possibly have caused a fall from grace. As far as he could tell there was nothing. Not even his most ambitious subordinate could have found an action or a speech that could possibly have been construed as disloyal. If they had made something up, they would swiftly discover the folly of spreading lies to the Witch King. Malekith had his own sources, and he checked and double-checked everything.

No. Dorian had performed his duties in an exemplary, some would say superlative fashion. He had held the border against Chaos for decades and he had overseen the arrival of the new allies Morathi had recruited as well as it was possible to do. There had been a minimum of fuss and trouble with the followers of the Dark Gods since their unexpected conversion to the cause of the rightful heir of Aenarion. If they planned treachery while within Naggaroth they would find themselves swiftly manoeuvred into a position where they could be destroyed by the druchii armies shadowing them.

Dorian knew that even the most diligent performance of one's duties did not always guarantee Malekith's favour, but it was unusual for the Witch King to take against those who served him well. Still, like every other dark elf he had skeletons in his closet that could be held against him. There was always that business with his accursed half-brother Urian which ensured that the whole family would be forever tainted, and then there was his relationship with Cassandra, sorceress and follower of many secret paths, not all of them particularly favoured by Malekith.

He doubted that even those meant that much. If Malekith had been going to punish him for Urian's transgressions he would already have done so. He had made his displeasure with Poisonblade known in the most spectacular fashion possible. For a thousand years druchii would talk about his fate in fearful whispers.

Dorian shuddered when he thought of his last sight of his brother hanging half-flayed from hooks over that blood-filled cauldron. Leather-clad torturers had driven truesilver spikes through his empty eye-sockets into the pleasure centres of his brain, and then muttered spells which turned agony into ecstasy and pleasure into pain. They had done it randomly so that the most awful torture became orgasmic pleasure, and the most gentle painkillers turned into nerve-wracking toxins.

Of course, Urian had gone mad many times, but he had always been nursed back to health. His body had hung there for thirteen months in the antechamber, kept alive by food and water pumped into his stomach through leather tubes and transfusions of blood from dying slaves hooked up to vampiric engines. Then one day Urian was just gone. Never mentioned again in Malekith's hearing, his body tossed unmourned on some rubbish heap in Naggarond.

All because of one ill-considered joke. And he had been a favourite of Malekith's up to that moment. His skill as a pit fighter and his wit and scholarship had all contributed to making him so. Malekith had made an example of him though, and now few considered speculating on how the armoured Witch King entertained himself in the privacy of his personal chambers.

Dorian had never liked his younger brother but it was a waste. Urian had been perhaps the greatest swordsman Naggaroth had seen in twenty generations. He had been a scholar of peculiar lore, an expert on poisons who had delighted in demonstrating their uses in the pits in which he had fought and made his name. He was merry and terrifying and entirely too self-confident. Dorian did not mind admitting now that he had feared him in a manner in which it was not entirely seemly to fear a younger sibling.

And yet he found he still missed him sometimes. They had come from the same place, poor scions of an impoverished ancient line. They had chosen different paths to fame and fortune at the court of Naggaroth, Urian in the fighting pits and bedchambers, he on the battlefield. They had both achieved success. One of them had gone on to demonstrate how transitory that could be. Dorian hoped he was not about to do the same.

SWORD OF CALEDOR 369

Had he said anything about this to Cassandra, he wondered, and had his sorceress lover betrayed him for it? She was loyal to Morathi, in the same way as he was loyal to Malekith, but that meant nothing. The mother and the son shared information about their minions even as they manoeuvred for advantage against each other. It had been that way in Naggaroth for millennia.

He wondered whether Cassandra could be the cause of this summons. Had he said anything outrageous to her when they were drunk on narcotic wine? He somehow doubted it. His tolerance for such things was better than his lover's. Of course, she was a sorceress, a follower of Morathi and that was automatically suspect, but Malekith knew about this. Dorian had reported the contact as soon as it happened. He was as much a spy on Cassandra as she was on him. It was the way the realm functioned.

There was always the chance he had missed something, or Malekith was going to bring up some long-forgotten – by Dorian anyway – indiscretion and punish him for it. It would not be the first time it had happened. He had known generals summoned to the royal presence who fully expected a promotion, only to have a centuries-old conversation repeated verbatim to them, and a treasonous slant put on it. His old commander, Hartelroy, had gone that way, which was a pity for he had been a good general and a decent enough druchii.

Dorian knew it was pointless looking through his past for acts of weakness or sins of treason. If Malekith wanted to find them, he would, no matter how blameless a life Dorian had led. And their entire system was set up so that no one could lead an entirely blameless life. If you did not criticise the king, you criticised his enemies in the Cult of Khaine, only to discover a decade later that those enemies were now trusted allies once more and your criticism of them could be construed as treason.

It was better to keep your mouth shut and say nothing at all, but what druchii could do that? There were so many parties, so many orgies, so many great public festivals at which drunkenness was not only expected, it was practically mandatory, as was narcotic indulgence.

And after all, if you were sober what was it you were trying to hide? And once you were drunk, tongues always wagged. In private gatherings, with friends, under the warming influence of the black grape, people suddenly felt compelled to speak things better left unsaid. And ears were always listening. No matter how small the group, how trusted the friends, there was always someone who saw some way of gaining some advantage from an indiscretion.

Dorian liked to think he could hold his drink, and with the example of his brother constantly before him he had every reason to, but even he had sometimes said things, let words slip that might be used against him. Perhaps that time was at hand.

The massive stone door to the great throne room slid open. The chamberlain, sumptuously garbed in ermine and purple silk, emerged. 'His majesty will see you now, General Dorian,' he said. There was no clue in his manner whether Dorian was going to reward or execution. It was always the same.

Dorian entered the great audience chamber. It was cold. No fires burned. Malekith did not need them and it would have been in bad taste to remind him of the time he had attempted to pass through the Flame. Icicle stalactites clung to the ceiling. Dorian's breath came out in chilly clouds. He pulled his cloak tight about his shoulders and began the long slow march towards the throne. He kept his back straight, determined to be a soldier to the end.

The audience chamber was vast and empty and his metal-shod footsteps echoed within it. He walked between lines of bodyguards who might have been statues for all the movement they showed. Doubtless some of them were elves he had once known, who might even have served under his command in the old days, but none of them showed the slightest flicker of recognition, which was as it should be.

Even at this distance, Malekith dominated the chamber. He was huge, out of all proportion to his surroundings. His bodyguards looked like children. His massive armoured figure looked even more like a statue than his guards did. Only the cold flicker of his eyes showed there was something living in there, an intelligence that had outlasted the millennia.

It was not just by sheer physical size that the Witch King dominated the room. He had an aura about him such as a dragon had. He radiated power and a force of will that was terrifying. He was god-like in his way. You only had to get near him to realise it. There could be no doubt that you were in the presence of a king, and something more than a king.

Another figure flanked the throne, an elf woman of astonishing beauty. Chains hung from her limbs that contained powerful, binding magic. Dorian was surprised that he had never seen or heard of her before. Hers was the sort of loveliness of which poets would sing. She studied Dorian with languorous eyes, erotic interest all too visible. He did his best to ignore it. She was standing beside Malekith which would make any such encounter dangerous, no matter how exciting it might prove to be.

'General Dorian, it is good to see you' said Malekith. His still-beautiful voice boomed out. It was not exactly jovial. It was always going to be too cold and remote and impersonal for that, but at least there was no anger in it which was a good sign, unless the Witch King was playing with him as a cat toys with a mouse.

Dorian bowed. 'It is kind of you to say so, sire.'

'You have done a sterling job protecting our borders and your work supervising the arrival of our new allies has been exemplary.'

The terror started to lift from Dorian's mind. It was as if a massive downward pressure on his whole body had been removed. Evidently he was still in the Witch King's favour.

'I live only to serve you, sire,' he said.

'If only more of my subjects felt that way,' said Malekith. Was he making a joke, Dorian wondered? It seemed very unlikely. Be careful, he told himself. He felt like he was moving onto very new, very uncertain, very dangerous ground.

'I am sure they are all as loyal as I, sire.'

'Spoken with true druchii ambiguity, Dorian,' said Malekith. 'But I can assure you that very few are, which is why you are standing in front of me now. I have new duties for you, more important than any you have been assigned in the past. If you carry them out to my satisfaction you will be rewarded as no elf has ever been rewarded before. If you fail you will be punished as no elf ever has been.'

It was typical of Malekith that he had to mention punishment, Dorian thought. He could have left it unsaid. They both would still have known it was the case anyway, but the Witch King liked to remind his subjects and himself who held all the power.

'I shall not fail you, sire,' said Dorian.

'See that you don't. Say nothing of what you hear today to anyone until I give you permission to do otherwise. Is that clear?'

Dorian knew he was expected to speak. He nodded and said, 'Yes, sire.'

'Very good, Dorian. Now I will satisfy your curiosity as to why you have been summoned.'

The Witch King spoke on then, and Dorian knew why he had been sworn to secrecy. His heart filled with wonder and terror as Malekith outlined his plan and Dorian's part in it. Truly nothing like this had been attempted in all the long years of history. By the time Malekith finished, Dorian was holding his breath. He also knew that the Witch King was not joking. If he succeeded in playing his part he could name his own reward. It was that important.

'Rest assured I shall not fail you, sire,' he said. 'And I would like to thank you for selecting me for this.'

'The only thanks I require will be your success,' said Malekith. 'In a few hours there will be a general staff meeting. You need not attend it. You will be selecting the troops you need and equipping them with the special amulets I have prepared.'

'As you wish, so shall it be, sire.'

Malekith studied his assembled generals. They represented the most powerful elves in his kingdom. They were feared throughout the lands of Naggaroth. They were soldiers, sorcerers and skilful politicians without equal. Yet here, in his presence, they quivered with barely restrained terror.

He would have preferred it to be different. Yet he knew there was no way that it could be so. He was no longer like any other elf, if he ever had been. His armour saw to that. It did more than protect him. It was a barrier to any natural contact between him and any other member of his race. Sometimes that had its advantages. Sometimes he wished things were otherwise.

He dismissed these feelings of weakness when he saw that the daemon's eyes were upon him. N'Kari watched him intently as always, even when he appeared not to be doing so. Malekith did not need his own eyes to know this. He could sense the daemon's attention through the bond they shared, the bond that had been created by the binding.

He became aware of the fact that more than the daemon were looking at him. All of the dark elves present gazed upon him expectantly. They knew that something of great significance was planned. They knew that he was about to reveal some great scheme to them. Why else would he have called them all to this conference? Why else would there be so many powerful nobles in the one spot?

Malekith let his eyes scan the chamber. It was a vast war room containing maps of Ulthuan, the most detailed that could be put together by his spies and by use of magic. On it was marked every major fortress, city, town, waystone, garrison and wizard's tower. The mobile forces of the Phoenix King were indicated by small jewelled statuettes. As yet, none of his own forces glittered on the huge map that dominated the centre of the room.

Sometimes eyes strayed to the daemon. They did not know who it, or rather she in her present form, was. They were curious as to why she was present. The sorcerers among them would get some sense of the daemon's power and of the power of the restraints holding it, and that would give them pause for thought.

His mother would have known in a moment, of course, which was one of the reasons she was not here. He had sent her to oversee her barbarian army, letting her believe she was gaining a new lever to use against him while he changed the delicate balance of power within his kingdom forever.

He allowed himself a moment to savour the sensation of the fear and respect and wonder and then he strode forward, knowing that all eyes were completely focused on him though and all of those present were wondering exactly what he was going to do and say.

'We are going to Ulthuan,' Malekith said. 'All of you already know that. All of you know that I intend to reunite the kingdom under my righteous rule and crush the rebels who defied my father's will.'

Dark elves were not usually given to shows of emotion but a few of those present applauded and a brief mutter of excited chatter flowed around the room. Malekith smiled inwardly. By stating the obvious he had piqued their curiosity and got them wondering about what he was really going to say.

All of them knew that he had failed to conquer Ulthuan before and were wondering what was different this time, whether they would come out of the experience better than their forebears had. They all knew that invading the island continent was a titanic risk with commensurate rewards. They were wondering how to minimise the risk to themselves and maximise their potential gains.

They felt themselves to be standing at the centre of things, to be gaining an advantage just by being here. Being nobles, all of them felt that they were entitled to as much as they could grab and all of them felt that they were clever enough to exploit the situation. Malekith did not care. In fact he was counting on it.

'You will be the spearhead of a plan that has been centuries in the making,' said Malekith. He paused to let them consider that. 'I have been planning and forging weapons and binding supernatural allies to aid us. The day that you have all long awaited is at hand. All of you will lead mighty forces to great victories and for the best of you, for those of you who serve me well, the rewards will be gigantic.'

He paused again for a few heartbeats to let them consider that. Some of them were licking their lips. They knew that he did not waste words and they knew that he did not make empty promises any more than he made empty threats.

'My mother, most blessed of matrons, has won us potent allies. From the far northern Chaos Wastes, hundreds of thousands of the followers of the Dark Gods have come to enter our service – although they do not know that yet.'

His last remark was met with a storm of cruel laughter. All of them knew that the humans were mere spear fodder for their asur kindred. The humans would not share in the rewards, Malekith intended to see to that. He had a plan for dealing with them at the end of the campaign that would ensure that was the case. He had no intention of letting his mother keep that particular sword hanging over his neck.

'The force that will accompany us is only a small portion of the human strength. The vast majority of it already sails towards the northern coast of Ulthuan. Of course, it will be spotted by the patrols of the false Phoenix King. The rebels think that that is where the blow will fall and a large proportion of their strength is being diverted to meet that threat. It will be a long time before they realise what is truly happening.'

'I do not intend to rely upon humans to reclaim my rightful kingdom. The honour and duty of that falls upon you, my loyal subjects. You are the ones who will lead in my righteous conquest and reunite the kingdoms. You are the ones who will do the important fighting and you will claim the true rewards of victory. You are the ones upon whom failure will press most heavily.'

All mirth vanished as he spoke the last sentence. They had heard him promise rewards. They knew that he would punish failure as he always did. He had let them know who their master was. It was a task that needed to be performed on a regular basis given the nature of his subjects and their ruthless ambitions.

'Your forces are smaller in number but much greater in skill. You are the ones who will conquer cities and fortresses and claim them for your own.'

Once again he dangled the rewards in front of them and watched them salivate. He had specifically stated that they might claim what they conquered for their own. He could see them performing the calculations almost visibly. Here was a chance that would not come again in their lifetimes to extend their estates, increase their flocks of slaves, bolster their fortunes and surround their names with glory.

'Some of you will lead armies overland in pursuit of great strategic goals. Some of you will have other duties.'

They were wondering now what he meant. Did he mean to punish some of them by denying them the right of conquest and holding them back from the front line of the war? Or did he mean something else? He let them wonder for a few more moments while he let his eyes rest upon each of them in turn.

'All of you must know now that I have made great magical allies and summoned them from the realms beyond our world. All of you are wondering why I have done this when I can rely implicitly on your own warlike skills. The answer is very simple. One of the allies that I have summoned will give us the keys to victory, will let us overcome every enemy army, take every enemy fortress and reach the furthest extent of the rebel kingdom, before our foes even know that we are there.'

A look of concentration passed over every face now – they were all wondering exactly how he proposed to achieve this miraculous feat. It was something that had eluded the greatest of sorcerers through all of the ages and they were wondering whether their king had finally gone mad.

'All of you must know this. I, your king, have bound one of the greatest foes of our people into my service.'

He gestured and N'Kari's true form was revealed. The great four-limbed monster towered over every living thing in the room. It flexed claws that could shear through the thickest armour. It roared and the very sound was thrilling and terrifying.

All of the druchii present, even the bravest, flinched. They wore the same expressions on their faces as they would have if he'd introduced a pack of starving lions into the room.

'Before you stands N'Kari, the Keeper of Secrets, the daemon defeated and banished by my father, who led the Rape of Ulthuan, who was once the greatest foe of all our people. I, Malekith the Great, son of Aenarion, have bound this beast to my service. I have done this knowing full well that given the chance, this foul thing will betray us if it can and knowing that, I will not allow it to do so. I have bound this creature not because I need it to fight for us, although it will kill anyone I tell it to.'

Malekith paused for a beat to let them consider that piece of information. None of them wanted to be the victim of a greater daemon. None of them would go against him in any way while they thought that was a possibility. He wanted them to fully consider the consequences of any rebellion against him.

Particularly, given the fact that he had bound a daemon that was a sworn enemy of their people. He thought it best to get the information out there in the open and to use it for his own advantage.

'The reason I have taken this creature into my service is because it knows the secrets of how to pass swiftly, secretly and unstoppably through the island-continent of Ulthuan. It has done so before and it has taken an army with it. Cast your minds back over a century to the rumours that came out of Ulthuan then. I am in a position to tell you that those rumours were true and that what the merchants of the marketplace whispered is exactly what happened.'

He could see shocked looks passing around the room now. He was giving them a lot to think about in a very short space of time, but he knew they were capable of absorbing it. He also knew it was best to give it to them all at once on his own terms, rather than wait for it to come out piecemeal.

'Of course, my servant failed then because it did not have the force that we have, or the skill at warfare, or the knowledge of when and where it is appropriate to attack. We can succeed where N'Kari failed and we will do so because it is our destiny.

'With the service of this bound daemon we shall be able to move so swiftly that our enemies will not know where we are or how to stop us before it is too late. We will be able to amass our forces to overwhelm our enemies before they know what has hit them. This more than anything else will give us a victory. This time all of Ulthuan will be ours. This time we will succeed. This time victory is inevitable.'

Malekith allowed some of his own enthusiasm to show in his voice. He could see that it was being communicated to his followers by his words and his gestures. All of them had sufficient knowledge of matters military to understand what an enormous advantage N'Kari would give them. All of them were nervous about the presence of the daemon but all of them could see exactly why it was there. There was silence for many heartbeats and even Malekith felt the tension in the room.

After a silence of long moment, all of them cheered. After an initial hesitation all of them were as convinced as he was that victory was their destiny.

'On the table,' Malekith said, 'you will find your orders. These are sealed and you will communicate them to no one except where you are authorised to do so. All of you have a part to play in this great victory. All of you will share in the spoils of victory. All of you will be part of the great historical process of reuniting the kingdom. All of you will be remembered for as long as that kingdom exists and elves gather to talk about great military triumphs.'

The elven nobles present almost came to blows in their haste to reach the table. He knew then that he had them. Then he saw the smile on the face of the daemon and wondered why it looked so happy.

◄ CHAPTER EIGHT ►

Weary almost beyond belief, Tyrion and his companions emerged from the swamp. The last few leagues had been the worst part. They had wandered from the jungle into the marshes surrounding Skeggi. The ground had become treacherous quicksand, mud and stagnant pools filled with the spores of the worst diseases.

All of them except Teclis were covered in filth. His magic had protected him from that. Yet, despite the weariness, despite the dirt, despite the loathsome nature of their surroundings, all of them were triumphant. They had made it all the way back from Zultec without losing anybody else. And the humans were filled with the knowledge that they were rich, while the elves knew that they were going to be even more famous very soon.

Ahead of them they could see the strange wooden longhalls that made up the bulk of the dwellings in Skeggi. They resembled the halls of the Norsemen back in the Old World, but in one important respect they were different – they stood upon stilts that raised them above the mud. Those buildings on the outskirts of the city needed them. Some of them sat in small algae-scummed lakes that resembled moats. The only way to get to them was either by small boat, rope-bridge or by jumping across the stumps of chopped down trees that made up a kind of stepping stone.

Right now the party was up to their waists in muddy water and starting to draw attention from the natives. They were very conspicuous – two tall elves and a small group of survivors from what had been a much larger party when it set out. Some of those present recognised Tyrion, some of them recognised Leiber. All of them were curious as to what the party had done and how they had survived.

Now came the tricky part. Skeggi was a dreadful place, lawless, ruled by feuding warlords and bandit gangs. It combined the worst aspects of Norse society and that of the theoretically more civilised

Old World. Some of the people greeting them now might decide to rob them in a few moments, once a sufficiently large gang of allies had assembled.

They would make formidable foes too. Most of those present were tall, strapping warriors descended from the Norse. They were blond-haired with golden, tanned skins and broad-shouldered, muscular bodies. All of them were armed with heavy axes or sharp swords. After the rigours of the past few weeks Tyrion should not have been too bothered, but he knew the perils of over-confidence and he did not want to fall victim to a random robbery when he was so close to returning to Lothern in triumph.

'If we are attacked, burn as many as possible with the most spectacular magic you can summon,' he said to Teclis in elvish. 'If you should happen to set a few buildings alight in the process so much the better.'

'And what will you be doing while I commit these theatrical acts of arson?'

'I will be killing as many people as I can in the most disgustingly bloody fashion I can manage. If we make an example of enough of them, the rest will leave us alone.'

'It's nice to hear you being so cheerful now that we are so close to safety.'

'No one is safe in Skeggi,' Tyrion said. 'The priests of the goddess of mercy will pick your pocket while they stick a dagger in your back.'

'They are somewhat unorthodox in the way they practise their faith,' said Teclis. 'It's always the way. Heretical sects breed in these out of the way places.'

'Joke about it all you like but be ready...' Tyrion said.

In the distance, Tyrion could see the monstrous brutal structure of the fortress. It was the size of a small town and had been built by a dozen generations of raider lords on the site of the original keep of Losteriksson, the town's legendary founder. The only thing that came close to being as noticeable was the giant barrow that had grown over the spot where Losteriksson had first set foot on this land.

As they progressed deeper into town, more and more people swarmed around them. Some were menacing-looking Norse warriors, others were the sort of shipwrecked wharf rats from the Old World. A few tired looking prostitutes shouted half-hearted terms of endearment at the elves and their companions.

'Leiber, you made it back, I am surprised,' roared someone who obviously recognised their guide. 'You finally find all that lost gold you always raved about?'

It was a leading question if Tyrion had ever heard one, and it was the one most likely to trigger a bloodbath if the wrong answer was given. They had talked about this all the way back but there was no telling what the humans would do now that they were back among their own kind.

In a way Tyrion was glad they had only taken the sword and a few keepsakes. There was not very much for their companions to kill them over. The humans were more likely to get themselves into trouble than the two elves. Of course, that would not make very much difference if they got dragged into a needless fight.

'I got more than enough to buy your mother,' said Leiber. 'But then that only ever cost a couple of coppers anyway, and she would give change.'

It was a good answer. It told the listeners that it was none of their business what Leiber had found and that they could expect only insults if they asked. The question was whether it would be enough to ensure they were left alone.

They pushed through the teeming streets of the town, trying to ignore all of the people staring at them. The fortress loomed over them, bringing back memories of a previous visit that Tyrion would have preferred to forget. He had spent some time in chains in that horrible place and he was determined that it would never happen again.

As they walked on, a sense of ending came over him. He was soon going to have to say goodbye to the humans. Most likely he would never see any of them again. The people he had known on his previous visits to Skeggi were all dead or withered ancients. Human lives were so brief that once their paths separated he was unlikely to come across them again, or if he did they would be so changed as to be almost unrecognisable.

He was not sure why this troubled him. He felt a certain attachment to these men as he would to any comrades with whom he had shared dangers. It seemed that the humans felt the same way because one or two of them were staring at him sidelong.

He sensed that they were at once relieved and saddened by this parting of the ways. They had found what they were looking for. They were wealthy men. Perhaps they felt grateful to Tyrion and his brother for providing them with this wealth or perhaps it was something else entirely, he could not be sure. All he knew was that by the time they had reached a crossroads at the centre of the town, all of them knew that their quest together was over. They were walking more slowly, starting to look at each other in a vaguely embarrassed way.

Leiber was the first to speak. 'It looks like we will be going our separate roads. I just want to say that it was an honour and a privilege travelling with you. I hope one day that we might be able to do it again.'

If he did not sound entirely sincere, at least he was trying to be polite, Tyrion thought. He felt like he was being called upon to answer on behalf of himself and his brother so he said, 'We could not have asked for better travelling companions.'

The humans all nodded and Tyrion found himself shaking hands with his companions. A few moments later they had started to drift apart, most of the humans heading towards one of the low taverns which filled the streets of Skeggi. Tyrion looked at Teclis and smiled sourly, 'It will not take long before word of our discovery is common knowledge in this port.'

'What do you propose we do about that, brother?'

'There is nothing we can do. We just need to hope that the local robbers don't decide to pay us a visit. It would not surprise me to find out that Leiber and the other lads were found in the gutter with their throats cut by this time tomorrow.'

'And you want us to avoid that fate?'

'It would seem sensible, wouldn't it? After all, it would be bitterly ironic if we survived all our adventures only to get ourselves killed in some back alley in this gods-forsaken place.'

'Then I think the first thing we should do is look for a ship out of here.'

'That might just be putting ourselves at the mercy of one of the local pirate captains. They are as much cutthroats as most of the people around here, probably more so.'

'Then perhaps we should look for a trading ship that will take us all the way back to Ulthuan.'

'I suppose that means that you're going to suggest we head down to the docks right now.'

'No time like the present!'

The harbour at Skeggi was a makeshift place of rickety wooden piers flanked by the local longhouses. There were no great warehouses, only the fortified dwellings of the local chieftains. There was a white sand beach on which long ships were drawn up.

Looking as out of place in the harbour as a swan among a flock of ducks was an elven clipper bearing the arms of House Emeraldsea, a golden ship on a field of green. Tyrion was even more surprised by the fact he recognised the vessel. It was the *Eagle of Lothern*, on which he had voyaged during that long ago time when he and his brother had first been summoned back to Lothern.

It was the last thing he would have expected to see in this shabby human town. There was only one reason for one of the great trading vessels belonging to their mother's family to be here – it was seeking himself and his brother. Then he noticed something else. The vessel was flying a black flag.

Someone very important had died.

A sudden shock passed through him as he wondered who it could be. He hoped it was no one in his own house. He had not seen such a flag since his grandfather had died. He hoped it was not someone else that he loved – like Lady Malene.

Two other possibilities sprang immediately to mind – it might be the Phoenix King or the Everqueen. It seemed unlikely that Finubar was dead. He was still very young for an elf and it was unlikely that anything but violence could have killed him.

It was not unknown for a Phoenix King to be assassinated or killed in battle but, as far as Tyrion knew, the elves were not at war with anyone. At least they had not been when he and his brother had left Lothern. Had some major conflict blown up that he had missed? It galled him that he might have lost a chance to win glory for himself and his family.

He saw that someone on the crow's nest was waving at him. They had already been spotted through a spyglass and it looked as if someone on the ship wanted to make contact with them.

Teclis came up beside him and spoke softly. 'This does not look good.'

'I fear you are right, brother. Let us find out what the bad news is.'

'Captain Joyelle, it is a pleasure to meet you once again,' Tyrion said as he pulled himself over the side of the ship. He could tell the captain was pleased that he remembered her name. He was quite famous now and he supposed that meant something.

'I wish it was under more pleasant circumstances,' she said. 'I bear terrible news.'

'What is it?' Teclis asked. He was being lifted up on a bosun's sling. He did not like to scamper up the web of ropes draped over the side of a ship unless he absolutely had to. 'Nothing has happened to Lady Malene, I hope?'

'No, Prince Teclis, the lady of the House is well and sends you her greetings. The bad tidings are that the Everqueen is dead.'

'The Everqueen?' Tyrion's mind reeled. He felt grief well up within his heart. She had been the spiritual leader of the elves for as long as he had been alive and considerably longer. Her blessing was invoked at the start of every major venture, every voyage, every season's crop planting.

'That is terrible news indeed,' Teclis said. 'It is a strange coincidence that you should be waiting here to give it to us.'

'It is no coincidence at all, Prince Teclis,' said the captain. 'I was dispatched to bring the news to your brother and to summon him home.'

Tyrion tilted his head to one side as he concentrated upon the captain. 'Why?'

'A new Everqueen will soon be crowned and a new Everqueen must have a new champion.'

'And what exactly has this to do with my brother?' Teclis asked. These days, he really had not the slightest sensitivity to any of the nuances of politics outside those of the Tower of Hoeth.

Tyrion understood at once. House Emeraldsea wished to have a candidate of their own as the champion of the Everqueen and he was the best possible candidate they could put forward.

Even for one so comparatively young for an elf, he was already a famous warrior. He was good-looking, well spoken, intelligent, diplomatic and he knew all of these things about himself. As the Everqueen's champion he would be ideally placed to help influence her decisions and that would give him, and through him House Emeraldsea, considerable political influence. He understood at once exactly why he was being summoned home.

He was not sure how he felt about this himself. He had plans of his own. There were things he wanted to do with his life. The position would entail a great deal of responsibility and an enormous curtailment of his freedom.

Wherever the Everqueen went her bodyguard went. Her champion was always at her side, ready to protect and fight for her honour. The position had existed ever since the reign of the second Phoenix King. Prior to that no one had ever thought that the

Everqueen needed a bodyguard. But the first Everqueen, Astarielle, had been slain by the followers of Chaos and ever since then
the Everqueen had had a champion at her side.

'Our family wants me to enter the great tournament,' he said.
Captain Joyelle nodded. Teclis's expression suddenly changed. He
understood now. He smiled at Tyrion.

'It is a very great honour,' he said.

'I am fully aware of that fact,' said Tyrion. His sour expression
must have told his listeners that he was less than thrilled by the honour implied. Teclis's eyes narrowed. Captain Joyelle looked slightly
embarrassed.

'I was instructed to bring you this news and to take you home
to Lothern. Lady Malene told me you would eventually find your
way back to Skeggi.'

It was the only possible place they could get a ship out of this part
of Lustria so it was a fair bet. Not that Lady Malene was incapable of
locating them by magic if she wanted to. She was a mighty sorceress.

'Fortunately,' said Teclis, 'our business in the jungles of Lustria is
concluded and we have found what we came for.'

'You have found it?' Captain Joyelle asked.

Tyrion drew Sunfang with a theatrical flourish. Fires danced along
the length of the blade. Captain Joyelle's eyes widened and her
mouth fell open. All of her officers looked stunned. As well they
might, thought Tyrion. They had just come face-to-face with one
of the great legends of the first and mightiest kings of the elves.

'Is that...' asked Captain Joyelle.

'It is Sunfang,' said Teclis. He could not keep his satisfaction from
showing in his voice. 'The sword of Aenarion, forged by Caledor
Dragontamer himself at Vaul's Anvil in the dawn ages of the world.'

'I never thought that in my lifetime this blade would be recovered,' said Joyelle. 'You have brought us some happiness in this time
of great distress, Prince Tyrion. May Isha bless you.'

Teclis's sour expression showed that he understood what was
going on. He was used to the fact that his brother would get the
credit for any of their joint ventures. Tyrion wondered if he really
cared about it all that much. He supposed that it might get annoying, but there was nothing either of them could do about it. It
seemed sometimes as if there was a conspiracy among the elves
to ignore any of the achievements of his brother and heap praise
upon him. There were times when Tyrion felt very guilty about
that.

He did not have time to feel that way now. There were other things he needed to consider.

Morathi strode into her son's audience chamber aware that all eyes were upon her. The courtiers stared. The assembled warlords of the great Houses looked at her with lust. She kept her face impassive, giving no clue to her inner turmoil.

When she had heard the stories she had left the Chaos horde and her own army and taken the fastest ship she could find back to Naggaroth. She needed to know whether the tales her spies had brought were true and one glance was enough to tell her that they were.

Morathi stared at the daemon that looked like a girl and found that it was as bad as she had feared. She could not quite believe what her son had done. She did not know whether to be proud or angry so she settled for both. Malekith had bound a Keeper of Secrets to his will. It was a feat of astonishing boldness. Such creatures were treacherous and powerful beyond belief and could turn on their summoners with fatal consequences in the space of a heartbeat.

And yet, he had done it.

The daemon was there and appeared to be under control, standing amid a crowd of dark elves who had no idea of how close death hovered.

The infernal thing was well bound by those strange alien shackles and yet Morathi still did not feel entirely secure. It was like being in the same room as a chained lion. The beast might not be able to get free, but you still would not want to put your hand into its mouth. Morathi glanced around at the elves present.

'Beloved son, I would have words with you in private.' All eyes moved from her to Malekith. She could see the druchii present were afraid and rightly so. None of them wished to offend her, but disobeying her son would be instantly fatal.

Malekith nodded. The elves began to filter out of the chamber, leaving mother, son and bound daemon alone. Morathi looked at the daemon and then at Malekith. She kept her anger under control, not a thing she would normally have any cause to do, but it was always counter-productive to rage at her son. He only became more icy and controlled.

'What have you done?' she asked eventually.

Malekith merely loomed over her. The armour gave him awesome presence. He seemed less like a living being than the daemon he had bound. He said nothing. It was obvious he was going to force her hand.

'You have bound a greater daemon of Slaanesh to your service. Do you know what that means?'

'It means I have found the key to unlock the defences of Ulthuan.'

'Maybe. It also means you have acquired the eternal enmity of an infernal being.'

Malekith surprised her by laughing. 'I had that anyway. This is the creature that had sworn to wipe out the line of Aenarion. That is what makes this so amusing.'

'You find this amusing?'

'N'Kari, Chosen of Slaanesh, meet my mother, Morathi, consort of Aenarion. The two of you should be friends. You have much in common.'

The daemon and the sorceress exchanged looks. Malekith's metallic laughter grew louder and colder. It was worse even than she had imagined. This was the creature that had led the Rape of Ulthuan, who had twice been beaten by Aenarion, who had every reason to hate her son and work his undoing.

'You will destroy us all,' said Morathi.

'I think, dearest mother, that is your plan, not mine.'

Morathi gave Malekith a searching look. How much did he really know? How much had he guessed? The fact that he had bound this abomination showed one thing. He had come a very long way as a wizard. He was to be numbered among the greatest mages, living or unliving, since these days one had to take into account certain undead abominations when making the calculation.

The daemon merely looked at them and smiled. She guessed that Malekith might be doing the same beneath his metal mask but she could not be certain.

'Oh yes, mother, I know of your schemes. I just wanted you to know that I will not allow them.'

'You will not... allow them!' Her anger showed in her voice this time. At once she knew it was a mistake but she could not help herself. Her pride and her fear had both been aroused. Any other living thing in the world would have cowered before her unveiled wrath. The metal monster her son had become just stood there impassive as a statue. 'Who are you to forbid me to do anything?'

'I am your king. I think you forget that sometimes. I am the absolute and unchallenged ruler of Naggaroth and soon of the whole elven world.'

Morathi wanted to rage, but something about the confidence that gleamed in his voice gave her pause. 'And when did you propose to tell me how this will be accomplished?' she asked.

'In good time, mother, although I am sure you can work it out for yourself given your undoubted knowledge and your gift of fore-sight. Or your spies will tell you. I just want to make sure there are no misunderstandings between us.'

'I am sure I do not know what you mean?'

'Let us say that if I find you have been disturbing the pattern of Caledor's work, I will give you to my pet here as a plaything. You would like that, wouldn't you, N'Kari?'

The bound daemon smiled and nodded.

'You will have to forgive her for not being more conversational,' Malekith said. 'I have forbidden her to speak until I am convinced she will be civil.'

Rage and fear warred within Morathi but she let neither show on her face. The fact that her son knew or had guessed her plans made no difference to her determination to carry them out. It would only make the process more difficult and the stakes higher. She smiled a genuine smile this time. This only made things more interesting.

'Return to your barbarian army, mother, and see that it carries out its duties well.'

'Of course, beloved son. How could I do otherwise?'

'Soon the invasion begins. You will be queen once more in Ulthuan.'

And more than queen, my son, Morathi thought. The daemon smiled as if it understood what was going through her mind.

⫷ CHAPTER NINE ⫸

'So what now?' Teclis asked.

Tyrion stared off into the distance. The sea stretched as far as the horizon, black, oily, reflecting the moon and the night sky. Already Tyrion felt better for being out of the jungle. He was wearing clean clothes for the first time in months. He was not being eaten alive by mosquitoes as he slept. He had eaten shipboard rations and even though it was very basic by most standards, it was food that he liked. He could hear elvish being spoken all around him, and he was reassured to be once more surrounded by his own people.

For the first time in a very long while, he felt like he could go to sleep securely and not have to fear waking in some terrible peril. And of course, because this was the case, for the first time in months he was having difficulty sleeping.

It did not surprise him to find his brother upon the deck. Teclis was a night person. He liked to be awake and studying while others slept. It was a habit he had acquired in their youth when he had difficulty falling asleep because of his numerous illnesses. It had never left him, even now after he had used alchemy to acquire almost normal health.

He was glad that Teclis was awake. He felt the need to talk to someone about what troubled him and his brother was one of the few people who he could do that with, even though they were no longer as close as they had once been when they were children.

'I could not sleep,' said Tyrion.

'That is strange,' said Teclis. 'Normally by now you would be lying there snoring, keeping the rest of us awake. Do you miss the jungle? Is the alarming absence of danger getting on your nerves?'

'Something like that,' said Tyrion. 'I have been thinking about the future.'

'I know how thinking always disturbs you. I am not surprised that you cannot sleep. My advice to you is give up on that. Thinking is not something that suits you. Doing is more your style.'

Normally Tyrion would not have minded his brother's teasing but right now he was not in the mood for it.

'I am serious,' he said. 'I am not sure that I like being summoned home in order to be put forward as a candidate in some political contest.'

He spoke softly so that no one might hear them. He did not want word of his doubts getting back to the ruler of House Emeraldsea, at least not until he was certain that he wanted them to.

'Would it be so bad being the champion of the Everqueen?' Teclis asked. 'It is a great honour. One of the greatest that any elf could ever aspire to.'

Tyrion considered his words carefully. He had rarely even hinted at his secret ambitions to anyone, even his brother, over the past century. He was not sure that he wanted to do so even now. His grandfather had been the only elf he ever really talked to about them, and Lord Emeraldsea had shared them. 'I know. It's just that I am not sure it is an honour I want. I have been thinking about other things.'

Teclis raised an eyebrow. 'Such as?'

'You remember when we were young, you dreamed of being a great wizard. I dreamed of being a great warrior. I wanted to be a hero.'

'You *are* a hero,' said Teclis. For once he sounded serious. There was no mockery in his voice. Tyrion was surprised and rather touched.

'That was the dream of a boy,' said Tyrion. 'I have other dreams now. I want to lead armies. I want to do something to help our people in this world.'

'You want to write your name in the history books,' said Teclis.

'Not just that.'

'You have... political ambitions? You have set your sights on the Phoenix Throne?'

'What if I have?' Tyrion asked.

'I am not judging you, brother,' said Teclis. 'I thought you were happy to be a simple warrior. I had not dreamed that you aimed so high.'

'Neither did I, not really. And I'm not even sure about them myself. I would just like to keep my options open.'

'And you think that becoming the champion of the Everqueen would limit you in some way.'

'You know it would! The champion must be at the Everqueen's side. The only time he can ever leave it is when she dispatches him on a mission. Being the champion of the Everqueen is to be nothing more than a glorified lackey. That is not what I imagined my life would be like.'

'Then don't do it. You don't have to. You don't even have to enter the lists if you don't want to.'

'You're being very simple, brother. House Emeraldsea has made an investment in us. They want to see it repaid.'

'I am astonished to hear myself say this but I think you are being too cynical. You are an ornament to the House. You add a certain lustre to their name just by existing. You are a hero of the blood of Aenarion. Without you they would be known only as the wealthiest merchants in Lothern.'

For such a clever elf, Teclis could be astonishingly naive when it came to politics. 'Our beloved relatives are playing a very long and deep game. Like all the great Houses, they seek power not just prestige. You and I are counters in that game, pieces on a board. They want us where we will be most useful.'

Teclis steepled his fingers and smiled coldly. 'And you think you would not be useful as Phoenix King.'

'I have never said I want to be Phoenix King.'

'You have all the qualifications. You have the looks, the charisma, the intelligence, the reputation...'

'The gold? The political support?'

'So you *do* want to be Phoenix King.'

'What male elf does not?'

'I, for one.'

'You are a special case. You love nothing more than magic.'

'There are many other special cases.'

'Look, brother. I do not know whether I want to be Phoenix King, or whether I have what it takes to be one. I do know that in order to become Phoenix King, you need a lot of powerful political allies and a lot of money. A good deal of horse-trading goes into the making of our ruler. If I wanted to be Phoenix King, I would need the support of Emeraldsea, and a great deal more.'

'I understand.'

'I will never get that support if I alienate Lady Emeraldsea now.'

'I understand that also. What I don't understand is why you think she would not want you to be Phoenix King.'

'I don't think that. What I think is that Finubar is young and already a powerful ally of our kin. He is not likely to die any time soon. And in the meantime I think she would prefer to have a definite hold on the Everqueen than a warrior who might never become Phoenix King many centuries hence.'

Teclis nodded slightly, as if he were finally seeing the point. 'A bird in the hand beats a Phoenix in the future.'

'Yes.'

'It does not matter.'

'I can assure you it does.'

'Your life will be long, Tyrion. You can't predict how things will turn out.'

'I can predict that if I do not do what is asked of me now then Malene will never support me, nor will any of her successors.'

'Then do what she asks, go to the tournament and lose.'

Tyrion looked at his brother in wonder. Was it possible that even after all these years Teclis did not understand him?

Teclis smiled again. 'No, you could not do that, could you? You have never liked to lose at anything. Is that what is really bothering you? The possibility that here is a competition you might not win.' The mockery had returned to his voice.

Tyrion shook his head. 'The thing that bothers me is the possibility that I *might* win.'

Teclis lay on the deck and stared up at the stars. The gentle rise and fall of the ship helped him relax. He remembered how, long ago, he had been plagued by seasickness and what a torment that had been. Now, like most of the other ailments, it was just a memory. It was odd how things that had dominated his life for so long could just vanish, leaving behind only strange dream-like recollections.

Of course, yesterday he and his brother had been in the jungles of Lustria. Now they were aboard the *Eagle of Lothern* scudding across the ocean. The jungle was the dream now, the ocean the reality.

Strange thoughts raced through his head. What was time? How did it work? What is this process that keeps us moving inexorably into the future at the same rate every day? Is it true that gods and daemons live outside time and are aware of multiple selves, in all places, at all times? Is that how their prophets are sometimes given glimpses of the future?

He considered Tyrion. To most people his brother always seemed the very epitome of the devil-may-care warrior, living life to the fullest now, because tomorrow he might be dead. Teclis knew his twin was cleverer than that, and much more thoughtful.

Did Tyrion really aspire to the Phoenix Throne or was this about something different entirely? Was he simply afraid of being tied down, of assuming responsibility? Teclis doubted it was the latter. Tyrion had commanded troops in the field. He was not frightened by that sort of responsibility at all. Perhaps it was the loss of freedom of action that he feared, of being drawn into the web of social entanglements that all elves eventually found themselves ensnared in.

Both he and Tyrion owed House Emeraldsea a debt. Their kindred had aided them, supported them, paid for their education, given them their start in life. Lady Malene had seen to it that Teclis had received the best training at the White Tower. Both of them were aware that one day those debts would be called in and need to be repaid, his own as much as Tyrion's.

Teclis was not troubled by that. When the time came he would worry about it. Right now he had other things to think of. Perhaps that was Tyrion's problem. He could lose himself only in action, in doing. When he was not, he fretted. His was not a nature suited to being at rest. He craved action, distraction.

Perhaps his brother was not really suited to be Phoenix King because of that. The elves did not need another war-seeking ruler. The thought seemed disloyal but it haunted Teclis for the rest of the night.

'I would like to look at that sword,' Teclis said. He had entered his brother's cabin in the dawn light. Tyrion was already awake, lying on the bunk, staring at the ceiling.

Tyrion shrugged, unfastened the sword-belt and passed it over to him. He did not seem particularly self-conscious about disarming himself in the way most warriors would. Teclis supposed it was because his brother trusted him, and also because he had no doubts he could get the weapon back if it was needed.

Teclis pulled the blade from its scabbard. For a moment, it felt as heavy to him as it really was. He had managed to restore his health by the use of alchemy but he would never be strong. He could feel Sunfang straining his fingers and his wrist. Only for a moment though, then the blade glistened, glowing as if flames were trapped within the metal, and it felt light enough even for him. Teclis smiled with pleasure.

'So it works for you too,' said Tyrion.

'Of course,' Teclis replied. 'Very useful.'

'It takes some getting used to,' said Tyrion. 'The weight and balance seem to adjust as you wield it. It's like a living thing.'

Teclis swept the sword through the air. It left a glowing trail behind it, faintly visible even without the use of his magesight. He smiled with pure pleasure.

'Careful,' said Tyrion. 'I don't want you taking my head off accidentally.'

'It might make you smarter,' said Teclis.

'Think of the pain it would cause the ladies of Ulthuan.'

Teclis would have responded but he was too busy concentrating on the sword. The enchantments designed to make it easy to wield were only one part of the complex web of magic pinned in place by the runes on the blade.

There were other spells present, fascinatingly complex ones which hinted at great power. Filled with curiosity, he extended his thoughts and activated one. A jet of flame blasted from the point of the blade. Only Tyrion's lightning reflexes kept him out of the way. He sprang to one side and the flame hit the porthole setting it glowing.

Panicked, Teclis sought to bring it under control. The jet of flame set the bedding alight before he managed to douse the fire blazing from the point of the blade.

Tyrion threw the porthole open, picked the burning blankets up and cast them through the window. He blew on his slightly burned hands. His face was sooty, his jerkin singed.

'How much is House Silverbright paying you for my assassination?' Tyrion asked. 'Tell me, I will double it.'

It was a line from a melodrama popular in the theatres of Ulthuan when they had left. He was smiling as he said it.

Teclis was anything but amused. He was embarrassed and frightened by what he had done. He could easily have hurt his twin, possibly injuring him permanently. 'I am so sorry,' he said. 'I did not mean to do that.'

Tyrion grinned. 'If I thought you had, you would not be holding that blade. Nor would you be conscious.'

He did not say it as a threat, simply as a statement of fact. Teclis knew that it was exactly the case as well.

Tyrion spoke more softly now. 'Learn a lesson. I saw that look of concentration come over your face, the one you get when you are lost in the contemplation of the wonders of magic and I knew you were about to do something extremely stupid. When the point of the sword started glowing I was certain of it. Was that you or the sword that did the trick with the flame, by the way?'

'It was the sword. There is a spell woven into it. At the blade's heart, Caledor trapped one of the elemental spirits of the volcano. It burns in there, its life force powering the blade. You can unleash part of it by contacting the spirit.'

'Useful. Having a sword that lets you breathe fire like a dragon, I mean. Nice to know the trick is still possible. I had always thought the ancient tales exaggerated.'

'You would not want to do it too often. You might over-draw the life force of the elemental and unravel all the magic in the sword. If you use it, you need to give the sword time to regain its health. Using its magic in that way is like an elf losing a lot of blood. It takes time to recover.'

'You think I could learn to use it then.' Teclis knew his brother had noted away what he was saying but as always seemed concerned only with his own purposes. They were very alike in that way.

'Undoubtedly. It was intended for use by a warrior, not a wizard.'

'Excellent.' Tyrion sounded genuinely pleased. 'How do I do it?'

'I will endeavour to find out if you will allow me to concentrate.'

'Just don't concentrate too hard. I don't want you stumbling on some new way to accidentally kill me.'

Teclis nodded. It was not a mistake he was going to make again. 'If I do find a way to kill you, it won't be accidental,' he said. It came out more ominously than he meant it to. Tyrion just grinned his idiot grin, as if certain that nothing in this world could really harm him. Teclis sincerely hoped that really was the case.

He was embarrassed and angry at himself and displacing it onto his twin, which was not fair. 'I did not mean that,' he said.

'I know,' said Tyrion. 'Just find a way to let me use the sword. I will leave you to it. Try not to set fire to the ship. It's a long swim to Ulthuan.'

'I can't swim,' said Teclis.

'All the more reason for being careful then,' said Tyrion as he left the cabin.

Urian stared into the mirror and waited for contact to come. How many times had he stood here over the past few centuries, he wondered? How many times had he made the strange pilgrimage through the underground labyrinth beneath the Silvermount Palace to find this place? How many more times would he have to do so?

The answers did not come. At the moment, his master did not seem to want to put in an appearance either. Urian made himself look devoted and alert. He was never sure exactly how the magical mirror worked, whether Malekith could see him even when he could not see the Witch King. Knowing the way his master's mind worked it was entirely possible.

Suddenly the colours in the mirror swirled, Urian's sardonically smiling reflection vanished to be replaced by the monstrous armoured figure of his master. He lounged like a massive, animated statue on his gigantic metal throne.

Standing beyond and behind Malekith, held on chains like a hound on a leash, was the second most astonishingly beautiful elf woman Urian had ever seen. Only Morathi was more lovely and she was not there to be compared, so it was possible this one's beauty exceeded even hers. She looked much younger and much more innocent than Morathi, but that meant nothing. Urian was well aware of how deceptive appearances could be.

There was something about the chains on this one's limbs that worried him, a magic that dazzled the eye and tired the brain. He let his eyes linger on her, wondering who she was. From behind Malekith's back, she winked at him. So she could see him and was aware of who he was. That might prove to be a bad thing in the long run.

'You are to be congratulated, Urian.' Malekith's voice emerged from the mirror with perfect cold clarity. The Witch King sounded as pleased as Urian had ever heard him. 'The Everqueen is dead. Your reward will be extraordinary.'

'Serving you is reward enough, my liege.' Urian was proud that he managed to keep any trace of irony from his voice. There were times when he could get away with that in front of his master but instinct told him that now was not such a time.

'Please, Urian, let us not even pretend that is so,' said Malekith. 'I am your liege, and it is my duty and my pleasure to reward my favoured vassals.'

'In that case, I await your magnanimity with breathless anticipation, my lord.'

'You shall not have to wait too long. Within this year I will have vast new estates to disburse to my most loyal subjects.'

Despite the fact he had long awaited this moment, excitement stabbed at Urian's vitals. So it was finally going to happen then – the long-awaited invasion of Ulthuan for which secret preparations had been going on for centuries. 'I am thrilled to hear it, my liege.'

'It pleases me that you managed to carry out your last task without being discovered. It means you will be in place to exceed yourself when our forces come to Lothern.'

'You have given the orders for the re-conquest of Ulthuan, sire?'

There was an eerie, evil joy in Malekith's voice that Urian had never heard before. 'I have. Hold yourself in readiness for further instructions. Within a moon, the world will be changed forever for the better. Perform your duties well and I will give you Lothern for your fief.'

It was astonishing generosity on Malekith's part. He would be satrap of the richest and most glamorous city in the world. The opportunities to become wealthy would be limitless and he was already intimately acquainted with the citizens. They would hate him of course, as a traitor and a turncoat, even more than they hated the Witch King. He wondered how long Malekith had planned this for. From the beginning was Urian's guess.

'What do you have to say, Urian?' It was clear that an answer was required.

'My apologies, liege. I was simply overwhelmed by your generosity. It rendered me speechless.'

'Then I have been generous indeed to achieve such a miracle,' said Malekith laughing.

His good humour was even more terrifying than his wrath.

Tyrion strode into Lady Emeraldsea's audience chamber. It was his grandfather's old office and little had changed since that ancient elf had occupied it.

Malene looked up from the account book she had been reading as he entered, her amber eyes hidden behind copper-framed bi-focals. She was as beautiful and severe-looking as ever but there was something different about her, something that made her seem older, even if she did not look it. She had been that way since her father died and she had taken over the running of the House. The responsibilities pressed down heavily on her.

'You wanted to see me as soon as possible and here I am, aunt,' Tyrion said. 'I have come straight from the ship. My brother has gone to our old house since you stated you wished to see me alone.'

Malene looked a little hurt. She had always preferred Teclis to him. 'Prince Tyrion, how good of you to join me. We have been wondering where you were.'

'We were in Lustria, aunt,' said Tyrion. 'As well you know.'

'And I trust you found whatever was so important as to take you there at this critical period in history.'

'Yes, my lady, we did. We found Sunfang, the sword of Aenarion, believed lost centuries ago.'

'Where is it?'

'Teclis has it. He wished to inspect it, to divine its mysteries. You know what he is like when it comes to new magic.'

'It has been a long time since anyone saw that blade,' said Malene. 'May it bring you more luck than it brought its previous bearers.'

'I was grieved to hear of the death of the Everqueen,' said Tyrion, wanting to get down to the true business of the evening.

'As were we all, Tyrion,' said Malene. 'We are all deeply grieved by the loss. However, life must go on. A new Everqueen has been crowned and her new champion must be chosen.'

'And you believe me to be a suitable candidate for that position,' said Tyrion.

'There is no one in our House better qualified. It is a great honour to be the champion of our new queen. Do you consider yourself worthy?'

Tyrion did not like Malene's tone. 'I should think that there is no honour in Ulthuan that a descendant of Aenarion is unworthy of.'

'It is good that you take such pride in your lineage. However, these are new times, and being of ancient blood is no longer sufficient qualification for any position in our realm. Merit counts for something as well.'

'I believe my deeds speak for themselves,' said Tyrion.

'I'm glad that you feel that way – you will soon have a chance to prove those words.'

Tyrion felt inclined to rise to the challenge just so he could prove her wrong, but he fought down the urge. If he was going to do something, he was going to do it because he wanted to, not because someone had played on his emotions.

'I take it then that you wish me to enter the lists,' said Tyrion.

'You take it correctly,' said Malene. 'I don't think it would do you any harm to be settled down in a position of responsibility. You have developed a reputation for being something of a rake and a brawler recently and it reflects badly on both yourself and this House. And there is no greater responsibility in all of the realms than the safety of our queen.'

Tyrion was not pleased by her comment about his being a rake. It stung a little, not least because there was some truth to the accusation. He knew his relationship with the Lady Valeria had put one of his family's oldest and most precious alliances in peril. Of course, he was not the only party who had caused that particular crisis.

'But there is more to the position than merely being her bodyguard, isn't there?' Tyrion said.

His aunt gave him a wintry smile. 'I don't think you will find some of those duties particularly onerous. Many would consider them a pleasure, in fact. They say the new queen is very beautiful. But then they always do.'

'But that is not why you want me to seek this position, is it?'

'Of course not, Tyrion. If you become champion, you will spend a lot of time in the company of the Everqueen and your opinion will become of considerable importance to her. The new Everqueen is very young and very impressionable and you are a very impressive elf.'

'And I should make sure that her opinion of House Emeraldsea is a good one.'

'As ever, your understanding of the situation is swift and accurate. But there are other good reasons for wanting you to take this position.'

'And what would those be?'

To his surprise, Malene lowered her voice. A worried look flickered across her face. 'Something bad is happening, Tyrion. I can feel it. I don't know what it is yet but I want us to be ready when it comes.'

'What do you mean?'

'We insure a lot of ships. The number of ships lost on the northern routes is so low that we have made more money than at any other point in my lifetime even after reducing the premiums.'

'And you think this is a bad omen?'

'It is unnatural, Tyrion. We normally count on losing some ships to druchii piracy. We have lost nothing for years. Nothing at all.'

'They say the druchii are dying out.'

'I do not believe it. I think the Witch King is merely quiescent.'

'I hope you are wrong.'

'So do I, but I am not. Something has changed in the world, something about the winds of magic. They blow stronger than they have during my lifetime and they are strangely tainted. I am not the only mage who has noticed this. Others are as troubled as I am.'

'This is more my brother's field than mine.'

'I fear it will disturb all our lives before long. I fear we must be prepared for the world taking a darker turn. That is why I want you with the Everqueen. She is young and has much to learn, and she may not have much time to get ready.'

'Ready for what?'

'I don't know but whatever it is, it will be bad. We have lived too long, too peacefully. We have grown lax. The cults of luxury are growing strong again. More of our young people than ever are joining them.'

Tyrion wondered whether Malene, all appearances to the contrary, was starting to succumb to the weaknesses of old age. Perhaps soon she would be explaining to him how much better things had been in her youth. He pushed these thoughts to one side. He knew his aunt better than that. There were other things he wanted to talk about.

'My grandfather always claimed, in private and to me at least, that he had ambitions for me,' Tyrion said.

'I know he did.'

'One day he wanted me to be seated on the Phoenix Throne.'

'That is not in the least surprising.'

'How do you feel about that?'

'I would be proud and happy if that happened.'

'I do not see how it can if I am to be a servant of the Everqueen.'

'So that is what is troubling you – I was wondering.'

'You must admit it would be difficult for me to go from being the champion of the Everqueen to the throne itself.'

'Difficult, yes. Impossible, no. Contrary to what you appear to think, Tyrion, you would not be her slave. Nor would your service to her be eternal.'

'Most champions serve until they or their queen dies.'

'Most do, it is true, but not all. You can resign the position.'

'That is not very honourable.'

'True, but if you had duties to your family that required you to be present or if you were summoned to be a candidate for the throne...'

'I don't think it would be good for my reputation.'

'And you must always keep that in mind, mustn't you?'

'You know I must. If your father's dream is to be fulfilled.'

Malene laughed. 'And yours, of course.'

Tyrion tried to voice his frustration. 'I do not even know if I truly want to be Phoenix King but I would like to have the option open to me, if I decide in favour.'

He wondered if he should mention the prophecy that had been made about him by the priests at the Shrine of Asuryan when he had been tested long ago. He decided not to. He had never mentioned it to anyone but his brother.

'I understand, Tyrion. But Finubar is young and may reign for a thousand years. In the meantime, you can best serve your House by doing what I ask.'

'What if I don't want to?'

'All of us have to do things we don't want to, Tyrion. I would rather be studying the Art, or aiding Teclis with his inspection of the sword of Aenarion right now, but my father is dead, and someone must look after our interests. In a few centuries you will be better qualified to do that than I.'

'I am not sure I want that position either.'

'You may not have much choice if I am not here. Who else will look out for your brother's interests or your father's? Prince Arathion has burned through all the money you left for him, buying materials to repair the dragon armour of Aenarion, performing more research into its history. So far I have covered his notes of hand, but I cannot keep doing so forever.'

And there was the stick, Tyrion thought. Someone was always going to have to look out for his father. Tyrion had left him enough money to keep a noble house in luxury for decades and already it was gone. He supposed he could have words with his father, but he knew how useless that was. His father would simply forget them as soon as Tyrion was out of sight.

'And what is my reward to be, if I am successful?'

'I should have thought that becoming the champion of the Everqueen was reward enough. But, in case that is not enough for you, my young horse trader, be assured that you will have our gratitude.'

Tyrion knew exactly what Malene meant. He was sure that the House would show its gratitude whenever he did something to its advantage. He was also beginning to become aware that the position was one that came with a measure of power attached to it. It was not the sort of power that he cared for or that he wanted to have, but he could see that it might be useful to him in the future. More to the point, it was a source of power completely independent of Malene and his kindred. It would be his and his alone.

'When do I leave?'

His aunt nodded, gratified.

'A ship is being prepared to take you to Avelorn. Anything that you require shall be provided for you. Clothing, gifts, horses – name it and you shall have it. We want you to make a good impression, after all.'

'I shall do my best, since it is so important.'

'And Tyrion...'

'Yes?'

'It might be best if you did not see Lady Valeria before you went.'

Tyrion grimaced. Something else was on his mind. 'How much would it take to cover my father's debts?'

Malene named the sum.

'Transfer it from my account to his. And add a further thousand in gold.'

'But Tyrion, that is almost all you have.'

'It is only money,' said Tyrion. 'I can always get more.'

She looked at him, and saw at once the point he was making. His aunt was a clever woman. He was letting her know he could only be pushed so far even by threats to his father.

'Not all elves are so lucky,' she said.

Carrying Sunfang, Teclis entered the family home. Tyrion had already gone to the Emeraldsea mansion to talk with its mistress. Teclis was hurt that Malene had summoned Tyrion and not him.

He had always felt that she preferred him to Tyrion but since she had become the head of the House she had spent more time with his brother than with him. Of course, Tyrion showed a great deal more interest in the business of the House and spent a lot more time in Lothern than he did.

'Greetings, Prince Teclis,' said Rose. She curtseyed respectfully, as any retainer to a noble elven household was expected to. She was a human, an indentured servant, a slave by any other name. It was all the fashion in Lothern these days although still illegal in the rest of Ulthuan. She was pretty too... for a human. She looked at him in a way that no elf maid ever had. 'It is good to have you home.'

'It is good to be home,' Teclis lied. He was not glad to be back in Lothern, even after a week at sea. He was certainly not glad to be back in this place.

The walls of the old family house hemmed Teclis in. Childhood memories of sickness and pain came surging back. He had never liked this place and yet it was part of the fabric of his being. With the wealth Tyrion had acquired raiding and trading, they could afford to re-open it. They could afford to have retainers and indentured servants. Their father had moved in and shipped all of his research material back from the wild mountains of Cothique.

'Can I get you anything?' Rose asked.

'See that a fire is lit in my bedchamber and please notify Prince Arathion that I am home.'

'Your father is out, visiting Korhien Ironglaive I believe, sir.'

'Thank you. Perhaps you could have a light supper prepared and sent to the first floor living room.'

'At once, sir.'

Teclis made his way into a richly appointed waiting room, laid Sunfang down on the table, poured some mildly narcotic wine into a golden goblet and stretched out in a comfortable leather-bound chair beside the fire.

It was all very different from the grinding poverty he remembered from his early childhood. Here in Lothern he found all sorts of thoughts and resentments came crowding in.

It was funny that his brother had the gift of managing money so easily and so well. He and his father had always seen Tyrion as the least intelligent one of them, but the truth of the matter was that his brother was much cleverer than they were about many things. As with everything he set his mind to, he did it well. He had mastered the making of money as easily as he had mastered the use of weapons, perhaps because in this day and age, the two were so closely connected.

Tyrion had made a small fortune during the raids on Naggaroth and he had invested the proceeds in some spectacularly successful trading voyages and the purchase of land which had been leased at high rents to the new breed of human trader down in the port.

Tyrion was now part owner of a number of trading ships and shared the profits of all their voyages. Having re-established the foundations of prosperity for their branch of the family he seemed to have lost all interest in the subject, delegating the management to competent retainers recruited from House Emeraldsea.

Teclis liked to think that he could have done the same, but he found the process too dull to bother with. His interests were magic and scholarship. He was grateful that his brother was generous enough to share his wealth but he resented it. It was just one more way in which he was beholden to his twin. He sometimes felt there would be no end to his obligations. His brother was an expert in using his generosity to bind people to him. Even his kindness came with invisible strings attached.

By Isha, he was in a sour mood tonight. He took another sip of the wine. It tingled on his tongue. He knew he was simply a little depressed. The great Lustrian adventure was over and he was back in Lothern with work to do and all the tiny, encroaching obligations that entailed. He should start inspecting Sunfang but at this moment he struggled to find the energy.

It was a mental thing not a physical one. Drugs, diet, sorcery and a regime of exercise had done much to compensate for the weakness and physical handicaps the diseases of his youth had caused. None of these things could rid him of the mental lassitude he now felt, nor make him any less of an outsider in society. All of them still looked at him sidelong, with secret contempt. He was sure of it. They had done ever since he was young, and would do so until the day he died.

In Lustria, with Tyrion and the humans, he had felt at ease. His brother had never held him in contempt and to the humans he was just another elf, a blessed immortal. If anything, his magical talents had made him seem even more god-like than Tyrion to them.

Perhaps that was why his initial reaction on his return was to come back to this house and lock himself away. He wanted to keep himself from view. To be out of sight of other elves. He let out a long breath. He was back and he had work to do.

A sound in the doorway alerted him. He looked up to see his father standing there. Prince Arathion looked older and even more decrepit than Teclis remembered. His cheeks were sunken and hollow and his eyes had a bright mad gleam to them.

'I heard you had returned, my son,' his father said. His voice at least was the same as Teclis remembered it. Light, aristocratic, a little sad, with something of the fussy air of the life-long scholar. 'I came back as soon as the news reached me.'

'It is good to see you, father,' said Teclis. It was too. He had always been fond of his father, who was one of the few elves who never seemed to judge him, and who, if anything, judged in his favour.

'Do you have it?' his father asked. The excitement was unmistakable in his voice. There was no need to ask what *it* was. Teclis nodded. He gestured to the table on which the blade rested.

His father crossed the distance in two strides and lifted Sunfang. He was getting weak in his old age, and needed the use of both hands to do so until the magic of the sword took over. He unsheathed the blade, and flames danced along its length. The brilliance of the illumination sent shadows skittering away to the far corner of the room. His father smiled and in that moment, Teclis found that all of the hardships of his long quest were repaid. A look of combined awe, wonder and pure unalloyed happiness passed across his father's face.

He twisted the blade back and forth in front of him, inspecting it from every angle. 'Astonishing,' he said, at last. 'Absolutely astonishing. I would not have thought it possible after all these years but you did it. You found it!'

'Indeed we did, father. There were times when I did not believe we could either.'

Prince Arathion looked as if he wanted to jump for joy. He shifted his weight from one leg to the other as if he wanted to dance. 'It still functions,' he said, as if he could not quite believe it. 'The fires of Vaul's Anvil are still bound within it.'

There was something about his excitement that was contagious. Teclis found himself nodding enthusiastically. His father sheathed the blade and placed it reverentially back on the table. He looked at the glass of wine in Teclis's hand, nodded and poured himself one. He drank it down in one long gulp, and then poured another glass which he just held in one trembling hand, as if he had suddenly forgotten all about it.

'I can't believe it,' he said again. He sounded as if he wanted to cry. He placed the glass down, walked across the room and ruffled Teclis's hair. Teclis recoiled, surprised and embarrassed by the physical contact. His father had never been the most demonstrative of elves and they were not the most demonstrative of families. 'I can't believe it.'

'Well, it's done and now the real work begins,' said Teclis.

His father did not seem to be paying him much attention. He walked back over to the table, put down the glass, picked up the sword, partially unsheathed it and then slammed it back. 'Just think, my son, once Aenarion held this blade in his hand. Aenarion! The first Phoenix King carried this sword through most of his early battles with the forces of Chaos.'

'I know, father,' said Teclis gently, now starting to get slightly worried by his father's excitement.

'I am holding in my hand the sword that Aenarion once held.'

'I am sure he probably held it a lot better,' said Teclis.

His father gave a small start and put the sword down once again as if he was frightened of breaking it. Silence filled the room for long moments until Rose brought in Teclis's meal. She put it down on the table beside the blade. It seemed somehow sacrilege to place something so banal beside something so sacred, but it restored a feeling of sanity to the proceedings.

Both Teclis and his father laughed, much to Rose's incomprehension. She had no idea of the significance of the sword, Teclis realised. Prince Arathion apologised for his rudeness. Teclis said nothing until the retainer had retired from the chamber.

'You have inspected it, of course,' said Prince Arathion.

'I have looked at it,' said Teclis, 'but I needed to bring it here, to have the tools I need to analyse it in depth.'

'How long do we have it?'

'Until Tyrion departs. It will be going with him to Avelorn. It is his.'

'He claimed it, of course.' There was some resentment in Prince Arathion's voice. Teclis told him how Tyrion had taken up the blade. As he did so, it struck him that his father had never asked how it was found and was showing very little interest now. He was only half-listening, his eyes constantly drawn from Teclis's face to where the sword lay on the table. When Teclis finished he said, 'Very good. Just think. We have the only surviving functioning artefact of the Archmage Caledor here in our home.'

'There is the Vortex, father,' said Teclis, surprised to find that he was somewhat annoyed by his father's lack of interest in the hardships that he and Tyrion had endured.

'Of course, of course,' said Prince Arathion. 'I meant things created by his own hand, like this weapon, like the armour, like the amulets he is said to have made for the Everqueen's children.'

He paused for a moment and went over and picked up the sword again. He unsheathed the blade slowly, so that the flames gradually underlit his face with ever more brilliant radiance. It made him look somehow daemonic. 'It still works, even after all these millennia.' He was repeating himself but did not seem to care.

'Yes,' said Teclis. 'And now our task is to find out how!'

'We had better adjourn to the laboratory,' said his father.

'Indeed,' said Teclis. 'Let me mix myself another potion. It's going to be a long night.'

Tyrion strode into the living room and smiled at his father and Teclis. In spite of his cordiality, Teclis could sense his twin was troubled and angry.

'Things went well with Lady Malene,' Teclis said, knowing full well that they most likely had not.

'Yes,' said Tyrion with his customary smoothness.

'That is good,' said their father, taking things, as always, at face value.

'You are going to Avelorn?' Teclis said.

'Indeed,' said Tyrion. He looked long and hard at their father, as if he wanted to say something. Their father never even noticed.

'Then your brother and I had better get started on Sunfang. You'll be wanting to take it with you, of course.' Their father sounded hopeful that Tyrion would say no. Teclis already knew the answer.

'Of course,' said Tyrion. 'I wish you good luck with your researches. I am going to change and then I am going to visit the taverns.'

He swept out of the room. Their father smiled. 'Always the care-free one,' he said, almost fondly.

You just don't understand, Teclis thought. He said, 'Let us get down to the laboratory. We need to map the spells on the sword and get the notes down in record time.'

'Let's get started then,' his father said enthusiastically.

With his twin's departure, Teclis set to the serious business of really examining the ancient blade. He and his father went down to the laboratory in the basement. He made sure that there was a plenti-ful supply of parchment and ink and then began.

He set the blade on the floor and inscribed a chalk circle around it. Swiftly he inscribed runes around the edges of the circle, mak-ing the signs of Isha and Hoeth and numerous minor deities of knowledge. He relaxed and began to chant. His heartbeat slowed, his breathing deepened, his spirit hung loosely within his body. He inspected the aura of the old sword.

And it was *old*, he realised, an artefact of the ancient time when mortal gods had walked the Earth. It had been made when magic flowed much more strongly through the world. He could tell from the brutal strength of the spells, so difficult to replicate in the mod-ern era, that magic had been more abundant when this weapon had been made. The world had been fundamentally different.

Slowly, it seeped into him, the realisation that his father was right, Aenarion had held this blade. He had fought and killed with it. He had trusted his life to it. It was a weapon intended to be wielded by a hero, one touched by the power of the gods. He was not sure that his brother would ever be able to use its full power. He did not lack the heroism. He simply had not passed through the Flame of Asuryan as Aenarion had.

Teclis had touched the Flame, using his own magic, during the final battle with the Keeper of Secrets. He could sense resonances of it within the blade, most likely simply traces of the fact that Aenarion had handled it. There had been a direct link between the Phoenix King and this weapon. Echoes of Aenarion's blazing ferocity could be felt by someone sensitive enough.

Beneath that there were echoes of another personality, one of more interest to Teclis. The presence belonged to one infinitely sad-der, wiser and far less bold, the first of the true Archmages, Caledor. He too had handled this blade and he had done so before Aenar-ion. The spellwork flowing through it was his.

Teclis looked at it, fascinated. It was as individual as handwriting. That was always the case. Two mages could cast the same spell and it would look and feel different to the knowledgeable observer. It would flow in a different way, be cast with different levels of energy, sometimes would get different results. Magic was always personal.

What could he tell about Caledor from his work?

The elf had been meticulous – the runes on the blade had been inscribed with care, and the flows of fire magic through them were still bound as tightly today as they were the day the sword had been forged.

He had been strong-willed. No one could have bound one of the Elemental Spirits of Vaul without being so. He had not been at all artistic. The magic was utilitarian. There was none of the florid scribblings of trace energies that many mages used to leave their own mark on spells and artefacts. The elf that had made this sword had been grimly determined to create the most powerful weapon he could for his friend. He had not been concerned with imprinting his own personality on it.

And, of course, that single-minded determination had left the strongest mark possible. Now he had a sense of the wizard as if he had been standing in the same room with him, of the indomitable will, the desperate courage, the despair.

Caledor had not been a warrior. He had never wanted to fight. It was not in his nature. He had been driven to it. He had been a maker where Aenarion had been a destroyer. He had made even this sword with reluctance, but having been driven to it he had made it to the best of his ability. He had put all of his genius into the creation of something whose purpose he despised.

We live in the shadow of titans, Teclis thought. We live in the world that destiny-cursed pair created. This sword is like the whole history of our people. It bears the stamp of Aenarion and Caledor.

He thought about the Vortex, which, even to this day, protected and maintained Ulthuan, channelling its magical energies, keeping the continent above the waves, draining the fatal power of the winds of magic from the world. Caledor made their land, in the same way as Aenarion shaped their people. The whole continent was part of his vast geomantic design.

Teclis considered the scope of the mind that could do that – plan and execute the most powerful spell in the history of the world in the midst of fighting the greatest war ever. The same elf who had forged this blade had forged a continent. The world had been fundamentally different when Sunfang had been made, and Caledor had been the one who altered it when he created the Vortex.

Surely there was something to be learned from understanding this spellwork. So thinking, Teclis threw himself once again into studying the weave and pattern of the magic and imprint of the elf who had made it.

Hours later, grimly elated, exhausted and at the end of his strength, he felt that he had grasped the essential nature of the magic. He thought that perhaps one day he would be able to forge a weapon, if not as powerful as this one, at least of a similar level of sophistication.

'You have penetrated the blade's secrets?' his father asked. It was not really a question.

Teclis took up his pen. 'I have discovered a very great deal. Let's get it all down while it is fresh in my memory.'

Teclis slumped wearily into his armchair. He looked over at his father and saw that the old elf was transformed. His face had lit up with something approaching joy. He looked as if he was about to burst into dance. In his hands he held the scrolls containing the notes that Teclis had made during his examination of Sunfang. He kept running his gaze over the runes again and again, as if he could not quite believe what he was seeing.

'What is it, father?' Teclis asked. His father looked as if he was about to burst into tears. He did not seem able to force the words out.

'I think we have found it, my son,' he said. 'I think we have found what I was looking for over all these centuries. I think we found the missing piece of the puzzle.'

Teclis found his father's excitement contagious. Weary as he was, he rose and limped over to where Prince Arathion stood. He looked over his father's shoulder at the complex mass of magical notation that he had left on the parchment.

For once, his father was ahead of him when it came to understanding magic. He simply could not see what it was that the older elf was so excited about. Then again, he told himself, he was tired and he did not have his father's long experience of studying this sort of spell. It was quite possible his father was the greatest expert on this sort of thing in the world. He had concentrated obsessively on it for centuries.

'I don't see it,' Teclis said.

'There,' his father said, his finger stabbing towards one section of the inscription. 'Do you see it now?'

'I'm afraid not.'

'I think this is the missing part of the weave, the thing that has prevented me from being able to reactivate the armour over all these centuries. I think this is the magic that will enable me to bind all of the complex spells together and make them work. It will be expensive and it will take time but I think I can do it.'

Teclis began to vaguely see what his father was getting at. It was not something that would have excited him, or even have got his attention had it not been pointed out to him. It was a relatively simple thing but once he looked closely at it he could see the cleverness of it.

It was a small, intricate piece of spellcraft, designed to link together a mesh of other spells, reinforcing them and letting them draw on each other's power. Anything inscribed with this particular rune would be much stronger and yet much easier to use. It was something that was difficult to spot because it was so embedded in the rest of the spells on the blade, but once you saw it...

'I see it now,' Teclis said.

'I knew you would – eventually,' said his father with a smile. 'It is quite brilliant and I can see how it has eluded me for so long. It will take quite a bit of work to recreate the links in the armour but once that is done, I should be able to bring it back to life. Of course, I won't be able to make the spell as strongly as Caledor did. There's less magic in the world now.'

When he said that his father looked troubled. 'Although that may be changing. The winds of magic have been blowing much stronger recently and there is an odd taint to them. You must have noticed that.'

'I have only just returned to Ulthuan, father, and all of the spells I have worked have been in this shielded laboratory.'

'Of course, but you will see what I mean the first time you try to work magic outside.'

'I'll take your word for that but now I'm going to bed. It's been a very long night and I am very weary.'

His father did not look tired. He looked younger and more energetic than Teclis had seen him look in decades. He looked keen to begin working on his lifelong project once more. Suddenly and ominously Teclis was reminded of Leiber. What if his father did succeed? What if he lost his life's purpose? What would happen then?

He told himself it was just the tiredness speaking, that there was nothing to worry about, but he had a very strong foreboding that this discovery would prove bad for his father. He was a wizard and he respected his forebodings for they very often proved correct.

'Drink!' said Orysian. He handed Tyrion a skin of wine. He was already quite drunk. Wine had spilled from the corners of his thick-lipped mouth and dribbled down his chin. A challenge glittered in his narrow eyes. It was obvious in his wine-thickened voice.

'Don't mind if I do,' said Tyrion, seizing the wineskin and tipping its contents down his throat in one long, theatrical swig. The rest of his companions laughed. All of them except the human slave who carried the lighted lantern seemed vastly amused.

Tyrion loved this, striding through the night-time streets of Lothern with his pack of friends, elves with whom he had spent many a night carousing down by the docks or in the taverns and brothels of the old city. Looking at them he understood his aunt's words about the bad reputation he was getting for himself.

They were all about his age or younger, heavily armed and ready for a fight with members of any other faction they might encounter in the streets of the city. Of late, such running street battles had become part and parcel of life in Lothern – what was worse, in various areas the humans seemed to be getting involved, fighting proxy wars on behalf of their patrons.

Lothern had become a much more violent place in the last century than the relatively peaceful city-state Tyrion had known in his youth. He had to admit that he was part of that problem.

He was one of the elves who took joy in street-fighting. He had a reputation for it and he was seen as a champion of House Emeraldsea. His grandfather and his aunt had disapproved but they were of an older generation, born in a simpler time.

They did not really understand the new world bred of riches and foreign trade and the opening of Lothern to a tidal wave of new money and goods.

At this moment, with the wine burning in his belly like liquid fire,

Tyrion did not really care what his aunt or anyone else thought. He swaggered along with his hands hitched into his sword-belt, daring any passer-by to look at him the wrong way. Very few could look him in the eye. They were afraid and there was something intoxicating about their fear.

This was not his usual practice – he liked to think of himself as a peaceful elf except when provoked, but at this moment in time he would welcome some violence. His companions sensed that. They were going out of their way to be provocative to anyone who got in their way, knowing that when Tyrion was in one of these wild moods there were very few people in the city who could stand against them. Merchants hastened into their shops, passers-by scuttled across the streets.

Only the soldiers of the City Watch held their ground and even they looked nervous, for they were outnumbered by this mob of richly garbed young elves. They knew also that these wealthy trouble-makers had the influence to avoid the consequences of breaking the heads of a few poor guardsmen.

The sight of them gave Tyrion pause. The guard were just doing their jobs, trying to keep the streets safe. They were not the enemy. They did not need trouble from the likes of him. They were the sort of elves he had led on battlefields. He had no quarrel with them.

There was something ugly about the faces of his companions, an expression of brutality and superiority that did not sit well on their fine features. Tyrion realised that exactly the same expression was on his face and he did not like that. He did not like to think he was simply part of the herd.

He forced himself to pause and smile and consider the reasons why he was doing this. He knew that it was not wise. No matter how tough an elf was it was still possible for anyone to be killed in the rough and tumble of a street brawl. He had lost a number of friends that way over the years.

It was wasteful and it was stupid. There were few enough elves as it was and with more humans appearing in the city every year it set a very bad precedent and example. The humans would see that the elves were fractious and divided and they would realise that it was a weakness. It was one that the elves really could not afford to display in a city where they were even now outnumbered by strangers.

He wrestled with his own anger, looking for the reasons and finding them easily enough. He did not like the way his aunt had spoken to him and he did not like being treated as if he were some sort of lackey – he was of the blood of Aenarion, after all. He smiled with genuine mirth; he certainly had the mad pride associated with that particular bloodline. It was coming out now. The wine had made sure of that.

His aunt had her own reasons for doing these things. Tyrion understood that. The trick was going to be to make sure that he did not do anything rash because of that. Knowing her motivations, he could put these to good use and manipulate his aunt for his own purposes, or at least he hoped so. It was never wise to assume such things with elves who were so much older and more experienced than he was. Although he was already very confident of his own gifts in that particular area.

He looked around at his friends. They were taking their cues from him. They seemed to sense the conflict in his mind. A few of them still looked angry and spoiling for a fight, a few of them looked as if they were waiting for him to say something funny; most of them just looked confused.

He grinned at them and spread his hands wide and said, 'Come, let us visit the Golden Lion and I will buy you all some fine wine – there is much to be celebrated. I have found the blade of Aenarion, a thing lost for many centuries. It is an omen of great things.'

Most of them laughed but Orysian said, 'I thought you wanted to blood it this evening. Our enemies have been casting aspersions on the bravery of House Emeraldsea in your absence. I thought you would have brought this fabled blade. We are all dying to get a look at it.'

Orysian was a brute, Tyrion thought. He wanted to be thought tough and he was. He wanted to be the centre of attention the way Tyrion was, but he could not be, because he lacked Tyrion's good looks and charm. Tyrion knew the other elf would have challenged him to a fight, if he had not been so certain he would lose. Instead he contented himself with sniping resentfully at Tyrion. Still these things made him easy enough to handle.

'It would be a very bad omen to blood the blade of Aenarion on asur,' said Tyrion. 'That is why I have left it with my brother this evening – so that I will not be tempted! Anyway, I have had enough fighting over the past few months to last me for at least an evening. While you were drinking in the taverns of Lothern, I was fighting lizardmen, carnosaurs and flesh-eating plants in the jungles of Lustria.'

A look of disappointment passed over Orysian's coarsely handsome features and he said, 'Doubtless you will bore us with all the details before this night is out.' Tyrion could see that Orysian was going to be the problem here, so he singled him out for attention.

'Don't worry, I will regale you with endless tales of my own heroism and bravery which you will, by the end of the evening, envy even more than my startling good looks and wit and charm.'

'I have heard it said that words can be just as deadly as swords and our friend Tyrion is about to prove that by boring us all to death,' said Orysian, rising to the bait.

'As ever, jealousy is an ugly thing,' said Tyrion. 'I have seen you bore a few of your enemies with the sword. The last time I saw you fight I thought it was your intention to watch your opponent die of old age... and let us never forget that they were elves.'

'It would still probably have been preferable for them than listening to your stories,' said Orysian.

'Then imagine what it would be like for them to listen to yours. Heroic tales of the number of courtesans you have kissed and bottles of wine you have drunk interspersed with stories of the cakes you have knifed to death.'

All of the others were laughing now. Even Orysian was amused and flattered to be singled out by the hero of the hour. Tyrion smiled at them all, having turned the mood to his own wishes. He kept it up all the way to the Golden Lion. He did not want to fight tonight. He had too much to think about.

Like a conquering army, Tyrion and his companions burst through the doors of the tavern.

'Drink!' Orysian shouted.

The Golden Lion was crowded. Glittering elven courtesans glided from table to table. Glowstones shimmered in chandeliers illuminating everyone. Servants carried goblets of hallucinogenic wine to gold-inlaid tables, or hookahs of Arabyan kif to those elves who desired it.

It was a vast place, furnished with articles from every corner of the globe, carpets from Araby and clockwork automatons from the Worlds Edge Mountains. Hanging from the ceiling was the huge skeleton of some aquatic monster harpooned by the tavern's owner back when he was a simple sea captain, or so he claimed.

It lay on the edgy territory between the human quarter and the Great Dock. It had once been a warehouse as could be seen by its huge internal area, with an enormous ceiling and many landings looking down over the central pit. On these landings there were still the loading bay doors where hauliers had lifted cargoes into the warehouse.

Most of the serving wenches and staff were humans. That was increasingly the way with all menial labour in Lothern. Some of the great trading houses had even started using slaves as labourers in their warehouses, although technically it was still only permitted to sell slaves in Lothern for purposes of transhipment. There was no business in this world that could not be pursued in this greatest of port cities. The merchants of Lothern did not want to miss out on the slightest copper piece of potential profit.

Tyrion glanced around to see who else was present. The place had gone quiet for a moment when the patrons had noticed his entry. It pleased him that he was so well known here. The tavern's owner came to greet him.

'Prince Tyrion, I had heard you were back.'

'News travels fast, Garion,' said Tyrion.

'In Lothern, always.' The owner led them to a massive platform where they could stare down on the less wealthy and famous below. Drinks were brought. The most beautiful courtesans began to drift away from other tables towards their own.

Tyrion sipped his wine and studied his friends. They were a typical cross-section of the young, outrageous and wealthy of Lothern; part of the new generation that had grown up over the past century as Lothern was transformed from a half-dreaming city into the hub of a global trading empire. They had the swaggering, piratical look of young merchants on the make. Many of them had captained ships to the far corners of the globe.

Here was Lucius, whose family had grown wealthy in spices and silks from Cathay and the Mystic East. He affected long flowing wizardly robes of the Cathayan upper echelons. It was intended as a joke, a parody of the self-importance of the mandarins but somehow it suited him.

Here was Kargan, who had made a fortune raiding the coasts of Naggaroth and the dark elf colonies. He was lean and scarred with a vulpine look to his features and two dark elf blades strapped to his sides. He hated the spawn of Naggaroth with a black passion that matched that of the druchii. He had lost a beloved sister to their slavers and was taking a lifelong revenge. Tyrion had made his first real gold shipping out with him and raiding the coasts of Naggaroth. Although he was very far from squeamish about these things himself, Tyrion found Kargan's bloodlust somewhat disturbing.

Here was Drielle, a she-elf who prided herself on being every bit as ruthless and tough as her male companions, who wielded a sword in battle with the same skill as they did, and who never refused a bet or a challenge. She was also reputed to be the best navigator in Ulthuan. Tyrion had funded several of her voyages and turned a huge profit on all of them.

There were others cut from the same cloth, spending freely, gambling unwisely, drinking all they could. They were all part of the same social group, all useful to each other. Tyrion had made small fortunes on the back of bits of gossip picked up from one or the other, and made sure to return the favours whenever he could.

These elves were not the powers in their Houses now, but they would be one day, and it did no harm to cultivate them. They could all be useful to him for as long as he was useful to them. In the future they would provide the spine of a very strong power base. One day these people would rule Lothern, and through Lothern the rest of the world.

Of course, they were not without rivals. There were other cliques and factions in the city, many of whom hated his friends or found it necessary to pose as if they did. In some cases, as with young Paladine Stormcastle over there, it was because they belonged to families who were hereditary enemies of House Emeraldsea. Tyrion suspected that under most circumstances he could have liked Paladine, but it looked as if they were doomed to be at each other's throats by an accident of history or birth. They were rivals in business, for the favours of courtesans and the notice of the Phoenix King. It could be no other way, and there was no sense in regretting it.

Paladine rose from his table and walked over to Tyrion's accompanied by a couple of his swaggering hangers-on. He had a new pet, Tyrion noticed, a small monkey dressed in the britches, tunic and exaggerated codpiece that the humans liked to wear. It even had a broad-brimmed feathered hat. It was a joke at the expense of the humans, an expression of contempt that Tyrion was not sure was at all wise in this new era. The monkey waddled over and bowed to Tyrion, as it had obviously been trained to do, then began to scratch its private parts. All of the elves laughed except Tyrion.

'Prince Tyrion. I had heard you were back.'

'And if you had not heard, you could see it with your own eyes.'

'I hear you found the blade Sunfang,' said Paladine. Tyrion nodded and waited for the inevitable sneer. He did not have long to wait.

'Your crippled brother has a gift for sorcery and forgery, I have heard. It would not surprise me in the least to learn that the blade you bore was some sort of fake.'

A gang of other young elven blades was closing in. Tyrion did a swift head count. His own group would be outnumbered unless some of the others here came to his aid. Most of them were looking on, waiting to see what happened. There was an atmosphere of tension, of barely controlled violence about to explode. Tyrion shrugged and forgot about his good intentions from earlier. It looked like a brawl was inevitable. That being the case, he thought, he might as well enjoy it.

Tyrion yawned. 'I have been having some difficulty sleeping of late. I am glad you have come over to bore me. It is very relaxing. And what have you been up to while I was in the jungles of Lustria? Bravely keeping your father's account books, wielding that razor-sharp pen of yours to good effect, terrorising the clerks in the counting house with the prospect of listening to your jokes.'

Paladine flushed and stepped forward. His monkey shrieked and capered, obviously disturbed by the anger in the voices around him. Out of somewhere a flagon of ale came flying, tumbling towards his head, soaking his clothes. Within seconds a brawl had erupted. Tables were smashed, punches were thrown.

'No blades, lords and ladies, no blades,' Garion shouted. Tyrion wondered if anyone would pay the slightest attention.

Standing on top of the moving mountain that was the Black Ark as it ploughed through the waves, Malekith studied the horizon. The sea was dark with ships. Every one of those ships contained troops loyal to him, or as loyal as elves and fickle Chaos worshippers were ever capable of being. It did not matter. They would serve his purposes in the end. He was not going to let anything spoil the mood of triumph this day.

He was returning home after all these years. That was what it felt like. He had dwelled in the cold northern lands for a much greater portion of his millennia-long life than he had spent in Ulthuan, but still it was so. He had brooded over the fate of the island-continent far more than he had over the lands he had seized so long ago.

His first memories were of the blue skies of Naggarythe. He still had vivid recollections of his first horse ride, the sight of dragons moving across an empty sky, the cloud-girt mountains, the emerald seas. He could remember talking with his father in their few quiet moments together when he was young.

Much had changed since then and he had been the one who changed it. By his actions he had sunk part of the ancient land. He now believed his mother had tricked him into that as part of her own secret plans. It was difficult to truly remember. It had all been so long ago.

This enormous sea-going vessel had once been part of a mountain citadel. Mighty magics kept it afloat. Without the power of the ancient sorcery that pulsed all around him, even now it would be on its way to the monster-haunted ocean bottom. It was not a ship. It was an enormous berg of hollowed-out stone, filled with warriors.

The sea seethed with the crude vessels, carrying the army of savages his mother had recruited in the Northern Wastes and bent to her will. Their guttural chanting and bestial bellowing drifted across the waves as they tried to placate their crude daemon gods. Sharks and smaller sea monsters swam in their wakes, devouring the offerings the barbarians made, living members of their own tribes sent on as messengers to the afterlife they thought they were going to.

The joke was on them. Long ago, when he had been little more than a child, his mother had told him the truth. There was no paradise, no afterlife such as the priests spoke of. There was only the black horror of the realms of Chaos in which daemons devoured the souls of the dead, feasting on them, as they feasted on the strong emotions of the living. His father had hinted confirmation of this, and his father had seen more of the workings of the universe than any living being before or since when he passed unshielded through the Flame.

Malekith himself had caught no glimpses in the hazy, agonising time when he had attempted that feat himself. He had caught sight of the presence of Asuryan and the god had rejected him... That fact still burned as much as the pain of his wounds.

Behind him, emerging from the bowels of the Black Ark, he sensed the chained malevolence of the daemon he had bound to his will. N'Kari still wore the form of an astonishingly beautiful elf maiden, naked, but now forged from steel, tattooed with runes that parodied those on Malekith's own armour. Normally Malekith would have brooked no mockery, but there was little more he could do to punish the daemon than what he was already doing. Let it have its little joke. In the end, it too would do his will. That was what was important.

Sometimes he let it shift to the form it was most at home in, that of a monstrous four-armed denizen of the deepest hells. At all times, the chains of cold iron and truesilver glittered on its limbs, the jewels on each of the alien bracelets pulsing with the power of the spells that bound the daemon to his service.

It was temporary, Malekith knew that. Not even his spells and that ancient alien artefact could hold the daemon enchained forever. He could feel its evil and its hatred where he stood. It was a palpable force, radiating outwards like heat, curdling the erotic, narcotic clouds of vapours that billowed always around N'Kari's form.

'Brooding, Malekith?' the daemon asked. Its voice was innocent and beautiful and completely at odds with its appearance, but then it could look and sound like anything it wanted. Malekith envied it. There were times when he thought he would give anything to wear the body he had once possessed, to feel cool air on his skin, not to be entombed in iron. He pushed that weakness aside.

'Dwelling on the past?' the daemon asked.

Malekith did not ask how the daemon knew. In some ways it was preternaturally sensitive to the thoughts of others, in other ways completely blind. Also, it would never do to lose sight of the fact that the daemon was not of this world. It had gifts, in some ways like his mother's.

'That is my business, daemon.'

'For the moment, your business is my business,' said N'Kari. It brandished its chains. 'You have made this very clear to me.'

'This does not mean I have to discuss it with you. Do not make me sorry I granted you permission to speak once more.'

'Who else are you going to discuss it with, Witch King – those idiots out there on their pathetic ships?'

'I do not require to talk about it with anyone, least of all you, lackey.'

'Then you are most unusual among your kind. Always they need to talk, to boast, to vaunt their pride. They are worse than humans in their way.'

Malekith was inclined to agree, but he was not about to admit it to this creature. 'You were thinking about life and death and the gods,' said N'Kari.

Malekith wondered if the daemon had been reading his mind. He did not think it was possible. His helmet was inscribed with very potent runes to prevent exactly that sort of thing from happening and he had shielded his thoughts for millennia using magic.

No, he thought, the daemon was simply making an obvious

insinuation and attempting to unsettle him, and that was not something he was going to allow.

'That shows no great gift of understanding,' said Malekith. 'It is what most elves would do, standing on these heights, and looking at this view.'

'While engaged in an exercise on this vast scale...' said N'Kari. 'It is what you mortals are like.'

'I am no mortal,' said Malekith.

'That remains to be proven,' said the daemon, allowing some malice to creep back into its voice.

'By you?' Malekith allowed his contempt to show in his voice. An elf or a human would have quailed.

The daemon merely smiled. 'My time will come.'

'If ever it does you will find me ready.'

'I did this once,' said N'Kari. The daemon sounded thoughtful. 'Invaded Ulthuan. Even in the time before your father arose to oppose me.'

Malekith laughed. The sound was iron, cold and biting as a blade. 'It seems mortals are not the only ones compelled to talk, to boast, to reminisce.'

'It is a weakness of being bound in this form in this world,' said N'Kari. 'Every day I become more like you. I live. I breathe. The realm of my birth becomes an ever fainter memory. But then you understand that too, don't you? We have some things in common, you and I.'

'I very much doubt that.'

'You are attempting what I once did. I suspect your results will be much the same.'

'I will prevail. I do not seek to destroy the world and enslave my people. I am merely reclaiming what is mine by right of birth.'

'Are you certain of that?'

'Of what?'

'That you are Aenarion's son? Your mother was, to say the least, promiscuous. I lay with her myself many times in many different forms. More than even she is aware of.'

Malekith knew the daemon was merely trying to goad him. He would not let it.

'The Flame rejected you. It did not reject Aenarion.'

There was nothing Malekith could say to that, so he let it pass. He knew it was pointless debating such things with daemons.

'Why do you think that was?'

Malekith exercised his will. The bracelets that bound the daemon pulsed with energy. It stood frozen in place, unable to move or speak until he willed it. He returned to contemplating his fleet.

Soon, he thought, he would be home and there would be a reckoning: with this daemon, with the elves of Ulthuan and with their gods.

◄ CHAPTER TWELVE ►

Teclis woke from an unpleasant slumber. Strange dreams had haunted his sleep, filling his mind with images of destruction and slaughter. In every nightmare was the hideous image of Morrslieb, the Chaos moon, blazing brightly in the sky. Something had transformed it into an eye through which a daemonic god looked down on the world.

He washed, pulled on his robe, and went down to breakfast. He had barely sat down at the table when there was a knocking at the door. Moments later Rose entered and said, 'A messenger from the White Tower wishes to see you, sir.'

'Send them in,' said Teclis. He was surprised to see a Sword Master of Hoeth, a tall slender woman with a great two-handed blade strapped to her back. He recognised her at once. 'Izaraa,' he said. 'What brings you here this fine morning?'

'The High Loremaster has summoned a conclave at Hoeth. I was dispatched to give word to all associates of the White Tower. I heard you had returned so I brought you the message.'

'What business is so urgent that the High Loremaster would summon us all back to the tower?'

'I do not know, Prince Teclis. All I know is that it concerns the Chaos moon. Many dark portents have been observed and perhaps the realm is threatened.'

'Omens indeed abound. I dreamt of Morrslieb this very night and awoke from a vision of it just before you arrived.'

'Such things are not uncommon at the moment, prince.'

'I had not noticed them before I returned to Ulthuan.'

'Rumour has it you were in Lustria, far south of here.'

'Rumour for once speaks truth and you are right; perhaps I have only recently returned to the area wherein these baleful omens hold sway.'

'You will come to Hoeth, Prince Teclis?'

'Most assuredly. I was returning anyway to consult the library. This only makes the errand more urgent.'

'How will you get there?'

'My brother is due to sail north very shortly. I can arrange to travel with him.'

'Good, then I shall bid you farewell. I must travel on and summon others.'

'I understand you just came back from Avelorn,' said Tyrion to Prince Iltharis. His head hurt a little from all the wine he had drunk the previous evening. He had a few bruises from the brawl. He needed this sparring session to get rid of the grogginess and work the stiffness from his limbs. That was why he had come to the courtyard of the Emeraldsea mansion. Around the ancient fountains members of his family's faction practised their skill at arms.

Was it his imagination or did Prince Iltharis flinch at the mention of the forest realm? Tyrion continued to strip off his shirt and don his practice armour. Iltharis paused and looked at him and then said, 'Yes, I have. Why do you mention it?'

'My aunt wants me to go there and take part in the great tournament to become the champion of the new Everqueen.'

Prince Iltharis let out a long breath that sounded suspiciously like a sigh. 'Of course. Of course. I thought for a moment that you too had become overcome by morbid curiosity, like so many of my fellow citizens of Lothern.'

'Morbid curiosity?' Tyrion began strapping up the padded tunic. He looked directly at his friend as he did so. It was plain that the prince was a little upset, which was very unusual because he was normally the most self-possessed of elves.

'I was one of the last people to see her alive. I was talking with her about my latest history when she was taken ill.'

'I did not know,' said Tyrion. 'I was in Lustria when all of this was happening. I was summoned back because of the death.'

That certainly explained why Prince Iltharis found his question so upsetting, Tyrion thought. It could not have been pleasant to be there during the last moments of a woman so beloved by all. In some ways, witnessing the death of the Everqueen was like witnessing the death of a god.

Prince Iltharis continued to don his own training gear. 'So I have heard. In a way I am grateful for your return. The fact that you have come back bearing the sword of Aenarion has given all of the gossips something else to talk about.'

'I thought you liked to be talked about,' said Tyrion with a smile. Prince Iltharis spread his hands wide.

'What elf does not? But I prefer to be talked about for my good looks, my charm, my skill with a sword, the beauty of my prose. It is not really pleasant to be gawped at like a trained monkey simply because you were present at the last moments of a famous woman.'

'I have never seen you like this,' said Tyrion. 'I believe the death of the Everqueen has really upset you.'

It was not something that Tyrion would ever have suspected of Prince Iltharis. He was very good at giving the impression of caring for nothing.

'Now my dear Tyrion, please don't start accusing me of being sentimental. That would be just too much.'

'I suspect you do have a sentimental streak, Prince Iltharis.'

Iltharis picked up a wooden practice sword and began to limber up with it. 'I shall have to beat that suspicion out of you then, Prince Tyrion.'

'I wonder if you still have that in you, or whether old age is creeping up on you.' Tyrion began to perform a few exercises designed to loosen his own muscles.

Prince Iltharis laughed. 'Ah, the cockiness of youth. To tell you the truth, I am glad that you have come back. I have missed the opportunity to put you in your place. Simply because you have won a few duels you overestimate your own skill and underestimate everybody else's.'

'I do not think it would be possible to overestimate your skill,' said Tyrion. It was true too; he had never encountered another elf as good with a blade as Prince Iltharis. Tyrion knew exactly how good he himself was with a sword. There were few people in Ulthuan capable of matching him, but Prince Iltharis was even better. He learned something new every time he faced off against the prince in one of these practice bouts. It was one of the reasons he still went in for them.

'Do not think this late showing of humility will save you from another thrashing,' said Prince Iltharis. 'Although, it is nice to be able to practise with someone other than Korhien who poses a bit of a challenge.'

'I see you have regained some spark of your customary insouciance,' said Tyrion. 'I was starting to think that you had entered a new and morbid phase of your decrepitude.'

'Decrepitude, is it? I'll give you decrepitude! Ready?'

'Ready.'

'Then defend yourself,' said Prince Iltharis. He lunged forward, fast as a striking serpent and Tyrion was hard put to parry. As always, when fighting the prince, he found himself constantly on the defensive, rarely able to take the initiative and mount an attack of his own.

Prince Iltharis was astonishingly swift and moved with a fluid ease that Tyrion envied. He seemed able to anticipate every one of Tyrion's counter-attacks and neutralise it easily. And he did all of this with the infuriating air of an elf who was not really trying, who could easily raise his performance to a much higher level if he wanted to.

Tyrion understood enough of the psychology of combat to know that this was as much a part of Prince Iltharis's arsenal as his superlative technique with a sword. It gave him a huge edge over his opponents, even ones as confident as Tyrion.

Tyrion was no longer the youth who had provided Prince Iltharis with such easy victories when they first met though. As his hangover cleared he unleashed the full fury of his sword arm, attacking with a combination of brute strength, lightning reflex and sheer skill that few could match. He forced Iltharis to take first one step back, then two. He struck at the blade and by sheer fluke managed to knock it from the prince's hand.

For a moment, triumph filled him. It looked like he was going to defeat the prince for the first time ever. That blow must have numbed his sword hand. Then Iltharis plucked the blade from the air with his left hand and returned to the attack. Tyrion could tell that his right hand was hurt, but it did not even slow him down. Within a few heartbeats, he found the wooden practice sword at his throat.

'You really are improving, Prince Tyrion,' said Prince Iltharis. 'I don't know what it was you were doing down there in Lustria, but I don't believe I have had such a good workout in the past two centuries.'

'I was still not good enough to beat you,' said Tyrion.

Prince Iltharis smiled. 'In another two centuries you will be much better and I really will be old. Maybe you will be able to beat me then.'

'That is not much comfort,' said Tyrion. He suspected it was not intended to be.

'You are good enough to become the Everqueen's champion though, at least when it comes to swordplay.'

'Not if you compete.'

'There is more to becoming champion than using a sword. You must be proficient with all weapons and fighting from horseback. You must be able to sing and dance and play the part of the dashing hero. Being champion is as much about looking good as it is about being able to fight and there you have the advantage, my young friend.'

'I am surprised to hear you admit it.'

'An ability to realistically assess one's own strengths and weaknesses is useful for every fighter,' said Iltharis in his most professorial mode. It was a manner he sometimes assumed with Tyrion, master speaking to pupil. Tyrion could not find it in himself to resent it.

'You seem less excited about taking part in this great contest than I would have expected,' said Iltharis. He sat down on a nearby bench and took a glass of wine from the tray a human servant was holding.

'I like the idea of competing. I am not sure I like the idea of the prize.'

'They say the new Everqueen is a beauty.'

'It is being her servant that I do not like.'

'Ah, the pride of the line of Aenarion...'

'Mock all you like, my friend, but I had become accustomed to the idea of being my own master.'

'We are none of us that, prince.'

'You are the last person I would expect to hear preaching sermons about duty. You spend your time doing exactly what you want.'

'Just because I deplore responsibility myself does not mean I cannot appreciate its benefit in others. Our society would fall apart if everyone was like me.'

Prince Iltharis seemed suddenly serious. 'Believe me, Tyrion, I have had my share of unpleasant duties in my time.'

Tyrion knew Iltharis had fought many duels on behalf of the political interests of his House. He talked about them flippantly, but being known as someone who was little better than a paid assassin must take its toll.

Tyrion laughed. 'I had not thought to find you so mournful.'

Iltharis gave a rueful grimace. 'I cannot help it. I look around me and see everything is in flux. The Everqueen is dead and it makes me uneasy. The world is changing, Tyrion, and I do not think it will be for the better for the people of Ulthuan. I cannot help but feel that my life and everybody else's will soon be very altered.'

'You are serious. The world *is* changed.'

Iltharis smiled. 'Indeed. I am filled with odd forebodings. If we do not meet again after you go to Lothern, remember that I wish you well.'

Tyrion wondered what had brought this on. 'And I you, Prince Iltharis.'

The prince gave him a strange sour smile. 'Come, let us leave this gloomy place and go and get something stronger to drink.'

He seemed his old self again. Tyrion wondered what was really bothering him.

After he left Tyrion, Urian cursed himself. He was getting sloppy, weak and emotional. He had been startled when Tyrion asked about the Everqueen, had felt certain that his guilt must show on his face. It had taken him most of the practice duel to become accustomed to the thought that Prince Tyrion did not suspect him and did not need to be killed on the spot. He probably could have done it and made it look like an accident, but he liked Tyrion and he had not, so far, been ordered to kill him.

It was more than the shock and the guilt though. He realised that over the centuries he had been here, an agent in place, he had grown accustomed to his life in Ulthuan.

He liked it, found it pleasant and would have been grateful for it to continue indefinitely. Instead, he knew now for certain that it would be ending soon. Malekith's plans were close to fruition and, despite the fact he had no idea as to the specifics, he knew they could not bode well for the high elves.

His forebodings for the future were based on that knowledge. Many of the elves he knew here would be dead soon, or under the iron heel of the Witch King's rule. He would be revealed as a traitor in their midst and one of the new rulers. There had been a time when he had looked forward to that with great glee. He no longer did. He now thought that when Ulthuan fell, something great would be lost and the world would be a poorer place for it.

He tried to steel his nerves by telling himself the high elves were foolish and degenerate, weak and easily deceived, but he could not even deceive himself about that. He had lived too long among them, had become more like an asur than his druchii kindred. He was an odd creature now, caught between two worlds, deceiving both as to where his sympathies lay.

He had not been lying to Tyrion, he realised. He really did feel a dark and terrible foreboding about the future. Everything *was* going to change for the worse. He told himself that he had better get used to the idea. Soon Malekith would rule this place, and he had no sympathy at all for those who were not utterly loyal. Urian had better be absolutely certain where his loyalties lay.

'Greetings, doorkeeper,' Korhien Ironglaive said. 'Welcome to my humble chamber.'

Tyrion presented Korhien with some wine from his father's cellars and looked around. Korhien's chambers were simple by the standards of the Phoenix King's palace, which meant they were luxurious beyond belief even by the standards of Lothern. Carpets from Araby covered the floor. The hangings were ancient silk tapestries. Paintings from the golden age of art during the reign of Aethis hung on the walls. The crystal window had an astonishing view of the harbour.

Tyrion took a seat on a divan and looked across at his father's oldest friend. Korhien looked almost the same as the time when they had first met over a century ago. He had a few more scars but the agelessness that the vast majority of elves possessed until extreme old age was still his. He was as tall, fit and muscular as a youth, and moved with the easy grace of the very highest echelon of warriors.

'I hear your quest to the world's far edges has been successful.'

'We found it, Korhien. We found the sword Aenarion carried in his youth.' For once Tyrion could allow all of his enthusiasm to show. He could not with his other friends, even Prince Iltharis.

Korhien raised an eyebrow.

'What?' Tyrion asked.

'Nothing,' Korhien said.

'Spit it out. There's never been any need for restraint between us, why start now?'

Korhien laughed. 'Very well, since candour is what you demand. I was thinking that I am not sure whether it's a good omen that you have found that sword.'

'Why?'

'Aenarion started with that blade. He moved on to another one.'

'You are not seriously suggesting that I am interested in drawing the Sword of Khaine?'

'What I am suggesting, doorkeeper, is that it would not matter whether you are or not. If it is your destiny to do those things you will, and you are very clearly someone marked by destiny.'

'I would never have believed you were so superstitious, Korhien.'

'Nor would I. But sometimes I look at you and I wonder into what pattern the stars are aligning behind your head. I wonder how much of it is deliberate, and how much of it is Fate, the gods, whatever you want to call it.'

He sounded unusually thoughtful. No, Tyrion thought. That was not fair. The White Lion had always been much more thoughtful than most elves ever gave him credit for being. It was just that his thoughts did not usually drift down such strange channels.

'You are serious, aren't you?'

Korhien nodded. 'A god reached out and touched your life once, Tyrion. It intervened to save you. How many elves has that ever happened to? I can count it on the fingers of one foot and contrary to the opinion of some I am not a Chaos mutant.'

'We were in the Shrine of Asuryan. The god was protecting his own.'

'Asuryan did not save any of the warriors with you, or any of the priests guarding his shrine. He lent his power to you and your brother. I would respectfully submit that he most likely did it for his own reasons. Now you return from the blighted edges of the world carrying a blade that was forged by Caledor and borne by Aenarion himself. I can almost feel the forces of destiny lining up behind you.'

'You are unusually full of forebodings this fine morning. And to think I only came over to offer you a cup of wine.'

'You are of the blood of Aenarion, doorkeeper. That means something.'

'It means I belong to a select group that has been prodded and tested and manipulated by its own people, hunted by daemons and secret cults, whispered about behind its back and accused of all manner of unspeakable crimes. I did not ask for any of this, Korhien.'

'Ah, but you did. No one forced you to go seeking that blade. And yet you did.'

'You think I have some ulterior motive?'

'Don't you?'

'What do you mean by that?'

'I think you are not without ambitions. I think you are interested in a career in politics and you, or the people behind you, are using your resemblance to Aenarion to build a legend around you.'

'The people around me? You mean my grandfather in his time or my aunt now?'

'And their faction, yes.'

'Are you talking for Finubar here? Does he think I threaten him?'

'No, doorkeeper. On both accounts. I am speaking for myself, based on my own observations. You are not a threat to Finubar, because he is the Phoenix King and only his death will change that. And you are not the sort to try your hand at assassination, nor is your aunt.'

Tyrion was annoyed but he did not let that show in his voice. 'I am glad you think so.'

'You asked me for honesty, doorkeeper. Would you prefer that I did not give it to you?'

Tyrion shook his head then smiled, seeing the absurdity of the situation. 'No. I prefer you as you are, Korhien, and I prefer you to say what you think. I am just surprised you have such a low opinion of me.'

'That I do not. It is just that I sometimes look at you and wonder how it is all going to end. Your life is taking on a strange shape and so is that of your brother. I worry about you both.'

'It would be best not to mention that to him. He likes to think he can take care of himself.'

'You both can, but that does not stop me from worrying. Now tell me about your aunt. How is she these days?'

Korhien and Malene had been lovers once, but the decades and politics had pulled them apart. He still seemed interested in her though. Perhaps she was in him. They were still friends.

'She seemed a little worried when I last talked to her,' Tyrion began.

'It is good to see you again, aunt,' said Teclis with what he felt was a little too much formality. He was unsure of his reception so he had fallen back on good manners. It was unusual for him.

Teclis looked at Lady Malene. Physically she did not look any different from the beautiful elf woman he had first seen the day before his sixteenth birthday over a century ago. She was still beautiful in a severe way and as ageless as any other elf. She looked somehow older though.

There was something to the set of her shoulders and the way her lips compressed. A slight frown was always present on her forehead. Responsibility had changed her. Just the way she sat hunched over her father's old desk made her look different.

Tyrion would have been able to tell him in exactly what ways and quite possibly explain why, but he had always lacked his brother's gift for reading people.

She looked up and smiled with a genuine warmth that surprised him. He never really expected anyone but his father and his brother to look at him like that.

'Prince Teclis,' she said. 'This is a pleasure.'

'Not entirely an unexpected one, I hope.' Try as he might, he could not keep the hurt from his voice. He had always thought she preferred him to Tyrion, the only person other than his father who had ever done so. It hurt him, more than he cared to admit, that she had summoned his brother first and in private.

'I knew you had returned along with your brother. I saw him yesterday evening.'

'I know.'

'It was business of the House,' she said, as if that explained everything, which he supposed it did. She took her duties as the new ruler of House Emeraldsea very seriously.

As she said it she rose from behind the desk, walked around it and hugged him. The intimacy of the gesture was startling. He was not used to any physical displays of affection. He returned the hug clumsily and backed away as quickly as he could, staring at her from arm's length.

'I understand you have become quite the adventurer,' she said, returning to her place behind the desk as if she understood his embarrassment. 'You have found the sword of Aenarion.'

'Not the blade everyone thinks of as Aenarion's sword,' said Teclis. 'But, yes, we found Sunfang.'

'Many said it was impossible,' she said. 'I knew you would succeed. You and your brother always do at anything you truly put your minds to.'

'I wish I shared your faith in my abilities. You are, of course, correct about Tyrion.'

'You always sound so sour these days when you talk about him,' she said. Teclis thought it certainly was so when he talked to her. He could not help himself. He did not wish to be displaced in her affections. He could never bring himself to say that openly though.

He realised he was being unfair to Tyrion as well, which galled him, for he knew his brother would never behave so towards him. It was just one more way in which he was better.

'I do not mean to, but it is hard sometimes,' he admitted. 'I live on his charity, me and father both.'

Malene studied him. 'You do not live on his charity. He has given most of what he owns to you and your father. It is all yours now, not his. He told me to tell you that if the matter ever came up.'

'Why would he do that?'

'He knows your father needs the money and he was letting me know something as well.'

Somehow this did not make Teclis feel any better. 'He earned that money with his raiding and his trading. He did it while I was studying at Hoeth. I think sometimes he does these things to make me feel bad.'

'You think your brother gifts you with gold in order to make you feel bad?' Malene's smile was curious. 'Explain!' For a second, she was the old Malene, his tutor in magic and alchemy.

'Even Tyrion's generosity is a weapon. Or rather, a display of superiority. He is saying he is the one who is in a position of power. He is always the one who helps us, helps me. It is never the other way.'

Malene steepled her fingers. 'I am surprised it has taken such an intelligent elf so long to realise this,' she said.

Teclis smiled sourly. 'I have never been good with people.'

'Better than you think.'

'You agree with me then?'

'Of course. The question you really should ask yourself is why your brother behaves this way.'

'Because he likes to feel superior.'

'No. Because he still feels inferior.'

'Why should he do that? Everyone always praises him. He is probably the best-loved elf in Lothern.'

'It was not always so.'

'I do not remember it any other way.'

'I do.'

'Your memory is better than mine then, lady.'

'We both know it is not. But I can still remember a day that you seem to have forgotten.'

'What day is that?'

'The day I first saw the pair of you.' Malene smiled fondly, as if recalling something that was special to her.

'You saw a sickly child and a perfect elf boy.'

'I saw a father who doted on the sick son who resembled him and who shared his interests. I saw another boy who was excluded because he had no interest in or talent for the Art, only for things his father despised or considered of no consequence. It was a small house and there was only one parent.'

'You think Tyrion still remembers that?'

'Probably not, but it does not matter. It set his feet on a certain path and he probably cannot even remember now why he still walks it. What matters is that he does.'

Teclis turned this thought over and over in his mind. He had been so lost in his own bitterness that he had never even thought that Tyrion might have some of his own. He always seemed so happy and secure. 'I am not sure I believe that. He has never said anything to me.'

'He is even more self-contained than you are, though you may not believe that. And he has said something to you. He says it by his actions.'

'You are as wise as you are lovely, lady,' Teclis said eventually.

'And it is pleasant to discover you have acquired some elven graces over the years. Now I presume this is not purely a social call. You have something you wish to discuss with me.' It had been a social call really. He had just wanted to see her and reassure himself, but he could not say that out loud.

'Tyrion told me you were troubled about something before he went to visit Prince Iltharis today. He said you told him that the winds of magic have changed. He did not know what it meant, but he said it sounded ominous. My father has been saying similar things. And I had a message from Hoeth this morning. It seems the High Loremaster shares your fears.'

'I am troubled, Teclis. More than I can say. There is something not right with the world, and not right with the flow of magic, although I cannot put my finger on exactly what.'

'Then I have something that may disquiet you more. In Lustria I found a slann prophecy. I feel it may be of grave importance. If I am not mistaken, it concerns the return of Chaos to our world, and if I understand the slann dating system, it is due to happen soon.' Teclis took out the drawings he had made and showed them to her.

'It does not strike me as chance that this sort of thing would fall into your hands right now,' said Malene. She looked thoughtful. 'I know very little of slann pictoglyphs, otherwise I would offer to help.'

She sounded wistful, almost as if she were looking for an excuse to get involved in some magical research again.

'I need to know who the best person to discuss the matter with would be,' Teclis said.

'High Loremaster Morelian is the greatest expert we have in the slann languages.'

'I suspected as much but it is nice to have that confirmed. Do you think he would help me?'

'He'll probably tear your arm off trying to get those out of your grip. A new and authentic slann text – it's the sort of thing he dreams about. I've known him since he was my tutor at the tower. The slann have always been an obsession with him.'

'I am familiar with the type,' said Teclis thinking of his father.

Malene could obviously tell the way his thoughts were running.

'Do not confuse Morelian with Prince Arathion. You do not get to be High Loremaster without being perceptive, ambitious and politically minded.'

'I know him by sight, of course, but not that well.'

'He will know you too, but, of course, I will write. It can't do any harm.'

As the head of House Emeraldsea, his aunt was one of the richest and most influential women in Ulthuan, a personal friend of the Phoenix King. Since she was a mage, she was also a powerful ally of the White Tower at court. Again, almost as if she could read what he was thinking, she said, 'I see you are becoming quite political yourself.'

'I have a long way to go before I can match my brother.'

'You'll get there in the end.'

'I am not sure I want to.'

'You'll be High Loremaster one of these days. I am sure of it.'

'It is not an honour to which I aspire.'

'Now you really do sound like your brother,' Malene said. Teclis wondered what she meant.

The shores of Ulthuan glittered on the horizon. Malekith saw the shimmering haze in the air that he remembered so well. It was the glow of magic that hovered perpetually over the island continent and had done ever since the time of the Archmage Caledor. The whole mighty fleet cruised along the coast now, heading for their goal.

Beside him his generals looked grim or pleased or filled with anticipation according to their temperament. Some of them directed lustful bemused looks towards N'Kari, who now wore the form of a lustrously beautiful elf maiden. Her shackles in particular seemed to focus their attention. Malekith easily guessed which direction their thoughts were taking.

Slaves walked through the chamber bearing platters of food and drink, their eyes downcast submissively as they attempted to avoid drawing any attention to themselves. Today it worked. The assembled nobles paid them no more attention than they would any other piece of furniture.

There was a certain febrile festival atmosphere about the command chamber. All of those present knew that war was about to begin and that it was going to be hard, but all of them also believed they were going to win. None of them knew the full extent of his preparations but all of them knew him, and they knew he would not have launched this attack unless he was utterly certain of victory.

They sipped drugged wine and smiled and calculated spoils. A few of them discussed reclaiming ancestral estates that had been lost millennia ago.

Malekith deliberately said nothing to damp down the conversations about reward. He wanted to foster this atmosphere of feverish competition and greed. His lack of intervention was duly noted by those who had spent a lifetime watching him for the slightest clues as to his whims. He knew that eventually the message would spread to all present in the fleet.

Sometimes he noticed the sorcerers turn their gazes on N'Kari for a moment. The most powerful present blanched and fell silent and that too was noted by the audience he had assembled. And that too was good. He was giving them all a demonstration, making a statement of how powerful he truly was. Word of that would get out too.

And in the inevitable druchii fashion it would filter its way down to every rank of the army. All of them would know that their lord and master had bound a greater daemon of Chaos to his will. They would wonder about what other allies he could command.

He felt something like happiness at this moment. His plans were under way and he was confident of eventual victory. So far everything had gone as anticipated. He was not foolish enough to think there would be no setbacks or that everything would go according to plan, but he had amassed a sufficient concentration of resources and power to counter any threat that might arise. It was only a matter of time before Ulthuan fell, and after that he would deal with his remaining enemies.

Not a few of those present were his mother's lovers and secretly sworn to her service. They thought him unaware of that fact and the time had not yet come to apprise them of their error. That day would dawn soon enough and Malekith was looking forward to it with relish.

One of the things he abhorred most was disloyalty.

'It seems as if you have become a person of some importance,' said Atharis. Tyrion looked at his old friend. They sat together in his office in the Emeraldsea palace. Physically, Atharis had not changed much from the young fighter Tyrion had met when he first came to the city all those years ago. His nose was still broken and he refused to have the healers use magic to set it properly. He was higher ranked in the House now and trusted with many secret duties.

'While you have steadily been working your way down in the world,' Tyrion said, smiling to take the sting out of his words. Atharis had made quite a name for himself among the brothels and stews of Lothern. He was also a very successful merchant, representing the family interests whenever their grandfather had chosen to send him.

'We cannot all be blessed with the blood of Aenarion,' said Atharis. 'Some of us have to get by using only our natural intelligence and charm.'

'That explains why you have been doing so badly then,' said Tyrion. Atharis punched him on the arm playfully.

'It is good to see you again,' he said. He sounded sincere. Once, long ago, they might have been considered rivals but Atharis no longer seemed to see things that way. Tyrion was glad.

'It's good to see you too,' said Tyrion. 'I understand that we are to be travelling together.'

'Your aunt could not allow you to travel to the court of the Everqueen unescorted. I am to be in charge of your retinue. I am responsible for seeing you don't disgrace House Emeraldsea.'

And doubtless you are also responsible for reporting my actions to my aunt, Tyrion thought.

'And how big is this retinue of mine going to be?'

'Well, Lady Emeraldsea feels you need at least fifty warriors to protect you from the marauding deer of Avelorn. You also need servants in order to make sure that your clothes look sufficiently impressive and that your hair is properly combed. So, you're probably being accompanied by the crew of an entire fighting ship. Let's hope that your participation in this tournament proves worth it.'

'Let's hope,' Tyrion agreed sourly. 'So am I getting a ship to go with the crew?'

'Of course you are. Your aunt has rerouted one of our Inner Sea traders to make sure that you get there in time. We are even supposed to row you if the winds prove unfavourable.'

'That's good,' said Tyrion. 'Because you look like you could use the exercise.'

'I'm still capable of giving you a good run for your money with the sword.'

Tyrion laughed. 'I'm surprised my aunt isn't sending you then. You could represent our House just as well as I can.'

'Alas, Lady Malene does not see things that way. Otherwise I would gladly do so. Our new Everqueen is supposed to be quite the beauty.'

'I have never heard of one who wasn't,' said Tyrion. 'All of the poets always sing praises of their good looks and all of the books say how lovely they are.'

'And, of course, no poet ever lied and no scholar ever propagated a falsehood,' said Atharis. 'You know this as well as I do.'

'Is there anything else I should know?'

'The protection of your sacred person is not the only reason that you're being allocated so many fighters. You are bearing some coronation gifts for the new queen of the forest. Your aunt feels that she must be sufficiently impressed with the wealth and generosity of our House. Obviously the poor rustic girl is going to be swayed by our silks and gold and some pretty mirrors brought all the way from the dwarf lands.'

'I imagine that we will not be the only ones bringing gifts,' said Tyrion. 'Every noble family in Ulthuan will be taking this chance to demonstrate its loyalty and generosity.'

'Indeed. I often think it would be more profitable and sensible if we came to some arrangement with all of the other families not to do this sort of thing. Then we could keep the gold for ourselves.'

'But gold is only a means to an end. How would we prove ourselves to be richer and more generous than all of our rivals if we did not give such gifts?'

'Doubtless we would find a way. We are elves after all, famous for our ingenuity when it comes to proving our superiority.'

'In the meantime,' said Tyrion, 'I suppose we shall have to go about doing so the old-fashioned way. After all, if it worked for our ancestors it should work for us.'

'Indeed. We're leaving with the tide. Let us head down to the docks and watch some other people working. I always find work very stimulating when I am not the one who has to do it.'

Tyrion watched as the crew loaded the ship. How often had he done this in the past, he wondered? There were times when he felt like half of his life had been spent aboard ships, going somewhere or returning to Lothern.

The vessel was anchored on the pier at Lothern's northern docks. The Inner Sea was a different sea from the wild outer ocean. It was superficially calmer and safer, bounded on all sides by the land-mass of Ulthuan, surrounded in its entirety by lands. There was less trade here, so the docks were smaller and less busy, but still bustling. Goods were shipped out to the rest of Ulthuan from here, and the produce of Saphery and Chrace and other places found its way to the great port, and from there to the rest of the world.

The ships here were smaller and more homely-looking than the great ocean-going clippers.

He saw his brother riding down to the harbour. As ever, no one paid too much attention to him. He was just another tall slender elf mounted on a fine steed. He was a terrible rider for an elf but still stood out less than usual. His limp made him noticeable when he walked. His twin rode right up to the pier and paused for a moment to study the ship. He waved and Tyrion waved back.

'I see your brother has deigned to join us,' said Atharis.

'You don't like him, do you?' said Tyrion.

'He never gives anyone much of a chance to like him. If he were less caustic, he might have more friends.'

Tyrion could not deny the truth of that. 'His life has been hard. It is not easy to be less than perfect among elves.'

'None of us are perfect,' said Atharis. 'Not even you. We don't use it as an excuse to be rude to everyone else.'

'I think he got into the habit of getting his retaliation in first when he was young. People were often rude to him because of who and what he was.'

'I can tell you are going to go on making excuses for him,' said

Atharis. 'He is no longer a sickly youth. He is a powerful mage and regarded as something of a hero among his kind.'

'His kind?'

'He is a wizard.'

'He is an elf.'

'It is possible to be both, my dear Tyrion.'

'Mages are not a breed apart.'

'You may want to explain that to them, my friend.'

Teclis limped up the gangplank, leaving his horse in the care of one of House Emeraldsea's dockside factors. He saw Atharis and made a sour expression. Atharis responded in kind.

'A pleasure to see you,' said Teclis ironically.

'I am as pleased to see you as you are to see me,' Atharis responded. His smile was insincere, and obviously so.

Tyrion wondered at his brother's talent for making enemies. Atharis was not the least amiable elf in the world. It would not take an enormous effort to keep on the right side of him. Instead Teclis seemed to take pleasure in being disliked.

'You are ready to depart?' Tyrion asked his brother, to forestall any further sniping. 'You do not seem to have brought much gear with you.'

'It is already on board. The servants brought it this morning. How about you? Are you ready to woo the Everqueen?'

'If she is as beautiful as everyone says, yes. I am just not sure I am ready to be her champion.'

'There are others who may have a say in that, your fellow competitors for the great honour of being in her service.'

'You are in an unpleasant mood today, aren't you?'

Tyrion wondered whether Teclis was being deliberately rude and abrasive because Atharis was present. He tended to adopt such a persona in public, even with his own brother. It was one of his less engaging habits.

'Forgive me,' he said. 'I have had a rather disturbing and sleepless night.' He shot Tyrion a warning glance so that his twin would know for certain that he did not want to discuss this further in public. 'Now if you will excuse me, I would like to go below. There is some reading I must catch up on.'

'Don't let us keep you from your books,' said Atharis. 'I am sure you have matters of earth-shattering importance to consider.'

'Oddly enough, I do,' said Teclis airily. 'I am sure you will hear of them soon enough.'

'I cannot wait,' Atharis said softly to the wizard's departing back. Once Teclis was gone, he said, 'It is hard to believe you are twins. You seem to have got all the good looks and charm in your generation of your family.'

'Possibly,' said Tyrion. 'But he got the brains and the magical talent.'

'I think you got the best of the deal.'

'That might be part of the problem,' said Tyrion.

'You are not as foolish as you look,' said Atharis.

'Why do you keep taunting Atharis?' Tyrion asked. He stepped into the small cabin as soon as Teclis opened the door.

'I don't like him and he does not like me,' his twin replied.

'Perhaps if you were more pleasant to him, he would be more amiable.'

Teclis laughed bitterly. 'Do you really think so?'

'You do this to everybody. Most elves just ignore it but some of them respond very badly.'

'And you think they might respond better if I was nicer to them?' A note of mockery entered Teclis's voice.

'There is that possibility.'

'There is no possibility,' said Teclis with flat certainty. 'Atharis does not like me because I make him uneasy. Most elves do not like me because I make them uneasy. I do not look right. I do not talk right. I am a cripple. I should have been exposed at birth. You know there is something to be said for the old ways.' By the end of his speech, Teclis's voice had become a high-pitched parody of the way most elves talked in polite conversation.

'You are not a child any more,' Tyrion said. 'No one talks to you that way and you do not have to talk to them as if they did.'

'You really don't understand anything, do you?'

'Then make me,' Tyrion said.

'I am an outsider in my own country, Tyrion. I do not belong here and I never will. I am not beautiful. I am... flawed. I know it. Everyone else knows it. Elves do not like to be reminded they are less than perfect, that there is even the possibility of it.'

'You exaggerate.'

'Alas I do not. And you are in no position to tell me otherwise. They like *you*. You are what they think they themselves to be. You are perfect.'

'No I am not.'

'Perhaps, but you look it, and this is a place where appearances are everything. You are a butterfly. I am a moth.'

'Now I really don't follow you.'

'People like butterflies. They are bright, vivacious, good-looking. They are creatures of the day. People hate and fear moths. They are dark, night-going. They do not like to feel a moth's wings on their face. Look closely at them and moths and butterflies are very similar creatures, but people feel quite differently about them.'

Tyrion laughed. 'I am trying to talk to you about the way you treat other elves and you start talking about moths and butterflies. Do you realise how strange that makes you sound?'

'I am strange, Tyrion. I am an outsider. I am a magician.'

'You are sure you are not a moth now?'

'Don't play the fool, brother. It does not suit you. You know what I am talking about. It's cockroaches and ladybirds.'

'Go on...' Tyrion could not keep a certain amount of mockery from his voice.

'They are both insects. People think one looks sweet. They are repulsed by the other. Look at them closely and they are the same except for colour. My basic point is that appearances matter. They colour what people believe. You look one way and I look another. You could be as rude as I am to any elf, and you would still get away with it. I could be polite as a courtier at the court of the Everqueen and they would still hate me.'

'So you are using this as an excuse not to try?'

Teclis looked shocked. 'Don't you think I've tried? I tried so hard for so long that my face was frozen in a permanent grin. I might as well have had lockjaw. I tried as hard as I could and no one wanted to know. They still don't. Keep that in mind before you judge me and come down on the side of *your* friends.'

'I do not judge you and I never take anyone's side against you. Surely you know that?'

'I do not know that. You started this little conversation telling me not to be rude to your friend Atharis.'

'I merely suggested that you might try being politer to him, and you might get on better. I am trying to help you.'

'I will thank you not to.'

'As you wish,' Tyrion said. 'But I think you will find that if you give other elves the chance, they will give you one.'

'You never give up, do you?'

'That is my nature.' They looked at each other for a long moment, their expressions frozen in looks that were almost of hostility. Tyrion did not quite understand how, but his well-meant advice seemed to have pushed them to the brink of a serious disagreement. He realised that he had misjudged things and that he did not know his twin as well as he thought.

Another idea occurred to him. They had got on well enough when they were adventuring on their own. Since they had returned to Lothern, they were at odds.

It was the situation, not them. Now they had returned to the homeland of the elves, he was once again accepted and his brother was once again an outsider. The centre of power in their relationship had shifted and they were both responding to it.

He suddenly understood why Teclis was so much happier travelling and adventuring and why he spent so much time isolated. At least he partially understood. He doubted he could grasp all of the situation because he was not his brother.

Teclis smiled at him and the tension was broken. They laughed, but both of them knew that things were different now that they had come back to Ulthuan. Tyrion knew that it was because he had returned home and Teclis never could.

'Since you have asked me, I will try and be civil to Atharis,' Teclis said. 'Watch and see what happens.'

Tyrion said nothing. He felt that Teclis was right. Atharis would not be his friend. He would go on being an outsider. Whether by reason of his appearance or his manner, or because he now chose to be. It was his brother's role in life.

He thought about what Korhien had said about destiny and he was more troubled by it than he ever had been before.

After days at sea, Tyrion was glad as the ship approached the harbour at Cairn Auriel. The sun beat down on the deck. It was not as warm as it had been in Lustria but it was still very warm. A cool breeze blowing in off the sea gave some relief from the heat. Tyrion stood in the shadow of the command deck and watched the shore come closer.

Cairn Auriel was not a large port by the standards of Lothern but it looked like a pleasant place, a natural harbour cut into the high cliffs on the western coast of Saphery. A silver lighthouse watched over it. Long marble piers protruded outwards from a beach of golden sand. The town itself was a place of graceful white towers tipped with golden domes. Dock workers helped moor the ship and get the gangplanks into place so that Teclis could get off.

Tyrion strode over to where he stood. He let his smile widen and said, 'Once again, brother, we must say farewell.'

'We shall see each other again,' said Teclis. 'All that remains is for me to wish you good luck in the upcoming tournament. See that you do not disgrace our family too badly.'

'I shall do my best,' said Tyrion.

'Doubtless I shall hear how well you have done from passing minstrels and other travellers,' said Teclis. 'You might even consider sending a messenger to let me know how things go.'

'I'm sure the wizards of the White Tower have ways of receiving news much more swiftly than by letter,' said Tyrion. 'But I shall write.'

'It always comes as a pleasant surprise to find that you're capable of it,' said Teclis. The ship was tied up now and the gangplank was firmly in place.

Teclis's baggage had been carried down by sailors and lay on the white marble of the pier. The two brothers clasped hands. The wizard left the ship and strode off in search of horses.

Tyrion watched him go until he was out of sight. By that time, the crew had cast off the moorings and the ship was being washed back out to sea.

Tyrion was suddenly struck by the ominous foreboding that it might be a long time before he saw his brother again.

Morathi stood on the prow of the great wooden ship and watched as her followers raced ashore. Tens of thousands of Chaos-worshipping barbarians leapt from their ships into the roaring surf and raced up the black sand beaches. Behind her, thousands more ships crowded the seas. Most of them carried humans and beastmen and less wholesome followers of the Dark Gods. Some of them were packed with her own followers, from the Cults of Khaine and the Cults of the Pleasure God. They were the druchii who would form her bodyguard amid the humans. Not that she needed one.

The chieftains of the great horde gazed upon her with worshipful eyes. They would do what she required of them in return for her approval and her caresses. They would fight with each other for her favours if she wanted. Perhaps she would have them do so at some point, but right now she needed them to cooperate.

There were elven fortresses nearby that needed to be taken, and elven cities that needed to be conquered and enslaved. Soon she would set this land ablaze from end to end and teach the people to fear and adore her as they had done in the past. In an odd way it felt good to be home.

Naked, she plunged into the sea and let the cool water flow over her. Like a goddess she emerged dripping from the surf, aware that all eyes were upon her. In the distance she could see a beacon fire had been lit. It looked as if the asur were aware of her presence.

And so it begins, she thought. She was curious as to how it would end.

◄ CHAPTER FIFTEEN ►

Teclis found the agent of the White Tower easily enough. The elf recognised him at once and knew what he needed. Swiftly he provided Teclis with a satchel of supplies, a saddle and two horses which he could use in relay.

Teclis rode up the pathway out of Cairn Auriel and followed the trail that he knew would eventually lead him to the Tower of Hoeth. It felt odd – for the first time in months he was on his own. Ever since he and Tyrion had set out on the quest to find Sunfang, he had been in the company of his brother and quite often many others. He had not had time to think or to study or to brood or to plan. As he rode along, he found that he quite enjoyed the quiet of the woods and the respite from having to constantly deal with other people.

He felt better now that he was on his own. He enjoyed Tyrion's company but several months spent daily with his twin had proven tiresome in the end. It was simply too much for an elf as solitary as he was. He loved his brother but he did not want to spend every waking hour of every waking day in his company.

Now at last he had time to think. He was pleased with the way the adventure had turned out. After decades of searching they had finally found Sunfang. His brother now had a weapon that was worthy of him and had burnished his reputation as a hero of Ulthuan.

Teclis did not really care how this victory affected his own reputation among the general populace. It might redound to his credit amongst the wizards of the tower but only insofar as it reflected upon his scholarship. His theories as to the sword's whereabouts had been proven correct. He felt certain that many of his fellow wizards would be as interested in the slann text that he carried as the details of the search for the sword. Of course, he would leave a record of it at the library so that future generations would have access to the knowledge. That was part of his duty as a scholar.

At the moment it was the slann text that troubled him. There were people at the tower who knew far more about slann hieroglyphics then he did and he wanted their help translating it. He had understood enough of what was on the thing to know that its portent was ominous. More than that, since he had returned to Ulthuan, he had started to sense that time was running out. He was uneasy and he did not know why. He was a wizard, though, and he trusted to that strange sixth sense that had so often warned him of trouble in the past.

He was not the best of riders and he had to concentrate on following the trail through the woods. Occasionally, he paused to re-weave his protective spells. The forests of Saphery were not without their dangers.

There were subtle protective spells woven onto the milestones that marked this pathway. They would keep the most dangerous beasts away and ward off some of the strange magical dangers that were to be found in these forests. He did not want to stray too far from this trail though and he did not want to rely on its magic alone to protect him.

In some ways, he was pleased that Tyrion was not here. It meant that he needed to rely upon himself. His brother had a genius for organisation that would show up in even the littlest of things, such as making a camp or pitching a tent. While Tyrion was around there had been very little need for him to do anything but now he needed to do everything for himself.

He was quite looking forward to that. He was not good at any of it but he enjoyed the practice. When he thought about how sick he had been in his youth and childhood, this was not an unexpected pleasure. He could never have foreseen that one day he would be riding alone through this distant, dangerous forest with nothing but his spells to protect him.

It was quite something. He meant to take advantage of every single moment of it while it lasted.

Teclis gathered up some moss and twigs to make a fire. He came back to where he had staked out the horses with a bundle of kindling held in his robes. He opened his hands and let it fall to the ground and then started to arrange the sticks in the same way as he had seen Tyrion do, although not so neatly or so well. Tyrion would have used a flint to get the fire going but Teclis did not have to. He spoke a word and called upon the winds of magic and the moss and twigs burst into flame.

He sat down by the fire and opened the satchel of supplies that the agent had given him. Inside he found dried fruit and beef jerky along with a selection of waybread. He never had the greatest of appetites at the best of times, so he took the tiniest morsel of waybread and began to chew it. He had already filled his canteen from the nearby stream when he had chosen the campsite. As he ate, he pondered the odd thing he had sensed when he lit the fire. It made him even more uneasy than he had been all day.

The winds of magic were tainted even here. He was not sure that most wizards would have noticed this thing – few of them were as sensitive as he was. His skin tingled slightly when he worked a spell and he had felt a twinge, only the faintest of twinges, of nausea. He suspected that the alchemy he used to maintain his health made him more susceptible to such things.

What was happening, he wondered?

It was possible that there was something nearby, some trace of old Dark Magic from the first Chaos incursion that still tainted the area. That might explain why it was so weak. Such influences had been fading for a very long time. That was the best explanation he could think of. He did not like to think what else it might portend.

He lay on his back, with his hands behind his head, and stared up at the stars visible through the gaps in the branches overhead. The woods did not seem as quiet at night as they did during the day, but he knew that that was an illusion. It was simply that his hearing was keener because his sight was dimmer.

It was good to be beneath the familiar stars of Ulthuan again. He could see one of the constellations that his father had taught him to recognise when he was a boy. Aenarion's Sword Belt it was called. It glittered above him cheerily.

He could hear something moving off in the woods. Most likely a fox he thought, certainly nothing larger. Not that he was any expert on such things, he thought sourly. It could be a beastman attempting to creep up on him for all he knew. He sat upright and rummaged in his saddlebags until he found a small group of stones that he had etched with runes.

He placed them around his campfire and spoke the words of an old spell. The runes on the stones glowed and small rainbows of light arced from one to the other and then faded. The wards would protect him and alert him if anything passed between them, bringing him awake instantly if it was larger than a rat.

Of course, that would not protect him if it was an arrow or a spear.

He told himself that he was being unnecessarily cautious but that was his nature. He arranged his saddlebags under the blankets and then spoke the words of another spell so that to any onlooker they would look like a sleeping elf.

He positioned himself a lot further from the fire and wrapped himself up in a blanket and wove an illusion that would make him blend into the landscape. He lay there in the darkness thinking if there was anything that he had missed, if there was something that he should do to increase the security but nothing came immediately to mind.

He began breathing exercises to enable himself to relax, to drift off into sleep. It was a long time before he could stop listening to the small noises of the forest and allow himself to slumber. Before he fell into sleep, he thought he felt again some taint to the magic around him. He hoped it would not affect the wards that he had placed on the other spells that he had worked for its protection.

He opened his eyes after what seemed like only a moment. The fire had burned down but he sensed a presence. It was odd because his wards had not woken him. He looked up and a shadow figure loomed out of the darkness, tall and slender, with a high forehead and a receding hairline unusual in an elf.

There was something immeasurably ancient and immeasurably sad about the stranger. He did not appear to be threatening. He was staring off into the distance, as if looking for something. When he turned to look at Teclis, it was a shock. He had no eyes. Where they should have been was only darkness, inside which something blazed.

Teclis felt as if he was falling into those eyes, and as he did so he could see that the lights formed a pattern, enormously large and astonishingly complex. It reminded him in some ways of the layout of Zultec. He could see that the pattern was flickering and unstable and starting to unravel in parts, and for some reason Teclis found this to be hugely threatening, as if his life depended on that not happening.

For a moment, everything appeared to be on the brink of dissolution, and he shouted for it to stop. He came awake with the echoes of the shout ringing through the forest. Panicking he glared around, seeking the tall stranger, but there was nothing there and his wards were undisturbed.

'Just a dream,' he told himself as he rose to see to his disturbed horses. He felt sure that was not all it had been.

* * *

As he rode, Teclis could feel the magic all around him. It was subtle, sly, hidden from most people, even the most sensitive of elves, but it was there. The defences of the Tower of Hoeth were ancient, powerful and strange.

There were no walls. Daemonic guardians did not patrol the woods around the tower. Spectacular magic did not blast intruders from the cloudless sky. Instead, the ancient wizards who had built the tower had protected it in a manner befitting their cleverness.

If you were a threat to the tower, you simply would not find it. You would wander lost in the woods, sometimes catching a glimpse of the mighty structure but never arriving at it.

Teclis had often wondered how this effect had been achieved. He could understand some of the components of it. Obviously there was an enchantment of divination present. The spells that guarded the tower needed to be able to detect any evil intention in those who approached. They needed to be able to reach into an enemy's mind, or perhaps even their very soul, to find this out.

And after that they needed to be able to twist that person's perceptions so that they could not find a way into the heart of the wood. The basic theory was simple enough.

Like many other scholars at Hoeth, he had pored over Bel-Korhadris's notes. He had caught glimpses of the workings of the Scholar-King's mind, but he had not been able to follow the whole process. No one had.

Bel-Korhadris had been the greatest geomancer since Caledor Dragontamer, with a gift amounting to genius when it came to the building of magical structures. When Teclis looked at his notes he was in the position of a peasant looking at a pile of bricks and an architect's plans for a mansion and then at the mansion itself.

He could see that the two things were connected, that they could somehow be used to create something magnificent. He just did not understand how.

Yet.

One day he would. Just as one day he would understand how Caledor had created the Vortex. If he lived long enough he would manage it. His thirst for knowledge was so great that it would not be denied.

Always when he studied the work of the great ancients, he felt this nagging sense that if only he worked harder, was just a little bit cleverer, understood just the tiniest amount more, he would gain the insight that he needed. So far it had not come, but he felt that one day it would.

He had heard some people claim that there were sophisticated tel-eportation spells involved in the tower's defences, but that seemed like nonsense to him. He knew that it was possible to warp time and space but it took an enormous amount of energy, which would be detectable by the most unsophisticated mage. Working on the minds of travellers would be far more efficient and far more difficult to detect. Of course, understanding the basic principles of how such a thing could work did not qualify him to be able to work the spell.

There were other things to be considered about it. The spells cov-ered an area of leagues around the tower. They were always in effect and had been ever since the tower was built.

Something maintained them and there were no obvious runes or points of focus that he had ever found. Perhaps elementals or dae-mons had been bound into the spell. After all, something at some point was making a judgement as to whether the approaching trav-eller was hostile or not. One possibility was that the judgement was left up to the traveller themselves. After all, who would be in a bet-ter position to know?

In any case it was magic of enormous sophistication and power. In its way it was a feat that was quite the equal of the building of the Tower of Hoeth itself, or of the creation of the vast web of spells that covered the Eastern Sea approaches to Ulthuan. The fact that it had been woven so discreetly into the fabric of this normal-seeming forest made it all the more impressive.

He tried to avoid thinking about the magic and simply concen-trate on enjoying the ride. The woods were beautiful in a quiet way. It was cool under the shadow of the trees and the air smelled fresh. Birds sang among the branches and the brilliant sunlight of Ulthuan poked its fingers through the canopy of leaves. It was all enormously different from the jungles of Lustria. It lacked the smell of rot and the overpowering heat and humidity against which the only pro-tection had been his magic.

He found that he was humming an ancient tune to himself. In some ways he was nearing the closest thing that he had to a home in the world. The tower was a place where mages gathered to study together and work spells and use the ancient library, easily the best in the world. It was a community of kindred spirits all sharing goals and ide-als. It was a place where everybody understood him in a way that was simply impossible for the non-magically adept to do. It was the one place in the world where he was not an outsider, and where his phys-ical handicaps were not held against him, at least some of the time.

Nonetheless, he found himself ambivalent about the place sometimes. He had grown accustomed to being an outsider, even enjoyed it in a perverse sort of way. It was, to a certain extent, the core of his own identity, of his view of himself.

Of course, sometimes having other people around could be pleasant. He was going to enjoy the sensation caused by his announcement that he had found the sword of Aenarion. He was going to enjoy talking about his discovery of its enchantments with his colleagues. He was going to enjoy sharing with them the knowledge that he suspected was in the ancient slann inscriptions he had brought back with him, even if that was knowledge of the disaster. There was something about being the centre of attention that he sometimes enjoyed, and he knew that he did not really care how he became the centre of attention when he was in this sort of mood.

Whistling to himself, smiling happily even though he carried news of impending disaster, he approached the White Tower. For whatever reason, the defences did not turn him away.

Teclis could really see the White Tower now. It was an enormous ivory spear, aimed at the underbelly of the clouds, easily the tallest structure that he had ever seen, quite possibly the tallest building in the world. It stood astonishingly high, immensely thin, tipped with a pointed cupola from which the High Loremaster could look down upon the vast width of his domain.

It was an awe-inspiring sight, at once fragile-looking and monumentally impressive, the sort of thing that could only be created by magic of the highest order. Many claimed that this was the crowning achievement of architecture and Teclis was not inclined to disagree.

Ever since he had first seen this building, he had loved it. It symbolised to him everything that was good and worth preserving about his people. When people talked about being willing to die to save their country, Teclis had never understood it. He could understand talking that way about this place though.

The Tower of Hoeth was not just a tremendous feat of architecture. It was the centre of learning for the entire island-continent of Ulthuan, the greatest repository of knowledge that the elves had ever created, greater even than the fabled library of Caledor the Archmage back in the dawn of the world. Hundreds of the greatest sorcerers from all across the continent came here to consult the library, talk with colleagues and share their knowledge with the students, among whom Teclis had once been numbered.

He was no longer a student. He rather missed that. In some ways it had been the happiest time of his life. He had had nothing to do but to study ancient texts and scrolls, to learn magic under the tuition of its greatest practitioners. There had been a time when every day revealed a new wonder and every night had been given over to learning how to work the small miracles of magic.

It had been an innocent time when he had nothing more to think about than which area of study he wanted to dive into next. He had been flattered by the attention of great wizards who found it worth their time to school him. He had been overcome by the sheer scale of the library, whose shelves and corridors filled the entire bottom of the tower, and the huge labyrinth of tunnels and cellars beneath it. He had been even more impressed by the complex labyrinth of spells that made the experience of studying in the library different for every person who visited it.

He knew he had seen shelves that had not been visited since the library was built and he knew that other people had found their way to parts of the library that he never would. The library showed each scholar what they needed to find when they needed to find it. It was as if some guardian spirit presided over it and gave to each student what was required.

As he wound ever closer to the tower, he began to notice the other guardians. In the shadows of the trees and bushes the Sword Masters of Hoeth waited. Each of them was equipped with a huge two-handed sword and each of them knew exactly how to use that weapon. Tall helmets shaded their eyes and heavy leather armour covered their bodies. One or two of them waved to Teclis as he rode by but most of them ignored him, concentrating on watching the approaches to the tower, even though no threat had ever managed to penetrate this far.

If one should perchance manage to do so, they would find armed warriors waiting for them and that would not be the least of the defences that they would encounter.

Potent spells walled the tower, protection against supernatural intrusions and divinations. The Loremasters did not want anyone spying on them and it was within their power to see that that did not happen. The spells were almost unnoticeable when they were dormant save, perhaps, to a wizard as perceptive as he was, but they were there, omnipresent and ready to be activated at the slightest sign of an intrusion.

As he got closer and closer to the tower, he found himself moving through larger and larger clearings. In some of the clearings were the glasshouse farms which provided food and drink for the wizards. In others were small villages where the retainers lived. Nearer to the tower, the open spaces held small groups of wizards. Some of them were scholars gathered together to discuss matters of research. Others consisted of a Loremaster and his students, engaged in the business of teaching and learning magic.

A few of them noticed him as he passed and pointed to him. He was well-known here, recognised as one of the most powerful of the new generation of wizards. His deeds were already discussed where mages gathered and he was sure that when word of his latest exploit got around, he would once again become the focus of all attention in the White Tower of Hoeth.

He waved at one or two of the academics that he knew and acknowledged others with a nod of his head. There were people here that he would need to talk to soon – scholars of ancient slann lore and wizards specialising in their odd means of divination.

He would also need to talk to artificers about what he had learned about the spells woven into the forging of Sunfang. He had an idea that he wanted to implement. He wanted to make his own blade using some of the techniques he had learned from the study of Caledor's work.

He did not want to copy that ancient masterpiece, though there were things that he could use, and possibly even improve on. He was being arrogant when he thought that, but a certain self-confidence was the mark of the true master wizard. After all, it was not enough to simply duplicate the work of the ancients, one had to engrave one's own signature on the work and leave one's own mark in the history of magical scholarship.

He dismounted from the steed and it was led away by a retainer, who seemingly had materialised there just for the purpose of doing so. He walked into the tower and made his way to the chambers that had been assigned to him. They were as he had left them, his books still strewn on the table, a scroll on which he had been penning magical formulae partially rolled up beside them.

He limped over to his bed, threw himself down upon it and looked up at the ceiling, knowing that above him the spire of the tower raced towards the sky. He was home. He had time to rest and gather his wits before he began to face the challenges awaiting him.

There was work to be done, and, for some strange reason, he did not feel like he had much time left to do it in.

* * *

Malekith strode up to the waystone. Tens of thousands of eyes were upon him. Most of those present were confused, wondering why so great an army had come ashore at this remote spot. They had expected to be besieging a city like Lothern by now.

Let them wonder, he thought. They would find out what the plan was soon enough.

He surveyed the land, drinking in the landscape of Ulthuan from which he had been so long away. He had a fine view out to sea where his ships lay at anchor and the Black Ark of Naggaroth sat like a volcanic island newly emerged from the waters of the bay. He could see the local farmers his warriors had captured and crucified for entertainment.

He shook his head at the stupidity of it. What a waste! Those elves could have been sold as slaves or made servants, or even simply put to death if they had committed some crime against Malekith's laws. It was not the way with the druchii though; they had to outdo themselves in proclaiming their decadence and cruelty. He blamed the influence of his mother and the cults she had introduced so long ago for that. The time would soon be here when he would bring them to heel.

Let them have their sport, they would be fighting soon enough and under the iron discipline he expected from the soldiers. They could indulge themselves – for now.

He inspected the waystone, studying the ancient runes marked in its side. He could feel the power surging through it, tapping into the ancient spell Caledor had cast on the last day of his life.

He could only see a tiny part of the vast network of energy that radiated out from the spot but he understood how it worked and just how awesome the concept was. This was probably the greatest feat of magic ever achieved by elves. It was difficult to see how it could be surpassed, although that would not stop him trying.

Once he had reunited the elves he would need to find some great projects to unify them behind him. Wars against the rest of the world would do to begin with but after that, once the world was reconquered, he would need to find some other great works to keep his subjects busy and prevent them from plotting against him, as elves always would if given the time and the opportunity. There had to be a way to improve on what Caledor had done, to use it against the powers of Chaos. If there was, he would find it.

That was for the future though. Right now he had other things that he needed to be doing. He gestured for N'Kari to approach. 'This is what you need, isn't it?' he said.

The daemon nodded. 'From here I can do all you require.'

'Then I suggest you proceed,' Malekith said. 'The sooner you are done, the sooner you can have vengeance on those you hate.'

'Let it be as you say,' N'Kari said, a measure of irony showing in its tone.

The daemon set to work, weaving a very intricate spell around the waystone that somehow tapped into its energies and the energies of something beneath it. Malekith watched fascinated, trying to understand what was being done.

Even with his vast knowledge of magic it was not quite possible. He wondered how much of what the daemon was doing was true magic and how much of it was deception, purely for show. He did not doubt that some of it was a trap that would have fatal consequences for anyone who tried to emulate the spell exactly as it was being performed now. It was what he would have done under the circumstances. He could expect no less from a Keeper of Secrets.

Soon a shimmering gateway glittered in the air before them. The assembled ranks of dark elf warriors eyed it uneasily. They did not quite understand what was going on, although they could see some powerful magic being cast. Only his generals were completely familiar with the plan and he suspected that even they had not really believed it was possible until they had witnessed it.

Malekith turned his cold gaze upon his army. He let them feel the power of his will. Not a single soldier present could hold his glance for more than a heartbeat and none of them dared even attempt it. All of them were thoroughly cowed. It pleased Malekith to note the result. It was possible for one being such as himself to intimidate tens of thousands. All it took was courage and iron will.

He raised his hand and gave the signal that the first phase of his great plan was about to begin.

His generals gave orders to the officers. His officers gave orders to their warriors. One by one, a unit at a time, the soldiers advanced into the gateway the daemon had opened and disappeared. Malekith turned his glance upon N'Kari. If the daemon planned treachery, this would be the time to attempt it: when it would cause the maximum damage to Malekith's plans. Once again, he ran over all of the binding spells and oaths he had placed on the daemon, looking for a flaw, but he could not find one. It was too late now anyway if there was.

This was just the first portal of many that it would open. If the daemon planned treachery it would have many opportunities. Still, within days, if all went well, his army would be in position to make the greatest surprise attack in history.

Now the Great War had truly begun.

Tyrion smelled Avelorn before he saw it. Even over the salty tang of the Inner Sea, he caught the scent of pine and a hint of the fresh air of the forest that lay just over the horizon. And there was something else in the air, some kind of magic, faint yet tangible, that set his skin tingling and made him feel more alive than he had in a very long time.

Soon, green was visible right across the horizon. Enormous trees overhung the water, packed so densely that it was difficult to see what was beneath their eaves. It was a forest, ancient and primordial, of the sort that had existed when the world was young, before the coming of Chaos changed everything. Perhaps some of those trees over there had existed during that dark time. It was possible that he was looking upon a thing that had existed when Aenarion was young.

The ship sailed on, leaving white foam in its wake. Gulls circled overhead. Atharis came up beside Tyrion and said, 'We shall be there soon. I hope you're prepared for your first look at the legendary Everqueen.'

'I'm sure she will be beautiful,' said Tyrion sardonically. 'Everybody tells me this.'

'Why do you sound so sour about it? Anybody would think that you did not want to be her champion.'

'Perhaps I just want to be different. Perhaps I just want to make up my mind for myself, not believe what everybody tells me.'

'You're starting to sound like your brother,' said Atharis.

'I am sorry if that disturbs you. It's just that everybody speaks about the Everqueen in the same tone of voice. Everyone who has ever met her sounds like they worship her, except Prince Iltharis.'

'Yes, he only ever sounds like he worships himself.'

Tyrion laughed. 'You know him too well.'

'He was one of the last people to see the old Everqueen alive,' said Atharis. 'She probably wasn't very happy that one of the last faces she ever looked on was not one of her devotees.'

'I think even he was disturbed by that event.'

'You talked to him about it, did you?'

Tyrion nodded. 'It was the most upset I have ever seen him.'

'You're probably the only person who has ever seen him upset then,' said Atharis. 'He is the most cold-blooded elf I have ever met.'

'You don't like him?'

'I never said that,' Atharis said. 'He is amusing enough in his own way and I don't suppose he's any more self-centred than most of us. I just don't think he liked me all that much.'

'I don't think he likes anybody all that much.'

'He seems to like you well enough. Probably because you are one of the few people that he can spar with and still get a bit of exercise.'

In the distance a bay was visible, the mouth of a river merging into the sea. The forest around the estuary had been cleared a little and there was what passed for a port in this part of the world. 'It looks like we have arrived,' said Atharis.

Tyrion could see that there were many ships in the harbour, a much greater number than there really ought to have been in a port this small. A large number of people had sailed here for the tournament, judging by the amount of ships that he could see riding at anchor.

'We shall need to head on upriver to find the tournament grounds,' said Atharis.

'It looks like we won't be the only ones,' said Tyrion.

'We'll be ready to go soon,' said Atharis.

'Good,' Tyrion replied. 'We don't have much light left.'

It had taken most of the day for his party to unload their horses and gear from the ship. They had to go as close as possible to the shore and then lower the horses into the water with winches and cranes, which was always a tricky proposition at the best of times.

While they were doing this, Tyrion waded ashore and explored his surroundings. The small village was right by the waterside. It had no walls and was built from logs with wattle and daub roofs. It looked very primitive for elven building but it somehow fitted in with the landscape. Perhaps this was how elves lived in ancient times. This was one of the few permanent settlements to be found on the coast. Most of the elves that dwelled within Avelorn were nomadic or lived deep in the woods.

'You seem unusually thoughtful,' said Atharis.

'This place is making me so. It's all very different from what I imagined.'

It all seemed stranger and older and wilder than any place he had ever been. The trees were hoary and ancient. Panthers stalked beneath the canopies of leaves. Somewhere off in the distance he heard the growl of an even larger predator, a manticore or a griffon perhaps. This would be a great land for hunting, he thought. It would be something to come here with a bow and some trusty companions and live off the land.

'Mount up,' said Atharis. 'We have a long way to go.'

'The sooner we start the better then,' Tyrion said. At the head of a force of fifty warriors and an equal number of retainers, he took the trail into the heart of ancient Avelorn. He could tell from the tracks that they were not the first to take this route in recent times. The thought was to occur to him more than once in the days of riding ahead.

In the distance, Tyrion could just make out singing and the sounds of flutes, lutes and other traditional elven musical instruments ringing out through the forest. The sounds drifted on the wind, carrying the sad, sweet music of the elves to his ears.

Tyrion's company rode down into a clearing crowded with musicians and archers and groups of elves that were cooking, singing and dancing. It was as if a city had suddenly sprung into being under the eaves of the trees. The ancient woods were crowded with people. There were elves everywhere under the boughs of the great oaks.

There were hundreds of tents visible and quite possibly thousands more hidden just out of sight among the trees and dells. They ranged from mighty pavilions, large enough to house companies of bowmen, to small lean-tos set up by poor elves with nowhere else to stay during this great festival.

The sound of musical instruments filled the air. A hundred songs mingled into one vast chorus. Thousands of voices sang the praises of the woods and the sun and the most beautiful queen who had ever lived.

There was an underlying note of sadness to the song that told the listener that the singers mourned the passing of someone who had been deeply loved, even as they celebrated the ascension of her cherished daughter.

Tyrion reined in his horse and paused to listen, drinking in the sound, surprisingly touched by what he was hearing. The rest of his party paused to listen as well, moved as much as he was.

As they stood there, a group of female elves armed with bows and dressed in leather armour came towards them. These were warriors of the Maiden Guard. They inspected Tyrion's party closely and their leader, a tall, stately beautiful elf said, 'You are here for the tournament?'

'Yes,' Tyrion said. 'I am Prince Tyrion and I have come from Lothern to take part in the competition.'

'You're very welcome here, Prince Tyrion,' the elf maiden said. 'We shall guide you to your campsite. You will want to be near the rest of the competitors.'

The Maiden Guard showed them to a place overlooking a stream. It was on a slight rise that gave them a good view of the vast open field on which the tournament would take place. Tyrion could see that there were many beautiful pavilions scattered around the area. Outside each of them stood a tall proud banner which told of the presence of a champion within.

Some of these little clusters of tents were the size of small villages. Some of those champions had a much larger retinue than he did. He wondered why they had brought small armies with them. Did they expect to be fighting a war for the favour of the Everqueen? Or was it all simply part of the great game of making a good impression, not just upon the new queen, but upon all rivals present?

He did not know and he did not really care. His own ego was not daunted by their presence, nor did he compare the size of his own retinue to those of his potential rivals and feel in the slightest intimidated.

He did, however, realise that the game had begun the moment he arrived, if not before. All of these things were moves on the board. He realised that his aunt had carefully calculated the size of his own retinue to be large enough to make an impression, but not so large as to seem ostentatious.

His followers went about their work under Atharis's careful eye and they were soon erecting his pavilion. Tyrion joined in. He always enjoyed using his hands and there was something about setting up these temporary structures that appealed to him. He helped drive the central post of his great silken tent into the dirt and then aided his fellows to throw the fabric shell into place, pull the hawsers tight and then drive in the pegs. He could see that some of the watching nobles were appalled to observe him performing manual labour and rushed off to tell their friends the gossip. He did not care.

When his own small village of tents was in place, he took the Emeraldsea banner himself and drove it into the ground outside his pavilion, like an explorer claiming a new land in the name of the Phoenix King.

He was not sure this was entirely appropriate behaviour or an entirely appropriate image to have in mind as he did it, but it suited his mood and he was pleased to see the green ship on a gold background flutter in the breeze before him.

He felt like he had staked a claim to his own place in this vast temporary city.

'Who is that?' Tyrion asked Atharis as they sat together on the slope outside his tent.

He pointed towards a tall, noble-looking elf, garbed in glittering armour and riding upon a most impressive steed. The warrior was accompanied by a group of knights almost as stern looking and impressive as himself. He waved in a friendly fashion as he passed.

'I believe that is Arhalien of Yvresse, judging by the device on his shield. He is widely regarded as the most likely winner of this tournament.'

'Why?' Tyrion asked.

'He is a great warrior. He has slain hundreds of dark elves. He has never lost a tournament with lances. He rides like he is from Ellyrion and fights like a Shadow Warrior. He is brave, noble, of ancient lineage, a noted poet, a fine dancer, a bold war-leader. He is everything a hero should be – sickeningly dull.'

'You sound as if you have studied him.'

'I have been forced to learn the life stories of all of your likely opponents. Your grandfather was a believer in thorough preparation. Your aunt is keeping that proud family tradition alive.'

'He knew this day would come?'

'Of course he did. The old Everqueen had to die sometime and it was a fair bet that her champion would not wish to serve her successor. Your grandfather had plans for all contingencies and your aunt is his daughter. Although I must admit that neither of them expected this to happen so soon. They would not have allowed you to go gadding around the world with your brother otherwise.'

'Is he a better warrior than I am?' Tyrion asked.

'I don't know. I doubt anyone except Prince Iltharis is better with a sword than you are, but if anyone is it will be Arhalien, or perhaps Prince Perian of Valaste. In addition, Arhalien has had far more practice with a lance than you have, and far more experience of tournament fighting. It is something of a sport where he comes from.'

'That is not real fighting,' said Tyrion.

'Perhaps not,' said Atharis, 'but it is the sort of fighting that will be going on here. And don't underestimate how vicious these contests can be. Competitors have died before now and not always by accident.'

'You don't think that is possible here? In the tournament to decide who will be the Everqueen's champion? That would make a mockery of everything the tournament stands for.'

'My dear Tyrion, there are times when I wonder whether you are really an elf. The forms will, of course, be observed, but there is a great deal of power and prestige at stake here, and you know how elves can be over those. This is a deadly serious matter. Deadly serious. I suggest you treat it as such.'

'I will bear that in mind.'

'We have found a poet to compose verses for you. You will merely need to memorise the couplets he writes and recite them.'

'I will not do that,' said Tyrion. 'I am here to compete on my own merits.'

'I have never known you to court failure. You are no poet, my friend, whatever else you might be. Many of those warriors over there are almost as adept with a pen as they are with a blade. Those who are not will have their own pet minstrels to compose verses for them. Why should you be any different?'

'Because I *am* different. I will win this in my own way or not at all.'

'It may well prove to be the latter.'

'If that is the case, let it be so.'

'You do not seem at all determined to win.'

'Let us rather say that I am not determined to win at any cost.'

'Then you start at a grave disadvantage.'

'So be it. You mentioned Prince Perian of Valaste as being good with a sword.'

'He is. Very good indeed. He fancies himself a bit of a wit too. A thoroughly unpleasant character if you ask me.'

'I do ask you.'

'He's vain, arrogant, spoiled–'

'A typical elven noble then...'

'Wait until you meet him. He is a veritable paragon of elven flaws. If I wanted to pick one elf to exemplify all that is bad in our people, it would be him.'

'I am starting to suspect you don't like him.'

'And to think people call you slow of mind. Such perceptiveness, Prince Tyrion...'

'Most people assume that no one so beautiful could be so clever,' said Tyrion.

'I see you are ramping up your egotism to compete with Prince Perian,' said Atharis. 'A bold strategy.'

'I am going to have to, aren't I? It's going to be like rutting deer competing to see who leads the herd, isn't it?'

'Not the metaphor I would have chosen, but yes. We really should get our tame poet working on your verses.'

'Is there anyone else I should know about?' Tyrion asked.

'At least a dozen, if you can stand being bored with the details. And I am sure there will be those I have missed. There's always some dark horse who enters these tournaments.'

'You'd better get started then...'

Tyrion and Atharis sat inside his tent, lounging on pillows and sleeping mats and drinking fine old wine from filigreed silver goblets. Tyrion could smell food being cooked and hear his bodyguard sitting around gossiping outside. They had spent most of the afternoon discussing Tyrion's potential opponents. There were no shortage of them.

'Well, we are here,' said Atharis, raising his goblet in a toast.

'Yes. Our epic quest has been accomplished,' said Tyrion. 'After many hardships we have finally reached our goal. I wonder how we managed to survive days of riding through these deadly forests. I think I saw some particularly savage-looking sheep at one point that filled my heart with dread.'

'There is no need to sound so satirical, my prince. We *are* a long way from civilisation now.'

'How will we endure life among these rustics? Missing Lothern already, Atharis?'

'I would not speak too loudly about the rustic charms of our present neighbourhood. Those Maiden Guard look as if they might carve you up for it. So do many of the yokels.'

Tyrion wondered whether his friend really felt that way, or whether he just felt out of his depth away from the city he knew and loved, and surrounded by the great woods and their inhabitants.

'This is a lovely place,' Tyrion said.

'It might be lovelier if it were not so crowded. I swear there are more people here than in the streets of the Foreigners' Quarter.'

'There are certainly more elves. So this is where our people have been hiding all this time. I was wondering.'

'This is probably the largest gathering these woods have seen in centuries. Warriors have come here from all over Ulthuan for the tournament. There are probably many still here from the coronation. They just can't be bothered to set off home yet. The lazy bastards.'

'I can understand that. There is something in the air here that encourages lingering.'

'I trust you, too, are not going to go all rustic on us? I think that would be just too much.'

'I meant it literally. I think there is some magic in the air here that clouds people's minds. Can't you feel it? There is a pulse of tranquillity about us.'

'I thought that was just all the dreamsmoke in the air. I wonder where I might get some. It may make our stay here more endurable.'

'I shall leave you in charge of that. I am going to take a look around.'

'Don't get lost, and try not to fall in with any of the local enchantresses. You may find that you never want to leave.'

'I don't think there is much danger of that,' Tyrion said, rising to his feet and striding towards the doorway.

'If you find any dreamsmoke vendors, bring me back some,' said Atharis.

'Find your own,' said Tyrion.

Tyrion wandered through the vast city of tents, feeling very much a stranger. In some ways it reminded him of the jungles of Lustria. All around were trees, some of the gigantic ancient things thousands of years old.

It did not feel as close or threatening as the jungle had and there were no poisonous snakes or biting insects that he could detect. Instead there were lots of elves. They had come from every corner of Ulthuan to attend the court of the Everqueen.

He wondered how many of these people attended on the Everqueen and how many of them were here for the tournament.

As always, people stared at him. He was used to this and paid it no more mind than he would have in the streets of Lothern. He rather enjoyed it as a matter of fact, particularly when the onlookers were women. He smiled at anyone who caught his eye and did his best to look amiable.

Teclis would hate this place. His brother did not like being the centre of attention or being surrounded by crowds of people. He would doubtless have something sarcastic to say about all of these happy, thoughtless revellers. He wondered how much of what he was seeing was the product of magic. Teclis would have known, of course, but he lacked his brother's sensitivity to the flows of the winds of magic.

Even he suspected that some spell was at work here. The people looked too happy, too energetic, too thrilled, even for elves in the mood for merrymaking. An atmosphere of almost complacent contentment hovered over this place. Every single person that he saw really wanted to be here and was really happy with the fact that they were. He could not think of any other place he had ever been in his life where that was true. Over the city of Lothern, for all its thrilling commercial energy, a certain melancholy brooded, shadowing even the happiest festival days.

This place reminded him, in an odd elliptic sort of way, of the atmosphere in the Shrine of Asuryan. There was the same sense of some ancient power touching the world. A girl danced by, flowers in her hair and a smile upon her lips. She blew him a kiss as she passed and, smiling, he answered in kind. She skipped back over to him and looked at him closely, examining him frankly and with considerable appreciation. He looked back at her in the same way, unembarrassed. He had heard tales of the way people behaved at the court of the Everqueen and he was determined to fit in as well here as he did everywhere else.

'You're here for the tournament?' the girl asked.

'I am indeed,' Tyrion replied.

'You hope to become her champion?'

'I am unsure about that,' he replied.

She laughed. The sound was like the tinkling of silver bells. 'You're unsure? How is that possible?'

'It is a very long story,' Tyrion said.

'We are elves. If we do not have time for long stories, who does? My name is Lyla.'

'Mine is Tyrion.'

'Like the hero of the Shrine of Asuryan?'

'Exactly the same.'

'I had heard he was as good looking as you.'

'That is quite possible.'

'You are he, are you not?'

'I was at the Shrine when it was attacked. I do not think I was all that heroic. I was hiding in it at the time the daemon came.'

'Do you have a twin brother who is a great sorcerer?'

'I have a twin who is studying at Hoeth. Although I am not sure he is all that great a sorcerer. He would probably tell you he was.'

'Let us drink wine. I am curious about you now.'

'Lead on,' said Tyrion. Ten minutes later they were naked in her tent. There was something to be said for the festival atmosphere of this place, he thought.

Tyrion took leave of Lyla and continued on his way.

As he walked through the cool shadows of Avelorn, Tyrion studied the people around him in a more leisurely fashion. This was a place utterly unlike Lothern. It moved to a different rhythm. Its people had a different attitude to time. They seemed more relaxed.

He watched a circle of elves gathered round a poet declaiming the ancient epic of Caledor the Conqueror. They knew the words, mouthing them silently as the poet spoke.

Tyrion watched them watching the poet. He knew the work and knew the reciter had been about his business for hours and most likely would still be speaking at sunset. These people had the time and the interest to do this, to watch the performance while other elves, selected by lot or from the family retainers, brought them food and wine. It was the sort of reading that you only saw in abbreviated form among the busy money-making elves of Lothern. It was like stepping back into the past, into the golden age of the first Everqueen, and he knew it was deliberately so.

He looked for notes of falseness and because he was looking, he found some. Here and there, some of the audience were asleep. Others paid no attention and inspected their nails, but this had probably been so during the golden age as well. Perhaps this was part of a different golden age, but a golden age nonetheless. These elves were keeping the old ways alive. They saw themselves as guardians of a certain sort of elfness, and he did not doubt that they were correct to do so.

Lothern was the future, if the elves were to have a future. It was commercial, home of an outward-looking, sophisticated, mercantile Phoenix King. It was a city of trade, a hybrid cosmopolitan place where the elves mingled with other peoples and learned from them and adapted to the new and altered world.

In Avelorn, the elves were behaving as they had before the age of Aenarion. It was beautiful and moving and rather sad. Sad because all of this took an effort to maintain and it was dying away. It was an enclave frozen in amber.

No, he told himself. That was not fair. This place still lived. It was the beating heart of asur society. It was where artists and poets and dancers came to compete, to find an appreciative audience, to seek fame and a certain kind of glory. It was not the sort of glory that he himself was interested in, but he could understand why some elves were.

He moved into another glade. Elves in green raiment practised archery, drawing and firing at targets hundreds of paces away. He realised these were not competitors in the tournament. These were just ordinary citizens of Avelorn, training with their weapons as was their right and duty. The practice made them the finest archers in the world, and the backbone of the elven citizen-armies.

He inspected them, as a general might inspect his troops. Each of them was an elf in his or her prime. All of them must have handled bows for decades, if not centuries. All of them were hale and hearty and would remain so for hundreds of years.

No other troops would or could have their skill, their discipline or their experience. Simply by virtue of still being alive for so long, they would have fought in dozens of skirmishes and battles. They would have survived encounters with numerous foes.

Like the poets he had just witnessed, they too were part of an older Ulthuan, one that dated from the age of Morvael, of the first great citizen-soldier levies. They were part of the culture. They too moved to a different beat than the elves of Lothern.

It came to Tyrion that elves like these could be found all over the island-continent. In aggregate, they must far outnumber the elves of Lothern although they had no single town or city that was even a fraction of the size of the city-state. Probably they were much more representative of the people as a whole. And they looked at least as much to the Everqueen as to the Phoenix King for leadership.

Perhaps for the first time in his life, in this place, he started to get a sense of what his own people were like, all of the folk beyond the city in which he lived and the mountains he had called home from his earliest youth.

For these people here, the folk of Lothern were something new and strange. The people here were the ones who represented the mainstream of life. Looking at them, he saw the majority of the elves as they wanted to see themselves and he realised that he was not at all like them.

He passed on, entering a vast clearing in the forest filled with silk pavilions and corrals for proud elven steeds. The symbol of the Everqueen was on everything and he realised that this must be the place in which she currently dwelled. Maiden Guards strolled everywhere, but no one looked at him suspiciously. It was inconceivable that anyone would want to harm the ruler of Avelorn.

Magic shimmered in the air, the sort of powerful conspicuous magic his brother could work. Beneath it he sensed the presence of another type of magic. The air was thick with it, a constant stream of something living, beneficial, potent. He remembered again the atmosphere of the Shrine of Asuryan, and the feeling here was of the same kind, although not produced by the same being.

In Asuryan's Shrine the being had been of fire, powerful, destructive, mercurial, somewhat akin to Chaos. Here, whatever was present was slower, more placid, enduring, fertile. It was a spirit of earth and forest, and its locus of power was in this place. Or perhaps in the person of the Everqueen.

A thought struck him. Perhaps Lothern was a place of water. If the old magical schemata of the elemental universe was to be believed, then there must be a place of air as well. He wondered where that could be, and it struck him that maybe the place was in the north, a place of cold and storm winds, perhaps where Malekith was.

He amused himself with such idle fantasies as he passed through the shadow of pavilions and onto the grounds where scores of elven artisans were at work creating the tournament fields.

A pulse of excitement started to beat in him. There was going to be a great contest here and he was going to take part in it. It was a ritual that had been enacted only a dozen times during the course of history, and it was one that had a significance that was embedded deeply in the nature of his people.

He understood that perhaps he was seeing things at an unusual time, during a change in reigns. The old queen was dead. The new queen was just that – new. The tone of her reign had yet to be set. Her likes and dislikes were as yet unknown. There were those who had known her as a child, and who thought they knew her as a woman, but they could not know what she was going to be like as the Everqueen. She was a butterfly newly emerged from that particular chrysalis and she might be changed as utterly as her relationships with those around her were going to be.

If he won the tournament he really would have a chance to influence the tone of this new age. He would have his chance to be part of her court, to sway her choices. It was not the sort of power he wanted, or the sort of role he craved. He was a warrior, not a courtier.

And yet, he had to admit to himself, despite his reluctance to do so, there was something here that appealed to him. This felt like the setting of one of those tales of heroism and chivalry he had so loved as a child. It was glamorous and full of intrigue. It was beautiful. There was pageantry and magic. He could picture himself as a knight at the court of the fairest of elf queens. It was the sort of role he had delighted in imagining as a boy. It still had its appeal even now, although he could see the folly of it.

In spite of all his reservations, like all those others, he was happy to be here.

◀ CHAPTER SEVENTEEN ▶

In the morning sunlight, Tyrion watched the gathering of heroes. More and more warriors arrived on the tournament grounds, great champions shorn of their retinues, single fighters who had come alone, perhaps following a dream, perhaps merely to test themselves against the best the island-continent could provide.

He stood on the field itself, where today only contestants and representatives of the Everqueen were allowed. Atharis and his retainers watched from the surrounding hillocks along with the followers of all the other champions present. He saw Arhalien of Yvresse turn and bow to his followers before he passed through the arch and onto the tournament field. His retainers cheered him but could go no further.

Tyrion saw proud armoured riders from Ellyrion mounted on their matchless, prancing steeds. He saw a lovely woman warrior from Tiranoc, staring around with fierce wary eyes. There were grim-faced soldiers from Yvresse, and tall, hard-faced elves from the Shadowlands, as harsh and craggy as the land that bore them.

They looked at him as much as he looked at them, and there was a challenge in their stare. They knew instinctively that he too was here to compete and that he would be a rival, and they could tell just from the look of him that he would be a worthy one.

In some glances there was hostility but in most of them was an odd form of comradeship. They were all here for the same reason, and by the nature of the contest, they were set apart from the mass of other elves. It was something that they shared, a kinship of spirit born of rivalry, yet forging a bond. That was the way he felt at least, and he suspected that for those he saw it would be the same.

He looked at his potential rivals and wondered about them. What were their stories? What sights had they seen on the way here? What drove them to compete? What was it they sought?

He felt like simply going over and asking. He was endlessly curious about these things. He could not do so though, not out of shyness, but because he knew that it would be misconstrued. Perhaps they would see him as only seeking an advantage, as attempting to uncover weaknesses, and perhaps he would be.

There would be time enough to get to know a small fraction of these warriors. There would be drinking bouts and dances and all manner of merry meetings. It was something he could wait for with anticipation, part of the pleasure of being here.

He could tell by the way some of them looked at him that his reputation had preceded him. They had heard of the battles he had fought and the way he had survived an encounter with a Keeper of Secrets while still only a callow youth. They knew he had crossed blades with a monster that had fought against Aenarion himself, and that he was of Aenarion's blood.

That thought cast a shadow over his happiness. One day the monster would be back and it would come looking for him, and it occurred to him that it would come looking for the new Everqueen as well. Like every Everqueen before her, she was descended from Aenarion's lost daughter, Yvraine. She too would be a target when N'Kari returned to pursue his infernal vengeance quest.

Tyrion tried telling himself that he might live his entire life without ever encountering the daemon. There were over six thousand years between its last two appearances in history. He could live and die and his descendants unto the tenth generation might do the same, before the daemon reappeared.

He doubted that things would be that way. He had a feeling that he and N'Kari were destined to meet again, that their paths were due to collide during his lifetime and, if that happened, he would need to find some way to banish the daemon forever, not just for his own safety but for the safety of his children and their children beyond them. He needed to find a way if he could. He let his hand rest on Sunfang. Perhaps the great blade held the secret. He prayed that it was so.

Horns announced the coming of the Everqueen. Surrounded by her Maiden Guard, she made her way into the massive stand that had been erected overlooking the tournament field. At this distance it was hard to see anything but a tall, stately golden-haired figure, graceful of movement, wealthy of dress, carrying a mystical staff in her hand. There was something about her though, a sense of power, deeply hidden, that commanded attention.

Tyrion was not the only one watching her arrival. Every eye on the field was drawn to the stand and its new occupant. It was understandable. She was after all the reason they were here. He glanced around and saw something odd. Everyone present was looking at the Everqueen with an expression that combined awe, religious reverence and love. He had not realised they all felt quite that way, and then it dawned on him that they probably could not help themselves. What he was seeing was most likely the result of a very powerful spell.

He wished Teclis were here to advise him. He was genuinely curious now.

Horns sounded again. This time the sequence of notes was different, a summons to battle, a challenge, a demand for attention.

The herald of the Everqueen took up his position on the great dais in front of the stand. All eyes were upon him now. He spread his arms wide with a flourish. Then he paused, dramatically, in order to focus attention before he launched into his speech.

The herald was a tall elf with silver hair. His features were very fine. He carried himself with great dignity. And yet beneath this, there was something else, a suggestion of the mountebank, of the need to please and the need to be at the centre of attention that was somewhat at odds with his majestic air.

'Friends, fellow elves, subjects of our beloved Everqueen,' he said, turning with a flourish to the stand. His voice carried over the murmur of the great crowd. He gave the impression of speaking in a conversational tone, but there was some magic at work that carried his voice to every corner of the field.

'We are gathered here at the start of the reign of a new Everqueen to select her champion. Unto that champion will fall the duty of guarding our kingdom's greatest treasure. Into his hands will be placed the life of the Everqueen. He will be called upon to defend her from all threats and all challenges and to protect her from harm, even if it costs his own life. The victor of this great tournament will be participating in a grand tradition that stretches from the earliest days of our realm.'

Tyrion thought the herald very self-satisfied and pleased with the sound of his own voice, but the words resonated anyway. He realised that up till now he had been thinking about this tournament simply from the point of view of his own needs and desires.

He had known about the responsibilities the position of champion entailed but he had never really thought about them and about the place implied in history and culture. Now he was forced to.

If he did win, he would be subordinating his own life to that of the Everqueen. He would be expected to give up his own life to save hers if need be. Was he really up to that challenge?

The answer was fairly simple given his personality. If the duties of champion fell to him, they would be performed to the best of his ability.

He had risked his life before on behalf of the kingdoms and for lesser reasons. He was certain that he was capable of doing so in the service of something much more important.

While he was thinking this, the herald spoke on, invoking the names of famous champions of the past and recounting their deeds and their sacrifices.

Tyrion was stirred, as were the people round about him. There was magic in the air again and he knew that the herald was using it. There was something about the elf's voice indeed. It was not just a spell, although there was an element of that. It was simply that the way that the elf spoke touched something deep within the soul. It went beyond his choice of words and the beauty of his speaking voice. There was something in Tyrion and in the others present that responded to it on a level deeper than thought.

It was a talent worth possessing, Tyrion thought. To be able to address troops in this manner would be a gift indeed. One of the most important things for a leader was being able to motivate the warriors who followed you and this type of magical speaking would be invaluable for that.

The herald continued. 'Today, friends, mighty and worthy warriors have come together from every corner of Ulthuan to compete in a contest to find a worthy heir to those mighty champions of the past. By the time this full moon has passed, a new champion will have been selected to guard the peerless treasure of our realm.'

The herald gazed upon the assembled competitors and smiled. 'Looking out at all of your faces, I can see there only the noblest of intentions...'

That beautiful voice carried no note of irony and yet it was there. Tyrion sensed it.

'Selflessly you seek to enter the service of our great queen. Selflessly you are putting aside personal ambition in order to take up a duty. It tells me something about the greatness and nobility of the spirit of our people and our kingdom that so many of you have come together here with no other desire than to serve.

'I can see that all of you are worthy. It saddens me that only one of you will, at the end of the contest, be able to take up the role of champion. However, the elf to whom this great honour falls will know that he has faced and bested worthy opponents indeed. You represent the best of the people, their great spirit, their great desire for self-sacrifice, their great love for their queen. I am proud to stand here before you and tell you what you need to know to participate in this contest.'

The herald was really milking the moment. And why not? It was the sort that only came once in most elves' lifetimes. How often was a new Everqueen crowned? How often was a new champion chosen? This might be the only time this contest would take place in Tyrion's lifetime or the herald's. The winner in the next few days would be remembered for as long as there were elves in the world.

He realised that this was important to him. Glory was important to him. More than wealth, he craved renown. He wanted to prove himself worthy. The question was – was he willing to pay the price?

'Today we begin with the tournament. The first round will decide who continues into the next rounds. Today every participant will prove his worthiness with a blade and shield. These are the most basic weapons of the warrior.'

Tyrion thought that the bow was actually the most basic weapon of the warrior, but he could see why the stress would be laid upon using sword and shield. These were the sort of weapon that a bodyguard was much more likely to be called upon to use.

The herald held up a small brooch. It was in the shape of a leaf and the bronze suggested the colours of autumn. 'Each of you will be issued with a bronze leaf and each of you will be matched against a worthy foe. The winner of the contest will be awarded his opponent's leaf. He should return it to the heralds and progress to the next round of combat. The winner of that contest will be awarded his foe's brooch to return to our watchers and progress to the next round. This will go on until there is only one winner and only one brooch. And it will set the pattern for all of the other contests that will take place. Once the horns sound, you will go from here and collect your brooches and proceed to the fields of trial, where you will be assigned your opponents.'

Everyone seemed light-hearted now and ready to begin and Tyrion felt the same way. After all these days of waiting, he was about to step forward into the contest. He found that his heart lifted at the prospect of a fight. Whatever happened, he was determined to enjoy himself today.

Smiling, he walked off towards the trestle tables at which lesser heralds were waiting to distribute the tokens of the contest. He collected his and pinned it to his breast. All the other warriors present were doing the same.

Tyrion entered the roped off area in which the first round of the tournament was to take place. He walked across to the sergeant-at-arms and was issued with a blunted sword, armour and a shield. He swiftly donned the armour. It was heavier than the very fine mail that he was used to, but it was adequate and he did not doubt for a moment that it was capable of resisting the blunted edge of the weapon he was carrying.

Of course, that did not mean that injury was impossible. The weight of a blade swung in combat practice could still break an arm or a rib. It was not unknown for elves to be killed during such trials. He knew that he would need to be cautious, because any sort of broken bone would disbar him from the championship and immediately end all hopes of winning.

Next he tried the blade and found it reasonably well-balanced. It did not harmonise with his movements with the supernatural grace of Sunfang. It was not even as close to being as good as the sword he'd carried most of his life, which had been a gift from Korhien. But it would do. Given a few moments he could habituate himself to its use. The shield was the fairly large kind commonly used by infantry. He strapped it on to his left arm. He had worn this kind of shield many times over the course of many battles. It felt like donning a familiar pair of old boots.

Once all of these preparations were completed he began running through a few practice exercises of the kind he had performed almost every day of his life. As he did so he was aware that he was being watched by a number of the warriors around him.

A few of them made favourable comments on his technique, a few of them looked jealous, most of them simply watched as if hoping to gain some advantage from studying their rival. He considered pretending to be slower and clumsier than he was but decided against it. He knew that some of his foes would be intimidated by witnessing his performance which would give him an advantage of a different sort.

The sun had risen quite high in the sky before the last competitor had given his name to the heralds and been announced. At last, though, everyone was armed and equipped for the first stage of the great contest. An atmosphere of excitement began to palpably form over the assembled host of warriors.

Thousands of spectators had gathered on the hillsides surrounding the competition glade; their presence as much as the presence of the Everqueen gave the tournament an excitement all of its own. It was very different from the atmosphere that Tyrion had experienced before a battle. Then the only audience consisted of your comrades and your enemies and the former were too concerned with their own survival to pay much attention, while the latter were only interested in killing you.

The onlookers gave this contest a very different tone. They made it special in a very different way. This audience was interested in every competitor and were here as much to be entertained as to witness the outcome of the tournament for the favour of the Everqueen.

Tyrion was very aware that eyes were on him. He knew that he was a striking figure and easy to pick out from the crowd of other contestants, and he had absolutely no doubt that his own name would be known among those who had come to watch.

This contest was open to all. There was no selection process other than volunteering. The role of the Everqueen's champion was one that many legends were attached to. Commoners and freeholders had held it, at least according to song and story.

Tyrion wondered about that. In practice the sort of weapons and gear that a champion was required to be capable with required gold and lots of it, and the qualifications concerning poetry, music, dance and courtliness were ones that the wealthy would have a much greater chance of acquiring than the less well off.

Looking around, he could see that there were many dreamers here today. Some of them perhaps believed they had a chance at being the hero of a storyteller's tale. Others were most likely only here because they wanted to take part, to have a place in a legendary elven festival. Long-lived as elves were, there would not be that many opportunities to do so for anyone.

The horns sounded again to announce the contest had begun. At this stage there would be multiple competitions at once. There were too many involved to allow the luxury of single combats taking place one at a time before the crowd. Heralds paired competitors off against each other.

Tyrion was drawn against some peasant swordsman from Chrace. He made short work of the contest, beating his first opponent in the initial swaggering of blades. After the combat was over, he bowed to his beaten foe and accepted the beautifully worked copper brooch, then walked around to watch the other competitors. The losers went out to swell the crowd.

The second round took place between those who still wore copper leaves. Tyrion found this just as easy as the first round and took his opponent's brooch from him at the conclusion of the fight.

As the day wore on he acquired more and more brooches. By late afternoon, the contest was down to the last four. Tyrion found himself facing Arhalien. It was something that had to occur sooner or later and he welcomed it.

The Yvressian lord was standing at the barrier chatting with his retainers. A herald came forward to introduce them and witness the fight. Arhalien looked just as interested in Tyrion as Tyrion was in him. His manner was aloof but polite and not unfriendly. He was the very model of a warrior lord.

'Prince Tyrion. I have heard a lot about your prowess with a blade,' he said.

'Poets everywhere sing of your skill,' said Tyrion, determined not to be outdone in politeness.

'I have heard you are but recently returned from Lustria, where you have added another glittering chapter to the tale of your deeds. Rumour has it that you have found the sword of Aenarion.'

'That is the case.'

'It is a pity that you are not allowed to use it in the tournament,' said one of Arhalien's retainers with a sneer. Arhalien looked at him as if appalled by his bad breeding.

'I do not need a blade like Sunfang for a tournament like this,' said Tyrion.

'The very fact that Prince Tyrion is standing here is testimony to his skill,' said Arhalien with a warning look at his follower. 'Boriane meant no disrespect,' he added to Tyrion.

'I am sure,' said Tyrion.

'I must say I am looking forward to this contest,' said Arhalien. 'It will be fine sport to encounter so worthy an opponent.'

'Your reputation as a duellist precedes you,' said Boriane. The sneer was better hidden this time, but it was still there. Beyond Lothern, duelling to the death was very much frowned upon. It was regarded as more of a tool of assassination than a contest of honour.

Tyrion could understand why. It was a formalised way of removing political enemies that resulted in the fewest comebacks against its practitioners. On Lord Emeraldsea's instructions he had provoked fights with almost a score of political enemies. He himself had been challenged dozens of times. He enjoyed the fighting, the killing and the victories, but he did not like being a political instrument. He was not sure why. He had been a soldier often enough and had killed under orders in that context. What had made it so different when he duelled?

The answer was simple. As a soldier he was killing the enemies of the realm. As a duellist he had killed other elves who were citizens of Ulthuan and subjects of the Phoenix King and the Everqueen.

'You look thoughtful, Prince Tyrion,' Arhalien said.

'I was remembering the last duel I fought,' said Tyrion.

'Now is a time to fight, not reminisce,' said the herald. 'Are you both ready to begin?'

'Yes,' said Arhalien. Tyrion nodded.

Tyrion raised his blade in salute to Arhalien. His opponent did the same then closed his eyes in a brief prayer to the gods.

The fight was not a long one. Prince Arhalien was indeed very good with a sword, but Tyrion was better. Arhalien did not seem to take his defeat badly.

'I shall just have to do better with my lance,' he said. Tyrion found that he rather admired the Lord of Yvresse. He felt sure the Everqueen would not find a better champion.

'I look forward to meeting you again,' said Tyrion.

'And I you. We will have the opportunity soon,' said Arhalien. 'Our position in this contest gives us both the honour of sitting at the Everqueen's table this evening.'

It was the last fight of the opening day. The sun was low in the sky. All eyes in the huge crowd were focused on Tyrion and Prince Perian. All of them were expectant. They knew two masters of the blade were fighting here.

After the first passage of blades, Tyrion knew Prince Perian was the best swordsman he had faced since he sparred with Prince Iltharis. The elf had a natural gift for the blade and many centuries of practice. He knew how to use the heavy shield of the elven warrior. He was fast and very strong and he had a great deal of experience on the field of battle.

Looking at his proud face, Tyrion wondered whether he really should be fighting against this elf. Prince Perian would make a much better champion for the Everqueen. He was a believer. He was dedicated to the woman and he truly, truly wanted to be her champion.

His heart was in it in a way that Tyrion's was not. It might be best for all concerned just to let him win. He could return home having done his duty as far as his family was concerned. No one except himself would ever know what had happened.

It would take a warrior as skilled as Iltharis, and one who knew him as well as Korhien, to know exactly what he had done and even they could never be sure. So much of combat was a matter of luck when it got to this level of skill. The slightest misjudgement, the slightest lapse of concentration, could see the contest go either way.

For a moment he considered it. Then he heard the crowd chant his name and sensed the adulation of the women. Part of him wanted to win, and worse than that, part of him was not sure that he could. Prince Perian was a great swordsman. They really were in the same class when it came to the use of their weapons. Prince Perian might even be better. Perhaps his sneering look was justified.

Something in Tyrion resisted that notion with every fibre of its being. He was not prepared to let anyone beat him while there was still breath in his body. If he was going to lose this fight then he would need to be defeated fair and square. His opponent would win because he was the better warrior, not for any other reason.

The crowd roared as Tyrion went on the offensive. He smashed aside Prince Perian's shield with his own, stepped inside his guard and stabbed. Prince Perian parried desperately, padding backwards, obviously taken off guard by the change of pace and tactics.

Tyrion pressed home his advantage, sensing that he was never going to get a better opportunity to go in for the kill. He closed the distance, striking out at Prince Perian's shoulder, numbing a nerve and causing the blade to drop from his hand.

It was over. Tyrion had won. He was the victor on the first day of the great tournament. The crowd chanted his name. It was more intoxicating than wine.

As he was taking the applause the herald beckoned him over. 'Join the other contestants. The winners on today's field are to be presented to the Everqueen.'

The Everqueen and her entourage entered the field. The face of every elf present changed immediately, taking on a glow of love and worship. They stared as if a goddess had just manifested herself in their midst.

Alarielle was beautiful, Tyrion did not deny that for a moment – she was tall, fair and possessed the most striking green eyes that he had ever seen – but he could see nothing to justify the adoration in which she basked. Powerful magic indeed was at work here. Was he the only one unaffected by it?

Even as the thought crossed his mind, their gazes met. A shock passed between them. She turned and looked away first. She seemed to have picked his face out of the entire crowd, possibly because it was the only one not wearing an expression of undying love, he thought sourly.

One by one, all of the final candidates for champion stepped forward to be introduced to her. She accepted their greetings graciously and as if it was her due. Tyrion found himself resenting this more and more as the ritual progressed. He tried to control his emotions, a thing he was normally very good at.

He struggled to make his expression bland and place a smile upon his lips but it felt unnatural and stilted. Whatever sorcery was being worked on the crowd was having the opposite effect on him.

He was not used to feeling such emotions. He was normally amiable. It was not because he was self-conscious around women that he felt this way either; there were few elf males who were less so. He greatly enjoyed female company. There was magic at work, he felt sure of it. And that in itself was unusual, for he was normally the least sensitive of elves as far as magic was concerned.

As she came ever closer, he began to get some idea of what he thought might be happening. There was an aura about Alarielle and it did seem to command love and respect. He suspected that whatever sorcery was present affected him differently. For some reason, something in him resisted it, and perhaps this anger was part of that process of resistance.

Suddenly they were face to face. Tyrion was a head taller and he bowed to her, not fully and formally as was expected but in the social manner in which one greeted an equal or near equal. He could hear gasps of outrage from the crowd and he suspected that if he was not careful he might get lynched.

The Everqueen did not seem to mind though. She seemed more intrigued than outraged, although that might simply have been good manners and self-control. Members of the Maiden Guard glared at him. They looked as if they would like to knock him to his knees with the butts of their spears. It was not something that you could do to a freeborn elf though. The Everqueen placed her hand on the arm of the captain of the guard to emphasise it, he thought.

A chamberlain leaned forward between them, stared coldly at

Tyrion then made the formal introduction as politely as ritual demanded.

'So you are the Prince Tyrion we have heard so much about,' said the Everqueen. Her voice was low and pleasant but it irritated Tyrion, as did her condescending manner.

'I am afraid I do not know what you have heard about me, your serenity,' he said.

'I confess I was expecting someone a little more polished,' she said with a trace of acid in her voice.

'I am sorry to disappoint,' he said. Out of the corner of his eye, he caught sight of Prince Perian smirking and he realised that he was not doing his own chances of becoming champion any good and that was giving his rivals cause for amusement.

He liked that even less. He was getting off to a bad start. Perhaps he was sabotaging his own chances of winning because he did not want the prize.

Already the Everqueen was moving along the line, and he noticed that Prince Perian was following through with the ritual with polished aplomb. He noticed also that the captain of the Everqueen's guard was staring at him coldly as if memorising his face.

He suspected that he had made an enemy there by his disrespect for her mistress. He smiled cheerfully at her in a way that he could not have managed with Alarielle and which was, as he knew, very provoking under the circumstances. The captain turned her head away quickly as if to hide her anger, but he saw that there was a red flush on her cheeks.

Very good, Tyrion thought to himself, very suave. He did not think he could have done worse in this situation if he had tried. In fact, he suspected that he would probably have done better. He told himself that he did not care, that he did not want to be part of this herd of worshippers, that he was quite happy that he was immune to whatever magic surrounded the Everqueen. He suspected, however, that he was not really immune, but rather it simply affected him differently.

Some of his fellow candidates looked as if they wanted to challenge him to a duel there and then. Some of them looked satisfied that a potential rival had eliminated himself from the competition so early, and some of them simply looked confused, as if they could not understand his behaviour. They looked at him pityingly which made him even angrier.

Tyrion knew he needed to get a grip on himself. If he was going to be eliminated from this competition he wanted it to be because he was beaten by his opponents, not because he had allowed himself to be beaten.

He resolved to do better. If he was going to lose, he was going to lose openly and fairly after he had done his best. There were still tournaments to be entered and fights to be won and he had no intention of losing any of those, even if he could win nothing else. This was his chance to prove that he was among the best warriors in elvendom, if not the best.

Tomorrow he would find out.

◄ CHAPTER EIGHTEEN ►

N'Kari could tell the druchii troops were nervous. He could tell they hated him. He rather enjoyed the sensation. He wore a form appropriate for the situation, an armoured female parody of Malekith, which amused and served him in multiple ways.

It mocked the Witch King while at the same time reminding his followers from whom ultimate authority flowed. It pained N'Kari to admit that he needed that. The spells binding him prevented him from bringing his full powers to bear. Without Malekith's permission, he could not unleash them.

Fortunately, the dark elves were in the habit of obeying their king. Malekith had ensured that it could not be otherwise, at least when his eye or the eye of his direct representative was on them.

A delicious aroma of fear rose from the assembled soldiery and their leaders. None of them wished to invite, or even give the excuse for, punitive action. There were many ways that could be turned to amusing advantage, N'Kari thought. If he wished.

At the moment, he did not really want to. Malekith had calculated things very finely. N'Kari did not want to interfere with his plans to ravage Ulthuan. He wanted very badly to see that happen and had made up his mind to do everything in his power to help in this one area.

He wanted to kill high elves and the best way of doing that was to see that their savage kindred were in a position to do as much damage as possible. That was why he had spent the past few days in the ultimately tedious business of shipping the Witch King's troops to various points around Ulthuan.

He paused for a moment, wondering where this sudden complacency had come from. He examined the nature of the spells binding him for what felt like the millionth time. There was indeed an element of subtle compulsion woven into them, guiding his thoughts

into these paths. This increased his anger but even that was channelled. He laughed and allowed himself to enjoy the mind-altering
sensation. All that was happening here was that certain aspects of
his mood and personality were being amplified. It was strangely
enjoyable, a thing which was also a component of the spell.

In his deepest secret heart, N'Kari understood the insult and
resented it. One locked-off chamber of his mind plotted vengeance and began to muster its resources. Other chambers of his
mind entered into the spirit of things and plotted how it could aid
in this new Rape of Ulthuan. He gave his attention back to the dark
elves.

He let his stern gaze rest on every watching druchii in turn. They
kept their faces impassive but inwardly they quailed under the gaze
of one who so resembled their much-feared leader and at the same
time was rumoured to be a daemon straight from hell.

All of them, except perhaps General Dorian, were wondering
exactly why they were here and exactly what was going to happen.
Being what and who they were, they must be half-expecting a trap.
They must be asking themselves whether Malekith had resolved to
dispose of them in some new and horrific way. They were the last
of the original force that had landed in Ulthuan. All of the rest of
the soldiers had been deployed near their objectives. They were the
only ones who had been issued with special amulets. Most of them
had no idea of the purpose of those charms save perhaps the sorceresses and their commander.

Being who they were, all of them in their secret hearts knew they
were guilty of some treason and N'Kari gave them time to dwell on
their own particular variations on that theme. Once the fear and
anticipation had reached a crescendo, he opened the portal in the
flashiest and most terrifying way he could. The basic composition
of the gateway was unchangeable but he could use his magic to
add little touches of his own to the spell.

The air chilled, thunder rumbled and the stink of ozone drifted
into every nostril as the gateway appeared illuminated by crackling
lightning. The area within shimmered with multi-coloured light.
There was no way they could see through it and know their ultimate destination. They could be going across Ulthuan as they were
told, or to the deepest hell. They would not know until they passed
through and their well-controlled terror was delicious.

General Dorian gave the order to move. In lockstep, the first of
the units began to march through the gateway he had opened in

the fabric of reality. Even N'Kari had to admit that their discipline was impressive.

Dorian studied his bodyguard as they marched with him into the portal. They were the elite of his force, a fine selection of druchii heavy infantry, disciplined and capable. They would stand and fight while others died or fled because they were proud of themselves, their heritage and their bloodlines. It was this pride that made them the finest heavy infantry in the world. It was what allowed them to march through the gateway under the daemon's terrifying gaze without any apparent show of fear.

He understood them because he was like them. From birth, he had been brought up to see himself as one of the born rulers of the world. He had trained alongside his brothers for hours with sword and spear and shield and crossbow. He had learned to fight and to compete. His brothers had been both comrades and rivals. He wanted to outshine them and he had, with the possible exception of Urian, but that very rivalry had provided him with the motivation to excel. The same thing applied through the entire vast army on a very different scale.

Each soldier attempted to outshine every other soldier in his company. Every company tried to surpass every other company in the regiment. Every regiment tried to outclass every other in the army. And the army must prove itself against every foe.

Glory was both personal and communal. The Witch King looked down on all and distributed his rewards. He was feared and hated, but his favour was sought out as the ultimate source of power. It was not a pleasant system, Dorian thought, but it worked. And it worked because at the end of the day, Malekith was fair.

He was proof of that. He had started off as a common soldier, or as common as any soldier ever was in his elite unit. His family had provided him with his weapons and his basic training. He had learned the hard craft of raiding and slaving along the coasts of the Old World for himself.

He had earned his rewards and the respect of his warriors. When the warhorns summoned the dark elves to battle against the hordes of Chaos, his retinue had proven themselves against the tattooed marauders with whose distant descendants they were currently allied. He had distinguished himself in raids on the slann lands of Lustria, and acquired much gold as part of the plunder.

On the greater battlefields he had come under the eye of Malekith himself and by a combination of ferocity, fearlessness and fighting skill he had attracted the Witch King's attention. He had risen eventually to become an honoured general in the armies of Naggaroth, being rewarded with the lands of fallen rivals, building his wealth on his share of the plunder.

Yes, Dorian thought, he had done well under the Witch King. But he was not sure about this invasion at all. Oh, there was nothing wrong with seeking to reclaim the lost lands of Ulthuan. The spoils would be immense, ancient estates would be restituted, new ones earned. Many slaves would be taken and the most hated enemies of the druchii would be humbled. He had no problem with any of this. In truth, he looked forward to it.

It was not that he resented the vast use of magic instead of force of arms either. Sorcery was an integral part of the way the dark elves fought their wars, part of the strength of their nation, one of those things that made them superior to all other races. He appreciated both the tactical and strategic uses of wizardry and he knew that both Malekith and his divine mother were masters of it.

It was this business of relying on Malekith's bound daemon and travelling through the mystical gates it summoned that troubled him. There was something about these pathways that made his elven senses scream at the peril. He sensed the presence of daemonic things very close by.

What if something went wrong?

He glanced across at Cassandra. His sorceress lover looked calm, but he knew her well enough to spot the small signs of nervousness: the way she kept toying with the rune-inscribed ring on her left hand, for example. She claimed they were passing through the realms of Chaos when they went through these portals and, if that was the case, terrifying, ancient horrors were close, separated from them by a barrier thinner than the skin of a bubble. Even more than their lives, their souls were at risk.

And that was not the only disturbing thing about this business. Cassandra had whispered other things in his ear at night as they lay in their sleeping silks, spent from their wild lovemaking.

She claimed that the Witch King's new pet was a creature whose strength might conceivably be greater than Malekith's and which might break free at any moment. Of course, Cassandra was Morathi's creature, and he suspected that at this moment the Hag Queen was not best pleased with her son, but that did not mean she was wrong. If N'Kari truly was what Malekith claimed, it was one of the greatest enemies of his people in history, if not the greatest.

It made him fear that after all these long millennia, the Witch King's sanity had finally cracked, that this expedition might be doomed by that alone. Worse was the thought that such a powerful, malign and barely controllable being was the one opening these gates and leading them through these hellish realms. The possibilities for disaster were enormous. The lives of all his troops were in the hands of a creature that could and would, if given the opportunity, snuff them out on a whim.

But what could he do? Rebellion against the Witch King was near unthinkable at the best of times, and this was a time of war, when any disaffection in the army could be disastrous. And there were other things to be considered.

Malekith *had* bound the daemon. It *was* serving them, and the strategic advantages of being able to move huge forces across Ulthuan so swiftly and unknown by their enemy were enormous. The task he had been set was proof of this.

It was a gigantic risk but it could so easily pay off, and if it did... This would be a victory still talked about in ten thousand years. The spoils that would go to the victors would be fantastic.

Dorian knew too that this was a campaign that had been centuries in the planning. The Witch King must know what he was doing. Their foes would be taken utterly and completely off guard and in a war like this, the advantage of surprise would be worth legions of warriors.

For the moment then, Dorian was determined to follow, but if things went wrong, then it would be time to consider the possibility of a new ruler of Naggaroth and exactly how that might be arranged.

N'Kari looked around. His magical senses told him that they were in Avelorn. Not much had changed in these forests since he had rampaged across Ulthuan all those millennia ago. It would have given him as much pleasure as ever to watch them burn, but he could not make it happen. He was constrained by this accursed chain and the Witch King's spells not to invoke his power, even in self-defence. If he were attacked now, he would have to rely on the natural resilience of his daemonic incarnation to save him, nothing else would.

The winds of magic brought something else to his spiritual senses than the scent of the forest's old magic. He could tell that somewhere relatively close at hand were at least two descendants of

Aenarion. Their psychic stench was quite unmistakable. One of them was even familiar, although it had been over a century since N'Kari had last smelled it.

It belonged to Tyrion, the elf who had helped in his ignominious undoing at the Shrine of Asuryan. Just the faintest hint of that spiritual aroma set N'Kari to flexing his hands like claws. He salivated at the thought of tearing that particular prey apart. This time he would not toy with his victim until after he was certain it could not escape doom.

Of course, right now there was nothing he could do. He was constrained to pass back through the portal he had opened and return to Malekith's side. He would need to do something to ensure that this situation did not last indefinitely.

His thirst for revenge on the whole line of Aenarion burned stronger than ever.

As soon as N'Kari vanished, a weight lifted from Dorian's shoulders even though the portal remained where the daemon had opened it, glowing in the air. He took a deep sniff of the pine-scented air. It was fresh and pure and smelled of living things. It was quite unlike the chill air of Naggaroth and yet there was something about its purity that reminded him of his homeland. He looked around and could not help but smile.

It was said that long ago the first elves had been born in the forests during the long golden reign of the first Everqueen. It was still thought by many that the forests were the true home of his people and at this moment he could believe it.

This was indeed a magical place. He could feel it in the air. Powerful sorcery surrounded him. For a moment that made him fearful, but only for a moment. This was not the sort of magic that was intended to harm. It was the magic of growing things, of life, of this most ancient forest. Potent though it was, it had nothing to do with warfare or death or killing.

He looked around at his warriors and could see that their faces were similarly transformed. Just for a moment they had all returned to childhood. There was something about this place that would do that to even the most cynical dark elf. Druchii who had hated each other and been rivals for decades exchanged smiles and then looked away from each other as if embarrassed, not quite understanding what was happening to them.

Perhaps he was wrong, Dorian thought. Perhaps this place did have the means to protect itself. Perhaps they were coming under its influence right now. If that was the case, he would soon put a stop to it. He bellowed instructions to his soldiers, telling them to form up in ranks, to set up a defensive perimeter, to be ready to protect themselves from any high elf who might stumble upon them.

Dorian looked at Cassandra. He could see from her look that she understood what had happened here. She understood how close they were to victory. They had established a beachhead in the most sacred heart of elvendom. They could use the daemon's portal to bring in an army and seize this land and its ruler.

Already scouts were fanning out from the point of arrival. If they encountered any rangers in the woods, they would capture or kill them. It would not do for word of their arrival to leak out before they were ready and the full force of the dark elf army had arrived.

No matter, Dorian thought. He knew that they were going to be blessed with success. The most difficult part had been achieved. He was walking where no druchii had walked in a thousand years and he knew that they were within striking distance of the Everqueen herself, if she was at the tournament ground as Malekith had predicted.

The Witch King had got it right. His plan was going to work and Dorian felt satisfied that he had been chosen to lead the force that was to execute this part of the great work. He knew that he was going to cover himself in glory and the rewards for his success would be immense.

He could see that Cassandra looked at him in a different way now. There was more than simple calculation in her eyes. She realised what he was going to be and what she herself might achieve by helping him. The two of them were going to become immensely rich and powerful.

There and then Dorian committed himself to Malekith once more. He would do his absolute best to see that this succeeded and nothing had better stand in his way. He walked around the perimeter of the camp that was coming into being. Cassandra and her fellow sorceresses were moving over to where the sacrificial slaves waited. They would need to expend a great number of lives to keep the daemon's portal open, but that was a small price to pay for their inevitable victory.

Screams rose above the camp. The portal flickered and shone. Every now and again its surface shimmered and rippled and a new force of dark elf infantry arrived. With ordered precision, they took up their places in the vast armed camp that Dorian was building right in the heart of this most sacred forest. It was astonishing to think that such a feat could be achieved without anyone noticing it. And yet it was happening, he told himself. Nothing could stop them.

More and more dark elf soldiery arrived. Units of cavalry mounted on huge lizard-like Cold Ones emerged from the portal. The great beasts looked strangely dormant and docile for a few minutes after they arrived, obviously disorientated by their passage through the pathways the daemon had opened. After that, as if in compensation for their docility, they became even more savage than normal and their riders had to apply discipline with sharp prods and metal implements.

Dorian smiled. Victory, promotion, wealth and riches were all within his grasp. All he had to do was reach out and take them.

'I heard you had returned,' said High Loremaster Morelian. 'I trust you were successful in your quest.'

Teclis studied the older elf. Morelian was very ancient looking. He was tall and stooped and very, very slender, with skin as coarse as a human's and hair so silver it appeared positively metallic. He had a small forked beard of a type very unusual among elves, who were normally clean shaven. He gave the impression of great wisdom and knowledge, but there was a twinkle in his eye and a cheerful smile quirked his lips.

His chamber was austere. There was a large desk and many scroll racks around the walls containing a selection of ancient lore. Books lay in a pile upon his table along with blank parchment, uncut quill pens made from the finest goose feathers and a jar containing black ink. The High Loremaster had been making notes about the books open on the table before him, that much was clear from even the most cursory inspection.

'My brother and I found Sunfang but that was not all we found,' said Teclis.

Morelian raised an eyebrow.

'You say that as if you found something even more important than Sunfang,' he said.

Teclis opened his pack and placed the slann inscriptions on the table in front of him.

'Perhaps we did,' he said.

The High Loremaster looked at the scrolls with something like awe. 'Is this what I think it is?'

'I'm not a fortune teller so I don't know,' Teclis said. 'I can decipher enough to see that it contains knowledge that might be important. That is why I have brought it to you. I know of your interest in these things.'

An expression of wonder passed over the High Loremaster's face. It reminded Teclis of the expression he had seen in his father's when the old prince had looked at Sunfang. Instantly he began to flip through the copies Teclis had made.

'You know what it is?' Teclis asked after a few minutes had passed.

'It is astronomical and astrological,' said the High Loremaster. 'It is written in a very compressed form of their hieroglyphic script. You were right to bring this to me. I think that your suspicions about its importance are correct. It is, among other things, an astrological calculation of the orbits of certain planets and moons and the way they are connected to the fluctuations in the cycles of the polar warp gates.'

Teclis was amazed that Morelian had been able to divine so much from such a cursory examination. Of course, this was his specialist field of knowledge. It galled Teclis to think that there was so much he did not know. This just reminded him of that fact. 'Is that all it says?'

'That is as much as I can make out in this short period of time,' the High Loremaster said. 'And I may not be correct. I am guessing as to the interpretation of quite a lot of the things inscribed. If you leave this with me I can probably have it translated fully in a few hours. There is something hidden here, I feel sure of it, something of great mystical significance.'

Teclis felt a reluctance to let the scrolls out of his sight, particularly if there was a mystical secret connected with them. He did not like the idea that someone other than himself would discover this hidden truth. He was fighting with his own personal daemons here, he knew. There was nothing he could do with the texts himself unless he was prepared to spend several decades improving his mastery of the slann language, and he did not have time for that.

'Of course, you may have them,' Teclis said. 'I am grateful for any help you can give me in this matter. I have been both troubled and puzzled by the little I have been able to deduce about what they contain.'

'It may be of the greatest importance to all of us,' said the High Loremaster. 'I suspect it concerns the times we now live in. I also suspect that the fact that you found it at this time is no coincidence. All things are connected, and mystical objects are more connected than anything else.'

Teclis had heard such things said before but he was not entirely sure that he believed them. Wizards tended to enjoy the benefits of exceptional hindsight, and pointing out the connections between things and events afterwards was much easier than spotting them at any given time.

'I'm not sure I know what you're talking about,' Teclis said.

'You should go and speak to Belthania,' the High Loremaster said. 'I know she wants to talk to you and she will be able to tell you more about what is going on than I can.'

Teclis felt certain this was not the case, but he could also see that the High Loremaster was like a child with a new toy. He was desperate to get to work at once and Teclis understood the benefits of being able to harness that enthusiasm.

'I shall see to it at once,' he said.

'That would probably be for the best,' said the High Loremaster. He was already focused on the scrolls in front of him and hurriedly scribbling down notes about their contents. Teclis knew that he had already been dismissed from the master of his order's mind.

Teclis entered the chambers of Belthania. Warriors in the livery of the archmage guarded a doorway that was carved from a sliver of the ivory fang of some great sea monster.

Why had she summoned him? They had met many times at social functions in Lothern and when he was studying at the tower, but he would not have said they were close. Perhaps there was some research she wanted to discuss with him.

A servant in black and gold showed him into a glasshouse protruding from the side of the tower, where it could catch the sun. It sat high in the tower with a magnificent view out over the forest. The floor was translucent crystal and he could see the grounds a long way below. The view made him nervous. The heat in the place reminded him of the jungles he had just vacated. Belthania was garbed in thin flowing robes of greenish silk that clung to the curves of her body. She smiled grimly as he entered. She had a faintly drugged, somnolent air to her, as always.

'Prince Teclis,' she said. 'It is good to see you again.'

She did not sound as if it was. The words were purely spoken from politeness.

He decided to match the tone. 'The High Loremaster suggested I pay you a visit. He said you wanted to talk with me.'

'Word has it you have recently returned from the jungles of Lustria, from the slann city of Zultec, and that you brought with you the sword of Aenarion.'

'My brother has it. He goes to offer it to the service of the Everqueen.'

'He may have need of it soon.'

'Why do you say this?'

'I have been studying the skies and performing other divinatory rites and the signs have not been good.'

'How so?' Teclis was curious. Divination was a famously imprecise school of magic. Its practitioners were regarded as little more than charlatans by serious scholars. Except Morathi. Her gifts had been proven again and again.

'The winds of magic are becoming increasingly contaminated by the powers of Chaos. You can feel it if you try any of the greater spells.'

'I have sensed something even when working minor spells of the Art.'

'You are certainly more sensitive than most to such things.'

Teclis wondered if she was sneering at him, but he saw none of the usual signs of contempt. 'Why am I here?'

'You saw no signs of anything similar in Lustria?'

'I noticed nothing of the sort.'

'Good, then perhaps things have not progressed too far then.'

'Too far for what?'

'I believe we may be entering a new age of catastrophe, Prince Teclis. The polar warp gates have long been dormant but they have started to erupt once more. The signs are all there if you know how to look.'

Teclis nodded to encourage her to keep talking. 'This is dire news if true.'

'It is true enough, I fear. Ships sailing off the northern coasts of the Old World have reported great drifts of tribes down from the Northern Wastes. They were accompanied by daemons and all manner of monsters. Agents have reported rumours that the Hag Queen herself was sighted there mere months ago.

'The Vortex has become progressively more unstable. The ghosts of Caledor and his companions have been sighted at many places close to the waystones. The land trembles. The mountains begin to burn.

'The winds of darkness blow hard again. The Everqueen is dead. A new Everqueen is not yet steady on her throne. I do not think this is all simply coincidence.

'The dreams of the Wise have been troubled. I wished to ask you if yours had been.'

So that was what this was about. Teclis mentioned his own vision in the forest en route to the tower. Belthania nodded as if she had expected to hear something like this. 'Did you have any such dreams before that?' she asked.

'No. But I have been far from Ulthuan in recent months. Have you done anything about these signs? Surely the Phoenix King should be warned.'

'We have sent messengers apprising him.'

'What has Finubar done?'

'Nothing as far as we can tell. But then what can he do until there is some definite threat?'

'From what you are saying, one of those will not be long in coming.'

'I would love to be proved wrong but I fear I will not be. I also feel that you have an important role to play in all of this.'

'What makes you say that?'

'It is a feeling I have. Things have been strange ever since the Keeper of Secrets returned.'

'N'Kari?'

'Yes. I fear he was a harbinger of a new age of terrors for the elves. He almost destroyed us once.'

'He certainly almost destroyed me once,' said Teclis, thinking back to the brief terrifying time over a century ago when he had faced the daemon.

'And yet you are still here. Perhaps that is why I think you and your brother are important. How many elves have ever survived an encounter with one of the greater daemons of Chaos?'

'I am not sure I could survive another. It was Asuryan who protected me then. If ever I meet N'Kari again, I doubt he will be foolish enough to attack me in the Shrine of the Phoenix God.'

'No doubt you are correct.'

'You think N'Kari may be behind all of this then?'

'I don't know. I do know that it is well past the time when he could have incarnated a new avatar and come back to seek his vengeance on you.'

It was a chilling thought, and most likely the real reason she had wanted to talk with him. 'I have suspected as much myself,' said Teclis.

'Be on your guard, Prince Teclis.'

'I shall be. I go now to perform some divinations of my own.'

Teclis glanced around his chamber and wished there was something more he could do. He had performed every simple divination he knew and the results had always been bad.

The hexagrams of the *Book of Change* had given a trigram indicating catastrophe. In the cards, the Plague Lord had appeared over the Changer of Ways, the worst possible conjunction it could display. The blood spray patterns of the White Bird ritual had been particularly ominous. Something terrible was going to happen, perhaps was even happening now.

He would find out soon enough what was destined to be. They all would. The sense of foreboding nagged at his mind. If he only had the slightest hint of what was going to happen, he could perhaps prepare for it, let those around him know. In any dangerous situation, even the smallest possible advantage could prove useful.

He felt like a prisoner awaiting execution for some unspecified crime on some unspecified date. The prospect hung over his head, colouring all his feelings, darkening his days. After performing the divinations, he found it very hard to return to his studies.

'It is very bad,' said High Loremaster Morelian. He looked very worried indeed, which given his normally cheerful nature was quite dispiriting. Teclis just stared at him unsure of what to say next. The High Loremaster looked at his notes and then back at Teclis. He steepled his fingers and then ran them through his hair.

'What did you find out?' Teclis asked.

'You were right to bring this to me. And you are right to be disturbed by it. I had not realised you were such a good scholar of the slann language.'

'I know only the very basics,' said Teclis.

'Even that is impressive,' said the High Loremaster. 'It normally takes decades for an elf to achieve that. The ancient slann language is not like ours. It is the tongue of a race so alien as to be almost incomprehensible. The hieroglyphs change meaning depending on their position with relation to each other. They imply shadows of meaning projected beyond and above themselves, an entire alien system of logic that it is very difficult to grasp even for one trained in the mysteries of magic. Their runes are language and mathematical and magical notation all rolled into one.'

'It surprises me that the primitive lizardmen that Tyrion and I encountered in the jungle could grasp such a thing.'

'I very much doubt that they can. They are warriors and labourers. It is the priestly caste that are literate, and more than literate by our standards. They and their masters, the ancient toad-gods of the race, are the only ones who could comprehend this fully.

It is impossible for an elf or a human, or a dwarf for that matter, to grasp their thoughts. Even now I am only guessing some of the content. The only one who ever even came close was Caledor and I suspect that this was one of the reasons he became the supreme mage that he was.'

The words hit Teclis with the force of a blow. He suddenly realised that if it were to take a lifetime to master this language he needed to begin to study it soon. It seemed like it was the key to understanding so much and might even allow him to surpass those ancient masters of magic who had done so much to shape the modern world. All of this was for the future. Right now he was more curious about what the inscription actually said. The High Loremaster seemed to sense this.

'As far as I can tell this text deals with our present time. Certain astrological references contained in it allow me to date the prediction with reference to the current position of the stars and planets. It is often the way with slann writing.'

He indicated the position of certain hieroglyphics. They were arranged within multiple etched circles which intersected in different places. Teclis knew that certain of the runes, under certain circumstances, indicated the names of planets and quite possibly the gods or daemons who ruled the movements of those planets.

The High Loremaster continued to speak. 'These runes indicate catastrophe of the worst sort. They refer to the polar warp gates and the gods of Chaos and the connection between them. I believe that the gates will open the same way now as they did during the first Chaos incursion and I don't think I need to tell you that that bodes no good for any of us.'

'Belthania says the same thing,' Teclis said. 'She has different reasons for thinking so, but she has come to much the same conclusions.'

'She is not the only one. The winds of magic blow strangely. Certain ominous portents have been observed by wizards as far apart as Cothique and Lothern. I have even been getting reports of such things from as far away as the Citadel of the Dawn.'

'What can we do about this?' Teclis asked.

The High Loremaster shrugged.

'I have written to the Phoenix King suggesting that we send an expedition into the Northern Wastes to discover exactly what is going on there.'

Teclis nodded. This certainly made sense. It was all very well talking about corruption in the winds of magic and strange signs in the stars, but the easiest way to confirm the truth would be to send observers to the place where actual events were happening.

'And what did he say?'

'I am awaiting his response.'

'Let us hope he comes to a decision soon. Otherwise it may be too late.'

Teclis and the High Loremaster walked through the vaults of the Tower of Hoeth in silence. They had spent the past half hour discussing Morelian's researches on the slann inscription and seemed to have said all that was needful. He carried the High Loremaster's partial translation with him.

They passed cases full of wondrous artefacts dating to an earlier age. Teclis loved this place. It always calmed him. He tried to spend some time here every day when he was at the White Tower.

He passed the Staff of Kaladreon, once borne by the white herald of Bel-Hathor, wound round with spells that generated an aura of calm and peace. It was a beautiful thing, but not much use for it had been found in the modern world. He admired the spell-work as much as the intricate carving of the winged goddess of mercy woven into it.

He glanced at the Oracle of Mammakis, a statue in the shape of a lion which was said to come to life once every ten centuries and answer any question asked of it truthfully although not always to the liking of the hearer. The inscription said it would be another two hundred and twenty years before it spoke again.

Teclis stopped to look upon the War Crown of Saphery. It was beautiful in a way that very few objects were, and it was potent, worked around with mighty enchantments to aid its wearer when casting powerful spells. It was one of the most powerful artefacts possessed by the Loremasters of the White Tower. Whoever wore it would be able to achieve wondrous feats.

His hands itched to pick it up and place it on his head. There was something about it that almost compelled him to do so. He had rarely felt so drawn to any object. It felt as if it belonged to him and had done all his life and always would.

The High Loremaster saw the expression on his face. 'What is it?'

Teclis wondered whether he should confess his desire to own this object. He hesitated only for a moment and then said, 'I feel drawn to the Crown. I feel as if it belongs to me.'

'It is one of the most powerful artefacts in our vaults,' said the High Loremaster. 'It was intended for use in battle by a war mage. It helps the wearer concentrate and manipulate the winds of magic, and it protects him from some of the worst side effects of miscasting a spell. It has other powers as well. It is said to amplify the senses and shield the mind from the temptations of Chaos.'

The High Loremaster looked at Teclis oddly. Teclis felt almost embarrassed by his scrutiny. It was as if the High Loremaster suspected him of wanting to steal the helmet. 'Sometimes,' he said, 'one has a feel for certain objects that are involved with one's destiny. This may be the case with you and the Crown.'

'It is a beautiful thing but I hope I never have any use for it,' said Teclis. 'It is something for a warrior, not for a wizard like myself. I do not see myself going to war at any time in the near future.'

'You can never predict what your fate might be,' said the High Loremaster. 'It is not something that even the greatest of wizards has any control over.'

Teclis doubted this, but he did not want to get into an argument with the head of his order.

'What do you plan to do now?' the High Loremaster asked.

'All this talk of the alignment of moons and stars and Chaos gates has made me curious. I wish to do some research of my own in the library.'

'That is a dark and serious subject. In theory, you need the permission of the High Loremaster to pursue it.'

'Do I have it?' Teclis asked.

'I think it is safe to say that you do.'

'I thank you for the work you have done on the slann text.'

'I should thank you, Prince Teclis. It is not often I have had such a fascinating subject to study.'

Teclis walked down the steps into the Great Library. Over the arched doorway was the symbol of the moon, the same symbol that appeared on the War Crown of Saphery and was the mark of the ancient princely realm. Sword Masters guarded the entrance.

Within this place were treasures uncounted: ancient books and scrolls, tablets of forbidden knowledge, palimpsests and metal etchings. It was said to be the greatest treasure houses of knowledge in existence.

Of course, the guards were symbolic because it was very unlikely that any thief would even find his way into the tower. Not impossible though, Teclis thought, or else the Sword Masters would be deployed elsewhere. Or perhaps they were there to report on the mages studying within. It was not unknown for them to seek forbidden lore.

He nodded to the guardians as he limped past. They acknowledged his presence and a clerk wrote down his name in the register. If he checked that huge leather-bound book he would find the names of the greatest magicians that Ulthuan had ever produced. Out of curiosity he had done just that in the past. It thrilled him to think that he was walking now where once those legends had walked.

He entered the main hall of the library. It was gigantic, eight storeys high, with books running all the way to the ceiling. On each level was a balcony that ran around the entire chamber. Steps led up to these balconies. In the centre of the room were many tables at which wizards and scholars sat studying ancient volumes of lore.

At the far end of the chamber was another exit which led to a room very similar to the first. He progressed through a dozen such chambers until at last he came to a room with a much lower ceiling and several exits.

This was where things started to get tricky. In the main chambers of the library, which he had just passed through, nothing ever went astray. It was easy to navigate them and no one ever got lost. Once you passed through this area you were into something else entirely. Soon he would be in the Maze of Books.

From here there was a labyrinth of corridors and tunnels walled with volumes of lore which seemed to stretch off in every direction. He had walked through this place on many different occasions and had come to the conclusion that this part of the library was several times greater than the area of the tower which contained it, impossible as that was.

He knew that some sort of magic was at work but, as with all of the magic connected with the tower, it was infinitely subtle and very hard to detect even if you were looking for it. Occasionally he felt the flicker of some spark of power when he passed from one room to another but he never quite worked out what was happening, which annoyed him, for he was very proud of his skill as a wizard.

When he entered these corridors, he was entering a realm where the normal laws of the world did not apply. He had known other mages to claim that they were in the same room as he had been in at the same time as he was there, but he had never seen them and they had never seen him, even though they had been studying books that were barely a few strides apart on the shelves.

He knew that the Master Librarian of Hoeth kept a catalogue which purported to show the location of every book on every shelf, but that catalogue could not be copied and it appeared different to everyone who studied it. Teclis himself had made notes and drawn sketches but they had never agreed with the notes and sketches of other scholars. Nonetheless, anyone who followed the guidance of the catalogue could find the books he was looking for.

Once, as an experiment, he and a fellow mage had sought the same book using different directions and had walked into the same corridors at the same time. Somehow, without ever realising how it had happened, they had become separated. Teclis could very distinctly remember looking back over his shoulder and discovering that the person he had been talking to just a few heartbeats before was not there.

And yet, when he had arrived at the book he was seeking, his fellow scholar was also there. It was the sort of thing that new students to the tower were always doing out of curiosity and probably always would do until the end of time.

He was looking for knowledge concerning the coming of Chaos, which meant searching all the way back to the time of Caledor. This was located in the deepest section of the Maze. He passed through numerous galleries, in which students of magic studied and library servitors went about their business, and then he entered an area in which fewer living presences were visible. The corridors were dustier, and cobwebs hung in corners even though there were no signs of spiders anywhere. It was as if they were spun by his imagination. Sometimes, out of the corner of his eye he even seemed to see them take form.

He went down a flight of stairs he could not recall ever seeing before, and turned a corner and went down another. He was far beneath the tower now, in its very foundations. The place felt old. There was an air of antiquity about it, and the books that surrounded him. The niches in the walls contained small statuettes in an archaic style, depicting elves in garb that had gone out of fashion millennia ago.

He kept walking, feeling that he was getting ever further from his goal. The walls of books seemed to be closing in around him.

For the first time in his life, he felt menaced by their presence, and by the library itself. He tried to turn back to retrace his steps, but when he followed the path backwards he could not find the stairs he had entered by, and after what felt like hours he thought he had passed the same statuettes of the goddess of wisdom several times.

What was going on here? Had the library turned against him? Had it decided that he was a threat or had become one for some reason since his return? Was this some variant of the spells that caused people to become lost forever in the woods around the tower? He breathed more deeply and fought against mounting panic. He guessed it was possible to be lost down here forever, if whatever power ruled over the Maze wished it.

He took another turning, trying to retrace his steps, and found himself in a chamber he had not been in before. Had he taken a wrong turning, become disorientated, or was something else going on?

He noticed that the room was lit by a small lantern and contained a table on which were several books. One was a volume of ancient poetry concerning the life of Aenarion and Caledor. The other was a history of Saphery. The last appeared to be a book of spells. It was this he reached for first. Also on the table was a game board that looked as if the squares were inscribed with slann runes. The pieces had already been moved, as if the players had only just left the room and intended to come back.

Weary and seeing nothing else better to do, Teclis sat down at the table. He placed the copy of the High Loremaster's translation of the slann tablet on the table. He opened the spell book. It contained a number of incantations written in old script. The hand was very fine. There was something familiar about it. Even though he was certain he'd never actually seen this writing before, there was something about it that reminded him of someone.

He turned to the opening page of the volume where he saw a famous mark. It was one that he recognised from the inscriptions on Sunfang, the rune that identified the sword's maker. This was a volume written in the hand of the Archmage Caledor. It contained spells that he had personally inscribed.

Excitement filled Teclis. This was a treasure he had never hoped to find. He felt sure somehow that no one except himself had ever seen this particular book. He was the one who was meant to find it, even though he was not sure why.

He continued to leaf through the volume, until his eyes came to rest on one particular spell. He could not say why exactly he was compelled to look at it. He was sure that it was not magic that made him do so. He would have felt that. He would have been able to resist the compulsion to read it as well. It was as if this particular spell was somehow intended to appeal directly to him. It was written in slann runes and yet he somehow understood them.

Something about the words embedded them in his mind immediately and set his lips forming them and his hands moving through the gestures of casting before he could even stop himself.

Even as he did so, he felt his eyes grow heavier and his voice grow throatier. His words became slurred and he started to mumble in a way that he had never done when casting a spell before.

Fear filled him. This whole episode was too strange. He felt as if he was caught in some vast intricate trap. This was not supposed to happen. It should not *be* able to happen. The Tower of Hoeth was supposed to be a safe haven for wizards.

Had he stumbled onto something strange and deadly? Had this happened before to other wizards? Would he simply be the last in a long line of people who had disappeared and were not remembered? He supposed it was possible. After all, the magic of the tower warped the minds of all who came into contact with it.

Even as these thoughts occurred to him, a wave of dizziness overcame him and he slumped forward over the books.

Teclis opened his eyes and wondered where he was.

The chamber was not like anything he had ever seen before. It looked as if it had been furnished by elves, but not any of the sort of elves he knew. The workmanship was crude, although still beautiful and still the product of a fine sensibility. Everything looked hastily made, as if the craftspeople had not taken the time to give it the requisite level of polish.

Scroll racks and bookcases covered the walls of the chamber. On a table in front of him was a game board inscribed with slann runes similar to the one back in the library, but this was the most fantastically complicated game board he had ever seen. Pieces that looked like elves and daemons, and dragons and monsters were strewn across it. One of the pieces even looked like him.

In the centre of the chamber stood a tall, stooped elf. He was almost skeletally thin, with receding hair and an oddly-shaped head. A woven carpet covered in a pattern that looked strangely familiar lay on the floor beneath his feet. He turned to face Teclis and there was nothing in his eyes except flaming light.

'You should not be here,' said the figure. Its voice was gentle and soft and very sad. 'I should not be here either.'

'And yet we are,' Teclis said. 'A strange meeting.'

The stranger's flesh was almost translucent. Tendons and sinews moved visibly beneath it. His face was a mask of strain and his expression was that of someone constantly in pain. Teclis recognised that expression only too well. He had often seen it in the mirror.

'Stranger than you think and later than you think,' said the elf. He limped over to the table and slumped down in a chair. He contemplated the game as if he were about to make a move, then tipped his head to one side and studied Teclis for a moment. 'You look like him, you know.'

'Like who?'

'Aenarion. You are one of his blood, aren't you?'

Teclis nodded. 'How can you tell?'

'Your face and your manner and something else, something about your aura, gives it away. You are a wizard too, aren't you?'

'And so are you,' Teclis said. He knew who this was now and he had a suspicion that he knew where they were. 'Your name is Caledor.'

'It was. At least I think it was. I sometimes forget. I sometimes forget everything except the task, and there are dangerous moments when I forget even that. Even now I am neglecting it. My fellows must take up the slack and carry my burden for me. We do not have long here you and I. I must return to my duty. It is all there is for me now.'

The conversation had a strange logic that reminded him of something.

'This is a dream, isn't it?'

'I have difficulty telling dream from reality,' said Caledor. The muscles on his face twitched a little. Teclis wondered if he was quite sane.

'I read something. I cast a spell written in slann runes. It was written in your hand,' Teclis said.

'That sounds about right. I found the secret of the Vortex written in slann runes. I found it in the burned-out rubble of one of their ancient cities. I saw the pattern of it and I saw the way it tapped into the magical structures that lie beneath the surface of reality. I saw how it could be used to save the world and that is what I tried to do. How long has it been... since I died?'

'Over six thousand years,' said Teclis.

'So long,' said Caledor, his soft voice sounded wistful. 'If I'd known...'

Teclis did not dare ask him what he meant. He suspected he already knew the answer. Caledor and his fellow wizards had given their lives to create the Vortex. Would they have done so if they had known what was waiting for them?

What must it be like to spend six thousand sleepless years weaving a spell that was constantly trying to unravel itself, to have to protect it from the forces that would destroy it?

'We have met for a reason,' Teclis said. 'At least, I would like to believe that this has not happened by chance.'

'It is hard to say what happens by chance and what does not,' said the first Archmage. 'Once I thought there was a pattern to everything, that it all made sense somehow and that I could understand it and it would be wonderful. I'm not sure any more. I am not sure of anything.'

'You've spent millennia maintaining a pattern, preserving the order of things.'

'I think that is what has changed me. If we were not here, if we did not constantly keep re-weaving our spell, there would be only Chaos now. And that is perhaps one of the reasons why you have been called here.'

'What do you mean?'

'The pattern is starting to unravel. It is sliding out of our control. The power of Chaos is growing stronger. The Vortex is becoming tainted by its energy and there are those out there who seek to accelerate the unravelling.'

'That is madness,' said Teclis. 'What possible benefit could be had from doing that? It would destroy Ulthuan and eventually the world.'

'It is good that you understand this,' said Caledor. 'But there are those who do not see things as you do. There are those who see the unmaking of the Vortex as an opportunity. They think that they can control the power of Chaos and remake the world as they want it to be.'

'Is it possible?' Teclis asked. It seemed that someone desired to transcend their own mortality, to have power like unto a god.

'In theory. In practice, I doubt that things would work out the way that Morathi expects.'

'So it is the Hag Queen that we are talking about.'

'Yes, and possibly her son, Aenarion's child, Malekith.'

The scale of the ambition revealed by Caledor's statement was breathtaking.

'How would they do it?'

'Tempted?'

'Who would not be?'

Caledor's smile was strange and sour. The complexity of the emotions in it made Teclis feel ashamed. The old wizard spread his hands wide and shrugged. 'Indeed. Who would not be?'

'What do you think they are planning?'

'If the pattern of the Vortex is destroyed, Chaos will overflow into your world. Eventually, matter itself will become mutable, the very structure of reality will become fluid as the powers of Chaos exert themselves. Once that happens, a mage of sufficient power and skill would be able, in theory, to remake the world in an image created by themselves.'

'Is that really possible?'

'Truthfully, I doubt it. We are talking about magic on a scale that only gods or daemon princes could work. Nonetheless, possible or not, I think that is what Morathi intends. I think it is what she always intended, even before she met Aenarion.'

'She must be stopped,' said Teclis.

'Indeed she must. You are here because we need a weapon against those who would swallow the world. You will be our sword.'

'Me?' Teclis felt suddenly very vulnerable. It was all very well saying that someone had to stop the most powerful sorceress of all time. It was an entirely different matter when you yourself might be the one chosen to do it.

Caledor's expression was bleak. 'We all feel that way when destiny taps us on the shoulder. I never thought that one day...'

He looked away and shook his head. The walls of the chamber faded, and Teclis looked out onto the vast, glittering space beyond. As far as the horizon an enormous pattern of light blazed. At its centre a cancerous darkness was eating away at it. Around that darkness blazing figures, elf-like but sky-tall, worked spells to keep it contained. Even as they did so, the darkness threatened to erupt in a different part of the pattern.

The walls returned. The chamber coalesced around them. Caledor, who had seemed for a moment to be one of those distant gigantic figures, was once more his stooped self, small and infinitely sad. 'We cannot do it. We are trapped here. We have screamed warnings in the dreams of the Wise. We have woven spells to summon aid to us. You are what we have been sent.'

'So she must be stopped,' Teclis said softly. 'What must I do?'

'You must return and tell the wizards of Hoeth to prepare for war. And you must prepare for war yourself.'

'Me? I am not a fighter.'

'You are of the blood of Aenarion. I doubt you will have a problem with killing.'

'It's the being killed I have a problem with.'

'Everything that lives has that problem.'

You do not, Teclis wanted to say. It was almost as if the old wizard could read his mind. 'I am no longer alive,' he said.

'I am sorry,' said Teclis.

'That makes two of us,' said Caledor. He tilted his head to one side, as if listening to something or someone very far away.

'Our time here is over.'

He rose from his chair with very great reluctance and walked as slowly as a prisoner going to his own execution towards the door. Every step seemed to take him a prodigious effort of will. He turned when he reached the door, his hand trembling on the handle.

'Farewell, Teclis, son of Arathion. Make sure your brother stays alive. If he falls, you fall and our world falls with you.'

Teclis did not know what to say. Caledor opened the door. The blazing inferno of the Vortex sprang into being behind him. Blast furnace heat washed across the room. Caledor stepped through the doorway and walked out onto the pattern, every step agonisingly slow. His body started to shrivel and burn as it had burned for over six thousand years. He raised his arms as if to cast a spell, a blazing figure crucified against the light, a weary ghost returning to hell to perform its final duties, of its own free will.

Watching him, Teclis knew he could not ever do that.

The scouts reported back early in the evening. Dorian greeted them in his command tent. They were the best of their kind, males, trained from early childhood when they were abducted from their kindred on Death Night. They had proven early their gift for survival by living through being tossed into a cauldron of boiling blood. That had been the start of a lifetime of hardships that made them among the best killers in a nation famed for its murderousness. Assassins of the Cult of Khaine.

'We have found the tournament ground, general,' said the assassin. 'It is where the king said it would be.'

'Did you ever doubt it?' Dorian asked, not because he thought the assassin ever had, but because he disliked him and his entire breed. They made him too nervous. They belonged to the Cult, body and soul, and it belonged to Morathi. It formed part of an extensive and alternative system of government to Malekith's. Rumour had it that the cults of pleasure performed the same function albeit in secret.

'Never,' said the assassin blandly.

'And they did not spot you or your brothers?'

'No, though we were close enough to the sentries to reach out and pluck hairs from their head.'

'I trust you engaged in no such frolics.'

'You seem determined to wilfully misconstrue everything I say, general. Do we have a problem, you and I?'

There was an obvious threat in the assassin's voice. Dorian would have had any one of his soldiers who spoke to him in such a way given over to the torturers but he could not do it to this elf and both of them knew it. Dorian felt compelled to let the assassin know he was not afraid of him either. 'If we did you would not now be standing here.'

The assassin inclined his head. 'That is the truth.'

He let his posture and his expression show that he believed that the reason for that would be that Dorian was dead, but the ambiguity of the response left honour satisfied on both sides. Dorian smiled to show that he understood this too.

'What did you find?'

'It is a vast tent city, full of armed elves but disorganised, more like a country fair in Bretonnia than an armed camp.'

'That is because it *is* a fair,' said Dorian. 'They do not expect an attack here of all places. Let us see to it that it remains so.'

'Quite,' said the assassin. 'My brothers scouted through it under cover of shadows. We have located the Pavilion Palace of the Everqueen.'

'It is guarded.' It was not a question.

'Yes, general, subtly and well. And even as we speak there is a great feast in which the Everqueen is surrounded by the pick of her potential champions.'

'Individually they will be formidable, but they are not a military force.'

'True. There are a number of smaller forces, armed bodyguards of nobles and such. It amounts to a small army of warriors but it is not organised as an army. It is a collection of retinues.'

'Nonetheless, they will be able to fight.'

'And fight well, I do not doubt. But they should not be able to stand against a competently led attack.'

Dorian smiled, knowing the assassin had said that to cover his own back. He would have his own reports to make, to his own masters, and ultimately his mistress. Blame would need to be apportioned in case of failure and the assassin would see to it that it would not fall on him.

'You need not worry about that,' said Dorian, letting irony show in his own voice. 'I will see to it that everything goes according to plan.'

'I never for a moment doubted that, general,' said the assassin. 'Khaine's blessing on your blade.'

'And yours, and all your brethren. Tomorrow we will reap many souls for your master.'

'I look forward to making the offerings,' said the assassin. His smile was disquieting.

All of the elves competing in the tournament gathered in the great Pavilion of the Everqueen. It was a massive tent made of spider-silk and spiralborne thread, large as a palace and big enough inside to hold a full grown tree. Only magic made a structure of such enormous size possible.

Beneath the branches of the great oak, in the glow of magical floating lanterns, hundreds of trestle tables were set. They groaned under the weight of food and drink. Minstrels moved everywhere, singing the old songs and playing the old tunes. Over everything an air of almost feverish festivity hung.

Tyrion sat at the high table with the Everqueen, the captain of her guard and a number of her highest advisers, along with those candidates for the post of champion who had performed best in today's contest.

This was part of the test. They were under observation to see how they fitted in. They were being judged by the Everqueen and her advisers for their suitability in the role of companion and defender.

All of the elves were on their best behaviour, showing off their most polished manners, making their wittiest quips, eating and drinking sparingly and watching their rivals like hungry hawks.

It was fascinating for Tyrion to watch. Seemingly polite conversation was filled with traps designed to give one elf a chance to show off his knowledge and display the ignorance of his rivals.

One after the other, a number of conversational set pieces took place, each wittier than the next and each showing a dazzling knowledge of history and culture on the part of the person who inaugurated it.

It was like watching a sword fight. All of the competitors were very good at this sort of thing, Prince Perian perhaps most of all. He had a sly wit that reminded Tyrion of Prince Iltharis and he used it expertly to needle his fellow competitors before despatching them with an effortless quip.

Only Prince Arhalien was able to match Prince Perian and he did it politely, persuasively and without giving offence. Somehow he always seemed to be able to extricate himself from the most cunning conversational snares and all the while managed to maintain his image of good grace and good breeding.

Perhaps he came across as being a little stiff but that was no bad thing under the circumstances, Tyrion thought. He did not seem determined to put down his rivals and that made him seem refreshingly different and perhaps more diplomatic. If it was a strategy, it was a very good one.

Eventually, as he knew it must, the conversation settled on him. Prince Perian looked over at him and said, 'You're very quiet, Prince Tyrion.'

Tyrion felt all eyes upon him. He was very aware that the Everqueen was looking at him, as was the captain of her guard. Normally he did not feel particularly self-conscious. He was used to being the focus of attention but there was something about the gaze of the Everqueen that rankled him.

'I do not have very much to say,' Tyrion said.

'Prince Tyrion prefers to let his deeds speak for him,' said Prince Arhalien.

'I have never heard that being a great warrior was incompatible with being able to speak,' said Prince Perian.

'Certainly being able to speak is not incompatible with being a great warrior, as you have proven,' said Prince Arhalien.

'Surely, Prince Tyrion wishes to take part in the general conversation. We have not yet seen any examples of his scholarship.'

'Save with a blade,' said Arhalien.

'I cannot claim to be a great scholar,' said Tyrion. 'In my family that honour belongs to my brother.'

'And why has your twin not chosen to enter the competition?' said Prince Perian. There was a sly smile on his lips. He had obviously heard about Teclis's infirmity.

'My brother is studying at the White Tower of Hoeth,' said Tyrion.

'I have heard he has good reason to hide away there,' said Prince Perian.

'I did not know he was hiding,' said Tyrion. 'He certainly wasn't hiding when he went with me to Lustria and reclaimed the sword of Aenarion.'

'You "reclaimed" the sword of Aenarion. That's an interesting way of putting it,' said Prince Perian. 'Do you claim it is yours by right?'

Tyrion saw the trap waiting for him. To make any claim to the mantle of Aenarion would be boorish in the extreme, not to mention foolish. None could compare to the first Phoenix King. 'I claim it is mine because I found it and all those with any other legal claim are dead.'

'A scavenger's claim,' said Prince Perian. 'It is said your father has the dragon armour of Aenarion, you have his sword. It is a pity that the first Phoenix King never left a crutch. Your brother might have had it...'

It was a cruel joke and had obviously been long prepared. Tyrion merely smiled. 'You think Sunfang would have been better left in the hands of the lizardmen?'

Clearly it was not the response Prince Perian was expecting. He remained silent. Tyrion continued to speak.

'Or perhaps you think it ought to have been found by someone more suitable, such as yourself. If that is the case, all you had to do was spend ten years looking for it and venture into the jungles of Lustria, as my brother did.'

'I see you are determined to tell us the tale of your adventure,' said Prince Perian. 'You have picked a roundabout way of introducing the subject but nonetheless...'

'You talked about my brother needing a crutch,' said Tyrion. 'It seems to me that he has, perhaps, done more than you have, while enjoying fewer benefits of good health.'

Prince Perian looked flushed. He obviously did not enjoy being told that a cripple was more heroic than he was, particularly since he was the one who had brought the subject up.

Tyrion looked around the table. It was hard to tell whether he had won or lost this particular sally. He suspected that neither he nor Prince Perian had come out of it looking particularly good.

It was going to be that sort of evening, he thought.

Still glazed in sweat from their furious lovemaking, Dorian leaned on one elbow and contemplated Cassandra's naked form. The sorceress was as beautiful as ever. He reached over from the silken bedroll and picked up some grapes and fed them into her mouth one at a time.

'Black grapes from the vineyards of Har Ganeth,' Cassandra said. 'And on campaign, no less. I never expected to encounter such luxury in the field.' Her voice was low and husky, out of keeping with her slender form. As ever he found it strangely thrilling. Like her, he was sleeping with the enemy. That too was arousing in its way.

'My slaves packed them in a metal container full of ice from Mount Ebonfang. They stored it in the ice-caves in the hull of the Black Ark to keep them cool. It has only been a few days since we left it.'

'And yet here we are,' she said. 'More than halfway across Ulthuan in a place I never thought we would see.'

Was she testing him, Dorian wondered, trying to draw out some sort of half-treasonous response so she could report it back to her superiors? She ought to know him better than that by now.

'I never doubted our king,' Dorian said.

'Never in public anyway,' she said with a smile. 'And never out loud. Nor will you ever. I said I did and I meant it.'

'Such words could be construed as defeatism,' he said. 'Treason in time of war.'

'Will you report me?'

Another test, he thought. Was she exchanging a confidence so that he would do the same? It was a time-honoured technique and he was too old to fall for it.

'I would if I thought you meant it.'

She smiled at his response. She looked a little sad tonight, he thought, which troubled him more than he cared to admit.

'Tell me, Dorian, do you ever tire of the ambiguity of our lives?'

He studied her face. He knew it very well. He had known it for a century. They had been on and off lovers for much of that time. There was an expression there he had never seen before. 'I am not even sure what you mean, Cassandra.'

'We fence. We lay traps for each other. We do not trust each other. We fear we will report each other to our masters. We watch every word we say, even here in a makeshift bed in an armed camp in an enemy land, and even though we may die tomorrow night.'

Her words hung in the air. He sensed they held more depth of meaning than usual, that their relationship was at some kind of junction, that something was in the air tonight that had never been there before. Or maybe that was just what she wanted him to think.

'Of course we do,' he said, choosing to make a joke of the thing. 'We are druchii. What else would we do?'

Her answering smile was brilliant and shallow. Her face had become a mask in the half-light, one he could not read at all. It was odd, like looking in the mirror and seeing the features of a stranger. A single bright jewel glittered on her cheek. Surely, it could not be a tear.

'I don't know. We live in the shadow of ancient terrors, you and I. We have spent our lives there. We trust no one because anyone could be the spy who undoes us – our sisters, our brothers, our parents, our lovers, our friends.'

'A druchii has no friends,' said Dorian. It was the punch line of an old joke which, like most jokes, had a core of uncomfortable truth to it.

'There are spies everywhere. The worst thing is that our system turns all of us into spies on each other. And even when we are not, we behave as if we were. That is very sad,' she said.

'You are in a strange mood tonight, Cass,' he said. He surprised himself by sounding almost sincere. 'What has brought this on?'

'I am frightened,' she said.

'There is nothing to be frightened of. Tomorrow we will win.'

'Tomorrow we go against a god. A very old god.'

'A very old god in a very new body which will not yet have learned to focus its power, and whose power is not warlike anyway.'

'And which nonetheless has survived since before the time of Aenarion. The Everqueen was sacred to our people once as well, Dorian.'

'Perhaps once, a long time ago, but we follow other gods now, stronger gods.'

It was strange to find himself arguing the religious line with her. She knew so much more about these things than he. Which perhaps was why she was so upset, assuming this was not just another one of the endless loyalty tests.

'Yes, I know,' she said, very softly, before burying her face in the pillow. He reached out to stroke her hair. The gesture was oddly tentative, with a tenderness he had never really felt before. 'Do you ever wish we did not?'

He chose his words with care. 'It is pointless. We are who we are. We do what we must. We follow the gods of our people because they are the gods of our people.'

She laughed and turned to look at him, her eyes shining wetly in the light. 'Loyal as ever, Dorian,' she said. He knew he had passed a test, but not one she had set him. He had failed that.

Perhaps the next time he spoke with the Witch King he would report her. Perhaps.

In the morning sunlight, Tyrion cantered over to the lists. Only twenty-four competitors remained today, those who had done best in the swordplay. He forced himself to relax and hold his lance in the upright position, pennon fluttering in the wind.

Each of the fighters drew lots to see who would face off against each other. Tyrion was pleasantly surprised to find out that he was drawn against Prince Perian. Seeing the draw, Perian smirked at Tyrion. He was obviously confident in his own prowess with a lance. All of the competitors then rode to the edges of the jousting area.

The first few bouts got under way with Prince Arhalien winning his easily. Tyrion had never seen another warrior use a lance so well. Prince Arhalien carried the lance as if it were an extension of his own body. He easily knocked aside his opponent's shield and then unhorsed the elf as part of the same flowing motion.

Tyrion had to admit that he was not nearly so good. When he was much younger, he had practised with a lance. It was part of his image of being a knight. As his career as a warrior had progressed, he had gradually stopped practising in favour of using weapons that would stand him in better stead on the sort of battlefields he was fighting on.

He had simply allowed himself to be good enough, by his own admittedly high standards, but he could see that he was little better than average with a lance compared to his fellow competitors. It was an odd sensation for him to be forced to admit to the possibility of losing even before he started.

He concentrated very hard on the technique of the other riders as the jousting progressed. One of his many gifts was that, when it came to combat, he was able to see things that would have taken other elves a lifetime to notice with just a glance.

It did not take long to pick up the finer points of using a lance from studying these experts. He was even fairly sure that he would be able to duplicate their technique when his own turn came.

Some people in the crowd were shouting his name. He was a favourite with a large section of the crowd. A lot of the women present seemed to like him. Only the number of Prince Arhalien's supporters seemed comparable. It was becoming obvious to Tyrion that on many levels and in many ways, Prince Arhalien was his true rival, no matter what Prince Perian thought.

After what seemed like an age, he and Prince Perian were called to face off against each other. Tyrion rode to one end of the jousting area and Prince Perian rode to the other. Tyrion waved at the crowd and was rewarded with cheers. Prince Perian did the same but his support was sparser.

The horns sounded. Tyrion applied his heels to the flanks of his horse and set it moving forward at a slow canter. It swiftly gained speed. The posts of the barrier blurred past.

Hoofbeats sounded like thunder in his ears. He was aware of the flow of muscles beneath him as his horse raced forward. The sun glittered on Prince Perian's helmet and the wind pushed back its crest. Tyrion leaned forward in the saddle to make himself a smaller target.

Prince Perian and his horse grew in Tyrion's field of vision. Tyrion dropped his lance into the attack position at the same time as his opponent. He angled his shield to deflect the blow that he fully expected to impact upon it.

This was as much about steadiness of nerve as it was about technique and skill. Now was the time when he would take the full measure of Prince Perian's ability.

Just before the moment when the point of Prince Perian's lance would impact upon his shield, Tyrion leaned slightly to one side and the lance skimmed past. Tyrion made no such mistake. His lance impacted squarely upon Prince Perian's shield and sent him tumbling out of the saddle and sprawling into the hoof-churned mud.

The crowd roared. Tyrion was through into the next round.

Tyrion faced Prince Arhalien. It was the worst possible draw. Arhalien was much better on horseback than he was and much better with a lance. Still, there was nothing he could do about that, other than his best.

He did not feel full of confidence as he rode up to the lists. Realistically, his chances of winning were very small, although he knew that there was always a chance that luck or a mistake by his opponent would turn things his way.

Things were not over yet. He would do his best. It was all he had ever done. It was all he would ever do.

The crowd were silent as the two warriors rode into position. They sensed that this was an important fight, that these two contestants were the most likely candidates to become the next champion.

Tyrion had already proved his mastery with the sword. Prince Arhalien had proved his mastery with a lance. If Tyrion won this contest then he would establish that he was the victor in combat, the best warrior among all of the contestants.

If Prince Arhalien won then the two of them would be equally matched and it would come down to the choice of the Everqueen and her advisers as to who would become champion. Tyrion suspected that in that case he would not be the victor.

He needed to win here if he was going to win the tournament outright, and all of his previous ambivalence returned. He was not even sure that he even wanted to win. He told himself that it was just an excuse he was making to himself as a cover for potential defeat.

He took up his position at his end of the lists. He raised his lance into the classic position and, knowing all eyes were upon him, made his steed rear and prance. Some of the crowd applauded, some of them waved, some of them cheered.

Prince Arhalien stood quietly at the far end of the tournament ground, waiting for the horns to sound with a quiet dignity. Tyrion envied the prince – it was an unusual feeling for him.

At that moment in time, he realised he had come to a crossroads in his life. Suddenly it was just there. The outcome of this contest was going to be very important for his future. All of his competitive instincts were engaged. He was going to win.

The horns sounded. The horses thundered forward. The two warriors crashed together like comets colliding. For a brief, ecstatic moment Tyrion thought that he had his opponent, but at the last second Prince Arhalien raised his shield and deflected the tip of Tyrion's lance.

Tyrion found himself flying through the air, twisting to avoid a bad landing. The wind went out of him as he hit the ground. The crowd roared and stamped and cheered and he realised that they were not roaring and stamping and cheering for him. They were chanting Prince Arhalien's name.

Tyrion lay on the ground and looked at the sky. So this was what defeat felt like, he thought. Clouds drifted across his field of vision. He felt strangely relaxed and depressed and not a little angry with himself. Nonetheless, he forced himself to get to his feet and walk over to where Prince Arhalien waited and saluted him with good grace. Prince Arhalien responded in kind and Tyrion resisted the urge to curse him.

Spectators ran onto the field to congratulate Prince Arhalien. They paid no attention to Tyrion as he limped away, pained and weary. For the rest of the long afternoon, he watched from the stands.

He had lost.

By the light of the full moon, Dorian watched the long columns of troops filter through the forest. The woods were dark and spectral, the trees huge and ancient. The druchii went without lights, relying on moonlight to illuminate their way. They moved mostly silently save for the occasional hissing of a Cold One. The great reptiles had been muzzled to stop them from bellowing.

Up ahead the assassins would be killing the sentries guarding the tournament grounds. Dorian looked over at Cassandra. Whatever doubts she might have had last night, there were none showing on her face now. She looked calm and poised. Power glowed within her. She was ready to unleash deadly magic at the first sign of trouble.

Dorian felt unease in the pit of his stomach. He had to work hard to conceal it. If anything was going to go wrong, it would go wrong now. All it would take would be for one assassin to make a mistake, for one sentry to give the alarm...

And then what, he asked himself? What did it matter? This army was a huge force, disciplined and well-trained. Even if the alarm was given, what could the asur do against them? Individually they might be great warriors, but this was not going to be single combat.

Dorian knew that on the field of battle individual bravery counted for little if the tactics and formations were wrong. Even the greatest of warriors could be surrounded and cut down, shot from a distance, immobilised with spells or poisoned crossbow bolts. His force was well-equipped with all of those.

Perhaps the Everqueen would work some strange sorcery, or the enchantments that were said to surround her would overcome his troops. Dorian discounted that possibility. That was why Malekith had equipped them with those protective amulets.

The greatest danger was that some warning might reach the Everqueen and her bodyguard might spirit her away out of reach. If that happened Dorian had better fall on his sword, for the vengeance of Malekith would be swift and terrible. The Witch King rewarded failure with painful death.

Again and again, he went over things in his mind. He had prepared for every contingency he could think of. At least six companies would converge on the Pavilion Palace of the Everqueen. More warriors waited in the woods to scoop up anyone who fled.

The worst thing that was likely to happen was that the snatch would be bungled and the Everqueen would be shot down while trying to escape. He doubted Malekith would be overjoyed with that eventuality. Still, it would be preferable to letting Alarielle escape.

Be calm, he told himself. Nothing can possibly go wrong.

The night was astonishingly quiet after the clamour within the Everqueen's Pavilion. Tyrion strolled through the darkness towards his tent. He felt odd after his defeat by Prince Arhalien. He was not used to being beaten, and beaten in such a public way. He had been subdued at the feasting and had not even risen to Prince Perian's taunting. Fortunately the other elf did not seem to have much heart for it either. His defeat by Tyrion had put him well out of the running. His sneers did not have their usual confident edge.

All around, the elves were still revelling. A group of dancers skipped by, flowers wound into their hair, male and female intertwined. They had wineskins in their hands. One of them carried a lute. They begged Tyrion to accompany them but he turned them down as gracefully as he could. Tyrion wondered if he should seek out Lyla and distraction, but he was not in the mood. He wanted to return to his own tent and simply sleep.

Tomorrow, he would feel better. He looked up at the great moon that filled the sky. It seemed brighter here in Avelorn than it did elsewhere in Ulthuan. This place was so peaceful, he thought, so different from the hustle and bustle of Lothern. There were aspects of this he liked, that calmed his mind in a way that he had never felt it needed to be calmed before. It occurred to him that he would miss this place when he went away.

Atharis raised a goblet to him as he approached the tent. He lay there on a rug with the other members of Tyrion's retinue, drowning his sorrows with narcotic wine. Tyrion smiled at them all and walked past. He was not in the mood for company.

He entered his tent and threw himself down on his sleeping mat. He pulled a blanket across himself and lay there listening to the sounds of the night. After the events of the day sleep would not come.

Being within the silken walls of the tent did something to him. By restricting his field of vision it made his other senses more keen. He lay in the dark, thinking about his life and what he was going to do with it after this.

If the Everqueen preferred Prince Arhalien, and it seemed only logical that she would, then he would return to Lothern and take up trading once more. He needed to rebuild his fortunes and some raiding off the coasts of Naggaroth seemed like a good way of doing that.

Druchii were on his mind, as he drifted off the edge of sleep's precipice.

Dorian's force exploded into the tournament camp. Many of the high elves were asleep alone, in pairs or in groups. Others were revelling still, drunk on wine and laughter. Most of them had no idea what was happening even as they witnessed it.

All they saw were warriors who looked like them coming out of the forest. No alarm had been given so they could not be a threat. But why then did the newcomers have naked blades in their hands...

The scene repeated itself a hundred times on Dorian's way to the Pavilion Palace. Asur looked up surprised, dazed, a little confused. Sometimes they would smile as if they were witnessing a joke or a hallucination. Only a few looked frightened. Even fewer reached for weapons. Why should they? They were safe at the Everqueen's court. No enemy could possibly reach them, and certainly not in such force.

Dorian had seen similar things countless times in the past on slave raids along the coasts of the Old World. It took time to adjust to bad news and no one wants to believe that terrible things can happen, even as the event unfolds before their very eyes.

The difference was that this time it was elves being taken off guard, knowing fear and surprise. It did not really make all that much difference. Taken off guard, most living things behave like sheep.

He led his guard company towards the great Pavilion, ignoring those who scrambled to get out of his way, knowing that the companies following him would deal with them.

Beside him, Cassandra's face was calm. A slight smile played on her lips. Like him, she could see that this was going to work, that everything was going to be all right. Her hand still played with the amulet that Malekith had given them, though.

He pushed on towards the tent, proud of the way his warriors marched in lockstep, spearing those asur who got too close, but otherwise concentrating on the objective and trusting in their comrades behind them to watch their backs. It was a very fine display of druchii discipline.

Somewhere off to the right someone screamed. There was a smell of burning on the wind. Things were starting to get out of control, he realised. People were starting to emerge from the tents to see what was happening. Many of them gawped. A few were cut down by crossbow bolts slashing out of the darkness. None of them seemed to have quite grasped what was going on yet.

The great Pavilion rose out of the darkness ahead of him. By Khaine, it was immense, the sort of thing Malekith might have taken into the field with him if he wanted to banquet his whole court. It was not a practical structure, not military, but it was beautiful. He could appreciate that as he looked upon it. The thing had been created with magic and with love to contain the living goddess of the asur.

A cruel smile twisted his lips. After tonight they would mourn the loss of their deity. She would be a slave of Malekith, bound to obey the Witch King's every whim. Dorian wondered what it would be like to have a goddess as his slave. Perhaps he would find out for himself, if only for a short time.

Female warriors guarded the entrance of the Pavilion. They looked up as they saw Dorian's force approach. Even at this distance he could see their eyes widen and read the expression on their faces. They were not quite sure what they were seeing, but they at least were on guard and they knew their duty. They raised warning horns to their lips to give the alarm. Crossbow bolts cut them down before they could sound it.

Dorian strode on, heading towards the entrance, pausing only to let his own guard precede him. As he did so, Cassandra gestured for him to halt, and cast a spell. The air glowed then she gestured for him to proceed. He was not sure what had happened but he had seen enough examples of her work in the past to know she did nothing without reason.

As they passed within, she said, 'No deadly wards, only alarms. The Everqueen is too kind-hearted to risk the chance of any harm accidentally befalling her subjects.'

Dorian nodded to show he understood. The same could certainly not be said of their own rulers. He wondered what it must be like to live in a world where the kings and queens did not fear violent death at the hands of their subjects. He guessed he would never know.

After this campaign Malekith would rule the world and his word would be law everywhere.

Tyrion awoke from a troubled sleep, wondering what was happening. He could hear screams coming from all around him. He could smell burning, which seemed somehow obscene in this part of the sacred woods. Then he heard something else, something that chilled his blood, something he had heard in other parts of the world but that he had never thought to hear here – the war cries of dark elves.

His first thought was that it was some sort of joke. It did not seem possible that the sons of Naggaroth could have been able to penetrate so far into Ulthuan without any warning being given. In fact, it *was* impossible. Unless an entire army had been cloaked by some sort of invisibility spell, it could not be done. Even then he was fairly sure that magic on that scale would have been detected by the wizards of Ulthuan.

He shrugged. It was all very well telling himself that what he was hearing was impossible, but he was still hearing it. He had known warriors to die from simply standing around trying to decide how to react during a surprise attack. He was not going to be one of those.

Having come to a decision, the rest was easy. He buckled on the armour that was within his reach, unsheathed Sunfang and stepped out into the burning darkness. Corpses lay everywhere. Two of his companions lay with spear wounds in their sides. Atharis stared at the sky. He looked as if he might have been drunk, but there was a huge gash in his throat from which blood poured.

Shadowy figures erupted from the bushes around him. Bloody blades stabbed out at him. A warrior less quick of reflex would have died in that moment. Tyrion sprang lithely to one side, twisting to avoid a blow that should have gutted him.

Sunfang lashed out in response, leaving a blazing trail through the darkness. It crashed into the helmet of one dark elf warrior, cleaving it in two and splitting the skull beneath. Blood and brains flew everywhere, splattering against Tyrion's chest and arm.

He did not let it slow him down. He kept moving, shifting his position to confuse his enemies, sending his blade flickering across their fields of vision, knowing that its light would ruin their night-sight and give him some slight advantage in the ensuing melee.

He was certain that his foes were dark elves now. They spoke with the accents of Naggaroth and their wargear bore its unmistakable stamp. They fought with the disciplined organisation so typical of the inhabitants of their dreary northern land.

These were hardened veterans. They responded to his actions quickly and well, not in the least taken aback to find themselves facing an opponent of his skill. The fury of his onslaught did not dismay them. They fell back before him, not panicking despite the fact that he slaughtered another two of them as they did so.

Lesser troops would have fled under the circumstances, to have the table so suddenly turned on them in the darkness, but these warriors held their ground as best they could and fought back with the fury of maddened panthers.

The foes he faced were only one small part of the attacking army. All around him he could hear the sounds of butchery taking place in the darkness and he could tell from the screams of the victims that most of those people dying were his own folk.

How many dark elves were there? Far more than there should have been, of that he was certain. Once again the thought returned to him that this was impossible, that these ruthless foemen could not be here, and yet they were.

Even as he killed and killed again, the sheer impossibility of it bothered him. An army could not move in secrecy the way this one had done. Not unless sorcery was involved, and sorcery on a scale that had rarely been seen in this world since the time of Aenarion. There was something about the situation that nagged at him though, something familiar and yet strange that he felt he should be able to remember, and that he might possibly be able to do so if he were not fighting for his life.

Mere heartbeats had passed since he heard the first screams. It seemed much longer, in the way that it always did when he was in combat. Time always seemed to dilate under the circumstances. He struck down another dark elf and tried to work out what was going on.

Why were the druchii attacking here and now? Forget about the impossibility of it – that was obviously an illusion. They were here for a reason and in that moment it struck him what that reason was.

They were after the Everqueen. It was the only possible reason why they would attack here and now. Their intelligence gathering must have been extraordinarily effective, he thought, to know her whereabouts and be able to dispatch such a force to find her.

Once again, this was irrelevant. All that mattered was that he prevent them from achieving their goal, no matter what the cost. If the Everqueen fell into the hands of the dark elves, it would be the most terrible blow to afflict his people since the time of Aenarion.

Nothing quite so dreadful had ever happened before. If the Everqueen died it would wreak havoc with the morale of the high elves. If she became a prisoner of the Witch King it would be even worse. With her as his hostage, he would be able to dictate terms in any subsequent peace that would be enormously to his advantage. That was if there was a peace and he was not seeking an outright victory and the total annihilation of the forces of Ulthuan.

Tyrion knew that whatever happened, he must find Alarielle and save her. His personal feelings counted for nothing under the circumstances. He must do his duty to his people. He must save the Everqueen.

Dorian burst into the inner chamber of the great Pavilion. Dead elf maidens lay sprawled on the floor, their swords close at hand. They had died like warriors, he thought approvingly, their wounds to the front. He hoped when his own time came he would be able to do the same.

At bay in the centre of the room, back to the great central pole, standing on a great carpet woven with scenes of grace and beauty, was the single most beautiful woman Dorian had ever seen, perhaps excepting Morathi. Even through the wards of the amulets protecting him, he felt the tug of reverence and even love.

He knew he was committing a sacrilege by being here and he wanted to beg her pardon and ask her forgiveness. He realised how clever his master had been launching the attack now. If this was how it felt before the new Everqueen possessed her full power, even through the protective spells of his amulet, what would it be like to enter her presence once she had her full strength?

Ruthlessly Dorian quashed his feelings of awe. 'Good evening, your majesty,' he said in his coldest parade ground voice. 'I bring you greetings from my master, Malekith the Great, true king of all the elves.'

The realisation of her predicament flashed across that beautiful face. In that moment, and just for that moment, she was no longer a living goddess but a frightened young elf woman realising that she was in peril, alone and surrounded by enemies who could only mean her harm.

He did not feel sorry for her. He felt only contempt for one whose pampered existence had not prepared her for even the possibility of an experience like this.

The confusion and fear was only there for a moment before command reasserted itself. For an instant something infinitely old and wise looked out of her eyes. She opened her mouth to say something, perhaps speak a spell. At that moment, two of his guards grasped her, immobilising her arms. Another placed his hands over her mouth. Cassandra swiftly gagged her. She was cast down on her sleeping silks, limbs bound with whipcord.

Dorian and Cassandra exchanged triumphant looks. For both of them this was the supreme moment of their lives. They had captured the Everqueen. Malekith would reward them with kingdoms. His mouth felt dry. His heart raced. His dark druchii nature asserted itself. He wanted to howl with exultation. Instead he clenched his fist and placed his foot on the recumbent form of the bound goddess. Part of him wanted to kick her until she was a bloody corpse, but that would not fulfil the terms of his orders.

Outside, screams filled the night. Smoke drifted on the air. There was the sound of weapons clashing. The massacre had truly begun. It would not end till morning.

Tyrion ran towards the Everqueen's Pavilion. He could see that the dark elf troops were densest around about it. The bodies of the Maiden Guard lay sprawled everywhere, staring at the sky with sightless eyes. Tyrion had no time for regrets, to feel sorry for the dead. His business was with the living, assuming that the Everqueen was still alive. He believed that she would be, for that was what would make more strategic sense.

Charging into a horde of armed soldiers would not serve either Alarielle or himself. All that was likely to happen was that he would die a quick death and that the Everqueen would remain a captive.

He needed a plan and he needed to come up with one quickly if he was to avert disaster. Mighty warrior though he might be, potent magical blade that Sunfang was, they were no match for an army. What was needed here was intelligence, not a strong arm.

He doubled back, moving away from the vast body of dark elf troops. He remembered the bodies of the warriors he had slain.

They were wearing the armour of his enemies and that was something he could put to good use.

Swiftly he chose the armour belonging to the corpse whose head he had split and stripped it off. It was bloody, but on a night like this that would not matter. It would simply add to the authenticity of his disguise. He took the helmet from another dark elf corpse and put that on.

He wished he had a mirror so that he could check how he looked, but that was like wishing for an army of high elves to come out of the forest and save him – it was not going to happen. He was going to have to trust in the darkness and confusion all around him and hope that he was not cut down by any surviving high elves who might mistake him for one of the enemy.

He took a deep breath, stepped out of the shadows and began to move confidently towards the Pavilion, as if he had every right to be among the attackers. He kept his shoulders pulled back and did his best to imitate the marching stride of one of the sons of Naggaroth.

In the howling confusion no one questioned him. No one paid the slightest attention to him being there. The fighting was all but over. The dark elves were triumphant. They grinned at each other like warriors who know they are in possession of the field. There was an exultant look in their eyes and cold smiles on their lips. That, more than anything, chilled Tyrion's heart. He knew those expressions from his own career as a soldier. He'd worn similar ones when he was victorious in battle and noticed them on the faces of his comrades.

If ever he had had any hope that the situation might be salvaged, it vanished then. He was on his own. If he wanted to, he could probably escape now, using his disguise to get clear of the dark elf force and vanish into the woods.

He considered it for a heartbeat, but knew that he could not do so if there was even the slightest chance that Alarielle was being held captive. He could not abandon this place without finding that out. It was the least he could do.

All around him, discipline was beginning to break down even among the hardened druchii. The certainty of victory affected even the cold-hearted children of the uttermost north. Soldiers were starting to collect loot and slaves. He could hear the screams of the prisoners.

Tyrion hardened his heart. Even if he could rescue those who were in pain, he could not do it now. He had a mission of the utmost importance and he could allow nothing to distract him. But he swore in his heart that the dark elves would pay with interest for every scream they extracted from the lips of one of his own people.

Much to his surprise, the Pavilion was still upright. It was surrounded by druchii warriors who looked alert and disciplined. They had the aura of elite troops, ones who might be entrusted with a mission of the gravest importance. Not for a moment did Tyrion doubt that he was in the right place. The question was how he was going to get inside.

One of the soldiers stared at him. It would be suspicious to back away now and he might be remembered if he returned in the future, so he squared his shoulders and strode confidently forward, as if he had every business being there, and was on a mission of some importance.

He must have looked the part because no one questioned him as he strode inside and made his way to the central chamber of the tent. There were several high officers, he recognised their rank from their garb. He had fought against that type before on many battlefields. In the centre, lying prostrate with her arms bound behind her back and a gag on her mouth, was Alarielle. She stared at him with hate-filled eyes as he came in. She did not recognise Tyrion.

One of the high staff officers turned to look at him. Tyrion strode forward.

'What do you want?' the officer asked. 'What are you doing here, sergeant?'

'I bring a message from the commander,' said Tyrion. He was almost within striking distance now.

'What?'

'It is of the utmost importance,' said Tyrion.

'It had better be or I will have you flayed alive,' the officer said.

'I do not doubt it.'

'Then spit it out,' the officer said.

'It concerns the Everqueen. There's been a change of plans.'

'Impossible!'

'No,' said Tyrion. He drew Sunfang and decapitated the officer. With two more quick strokes he chopped down his companions. In a flurry of blows, he struck down the remaining dark elves within reach. Most of them died clawing for their weapons, desperately trying to react to the sudden fury of his onslaught.

* * *

Dorian wondered what was happening. A burning blade chopped down Captain Aeris and slashed off half of Captain Manion's face. The stench of seared flesh suddenly filled the Pavilion. Had one of the druchii gone mad, or was this some kind of sorcery? Were the Everqueen's powers still at work?

Even as the thought occurred to him, Alarielle rolled away from beneath his feet, sending him tumbling backwards. That action probably saved his life, unintentionally, for he fell out of the way of that blazing sword. He felt the red heat of it mere fingers' breadths from his face. He saw the warrior wielding the blade leap among his guard, slashing left and right as he went.

Maniac or not, the newcomer was eye-blurringly swift. He made the hardened veterans of Dorian's guard seem like children. They could do nothing to stop him. They did not even appear to be trying. They had been taken completely off guard by the sudden, stunning savagery of the stranger's attack. He recalled his own thoughts about how people responded to surprise attacks earlier. It seemed his own troops were no more immune to it than anyone else. Sheep, he thought.

Cassandra raised her hand as she attempted to cast a spell. Somehow the stranger was aware of it before she even half began. He pounced like a great cat springing. The brilliantly glowing blade slashed downwards. The protective spells surrounding Cass overloaded, burning out in a blaze of power. The sword smashed into her, snapping bones like twigs, cauterising flesh as it passed through.

'No,' Dorian shouted, rising to his feet. This could not be happening, he thought. Life and victory could not be snatched away from them so quickly. He remembered Cass's forebodings of the previous night. It seemed they had come true, since Alarielle had summoned this daemonic warrior to her aid.

He ripped his sword from its scabbard and just managed to parry as the stranger was upon him. Dorian was gifted with a blade, and he knew it. He was considered among the best in the entire druchii army.

Somehow though, he instantly found himself on the defensive. It was all he could do to parry the newcomer's weapon. The light from it dazzled his eyes in the gloom.

The fury of the stranger's attack was astonishing. He struck with the speed and power of a lightning bolt. Dorian's arm was numb just from maintaining his increasingly desperate parries. He would have liked to have gone on the offensive. He would have liked to have avenged Cass but there was no chance of it. He could barely find the time or the energy to shout for help. It took all of his concentration merely to stay alive.

There was something about the newcomer's style that reminded Dorian of his brother Urian. It had the same fluidity, and the same tricky manner of placing a feint within a feint, so that you never knew where the true attack was going to come from. It was almost as if this newcomer had been a pupil of his brother. Was it possible that this was some incredible feat of treachery?

Even as the question entered Dorian's mind, the stranger's sword found its way past his guard. Volcanic agony erupted in Dorian's side and he fell forward into darkness.

So this was death at last, he thought, come when he least expected it.

'Quickly! Stop him! He's getting away,' Tyrion shouted, to send the guards outside sniffing down the wrong trail. He strode over to the Everqueen, tore off the gag, and cut her bonds. She stared at him for a moment then her eyes widened and he saw the flash of recognition. 'Prince Tyrion!' she said.

'None other.' He strode to the opposite side of the Pavilion and slashed it with his sword. 'Come with me,' he said. 'We are getting out of here.'

She nodded, and dived through the gap he had created. He followed her out into the night.

'This way,' Tyrion said. He grabbed her by the hand and began to drag her through the undergrowth.

'We need to keep low and not be seen. If we are lucky they won't pick up our trail for a while. I can't imagine they brought hounds with them and there's been so much chaos around here, it will be difficult to pick up our tracks.'

'Sorcery,' she said. 'They will have wizards.'

'I was rather hoping you could do something about that.'

She stared and he saw the black hopelessness in her eyes. 'Why? What chance do we have of getting out of here, Prince Tyrion? The dark elves are already in Avelorn. They have killed my guard, my friends, my people. I have already failed in my trust.'

Tyrion shook her. 'You are alive. And while you are alive there is hope. What chance do we have? I don't know. I do know we will have no chance at all if we give up.'

She nodded but she did not seem to understand. Tyrion had seen the same look and same reaction written on the faces of young warriors after their first battle in which they had lost friends and comrades.

It must be worse for her. She was the Everqueen. She had grown up in luxury. She had never expected to see war or its aftermath.

'Listen to me,' he said. 'You are our queen. You were chosen by the gods. You are the heart of our realm. If you give up, we may as well all just surrender to Malekith. He will become king after all these millennia of waiting. Is that what you want?'

Slowly understanding came back into her eyes. He saw a powerful will begin to reassert itself. The moment of weakness and panic had passed. She was herself again.

'There is no need to clutch me so tightly, Prince Tyrion. You have made your point.'

He let go of her arm. Tyrion had grabbed her so tightly that he had left the print of his hand on the flesh of her arm.

'You have a plan?' she asked.

Tyrion shrugged. 'I never thought beyond making sure you were alive and getting you out.'

'I have heard people say you had a gift for strategy,' she said. 'That you are a war leader of great cunning.'

'I did get you out,' he said.

She seemed to come to a decision.

'Where did you get that armour?'

'I stripped it from a corpse.'

'We need another set.'

Tyrion nodded. He understood what she was thinking.

'They might take us for deserters.'

'It will be enough if it gets us clear of this awful place. And I would feel somewhat less vulnerable.'

'Have you ever worn armour before?'

'I can learn.'

Tyrion knew how easy it would be to allow themselves to stand here discussing things until they were captured. It was a natural reaction. They had found a small island of safety. Their instincts told them to cling to its shores.

'Wait here!' he told her. 'I'll be back.'

'What?'

'If someone sees me, I am just another dark elf soldier. If they see you...'

He did not need to explain any more. Behind him he could hear the sound of one voice rising over the babble. It seemed like some-one was taking charge of the situation. It would not be long before the hunt began in earnest.

Dorian rolled over. His side hurt immensely. When he touched it, it was wet but with a clear fluid rather than blood. The burning blade had cauterised the wound even as it made it.

He had no idea whether he would live or how much internal damage there really was. Looking around the chamber he could see he was lucky to be alive. Every other druchii that had been present was dead, including Cassandra. She lay on her back, eyes open, but glazed as if she was staring in wonder at the tent ceiling. Her face looked normal but her body was ruined.

Dorian crawled over to where she lay and took her hand. It was cold. Soldiers flooded into the room, glaring around at the scene of carnage.

'What happened, general?' one of them asked. Dorian struggled to answer.

'An elf with a burning sword,' he said. 'He killed us all and took the Everqueen.'

His soldiers looked at him as if he were raving, but they could not see any other explanation. 'Find him,' Dorian ordered. 'Find him or you are all for Malekith's torturers.'

He was all ready for that himself, he realised. The stranger had done him no favours letting him live. He lay on the ground, holding Cassandra's cold hand, and found that he did not care all that much.

'Put those on,' Tyrion said.

He pointed to the body of the dead elf soldier he had dragged into the undergrowth. Alarielle looked at the corpse in distaste but she began to strip it of the wargear.

'Did you kill her?' she asked.

'I cut her throat,' said Tyrion.

She looked at him with distaste.

'That was not very chivalrous,' she said.

He understood why she was saying it. She understood the necessity of what he had done but she was still shocked by it. She felt the need to vent her feelings, to do something to relieve her tension and fear. If that meant she despised him, so be it. He could live with that.

'This is not a tournament,' he said. 'This is war. People will die. You will send them to their deaths and you will smile while you do it.'

'I already caused a death, didn't I?' She indicated the dead warrior with her foot. 'I killed her when I sent you to get me a disguise.'

'Get used to it,' he said, knowing he was being brutal, but knowing also that he needed to make her understand the reality of the situation. 'It will be the first of many.'

'You enjoy this, don't you, Prince Tyrion?'

The answer was too complex to be gone into here so he just said, 'Yes. It is what I was born for.'

'Blood of Aenarion,' she said softly. He was surprised to hear pity in her voice. She stripped and put on the soldier's undergarments then her leather tunic and then her armour. Tyrion stood close and helped her. She had no experience with this sort of gear, so much was obvious. As he helped lace up the jerkin, they were close as lovers. He was suddenly very aware of her presence.

They stepped apart. 'We need to go,' he said. 'They will be looking for us now.'

What had been a place of pleasure had become a place of terror. Corpses were strewn everywhere, cut down in flight, in combat, while they had slept, while they had been drunk. The dark elves had spared no one. They had killed like maniacs, as senselessly as a wolverine in a henhouse.

Tyrion felt his heart become colder. A great rage was building up in him. This was not how war should be fought. His expression became as cold and grim as a true son of Naggaroth. The Everqueen looked upon his face and shuddered. He did not care and he did not want to explain to her how he was feeling.

'This was not war,' she said. Tyrion agreed with her. This had gone far beyond war. It was a murderous venting of long suppressed rage.

'It is now,' he said. 'This is what war looks like now.'

She shot him a sidelong glance. 'Do they really hate us so?'

'Apparently.'

They followed a path deeper into the woods. Tyrion had no idea where they were going. He was not familiar with this place. He was merely trying to get as far away from pursuit as possible. 'Do you know where we are?' he asked.

She nodded. 'We are on the old game trail to the Glade of Promises.'

'Beyond that?'

'What do you mean?'

'We must find refuge for you. A place where you will be safe.'

She looked as if she wanted to cry. 'Avelorn was safe. If I am not safe in the heart of my own realm where will I be?'

'I don't know,' Tyrion said. 'But we need to find somewhere.'

'You sound very angry, Prince Tyrion.'

'And you are not?'

'I have not had time to feel very much of anything, except afraid.'

'It is our enemies who will be afraid by the time we are finished,' Tyrion said. He knew he sounded petulant, like a small boy telling his friends that one day he would get even with a bully, but he meant it. One day there would be a reckoning for the carnage here. He would make the Witch King and all his minions pay.

'How could this have happened?' Alarielle asked.

'We were too confident,' Tyrion said. 'We thought the threat of Naggaroth had ended. It had not. There is only one way it ever will be – when the Witch King and all who follow him are dead.'

'I meant how did they find me? How did they get such a force into the heart of Avelorn? It should not have been possible. Our scouts should have seen them. The eagles would have spotted them from afar.'

'Magic would be my guess, but what sort I do not know. It is a subject I know very little about. My brother would know more.'

'Chaos has returned,' Alarielle said. 'I feel it. It is always there now, far in the distance, a great cancer eating away at the heart of the world. The winds of magic are tainted. Shadows lengthen, even here in Avelorn.'

'You think this has something to do with the invasion?'

'All things are connected. There is more power and more evil in the air than there has been for a very long time.'

How would you know? Tyrion wanted to ask. You are younger than me and I am not old as elves measure time. He kept his mouth shut. He would have sounded foolish anyway, for the Everqueen had inherited more than a title when she was crowned. Who knew what hidden knowledge was available to her? Who knew what magical powers?

'Can you help us? Can you use your magic to shield us?' he asked.

'I will do what I can,' she said. 'My powers were not intended for warfare.'

'Anything you could do would help. We are on our own here.'

She seemed to realise the pressure that was on him. 'You have done your best for me, Prince Tyrion, and I will be forever grateful.'

'My best may not be good enough. There is an army out there

and they are hunting for you. Who knows what they will do when they find you?'

'Let us pray I never find out,' she said.

'Who shall we pray to?' Tyrion asked. 'Our gods seem to have deserted us.'

'One of your gods is still with you,' she said.

'Let us make sure it stays that way,' he said.

They set off deeper into the dark woods. Behind them Avelorn burned.

BANE OF
MALEKITH

The wizard looked over the gameboard at Death. 'You are not real,' he said.

'Come now, Caledor,' said Death. 'You are in no position to cast aspersions. After all, you are dead.'

The wizard touched the place where his heart should have been. There was no beat. He placed his hand over his mouth. He did not breathe. He touched his wrist. There was no pulse.

A small fragment of knowledge came back to him. He had died a long, long time ago, trying to save the world. He had died slowly, in great pain, while trying to work powerful magic.

Caledor – his name *had* been Caledor once, when he had walked among the living and still had use for such a thing. He had not known that until Death had mentioned it. He could remember almost nothing else about himself, but it was good to have a name once more. It was a beginning, something he could build on.

'Nonetheless,' Caledor said, 'you are not real.'

Death raised a long pale hand and removed his ivory mask. He knuckled the hollow space below his eye and he let out a long patient sigh that seemed to go on forever, as was the nature of even the least of the actions of gods. 'I suppose you are going to argue about the nature of a reality that allows you to be dead and yet be aware of my existence and of your own. You are one of those for whom there is no afterlife, only a negation, a non-being.'

'Not at all,' said Caledor. 'I merely doubt the reality of this whole experience.'

'Living things have been doing that since the world began,' said Death. 'I am surprised that you, of all the elves, should be so unoriginal.'

'Why am I here?' Caledor asked.

'You are here to play the Great Game and decide the fate of the world.'

Caledor considered Death's words as he considered Death himself. The dark god had taken the form of a tall elf, very pale of skin. His nails were black. His teeth were black. His eyes were pools of infinite darkness. He wore robes of spider silk the colour of the black grapes from the vineyards of the furthest south. On those robes, in silver thread, were inscribed the runes of all the names by which the elves knew him: Khaela Mensha Khaine. This was the Reaper of Souls, the Ender of Worlds.

Propped against the side of Death's chair, unscabbarded, was a tall black sword that Caledor had seen before, although it had not then been borne by Death. Hideous runes glittered on its blade. The remnants of the souls it had devoured clung to the naked metal in a scummy crust. It was an evil blighted thing, its aura of matchless malignity noticeable even in this odd place and even while the blade was quiescent. Caledor could not look at it for too long without feeling queasy.

Instead he studied the game. It looked something like chess but was played on a larger and infinitely more complex board. The squares each contained Slann runes pregnant with mystical meaning, symbols that governed the magic of time and space.

It was hard to tell the board's true size. Each square was like a hole in reality that looked out into some other section of creation. The patterns were not like that of a chessboard at all. The squares, the focal points of the action, were not beside each other. They floated in the air at different levels. They were connected by lines, ellipses— the whole mass of squares lay amid concentric circles which had their own mystical significance.

He knew somehow that each square represented a specific place, some of which he had known in life, some of which had been created since his death. This gameboard was a map of a very specific reality. There was an underlying pattern to it that he felt he could grasp if only he was given time.

As above, so below, whispered a small distant part of his mind. What we change here, we change in the true world. This map not only represents the terrain, in some strange way it *is* the terrain.

The game was already in progress. Pieces that represented kings and queens, wizards, demi-gods and daemons were already in motion. Some of them lay beside the board, removed by the effect of earlier moves. Just as the squares represented real places, the pieces represented real people.

Death's pieces were carved from bone ivory, of course. His own pieces were made of silver and gold. Many more of his than of Death's were gone. It was obvious to even the most cursory inspection that he was losing.

He knew that it was very important that he win. If he failed here, his world fell too and his entire life, his death and the deaths of all his friends would have been in vain.

Despair filled him. He was no player. Not the way Aenarion had been.

Aenarion. That was another name he had once known. Aenarion had been there when he had died. He had died himself shortly thereafter. Looking over at the sword, it came to him where he had seen it before. It had been Aenarion's once, a long time ago, in that different world the gameboard represented. In the world they had died trying to save.

He saw a resemblance in Khaine's features to Aenarion's. Aenarion had been half a god himself. Perhaps they were related. Or perhaps this was something else entirely. He was not sure what, but he knew it was as well to question all of his assumptions here.

'You are considering your move,' Death said.

'No. I am remembering Aenarion,' said Caledor.

Death smiled. 'He was my greatest servant.'

Even lacking all the knowledge that had made him what he was, Caledor sensed the lie in that. 'Aenarion was never your servant.'

'He bore my sword.'

'That still does not mean he served you. It was a tool which he used.'

'Perhaps you are right,' said Death. 'Let me rather say that his aims and mine coincided for a while.'

Caledor did not have the energy to argue. Death picked up the piece that represented Aenarion from where it lay beside the board. It was old now, marked by age, its surface rubbed away in places. It might have been tarnished silver or grubby ivory. It was difficult to tell.

'He was a very great killer,' said Death. 'Even the greater daemons, the firstborn children of Chaos, feared him.'

Looking down at the board, Caledor could see that a couple of his own pieces had similar features to the ones Death wore. One of them was tall, broad-shouldered and golden. Looking at the piece, Caledor saw him as he was in life. He could have been Aenarion reborn, but a smiling, good-natured Aenarion, without the weight of care that had always bowed the broad back of the first Phoenix King.

Tyrion, Caledor thought. That was this piece's name. Tyrion, son of Arathion of the line of Aenarion. Looking at Tyrion's face now, he could see it was twisted with uncharacteristic worry. He was wearing the armour of the druchii, which was not natural for him, for he was an asur, a high elf. It was a distinction that had not existed when Caledor had been alive.

Beside Tyrion was a woman of glorious beauty, whose life too had been touched by the power of a god. The piece that represented this woman's mother had already been removed from the board. She was a pawn promoted, a new Everqueen. This was all part of the pattern, he told himself, and he needed to understand it, as he needed to understand what was happening to him.

Before you can rule others, you must first rule yourself.

It was a law of wizardry and more than wizardry. Another fragment of memory bubbled to the surface of his mind. He remembered Aenarion talking to the young Malekith in the great armed camp at Skaggerak. The child had thrown a tantrum and his father, with a tender patience so different from the attitude he displayed in his dealings with all others, was explaining that law to his young son. Caledor remembered that even at the time he had found it ironic. Aenarion had been incapable of the least restraint, resented anything or anyone that tried to baulk his wishes.

Malekith was there upon the board now, no longer a small, watchful boy but a towering, terrifying armoured figure that reeked of death and ancient dark magic. He had turned out badly then. The thought saddened Caledor because he fondly remembered the child. Still, how could he have turned out differently, with two parents such as Aenarion and Morathi; a more self-centred, doom-torn pair of elves had never lived.

Morathi was still on the board too, as wickedly seductive as ever. She did not appear to have aged in all the long ages since Caledor's death. She was still much as he remembered her: dark-haired, sinuously lovely. Like every other elf who had ever looked upon her, he felt the erotic power of her beauty.

Unlike most of them, he could see exactly how much of it came from sorcery. Spells glittered in the air about her, obscuring her true self. Over the millennia a patina of evil magic had crusted around her. As with the Sword of Khaine, the residue of the souls she had devoured clung to her. In her case, they were the fuel for the spell that kept her alive.

She always had a great gift for magic, Caledor thought. More than that, there was a power in her. That which let her look into hell and the future had other side effects too. He could catch the resonance of her thoughts concerning him.

Do you watch me, old ghost? Do you shiver at the thought of what I do?

Caledor did not shiver. He was no longer capable of it. All he could do was watch, appalled, as she tried to destroy his great work once again. All elves were selfish, but she took it to an extreme. She was prepared to murder a world so that she could live forever.

Had she always been this bad, Caledor wondered, or had the madness slipped on her over the centuries? Did her son realise what she was up to? Perhaps he did, judging by the company he kept now.

Malekith was accompanied by something even worse than his mother, a daemon Caledor had known of in ancient times, a creature responsible for the destruction of half a continent and the killing of countless elves.

N'Kari, it was called. The piece on the board was a huge, four-armed monstrous thing, the sort of daemon that the texts referred to as a Keeper of Secrets. The vision that entered Caledor's mind was of a beautiful elven woman, chained by magic that might have bound a god. Malekith had indeed grown in power if he could do that.

Something told Caledor that this daemon was important, that its presence on the board was one of the reasons why Death was doing so well and he was doing so badly. It should not have been there.

'Are you going to move?' Death asked. 'Need I remind you that we are playing to a time limit, and that you forfeit the game if we do not complete it before the sands of time run out?'

Death indicated the hourglass that sat beside the table. Caledor could not remember it being there before. Perhaps Death's gesture had called it into being.

'I do not like this game,' said Caledor. 'It seems all the rules are stacked in your favour.'

'If you do not like the game, why did you agree to play?'

That was a good question. Why was he sitting here, playing an unbeatable opponent at a game he had no hope of winning?

'I had no choice,' he said at last. 'Nothing that lives does.'

'You had a choice,' said Death. 'You least of all can claim you were forced into this. You started the game when you created the board, wizard.'

Caledor reclaimed another part of his memory. The board was, at least in part, a representation of the vast spell he had woven over six thousand years ago and which had trapped him in this limbo. They were in the place where he had died, at the exact centre of the Vortex.

Contained within that truth was another one, a truth he was not yet prepared to face. It was still too terrible for him to contemplate.

Caledor picked up one of his pieces, the other one that resembled Aenarion. It was made of moon-silver. Teclis, this one was called. He blazed with power, power almost as great as that Caledor had wielded himself once, even though this one had been born into a world of far less magic. Teclis was Tyrion's twin, although physically they were nothing alike.

As he touched the piece he recalled other things. He had spoken to this Teclis before, had reached out to him through the Vortex and through other things. He had spoken to him of magic, the fate of the world, and of secrets long hidden and now become important once more.

He knew then how he could influence events and where. He could sense those who were close to the Vortex and close to the things he had once created. With this one, as with Morathi, there was something else. This one had studied Caledor's work, had deciphered its patterns and held them in his mind. This had set up a resonance of sympathetic magic between them.

'You have touched the piece, do you intend to move it?' Death asked.

Indecisively, Caledor returned the piece to the board. 'No. Not yet.'

'Waste all the time you wish. The sands of time are running out.'

Caledor glanced again at Death and at the powers arrayed against him. A daemon, a dark lord and a would-be divinity. They had all grown stronger over the millennia and he had grown weaker. Even at his mightiest he would have been hard put to stand against any one of them. Now, in order to preserve what he had made, he needed to defeat them all.

It was not a matter of power, he told himself. It was a matter of intelligence and strategy and the ability to think ahead. Even there he was at a disadvantage. Who had ever out-thought Death? Malekith was one of the greatest generals in history. Morathi could see the future.

There was nothing to be gained by complaining. Some things simply had to be done. He gathered the tattered remnants of his once near-immeasurable strength to him and raised the piece that represented Tyrion from the board.

'Come then, Ender of Worlds,' Caledor said, placing Tyrion decisively in his new position. 'Let us play.'

CHAPTER ONE

All around them the ancient forest burned. Shadows danced like mad ghosts at a daemonic revel. The air reeked of the fiery death of trees older than empires. The shrieks of the dying, the raped and the tortured mingled with the roar of the flames.

Instinct screamed at Tyrion to put as much distance between themselves and those awful sounds as they could while night lasted.

Those were his people being put to the sword. Those screaming voices belonged to asur, high elves. Their blood enemies, the druchii, had come upon them in the night. If he had not rescued Alarielle from the grasp of the dark elf general, the Everqueen herself would be in the hands of her most deadly enemies.

They needed to get out of here now, to flee, so that she might be spared capture and humiliation by her foes. That was the reason to run.

He glanced across at the Everqueen. He doubted that anyone would have recognised her as the proud and beautiful ruler of Avelorn now. Like him, she was garbed as a druchii soldier. Her face was bruised and her body blood-spattered. Her green eyes held fear and a courage that kept that fear contained, if only just.

Until a few hours ago she had been the pampered ruler of her people. The only fighting she had seen was at tournaments where warriors fought for her favour. Yesterday, he had been one of those warriors, if an ambivalent one, fighting in the great tournament to be her champion.

Today the position seemed to have fallen to him by default. All of the others sworn to her protection were dead, killed by a druchii army which had somehow, impossibly, managed to erupt into the very heart of the forest kingdom of Avelorn without any warning being given.

Other sounds interrupted the shrieks of torment – the blaring of horns and the bellowing of orders. Pursuit was being organised. He needed to get Alarielle to safety. Another chilling thought struck him. If a dark elf army could reach the heart of Avelorn, where else could it reach? Perhaps no place was safe any more.

The Everqueen looked at him, as if frightened by what she read on his face as by the possibility of pursuit.

'You look thoughtful, Prince Tyrion.' He could tell she had wanted to say something else but she was being tactful.

He caught her by the wrist and pulled her along behind him, his elven eyes following the shadowy path without difficulty. 'I was thinking that Avelorn might not be the only place the Witch King has attacked. In fact, it is very unlikely.'

Alarielle looked troubled. 'Of course,' she said. 'Avelorn is not the centre of the world.'

'Ah but it is, at least as far as the elves are concerned, your serenity,' said Tyrion. 'That's why we must get you as far away from here as possible come dawn.'

He was not sure how long these disguises would hold once the dark elves really started looking. He doubted either he or Alarielle could pass as druchii under even the most cursory of inspections.

As if summoned by that thought, a group of at least a dozen figures emerged out of the gloom, all of them dark elves and all of them female. They were beautiful in a savage sort of way – their garb consisted of leather straps, quivers, scabbards and very little else. Their hair was long and matted. Intricate, evil-looking tattoos marked their skins with shocking runes.

Crimson smeared their pouting lips as if they had been drinking the blood of their victims. Each of them bore two blades, and those bloody blades had seen use. Runes on the blades mirrored the ink on their skins. Into those swords, fell magic had been woven. Strange poisons dripped from their points, venoms capable of killing a warrior over a period of many days, making sure that he died in screaming agony.

Tyrion's heart sank. He had faced these women-warriors before in the cold dark lands of Naggaroth. These were witch elves, among the deadliest fighters of a deadly breed.

The women blocked their path away from the tournament grounds. Tyrion had no idea what they were doing out here. Perhaps they were already scouring the woods for high elf survivors fleeing the battlefield. He gestured for Alarielle to hold her ground.

The witch elves came closer, half surrounding them in a great semicircle. Tyrion did not like the way their leader looked at him at all. He liked the way she looked at Alarielle even less.

'Hail, brother,' she said. 'You seem to be going the wrong way.'

Her bright, mad eyes studied Tyrion. He smiled easily and said, 'we were just looking for a private place to do some celebrating.'

The witch elf smiled, showing small, sharp teeth. 'Is that so?'

Tyrion reached out and took Alarielle's hand and squeezed it. 'That is so.'

The witch elves moved closer, and it was all that Tyrion could do to keep from drawing his blade. That would give them away as nothing else would. No dark elf bore a sword like Sunfang. The magic of that ancient blade would mark him as a stranger among the druchii.

The leader reached out and stroked Alarielle's cheek. The Everqueen shivered a little at the contact. 'She is certainly a pretty one. I can understand why you would feel that way. On the other hand, now is not the time to be leaving the battlefield.'

'Perhaps you are right,' said Tyrion. 'Perhaps we should head back and report to our units.'

'And what unit would that be, my pretty boy with the so-strange accent?' The witch elf was suspicious. He knew that he did not sound very much like an inhabitant of Naggaroth even when he tried. He was always going to have the accent of Lothern overlaying the mountain twang of Cothique he had picked up as a boy.

'We are with Captain Ichmael,' Tyrion said.

The witch elf laughed, a high-pitched crazed tittering that set cold fingers running up and down Tyrion's spine. She reached out and stroked Tyrion's chin now. Her nails were long and sharp and enamelled black. She tilted her head to one side and her eyes narrowed. 'Captain who?'

Tyrion did not miss the faint gesture she made with her left hand or the response that the other witch elves made. They had begun to circle behind Tyrion and Alarielle and within heartbeats the two of them were surrounded. Somewhere in the witch elf leader's crazed mind a mad suspicion had bloomed.

Tyrion drew Sunfang in one eye-blurring motion. The sword blazed to life, flames flickering along its length. The woman's drug-enhanced reflexes were so quick she almost managed to parry the blow. Sunfang grated along her blade, sparks bursting out as the metal ground together, then buried itself in the witch elf's head with the sound of a butcher's cleaver hitting a hanging carcass.

Tyrion lashed out left then right, taking down two more of the witch elves with as many blows. The rest of them responded with the speed of elite troops and something else...

Surprise did not slow them. Something about the drugs they had taken made them accept the sudden eruption of violence in their midst as if it was a perfectly normal occurrence. Perhaps for them it was. He knew how crazed witch elves could be.

They swarmed towards him, blades stabbing. He danced through a whirlwind of razor-sharp swords, ducking, weaving and slashing. Within a few more heartbeats he had killed three more. Other elves might have turned tail and fled in the face of the carnage that he wrought, but not these ones.

A poisoned dagger flickered towards the Everqueen. Desperately, Tyrion twisted to parry the blade, striking it from the air. As he did so, he felt a stab of pain in his side. One of the witch elves had managed to penetrate his stolen armour. He could only pray that no poison had got into the wound.

Seeing his concern for Alarielle, his foes switched targets, two of them going for her and the rest of them striking at him, knowing that he would be distracted.

There was no way he could protect Alarielle and himself at the same time. If the witch elves were determined to cut her down, they would, and there was nothing he could do about it, short of throwing himself in front of their blades.

'Don't kill her! She is the Everqueen!' Tyrion shouted. It was the only way he could think of to slow them down.

The two witch elves attacking Alarielle paused for a second. Tyrion took advantage of it to stab one of them through the throat. Her flesh sizzled as Sunfang bit.

Alarielle raised her hands together over her head and spoke a word. There was a flash of greenish light and the witch elves reeled back, momentarily blinded. Tyrion leapt forwards into the blinded mass, blade slashing, leaving only dead and dying in his wake.

'You are hurt, Prince Tyrion,' said the Everqueen. Her voice sounded unnaturally loud in the strange quiet after the combat.

Tyrion's side stung where the witch elf's blade had bit. He took off the chainmail shirt, unlaced his jerkin and inspected the wound. It was nothing, a mere scratch that would not even require stitching.

'I took worse in practice matches when I was a boy.'

The Everqueen looked at him scornfully. 'I doubt you duelled with witch elf blades when you were a youth. There is no need for such bravado.'

She was right, of course. He had seen too much of what happened to those wounded by witch elves to want to take any chances now. He unstoppered the canteen that was part of the gear he had stolen. It smelled of potent alcohol. Trust a druchii to carry that in his water bottle. He poured some out onto the scratch. It burned as if he was being branded by a dark elf torturer. He kept his face calm, not wanting to give the Everqueen the satisfaction of seeing him in pain.

'Let me see it,' Alarielle said. Tyrion wanted to refuse but to do so would have seemed childish, so he stood there while she bent down to look at it.

'You might have been lucky, but I don't like the shadow surrounding the wound. If it gets worse, let me know.'

He looked at the wound again. There *was* a curious blackness around its edges that did not bode well, but there was nothing he could do about it now.

'What will you do, work magic on it?'

'I might have to.' She did not sound at all confident in her ability to do so.

In the distance horns rang out again. They made Tyrion think of hunters with packs of hounds. 'Not now. We had best be going,' he said. 'Run!'

They raced off into the night.

'A new day at last,' said Tyrion, looking at the red sun as it rose upon the horizon, clearly visible through a gap in the foliage. Birds had begun to sing. The grass was moist with dew. It all seemed strangely normal after the long night of flight and terror.

'Let us hope that it proves to be a happier one than the last,' said the Everqueen. 'I am not sure that I can endure another like yesterday.'

'I'm afraid you're just going to have to, your serenity,' said Tyrion. 'There will be many days like yesterday and worse ahead of us.'

'You're doing nothing to bolster my courage, Prince Tyrion,' said the Everqueen.

'I am trying to be realistic. We don't have an army. We don't have any friends. We only have the two of us to rely upon for our own safety.'

The Everqueen nodded. Her jaw tightened. Her eyes narrowed. She straightened her shoulders and stood a little taller. She was grim but resolute, and for the first time in a long time it seemed to Tyrion that here was someone he could follow.

'Where should we go?' the Everqueen asked. Just when she seemed ready to be a leader, she reminded him she was hardly more than a young girl. It was a strange mix.

'That's a very good question,' said Tyrion. 'We need to go in the direction that Malekith's minions least expect.'

'That's all very well, but it needs to be a direction in which we can eventually find refuge and get help.'

'Indeed. I say that we should strike out east.'

'How do we know that the dark elves are not waiting for us in that direction?'

'We don't – we will just have to take our chances.'

'What I still don't understand is how they managed to get to us. It should have been impossible for a force so large to penetrate so deeply into Avelorn without being spotted.'

'Magic,' said Tyrion. 'It's the only explanation.'

'Even so, I should have been able to sense such magic in the very heart of my domain. I may only have just become Everqueen, but in these lands nothing should be able to happen without me knowing it.'

'I am no sorcerer, but if you've only just inherited the power, perhaps you overlooked something.'

'You're not making me feel any better, Prince Tyrion.'

'I don't think it was a coincidence that the dark elves attacked so soon after your mother's death. I think that we have fallen into a trap that has been in preparation for a very long time. I think that we are very lucky indeed to have escaped it with our lives.'

The Everqueen looked thoughtful. 'The only reason that I am here, that we managed to escape at all, is because of you. I am very grateful for that. Perhaps I misjudged you, Prince Tyrion.'

Tyrion was very surprised to receive that apology. After all, he was the one who had been rude to her over the past few days. 'I do not think you were wrong about me at all, your serenity. And I think that the reason that we are here is that the gods have smiled upon us so far.'

'Then we are the only ones that the gods have smiled upon. I do not think there are many more survivors among our people.'

Tyrion felt cold rage spark within his heart. 'I left a number of friends back there cold upon the ground. The dark elves owe me a great debt, and I intend to collect upon it. But first we must get you to safety. As long as you are alive and free, the Witch King's plan has failed. Let us see that it continues to do so. If this is the only blow that we can strike against our enemies, it will have to do, for now.'

'Yes, Prince Tyrion. Let us do exactly that.' She began to collect some berries from the undergrowth. 'And now let us eat. We will need all of our strength and all of our wits about us if we are going to maintain our freedom.'

'How do you know these are not poisonous?' Tyrion asked.

Her smile was dazzling. 'I grew up here, Prince Tyrion. There is little I don't know about life in these woods.'

'I am glad one of us has that knowledge,' said Tyrion. 'I suspect it is going to prove necessary.'

—◀ CHAPTER TWO ▶—

Death looked at the witch elf piece and smiled. It was removed from the board now but the pawn had done its work. It had infected Prince Tyrion with a poison that would surely kill him before he could perform his purpose. If nothing else, it would slow him down until the pursuit could overtake him.

'A subtle move,' Caledor said.

Death smiled. 'I await your response with interest.'

Caledor focused his power on the square containing Tyrion and the new Everqueen. It was near a waystone. Of course it was. He saw another part of the pattern here.

Somehow his enemies were using the Vortex as part of their plans, or perhaps the mystical structures of the Old Ones that lay beneath. It mattered not at this moment in time. He needed to concentrate on making events run his way.

A vision danced into his mind, of a torn pavilion, a pile of corpses, an army running half out of control. The dead lay everywhere, elves. A huge number were garbed as if for a festival. Far fewer of the corpses wore the iron armour of the dark elves. It saddened Caledor that his own people should have taken to slaughtering each other, as if there were not enough enemies in the world. Somehow all of this was connected with Aenarion and his cursed blade. It would have been better for the elves if it had never been drawn from its altar.

Another image sprang into his mind – a great metal mirror, forged in the ancient manner, had been set up within the pavilion. Potent spells were woven into its magical glass, a strange intelligence glittered in the crystal eyes of the metal dragons that held the frame in their claws. The glass itself was many-layered and magical. It could be used to communicate across distances by those who knew how.

Before it stood a powerful-looking dark elf in the elaborate armour of a high officer. His head was bowed as if in grief. That surprised

Caledor. It was not what he would have expected at all. The dark elf was waiting for someone or something. He had already invoked a spell. There was a sense of a powerful cold mind being brought to bear through the mirror. Caledor knew that mind, or had done in the past, although back then it did not have the aura of ruthless evil it emitted now. It was Malekith, son of Aenarion, much changed from the quiet lad he had once been.

Caledor expended a morsel of his carefully husbanded power, disrupting the spell that the mirror contained, making it impossible for its master to look out of it or speak through it.

'Interesting,' said Death, 'although I don't see what good it does you. A messenger will work as well as that mirror albeit more slowly.'

Caledor smiled at him, knowing that in this game tempo was all-important. Time might work as well for him as it did for his enemy.

Death reached out to pick up a piece. 'I believe that was a mistake,' he said.

'We shall see,' said Caledor, wishing that he felt as confident as he tried to sound.

General Dorian, Marshal of the North, by Grace of Malekith the Great Commander of the First Army of Conquest, stared into the mirror bleakly. Cassandra was dead. The thought hit him harder than he would have expected. In some ways it weighed on him more heavily than his failure to capture the Everqueen; and that was most likely going to cost him his life.

What did it matter? Life seemed bleak and empty now. He felt the woman's absence in a way he had never felt her presence in life. Or perhaps he had, and had just never noticed until today, the way one never notices the presence of a limb until it is amputated. He told himself it was only a foolish, sentimental attachment – as a druchii such things were meaningless to him. He could not convince himself of the truth of that.

He glared into the mirror, willing it to come to life so that he could get things over with, but all he could see was his own reflection: pale, angry and scared, glaring back at him. His armour was dented, his face was bruised, his lip was split. His side was bandaged and bloody.

He did not look like a successful druchii general. He looked like the broken survivors he had sometimes seen after a great defeat. He wore the expression of one of the slaves he used to capture when raiding the Bretonnian coast immediately after it had been put in chains.

He forced himself to smile coldly, to make his face a mask of confidence and command. The expression was not convincing.

What was taking the Witch King so long? Dorian had already made the offering of blood and invoked the spell that should have let him speak to his master over the long leagues of Ulthuan. Why had Malekith not made contact? He had never taken this long before.

Was his master toying with him, like a great predatory cat tormenting its prey?

He thought about the warrior who had done this to him. It should not have been possible. One elf could not simply stroll through a formation of druchii soldiers, walk into the presence of its general, slaughter half the command staff and their bodyguards and then walk out again, taking their prisoner and prize with them.

It beggared belief.

It was the sort of thing that happened in old tales, in the legends of Aenarion and Caledor. It did not happen in reality.

Still, this had been a gathering of champions, where a group of the mightiest warriors in Ulthuan had come together to compete for the favour of the Everqueen and to become her champion. If ever there was a place for a hero to emerge from, it was here. It was not something that the Witch King had calculated upon, apparently. He could imagine it becoming the start of a new epic, a myth of the asur, if the elf who had done it got away with it.

He shook his head and his reflection in the mirror did the same, mocking him. He felt like striking the magical thing with his sword, but he doubted it would do any good. This mirror had been forged beneath Naggarond by Malekith himself. The mage-steel frame was marked with dragons and looked as hard as the Witch King's armour. The glass only appeared fragile. It had been made to survive being taken on campaign with an army. It was, after all, how Malekith kept in touch with his generals when they were in the field and needed his personal supervision.

He thought about his lord and master. Malekith was not forgiving. He despised failures and he punished them; up until an hour ago Dorian would not but have agreed with that policy.

Why preserve the weak?

They needed to be winnowed out so that the strong might prosper. Of course, that had been before he had become a failure himself.

Somehow he did not see the Witch King making an exception to his policy in this case. This was failure on a monumental scale. Dorian had imperilled a plan that had been a century in the making.

It was unfair. It had all gone perfectly. Right until the end. They had destroyed the great tournament camp and taken prisoner or slain thousands of the asur. They had captured the Everqueen. She had lain bound on the floor of this vast florid pavilion before him. The god-queen of the asur had been his prisoner.

For all of twenty minutes, he thought sourly. Before a solitary warrior had stolen her away.

As if that was not bad enough, his aides were bringing him news that some others had cut their way out of this trap. A group of elven knights under the banner of Arhalien of Yvresse had fought their way free.

Arhalien was a famous warrior. Was it he who had come back to undo Malekith's plans, slay Cassandra and lay waste to Dorian's life?

The Everqueen was a potent symbol to her people, their living goddess, an incarnation of their spirit. While she was free she would provide a rallying point for her people. They would not give in without a fight. It had been Malekith's master-stroke, capturing her. Or it would have been, if Dorian had succeeded.

At least it was peaceful here, he thought. He was alone with his grief and his sense of failure and shame. None of his officers dared enter this part of the tent. None of them wanted to catch the Witch King's eye when he was wrathful.

If Dorian had been reporting success, as had seemed so likely a few hours ago, they would have crowded around him, elbowing each other out of the way to come into the view of the mirror's great watchful eye. Now, there was no one except him there. Outside, all was silence. He knew the survivors of his staff were listening intently to see what transpired, to eavesdrop for any hints of their own fate.

He wondered if the sense of failure had started to ripple out through the army yet, if they realised exactly how bad things were or could be, if Malekith became really wrathful. They were hundreds of leagues behind enemy lines, in the heart of the oldest forest in the world. They were being supplied through a mystical portal created by an enslaved daemon who might turn on their master at any time. They were in a land they did not know and surrounded by an enemy who knew every inch of it. They had lost the element of surprise, which had been their greatest weapon.

He told himself not to be so defeatist. All across Ulthuan, the

Witch King's armies were striking unexpectedly in the heart of Elvendom. A gigantic host of Chaos marauders was descending on the elven realm from the north. This was the greatest invasion of Ulthuan since the time of Aenarion. It was not going to fail.

And yet, Dorian thought, he had. One solitary elf had turned the greatest of victories into the most disastrous of defeats. He glared into the mirror, willing his master to appear so he could report his failure. Nothing happened.

What was going on, Dorian wondered?

He reached out and touched the mirror. It felt cold and dead. It was inert, without the faintest trace of magic in it.

He waited for an hour. Malekith still did not communicate. Slowly it came to Dorian that he was not going to die immediately. If the delay was sufficiently long, he might not have to die at all. If he could just recapture the Everqueen...

And why not? He still had a powerful army at his command. He still had the advantage of surprise. His foe was only a solitary elf, in the company of an Everqueen who had yet to come into possession of her legacy of power. If he acted quickly, he might still be able to save the situation, his career and his life.

Filled with a renewed sense of purpose, he squared his shoulders and strode out of the tent, bellowing orders to summon his captains, his scouts and his magicians to him. At the very least, he thought, he would get revenge for Cassandra's death.

CHAPTER THREE

As the sun rose higher, Tyrion's natural good spirits began to assert themselves. He was still alive and so was the Everqueen, and that meant that whatever the Witch King had planned could still be stopped. Ignoring the pain in his side, he vaulted over a fallen log.

He was not sure what that ancient evil being had in mind for the Everqueen, but he knew that it could not be anything good. At the very least, having her in captivity would allow him to exert a great deal of pressure on her people, who would naturally be very concerned for her safety.

Perhaps Malekith thought that if he had the Everqueen in his hands, he could use her as a figurehead for his occupation. Perhaps, by the use of magic or torture or some combination of both, he might even be able to make her act the part.

It would be a very bad thing for the people of Ulthuan if the Everqueen was to fall into the Witch King's hands. The best thing he could do for his people might be to ensure that it never happened.

Looking at the beautiful girl walking beside him, he was not sure he was capable of killing her. She was not his enemy, she was his queen. It was his duty to keep her alive if he could, and that was a duty he intended to perform for as long as there was breath within him. The Everqueen caught him looking at her from the corner of her eye and looked at him quizzically. 'What are you thinking about, Prince Tyrion?'

'I'm thinking about my duty, your serenity, and what I may need to do to perform it.'

'I'm sure that you will do whatever needs to be done, Prince Tyrion.'

'There are some things that I hope never become necessary.'

'We all have had such duties to perform. When the time comes, you must put aside your personal feelings and do what is needed.'

Tyrion wondered if she knew that she was signing her own death warrant. He half-suspected that she did.

Sunlight dappled the path. Alarielle gave a shout and dropped downslope. She picked up something, studied it and nodded.

'What are you doing?' Tyrion asked. He was still taken aback by the suddenness of her action. He glared around, half-expecting some threat to emerge from the trees.

'I saw this,' said Alarielle, raising the long piece of wood in her left hand.

'Very good,' said Tyrion. 'You found a stick.'

'Not just a stick,' she said, already cross-legged and whittling away at the wood. 'I can make this into a bow.'

'I am not sure that will help us against the armies of Malekith,' he said.

She kept stripping the bark from the wood with her knife. 'No, but it will help us to eat.'

'Only if you can hit something with it,' he said.

She smiled. It was as dazzling as the sunbeams filtering down through the gaps in the leaves. 'I think I might be capable of that.'

'How long is this going to take?' He glanced around, as much to let her know that even now enemies might be creeping up on them as to give himself a chance to spot pursuit.

'A while,' she said. 'You may as well make yourself comfortable.'

'Let us hope our enemies are doing the same.'

'You were not brought up in Avelorn, were you, Prince Tyrion?'

'You know it.'

'It's easy enough to see. You do not move like an elf of Avelorn. You do not cover your tracks like an elf of Avelorn. You do not think like an elf of Avelorn.'

'I suspect all of this is leading towards the inevitable conclusion that I am not an elf of Avelorn, and that you are...'

'How long do you think this pursuit may go on?'

'I don't know. Weeks, perhaps months.'

'Indeed.' She inspected the bow which she had stripped of all bark now. 'Improvised, but it will do.'

'What has the time got to do with it?'

'How do you propose we eat?'

'We forage for edible roots, we bring down small game.'

She was making a string from the lacings of her dark elf tunic now and winding it around the bent piece of wood, drawing it taut. Tyrion could see a bow beginning to take shape.

'And how are you proposing to do that?'

'I was brought up in the mountains of Cothique. I can use a sling.'

Alarielle took some other pieces of wood and began to sharpen them. She was making very basic arrows.

'I don't see a sling,' she said.

'They are easier to make than a bow,' said Tyrion. 'You can use leather or cloth. Leather by preference.'

'And you are good with this improvised weapon?'

'I am good with any weapon.'

Alarielle took her hastily made bow and sighted at something in a nearby tree. She aimed, drew and fired. A bird fell, improvised arrow sticking from its breast.

'And I am good with a bow,' she said. 'All the children of Avelorn are.'

She walked over to where the bird's corpse lay, picked it up and began removing feathers. Tyrion already knew she intended to use them on her arrows.

'I could have brought that down,' he said, a little defensively, 'with a thrown stone.'

'You may not always be here to ward and feed me. I think it best to be prepared for that eventuality.'

As she said this, she turned and fired again. Another bird fell.

Tyrion could think of nothing to say. She was correct.

Dorian looked at the chief scout then at the dead witch elves.

'You see it?' Scout Commander Malak asked.

'The wounds have been cauterised.'

Malak nodded. 'Unless a passing torturer decided to mutilate the corpses with red-hot pokers, I would say they went this way.'

'Good. I want this elf found and I want him dead, and I want the Everqueen back in my hands before this week is out.'

'Perhaps you should simply leave the matter in my hands, general,' Malak said. 'I can do what needs to be done, and someone needs to be in command of the army.'

'You think to teach me my duties, or how to run my command?'

'Of course not, general.'

'Good. Let me explain something to you. There is nothing in the whole wide world more important than finding the elf with the burning sword and the woman who is with him. Is that clear?'

'Yes, general.'

'If he is not found, none of our lives will be spared. The Witch King will make an example of us all.' Dorian paused and studied Malak's expression. If the scout thought that the general had gone mad, no sign of it showed on his face. If he was laughing inwardly at Dorian's failure, it was cleverly concealed. He had spoken loudly so that his words would reach all nearby ears. Soon it would be communicated to the whole army. He thought he had better emphasise the point.

'If we find the Everqueen, our rewards will be unimaginable. If we fail, the tale of our deaths will cause druchii everywhere to shudder for twice ten thousand years.'

'We will not fail, general,' said Malak.

'Good. Now let us get about our business.'

Bending over the tracks like a hound sniffing at a trail, Malak looked for clues. After a moment, he said, 'There were only two of them, a male and a female. They were garbed as druchii or at least wearing the boots of our soldiers.'

'I think it safe to assume they are in disguise then...'

'Indeed. They fought against a dozen witch elves and killed them all. The weapon used by one of them was a magical burning sword. It is definitely the elf you want, general.'

'How long till we find them?'

'They are travelling fast and light but my scouts can overhaul them. I recommend we fan out our force on either side of the trail in case they are hiding. I will assign a tracker to each company. We can send scouts on Cold Ones ahead down the trail and hope to overhaul them.'

'So be it,' said Dorian. 'Let us get to it.'

Already he was thinking that it might be best not to rely on the skills of his scouts. It might be best to invoke sorcery. He would need to talk with the witches.

Tyrion added some more twigs to the fire. The night was cool and there were beasts about. He had made camp in a hollow which would put their fire out of sight. In the darkness, he did not fear that woodsmoke rising skywards would give them away, although perhaps the scent of it would if their enemies got close. They needed warm food and comfort more than that slight risk at the moment, he decided.

The Everqueen looked at home here. Her face was smudged with soot. She had dressed the birds she had shot earlier and was cooking them on an improvised spit, baking tubers in the same fire. He was glad she had turned out to be competent at this. He was not sure he was going to be able to get her all the way out of the forest. His side was paining him already and he did not know how long they would have to flee.

They sat in silence as the pigeons cooked, then ate quietly, stripping the birds right down to the bones. Afterwards they sat down by the fire. Alarielle stared into it.

'I used to love doing this when I was a child,' she said. The sound of her voice was surprising in the night.

'Doing what?' Tyrion asked.

'Staring into the fire I could see all sorts of things in it: castles, clouds, gods, elementals, daemons. I used to tell myself all sorts of stories.'

'I would have thought there was always someone there to do that for you.'

'You don't like me, do you, Prince Tyrion?' There was truth in that, but now did not seem like a time to say it.

'I don't know you.'

'And yet you still don't like me – why is that?'

Tyrion sighed. 'Does it trouble you so much that one person does not like you? I would have thought the adoration of all the rest made up for it.'

'Is that what bothers you? The way the people worship me?'

'Perhaps worship is too strong a word.'

'No, it is not, and the truth is that it bothers me too.'

Tyrion looked at her sharply. 'Why?'

'Because it was not always so. I was once an elf maid like any other. Now people treat me as a living goddess. Even you, in your strange, sullen way.'

Tyrion felt that was unfair. Her words stung. He was not used to being talked to like this either. 'Perhaps because you *are* a goddess.'

'It was not my choice.'

'Poor child.'

She smiled, and something in her smile made Tyrion feel ashamed of himself. 'No. Really. It was not my choice. And I would much rather my mother was alive than I was possessed by this thing.'

'Possessed? That is an interesting choice of words.'

'It is an accurate one, Prince Tyrion. I share my body with something else. I am not even sure what that something is.'

'It is the spirit of the earth goddess. Even I know that.'

'You may know the words, Prince Tyrion, but I very much doubt you can have any inkling of what they mean.'

'I have met the Phoenix King.'

'I have not. Do I remind you of him?'

'No. Yes.'

'You are not normally so indecisive.'

'There is a spell around you. Even I can see that.'

'Why do you say *even*?'

'Because my magesight is not good. It has always been worse than most other elves.'

'I would not have thought you had any flaws. You don't behave as if you do...'

Tyrion laughed. 'You don't like me either, do you?'

'It's difficult to like someone so hostile.'

'I am not always so hostile,' Tyrion said. He decided it was best to be honest. 'You bring it out in me. You did before ever I saw you, if truth be told.'

'Why?'

'I did not want to become your champion. I was blackmailed into it.'

'By whom?'

'By my aunt, a very great and gracious elf lady, not unlike yourself.'

'You don't like her either?'

'On the contrary, I like her very much. I just don't like being made to do things.'

'We are all made to do things we don't like, Prince Tyrion.'

'Now you sound like her. She said very much the same thing.'

'Perhaps because life is like that.' She sounded sad again. Tyrion did not like that. He did not like seeing her as a person.

'What would you know of that?'

'I was born to be the Everqueen.'

'And you did not want to be the goddess of an entire people, of course?'

'Of course I did. When I was a little girl I dreamed of it. It was only later, when I saw what it really meant, that I had my doubts.'

'When you saw what it really meant?'

'What it did to my mother and to me and my sister.'

'What do you mean?'

'My mother loved me, Prince Tyrion.'

'Is that such a bad thing?'

'And I loved her.'

'So?'

'We almost never saw each other. We almost never saw my sister either.'

Tyrion thought he already knew the answer but he spoke anyway – she seemed to need to talk. This was the odd intimacy of strangers met around a campfire, telling things to strangers they would not tell to their best friends. He had experienced it before on his travels. 'Why?'

'Because she was the Everqueen and we were her heirs and we could not all be in one place at one time in case we were all slain or captured together. There must always be an Everqueen.'

Tyrion saw the logic of it. 'Don't put all your eggs in one basket.'

'A crude way of putting it, but essentially correct. I was taken away from her and put in the care of my aunt when I was small. I never saw my mother until my sister was born.'

'So you both could not be killed at one time.'

She nodded. 'My sister and I were not allowed to be in one place together. My mother could see one of us only on special occasions under conditions of highest security, and only for very short times.'

'After the events of the past few days, I think you can understand why.'

'I always understood why, Prince Tyrion. It did not make it any easier. I never saw my mother again after my sister died.'

'Died?'

'An accident. She fell from a tree into deep water. There were rocks, they say. I don't know, of course, for I was not there.'

There was something shocking and accusing about her grief. He did not want to hear it. He felt like he was standing in for the world that had forced this young woman to live apart from her family. In Lothern, he had seen many examples of the way elven society made the people in it cold and distant. He had not expected to encounter the same here.

'You have a brother,' she said. 'The famous magician.'

'Yes.'

'Are you close to him?'

'Yes.'

'And your mother?'

'She died when we were born. It was a difficult birth, so they say – twins.'

'I am sorry.'

'Why? You never knew her.'

'Nor did you. Perhaps you would have been different if you had.'

He did not want this conversation to go any further. 'I am going to take a look around,' he said. 'Make sure there are no dark elves sneaking up on us.'

He moved off into the quiet of the night and did not return until she was asleep or pretending to be. He stared into the fire for a long time, thinking of daemons and gods, castles and the lovely stranger lying so close by the fire.

The fire had burned down and the sun had already risen when he came awake suddenly. The woods around them were filled with the noise of an approaching army. Alarielle was already awake, staring at him with fear-filled eyes. Sometimes he thought he saw something else staring out at him, something ancient and alien and strange.

'We need to run,' he told her. 'Now!'

◄ CHAPTER FOUR ►

'What's that?' Alarielle asked. Tyrion could understand why she was disturbed. He recognised that eerie high-pitched screeching sound. He had heard it before in the cold northern lands of Naggaroth. It was a sound that meant terror to the warriors of Ulthuan.

'Cold Ones,' Tyrion said.

'The great lizards that the dark elves use as cavalry? What are they doing here?' Alarielle asked.

'Looking for us,' Tyrion said. 'That would be my guess.'

'I mean in Avelorn.'

Again he understood her shock but he chose to wilfully misunderstand it. 'Doubtless they got here the same way as their riders. One day, if we are lucky, we will know how that happened.'

'Cold Ones,' she said softly, as if not quite believing either her own words or the distant bellowing of the great beasts.

'We need to move. They can smell warm blood. They are trained to be particularly receptive to the smell of high elf blood.'

Almost as if the creatures could hear him, the bellowing came closer.

'It sounds like there are a number of them,' Alarielle said.

'One would be too many,' Tyrion said. He was already starting to jog down the track, trusting to Alarielle to follow him. She kept up easily. His side hurt from where the witch elf's blade had bit home. It was going to be difficult for him to keep up any speed over long distances.

Tyrion could hear the sound of branches breaking as the Cold Ones' massive forms forced their way through the forest. Horns sounded, nearby and farther in the distance, as the dark elves exchanged signals. They were on the track of something and it seemed safe to assume that the trail which had been found was their own.

'They've caught our scent,' Alarielle said.

'Some of them can smell warm blood at a distance of a mile,' Tyrion said. 'I don't doubt that this is why these riders were sent ahead.'

'We can still lose them if we can find a way to water. That throws hounds off the tracks and wolves. It ought to do the same for them.'

'Do you know where we can find a stream?' Tyrion asked.

'I can do better than that,' Alarielle said. 'There is a river ahead. If we can reach it we can probably get them off our trail.'

'Lead on,' Tyrion said. Behind him he thought he already heard the sound of elves moving through the forest nearby. He doubted they would be friendly.

Tyrion looked out of their rocky hiding place and studied their enemies. Alarielle had chosen it because it would be impossible for their foes to track them over this ground. She had gone off and left a false trail beyond it and circled back to him. He had not liked letting her out of his sight, but he had no choice. She knew about these matters and he did not.

They had been running for most of the day and no matter how they tried, it seemed impossible to outdistance the pursuit. Always, the woods were full of the sounds of horns and druchii battle-calls, as the various components of the army kept in touch. Gradually, some of the noises had faded into the distance, but others had managed to keep up, no matter how quickly he and Alarielle ran.

Looking back now, he could see why. These were not standard infantry. They were lightly armed and armoured and moved with the easy authority of the highest echelons of combat troops.

Their very appearance here was shocking. The dark elves moved confidently along the trail. They gave every impression of being at home, of having utter confidence in their right to be there in the heart of the most sacred place in Elvendom. There was no fear in the way they walked. They were the hunters, not the hunted.

The cockiness in their manner almost compelled Tyrion to leap out and slay them. An insane anger burned deep in him, filling him with the urge to rend and slay. He wanted to wipe the confident smile off the smug face of the dark elf sergeant giving orders to his troops. He wanted to see fear blossom in the eyes of the two druchii warriors sharing a joke, doubtless at asur expense. His hand tightened on the hilt of Sunfang.

A hand gripped his. He turned and glared angrily at Alarielle. She shook her head. I can kill them all, he wanted to say. There were only a score of them. With the advantage of surprise, and the power of Sunfang, it was possible he could do it too, even with the Everqueen clinging to his arm.

He let out a long breath, realising how mad the thoughts cascading through his brain had suddenly become. Attacking a score of armed veterans was not a sensible thing to do. The chances were that he could not kill them all, even if he could he might be wounded or slain in the process. It was a mad risk and there was nothing to be gained from it, save the satisfaction of a bloodlust that he had never even suspected he possessed.

Was this the Curse of Aenarion finally coming on him in full force? Or was it something else? Had the wound from the witch elf's blade infected him with something else, a taste of their reckless madness perhaps? He stayed frozen in place, waiting tensely to see if the dark elves discovered their trail.

One of them bent down and said something to the others. Had he spotted a track? Tyrion readied himself to spring into action if that was the case. It looked like his bloodlust might be slaked after all. Part of him would have welcomed it.

He could feel Alarielle tense beside him. If the dark elves overcame him, she might end up their prisoner once more. If that happened, she would eventually end up within Malekith's iron-gauntleted grasp.

After a long moment, he felt her exhale. The dark elves moved on, still scanning the woods around them, hunters seeking prey. It seemed like a very long time before they were out of sight.

Tyrion and Alarielle lay in the undergrowth, slumped out of sight, close as lovers. Eventually they smiled at each other. It seemed that danger had passed them by for a while. Some buried instinct urged him to stay here, but he knew it was foolish. The horns in the distance were coming closer. It was only a matter of time before the larger force of druchii overhauled them and they would have the numbers to search thoroughly. They needed to get moving by another path than the ones the pursuing scouts had taken.

Reluctantly, he rose from the hard ground. He felt a small sharp pain in his side, where the witch elf had wounded him. It seemed to be getting worse.

Alarielle stopped walking, raised her head and looked around. 'What was that?' she asked. Her jawline was set tight and every muscle was tense. Tyrion reached out to touch her shoulder and he could feel the tightness of the muscles beneath. She shrugged off his touch and glanced around, wary as a deer that has caught the scent of a hunter.

He understood why. There was a sudden tension in the air that had not been there before. Fewer birds sang. Fewer small creatures moved through the undergrowth. He realised how tightly wound the Everqueen must be to spot this before he did. Normally he was the person most aware of his surroundings. She gestured for him to take cover and threw herself under a nearby bush. Tyrion burrowed into the undergrowth, not a moment too soon.

A group of druchii emerged into the clearing, moving carefully and calmly. They carried small hand crossbows and had wicked-looking blades at their sides. Their movement was stealthy. There was something shadowy about them. They looked like creatures of the night, feral, predatory and deadly.

Their leader studied the ground where Tyrion and Alarielle had stood. He made a gesture using hand signals that could have meant anything but which Tyrion suspected meant they are close, be careful. He looked around the clearing and seemed to pick up their tracks. Tyrion knew the game was up and that he could only hope that there were not too many other druchii nearby. Alarielle clearly recognised what was happening. She stood up with her bow aimed directly at the scout leader. All of them turned to face her.

'It seems we have found our prey,' the leader said. His voice was as cold as the winds of the north. He sounded like a true son of his harsh land.

'I will put an arrow through the first one of you who moves,' Alarielle said.

'Perhaps,' said the druchii. 'And then you will be pin-cushioned by the rest of us.'

'It will be better than the fate that awaits me at your hands.'

'Our king wishes you delivered to him unharmed.' The dark elf's tone was reasonable.

'That was the fate to which I was referring,' Alarielle said.

'Shoot one of us and the rest will shoot to wound you,' the leader said. Tyrion knew his words were aimed at his followers. He did not want them making any mistakes in this tricky situation. He was obviously a careful elf. He glanced around the clearing again, puzzled, and Tyrion knew that he was thinking about the second person who might be there.

He had no recourse but to act. He leapt from the bushes, driving Sunfang into the back of one of the scouts. He heard a scream from nearby and, turning, saw that Alarielle had put an arrow through the eye of the leader. The remaining pair of druchii were distracted for a moment, unsure who to shoot at, the sight of a warrior in their own armour bearing a blazing sword confusing them for a crucial second.

Tyrion covered the distance between him and the closest in three strides. The immediate threat made the druchii swing his crossbow towards Tyrion. Sunfang swept down and cleaved it in two. Tyrion dropped the dark elf with his second cut and turned in time to see the last scout's crossbow pointed directly at him. There was no way he could close fast enough to avoid being shot. The dark elf's finger squeezed the trigger. An arrow flashed through the air and took him in the side of the neck, sending him falling to one side, spoiling his aim. The crossbow bolt flashed past Tyrion's ear, so close that he felt the wind of its passing.

Tyrion sprang forwards and beheaded the scout before turning to face Alarielle. 'Thank you,' he said. 'You saved my life.'

She was not looking at him and she did not respond. Her face was very pale, and Tyrion turned to see what she was looking at. In the shadows beneath the trees hundreds of druchii marched, an army on the move; he did not doubt for a moment that it was seeking them.

Already crossbow bolts were starting to flash towards them. Fortunately the bushes, the shadows and the low branches interfered with their flight, but it was only a matter of time before they got the range.

'Run!' shouted the Everqueen. She did not have to tell Tyrion twice. They sprinted away through the trees with what must have been the better part of a regiment of druchii in pursuit.

Tyrion and Alarielle sprinted through the woods. Now and then they could hear the sound of the druchii screaming. The enemy had caught sight of their prey and felt it within their grasp. The woods echoed with the shouts and war cries of the dark elves. Tyrion's heart pounded within his chest. Alarielle looked back at him over her shoulder. She could run like a gazelle when frightened, and she was frightened now.

Despair filled Tyrion's heart. He could not see how they were going to escape the jaws of the enormous trap that were snapping shut. From all around now he could hear druchii voices. It seemed like an entire army filled the wood, stretched out in a vast crescent, like beaters driving pheasants before them on a hunt. Tyrion began to understand what it must feel like to be hunted in that way.

He stretched his legs and began to overtake Alarielle. He was already breathing hard, much more so than he ought to be for this amount of exercise. It seemed that the wound in his side was already beginning to drain his strength – he did not like that in the slightest. Just when he needed it most he was losing his fitness. He cursed the witch elf once again, hoping that her wicked soul rotted deep in hell.

A few crossbow bolts fell around him. They had come a great distance and lost much of their power. A bolt clattered off a tree in front of him. He could hear the *whoosh* of arrows behind him. He had heard the sound before on the field of battle but he had never known so many missiles to be directed at only two people. It seemed only a matter of time before one of them hit home and either he or the Everqueen was impaled. That would be the end of the chase.

He began to zigzag, moving from side to side to confuse the archers, but he realised that this was not such a clever plan. The people chasing him would be able to run directly after him and thus gain ground. Alarielle was pushing on and with great woodcraft was simply weaving in and out of the trees, moving in as straight a line as possible while gaining as much cover as she could. Tyrion decided to do the same.

He heard another terrifying sound now. It was one that he had heard before in the cold northern lands of Naggaroth. It was a high-pitched noise somewhere between a scream and a roar. He ran abreast of Alarielle.

He risked a glance backwards and saw some of the great lizards striding forwards through the massed ranks of the druchii troops. Cold Ones were bipedal wingless reptilian creatures who carried armoured knights upon their back. Their movements seemed oddly slow and bouncing but they covered the ground very swiftly with their enormous strides.

It was only a matter of minutes before the Cold Ones reached them, if that. He heard the running water up ahead. Just from the sound of it he could tell that it was a mighty river. It seemed as if they were trapped. Tyrion prepared to turn around and fight. Even a battle against hopeless odds seemed preferable to being captured.

'What are you doing, idiot?' Alarielle asked. 'That is the River Everflow. We have a chance to escape if we are swift.'

'They will shoot us while we try to swim across.'

'There is another way.'

'Lead on,' Tyrion said. 'I hope you know what you're doing.'

◄ CHAPTER FIVE ►

The Cold Ones were closing the distance with appalling speed, outpacing the soldiers behind them. Tyrion could hear them thundering along the trail even now. The screeching echoed out through the forest, terrifying the birds and sending them racing skywards in fear.

'How much farther?' he gasped.

'A few hundred yards, if I remember correctly,' Alarielle said.

'I don't think we are going to make it,' he said.

'Run faster,' she replied.

It was already too late. Three riders closed the gap swiftly. The creatures gave off an awful stink that Tyrion well remembered. They had gigantic jaws capable of ripping off a limb in one bite and crunching through armour as easily as flesh.

Alarielle sprang upwards, grasping a branch and somersaulting onto the one above. Tyrion considered doing the same, but he needed to hold the attention of their pursuers, so he held his ground on the track as the dark elf riders thundered closer.

They howled in triumph even as their beasts roared at the prospect of devouring prey. Tyrion could see saliva glistening on massive dagger-like teeth. He braced himself to face onrushing death. His heart beat a little faster. His grip tightened on the hilt of Sunfang as he ripped it from its scabbard. He raced towards the oncoming Cold Ones. If nothing else he might be able to distract their pursuers and give the Everqueen time to escape.

The jaws of the leading Cold One snapped shut. Tyrion sprang to one side. He could smell the foul beast's breath. Its rider struck down at him with his sword. Tyrion rolled forwards, lashing out with Sunfang, aiming at the Cold One's ankle. His blade bit home, drawing blood and sawing through the tendon.

The Cold One shrieked and turned to snap at him, lowering its

head to reach him. As it did so, its left leg gave way beneath it and
it tumbled to one side, hitting the ground with a thud. It tried to
rise, small arms waving desperately.

Its rider groaned and tried to wriggle free, his leg trapped beneath
the beast's great bulk. Tyrion rolled to his feet, favouring his side.
The poisoned wound ached. He struck out with Sunfang, catching
the dark elf in his thigh as he was trying to get clear, severing the
artery. Sunfang partially cauterised it, but blood still flowed from the
wound and the dark elf desperately tried to stop it with his hands.
Sensing the wetness flooding its back, the Cold One twisted to snap
at him. It could not quite reach him but the two of them became
progressively more entangled.

The other two riders charged towards Tyrion. Their beasts bellowed deafeningly. Tyrion watched the two massive monsters close
with him, following the play of muscles beneath their scaly skin,
readying himself to face them. A few hundred strides behind came
a company of druchii soldiers.

An arrow whizzed out of the background and took the left-hand
rider through the visor of his helmet. It was an awesome shot with
an improvised bow.

The rider slumped in his saddle but his beast kept coming. Tyrion
sprang, getting his foot into the stirrup of the dead rider's saddle.
He was just outside the range of the Cold One's snapping jaws. He
drew Sunfang across its throat, sawing with the blade so that even
the cauterising effect of the magic could not seal the wound on its
jugular.

As he did so, the last monster snapped at him and he just managed to pull his arm clear. Its teeth snagged on the sleeve of his
jerkin and pulled him from the saddle. He twisted as the sleeve
tore, dropping to the ground, facing the creature. Desperately he
parried the rider's attack. Steel clashed against steel as the blades
met. The beast bit at him again and he jumped backwards, away
from its snapping jaws.

Its rider applied his spurs to its flank and brought the Cold
One jogging forwards. Tyrion noticed how slow its stride seemed
compared to the distance it covered. Another arrow flashed past
overhead, but this one was not so accurate or so lucky. It buried
itself in the rider's chest but was partially stopped by his armour. It
put him off his stroke and enabled Tyrion to concentrate on avoiding his mount. He tried to hamstring the reptile but was too slow
and merely scraped at its taloned heel. The Cold One buffeted him

with its tail, sending him staggering backwards off balance. The strike hit him on his wounded side, and the pain was all but overwhelming. Sensing its advantage, the beast rushed closer, its jaws open wide, its foetid breath emerging in a poisoned cloud. Tyrion knew there was nothing he could do to stop it. He could barely move, so stunned was he.

Sunfang seemed to twist in his hand of its own accord until it was pointing directly at the onrushing Cold One.

Something sparked inside Tyrion's mind. A connection was made with the blade. The flames blazing along its length intensified for a heartbeat, turning bright red and racing towards the blade's tip, forming themselves into a sphere of fire. After a heartbeat, a fireball erupted from the sword, arced towards the Cold One and impacted in a huge explosion that sent the creature tumbling through the air to land in a fire-blackened heap.

Tyrion picked himself up groggily and stumbled over to Alarielle's perch. She dropped lithely to the ground and raced over to him. 'How did you do that? I thought you said you were no mage...'

'It was not me, it was the sword,' he said. 'Some sort of spell was woven into it.'

The flames along the blade had died down now. They did not blaze with quite their normal intensity. The blade did not feel so light in his hand. He remembered Teclis's warning that trying to summon the power within it too often would kill the spirits bound into it and make the sword useless.

'I still don't understand how you triggered it,' Alarielle said.

'Neither do I,' said Tyrion. In the distance he could hear more Cold Ones bellowing, and the shrieks of the druchii infantry as they came closer. 'We've got to go.'

They ran, with the hordes of Malekith howling at their heels.

Death looked over the gameboard at Caledor. He smiled appreciatively. 'A good move,' he said, 'triggering the sword.'

'Tyrion could have done that anyway,' Caledor said. 'I merely nudged his hand.'

'Still, it's fortunate that you did, or you might have lost one of your most powerful pieces.'

Caledor studied the board and the image of Tyrion sprang into his mind. The poisoned wound was still there, aggravated by Death's magic. It could kill the elf prince at any time. A horde of pawns was closing in around Tyrion's position.

'I still might,' Caledor said. 'You have been playing very subtly yourself.'

'Such is my nature,' said Death.

He reached down and began moving more pawns. The net of living steel around Tyrion and the Everqueen started to tighten.

Ahead, the wide rushing river swept past Tyrion in a great curve, disappearing under the shadow of titanic trees. The branches of the largest trees overhung the river. Vines dangled down almost to the waters.

Behind them, he could hear the sounds of pursuit drawing closer. Tyrion's side hurt from the running and the poisoned wound. He knew that he would not be able to go on for much further and still be able to fight – there was no chance of being able to overcome a force of the size that pursued them.

They did not have time to swim. The dark elves would be able to use their crossbows to shoot them before they reached the other bank. They might abstain from shooting Alarielle because she was the Everqueen, but they would certainly kill him.

He would have been willing to let that happen if he thought that it would enable her to get away, but he doubted that it would. They might shoot to wound her and that might have disastrous consequences. A wounded swimmer and a strong current were a recipe for disaster.

He looked over at Alarielle. She was as winded as he was from the long chase. Her breath came out in pants and sweat stained her clothes. Her hair was lank.

'This is the Everflow,' she said. 'We used to come here when I was a girl.'

He smiled sourly. 'That's nice. Perhaps you would care to share the story with the dark elves when they get here. I'm sure they will be charmed.'

'I think I will save my girlish reminiscences for more congenial company,' she said. 'We need to get across the river.'

'A short swim would seem to be in order,' said Tyrion.

'You are in no condition to cross this river while wearing full armour. I have seen strong swimmers sucked under by the current here. I would not give a crumb of waybread for your chances.'

'It is not beyond my wit to take off the armour.'

'There is another way,' she said. She looked up at the vines overhanging the river.

'Are you serious?' Tyrion asked.

'We used to do it all the time when I was a child.'

'I'm surprised your guardians let you.'

'I never said anything about them letting me,' she said, smiling.

'You disobedient child,' he said. Alarielle was already beginning to scramble up the nearest tree. Behind them he could hear the pursuit coming ever closer, the dark elves whooping with triumph, knowing that their prey was within easy reach and sensing the river had cut off their escape.

Tyrion followed her up the trunk of the great tree. Every time he tried to use his left arm, the pain in his side almost crippled him.

Slowly, painfully, he pulled himself up hand over hand. Alarielle was already poised, graceful as a gazelle, on the main branch above him.

He smelled the moss that clung to the side of the great tree. The tips of his fingers were green from the moist substance on the bark. His breath came in gasps.

He was grateful when she reached down and offered him her hand. She pulled him up with surprising strength. They stood looking into each other's eyes for a long moment, then she turned and sprinted along the great branch, leaping into the air, reaching out and grasping the first vine. Her momentum carried her out over the great river and at the last second she let go, reaching out to grasp another vine. On and on she went, lithe as an acrobat, until she reached the far side and landed in the bole of one of the enormous trees.

Her passage had made his more difficult by setting the vines in motion. Now they were swinging backwards and forwards. He took a deep breath. He did not have much time. The dark elves would soon be upon them and he did not want them to notice how he and the Everqueen had disappeared.

He offered up a prayer to whatever gods might be listening and ran out along the branch. It was as wide as a footpath and solid as a rock at the point where he was upon it. He saw the first of the vines ahead of him and he sprang, reaching out to grasp it. Pain surged through his side as he put strain on his left arm. That accursed wound was going to be the death of him yet. He began to rotate; he knew that that would be bad because it would put him in the wrong position when he needed to let go.

He twisted to get his line back and the pain in his side increased. He gritted his teeth and bit back a cry. Beneath him the waters of the great river surged. He noticed the rocks. If he let go now he would fall upon them and most likely be dashed to pieces.

He knew he was not doing this well. He was heavier than Alarielle and not in such good condition. He tried to judge when to let go through tears of pain. For a few seconds he was flying free over the waters far below, feeling out with his hands, desperate to grasp the next vine in the sequence.

There was a sickening feeling in the pit of his stomach when he caught nothing, then a heartbeat later his fingers closed on something slick and green. He felt as if his arm was about to be torn from its socket by the strain.

His fingers slid and his hands burned from the friction, but he refused to give up and let go until the time was right. There were a few seconds of relief while he swung forwards, and then it was time to let go again.

It seemed as if his fingers were not about to respond. He forced them open and once more was flying through space. He could see that the vine was still swinging from Alarielle's momentum. He prayed that it would move back into position in time for him to grasp it.

It began to swing back. He was still moving forwards. He was going to make it. He reached the furthest extent of his vine's swing and let go. The other vine kept coming back towards him. He stretched out as far as he could, trying to catch it.

Closer it came, its path converging with his own. He stretched out farther, extending his fingers as far as he could, as if somehow that would give him the extra reach. It came to him then that he was not going to make it. He had already begun to fall through space towards the water below.

The vines swished past overhead. He wondered whether he had time to twist into diving position and whether the water was deep enough for it to make any difference. He tumbled like an gymnast, trying to get his feet below him. He could see the moving water and the rocks and the far side of the river – it was much closer now. He thought he caught sight of Alarielle's horrified features. Everything seemed to slow down. He was abnormally aware of every motion and every muscle in his body.

The water rose to meet him. It smashed into his body with the force of a giant club. For a moment he thought he'd hit a rock, but then he was tumbling deeper and deeper into the water, his mouth filling with liquid, his eyes stinging.

All of the breath had been knocked out of him and he knew that he would not be able to survive long before drowning. He kicked out, hoping that his legs would still function, hoping that he was moving in the right direction, heading towards what he thought was the light.

His head broke the surface. He could feel the current pushing him downriver. He kicked out with his legs, trying to use his arms as little as possible to avoid irritating his wound. After what seemed like a very long time, he reached the far bank. Away on the other side, he could hear the dark elves shouting to each other.

It took what little strength he had remaining to pull himself up onto the bank and lie there, staring at the branches above him. Slowly, the sickening knowledge of his failure percolated into his mind. He had become separated from the Everqueen. She was out there now alone and hunted by her enemies.

Caledor studied the gameboard, his attention momentarily away from Avelorn by the complexity of the action. It was becoming intricate and ever more confusing to follow. Armies moved all across the continent of Ulthuan.

He saw the Phoenix King in Lothern, looking from the great sea wall of the city. Out in the waters of the bay beyond lay not one but three Black Arks, mountainous druchii ships with their attending fleets of smaller vessels and sea monsters. The hills around the city were full of druchii soldiers. Siege engines sent fiery death hurtling towards the walls of the city-state. Sorcerers aimed deadly spells. Legions of tightly disciplined druchii hurled themselves at the gates while the asur fought against traitors within their own walls.

In the mountains, hordes of Chaos-worshipping barbarians chanted outside the walls of the mighty fortresses built by Caledor the Conqueror. Their armies had already overrun much of thinly populated Cothique and were ready to move south.

Along the coast of Tiranoc, druchii warships controlled the seas. The great fleets of the asur were rushing hither and yon in confusion, while the dark elves knew exactly what to do and where to strike.

Caledor sensed the disruption to the fabric of reality caused by N'Kari's magical gates. The Witch King was using them to move his forces all too easily around Ulthuan. It gave him a great advantage, being able to take his foes by surprise and concentrate his forces wherever he wanted. Such mobility magnified the potency of his army many times over. Something needed to be done to neutralise it, but that could be achieved by nothing less than the destruction of N'Kari, and that was not a feat that many of Caledor's pieces were capable of, and none of them were in the area of the city.

He knew he should not allow himself to be distracted. There were things that needed to be done. He reached down and picked up the piece called Teclis.

Teclis woke. His mouth felt dry and his head felt fuzzy. His thoughts came with uncharacteristic slowness. On the table in front of him was a book of spells, and diverse other things including High Loremaster Morelian's translation of the Slann tablet Teclis had found in the ruins of Zultec. It all came back to him. He was in a chamber that was part of the Maze of Books below the White Tower of Hoeth.

Teclis shook his head. It was a mistake. The contents of his stomach roiled volcanically and for a moment the room tilted. It was more than just his physical frailty reasserting itself. It was something else, a reaction to his dream, if dream it had been, and he was enough of a sorcerer to very strongly doubt that. It had seemed so real, so concrete.

Had he really talked to the Archmage Caledor, an elf more than six thousand years dead? Had he spoken to the ghost of the creator of the Vortex, the huge spell that kept Ulthuan above the waves and the world safe from being overwhelmed by the dark cosmic magic of Chaos? Had the archmage really told him to protect his brother Tyrion, when all his life it had been Tyrion who had protected him?

It all seemed so unlikely, yet he did not doubt its reality for a moment. He had been given a warning and he had better deliver it at once to the head of his order. He had been sent to tell the High Loremaster to prepare for war.

He felt something else, a premonition of disaster even stronger than the one that had been hanging over him ever since he and his brother had returned to Ulthuan from the jungles of Lustria. He rose unsteadily to his feet, picked up the papers on the table and made for the exit of the small chamber, praying that this time he did not get lost in the spell-warped maze beneath the tower.

The corridors did not twist and turn around him in a way that would baffle his senses. Spells did not prevent him from finding the stairwell that led back up into the library.

Even as he emerged into the great book-filled chambers, his sense of unease grew stronger. The rooms were deserted. He had never seen that before. It seemed somehow unnatural that there should be no scholar in the Great Library at Hoeth. He doubted that such a thing had happened in an age of the world. There was always someone in the library, no matter at what hour of the day or night.

It was as if some great disaster had struck Hoeth while he was in the Maze of Books. For a brief moment, Teclis entertained the fantasy that some dreadful magical catastrophe had swept through the White Tower and he was the only survivor.

Impossible, he told himself. No enemy could have found their way to the tower. It was warded by some of the most powerful protective enchantments ever created, surrounded by spells that could deflect even the most terrible curses and destructive spells.

Nothing could possibly have happened. Could it?

As he emerged from the library, Teclis was relieved to see a Sword Master, one of the warrior-guardians of the tower. The elf seemed surprised to see Teclis. It looked like he had not expected to encounter anyone coming from the library.

'What is going on?' Teclis asked.

'Haven't you heard the news?' The Sword Master asked.

'What news?' Teclis asked.

'Avelorn has been attacked! The Everqueen is dead! So is everyone with her!'

Teclis's eyes narrowed as he stared at the guardian. He shook his head. 'That cannot be true! My brother is there.'

'The word just came in an hour ago,' said the Sword Master. 'It was brought by one of the eagles of the forest. The Loremasters have verified it with their scrying crystals.'

Unbidden, the image of his brother's body lying sprawled in a pool of blood came into his mind. He shuddered. He told himself that was only his imagination. It was not a vision. He took a deep breath and tried to calm his racing senses. He was sweating. His heart raced.

It was impossible that Tyrion could be dead without him knowing. And yet, what if he was wrong? The powerful wards that surrounded the Tower of Hoeth might stop him from sensing such a thing. Perhaps this was the reason he felt so bad and had such a strong sense of foreboding.

He refused to believe it. The bond that existed between him and his twin ran deep. There was no barrier it could not penetrate. He was certain of that. Tyrion could not be dead. He would not believe that until he looked upon his brother's corpse with his own eyes.

Even thinking that felt like a betrayal. It was admitting the possibility that the guard might be right and that he might be wrong.

'What happened?' He felt like taking the guard by the collar of his jerkin and shaking him until he answered.

'The dark elves attacked.'

'The druchii attacked Avelorn? Nonsense!' Teclis almost shouted. He could hear the almost hysterical edge to his own voice. It was simply impossible that a dark elf army could have got so far into Ulthuan.

'It was the dark elves,' said the guard. 'And they did not just attack Avelorn. Their fleets are at sea off our coasts and their armies have attacked in other places. The news keeps coming in and none of it is good.'

'Where?' Teclis demanded. He felt as if he were caught up in a nightmare. Last night he had gone to sleep in a land of peace and plenty. He had woken up in a land torn by war. His mind rebelled against the very thought of it. It was as if thunder and lightning had come out of an empty sky in which there had not been a single cloud. It was impossible, simply impossible.

The Witch King could not have prepared an invasion fleet without it being noticed. Naggaroth's ports were constantly watched. He could not have built up a fleet without it being noticed by the scout ships of the high elves. No army could have found its way into the very heart of Elvendom in so short a time without being spotted by a single person. A legion of Shadow Warriors could not have achieved this goal, let alone an army of heavily armoured dark elves. Even Teclis knew that and he was no soldier.

Yet, in spite of all this, there was a Sword Master standing in front of him telling him that Avelorn was invaded and that his brother and the Everqueen were dead. He forced himself to get a grip on his racing thoughts.

'I must have words with the High Loremaster,' Teclis said.

'Good luck with that,' said the guard. 'Everyone feels the same today.'

'Then I had best get going,' Teclis said. He strode off through the oddly deserted paths of Hoeth.

As he walked through the tower, Teclis understood where everyone had gone. All of the students, all of the masters, all of the guards and all of the elves who served them had gathered in the great open spaces. All of them were talking of the attacks and all of them looked frightened.

As well they might, Teclis thought. No such invasion of Ulthuan had happened in their lifetimes. Everyone has assumed the druchii were a spent force. No one had wanted to think otherwise.

Teclis overheard scraps of conversation. It seemed that rumour bred rumour and no one had any idea what might be true or false.

'An army of Chaos worshippers has landed in the north.'

'A thousand daemons lay siege to Lothern.'

'A million barbarians with Morathi at their head are riding to Hoeth and will not be turned aside by the warding spells.'

'The High Loremaster is working magic to scry the land.'

'The Vortex is failing. The ghost of Caledor himself has spoken to a dozen people in the tower.'

Crowds surged around the doorway of the High Loremaster's chambers. It seemed everyone wanted an interview. Everyone had questions. Everyone had something to say. Even in the most secure heart of the tower there was an aura of panic and fear.

Belthania emerged from the Loremaster's sanctum and caught sight of him. The tall sorceress gestured for him to come over. Teclis was not strong enough to elbow his way through the crowd and it would not part for him. Belthania gestured to someone within the office. Two Sword Masters emerged and began to force a way through the crowd for him.

A short minute later he was within Morelian's chambers. The High Loremaster looked up at him. He had looked old the last time Teclis had seen him, but appeared to have aged centuries within the past few hours. His already ancient frame seemed withered and bent almost double. The Sword Master slammed the door shut as soon as they entered and the hubbub from the corridors and chambers beyond subsided to nothing. A spell was at work there, Teclis realised.

'I can tell from your expression you have heard the news,' said Morelian.

Teclis said, 'My brother was in Avelorn.'

'Then he is most likely dead,' said Belthania.

'I would know if he was.'

'Where have you been? No one has seen you for hours. I have had people searching,' Morelian said.

'Why?'

'I had a peculiar dream concerning you.'

'What was its import?'

'The Archmage Caledor spoke to me. He told me you would be going on a journey, one very important to us all, and that I was to see you were prepared for it.'

'I too had the same dream,' said Belthania. 'As did every other Loremaster in the tower.'

'And all of those scattered across Ulthuan, for all we know,' said Morelian.

'I see,' said Teclis. 'If one Loremaster has a dream it may be meaningless. If all of them have the same dream – it is significant.'

'It was more than a dream,' said Morelian. 'It felt extraordinarily real. I stood near the centre of the world and watched the ghosts of the Five enspell the Vortex. And they were failing.'

'I saw the same thing,' said Belthania.

'When did this happen?'

'In the small hours of the morning. After we last talked.'

Teclis nodded. 'That would be after I cast the spell.'

'What spell?'

'I was lost in the Maze of Books. I found a chamber and in that chamber was an ancient spell. I was compelled to cast it by some force. I could not have stopped myself even if I had wanted to. I thought the spell affected only me but it seems that it reached out to all of you as well.'

'Those of the Loremasters who were not asleep fell into a faint,' said Morelian. 'When they came out of it, they too had seen the same thing as the rest of us. That would explain it.'

'It might mean nothing,' said Teclis. 'It might be the work of the enemy.'

'No inimical power has ever reached into Hoeth.'

'There is a first time for everything,' said Teclis. His two fellow Loremasters looked disturbed by that prospect.

'I do not believe it possible,' said Morelian eventually. 'And if it was, why afflict us with such a vision? Why not something that would be of more material assistance to our enemies?'

'Indeed,' said Belthania. 'I am willing to believe this spell of yours contributed to the vision, but I doubt anything hostile was behind it. I am more likely to believe it was the spirit of the tower itself helping us in our time of need. I don't think it's a coincidence that this happened at the same time as Avelorn must have been attacked.'

'Not just Avelorn,' said the High Loremaster. 'Lothern, Tor Yvresse, Mancastra and a dozen other places. All of Ulthuan is besieged by the dark elves and their Chaos-worshipping allies. The Everqueen is missing, presumed dead. There are rumours of treachery everywhere. Members of the Cult of Luxury have risen up to aid the invaders. This is the gravest threat Ulthuan has faced since the Sundering.'

'And yet in the middle of this, Caledor, if Caledor it was, chooses

to tell you that I will be going on a journey. You would have thought
he would have more important things on his mind.'

'This is not a subject for jest, Teclis,' said Morelian. 'The first
archmage must have known we would find out all the rest for ourselves soon enough. It is a mark of your importance in the great
scheme of things that he chose to speak to us about you.'

'Why me?' Teclis asked.

'You are of the Blood of Aenarion,' said Belthania.

'And you and your brother are heroes,' said Morelian.

'I am no hero,' said Teclis.

'If you are not now, I fear you will be before all of this is over,'
said Morelian.

'I am going to find my brother,' Teclis said. 'And to do that I will
need a weapon.'

'We shall see what we can provide,' said Morelian.

'I shall make my own sword,' said Teclis.

'Then you had best get started,' said the High Loremaster.' I shall
see that a forge is put at your disposal.'

Quickly Teclis took a fresh piece of parchment and sharpened a
quill before dipping it in ink and sketching out the runes and magical equations that would be needed to make the sword. For long
hours he sat hunched over the desk in his chamber, working swiftly
and easily.

He had studied Sunfang and he felt certain that he could duplicate at least part of the magic that had gone into creating it. The
basic spells that would go to making the blade sharp and deadly
would need to be every bit as potent and as well constructed as
the magic of Caledor.

As he worked he wondered why he was really doing this. He did
not have any great use for a blade – he was no warrior. He had no
plans to run around like his brother, cutting things up with a sword.
The only thing he was likely to be able to hurt was himself.

Anything that had got close enough to him that he would need
to use a sword upon was already too close. He did not need to do
anything as spectacular as the fire magic that had been woven into
the sword. That would be difficult to do without access to the volcanic fires of Vaul's Anvil. He was no warrior and he did not really
need the blade to do anything so spectacular anyway.

It was the creation of the sword itself that was important. It was a
test that he had set himself. If he could recreate this part of Caledor's

work, he could recreate other parts, at least that was what he told himself. He was setting himself on the same path as that great master-wizard. He was making a statement to himself and to the world about what he could do and what his intentions were.

In the end, it did not really matter what his motivation was. What mattered was that he completed the work he had set himself. The mystical diagrams and the potent incantations flowed freely onto the parchment, seeming almost to write themselves. He kept at work long into the night, using more and more parchment, constantly having to sharpen the nib of his quill, burning the candles in his chamber low.

Dawn was breaking by the time he had completed his work, but he did not feel tired. It was not merely the drugs that he used to give himself energy that made him feel so lightheaded. He had a sense he was becoming the person that he was intended to be; finally he was on the right path to fulfilling his destiny. Making this blade just felt right.

This was a sword that would never lose its sharpness no matter what it was used to cut and which would be able to cut through almost anything. It did not really matter to him that he had no real use for it – it was something that he could build upon, a structure into which you could eventually fit other spells in exactly the same way that Caledor had.

Yet even as he completed the design, a vague sense of dissatisfaction filled him. He was merely recreating the work of another. What he had done was a work of genius, but it was a work of someone else's genius. It pleased him to be able to do this, but he knew that he would never be truly happy until he had managed to create a work of equal magnitude of his own. He wanted to make his own masterpiece.

As that thought occurred to him, a sardonic smile twisted his lips. He could see where that path was eventually going to lead him. He was putting himself in competition with the greatest mage who had ever lived. Caledor's masterpiece was the Vortex, a spell that had saved the entire world and which even to this very day protected his homeland.

How could you compete with that?

He already felt certain that he was going to try and find a way. He strode down to the forges.

It took long hard hours wielding the heavy hammer, sweating at the forge, using all his strength while weaving potent enchantments into the metal. It required him to perform two very difficult tasks at once, and it taxed his mental and physical strengths to the limit. By the time the finished blade gleamed in his hand he was exhausted – it was all he could do to drag himself to his chambers and throw himself upon his bed. Sleep took him almost instantly. Visions of Tyrion and the Everqueen being pursued through dense forests by armies of druchii dogged him. Over everything loomed two gigantic figures: one was robed and cowled and radiated a chill aura of deadly power, the other was the Archmage Caledor. They seemed to be involved in some titanic battle of wills, and he knew he was part of that struggle.

He awoke with a growing sense that time was running out.

'I cannot say I am pleased to lose you,' said Morelian as Teclis entered his chamber. He glanced significantly at the new blade that hung scabbarded at Teclis's side. 'Your power and your skill could be of great use here in Hoeth.'

'The tower does not need another defender,' said Teclis, wondering why the High Loremaster had summoned him.

'That remains to be seen,' said Morelian, although he did not say it loudly lest they be overheard. 'In any case, I have some gifts for you to use on your quest.'

'Any help will be gratefully received,' said Teclis.

'I suspect you will need all of it by the end of your journey. I fear you go along a very dark road.'

'Your words are not calculated to improve my morale.'

'You are not riding into such circumstances that overconfidence would be justified.'

'I trust that your gift does not consist merely of advice, no matter how well meant. If you continue in this vein it may discourage me from departing entirely.'

'Hopefully you will find this a somewhat greater mark of my faith in you,' said the High Loremaster. From behind his desk, he produced a helmet that Teclis recognised. It was a winged crown that had once sat in the vaults beneath the tower.

'The War Crown of Saphery,' he said. It was difficult to keep the awe from his voice. 'You're placing a mighty trust in me.'

'Let us hope that it is justified,' said Morelian. He raised the crown reverently with both hands and placed it upon Teclis's head. Almost at once, Teclis felt a difference. His eyesight and his hearing both became much keener. He could see the High Loremaster's face in much more detail than he had ever been able to do before, with his weak eyesight. Concern was written in the old elf's face, and something else too, something like respect.

'I will do my best to see that it is,' Teclis said. His own voice sounded different now. It was louder and more decisive. He was much more aware of the flow of magical energy about him. He was not entirely sure of all that the crown was doing for him, but he was certain that it was enhancing his power in many ways.

'It is a princely gift,' Teclis said.

'Think of it more as a loan,' the High Loremaster said. 'For as long as you live, you will hold it in trust for the tower. On your death, it will be returned to us.'

'It shall be as you say,' Teclis said. 'And once again I must express my gratitude. Never did I expect to be granted such a boon.'

'It may well be that you carry the destiny of us all with you,' said the High Loremaster. 'It is the least that I can do. And it is not the only thing. Come with me.'

He led Teclis from his chambers and by devious and secret ways took him out of the tower, avoiding the throngs that sought audience with the High Loremaster. Two Sword Masters dogged their steps. It was a measure of the High Loremaster's worries that even here in the tower, bodyguards followed him everywhere.

Had things really come to this, Teclis wondered?

They emerged into the sunlight. The day was bright and beautiful and one would never have suspected that somewhere far-off wars were being fought and elves were dying. The High Loremaster trudged on, leaning on his staff, and Teclis was all too aware of how old Morelian was and what a great weight of responsibility pressed down upon his shoulders.

They came eventually to the open fields where many beasts grazed. They passed the corrals in which the steeds of the Sword Masters were penned. They came at last to an oddly constructed stable on the very outskirts of the tower's domain. From inside came the whinny of a great horse. It seemed to greet the High Loremaster as if the beast was welcoming an old friend.

'Peace be upon you, Silver Wing,' the High Loremaster said. The horse snorted in response, or at least Teclis thought it was a horse until he entered the stable. Then he saw it was something quite different.

In some ways it looked like a great white stallion, as noble a beast as he had ever seen. It looked old but still very strong. In one important way it differed from a normal horse. Two great wings were folded against its flanks and when it reared to welcome its master, the wings extended and their flapping sent great gusts of air billowing around the room, making the wizard's robes flutter.

Morelian said, 'Silver Wing and I are old friends. He carried me on many a quest when we were both younger. He will bear you on this one at least as far as Avelorn.'

Teclis knew that he should feel grateful, and he did, but he could not express his gratitude. He found the prospect of riding upon this great beast terrifying. It could bear him to Avelorn faster than any horse could. It would take him through the air with the speed of a bird.

That was the problem. Just the thought of getting into the saddle and riding through the sky almost paralysed him with fear.

'You do not seem entirely enthusiastic,' the High Loremaster said. 'I confess I had expected a somewhat greater display of gratitude. It is not every day that Silver Wing extends this privilege.'

Teclis considered his words with care. 'I am grateful to you both. I was merely overwhelmed by the immensity of the favour that you're doing me.'

'That and something else,' the High Loremaster said. He looked as if he was struggling to keep from smiling. 'I can tell.'

Teclis decided that it would be simplest not to conceal his reservations. 'I find the prospect of flying more than a little daunting. I might even go as far as to say I find it terrifying.'

'I felt exactly the same way the first time I ever had to bestride a pegasus.'

'Without wishing to insult Silver Wing or demean the generosity of your offer, perhaps it would be better if I took a normal horse to Avelorn.'

'I was under the impression that every minute, every second, counted.' Teclis got the impression that this evil old elf was rather enjoying his discomfiture. 'I thought there was not a moment to be wasted.'

'And indeed, this is the case,' Teclis said. 'On the other hand, it would probably be for the best if I actually arrived in Avelorn and did not fall out of the saddle as I streaked through the sky.'

'Fortunately, we have provided for that contingency,' the High Loremaster said.

'I suspected that you might have,' said Teclis. He did not entirely succeed in keeping the sour note from his voice.

'The saddle of a pegasus rider is not like a normal saddle. It contains an arrangement of straps designed to restrain the rider in place as much to keep it attached to the pegasus.'

'That goes some way towards reducing my reservations,' Teclis said. 'But I am forced to confess that I have some more.'

'Doubtless you're wondering how you will guide Silver Wing.'

'You show an understanding that verges on the telepathic.'

'Silver Wing is very old and very wise and will respond to voice commands. If I may say so, he is considerably more intelligent than many elves although he cannot speak.'

'I suppose you will have ready answers to any other objections I might raise.'

'I would deem such an eventuality very likely. Pegasus is undoubtedly the fastest way for you to get Avelorn unless you propose inventing a spell of long-distance teleportation within the next few hours.'

'Would that I were capable of such a prodigy of research.'

'I have taken the liberty of not only providing you with the special saddle, but also with saddle bags containing rations and enough space for any medicines that you might need to carry.'

'It seems that you have thought of everything. I wish I could find suitable words to express my gratitude.'

'You have done quite well enough so far,' the High Loremaster said.

'When do you propose that I depart?'

'Once again, I was under the impression that there was not a second to be lost. You seemed most insistent upon this the last time we talked about this matter.'

'Forgive me for saying so, but you seem to be taking some pleasure in using my own words to discomfit me.'

'When you reach my age,' the High Loremaster said, 'you will understand that one must take one's pleasures from what one can, no matter how petty those enjoyments may seem to those younger than you.'

'I hope that when I reach your age I should be somewhat more generous of spirit.'

'A noble wish, but I fear it will not be the case.' The old elf was smiling. 'I would like to be here to wish you a safe journey, but I do not have an infinite supply of time to take off from my duties.'

'It seems that you have prepared all that I need. All that remains for me to do is to wish you farewell.'

'And to mount your new steed,' the High Loremaster suggested.

'Indeed,' said Teclis. 'I would not wish to deprive you of the pleasure of witnessing that.'

Cautiously Teclis approached the pegasus. As he got closer, he realised exactly how massive it was. Its head was taller than his own. Huge muscles bunched as it moved. He reached out to gently stroke its muzzle, and it lowered his head as if accepting him and his touch. His hands trembled as he stroked the creature's cheek and looked into the huge, deep black eyes. There was an intelligence in them greater than in that of any horse he had ever encountered. The pegasus whinnied softly and stopped prancing.

The High Loremaster himself came forwards and fixed the saddle onto the beast. It was larger than a normal saddle, with far more straps holding it in position. At front and back, it was higher and the saddle posts were larger. As it was fixed in place, Teclis could see that there were a number of straps left unbuckled. Doubtless these were intended to hold the rider in place. Carefully, he put one foot in the stirrup, threw a leg over the saddle and got himself into position. The High Loremaster showed him how to fasten the restraining straps that would hold him in.

The beast shifted below him as it adjusted to his weight on its back. Its wings flapped. Teclis was all too aware of their motion very close to him, of the great muscles moving in the beast's flanks. Mighty as the creature was, he could not see how those wings alone could get it airborne. There had to be magic involved. He sensed a reservoir of energy within the pegasus and he suspected that it was as much needed to get the winged steed aloft as its pinions.

'Very good,' the High Loremaster said. 'You look as if you were born to do this.'

'I don't feel like it,' Teclis said.

'Desist from complaining and learn to simply enjoy the circumstances you find yourself in. That would be my advice to you.'

'It is easy enough for you to say that,' Teclis said. 'You're the one standing with his feet on the ground while I am trussed up like a prisoner awaiting torture.'

'Believe me, I wish I could take your place. There is nothing quite in comparison with the sensation of racing through the sky with the wind tugging at your robe and the ground a thousand feet below.'

'I find that I am inclined to let you take my place if you desire the experience so much.'

'My heart has already thrilled to that particular delight. I shall

leave the joys of flight to you. And there's no time like the present –
Silver Wing, take to the skies!'

On the High Loremaster's command, the pegasus raced from the
stable. Its wings beat steadily and Teclis felt the build up of magical energy within the creature's breast. It took a dozen strides and
then sprang. At first, Teclis thought that it was actually going to be
in the air. The leap went on for longer than any normal jump by a
normal horse, but the pegasus returned to the ground, took three
more strides and then sprang again. This time it stayed airborne for
a dozen heartbeats before returning to the ground. It made a third
attempt to get aloft, wings thrashing, and this time it stayed aloft.

Teclis watched the trees of the surrounding forest race ever closer.
He feared that his career as a flier was going to be cut short by the
brutal impact of their branches. At the very last second, Silver Wing
gained height and skimmed just over the treetops. Teclis clung on
desperately, his knuckles white against the saddle post.

Silver Wing circled, gaining altitude as it flew round and round
the tower. At first, it was all Teclis could do to hold on. He kept his
eyes resolutely closed and fought against dizziness and nausea.
When he looked down, the ground seemed a long way below and
the faces of those who stared up at him appeared tiny.

His weight strained against the harness that held him in the saddle. The fear that he was going to fall or that the leather straps would
break and send him tumbling to the earth far below dominated
his mind.

Every little creak that the harness made seemed an ominous
warning that it was about to snap and send him to his doom. It
felt impossible that an animal as large as Silver Wing could be kept
aloft merely by the thrashing of its wings. At any moment the power
of the spell could run out and the two of them would be sent tumbling earthwards...

After a few minutes, he managed to keep his eyes open despite
the tears from the roaring wind that threatened to blind him. He
had enough presence of mind to speak a shielding spell. It was the
same cantrip he used to protect himself against the heat of the jungles of Lustria, but it served just as well to protect them from the
passing breeze.

He saw that they had climbed far above the trees but still had not
managed to equal the height of the great Tower of Hoeth. It loomed
enormously before them. Seen from this angle he was able to appreciate both its massive size and its astonishing grace. It was indeed

true – there never had been a structure built upon the face of the world to match this tower in beauty or scale.

The High Loremaster waved to him. Teclis did not dare let go of the saddle posts to wave back.

Silver Wing soared northwards towards the distant forest of Avelorn.

It was mere minutes before the area surrounding the tower faded from view and Teclis found himself flying over the dense woods of Saphery. It was strange to see the world from this angle, to look down upon the tops of trees and watch the clusters of leaves swaying in the wind, to see the birds rising up from beneath him as they were startled by the passage of the pegasus's shadow. It was odd to find himself flying alongside flocks of starlings.

Teclis was not sure how long he was airborne before he started to get used to the sensation of flight. He doubted that he would ever become totally accustomed to it, but eventually his stomach settled and he lost some of the fear of falling to his doom. Silver Wing had managed to stay aloft for a sufficient length of time to reassure him that it was not an accident and that the pegasus was actually capable of flying for long distances.

He had grown accustomed to being able to work the most powerful spells of the magical art, but he was upset by simply being mounted upon a flying horse.

He had a suspicion as to the reason why that was. When working magic, control of the ritual was his. Flying this way, he was utterly reliant on the ability of his steed. He knew that there were spells that would slow the fall of anyone dropping from a great height, but he had never taken the trouble to learn any of them. He made up his mind to rectify this omission as soon as he was given the opportunity, if he ever was. It had been a lamentable oversight in his magical education. In fact, he thought, as he flew he would do his best to derive some from first principles.

The saddle creaked. He tried to push thoughts of the straps coming undone from his mind.

After many hours of flight, Teclis saw the curve of a vast silver river below him. From his memory of the maps he had once studied in the tower he reckoned this was the Everflow, which at this point marked the ancient boundary between Avelorn and Saphery. Here the rule of the wizard-princes gave way to that of the Everqueen.

WILLIAM KING

He knew the river ran a long way northwards to its sources in the mountains of Chrace, but it was at least a landmark to navigate by.

The forests beneath him were changing. The woods seemed deeper, older, the trees taller and darker. These woods were quieter than those of Saphery. There was a magic here just as deep but more still and subtle. In Saphery the magic felt like the product of intelligent intervention, of spells, old and well woven. Here the land itself was magical. Power flowed through it and sometimes formed deep pools. Not all of those pools were pure. In some places, Teclis sensed the taint of an evil as ancient as the world. It seemed somehow appropriate. No place was entirely free of the taint of darkness, not even ancient, noble Avelorn. He wondered if Tyrion had found this out yet.

The thought struck him that Tyrion might have found this out and died. He pushed that thought to one side. Such a contingency was simply not possible. He would know if it had happened. Another thought, just as discouraging, replaced it. This was a quest that was more difficult than looking for a needle in the proverbial haystack or a single grain of sand on a beach. Avelorn was a vast land, mostly wilderness, and he was no woodsman. How was he going to find his twin? Looking down from above, he could see almost nothing through the canopy of leaves and branches. Even being mounted on a pegasus was not going to be much of an advantage.

He could try a spell of location. Normally he would have been dubious of its efficacy over so wide an area, but he had some hope that given the strength of the bond between him and Tyrion he could make it work. Of course, that would mean returning to the earth and sacrificing the advantage of speed and mobility that flight gave him. The best bet seemed to be to head towards the tournament grounds and try and pick up the trail there.

He found that in an odd and half-scared way, he was coming to enjoy the sensation of speed, of skimming over the surface of the world and being able to see to the distant green horizon. He doubted that he would ever get used to it, but he was starting to find the wonder within the terror. As if in response, Silver Wing snorted, almost derisively.

'You stick to flying, and leave the sarcasm to me,' Teclis said softly. Onwards they flew over a land that was now in the hands of the enemy.

✦ CHAPTER EIGHT ✦

Tyrion lay gasping on the bank of the Everflow. His mail shirt felt as if it was made from a ton of rusting metal. His clothes were sopping wet. Water had almost doubled the weight of the tabard. It dripped into his eyes through the eye pieces of the helmet. His side burned, and with more than the effort of swimming.

He pushed himself upright with both hands and looked around. On the far side of the river, somewhat upstream, a company of Cold One riders had come into view. Their beasts were screeching with frustration. One of them, obviously the leader, started bellowing orders and they split up into multiple parties, some of them heading north along the riverbank, some of them heading south, some of them starting to swim across the river. They had obviously underestimated the strength of the current, for it started to sweep even the great beasts away, bringing them in Tyrion's direction. More and more dark elves came into view on the far bank of the Everflow. They halted, reluctant to press on across the water in the fading light.

The cold water seemed to have leeched all strength from Tyrion. He struggled to pull himself into the undergrowth before he could be spotted. He had to dig his fingers into the soil to gain purchase. Pain stabbed his side. His knuckles were scratched and the palms of his hands had friction burns.

He was not in any state to fight. Somehow, with as much effort as it would once have taken him to run several leagues, he managed to fight his way in among the roots of a bush. Twigs scratched against the outside of his helmet, monstrous fingers scraping against metal. He let himself lie there, more exhausted than he had felt in a very long time.

The Cold Ones emerged from the water upstream but still closer to him than he would have liked. He wondered if they were already on his trail, catching his scent with sensitive, bestial nostrils.

He just lay there, thinking that he ought to do something, but not sure what. The most logical thing to do was to lower himself back into the water so that they could not catch his scent, but he was not sure he had the strength to hold on if he did that.

He feared for Alarielle. She was alone.

What was she doing right now?

Hopefully she had sense enough to take cover or flee. He told himself not to worry. She had grown up in these woods. She was better at this sort of thing than he was, as she had already proved. He was the one he needed to worry about right now. He doubted that the magic sword was capable of saving him twice in one day. It seemed mostly luck that he had been able to trigger it in the first place. He had no confidence that he would be able to do so again.

He could hear massively heavy forms crashing through the undergrowth nearby. Something enormous bellowed its hunger and its hate. He had no choice. He had to get away before it caught his scent. Steeling himself against the cold, he pushed off, sliding down the bank back into the water with a splash that was louder than he would have liked. The cold water closed over his head again. Bubbles of trapped air emerged from his helmet and clothing. Instinctively, he pushed himself to the surface, making even more splashing noises that sounded as loud as the trumpets of an army in his ears.

Very good, Tyrion, he thought. Very stealthy.

He reached out and grabbed the root of a nearby tree to hold himself against the current. The cold of the water already seemed to be seeping into his fingers, paralysing them, numbing them, making it more and more difficult for him to hold his grip. He could see the vague outlines of massive forms moving through the undergrowth, displacing it. He could hear the jingle of harnesses and the bellows-like breathing of the monstrous animals.

Once, he saw the cold glitter of one of their eyes turned on him. He did not move, fearing that any motion would simply draw their attention.

Yes, he could see the outline of one of those great reptilian heads. It was turning backwards and forwards, nostrils flaring, as if attempting to catch his scent on the wind. Tyrion considered letting himself drop back under the water, but he resisted the impulse although his heart was pounding and his breath was coming in short, shallow gasps.

The beast stood there for a very long time, and he felt certain that

it knew he was there. It made a small mewling noise as if it was confused, then its rider hit it with the butt of his sword and it moved
on, followed by a long line of its scaly brethren. It seemed to take
hours for them to pass although it could not have been more than
a few minutes.

When they were finally gone, Tyrion pulled himself back out of
the water and lay there, too exhausted even to think about what
might have happened to the Everqueen. He knew that he had to
do something. He had to take off his soaking clothing before he
caught a chill. He needed to look after his armour or it would rust.
He prayed the dark elves would not cross the river and find him.

Tyrion pulled off his metal jerkin and place it on the ground beside
the tabard. He stripped off his shirt and britches and began to wring
them out. Water sopped over his scraped knuckles and abraded
palms. He was shivering from the cold and wet. He could hear the
dark elves receding into the distance but that did not mean he was
safe. It was possible that there were other silent hunters nearby. It
would be foolish to assume that the Cold Ones were the only things
looking for him.

He drew Sunfang from its scabbard and placed it on the ground.
Its flames blazed up, not as bright as usual but still enough to give
some heat. He drove the tip of the blade into the ground and sat
down beside it, letting its warmth heat his body and dry his clothes.

He draped his shirt and britches over a piece of wood so that they
would catch the heat and form a small windbreak which he hoped
would also shield the sword from view. He inspected the chainmail
shirt he had taken from the dead dark elf what seemed like a lifetime ago. It had been well oiled, but the water had removed that
protective coating and he could see that some of the links were
already beginning to rust. There was nothing he could do about it
since he did not have the tools needed for maintenance. Instead
he put the mail shirt to one side and thought about what he was
going to do next.

He had become separated from the Everqueen because of his own
weakness – even now she might be in the hands of the druchii and
he would not even know it. He had to fight down the impulse to
rise and run off into the woods and begin searching for her immediately. He was even tempted to shout her name, although that
would be madness since it would alert the children of Naggaroth
to his presence and possibly to hers as well.

He hated this feeling of weakness, of not being able to do anything. He clenched his teeth and fought down the urge to punch the
ground with his fist. That really would not do him any good at all,
given the condition of his hands. He was suddenly aware of what
a fragile thing his body was.

He had never felt this way before. It had not taken much to trans-
form him from an efficient fighting machine into something barely
capable of movement. All it had taken was a little hardship, a little
cold and the strangling strength of the river.

He looked at where the witch elf's blade had bitten into his side.
The wound had gone a strange colour around the edges, a sort of
blackish-purple, and the area was strangely tender. Worse than that,
it felt as if something in it was draining the strength from his body.
It seemed all too likely that he had been poisoned, and there really
wasn't anything he could do about it.

Perhaps his aunt or Teclis would know what to do – they were
alchemists after all. He had no such knowledge. He knew only
the basics of field medicine that any elven soldier picked up on
campaign.

Sitting here feeling sorry for himself was not going to achieve anything. He needed to do something. The heat from his sword had
given him back a portion of his strength. He would wait until his
clothing was dry and then he would set out in search of Alarielle,
although he had no idea where he could find her.

Having made that resolution, he felt a little bit better. He wished
he had something to eat but there was nothing. At least there was
no shortage of water, he told himself. He supposed that given some
time he might be able to catch fish in the river, although he was not
sure, given the speed of the current.

It was dark by the time his clothes had dried. His blade crackled with its flames, sending shadows dancing away from him. He
knew he really should put it back in its scabbard, for its light would
probably attract pursuers. The small windbreak that he had created from his clothing would shield it from certain angles, but all it
would take would be the Cold One riders to turn up the path they
had been following and they would see it. He did not fancy fleeing
from one of those hunting reptiles through the dark. It would be
able to track him by scent. There was something unnerving about
the prospect of being pursued through the night-shrouded woods
by one of those great cold-blooded monsters.

He rose and donned his shirt and leather underjerkin and then put on the mail shirt. It jingled slightly when he moved and the noise was all the more noticeable at night. He wondered why that was – why did sound always seem so much louder at night? No doubt Teclis would have some explanation – he always did. All Tyrion ever really had were questions.

He picked up the blade and put it back in its scabbard. Suddenly the night seemed very cold, colder than it ought to have. He was almost tempted to draw the blade again so that he would have more light, but that was madness. He stood there waiting for his eyes to adjust, letting himself become more accustomed to the shadowy mass of the woods around him. Nearby the river continued to race by. The sound of water on rocks was like quiet thunder.

Tyrion figured that he would need to head back the way he had come to pick up the Everqueen's trail. She had been north of him when they had tried to cross the river and it seemed only logical that she still would be. Of course, it was always possible that she had somehow passed him by in the darkness. He dismissed such thoughts from his mind. If he allowed them to influence his decision, he would never do anything.

Tyrion considered his options. It seemed foolish to be blundering around in the dark, wearing the armour of a dark elf. If Alarielle saw him she may put an arrow through him. If a druchii saw him, he might be mistaken for a deserter. His disguise certainly had not fooled the Cold Ones, so it was not a great deal of use to him under the present circumstances.

On one hand, the mail shirt was certainly useful as armour, but then again it was noisy and might give away his position when he was trying to move stealthily. Reluctantly, he decided that he would need to get rid of it. Stealth was more important than protection at this point, and the truth of the matter was that the armour was hurting his wounded side and its extra weight was slowing him down.

He decided he would keep the leather underjerkin because it offered a measure of protection and did not make any noise when he moved. The dark elf helmet was of a very distinctive shape and if Alarielle saw him it might cause her to mistake him for one of the enemy. He decided that he could not afford that either. She knew his face and it would be best if she could see it.

He took the armour he was going to discard, wrapped the helmet in the mail shirt and tossed it out into the river. He did not want to leave it here because it might give away his position to the Cold

Ones when they returned. It was best to leave as few clues as possible behind him.

He felt better for not carrying the extra weight, and made his way down onto the trail. He discovered some evidence of the Cold Ones' passage almost immediately. Large lumps of excrement, foul-smelling in the extreme, dotted the path.

He kept moving, keeping to one side of the trail, so that he could dive into the undergrowth as quickly as possible. His night vision was good, even for an elf, so he did not have much trouble picking his way along in the darkness now that his eyes had adapted to the lack of light.

He paused now and again to listen, filled with foreboding that some enemies might be creeping up on him in the dark. At night, small sounds filled the forest. A white owl passed by overhead, gliding on silent wings, seeking its prey among the shadows. Tyrion felt a certain sympathy for the creatures it hunted. Occasionally, he caught the glitter of bestial eyes in the undergrowth. A fox, perhaps or maybe a wild dog. Whatever it was, it was silent and it retreated as he approached.

As he marched along, a sense of futility overcame him. What was he doing? He was never going to be able to find Alarielle in this gloom. She must be leagues away, or perhaps she was in the clutches of Malekith's minions. He could pass her in the darkness if she lay sleeping, and the chances were that he would never spot her. Nonetheless, some instinct told him to keep moving. It was his nature to do so anyway. He preferred action to inaction. At least this way he felt as if he was doing something and he was, in some small way, master of his fate.

He wondered if he should call out to her in the darkness, perhaps just whisper her name quietly, but this too struck him as a species of madness. It was the counsel of desperation. He was infinitely more likely to give away his position to any hunters that might be looking for him in the night.

He told himself that he was over-thinking things. Why should the dark elves be abroad now? They would most likely be making camp and laying themselves down to sleep, which is what he would be doing if he had any sense. Nonetheless, by the light of the fading moon, he kept walking, and occasionally when instinct told him that he was safe, he whispered the name of the Everqueen as if it was a talisman or a desperate prayer.

In his hand he clutched a dagger, and held himself ready to lash out at anything that might spring upon him from the darkness. He almost hoped that something would attack. At least it would break the tension, and it would give him a sense that he was not alone in the night.

He wondered how many other people were abroad in the darkness. Not too many, he suspected. If they were, they were likely to be enemies. He told himself that he was being too pessimistic. It was possible that there were other elves friendly to the Everqueen in this forest. Not all of them could have been massacred or captured by the dark elves back when they attacked the great tournament grounds. Perhaps there were even natives of Avelorn in this area who had not been at the tournament.

Of course, if that was the case, it was more than likely that the Cold Ones had scented them and they were now dead. It galled him to be wandering on his own through the night when his homeland was under attack by their ancient enemies. He wished that he was with an army right now, getting ready to fight against the invaders.

Perhaps there was no army anywhere in Ulthuan capable of fighting any more. The enemy had reached the heart of Avelorn and had almost succeeded in capturing its queen without anyone opposing it. Perhaps the same thing had happened elsewhere. Perhaps the armies of the Phoenix King had been taken completely off guard and overwhelmed by the same sorcery that had allowed the dark elves to penetrate so far into the forest kingdom.

He dismissed such speculation as futile. It could not be so. There were not enough druchii in Naggaroth to overwhelm all of the elven lands. Somebody, somewhere must be fighting against them, and while they did so, there was hope. Tyrion smiled sourly. It was one thing to tell himself that logically this must be the case. It was another thing entirely to make himself believe it, in the night, while hunger gnawed at his belly, and the witch blade's poisoned wound sapped his strength.

From up ahead came the sound of voices.

Tyrion could see a fire and hear the muffled, rasping breath of the Cold Ones. He paused, fearing that it was already too late to avoid detection and that at any moment the creature's bellowing would give the alarm and warn their riders of his presence.

He froze, becoming just another shadow amid shadows. No alarm was given. No monster sprang to life. The rhythm of their breathing was undisturbed. They were either asleep or made sluggish by the darkness. He let out his breath in a long, soft sigh, and crept forwards. He could see a group of druchii knights gathered around a fire. Their great mounts were tethered to metal stakes driven into the ground close at hand.

Slowly, carefully, Tyrion moved closer, writhing along on his belly, balancing himself on his palms. He got so close he could make out the features of the dark elves around the fire. They had removed their helmets so they could eat, and that action made them seem strangely vulnerable. They could have been elf soldiers anywhere on the seven continents, fighting a war far from home. Just watching their familiar actions gave Tyrion an odd pang of homesickness for the camps he had known.

One of them was leaning forwards, turning the corpse of some small animal on a stick-spit. Another was passing around his flask. From where he crouched, Tyrion could smell the alcohol. Two more were lying on the ground, looking at the stars. Another, the loner of the group, sat on a log and whittled something from a twig with his knife. It did not seem possible, looking at this homely scene, that these were the same fierce invaders who had killed so many at the tournament grounds.

And yet, they were.

If he wanted, he could take them by surprise. He could kill them all before they realised what was happening. It would be easy. He would circle the fire and take the first two from behind, then kick the embers of the fire on the ones facing them. A few strides and he would skewer them, leaving only the whittler and the ones on the ground. He had no doubt he could handle them, even in his weakened state, provided their beasts did not wake and join the fight.

There was nothing to be gained from doing so though, other than the slaking of the thirst for revenge that burned in his gut. He might even get himself killed, which would do no one, not the Everqueen and certainly not himself, any good. He had established that Alarielle was not their prisoner at least, which was one thing. He could be on his way.

Yet something held him in place. Perhaps it was loneliness. He found himself drawn to the fire and to vicariously participating in the soldiers' comradeship, and he was reluctant to leave just yet and wander off into the darkness.

'Do you think we'll find them?' one of the dark elves asked.

'They are leagues away if they have any sense,' the whittler replied. Tyrion knew his type. There was always one in every group, the loner, the one who had to be negative, who needed to bring his comrades down.

'What would you do with the reward?' the drinker asked.

'Forget the reward. I would just like to get my hands on the Ever-queen for a few hours,' said another soldier.

'A few minutes,' one of his companions said.

'A few seconds more likely,' said Whittler.

'You had better hope those seconds are worth it,' said one with the voice of authority and the badges of a leader. 'She is to be returned to Malekith untouched and unharmed. I think the Witch King wants to bed her himself.'

This led to a burst of ribald speculation. 'Soon we might have two queens in Naggaroth,' Whittler said.

'The gods preserve us, one is enough,' said Drinker. 'Not that I would kick Morathi out of bed, you understand.'

'That's very generous of you,' said Whittler.

'I am free with my favours,' said Drinker, 'although not as free as she is.'

'You have not had seven thousand years of practice.'

'Well, tomorrow we have another chance at the reward, if the trackers have not already found our high, bitch-goddess majesty,' said the leader.

'I thought Morathi was in the north, selecting some new barbarian lovers for her harem,' said Drinker.

'I was talking about the Everqueen, as I am sure you would real-ise if you were sober.'

'Which way did the scouts go?' asked one of the sleepers lying on the ground.

'You know what they are like. They are always creeping about, going their own way without anyone seeing them.'

'I thought we had them today,' said Drinker. 'When old Sharptooth caught the scent. I didn't think anything on two legs could get away.'

'And yet somehow they did,' said Whittler. 'And they killed three good riders while they were doing it.'

'They say Harek and his boys were burned by magic,' said one of those on the ground. 'You think this famous warrior is also a sorcerer?'

'I don't know. I heard he walked into the pavilion and slaugh-tered the general's bodyguard all on his own. He was carrying a burning blade, just like the one Aenarion used to carry before he picked up the Sword of Khaine.'

'Maybe it was Aenarion,' said Whittler, with heavy sarcasm. 'Maybe he returned from wherever he flew off to just to save the Everqueen.'

The silence that fell told Tyrion that Whittler had said the wrong thing. Not even those sacrilegious druchii wanted to hear jokes about Malekith's father. Or contemplate the prospect of his return.

'We'd better set some watches,' said Leader. 'I would not want to be taken off guard, just in case this famous warrior comes for us.'

Tyrion knew a cue when he heard one. He left their corpses for the Cold Ones to feast on.

—◀ CHAPTER NINE ▶—

'You seem unable to resist slaughtering things, Prince Tyrion,' said a voice from behind him.

Tyrion turned to see the Everqueen standing there. She held her makeshift bow in her hand and she looked ready to use it. He was not sure whether she intended to use it on him.

'In case you had not noticed, your serenity, these are our enemies,' Tyrion said. 'Or they were.'

'You're leaving a trail of dead bodies around Avelorn that a blind elf could follow,' she said. 'Perhaps you ought to learn some self-restraint.'

'At least I had made it easy for you to find me,' he said. 'I presume you sought out the sounds of carnage.'

'I was looking for you,' she said. She moved over to the pile of corpses that Tyrion had left and inspected them distastefully. It was not a pretty sight.

'Well, you found me, though it took you long enough.'

'I was pursued by an army of dark elves,' she said. 'I had to flee before them and then double back.'

'How did you escape them? I thought those Cold Ones would never give up, once they got your scent.'

'I took to the trees. Some of them grow very high here, and I think that kept me out of range of the hunters' nostrils. I came back here by climbing through the branches over their heads.'

'Very clever,' he said. 'I see I was wasting my time worrying about you.'

'Here's an idea you might like to drive into your head, Prince Tyrion. I was born here. I grew up in these woods. I know how to take care of myself. More than you do, it seems.'

Tyrion thought back over the events of the day. 'You're right. I am more at home on a battlefield than being pursued through a forest. My instinct is to turn and fight. It galls me to have to watch these scum overrun our homeland.'

'As it does me, Prince Tyrion. But there is a time to fight and a time to flee, and I think we both know which time this is.'

'How did you find me?'

'I doubled back along the trail. I looked down the river to the place where it seemed most likely you had come out of the water.'

'Did you find my trail?'

'No. I am no great tracker. I could not follow in this light.'

'And yet you found me.'

'It was simple enough. I merely asked myself what I would do if I were you. And naturally I found you slaughtering dark elves, so my method was proved correct.'

'You're being too glib.'

'I thought you would head north, looking for me. You seem determined to be my protector.'

'And you obviously don't need one.'

'I think we both need one. I lack your talent for killing things. You leave a trail through the woods that a child could follow, at least a child of my people. We have to assume that the dark elves have trackers just as competent.'

'I stand chastened,' he said. 'What do you suggest we do?'

'I suggest we search these bodies for supplies. They most likely have some things that we need. After that, I suggest we leave this place as quickly as possible.'

'I could probably have managed to think of that all by myself,' he said.

'Once we're far enough away, we can build a sleeping platform in the trees.'

'I will leave that to you,' he said. 'It's not something I have a great deal of experience of.'

'Don't worry, I shall show you how it is done.'

'Well, this is novel,' said Tyrion, looking down from the bole of the great tree. The ground was a very long way below, but he had always possessed a good head for heights.

'Great oaks are good places for this,' Alarielle said. 'Their branches are broad and there are boughs where they join the trunk. Even better, there are often hollows such as this one.'

She threw herself flat inside the small cave-like opening in the tree's side. 'Out of the wind, see?'

She was showing off and revelling in her superior knowledge, but he did not mind. She had charm when she chose to use it, and anything that made her feel more confident was a good thing as far as he was concerned.

'What about beasts?' Tyrion asked. 'I would imagine some things use them as dens.'

'Tree panthers, oak hawks, leaf pythons,' she said. 'But there are none of them here. I checked. Nothing has used this place for a long time.'

'Perhaps there is a reason for that,' he said.

'The main thing is that we are off the ground, and away from the trail.' Tyrion wondered about that. They had clambered up a lesser tree and then made their way here following the broad branches. It had not been the easiest of feats in the moonlight but they had managed it.

'Won't anybody tracking us wonder that the trail suddenly vanished?' he said.

'That's why I picked a tree surrounded by rocks in a rocky area,' she said, 'and that's why we climbed up them first. If anyone can track us over that, they are using magic, and we have other things to worry about.'

'I am glad you reminded me of that. I think it's safe to assume that there will be sorcerers amid the dark elves.'

Her smile vanished like the sun behind a cloud. 'True. But we've done what we can.'

'Can't you work magic to hide us? I have always heard that the Everqueen was a great sorceress.'

'It is not so simple, Prince Tyrion. I have the power but I don't know how to use it... yet.'

'I would respectfully suggest that you learn.'

'If I could, I would. Anyway, that is a problem for tomorrow. Tonight we shall sleep.'

'You sleep first,' he said. 'I will keep watch.'

She looked as if she wanted to argue, but then said, 'Wake me in a few hours.'

'That I will,' said Tyrion.

General Dorian strode through the woods. He was coming to hate this place. He disliked being surrounded by the gigantic trees. He wished that he was home in the cold wastes of northern Naggaroth, fighting against a foe that he at least understood. He disliked being surrounded by gigantic plants that obscured his field of vision, and low bushes in which predators could lurk. He preferred the rocky wastelands.

This was like hunting for a shadow in a darkened room. Even his army, which had seemed so large when he set out, seemed inadequate to the task. He had hundreds of trackers looking for the Everqueen and her mysterious protector, all of them following different trails with different forces. He was starting to wonder whether that was wise. Already the queen and her protector had more than once turned at bay and slaughtered those who should have been hunting them.

He wondered if he was only doing this in order to lengthen his life. All he was really doing was putting off the evil moment when he would need to go back and confess his failure to Malekith.

No! He would not give up. He would find the Everqueen and where she hid, no matter how long it took. It was only a matter of time before the trackers found the right trail and he would be able to bring his overwhelming force to bear. Once that happened, he would be able to report to his master the good news and claim the reward that would be his due.

He suspected that he was not even fooling himself. He very much doubted that there would be any reward for him except a painful death. Malekith did not like to be kept waiting.

Even though it was not his fault that the mirror had not worked, Dorian knew that he would take the blame for it. He should have stayed at his post and waited instructions. He had not. He had taken it upon himself to go and seek the Everqueen. It was the only sensible decision. There was nothing else he could have done under the circumstances. That would make no difference.

Dorian decided that it was time to employ new methods to find the Everqueen and her guardian. Conventional scouting and tracking had failed, so it seemed that the time had arrived to use magic. He had been putting this off because normally he relied on Cassandra to perform the sorcery that he required or to pass on his commands to her fellow witches. Doing this reminded him of her absence and of his own weakness. Nonetheless, the time had arrived.

Alexandra, the chief sorceress, arrived flanked by her sister-witches. They stared at Dorian with cold, malevolent eyes. He matched them glare for glare. He knew they were used to intimidating most druchii, but he had not reached the rank of general by allowing himself to be intimidated.

'Yes,' Alexandra said. Her gaze was particularly cold. She had once been his rival for Cass's affections, and it meant that no love was lost between them.

'We need to find the Everqueen. She continues to elude our scouts.'

'And you wish us to use our magic.'

'No, I expect you to strip naked and race through the woods shouting her name until she answers.' That drew a laugh from the surrounding soldiery which was quickly quelled by the glares of the witches.

'You are not requesting our aid very politely.'

'I am not requesting your aid at all. I am ordering you to do it as your commanding officer.'

'I answer to Morathi.'

'You will answer to Malekith soon if the Everqueen is not found. I doubt even your mistress will protect you from his wrath.'

'Your failure is not our failure, general,' said Alexandra. She had clearly decided that this was the line to take.

'And I am sure the Witch King will take your assessment of that at its true value,' Dorian said. 'I will be sure to mention you specifically when he questions me about this matter.'

Dorian wanted to make it very clear that he was not going to go down for this alone. The witches were no more going to be able to wriggle out from under Malekith's vengeance than he was. He smiled coldly at her to emphasise his point.

'Accidents happen, general. You may not live to be questioned.'

'Some would say that would be a fortunate event for me, given the current situation. I am sure Malekith would conduct his own investigation should that eventuality arise, and he will be generous in apportioning blame.'

Alexandra clearly got the point.

'There is no need for this senseless bickering, general. My sisters and I will get you out of the mess you and your scouts have got yourself into.'

'I welcome your acquiescence.' Her glare told him he might be pushing things a little too far.

Alexandra led her coven out of the tent and Dorian followed. He was curious, and knew that watching her perform their rituals would provide him with distraction from his grief.

The witches scratched a hexagon six paces wide on the ground and then a circle that connected to its corners. Each of them then inscribed a smaller version of the same figure at a corner.

'Are you sure you want to stay, general?' Alexandra asked. 'If something goes wrong you may suffer from the backlash.'

'I am sure my amulets will protect me,' said Dorian, although he was not sure at all. He was simply beyond all caring. He took a few steps back though, to put some distance between himself and the ritual.

Alexandra started to chant. One by one the witches took up the chant. It was in the ancient elvish tongue interspersed with some words in another language which made the hairs stand on the back of Dorian's neck. He recognised some of them from Cass's grimoires. They were in one of the daemon tongues. Curious birds fluttered overhead, cawing raucously, obviously disturbed by what they saw.

As the witches repeated the words a cold breeze sprang up which carried on it strange odours. Small firefly-like points of light shimmered in the air around the hexagon until the witches were obscured by their swarming. The tones of the chant changed and the motes drifted outward. One of them touched a hovering raven. The bird let out an unearthly shriek. Its eyes glowed with the strange corpse-light of the mote. It began to move and circle with a new intelligence, buffeting some of its companions down into the cloud with its wings. They too were limned in light and shrieked loudly and were merged with the possessed flock.

The motes continued to drift outwards, touching animals and birds as they went. Every one that was touched joined the great swarm, and circled around the witches, a mass of birds, foxes, weasels and other animals, all moving in eerie unison, like a great shoal of fish changing directions in a current.

One of the motes drifted close to where Dorian stood. He was almost curious enough to reach out and touch it. It moved closer and circled him, coming close to the amulets he wore before veering away. He had a sense of malign intelligence in the thing. It buzzed into a nearby bush, and something shrieked and scuttled out of the undergrowth and headed back towards the ever-growing swarm.

Alexandra was talking to it, and it was responding in the same odd language, all of the creatures' voices blending together into one cacophonous roar that made the air vibrate with its words. He knew without being told that the witch was giving this composite creature its orders, telling it what to seek and what to do when it found its prey.

The roar sounded angry and defiant. Alexandra's tone was by

turns threatening and cajoling. Eventually some accommodation seemed to be reached. The birds fell upon the ground-based animals, pecking out their eyes, devouring their flesh and drinking their blood. As they did so, imprisoned sparks were liberated and drifted free to seek out another avian host. Eventually the air was filled with birds, swarming in a vast flock, which suddenly erupted skywards and hurtled east as if seeking a trail.

'Something is wrong,' Alarielle said. 'I can feel it in the air.'

She had been nervous all day, full of dire premonitions.

Tyrion just looked at her. Studying their surroundings, he could not see any threats at all. It was not that the woods were quiet. They were never really that. There are always some small animals or birds moving through them somewhere but he could not discern any threat, particularly compared to previous days when it had seemed that the surrounding forest teemed with dark elf soldiers. She tilted her head to one side and said, 'There is something wrong – it has something to do with magic. That is all I can say.'

Tyrion understood this – he had never been good at sensing the winds of magic. In fact, he was much worse at it than most elves. It was a species of blindness that he suffered from compared to most of his people, and he felt its lack now.

Even as Alarielle spoke, a dark cloud appeared overhead. It was a mass of birds, all flying together with a strange rigidity and precision in their formation. His magesight was not the best but there was nothing wrong with his eyes, and he immediately saw the sinister nature of the flock.

It consisted of birds that should not have been flying together, such as rooks, sparrows and swallows. Its composition was random and there was something strange and malevolent about the eyes of the birds. Looking closely he could see that they glowed with tiny pinpricks of red light. Even as he noticed this, they swooped down towards him and swirled around in a storm of wings. He could feel the wings beating against him, the feathery mass obscuring his vision temporarily. He regretted that he was not wearing a helmet for he feared that the birds would start pecking at his eyes. They did not attack, and shortly thereafter they withdrew. One of them was soaring off into the distance and he could hear it cawing with a strange intelligence. The birds returned to swooping above them in a holding pattern, circling overhead. If they had been on open ground he would have worried that such a strange formation of flying creatures would have given away their position at a distance, but he strongly doubted that anyone would notice that unless they were close enough to hear the birds shrieking.

'It is a spell,' Alarielle said. 'Those creatures are possessed, I can feel it.'

It came to Tyrion exactly what was happening. 'One of them has returned to whoever sent it.'

Alarielle nodded. 'And I do not doubt that there is a link between it and the rest of the flock so that it will be able to find where we are again.'

'We should kill them,' Tyrion said.

'And how do you propose to do that, Prince Tyrion?' Alarielle said. 'I have a limited number of arrows and they are flying among the branches and I doubt that we can even see all of them.'

'We have to do something,' Tyrion said.

'The best thing that we can do is to try and run ahead of them and hope that we can outpace our pursuers.'

Tyrion could not think of anything else to do, so he started to jog along among the trees while Alarielle easily kept pace beside him. Overhead the birds followed, mostly in ominous silence but sometimes cawing loudly as if to summon pursuers who might be lurking in the woods.

'There has to be some way to get out of their sight,' Tyrion said.

'I can only think of one,' Alarielle said. 'We could head for Winterwood Palace.'

'Where is that and how will it help?'

'Save your breath for running, Prince Tyrion. You'll see when we get there.'

The shadow of the daemonic birds fell upon them as they ran.

CHAPTER TEN

Impatience grew within Malekith. What was going on, he wondered? Why had he not heard from Dorian? He glared at the mirror once more and willed it to work. It stubbornly refused to respond, just as it had done for the past several days. He clenched his fist and fought down the urge to smash it. He knew that it would do no good – after all, he had designed the thing and caused it to be created. It was intended to be able to withstand much greater force than even his massive strength could bring to bear.

He turned his burning gaze on the rest of the druchii in the command tent. They quailed, sensing his mood. Only N'Kari, the greater daemon that he had bound to his service, refused to care. The daemon still wore the form of a beautiful, naked elven woman. Today, she was tattooed with the runes of Slaanesh.

Malekith rose from his throne, looming over every single person in the room. He strode down from the dais on which his seat had rested and marched across the chamber, wrestling with his own anger.

Be calm, he told himself. Restrain yourself. Before you can rule others, you must first rule yourself. There was no need to be impatient. Everything was still going according to plan. All of the reports coming in told him this.

In the north, the vast force of human Chaos worshippers led by his mother surged across the lands of Yvresse with fire and the sword. In Lothern, the rebellion his supporters had fomented was tying down the great city-state's military strength even as his fleet laid siege. In a dozen different places, armies led by his generals had seized crucial objectives, fortresses, mountain passes that dominated supply lines and ports. From everywhere came reports of uninterrupted success. The plan was working. As he had known it would.

Except in one aspect.

He had heard nothing from Dorian. It had been days now and still there was no contact. He did not know whether the Everqueen was his prisoner or not. He did not know whether the spiritual leader of the elves was alive or dead. He did not know whether his army was victorious or had been destroyed.

For the first time in centuries, the magical mirror he used to keep in touch with his agents and lackeys all over the globe had failed to make contact with its counterpart. It seemed ominous that for the first time, that potent magical instrument had failed. What did it signify?

Had his army been defeated? Was the mirror even now in the hands of his enemies? Had it been destroyed? He doubted it was the latter. He would have sensed that.

Perhaps there was some more reasonable explanation. Perhaps there was some form of magical interference. He knew that protective spells might be at work in the area of Avelorn where the Everqueen dwelled.

Partially, it was his own fault. He had let things slip. He had been too busy issuing orders to the force he himself commanded. He had been too busy overseeing the destruction of the ancient elven city of Mancastra. He had neglected his duties. It was his first field command in many decades. He had allowed himself to succumb to the pleasure of watching his troops smash through the walls of the ancient city and search through the streets, killing and enslaving the inhabitants. He had allowed himself to be overcome by the pleasure of destroying his enemies with his own hands. For the first time in many years he had killed using his own sword.

It had been a foolish mistake, he now thought. He pushed his doubts to one side. He did not know that any mistake had been made. He needed to find out what was going on. The capture of the Everqueen was a major part of his strategy. It had been stupid to delegate responsibility to any underling, no matter how competent.

He had let his own secret, nagging fears dominate him. It was something that he had trouble admitting even to himself. The prospect of facing the god-queen of the elves had worried him. There was always the possibility that he had miscalculated, that his spies had missed something, that there were ancient, potent spells in place in Avelorn that might be able to slay even him.

Perhaps that was in fact the case. Perhaps that was why General Dorian was not in contact with him. Perhaps some hidden magic had risen up and destroyed his follower and the force he led. Perhaps it had been wisdom, not fear, to avoid going to Avelorn himself.

In any case, it was no longer permissible for him to stand by and do nothing. He needed to know what was going on there. He needed to know what had happened to his army there. He needed the information so that he could deal with any problem that might have arisen.

He could not send another army just yet. In fact, it may not be wise to do so. If one army had already been destroyed, he would only be weakening his forces unnecessarily by sending them into the same trap. He needed to do something else. He looked at the daemon, wondering suspiciously if N'Kari had anything to do with what was going on here.

The daemon smiled blandly. Malekith knew he would need to use its services to get what he wanted done. A chamberlain announced the presence of those he had summoned. He turned his burning gaze to greet them.

Malekith inspected the four elves. They did not look immediately prepossessing. No one would suspect them of being among the most deadly elves who have ever lived. Which, of course, was the whole point.

These four were almost as dangerous as the great Urian himself. Each of them was only a hair's breadth less dangerous in his or her field. All of them now looked at their ruler expectantly. Malekith stared back, daring them to show the slightest quantum of defiance. They were all too clever for that.

Malekith walked around them, surveying them. Amara looked as beautiful and innocent as a maiden from the foothills of the mountains of Cothique. She might have been a dairy maid from some small elven village in the wilderness. Her hair was long and blonde. Her eyes were wide and innocently blue. Her nose was small for an elven aristocrat. Her lips were wide and pouting. She looked innocent, trusting and ever so slightly stupid.

She was none of these things.

To Malekith's certain knowledge, she had slain over a thousand elves. She had done it with daggers, poison, garrottes and even a long slender blade which she wielded very expertly when she needed to. She was one of his deadliest spies, a consummate actress who had travelled undetected across Ulthuan on hundreds of occasions. She could appear to be a merchant princess from Lothern or a barmaid from a tavern in some remote village in Yvresse just as easily.

She was an expert of winning the trust of other elves and seducing them to her cause. Now she was dressed in the raiment of an officer of his guard, which was the position she occupied at his court when she was not dispatched on some mission. She kept her eyes modestly downcast but he knew she was listening attentively and without flinching as his metal footfalls passed behind her.

Balial was big and brutal. He was almost as large as Malekith himself. He was enormously broad and enormously strong and he delighted in using his strength. He could break the neck of a human blacksmith with a twist of his hands. He could wrestle monstrous bulls to the ground. He could chop through an outstretched neck and a heavy wooden log on which it rested with one sweep of the giant double-bladed axe that he carried across his back, unusual in that it had an axe-head at each end. There was nothing subtle about Balial. He killed face-to-face in combat. He liked to feel blood splatter his face as he did so.

He had started off as a pit fighter who had attracted Malekith's attention through his sheer ferocity and brutality. For a time, Malekith had thought to make him his executioner until he had discovered that a sly intelligence lurked beneath his brutal mask. Balial was perhaps the deadliest warrior in Malekith's entire retinue. Strangely enough, he possessed a certain charm that was able to win the trust of other elves. Malekith had often infiltrated him into groups of captured slave gladiators to find out what they were thinking, to pick their brains for intelligence about their homelands and to motivate them to fight and win and thus put on a better show. Balial had an excellent memory and a sound grasp of strategy; he was utterly trustworthy, which was not something that could be said of most dark elves.

Khalion looked like he liked his food, his wine and his drugs too much to be a fighter. That was deceptive too. He was a master sorcerer. He was particularly good at spells of illusion and deception, and being good at such things, he did not often fall for them himself. Malekith often used him to bring rebellious wizards to heel or to death's door if they could not be disciplined. Khalion looked amiable but he was cruel almost beyond belief, even by the standards of dark elves. He liked to torture his victims and devour their souls or offer them up to daemons in a most unpleasant manner.

Vidor looked like an inhabitant of Avelorn. He could almost be one of the primitive asrai of the far eastern continent. He dressed all in leather, in a hooded jerkin. In his right hand he carried a great

longbow which he could use with a proficiency that would do credit
to even one of the elves of the forests across the ocean. He was a
deadly shot and just as deadly with a sword or knife. He liked to
hunt, and most of all he liked to hunt intelligent creatures such as
humans and elves. He was a famous tracker who often returned
escaped slaves to their masters. He delighted in doing such things.

Malekith knew his secret. Not only was he a great tracker, but
Malekith had ordered his sorcerers to alter the olfactory centres of
Vidor's brain. It had been an interesting experiment, a precursor
to the much more elaborate ones that he had worked upon Urian
and others. Vidor was capable of tracking like a hound. He had a
sense of smell as keen as a wolf. Something about the sorcery had
altered his brain and let him derive an almost sexual pleasure from
the hunt and kill.

Malekith said, 'You are being dispatched on a mission of utmost
importance. You will travel to Avelorn and ascertain what has happened to our army there.'

They knew better than to ask any questions at this point. If he
wanted to explain, he would. If he did not, they would need to interpret his wishes according to their own understanding.

Tersely Malekith explained the situation and gave them their
instructions. 'You are to seek out General Dorian's force and seek
an explanation as to why he has not been in contact. If this explanation is not satisfactory, you are to see that General Dorian is
replaced by his immediate subordinates. If the Everqueen is present, return with her to me. If she is not present, find her and bring
her to me if that is possible. If it is not possible, kill her and bring
back her head so I may use it as a standard for my army.'

He gestured to the small gemstone amulets in the shape of a bird
that lay on a nearby table.

'You are each being given a stone raven. Use it to communicate
with me if the need arises. I do not need to explain to you that it is
of the utmost importance that you succeed in this mission. So far,
the conquest of Ulthuan has occurred precisely as expected and
according to plan, with the single exception of General Dorian's
command. To you falls the great responsibility of bringing that part
of the plan back on track. Any questions?'

'Am I to take it that we have your authority to do anything we
require, sire?' Balial asked.

'You will be given black signets. You speak with my voice for the
course of this mission.'

Balial looked satisfied. There could be no greater mark of Malekith's trust.

'We may remove any who get in our way, no matter how highly placed or no matter whose favour they enjoy, sire?' Khalion asked in his annoying, high-pitched voice. He was well known to have feuded with several of Morathi's most devoted sorceress followers. He hated them with a passion, possibly because all of them had rejected his overtures.

'You do. No matter who they claim protects them. Your actions will be assessed afterwards. If they are found to be unnecessary, you will answer for them.'

Khalion smiled. He knew that success would absolve him of many sins. Malekith knew this too. He did not wish to state it overtly, however. There was no need to provoke his mother's enmity unnecessarily.

'How will we get there, sire?'

'N'Kari will take you. I have assigned her to this immediately. It is a sign of the importance of your mission.'

'I am ready to depart, sire,' said Vidor.

All of them nodded. 'Go!' said Malekith. 'Bring me the Everqueen dead or alive, and you may name your own rewards.'

That startled them. It was an offer of fantastic generosity. They hurried from the pavilion.

The four assassins stepped into Avelorn, leading their four large black steeds. They glanced around at what looked like a partially abandoned camp.

'Not a lot of people here,' said Balial.

'Very observant,' said N'Kari.

'I did not ask for your opinion,' said Balial.

'I did not ask to endure your stench and yet I must,' said the daemon. 'And now I must go. I apologise for not waiting until your slow wits could formulate a reply, but I do not have a month to waste.' With that the daemon was gone. The magical portal closed behind it.

'You!' Balial bellowed at one of the dark elf soldiers who stood nearby watching. The soldier marched over.

'Sir,' he said cautiously, for he was unsure who the newcomers were although he suspected they were important.

'Where is your commander?'

'Captain Marin is in the field, sir. We have heard nothing from him for several days. Our last order was to hold this spot and wait for the portal to open.'

'Where are your captain and the general?'

'They both went to the tournament fields, sir, to capture the Everqueen.'

'They are there now?'

'We have heard nothing from them, sir, since we received our orders.'

'They have captured the Everqueen?'

'I believe so, sir.' The soldier did not seem at all certain.

'Then why has the matter not been reported to the Witch King?'

'General Dorian does not explain his decisions to me, sir. Perhaps you should ask him yourself.'

'I will do that, soldier,' said Balial. Vidor had already picked up the track and was riding down it. Clearly he intended to be the first to report success if he could.

Balial mounted up and followed the rest of them. It was clear the army had not been wiped out, or at least this contingent of it – the base camp had not been either. He wondered what they would find at the tournament grounds.

'A remarkable number of slaves,' said Vidor, inspecting the captives. They had that beaten look he knew from the faces of new captives everywhere. There were hundreds of them. He had never seen so many enslaved elves in one place before. The smell was quite distasteful. These elves clearly had taken defeat badly. They were unwashed and stank like humans.

'A less than remarkable number of guards,' said Amara, in her soft, husky voice.

'There are enough,' said Balial. 'Dorian knows his business in this at least.'

'He seems to have let the Everqueen slip through his fingers,' said Khalion. He sounded almost disappointed. Vidor wondered what the sorcerer's plans were if he got his hands on Alarielle. Nothing pleasant, that was for sure.

'Taking most of his army in pursuit of her seems almost a dereliction of duty,' said Khalion.

Balial shook his head. 'It is entirely according to his orders. Taking the Everqueen dead or alive is of the highest priority both to him and us.'

'It seems he had her and she escaped.'

'Accompanied by a warrior with a burning sword, if the reports are to be believed,' said Vidor.

'I would like to meet this fighter,' said Balial.

'So would I,' said Amara, although she sounded as if she had a different purpose in mind to the burly warrior.

'Let us see what we can do about finding him,' said Khalion.

'It's not the easiest thing to see what was going on here,' said Vidor. 'Too many others have been around and spoiled the traces.'

'Surely the master tracker can tell us something,' said Khalion. The sneer was evident in his voice. Vidor looked at him as if he wanted to put an arrow through the sorcerer's throat.

'There are still some traces,' he said as if lecturing an idiot. 'Over here we can see where the Cold Ones were. Their breath poisoned the leaves above them. Their riders were sitting by the fire over here. They were talking or drinking or both.'

'Such a brilliant tracker,' said Khalion. 'He can even detect the fact that people were talking.'

'It's not a difficult thing to do,' said Vidor. 'From your tracks I could easily deduce that an idiot would be talking. Anyway, I can tell from the scent that the stranger came from over here. He was hiding in the bushes watching the knights. He came out of them and then he killed them.'

'He killed half a dozen knights on his own,' Amara said. 'Impressive.'

'Not quite so impressive if he took them by surprise,' said Balial. 'And I don't doubt that he did.'

'There was another one here. She was watching him. I can catch her scent too. She is the one we are looking for. The trace is very distinctive.'

'I will take your word for it,' said Balial. 'You think you can find their trail from here?'

'I can do that easily enough if I am not distracted by Khalion's inane ramblings.'

Khalion poured some black liquid into a small goblet and took a sip of it. He shuddered with pleasure after he swallowed the first mouthful. 'What reward will you ask of our glorious king?' he asked.

'I am tempted to ask for your head,' said Vidor, 'with the empty space inside it filled with gold. That would make me a very wealthy elf.'

'I think I will ask for copies of all Morathi's grimoires. I will be capable of astonishing things once I have mastered the knowledge in them.' He turned the words into a very ominous threat.

'I will settle for a mansion and a royal title,' said Balial. 'And the right to raise my own personal army.'

'How about you, Amara?' Khalion asked. He leered as he spoke. 'What does your heart desire?'

'Nothing that you could provide,' she said.

'I would not be so sure of that,' he said. 'The sorcerer's arts are not the only arts I have mastered.'

'I am sure many a maid has fainted under your caresses,' said Amara. Her tone made the words very ambiguous.

'We do not have all day to stand here,' said Vidor. 'We need to get on the trail as soon as possible, or the only reward any of us will get will be a painful death.'

All of them nodded in agreement and mounted their horses, following him off along the trail. Excitement filled them. It was only a matter of time before they overhauled their prey.

Malekith stared into the mirror. His mother looked as clear and steady as if he was looking at her through a crystal window rather than by means of a spell that crossed the leagues between them. She smiled sweetly so he knew she was about to place one of her daggers ever so delicately through some chink she believed she had found in his armour.

'It goes very well,' she said. 'The asur were taken completely by surprise. We have taken a dozen of their towns and villages. They are learning humility under the gentle caresses of our barbarian allies.'

'Good. It will make them all the more grateful when I restore the natural order of the world,' Malekith said.

'The barbarians may not take to discipline quite as easily as you imagine.' Morathi's smiled widened. She was about to deliver the bad news. At least, he felt certain it would be bad news from his point of view.

'What makes you say that?' He allowed the merest fraction of his annoyance to glitter in his voice. Anyone else would have blanched with dread. His mother was amused.

'They have their own priests, their own cults, their own ideas of destiny.'

'I would have thought it would not be too difficult for you to subvert all of those to our needs. You have a gift for such things, mother.'

'Under normal circumstances, I would have to agree with you, but these are not normal circumstances. The winds of magic blow strong and they are tainted by Chaos. That should tell you something.'

'It tells me I am about to hear you make excuses about why you cannot do what is required of you.'

'Do not sound so petulant, Malekith. It ill befits the greatest ruler of elves world has ever known.' How typical of her to mingle a compliment with a reprimand. Or perhaps it was a secret sneer at what she felt was his vanity. Even after all this time, with his mother, it was difficult to tell.

'Make your excuses, mother.'

'The winds blow so strongly because the northern gates awake from dormancy.'

'We both knew this before we started. In fact we counted on it.'

'What we did not count on, my son, is that those who lurk beyond those gates might also become more active. The old dark gods are reaching out and making their worshippers restless.'

'You are saying the daemon gods of Chaos are preparing to intervene.'

'They have intervened. They have spoken in the dreams of their priests. They are giving their followers ideas above their stations.'

'Why have you not discouraged this?'

'Our situation here is delicate, Malekith. I stand at the head of an army of ten thousand druchii. The barbarians have twenty times that number and that is but a fraction of their force. If we are to ride this whirlwind, we must be subtle. We cannot stand in its way. Not yet. We have unleashed a daemon that will be difficult to banish again.'

'We shall see about that in time.'

'The barbarians have started to act on their own account. The great army is splitting up into marauding hordes, bands of savages are following their own prophets, covens of magicians are going their own way. Many have headed south.'

'So much the better. They will still cause havoc and they will be much easier to deal with piecemeal than as one unified force.'

'Let us hope so. Many of their mages have already departed southwards. More and more of the barbarians are preparing to follow.'

Malekith understood. His mother was taunting him. She was showing him the mistake he had made in his calculations. She had planned this all along. She wanted him to know how clever she had been, organising it, working it into his plans. She was planning something herself, and doubtless would dispatch agents to work her will. The question was, what was she up to?

'It seems one of us has made a miscalculation,' he said, and broke the contact. Let her think about that for a while.

Signs of life became evident below Teclis as the sun lowered itself on the horizon. He did not welcome them. Large creatures prowled below, even as he looked for a place to put down for the night.

Silver Wing was weary – flying on by moonlight did not seem like the smartest of things to do.

Teclis found a clearing and patted the pegasus's shoulder and pointed down. Silver Wing had no difficulty understanding. The steed circled cautiously, as if looking for threats, and then descended.

There was a brief, half-terrifying, half-exhilarating sense of moving far too fast over the ground as the winged horse touched down. The pegasus beat the air furiously with its wings and they slowed. Teclis had a few moments to worry about Silver Wing stumbling on a hidden pothole and sending him tumbling to a broken neck before they came to a halt.

Nervously, Teclis unstrapped himself, dismounted and looked around. He felt alone and vulnerable, as he never had before in the woods of Ulthuan. It was more than simply the fact that he knew there was a hostile army out there that would gladly torture him to death if it found him. It was something to do with being on the ground again, away from the sky and the wind and the lonely heights where nothing could threaten him but the birds. He found that now the motion had stopped, he missed it.

He could see much better in the gathering gloom than he ever had been able to do before. That was obviously the War Crown's work. He took it off, and found the circle encompassed by his sight and hearing shrank. The world blurred and became far more difficult to see. Despite its weight, he put the helmet on again. Everything became sharp and clear once more. It saddened Teclis to know that he needed magic and artificial aids to make him the equal of a normal elf. It came to him that in some ways this quest was madness. He was not fit for this, but then if he was not, who was?

He began to rub down Silver Wing with a saddle blanket. The pegasus began to graze, occasionally pausing to sniff the air and whinny. The sound was not exactly fearful – Silver Wing was not the sort of animal that gave a sense of that – but it was uneasy, as if the pegasus was catching the scent of something it disliked.

Teclis moved to the edge of the forest and gathered wood. He returned to the centre of the clearing and piled it up. He put his body between the pegasus and the wood before he spoke the word of power that turned the kindling into a blazing fire. It was likely the flying horse was used to such magic, but there was no sense in taking the chance of spooking it.

The pegasus returned to where he sat and nuzzled him gently. Teclis patted its head, grateful for the company. The scent and warmth of the huge beast was reassuring. At night, Avelorn did not sound like the more domesticated woods of Saphery. Out there, huge beasts roared, and other animals shrieked as they died. A massive white owl glided across the clearing, and stooped on some small prey.

This was nature, Teclis thought, a place where living things ate each other raw. He did not much care for it.

He was contemplating setting his wards for the night when he looked up, startled. He was surrounded by elves. They did not look exactly menacing, but they did not look friendly either. Several of them had bows trained on him. It seemed the Crown had not amplified his senses quite enough. It came to him that perhaps he had a problem.

'I had heard the elves of Avelorn were stealthy. Let me congratulate you on living up to your reputation.' He was proud of himself. His voice was steady. He had managed a deadpan politeness worthy of Prince Iltharis.

'It does not look like a druchii,' said a voice.

'I am not a creature of indeterminate sex,' said Teclis. 'I would be obliged if you referred to me as he.'

'It does not sound like a druchii,' said another. 'More like an effeminate scholar.'

'This effeminate scholar will be forced to teach you manners soon,' said Teclis. He really was starting to sound like Prince Iltharis.

'And how will you do that? With that pretty slender blade at your side? It looks good but you must be able to use it.'

'So this is the legendary hospitality of Avelorn. It seems somewhat over-rated.'

'You do not sound as troubled as I would expect someone a heartbeat from death to sound.'

'If you use your eyes, you will notice I am a wizard. I am protected by several powerful charms against arrows. I am quite capable of killing you all with a word, which I would rather not have to do, since I have a natural aversion to killing simpletons. It does not seem quite fair somehow.'

Teclis was surprised by how calm he sounded, how easily the words came. He had a mission. He was not going to let anything stand in the way of his completing it. He was even prepared to put his fellow asur to death if they tried to obstruct him.

'I don't think a druchii spy would talk like that,' said one of the voices.

'You've met a lot of Naggarothi spies, have you?' asked the first voice, obviously the leader.

'I am Teclis, Loremaster of Hoeth. I am seeking my brother, Prince Tyrion, who will be, if he follows his usual lecherous habits, in the company of your Everqueen.'

A stunned silence followed that announcement. Teclis wondered if perhaps he had overdone the insouciance.

'The Everqueen is dead,' said the one who sounded like the leader. 'If he is with her, your brother is too.'

A shock ran through Teclis. 'You have seen this with your own eyes?'

'We have met those who were at the tournament grounds when the druchii attacked. They saw it.'

'I would talk with them,' said Teclis.

'We still have not decided whether you are a spy or not.'

'I come here riding on a pegasus and wearing the War Crown of Saphery, and you ask me if I am a dark elf spy?'

'Anybody can make outrageous claims,' said the asur. 'Talk is easy.'

'Obviously thinking is harder.'

'If he was a dark elf spy he probably would not be so rude,' said a voice from the gloom. Teclis could sense a shift away from outright hostility to something else. They did not see him as an immediate threat. Most of them seemed to be prepared to take him at face value.

'I am seeking my brother and the Everqueen. If they are alive, I can find them and help them. If they are dead, you will be doing no harm.'

'You might be trying to find out where our camp is.'

'Bring your friends here to me then and I will talk to them.'

The leader nodded. 'Jaq, go and fetch the survivors. We'll stay here and keep an eye on this fop.'

'If you have no objections, I will prepare my medicines.'

'Your medicines?'

'I require them for my health.'

'You carry some sort of plague?' the elf leader asked him.

'I have been troubled by ill-health since birth.'

'You are a strange one. I think I am starting to believe you.'

'I am touched,' said Teclis. He took out some waybread and offered it around. The elves refused although they looked hungry. He shrugged and ate, and began to mix his potions in their alembics. He removed the War Crown so he could drink. He had finished with them when the scouts returned with some stunned, haggard-looking elves. Their gaudy celebrants' clothes contrasted oddly with their staring, haunted eyes. A few of them were heavily armoured warriors leading huge warhorses. Their leader was a tall, noble-looking elf.

'Our friends here say you claim to be Prince Tyrion's brother,' he said.

'I am his twin, Teclis.'

'I am Arhalien of Yvresse.' He came closer and inspected Teclis closely. 'It is odd. You are much gaunter and darker than your brother, but there is a certain resemblance.' The other elves present relaxed when Arhalien said this, becoming a fraction less wary and on edge.

'You have seen my brother?'

'I bested him in a tournament a few days ago.'

'Then you are one of the few elves living who can say that.'

'That I can well believe. I have never seen a better elf with a blade. He used weapons as if born to them.'

'I would be grateful if you would not refer to him in the past tense.'

'It would be a miracle if he were still alive. The tournament grounds were overrun by a vast dark elf army...'

'And yet, you are still here...'

Arhalien smiled ruefully.

'It was good fortune. I was camped by the edge of the tournament grounds with my retainers. I could not sleep after the excitement of the day and I was checking our sentries when I noticed one of them seemed to be asleep. When I checked I found his throat had been cut. A moment later I was beset by assassins. I cut them down and shouted the alarm. Within moments the whole camp was a battleground.

'I rallied my warriors and we made a stand. After that I tried to cut my way to the centre of the camp but it was hopeless, there was an army between us and them. We were sore beset and only just managed to cut our way free.'

'So you never actually saw my brother fall.'

'I passed his encampment. I thought to join forces with him, but by the time I got there all were dead.'

'You saw his body?'

Arhalien shook his head. 'I saw a dozen of his friends, Atharis and others. Corpses were piled in heaps all around. It was howling chaos. But honesty compels me to say I saw no body, of Tyrion at least.' Honesty seemed to be something of importance to this elf.

'So you cannot be utterly certain that my twin is dead.'

'No.'

'Or the Everqueen? Did you see her body?'

'No. You are making me feel very foolish and guilty, Prince Teclis.'

'An elf is the best judge of his own conduct.' Teclis knew he was being rude and unsympathetic. Arhalien seemed decent and brave – he must be a very great warrior indeed to have beaten Tyrion and fought his way clear of the massacre.

'I will accompany you on your quest. If your brother and the Everqueen are still alive, they may need aid from both of us.'

Tyrion gestured towards Silver Wing. 'Unless your horse grows wings you will only slow me down.'

'You think it likely your brother and the Everqueen are still alive?'

Teclis shrugged and spread his hands wide. 'Since we were very young my brother and I have shared a bond. We have always known when the other was hurt or in danger. I have a terrible nagging fear concerning Tyrion, but I do not think he is dead. And if he is alive, the Everqueen may be too. I have no reason to say so but hope, however.'

Arhalien sighed. 'I had hoped your magic had given you a vision of something better. You are said to be a very great mage. And you are not without courage. These woods teem with druchii.'

'Have you any idea how they got here?'

'You are the wizard. I was hoping you could tell me.'

'Once again I must dash your hopes.'

'Perhaps you will uncover the secret on your travels.'

'It is a great one, if it has let the dark elves penetrate into the very heart of Avelorn and beyond.'

That got the attention of the elves around him. It came to him that they had all been trapped in these vast woods and could not possibly have had news of the rest of the kingdom.

'Beyond?' Arhalien asked.

'Ulthuan is invaded. A horde of human barbarians led by Morathi is in the north. Malekith himself leads an army to the west of here. Lothern is beset by traitors from within and fleets from without. That was the word at the White Tower when I left.'

A shocked murmur rippled away into the darkness. 'These are terrible tidings,' said Arhalien. 'The Witch King himself... He has not set foot on Ulthuan since the time of Morvael.'

'I suspect he has returned to claim his father's kingdom.'

'We respect Aenarion, but Ulthuan was never his fiefdom. He did not own it.'

'I doubt Malekith would agree with you.'

'What can we do?'

'You must fight,' said Teclis. 'And you must win.'

'How?'

'Ah... that is the hard part.' They laughed at that. They sounded like elves who had not laughed in a long time.

'Sleep, wizard, we will guard you,' said Arhalien.

'I will set my wards,' said Teclis. 'I was going to do so when you interrupted me.'

No one objected.

Teclis lay in the forest. His side hurt like fire. He sat up and looked at the beautiful woman sleeping nearby. He stood easily, much more easily than Teclis had ever found natural, and looked around with an eyesight that was keener than even that the War Crown gave to him. He was tired but he could not sleep. Somewhere out there in the distance the druchii were moving, coming ever closer.

Part of Teclis knew this was ludicrous. He was asleep and he was dreaming that he was Tyrion. It was one of those special dreams that had been very common when they were children but much less so as they got older. He was glad. His brother was still alive and so was the Everqueen. This was the first conclusive proof he had of it. He was not on a fool's errand then. There was still a chance of finding his brother before it was too late.

He tried to memorise any of the things that Tyrion could see, hoping for some clue as to where he was. It was hopeless. He was surrounded by trees, and all the different parts of the forest looked alike to Teclis. He could hear the sound of running water nearby. His brother was near a powerful river, that much was certain. The only large river that Teclis knew of that was near here was the Everflow although it was a river of great length. At least he had a direction to head in.

Things twisted, as was their wont in dreams, and he was no longer in Tyrion's body. He was standing on a high ledge, overlooking a vast intricate pattern. The pattern was starting to fade in places despite the efforts of the ancient ghosts who maintained it.

Things twisted again and he was standing in a chamber that seemed familiar, where Caledor leaned forwards over a gameboard and moved a piece. Opposing him over the table was a shadowy figure that Teclis knew it would not be good to look too closely at. As if sensing his presence, the figure turned its head and looked up at him with cold empty eyes. Teclis felt himself falling forwards into those eyes and into oblivion.

He woke in a cold sweat, feeling as if he had just had a very narrow escape indeed.

Teclis rose with the dawn. He felt like blasting the birds singing so cheerfully in the trees. His shoulders felt as if someone had been punching them all night. His back hurt and so did his hip. Sleeping on the ground did not agree with him.

Arhalien was already awake and inspecting Silver Wing with his knightly companions. The elves of Avelorn were not visible. Teclis put on the War Crown, although it felt like the weight of it might break his neck this morning. Immediately his eyesight improved and he saw a few elves asleep in lean-tos under the eaves of the forest. He suspected there were others out there guarding them.

Arhalien walked over. In the early morning sunlight, Teclis could see his surcoat was grubby and blood-spattered. His armour was dented. The links had been broken and hastily repaired in some places. The ornate working on the hilt of his blade was dented and damaged. His companions looked to be in similar straits. He really did look as if he had fought his way clear of a brutal battle and spent the last few days racing ahead of terrible enemies through muddy woods. Teclis invoked the spell that kept his robes clean and his gear sparkling bright.

'You woke bright and early with the woodlarks,' said Arhalien, smiling.

'If it was not for those damnable winged vermin I might still be asleep.'

'You intend to go ahead with your plan?'

'I dreamt last night of my brother and the Everqueen. I believe they are alive and in danger. Dark elves pursue them through the forest.'

'Do you know where?'

'Would that I did! I must go to the tournament grounds and try and pick up their trail there.'

'How will you do that?'

'Magic.'

'I wish that I could come with you.'

'I would welcome that, but it is not to be. Silver Wing can carry only one of us.'

'I believe I will take my warriors north and see if I can be of some help.'

'It might be better if you escorted the refugees southwards to the White Tower. It is the only place where they will be safe.'

'I am not sure any place is safe any more,' Arhalien said.

'You may well be right.'

'May Isha watch over you,' Arhalien said.

'May you live a thousand years,' Teclis responded, but with foreboding.

◄ CHAPTER TWELVE ►

Teclis felt strangely lonely as the ground fell away below him. His companions of the night waved farewell. Silver Wing circled, giving him a chance to respond. After that, they continued to fly northwards, following the line of the Everflow.

Teclis was as nervous as ever, strapped into the saddle, but he found he was able to concentrate on some of the things happening below him. It was fascinating, seeing the great forest from the air and noticing the way the river carved through it. There were a number of waterfalls and in places the current looked very swift.

After a time, he noticed that he was not alone. Below him he could see large bodies of elves moving. Logic told him that they had to be interlopers, druchii, the invaders of whom he had heard so much and seen so little of previously.

He nudged Silver Wing to descend. The pegasus responded reluctantly, as if it sensed danger. Crossbow bolts begun to whizz by, some of them only deflected by Teclis's magic. He caught sight of heavily armoured dark elf warriors firing up at him.

With the power of the War Crown of Saphery enhancing his eyesight, he could make out the decorative metalwork on their helmets and the insignia on their shields. He could tell that there was a magician down there because he felt the shift in the currents of the winds of magic. He readied himself for the attack that was not long coming. A bolt of pure magical energy lanced upwards towards him.

He invoked a swift counterspell and neutralised it.

Silver Wing whinnied and pulled upwards into a steep climb, instinctively avoiding the terrible magic that had been unleashed beneath it. A few half-hearted crossbow bolts succumbed to gravity behind him and there was no further spell from the wizard who had previously attacked them.

The pegasus flew on, northwards, leaving the line of the river, heading towards the tournament grounds. Teclis dreaded what he would find there.

Even before he saw the tournament grounds, Teclis was filled with a sense of wrongness. The winds of magic in the area were curdled, tainted by some dark power whose aura was ominously familiar.

He sensed the psychic stench of a powerful daemonic force. It had faded and he doubted that it was present now, but something of it lingered in the air, the way the smell of a rotten corpse hung in the air near a charnel house.

He saw that there were the remnants of a vast military camp below him. A powerful force of dark elves was still down there. At the moment, Silver Wing was flying too high to be shot at and it would have taken a very powerful wizard indeed to be able to propel a spell to this height.

He could see that his arrival had created quite a stir. Dark elves had emerged from tents to stare at the sky. He was tempted to send a wave of destructive magic raining down on them. He resisted the temptation. He needed to preserve his strength in case of an emergency. He was alone here, without bodyguards or friends, and it would not do to waste his resources in pointless shows of strength.

He could see that the dark elves were camped within the boundaries of what had been an even larger campground. This was certainly where the great tournament for the favour of the Everqueen had taken place. It looked as if the vast tent-city had been overwhelmed very swiftly indeed. There was a nasty smell of death in the air as well as tainted magic. He suspected that huge piles of bodies must have been burned. It certainly was not a pleasant aroma.

He kept Silver Wing circling. Guards watched over huge pens full of enslaved high elves. It was what he would have expected. It was what he had been half-dreading all day. The dark elves were not wasteful except when it came to making sacrifices to their daemon gods. Living, sentient creatures represented wealth to them. They were slavers. Those were his people down there, but he could not take the risk of trying to free them. He might just be throwing away his life.

From this height, he could see that the earth had been churned as if by the passage of thousands of feet. There were many tracks. They ran everywhere. From above, they looked like the outline of some mad maze created by an insane god. Teclis knew that he was looking at the paths over which units had marched and crowds had fled, but he was not skilled enough in tracking to understand what they meant. One thing was clear though: the largest path led away from the camp in the direction from which he sensed the strongest stench of dark magic. Instinct told him he might find some answers there.

He turned Silver Wing in that direction, following it outwards as it ran through the forest. Sometimes, he lost sight of the tracks where the trees overhung the path, but always it emerged again. Even if it had not, he knew instinctively that all he needed to do was follow the strange psychic spoor of the dark magic. After what was not a very long flight, he came upon another, smaller dark elf camp.

Nearby was a tall standing stone carved with intricate runes and patterns. It was a waystone – part of Caledor's vast, ancient spell. A company of dark elf soldiers stood near the point where the tracks vanished. They simply ended as if the whole crowd of people that had made them vanished. What was going on here, Teclis wondered? He knew it was imperative that he find out.

He directed Silver Wing downwards. The dark elf soldiers ran to meet him. They were clearly uncertain as to who he was, but they were wary and they were levelling their crossbows. Teclis spoke a spell and when they unleashed their bolts, the projectiles caught fire in the air long before they reached him. Teclis invoked another spell – chain lightning danced around him, leaping from dark elf to dark elf, sparking from blade to blade, killing everything it touched. The smell of scorched flesh filled the air, mingling with the ozone stink of the electrical bolt. The remainder of the druchii turned and fled. Teclis proceeded with his investigation.

The aura of dark magic was strongest near the waystone. It was also very familiar. His senses had grown much more discerning since the last time he had encountered this particular spiritual stink, but it was not something he would ever forget and it brought a chill of terror to his heart.

The Keeper of Secrets N'Kari had been here. The daemonic enemy that had sworn to destroy all of the descendants of Aenarion had walked on this very ground. Teclis glanced around warily, fearful that the daemon might suddenly manifest. Potent wizard as he was, he knew he was nothing compared to a greater daemon of Chaos. All of the confidence in his own power that had been building over the past few days flowed from him like wine from an overturned decanter.

If Malekith was in league with such a creature, it explained a very great deal. When he was very young, an army had been moved around Ulthuan with similarly astonishing speed by N'Kari. He had managed to lay siege to a number of elven towns and even the shrine of Asuryan itself within the space of one month. No one had ever worked out how the daemon had done this, but just the fact that it had done so showed that it was theoretically possible, at least if you were a greater daemon of Slaanesh.

Or had access to the services of one.

That thought chilled Teclis's heart. It was virtually impossible to imagine someone compelling a Keeper of Secrets, but if anyone had such a power, if any sorcerer possessed enough skill and knowledge, it was Malekith or his mother Morathi.

Teclis did not want to believe that it was possible, that this could have happened. His mind reeled at the possibilities. N'Kari was a daemon with a great thirst for vengeance, at least part of that thirst would be slaked by drinking the blood of Teclis and his brother. The daemon had sworn vengeance against them personally.

Was it possible that Malekith had known this and used it as a bargaining chip to win the services of the daemon?

But Malekith himself was of the blood of Aenarion, and N'Kari had sworn vengeance against all of the descendants of the first Phoenix King. Surely he would want to destroy Malekith as well as Tyrion and Teclis.

Those things were not mutually exclusive, Teclis thought. The daemon was a being of great cunning. It was perfectly capable of cutting a deal with the Witch King and then turning on him once it had achieved its vengeance on the twins.

The more he thought about it, the more Teclis thought that he had hit upon a potential explanation for what had happened, or at least part of one. The question was: what could he do with this knowledge?

He needed to tell someone – the High Loremaster was the best candidate for this, but how could he send the message? And after he had done that, what should he do – turn back to Hoeth with news of the discovery and attempt to find a way to thwart the Witch King's magic, or press on with his quest?

Teclis heard booted feet racing closer through the trees. He saw a group of druchii emerging from the forest. They raised their crossbows and sent a hail of bolts flashing towards him. His charms repelled most of them. One or two found their way through, most of their energies spent. The impact was still painful though, and the sharp edge of one sliced his hands. Nearby Silver Wing whinnied and reared. Teclis turned to see that a bolt had bounced off his protective charms and hit the pegasus.

Realising they could not harm him with their weapons, they were, with the merciless vindictiveness of their kind, concentrating their fire on Silver Wing.

Teclis raced towards the pegasus, hoping to envelop it in the protective globe of his charms. Before he was within range, the winged horse screamed again. A dozen bolts had penetrated his hide.

Silver Wing fell, gasping. Bloody froth emerged from its nostrils. Its breathing was like the wheezing of a drunk man. It was drowning in its own blood. The pegasus looked up with sorrowful eyes. Teclis could see the intelligence fading from them. It was like watching the death of another elf.

He could try speaking a healing spell, but he did not have the time to do so and to protect himself. He was not familiar with the anatomy of pegasi and he doubted that any of the spells that he knew would be of much use. Even as these thoughts crossed his mind Silver Wing gave one last gasp, its wings twitched as if its spirit was making one last leap for the sky, and then the winged horse was still.

Fear dried out Teclis's mouth. The fate of the pegasus would be his if the dark elves had their way. More than that though, he was enraged that he had failed to protect the creature. What was worse, he had lost the thing that would allow him to find his brother quickly. He was going to have to proceed on foot through the wilds of Avelorn, and this was at a time when speed was of the essence.

The war cries of the druchii were triumphant now. That they had killed something beautiful only pleased them more. A cold, cruel rage took hold of Teclis, burning away his fear, leaving him thinking with a terrible clarity that he had never enjoyed before.

He spread his arms wide and invoked his power, drawing the winds of magic to him with a force that could not be denied. It was as if he stood at the centre of a vast whirlpool of power, sucking all of the magical energy into himself. Once, such a thing would have killed him. Drawing on so much power so quickly might have burned out his gift for wielding it, overloaded his brain, driven him mad.

Perhaps that was happening anyway, perhaps he was deluding himself that he could handle so much of it. Blazing light surrounded him now. The patterns of the winds of magic themselves were visible in the air. Shimmering lines of light were drawn to him in all the colours of the rainbow and some colours that were not natural for the eye to see at all.

His body was on fire. He burned but he did not feel any pain. His skin tingled. When he breathed, the air he took into his lungs felt incandescent. He kept chanting, drawing more energy to him.

The shouts of the druchii faded. At first he thought it was because of the effects of the magic upon his hearing, but then he realised that they were silent out of dread and they were right to be so.

He was going to give them a lesson in the use of power that they would not live to forget.

There were wizards present among his enemies. They sensed what he was doing and tried to interfere. One of them sent a bolt of lightning arcing towards Teclis. It was like trying to put out a fire by throwing pitch upon it. Teclis merely drew on its energy and it dissipated harmlessly before it reached him.

He added it to his own and began to shape it. The other dark elf mage attempted to dispel the magic he was casting. Teclis squelched his spell as he would an insect underfoot.

He was drunk with power now. He was like a giant who could reach out and knock down the trees with his hands. He felt free for the first time in his life; free of all restraint, free of the restrictions he had placed upon himself out of fear of his own strength.

Hatred burned in his heart. It was not a new hatred. It had been there for a very long time. The druchii merely provided it with a focus. They were, after all, elves. They looked like the people who had sneered at him and tormented him all his life. They looked like every enemy he had ever had. Every female elf who had ever rejected him. Every male elf who had ever laughed at him or bullied him or sneered at his ill-health.

Living in Ulthuan, among the asur, he had needed to restrain himself. Even though he was an outsider, he was still a member of a society. The druchii were not his people. No law protected them. No one would punish him if he destroyed them. There was no need for him to restrain himself.

He laughed out loud, there was a wild, cackling evil in his voice. Some of those who heard it turned and fled.

He wove a spell of awesome, ominous power. Words emerged from his throat and seemed to take shape in the air, becoming glowing runes of light formed by the very vibrations of his voice. They swirled around him, forming ever more complex patterns, daemonic in their complexity, moving ever faster around him until they seemed to leave lines of fire behind.

Finally, when maintaining the spell was all but unendurable, he unleashed it. It flooded outwards, surging in lines of light towards the trees, lines dividing and re-dividing until there were hundreds of them. Each line sought out one living thing, one dark elf, and pursued it through the forest. Where those lines touched flesh, the targets screamed and died, becoming incandescent and then turning to dust which was blown away on the wind caused by the vortex of Teclis's might.

A few wizards tried to shield themselves, but Teclis's spell smashed through their defences like an axe through rotten timber. Within heartbeats all of the druchii were dead, and Teclis stood in the centre of the clearing, over the dead body of the pegasus, howling with mad exultation.

A small wary part of Teclis's mind realised something.

Part of the rage and part of the anger was most definitely his, but part of it came from somewhere else. It was fuelled by the dark taint on the winds of magic, the even darker taint of the place where he stood, on ground upon which a greater daemon of Chaos had once trod and woven potent magic.

He sensed a darkness creeping into him, blighting his spirit and making him into something he had not intended to become. He knew, for he had been taught by true masters of magic, that there was always a chance of daemonic possession when working high and powerful magic, that things reached out from the Realm of Chaos when a wizard drew upon them for power. Something was doing that to him now. He closed his mouth and stopped his mad laughter with an effort of will, and began to utter ritual words of cleansing and to calm his mind with meditation.

It was a long time before he felt like himself again, even then he was both thrilled and appalled by what he had done, by the murder he had committed on such an epic scale. He felt for the first time in a long time the very dark depths within his soul, the awful potential for abomination that was his. He feared it and he loathed it, but he was entranced by its possibilities nonetheless.

He was shocked to find that he had enjoyed smiting his fellow elves far more than he had ever done any other foes. It came to him then that there was within him a terrible potential for evil. He started to understand why the dark elves took such pleasure in tormenting their foes. It was a way of asserting their personal power in a universe that did not care for them. In that moment, he was surprised indeed to find in his heart the truth that he was more like the spawn of Naggaroth than he would ever have previously cared to admit.

He looked at his hands and found that they were shaking. His mouth felt dry. His heart beat faster. He felt certain that he had crossed some personal bridge, had stepped onto a path that was going to take him somewhere that he might not like but that he felt was his destiny. He was starting to see that in this war he might find a crucible in which he would be transformed into someone very different from the person that he had previously thought that he was.

He began to understand his brother better than he ever previously had. Perhaps this was how Tyrion felt when he stood alone on a battlefield with all his foes vanquished.

Teclis had killed all the other wizards. He felt good about it. He had proved his superiority. He had not started that particular fight but he had finished it. He wondered at the moisture running down his cheeks. He had expected his spells to protect his eyes from the effects of the wind.

◄ CHAPTER THIRTEEN ►

Teclis limped through the woods, heading east towards the Everflow as he had done for the past few days. Birds sang cheerfully. He felt like blasting them with magic because he was anything but cheerful.

Only now that it was gone did he really realise what the pegasus had given him. It had allowed him to travel with amazing speed across this vast wooded landscape. It had enabled him to cover in a few days what would have taken him months on foot and weeks on horseback, to navigate through a realm that had no major, well-marked roads. Now he was reduced to walking, and he was even slower at that than most people would be because of his limp and physical weakness. Only now did he have a real sense of the size of the forest he tramped through. It was as vast as many countries.

Even wearing the War Crown of Saphery, he felt trapped in a dense world where he could not see peril as it came towards him. The forest limited his vision, huge trees and dense undergrowth making it impossible for him to see very far.

Anything could be out there, creeping up on him, taking aim at him with a bow or spear, and he would not know it until it was too late. His magic protected him somewhat – he had charms against arrows and other missile weapons that would deflect things fired at him. That did not make him any less nervous though. He was not used to travelling on his own through such wild lands.

He had thought that Avelorn would be like the forests of Saphery, but that was not the case. Saphery had been domesticated by the presence of wizards. The roads there were protected by warding spells, and dark and wild creatures shunned the paths that were likely to be protected by magic. That was not the case here. Huge predatory cats stalked through the undergrowth. He heard them prowling at night. Sometimes, he could see their eyes reflecting his firelight as they watched him.

It was not just that. He sensed the presence of patches of old, dark magic in the trees around him. There were places that were blighted and had been since the time of Aenarion. Sometimes, he could sense powerful malign intelligences waiting for unwary passers-by to draw into their web of magic.

Sometimes he came across the signs of war. He passed bodies left on the ground where they had been slain. Sometimes, the corpses bore the marks of torture and they belonged to elves of Avelorn. It was obvious that the druchii were taking great pleasure in killing anyone they encountered.

That did not make any sense. The druchii were slavers. To them prisoners were wealth. They were looking for something and torturing the people they found for information. Part of him hoped that they were simply looking for the elves who opposed them.

Not all of the corpses he found belonged to high elves. Sometimes he came across the sites of ambushes where forces of dark elves had obviously been surprised by the natives of Avelorn. There, the bodies had been riddled with arrows and sometimes left nailed to trees as a warning. There was nothing honourable or chivalrous about the war being fought around him. It was savage, brutal, ancient hatred on both sides unleashed in the struggle.

He half-suspected that the dark elves were seeking news of Tyrion and the Everqueen just as he was. It was the only reason he could think of for them splitting their forces and searching through this vast, trackless wilderness with such fury.

No other military objective could be achieved by this invasion of the forests. Tyrion might have been able to tell him otherwise; his brother had always been a great expert on military matters. Teclis doubted it though. There were no fortresses here, no wealthy cities to be plundered, no towers full of magical knowledge.

This was the spiritual heartland of Elvendom but it was mostly empty and far from civilised. The only place that would be counted as such had been very civilised indeed. That was the court of the Everqueen, but the dark elves had already destroyed that and killed most of the people who had attended it.

In some ways this gave him hope. It meant that it was likely that his brother and the Everqueen were still alive. Why would the dark elves be pursuing them otherwise? That only made the slowness of his progress more frustrating. He felt as if time was running out and that every second counted – being afoot was putting him at an enormous disadvantage in a race that he did not have much chance of winning anyway.

He wished that he could encounter some of those marauding high elves himself. He could have asked them for news concerning the druchii or the passage of those that were hunted by them. He half-hoped that his brother had found refuge among the nomadic warriors who harassed the dark elf army. At least he would have found shelter among locals. In theory, they would know where to hide and have the best chance of avoiding the marauding druchii.

Of course, there were other threats now. He had come across a few bands of humans. He had no idea how they had got here so quickly, but he felt that magic must be involved somehow. Maybe not. Maybe they had infiltrated the woods a long time ago and waited for their opportunity to come forth. He resigned himself to the fact that he might never know and trudged wearily onwards, not even certain he was on the right path.

All he could do was follow the feeling in his heart that this was the right way.

Teclis looked up. Overhead he could see a group of wizards. They zoomed along on floating discs of light, leaving comet trails behind them. They were not elves, that was plain to see even at this distance. They were shorter and squatter – their robes could not conceal that. There was something about them that was deeply disturbing, a suggestion of dark magic worse than any Teclis had ever encountered among humans before. These were followers of Chaos at its most corrupt and wicked.

The thought that such creatures had found their way to the very heart of Avelorn was shocking. Such a thing had not happened since the time of Aenarion. They should not have been here. There should have been no way that they could have progressed so far.

Had they been carried here by daemons, or had they somehow found their way through with their own power? It was possible it was the latter since they could fly, but someone should have stopped them if things had been at all normal. They should not have been able to get here and they should not be travelling around unhindered. It was an insult to the high elves and the people of Ulthuan. Teclis supposed that they had probably come with Morathi and the huge horde that had appeared in the north.

It was clear that they were looking for something. He was not certain whether it was him or not. So far, it seemed like his spells of misdirection had protected him. Even as he watched, the formation split up and the wizards went their own way. They were definitely looking for something. This was the easiest way for them to cover more ground. Of course, it made them more vulnerable to being attacked. Teclis supposed that it was a mark of their confidence that they had done so. They did not feel threatened. He was going to have to see what he could do to change that if he encountered them.

He pushed that thought to one side. He was not here to brawl with wizards. He was here to find Tyrion and the Everqueen and save them if he could. He only wished he had a clearer notion of how.

Dorian watched as the wizards came closer. He could see that they were not dark elves. They were humans, albeit humans of a very strange sort. They were flying through the air above the dark elf army, mounted on some kind of flying disc that seemed to be made of light. As soon as he saw them, he felt the old urge to enslave and dominate come over him.

They descended, circling warily, a glowing order of magic surrounding them which spoke of protective spells. One of his captains looked at him as if waiting for the order to fire.

Dorian shook his head. There would be time enough for that if things turned nasty. He gestured for his own wizards to stand ready in case this was some kind of trick or trap.

A few seconds later, an eerie figure hovered in the air before him, standing on a disc of floating light. The wizard was tall for a human, almost as tall as Dorian himself, and almost as slender. He was wearing a long robe of red and purple and a mask of purple cloth covered most of his face, leaving only the eyes visible below the hood of his robe. His fingers were covered in leather gloves and were unnaturally long for a human's, tipped with nails that were almost as sharp as talons.

'Greetings, druchii, from the great sorceress Morathi.' As soon as he heard Morathi's name, Dorian was instantly wary. He sensed intrigue and something else. Whatever it was, he knew it could not be good. 'Who are you, human?'

'I am Ferik Kasterman and I am the leader of the Coven of Ten.'

'You are a wizard then,' said Dorian, stifling a yawn. The officers nearby laughed.

'Yes, my lord, I am a wizard and dedicated to the great powers of Chaos which we all serve.'

'I serve Malekith, Witch King of Naggaroth and rightful ruler of this island continent of Ulthuan. I do not serve the ruinous powers.'

The wizard tittered. The sound even disturbed Dorian, and he was used to such mad mirth. 'Perhaps not knowingly,' the wizard said. 'But be assured we all serve Chaos, even your king.'

'I could have you put to death quite painfully for suggesting such a thing,' Dorian said. 'Our king serves only himself.'

'Believe as you wish. Some do not know the truth even when it is slapping them in the face.'

'Unless you moderate your tone, *I* will be slapping you in the face.'

'That would be most unwise. You do not wish to provoke the enmity of my mistress.'

'So Morathi has taken humans as lovers now. I suppose it was only to be expected. She has tried everything else.' That got another laugh from the nearby druchii.

'I shall make sure that your words are reported back to her exactly as you said them. I am sure she will be very interested to hear your thoughts on this matter.'

'She will most likely be flattered. She prides herself on her degenerate behaviour. It seems you do not know your mistress as well as you would have us believe.'

Dorian's attitude seemed to have taken the wizard off guard. He did not seem to know quite how to take things. He was obviously used to having people cringe in terror before him. Dorian supposed his attitude must work quite well among the worshippers of Chaos. It was not something that cut any ice with a noble of Naggaroth.

'I have been sent to aid you in your search.' It was Dorian's turn to be taken aback. He had not realised that any beyond his own army knew the truth about what was going on. Of course, it came to him at once, Morathi had her visions. She was able to see the future and things that would happen at a distance. It seemed that she had divined something about what was going on in Avelorn.

'What search would that be?' Dorian asked to give himself time to think.

'You seek the ruler of this land. She is lost in the woods. Once you had her in your grip but she slipped away. An elf with a burning sword took her and now you're desperate to get her back before your master learns of your failure.'

Dorian considered ordering the human killed. He did not like the wizard's tone and he did not like being spoken to in this way. On the other hand, the wizard had just proved that he had been sent by the Hag Queen of Naggaroth in a way that made his credentials indisputable. Dorian suspected that if he put this human to death, Morathi would know, and she would find her own way to take revenge. The wizard was right in one way. She was a very dangerous person to get on the wrong side of. Dorian was also curious not only about what Morathi knew but about how these wizards might help him find the Everqueen. Also, he reasoned, it would be easy enough to have them put to death once they had helped him find Alarielle.

'You say you can help us find her – how?'

'We are wizards. I should have thought the answer was obvious. Magic.'

'I would be interested to see what you can do that my own wizards cannot. I do not lack sorcerers in my service. Even now they close in on those we seek.'

That seemed to take the wizard aback. He had not been expecting such a response. Then the human laughed, as if regaining some fraction of his mad confidence. 'I doubt any of them possess the same gifts from Chaos that I and my coven do. There is a reason our mistress has sent us.'

'Then I will gratefully accept your aid,' said Dorian. 'Be warned though, if you fail us, we will treat you as we would any other human.'

'You are not in any position to make threats, general. We both know that. Now I must go... We will need some prisoners for the sacrifices... Unless, of course, some of your own troops would care to volunteer.'

'Be careful what you say, wizard.'

'Both of us should be that, general.'

⚔ CHAPTER FOURTEEN ⚒

From up ahead Teclis could hear the sounds of battle. The full-throated roar of human warriors mingled with the shouts of elves. He had no idea who was fighting who here, but his trail led towards the fight. He could hear another sound – it was the rushing of water. Cautiously, he moved forwards. He left a trail and took to the trees, moving between them as quietly as he could. It did not really matter that he was not particularly stealthy. He doubted that anyone could hear him over the sounds of battle.

The air was getting moister. It swiftly became clear why. The rushing sounds came from the fast-flowing waters of a great river. He got down on his hands and knees and moved ever closer to the edge, poking his head out from the undergrowth.

By chance, it looked like he had picked a good spot. He could see that a large force of humans were trying to ford the river at this point. There were hundreds of them, mostly tattooed barbarians, with a sprinkling of dark, armoured figures who appeared to be the leaders. They were being ambushed by a force of elves. At least, Teclis thought they were elves. He had some difficulty making them out at first sight. They were extremely well concealed in the undergrowth. What gave them away were the great clouds of arrows emerging from the forest on the far banks of the river.

For once, it looked as if he was about to witness an elven victory. The humans were caught in midstream, slowed down by the fast-flowing currents of the river. They were struggling to get across and get to grips with their hidden attackers.

Already the river was red with blood and corpses floated swiftly downstream. Teclis felt like cheering. It was amazing how swiftly he had been reduced to a barbarism similar to that of the humans. A few months ago it would have been impossible for him to imagine himself doing such a thing. Now it came all too easily.

There was no doubt that the humans were brave. Some of their leaders, mounted on massive armoured steeds, were thrusting their way through the water, bow waves forced ahead of their mounts by the speed of their passage. It looked as if some of them might actually make the far bank.

It seemed that the elves who were fighting with them had realised the same thing as Teclis had. They began to concentrate their fire on the riders. Even the powerfully driven elven shafts bounced off that evil, rune-encrusted armour. Obviously, the mounted Chaos knights were protected by more than mere metal. Some form of magic, similar to the charms that Teclis himself wore, deflected the incoming arrows.

Teclis could hear the inhabitants of Avelorn shouting to each other in Elvish. They were preparing to retreat back into the woods, not wanting to have to face off against such heavily armoured foes. It seemed entirely sensible. They could withdraw in good order, outrun their foes and return to attack them stealthily at night.

Even as the thought crossed his mind, Teclis heard a strange whizzing sound from above. He looked up and saw a sorcerer mounted on a flying disc pass overhead. It was one of the same wizards that he had seen previously. The mage was already starting to cast a spell, bringing down death on the elves in the woods. More of the sorcerers flashed into the air above the ford. Teclis counted ten of them, and all were potent wizards. The air shimmered around them as they summoned the winds of magic.

Clouds of poisonous gas erupted in the forest. Rains of ice and fire descended upon the elven archers. Their screams filled the air. The brutal bellowing of the humans rose in triumph. What had seemed like an imminent defeat had suddenly become a potential victory.

As the hail of arrows ceased, the Chaos worshippers surged forwards across the river, brandishing their weapons, shouting challenges and curses at their enemies.

Teclis wondered whether he should do something. Hundreds of elves were being killed out there. It was not his task, he told himself. He had work of his own to do and he should not take any risks. His brother needed him and the Everqueen needed him. On the other hand, it was possible that those elves over there might be able to help him. Perhaps they even had some news as to the whereabouts of those he sought. More than that, he disliked the sight of those human magicians slaying the inhabitants of Avelorn.

Before he had really thought things through, he was in motion. He spoke a simple charm of dispelling. It sucked all the magic out of the air near three of those wizards who were flying overhead. The discs supporting them in the air suddenly vanished. They fell, suddenly and spectacularly, into the river below. He was not sure whether the fall had killed them or whether they were simply stunned by the descent from such a great height into the chill waters, but he was sure that they were out of the fight at least temporarily.

He spoke another word of power and a bolt of chain lightning knocked another two wizards from the sky. It was all so sudden that those he attacked had no chance to realise what was happening. They continued to invoke their deadly spells upon the elves below them. Perhaps some of the humans had some inkling that something had gone wrong, for they had paused and started to look around.

One or two of the tattooed warriors pointed in his direction. He cursed the visibility magic gave him. Wielding such power made his aura incandescent. Surely there must be some way to do something about that. Not today though. He had too much else to do.

A group of the humans broke off from charging the far bank and came towards him. It was foolish and brave. They had to fight against the current as they tried to swim upstream. More by luck than judgement he had chosen a good place to make his stand. It was something he was going to have to remember in the future. Position was important. Such stuff had always come naturally to Tyrion but it was not something Teclis had ever given much thought to.

The humans were not being stupid, he realised after a moment. The water provided them with some protection against any fire spells he might invoke; they dived beneath its surface, hiding themselves from view for a time before they surfaced. He could see only their savagely twisted faces and their broad, muscular tattooed shoulders – and then only sometimes.

Right now, they were not his main problem. One of the mages had also noticed something was happening and was skimming towards him, low over the surface of the water, his disc undulating over the wavelets like a woodlouse moving over a log.

Simply dispelling the disc would send him into the water, but it would not take him out of the fight as it had done the others. The human mage was chanting a spell, summoning a pulse of destructive Chaotic power to him.

Teclis invoked a spell of shielding just as the Chaos bolt powered

towards him. It impacted the shield spell with awesome destructive force. Teclis had to concentrate to maintain his defences. There
was nothing subtle about the magic the human was using, but it
was effective.

The human smiled as if he sensed he was putting his opponent
under pressure. Teclis laughed aloud at his naivety. With a short
chopping gesture he sent bolts of his own rocketing towards the
human. The mage attempted to dispel them but failed to catch
them all. One of the tiny circular spheres of energy hit the disc and
exploded, shattering the flight spell and taking the human's legs off
at the knees; he fell flopping into the water and vanished beneath
the fast-flowing waters. He did not become visible again.

Enough, Teclis thought, it was time to finish this thing. He spread
his arms wide and pulled a massive amount of magic to him. He
spoke words of elemental fury. The sky darkened, the wind howled,
the branches of the surrounding trees whipped backwards and forwards under its force.

It was as if an army of trees was giving a rustling war cry. The
surface of the river turned white as the wind drove it on. A cloud-
burst of rain descended, putting out the fires on the far side of the
river, wider and wider ripples appeared on the water's surface as
heavier and heavier raindrops hit. The force of the wind increased
till a hurricane ripped through the forest. Thunder cracked. Lightning flashed. A great tree toppled under the force of the wind. The
humans swimming towards him screamed in panic. The sorcerers on their flying discs turned towards Teclis. They struggled to
make progress in the teeth of the daemonic winds, as had been
his intention.

Chain lightning flared again, dancing from disc to disc, overloading the mages' protective spells, causing the flying discs to disappear
in a hail of sparks. It flashed down where armoured Chaos warriors
stood, and danced from massive metallic armoured form to massive metallic armoured form. It impacted in the river and flash-fried
those human warriors who were still trying to cross. They screamed
and died, their bodies floating lifelessly downriver like so many logs.

Within minutes it was over, the mage storm had cleared the Chaos
force from the river. Those humans who had made it to the far side
were killed by the remaining elves. Teclis allowed the sky to clear
and waited by the riverbank. It did not take long for the elves on the
far side to emerge. He waved to them and they waved back. Teclis
invoked a spell that let him walk across the water. He swayed as if

walking on a fluffy mattress but managed to keep his balance. The elves cheered him as he came towards them.

'Greetings, wizard,' their leader shouted. 'We thank you for giving us victory. Hathar Ford is a name the forces of Chaos will long have cause to remember.'

'My name is Teclis. I am a wizard from Hoeth. I come seeking my brother, Tyrion, and the Everqueen. Perhaps you have heard news of them.'

The elf looked wary for a moment. 'Join us in our camp and I will tell you what I have heard. It is not much, but it may be of some help.'

'I thank you for the offer. I have spent a long time wandering these forests on my own. Some company for the night would be welcome.'

Teclis warmed himself by the fire and drank wine, an honoured guest of the elves of Avelorn. For the first time in his life, he felt like a hero. Many elves came over to thank him for his intervention, and many more offered him drinks from their flask or some of their pitifully small supplies of food.

He wandered among them, healing those he could, brewing medicines for the sick, drawing poisonous humours from the wounded. He was touched by their gratitude but he found himself becoming colder and more distant with every word of thanks.

He did not know how to behave in situations like this. He was not used to being popular. No one had commented on his pallor, his thinness or his limp. Everyone present had endured a great deal of hardship – perhaps they merely assumed he had done the same. Or perhaps it was something about all being in this fight together. They seemed prepared to overlook his shortcomings. The only one present dwelling on them was himself, he thought sourly.

Alanor, the leader of these elves, sat down at the fire across from him. 'You saved us all today. We miscalculated. We thought we could hit the Chaos warriors when they crossed Hathar Ford and melt away into the woods before they could catch us. We never counted on Ferik Kasterman and his Coven of Ten showing up.'

'Ferik Kasterman?'

'He was the leader of those sorcerers, a twisted and evil human if ever there was one.'

'It seems like every twisted and evil human in the world has descended on the shores of Ulthuan.'

'You are right,' said Alanor. 'What are they doing here?'

'Helping the druchii, it would seem.'

'Why?'

'Because it suits their daemonic masters to do so.'

'What could they possibly want here?'

Teclis looked at the Avelornian. It seemed impossible that he did not understand what was happening here, but it was quite obviously the case. He sometimes forgot that not every elf was a magician or had access to the libraries at Hoeth. They did not encounter the maker of the Vortex in their dreams either. 'Nothing good,' Teclis said. The truth could not do any good here and would only help spread fear. 'You said you had something to tell me of my brother and the Everqueen...'

'Not very much, I am afraid.'

'Every little helps.'

'I know the druchii are still looking for them. Some of our scouts sneak in so close to their positions that they overhear them talking sometimes. We have our own people looking for them, but it is difficult for them to break through and seek among the dark elf soldiery. The last I heard, some dark wizardry was being used to hunt our queen. I do not know what.'

'They are sure of this?'

'Believe me, if General Dorian or his army had found the Everqueen, we would hear them celebrating all along the Everflow.'

'I guess you are right.'

'The druchii have split their forces in the hunt. It's the only thing that lets us strike at them, but they are getting more cautious. More and more of the humans are finding their way here as well. How are they doing so?'

'Some of them by magic, like Kasterman and his coven. The rest must be coming on foot.'

'How? How can they get through the mountains?'

'I think this is an invasion long planned. They have scouted well. The fortresses are besieged. It would be easy enough for warbands to slip by them under the circumstances.'

'Are things really so bad?'

'Worse.'

'You are not giving me much hope.'

'My brother is the great inspirational leader. I am merely a wizard.'

'There is nothing *merely* about that. You saved all of us today, and we are grateful. And we are grateful to you for helping the wounded as well.'

'Do you know where this General Dorian and his men are cen-tring their hunt?'

'To the east of here. The trail always seems to lead in that direction.'

'Do you have any idea why that would be? What is in that direction?'

'The Winterwood Palace.'

'Could you spare me a guide to take me there?'

'I will ask for volunteers. If no one can do it, I will take you myself, although I think these people need me.'

'If I can find my brother and the Everqueen, I can save them.'

'If you can do that, you will be more than a wizard, you will be a miracle worker.'

'Will you help me?'

'I will do anything within my power.'

'Then let us set out in the morning. Now I need my rest.'

'Sleep well. You have earned it.' Teclis felt a sudden sharp stab-bing pain in his side. He knew that his twin was feeling it too.

'What is it?' Alanor asked.

'Nothing good.'

Urian entered the presence of his ruler for the first time in many decades. It had been a long hard ride to the waystone. He had not trusted the daemon sent to collect him or the strange portal through which they had passed, but now it seemed at last he was here in the great hall the Witch King had commandeered for his headquarters.

He stepped forwards with what he hoped was the correct air of humility. It would have been when he left Naggaroth, but Malekith was given to shifts of mood and formality. Sometimes he wished to be treated as if he were a barbarian potentate, at others with the formal courtesy of an elven lord. There were times when he played the simple warlord that he thought his father had been. There were times when he oversaw revels that would have put Morathi to shame, indulging vices by proxy that he could not any other way.

Today it looked like he was the warlord. He was surrounded by soldiers, generals and mages. Messengers bearing dispatches came and went, and the great mirror through which he communicated with distant corners of his empire stood uncovered in the middle of the chamber.

They had gathered in a palace on the outskirts of Mancastra, the first city of Ulthuan to fall to Malekith personally in centuries. The full panoply of the conqueror had been unfurled. The banners of hundreds of druchii lords hung outside, and pens full of weeping, captured slaves filled streets, plazas and courtyards.

Urian enjoyed the shock that rippled across the vast audience hall as his name was announced. Everyone here thought him dead for centuries. The only ones who knew differently were Malekith and the mages who had transformed him. Malekith rose from his throne and gestured in welcome. It was an almost unheard-of sign of favour. The murmur of conversation died immediately. Everyone smiled at him, knowing that he was, at least for the moment, the favourite of their king and thus a personage to be cultivated while he enjoyed access to Malekith's favour.

'Welcome, Urian,' Malekith boomed. 'Step forwards that we may embrace you.'

Urian did as he was commanded and was raised from the ground by Malekith's vast metal arms. It was the greeting of a comrade for a comrade, a mark of Malekith's approval unheard of in the life-times of any of those present.

'Let everyone hear the words of Malekith the Great,' the Witch King boomed. 'Urian Poisonblade has returned from long and secret service among our rebellious subjects of Ulthuan. All marks of our disfavour are erased. He is our chosen champion, our her-ald, and when he speaks, he speaks with our voice and is to be obeyed. He has been our instrument in matters of policy deep and subtle – he has slain many enemies of our cause. All hail him and salute him as we do.'

The Witch King placed Urian back on the ground and banged his armoured fist against his breastplate in warrior's applause. All of the other druchii present did the same. The women looked at him with smiles, the men with calculation. All of them applauded, for it was their lord's desire. Urian smiled ironically as he accepted it for what it was worth – the mark of a momentary approbation.

Tomorrow, he would find out what Malekith's favour was really worth. Today, he might as well enjoy it.

Urian looked down at the armour Malekith had presented him with. It was, in some ways, a smaller replica of the Witch King's own. It was just as invulnerable. It amplified his strength in a similar way.

'You are my champion now, Urian,' Malekith said. His voice was confiding. They were alone in his huge pavilion aside from the Witch King's servants and slaves. No other druchii nobles were present. 'You must be armed and equipped as such.'

Urian bowed to indicate his gratitude. Malekith gestured for slaves to bring forward his gifts. Two hulking humans, blinded with their eyes sewn shut, brought forth a massive lead-bound, heavy wooden chest. They opened it and Urian saw two long black blades etched with runes that glowed greenly from within.

Malekith indicated that he should pick them up. 'Be most careful with these. Do not touch the blades with your unprotected hands.'

Urian would not have done so, even without the warning. There was something about the way the rune-embossed metal shone that reminded him of warpstone, the terrible substance that some said was the crystallised form of pure Chaos magic.

He took the blades by their hilts and lifted them. They were feather-light and razor-edged; he knew without having to be told that they would cut through the heaviest steel armour. Malekith pointed to the massive armoured slave and made a chopping gesture. Urian tested the edge of the blade on the slave's huge, metal-encased form. As he had suspected it went right through the armour, the flesh and the bone, shearing cleanly through. It had another unexpected side-effect. The victim writhed, his skin blackening where the blade had touched, liquefying and becoming corrupt.

'Now you are Poisonblade indeed,' Malekith said. It seemed like he had actually put some thought into this gift. It was flattering as well as frightening.

'I thank you for the honour you do me, sire,' he said.

'You have earned it. These weapons will overcome the strongest healing magic. Once you inflict a wound, it will not be healed and the victim will die in extreme and very educative agony.'

There was no need to ask who would need to be taught such lessons. Anyone who earned the Witch King's displeasure must be subject to the harshest punishment.

General Dorian awoke knowing that there were others in his tent. He sat bolt upright, reaching for his scabbarded blade. A strong hand grasped his wrist, immobilising it. Another hand covered his mouth. A very sharp blade nicked his throat. Was he the prisoner of some sort of mutant? Did the intruder in his tent have three hands?

'Hush, general,' said a quiet voice near his ear. It belonged to a woman. It was husky and sensual. Despite his position, or perhaps because of it, Dorian found himself becoming aroused.

'The Witch King sends his regards,' said another voice. This one was male, deep and resonant. It sounded somewhat familiar.

'Lord Vidor?' Dorian said. He knew he was in trouble. At least two of Malekith's pet assassins were in his tent – not a good sign.

'None other,' said the male voice. 'Our master has dispatched us to make enquiries.'

'It seems that you have not contacted him,' said the female voice. 'He's curious as to what you have been doing.'

'I have been seeking the Everqueen,' said Dorian.

'There have been rumours,' said Lord Vidor. 'People have been saying that you found the Everqueen and then lost her again.'

Dorian felt his mind racing. He was not sure what to say. He was not sure of what these deadly assassins knew. He was sure this was the way they had intended it. He decided it would probably be safest to tell the truth. 'I captured her as I was ordered to do. I had her bound at my feet.'

'Very erotic,' said a female voice. She sounded as if she meant it.

'We were surrounded by my warriors. There was at least a score of us.'

'And yet she managed to escape?'

'She was rescued. A warrior came in–'

'One warrior?'

'One warrior. He was armed with a magical blade. It burned, like Sunfang, the legendary blade of the first Phoenix King.'

'So one hero entered the pavilion and snatched her from your grasp.'

Dorian could not miss the fact that Lord Vidor knew that the rescue had taken place in the pavilion. Someone had obviously been talking. 'Quite so.'

'And you were the only survivor of this rescue attempt?'

'The guards saw him enter. He was dressed like one of us. He was wearing our armour.'

'Is it possible he was one of us? Is it possible that he was a dark elf? A spy?'

'Of course it is possible, but I don't think it likely. I suspect he was one of the asur. I think he was wearing stolen armour – I think he took it from a warrior he killed.'

'That is certainly a possibility,' said the female voice. Dorian recognised the pattern now. The male voice was mocking and had no sympathy for anything he said. The female voice sounded as if she believed him, as if she wanted to be convinced by his words. It was one of the oldest interrogation techniques in the book. That did not make it any the less effective.

'So, this one warrior, with his legendary magical blade, slaughtered your entire high command and their bodyguards, unbound the Everqueen from where she lay at your feet, and then casually departed from the tent while none of your guards did anything to stop him. Have I stated matters correctly?'

'I would not have placed the emphasis where you have, but yes. He slaughtered everybody present and damn near killed me. I'm sure you've noticed the wounds in my side. Inspect them closely and you will note that they were partially cauterised. His blade did that. He shouted instructions to the guards to confuse them, slit the side of the tent and departed.'

'And what were you doing all this time?' Lord Vidor asked.

'I was bleeding on the carpet of the Everqueen's tent. I suppose I could have attempted to make him slip in a pool of my blood, but I was drifting in and out of consciousness at the time and the thought did not occur to me.'

'When did you come to consciousness?' the female voice asked.

'It was only minutes later. My guards found me and helped revive me. Once I was up and about I gave orders for pursuit, but the Everqueen and the one who rescued her were long gone.'

'I am given to understand that they slaughtered some witch elves on the way out,' Lord Vidor said.

'That is correct,' Dorian said. 'We think the witch elves tried to stop them.'

'And got chopped down for their pains.'

'Quite.'

'So this warrior also killed a dozen witch elves on his way out.'

'So it would seem.'

'It's almost like one of the ancient heroes of legend has come to life and fights against us,' said Lord Vidor, the sarcasm obvious in his voice.

'Almost,' Dorian agreed.

'There are, of course, alternative explanations.'

'I would be glad to hear them.'

'There may well be traitors in your force who have betrayed us to the enemy. They might even be very high in the command chain.' Vidor's tone left no doubt that the suspicion rested on Dorian himself.

'An interesting theory,' said Dorian. 'If a little fanciful.'

'Perhaps then it was simply incompetence on your part or the part of your officers that let the Everqueen escape.'

'Then my officers paid for their incompetence with their lives.'

'You have not.'

'I suspect you are about to change that.'

'No. I am not, general. I believe your story. I have seen the tracks of this warrior. I have noted the fact he was capable of killing a group of our strongest knights all but single-handed.'

There was no need to ask why Lord Vidor had performed the interrogation. No druchii would have passed up such an opportunity to humiliate another. Dorian suppressed his anger. He still had no idea where he stood with these assassins. They might kill him yet. They could do it before his guards could respond to a cry for help, and disappear into the night to escape vengeance.

'You have authorisation from our king?' Dorian asked. He was already trying to work out how to have the pair of them killed if he could. They were not the only ones who were capable of cruelty here.

A black ring, the seal on which Dorian recognised only too well, was shoved under his nose. There was no question of having them assassinated then. Malekith would make him pay very dearly indeed for that.

'We are here to help you recover the Everqueen,' said Lord Vidor.

'That will not be necessary. Our sorcerers have already located them. Even now the net closes around them.'

'Perhaps they will perform another miraculous escape,' said Vidor.

'Their luck cannot last forever.'

'I should certainly hope not. Oh, and in case you have any odd ideas, we are not the only ones our master has sent. If anything happens to us...'

There was no need for him to complete the sentence. 'What can I do for you?' Dorian asked.

They told him.

◄ CHAPTER FIFTEEN ►

'Here,' Alarielle said.

'Where?' Tyrion responded. He could see nothing. This place looked like any other part of the great forest. Overhead huge ancient trees loomed. All around them was the tangle of massive, ancient roots. They were like the hands of wooden giants buried deep and trying to dig themselves out of the earth. The dismal birds circled overhead, cawing and giving away their location. They kept out of direct line of sight though, since Alarielle had taken to shooting them. The birds had pursued them for days, and once again Tyrion could hear the sound of Cold Ones closing in.

Alarielle stood like a statue for a moment and then danced over one of the roots, arms held wide, whirling like a child playing a game trying to make itself dizzy. She seemed unusually elated.

'I am glad you are so happy,' he said, 'but I don't see anything to be happy about. We are still lost in the woods. We are still pursued by enemies. We still have no aid.'

He did not mean to sound so angry. He felt very ill and his side was paining him. He was not sure how much further he could go without rest, and she did not seem tired at all. He was used to being able to go for days without rest if he had to. Now it felt like he could barely go for hours.

'I know where we are,' she said, her exuberance fading with her smile.

'Please, share the information with me!'

'We are at the Winterwood Palace.'

'I don't see any palace.'

'Perhaps that is because you do not know where to look.'

'If you would be so kind as to point it out to me...'

'I am standing on it.'

'I have always heard that the people of Avelorn were backward, but I never thought that even they could mistake a tree for a palace.'

'And I have always heard that the people of Lothern know nothing but stone houses.'

'I don't see any stone houses.'

She jumped down from the great root upon which she was perched and moved amid the tangle of them which formed something like a cave. She vanished from sight into the gloom and did not reappear.

'Alarielle!' Tyrion said. 'Alarielle!'

There was no answer. Tyrion walked forwards into the gloom, hands extended, expecting at any moment to encounter a rocky surface. Nothing happened. He kept walking, and ahead of him he heard mocking laughter.

'Wonderful,' he said. 'A tunnel for a palace. I suppose it's an improvement on a tree root, but not much.'

'Keep walking,' she said. Her voice echoed strangely in the darkness. He walked into something – a dead end. He moved his fingers along it and turned slightly, realising that the tunnel had reached a bend.

He repeated the process a number of times, all the while speaking her name and following the echo of her laughter through the darkness. It receded before him and then it got closer again until, reaching out, he touched her warm flesh in the darkness.

She laughed again and moved away from his grip and then spoke a word in the ancient tongue of the elves. A greenish glow emerged from the air itself and he saw something that took his breath away.

He stood in a vast cave, the roots of the trees thrusting out of the earth like beams in the dome of a great hall, forming a large arch overhead.

In the centre of the chamber was a huge dark pool, the surface rippling as if something in the depths was disturbing it. Clouds of steam emerged from it. The air was warm and slightly humid and it smelled of earth. Tyrion suddenly had a sense that they were deep underground. It was like being in the burrow of some great beast.

After a few further moments of inspection, he decided that was wrong. This place was the product of an elven sensibility. The earth had been shaped and sculpted to make this place exactly what Alarielle claimed it was – a palace.

They had not come through tunnels, they had come through corridors that resembled tunnels. This place looked as if it was the creation of natural formation at first glance, but you could see that the roots of the trees and the nature of the ceiling had actually been arranged to artfully suggest that. In fact, the whole chamber had a symmetry that could only be the product of intelligence at work.

Alarielle smiled. 'I used to love this place,' she said.

'I can understand why,' Tyrion said, surprised to find that he could. The chamber had an odd charm and the more he looked at it, the more he liked it. 'It is like nothing else I have ever seen.'

'We used to come here in the winter, when the snow lay deep on the ground, and be snug as badgers in their burrows. The hot springs keep the place warm. A certain amount of magic has been woven into the place as well.'

'Do you think that those who follow us will be able to detect that magic?'

'I don't know,' she said, looking thoughtful. 'This place was never intended to be a fortress or to be particularly secret. It was a refuge when the winters were hard, a place to come and sing and dance.'

'Let us hope that our pursuers can't spot us with their spells,' Tyrion said.

'This place is also a storehouse,' Alarielle said.

'Good. So we can find food here,' Tyrion said.

'And more than food.'

'What do you mean?'

'Wait and see,' she said.

'With bated breath.'

'We should be able to use the tunnels here to give our feathered pursuers the slip. There is more than one exit from here, and if we are careful and come out under cover of night, we can lose them.' She sounded more confident than she had in a long time. Tyrion wished he shared her confidence. His side hurt more with every step.

They moved deeper into the palace and each chamber was as large as the first, sometimes larger. Tyrion began to feel like a hunted animal that had found its way back to its burrow, a safe haven. He knew that feeling was deceptive though. It was perfectly possible that those who followed them could find this place just as easily as they had.

If that was the case, what Alarielle thought was a safe haven could easily turn out to be a very large trap. He told himself to stop looking on the dark side so much, but he could not help it. His side hurt. He felt weaker than he had at any time in his life; a sense of doom was creeping over him.

He felt as if great danger was approaching and there was nothing he could do to avert it. It had a nightmarish quality that was profoundly depressing. He started to understand his twin's temperament. For a great deal of his life, Teclis had laboured under ill-health of the worst sort. It was no wonder he was so sour.

'You look very thoughtful,' Alarielle said.

'I know that must be disturbing,' Tyrion said. 'But I am capable of it.'

'I never said you were not,' she said.

'I'm sorry, I was thinking about my twin.'

'You are very close to him?'

'Yes.'

'What were you thinking?'

'Nothing,' he said.

'You're not very forthcoming,' she said.

'You said there was more than just food here,' he said. She nodded. She gestured through some archways. Tyrion could see light springing into being within them. It was a greenish glow emitted by what looked like gems. Inside each chamber was a sleeping platform. Near each platform was a chest. Alarielle opened the chest. It contained bedding – furs and sheets.

'You said there are other ways in or out from this place...' Tyrion was curious as to how many escape routes they might have.

'There are many. You're thinking that we may be trapped down here, aren't you?'

'The thought had occurred to me.'

'You need rest,' she said. 'We both do. And this is the safest place we're likely to find in many leagues. We cannot be spotted from the air. It is difficult to find the way in if you don't know how. We will be safe here for a little while.'

'I hope you're right.'

'In any case, there are things here that we can use.'

'Like what?'

'You will see.' Her smile was enigmatic. She seemed to delight in having secret knowledge. He supposed he could not blame her for that. 'Wait here! Rest! I will find it.'

Tyrion wanted to protest. It would be dangerous for them to be split up again. It would be dangerous for her to wander off alone. She simply shook her head.

'I know this place. I grew up here. I can find you and I can get away from anyone who pursues me.'

'What if you're not the only one who knows how to find their way around here?'

'What do you mean?'

'This attack has been supremely well planned. I do not doubt that Malekith has had spies investigating your kingdom for centuries. It is possible that one of them has been here.'

'You're right, but what of it? Unless that person is here right now, the advantage will still be mine.'

'Who's to say that they are not?'

'Then I think I will recognise them and we will know who the traitor is, won't we? Now, stop fretting, lie down. I will be back soon.'

Tyrion lay down on the bed. He felt very dizzy. The room spun but only for a moment. He fell into a pit of sleep. There was nothing he could do to prevent it. If a legion of dark elves charged into the room at that very moment, he would not have had the strength to rise and fight them.

He knew that Alarielle was right. The best thing he could do was sleep and regain his strength, if that was even possible. He was useless to both himself and her in his present condition.

Tyrion woke feeling much better. Alarielle stood in front of him. She was garbed in fresh clothes and carried a tall winged staff which exuded an aura of power that even he could feel. She smiled and looked genuinely happy.

'What is that?' Tyrion asked.

'It is the Moonstaff of Lileath,' she said. 'It is an ancient artefact useful when you're casting spells. I hope that I will be able to find a use for it.'

'I hope you never have to,' said Tyrion.

'There are a number of other things that have proven useful. I found some of my mother's elixirs. I have been feeding them to you while you slept and sometimes when you were awake, although you do not seem to remember that.'

He ran his fingers through his hair and noticed that it was significantly longer. He had acquired the beginning of a beard, which was unusual because normally his chin hair grew very slowly. 'How long have I been asleep?'

'Three days.' She looked worried and he understood why. It was possible that their enemies were creeping up on them even now.

He sat upright very quickly. The motion made him feel very dizzy. He did not let that stop him though. He forced himself to stand although his legs felt weak and he could barely stay upright. He felt very hungry. The pain in his side had diminished somewhat, which was a blessing.

'Lie down!' Alarielle said. 'You need to eat and you need to get back your strength.'

'I have been unconscious for days?'

'Not all of the time. Sometimes you were conscious but raving. I needed to restrain you sometimes. I still have the bruises.'

She showed him her arms. They were patterned with small bruises that looked as if he had gripped them there very hard. 'I am sorry,' he said. 'I did not mean to hurt you.'

'You were not yourself. Think nothing of it.'

He sat down on the bed again and the room seemed to revolve. He lay flat on his stomach and waited for things to settle down. She touched him gently on the shoulder. 'Don't worry, you'll feel better soon.'

'I certainly hope so. I'm not used to this.'

'I found some new clothes. And some new armour. And a proper bow with real arrows. There is one for each of us.'

'You have been busy.'

'There is no need to sound so bitter. I have managed to collect some supplies as well. We won't be any worse off for the time we spent here. We might even be better off.'

'What do you mean?'

'I think the ones pursuing us may have passed us by. I saw no sign of them when I went up to take a look.'

'You saw no sign of them? When you went up to take a look? What were you thinking?'

'I was thinking that we need to know what was going on. I was thinking that *I* need to know what is going on. And I am thinking that I am your queen and it is not your place to use that tone of voice with me.'

'You could have got yourself killed or captured.'

'Why? Because you were not there? You were unconscious. I doubt that you could have protected me.'

'It seems like you have been protecting me rather than vice versa.'

'I would not be here now if it had not been for you. I am grateful. And I'm going to need your help again, if we are to get out of here alive.' She sounded a little embarrassed and a little defensive.

'I need something to eat,' he said, 'if it is not beneath your royal dignity to serve me.'

'I think I might stoop to that,' she said. 'Just don't expect it to become a habit.'

He could see that she had already prepared waybread and cold meat. He began to eat slowly. The magic in the food lent him some strength and settled his stomach. A few moments later he felt himself sinking back into sleep. The Everqueen seemed to be singing a song. It sounded like a lullaby, but there was magic in it. He wondered what it was for.

Tyrion woke, sensing the presence of someone near. He looked around and saw Alarielle stretched beside him, fast asleep. With her eyes closed she looked much younger and much more vulnerable. He rose as softly as he could and padded across the chamber, head cocked to one side, listening for the presence of intruders.

He found clean new clothes in a neat pile lying near the bed. He donned the underwear, the linen shirts and then the leather jerkin and trousers of an Avelorn woods ranger. It felt more natural and more comfortable than the dark elf equipment that he had been wearing for so long before they came to this place.

He had to lace up the shirt and jerkin very gently because his wound still pained him – less than it had for some time, but still he sensed that it had the potential to become agonising. It was only a matter of time before the poison in it claimed his life.

So far, nothing that Alarielle had attempted had managed to clear his system of the witch elf's deadly venom. He strapped Sunfang onto his belt and did some gentle stretching exercises. The waybread and the elixirs had done their work. He no longer felt weak.

He padded through the tunnel-corridors of the Winterwood Palace. The place was vast and empty. The air was damp but warm. He felt himself starting to sweat, but it was a natural sweat, not the sweat of fever. He understood Alarielle's need to get out of this place. He felt a craving for fresh air himself. He thought that he could find his way back to the chamber in which the Everqueen slept. He pushed on, back along the route that had taken them to the chamber in the first place. He was heading for the exit.

As he did so, from up ahead he heard the sound of voices, speaking in the accents of Naggaroth. Swiftly, he backed away along the corridor and made his way back to the sleeping chamber. He shook Alarielle. She murmured something and turned over in her sleep. He shook again, more violently this time, and put his hand over her mouth so that she would not make any loud noises. She started to struggle against him, as if she feared what he was doing.

'Hush,' he whispered. 'They have found us.'

She nodded understanding and he took his hand off her mouth, still aware of the warmth of her breath against his palm. 'Where are they?'

'Down the corridor.'

'How many?'

'I did not wait to see. More than one.'

'I'm surprised you did not just slaughter them.'

'I prefer having you as an audience while I perform my heroics.'

'I am gratified to find that I have some part in your life.'

She spoke softly and in a joking tone, but he could see the fear in her eyes. She had the hunted, wild beast look to her again. It could not be pleasant, knowing that Malekith wanted you as his prisoner.

'We need to get going. You'll have to show me the other way out. We can't go back the way we got in.'

'What if they are watching the other exits?'

'That's a chance we will just have to take.'

Alarielle strapped the Moonstaff to her back, and snatched up her bow and her quiver of arrows. 'This way,' she said.

Tyrion followed her out into the corridor. He glanced right to make sure that none of the intruders had found them and then raced off after her.

'There is another way out,' Alarielle said. 'We just need to–'

Tyrion pushed her back into the sleeping chamber. A crossbow bolt flashed past her head. He heard one dark elf shout at the other, 'Don't shoot, idiot! The reward is greater for taking her alive.'

Tyrion stepped back into the chamber. They were trapped. There was no other way out. The dark elves could simply shoot them if they stepped out into the corridor. All they had to do was wait and bring up more soldiers.

'We waited too long. I'm sorry,' said the Everqueen.

'It's not your fault,' Tyrion said. 'If I had not become sick...'

'I could give myself up and they would not hurt you,' Alarielle said. Tyrion shook his head. He heard footsteps coming closer down the corridor. It would not be long now.

He drew Sunfang. Caledor's magic sword blazed brightly in his hand. He had left the doorway open. A dark elf, armoured and carrying a crossbow, appeared in it. Behind him there was another, with even more out of sight. Tyrion sprang forwards, even as the druchii aimed. Sunfang described a blazing arc downwards and smashed through the crossbow, setting it alight, before burying itself in the dark elf's chest.

Slowed by his wound, Tyrion could not attack the second dark elf before he had struck a blow. Tyrion raised his blade to parry and the dark elf stepped back instinctively, flinching before the flame. The two blades clashed together.

Tyrion struck. The dark elf fell. He tumbled backwards into his friends, getting tangled in them. Tyrion pressed his advantage and stepped forwards, claiming another victim.

'Get out! Run!' he shouted. Alarielle stepped into the corridor behind him. He sensed her presence and roared, 'Get going! I'll be right behind you.'

He could see that there were only a few more dark elves left, and in the confusion they were panicking. Disciplined as they were, they were not used to fighting in these narrow tunnels deep beneath the earth against a foe with a magical blade.

Several of them had already turned and run. The last one faced Tyrion, only to be chopped down with one brutal stroke. Tyrion considered pursuing the fleeing dark elves, but that would mean losing contact with Alarielle; he was not going to let that happen again. He turned and was surprised to see that she was still there, aiming her bow. Tyrion stepped to one side. She let loose her arrow and was rewarded with a scream from the far end of the corridor.

'Now they'll know that they're not the only ones who can shoot,' she said.

'Don't you do anything that you're told?' Tyrion asked. She shrugged.

'You looked like you could use the help.'

He grabbed her by the wrist and tugged her off down the corridor, regretting it immediately when the wound in his side began to ache.

'Don't you want to know where we are going?' she asked.

'Why don't you tell me as we run?'

Alarielle ran like a frightened deer, speeding along, turning left and then right decisively as if she knew exactly where she was going.

It occurred to Tyrion that if the dark elves had found other entrances, there might well be a problem. They might run headlong into their pursuers.

The ceilings became lower. Tyrion had to crouch in order to keep going. Ahead of them, he could see a wooden doorway. It looked old and was covered in moss. The air here was colder and damper than it had been, and he felt as if the outside world was closer.

She reached out and touched the door, muttering a word of

command. It swung open even before Tyrion reached it. A draught of cold air hit him in the face and he caught sight of shadows and gloom outside. It came as a shock – he had somehow been expecting to see daylight when the door opened, and he realised now that it was night.

Alarielle paused for a moment and listened. Tyrion realised that she was learning caution. She had not bolted straight out into the night as perhaps she might have been inclined to do only a few days before.

He felt winded as he had never done in the past, and he realised that his wound and the poison in it were still affecting him greatly. He felt his face flush. He was not used to being the weakest person present and he found it both irritating and embarrassing.

He tried to listen over the sound of his own rough breathing, but he could hear nothing. Alarielle waited for a few heartbeats, looked at him, nodded and gestured to him to go ahead. He drew his dagger, not wanting to draw Sunfang in case the flame of the blade gave away their position to any watchers. He advanced, balanced on the balls of his feet, ready to strike at anybody waiting in ambush, but there was no one.

He surveyed the bushes close at hand and saw no waiting enemy. They had emerged onto a wooded slope. Beneath them was a river. It was not as wide as the Everflow and there was a path of stepping stones just below them, doubtless put there deliberately to service this doorway into the palace. He gestured for her to follow him, and they both ran down the hill until they reached the stepping stones and crossed the river.

He kept glancing to left and right, suspecting that every shadow might conceal a watching archer, expecting at any moment to feel a crossbow bolt plunge into his chest. He kept low, squatting down to provide the smallest possible silhouette, to make himself the most difficult target he could. Copying his action, Alarielle did the same.

Where were the dark elves? Surely they must be out there somewhere. He felt as if he was walking into a vast trap of which he did not know the full extent.

There must be enemies out there, for not all of the dark elves could have entered the palace. That would be foolish. There must be scouts here somewhere, watching things, hoping to prevent their escape. It was what he would have done if he was leading the dark elves, and it would be foolish to assume that their leader was any less competent than he was.

Alarielle held her bow, ready to shoot any dark elf she saw. He realised she had come a very long way in a very short time. She was no longer the scared girl he had rescued. Perhaps she never had been. Perhaps that had only been the way he perceived her.

They had to come to a decision, he realised. They could not just stand here waiting like frightened rabbits for the dark elves to pick them up. They needed to move.

Something quivered in the ground at his feet. A crossbow bolt. He looked around to see who had fired it. An arrow whizzed past his ear and into a bush. A scream rang out through the night. Alarielle's shot had found its target.

Answering cries echoed through the night. They were surrounded.

─◄ CHAPTER SIXTEEN ►─

She walked along a beach of black sand. Black gulls shrieked overhead, sometimes coming to rest on oddly shaped dunes. It took her a few moments to realise that the dunes were made of skulls, bones and ancient rotting armour. She was looking for something or someone she had lost a long time ago. She had been looking for ages and she had not found it. She feared she never would, no matter how hard she tried.

'Morathi...' The voice might have been the cold wind that blew in from the sea; it was just as monotonous, just as cold and just as cutting. Her cloak fluttered in the wind. A strand of her curly black hair escaped from beneath her hood. She turned around and could not see who spoke.

'Morathi...' She glanced back over her shoulder and still no one was there. Perhaps it was a ghost who taunted her. This was a haunted land. She felt the nearness of the Black Sword. It was a hideous presence, terrifying in its fatal potential and yet oddly reassuring. It reminded her of Aenarion. Its aura had always marked his presence. He had not been separated from the weapon in all the time she had known him.

Perhaps that was what brought her here so often. Perhaps something of him still lingered, unable to part from the blade even in death. She felt a certain bitterness. She had always thought the blade was more his mistress than she was. It was a more terrible rival than any mere elf woman could have been.

'Morathi...' She thought she had identified the source of the voice now, and began to follow it through the dunes of bones and wreckage, determined to confront whoever was its source and make it pay for mocking her.

She found him standing amid the rubble of some ancient broken shrine. The stone face of Khaela Mensha Khaine looked down upon him as he studied his reflection in the stagnant, scummy waters of the font. His back was to her but even before he turned to face her, she knew him.

His skin was near translucent. The muscles writhed below it like worms in a corpse. His eyes were mere pools of black light. His fingers were claws. He looked like an animated skeleton smeared with a thin layer of flesh. The expression on his face was a calm madness personified.

'Death does not agree with you, Caledor,' Morathi said. His lips quirked in a quiet, mad smile.

'I did not need you to tell me that, Morathi. He tells me that himself.' She studied him closely. His limbs twitched. He licked his lips. He looked shrunken and twisted and lonely.

'You have gone mad, old ghost. Avaunt, begone and trouble my dreams no more.'

'This is more than a dream, Morathi. You know that. You sleep surrounded by wards to shield your thoughts. And yet I am here. Why do you think that is?'

'You grow lonely in your dotage, perhaps.'

'You are in my land now, Morathi. In the place I made. You should be careful what you say, careful what you think...'

She started. What the wizard said was true. He should not be in her dreams and yet he was. Who knew what else he was capable of? In life, there never had been another mage as subtle and powerful as Caledor. Who knew what he was capable of in death. Best be wary.

'You have something to say to me, Caledor, so say it and begone!'

'I know why you have come to Ulthuan. I know why you lead your army of barbarian Chaos worshippers. I will not allow it, Morathi.'

'What can you do to stop me? You are trapped with all your former students at the heart of the Vortex. You cannot leave it or it will collapse, and that will serve my purposes just as well.'

'Are you sure?' In truth she was not, but it would never do to let him know that, so she kept quiet.

'Listen to me, Morathi, and listen well... I created the Vortex, and before I let you use it for your twisted purposes I will destroy it myself.'

'Then you are as mad as I always suspected...'

'No. The destruction will liberate an enormous amount of magical energy and I will use it for one purpose...'

'And what would that be?'

'Though it be the last thing I do, I will slay you. On this you have my word.'

The most frightening thing was the way he said it. There was no menace in his voice, just sorrow, regret and absolutely no doubt that it would happen if he so willed it.

Looking at him now, she recalled exactly who and what he was – the mage who had beaten back the greatest invasion of Chaos the world had ever known, who had shackled a continent with his power, whose will, even in death, preserved the spell that preserved the world.

Gazing upon the ancient ghost, Morathi discovered, much to her surprise, that there was still a being in this world capable of frightening her. She awoke covered in cold sweat, her scream awakening the barbarian lovers who shared her bed.

Caledor picked up the piece that represented Morathi and removed it from the board, then slumped forwards in his chair. His confrontation with the sorceress had left him feeling weary. It had been a task of near-insuperable difficulty to penetrate the wards surrounding her dreams. Talking with her had been worse.

Death looked at him and smiled. 'An excellent move. I thought your bluff about destroying the Vortex was masterful.'

'It was not a bluff,' said Caledor. 'I never make a threat I am not prepared to keep.'

'Interesting,' said Death. 'I will remember that.'

Caledor feared he had revealed far more than he had intended to or was wise. Death reached down and lifted another piece.

'You are doing what?' Malekith bellowed, barely able to restrain himself from rising from his throne. In the mirror, his mother shrugged. She looked pale and dishevelled and there was something in her expression at odds with her normal perfect poise and self-possession.

'I am leaving for Naggaroth.'

'You cannot do that! I forbid it!' His mother looked frightened, but not of him.

'I think you will find I have already done it.'

'Leaving our northern allies leaderless.'

Her smile was full of sweet malice. 'They are not exactly leaderless. They never were. They follow their own chieftains and warlords.'

'What new treachery is this, mother?'

'No treachery, my son, I swear it.' She sounded completely sincere, but then she always did when she wanted to.

'Then why abandon our human catspaws now and retreat when everything is going well?'

She gazed around nervously, that alone told him that something was wrong. Under normal circumstances, she would never allow the slightest trace of weakness to show. 'Caledor has spoken to me.'

'It must have been quite a conversation.'

'He told me he will kill me, if I proceed.'

'And you are still frightened of that ancient ghost?'

'You did not see him, my son. He has changed. I think he is mad.'

'And who would not be, imprisoned within the Vortex for six millennia?' His mother smiled ironically. She was clearly thinking that he had been imprisoned within his armour for almost as much time, although she did not say it. She did not need to. He knew her that well.

'You do not understand, Malekith. He spoke to me. While I slept. While my dreams were warded, through my strongest protective spells.'

That was troubling. The defences his mother had woven around her were every bit as strong as his own. 'He has not taken the trouble to appear to me. Are you implying he considers you more important than me?' There was a dangerous edge to his voice now.

'No. Who knows why he does anything? He defied your father when it suited him. Even in life he was a law unto himself. In death...'

Malekith considered her words and suddenly he understood. He knew why the ancient mage would threaten his mother and not him. 'Mother, if you have been tampering with his work, I swear to you that if he does not kill you, I will do it myself.'

'You may find that more difficult than you imagine.'

'And yet clearly you do not think that Caledor would have any trouble with that.'

'You do not yet have the power he has.'

'And what would that be?'

'The power to destroy everything that exists.'

Malekith slumped back into his throne and considered what she had said. It was true. He lacked the power of that ancient wizard, and while he did it would always hang over his head. He refused to acknowledge that anyone had that right, even the gods. And yet that was a problem for another day.

'Flee back to your kennel then, mother. When I have completed the conquest of Ulthuan, you and I will have words.'

'I wish you luck with that, my son, but I fear there are older and stronger powers working against you.'

The mirror went blank, leaving Malekith contemplating his own massive armoured reflection. He feared his mother was right. Everything was starting to unravel, all of his carefully woven plans. The question was, why? Who stood to gain from that? And what could he do in response?

Malekith faced the mirror for a long time, brooding. His mother's defection was an immediate problem. Without her to restrain them, her barbarian horde would fragment and rampage across northern Ulthuan. In itself that was no great problem, as he had once told her it would simply make it easier to deal with them permanently when the time came. However, that time was not here yet. He still needed their massive manpower to tie down the asur armies in the north. As things stood it was perfectly possible they might turn on his own troops and he would be facing a double threat.

Beyond that, he had no idea what their daemonic masters would put them up to. They needed to be restrained and either brought to heel or destroyed. There was only one person who was capable of doing that, who had the power and the charisma to force them to obey, and that was himself. He would need to gather his force, leave a garrison in Mancastra and head east to take control of the situation. N'Kari would open the gate to take his army there.

It niggled at him, being forced to abandon his carefully laid plans, and yet he had always known that such a situation might arise. No plan ever survived contact with the foe.

He summoned aides and began bellowing orders for departure. He would bring the rebellious barbarians to heel, then hunt down the Everqueen if need be.

◀ CHAPTER SEVENTEEN ▶

'Be still!' Tyrion said. Alarielle froze in place, becoming just another shadow. Tyrion listened – he could hear soldiers moving all around, but that was not what he was seeking. He knew there would be others out there, assassins, scouts and dark elf warriors, all capable of moving silently through the night. They would be the real danger.

He gestured with his left hand for Alarielle to start to move again. She did so slowly, like a hunter stalking a dangerous beast. He did the same, moving as cautiously as he could, paying as much attention to his surroundings as his senses would allow. She was keeping an arrow nocked in her bow. He could understand the reassurance that having a ready weapon brought. He dared not draw Sunfang in case the sudden blaze of light drew attention to them. Instead he kept a long hunting knife available in his right hand.

The woods around them were thick. The undergrowth was dense. He gestured for Alarielle to start moving through the undergrowth. He followed her, wriggling on his belly, pushing aside twigs and leafy stalks to keep them away from his eyes. The heavy tread of moving soldiers passed nearby. They were so close that Tyrion could hear them talking.

'I don't think they came this way,' said one voice.

'That would be our bad luck,' said another, obviously more authoritative. 'We could live on the bounty for the rest of our lives if we are the ones who find them.'

'I am never that lucky,' said the first speaker.

'Perhaps you should both be more attentive,' said a third voice, more sinister and quiet. What was startling was the fact that it had come from a point where Tyrion had not expected to hear anyone speak. Its owner was obviously capable of moving with great stealth. How long had he been there? Had he seen the fugitives as they took cover?

'Someone has been this way,' it said. 'Look at these tracks!'

'I don't see any.'

'You've obviously never stalked wolves in the wastelands of Naggaroth.'

'No, Kalysar, I was too busy fighting Chaos warriors.'

'These tracks were not made by Chaos warriors. They were not made by dark elves either. You can see these were made by leather moccasins, the sort that the natives of Avelorn wear.'

'Maybe they were made by hunters. Maybe they were made by scouts.'

'In that case you'd better keep your eyes open, hadn't you? And maybe, just maybe, they were made by the people we are looking for.'

Tyrion lay so close to the Everqueen that he could feel her heart pounding. He realised that they were not in a good position. It would be difficult to rise and fight while concealed in the undergrowth. He was lying flat on his belly. There was no way he could dodge if someone decided to put his spear through him.

'Maybe you should show your skill as a tracker, Kalysar,' said the second of the speakers, whom Tyrion was starting to believe was an officer. 'Maybe you can help us all get our hands on the general's gold.'

'I'll do just that if you give me some space and stop yakking. I need to concentrate.'

Tyrion tapped the Everqueen on the shoulder and gestured for her to move. Every wriggle, every furtive movement that they made sounded as loud as the blare of trumpets in his ear. It seemed impossible that the dark elf soldiers could not hear them as they moved. Behind him he could hear the faint ring of metal on metal as armoured soldiers moved around.

'Idiot!' Kalysar said. 'You've obscured the tracks with your booted feet.'

'At least we know someone passed this way,' said the officer. 'We should report that.'

Tyrion felt some relief. He felt his muscles begin to loosen and only then did he realise how tense he had been. He and Alarielle kept moving through the undergrowth and eventually emerged from the bushes, onto another game trail.

'That was a little too close for comfort,' Alarielle said with a tentative smile. She was trying to conceal her fear and doing it better than most.

'Best keep moving,' Tyrion said. 'There will be plenty more of the sons of Naggaroth about. We may not be so lucky next time.'

Alarielle nodded and started to lope along the trail, moving as quickly as was compatible with being quiet. She was definitely better at this than he was, Tyrion thought. It was an unusual sensation, meeting anybody who was better at anything. He was glad of it at that moment.

Tyrion crouched in the bush, watching another company of dark elves pass. There were dozens of the tall warriors, garbed in mail, clutching crossbows and longswords. They moved through the woods with the swaggering ease of conquerors.

Over the past few days, as they had followed the trail eastwards, it became obvious how lucky they were. They had to move very carefully, keeping always to the undergrowth for fear of daemonic birds. The woods were full of dark elves. They were thrown around the Winterwood Palace in a wide net. There were scores of companies amounting to thousands of elves. There seemed to be no doubt that the druchii had well and truly found their trail. A whole army had been deployed in pursuit of them.

He felt oddly vulnerable crouched down here in a hollow between the trees, with only a thin shield of leaves between him and detection. It seemed impossible that one of the druchii would not sense the pressure of Tyrion's gaze upon him and look round and give the signal that would result in his death and Alarielle's capture.

Several times they had turned at bay and attempted to double back through enemy lines, but each time the enemy had swept forwards and they had been forced back onto the eastward path. If this kept up they would eventually be forced out of Avelorn entirely. With no trees in which to hide, it would not take long for the dark elves to find them.

In the distance he heard the roar of a Cold One. They needed to get moving again soon, before the great lizard got close enough to catch their scent. Alarielle gestured for him to remain in place. It would not do to move now and attract the attention of the passing soldiers.

Tyrion's side ached. He was petrified that he would fall into another feverish faint while there were enemies close. There were times when he was barely strong enough to draw Sunfang, and the intervals of strength and ease of movement came and went with worrying rapidity.

He felt his fingers drumming against the hilt of the blade. It was a nervous tic that had emerged more and more often recently. Cold sweat ran down his forehead. He fought down the almost irresistible urge to cough. His throat felt dry. He wanted to unscrew the top from the flask of brackish water on his belt and drink it all down. Perhaps that would relieve the irritation in his desert-dry throat.

The Cold One's roar sounded again and was answered from a spot to the south of them. They had best not go that way then, he thought. A few moments later, he felt a hand shaking him.

'Tyrion! Tyrion!' Alarielle's voice held a hint of fear. 'Wake up. Move! They've gone and we need to do the same.'

Tyrion realised that he had been lost in a reverie of thoughts and plans for their escape. He had lost contact with his surroundings and he had no idea for how long. It was only going to get worse.

'Leave me,' he said. 'You will have a better chance on your own.'

It came to him then that this had been true for a long time. He was nothing but a liability to her. She might even have been able to escape by now if it were not for him. She was surely much better at woodcraft than any dark elf they had met.

'We will both get out of this together,' she said. 'We started it together and we will finish it together.'

He wanted to tell her to move, that she was not being sensible, but he could not find the energy. He understood why she was doing this as well. He would not have abandoned a comrade either. He forced himself to rise to his feet. The ground rocked. It felt like an earthquake.

'It's like being on the deck of a ship in a storm,' he said, then realised that she was not having the same difficulty. It was the fever, the wound and the fever.

Just put one foot in front of the other, he told himself. Ignore the movements of the earth. This will pass.

'There is a strange stink in the air,' Tyrion said. It was true too. It was the sort of smell he associated with old, damp houses in Lothern, with sickness and plague among humans, with rot. It was like the scent of waste composting in rubbish heaps in a human town mingled with the rotting jungle smell of a Lustrian swamp. He wondered for a moment whether it was the fever. The air seemed to be getting hotter, and there were more biting insects present. There was something else too, something that made his skin tingle in an unwholesome way.

A frown crossed Alarielle's face. 'We don't have much choice,' she said.

'Much choice about what?'

'We need to go on. The druchii are too close for us to go any other way.'

'I know. What has that got to do with the smell, or the bugs in the air for that matter?'

'If we follow this path we will come to the Darkwood.'

'I am guessing it is not called that because it is a place where flowers grow and baby deer frolic through sweet-scented glades.'

'Perceptive as ever, Prince Tyrion. It is a place where the taint of Chaos and the old dark magics are still strong. There are parts of Avelorn that have been that way since the Great Chaos Incursion in the time of Aenarion.'

'It sounds... interesting,' he said.

'Most people would say fearsome.'

'We are heroes, you and I, your serenity. We shall dare these dark lands.'

She smiled wanly. 'As you say.'

'What is this?' Tyrion asked. He glanced around at the forest with dazed eyes. The pain in his side was getting worse again. The poisoned wound that the witch elf had given him was getting far worse. He felt as if soon it would be impossible for him to go on. He gritted his teeth and forced one foot in front of the other. He was not going to give up. Not now. Not ever.

There was something about this part of the forest that daunted him, though. The trees were older and larger. Some of them were as thick around the bole as the tower of an ancient castle. Many of them were taller than any trees he had seen since he left the jungles of Lustria. Moss covered all of them like a thick fur. Thick vines dangled from the branches. Enormous mushrooms crowded the shadows beneath the ancient leaves. Some of them even clung to the sides of the trees parasitically. Over everything hung an aura of vast age. The air seemed thick and close. It felt damp and fusty. In the distance, the leaves and branches seemed to sway even though there was no wind. It was as if some vast invisible monster was making its way through the ancient forest.

'This is the oldest part of the forest of Avelorn,' Alarielle said. She looked thoughtful. 'There are many strange stories about this part of the wood. Even my people shun it. Not much has changed in there since ancient times. Since the first wars with Chaos.'

'Is it haunted?'

'Who knows. Powerful magic scorched these woods once. In some parts, ancient evil clings even to this day. The taint of Chaos causes mutation. Monsters are often born in these parts. They come out and hunt sometimes and it often takes a great effort to drive them back.'

'I have heard much of the great hunts of Avelorn. I was wondering what you used for prey.'

'Manticores, hippogriffs, half-dragons and other strange things.'

'It does not seem as if we have much choice though. We're going to have to enter these woods if we are to escape our pursuers.'

'Unfortunately, Prince Tyrion, you are correct. I would have preferred to avoid this part of the woods if we could, but we have no choice.'

'Then we had better hope that the monsters are all asleep or hunting for dark elves in other parts of the woods.'

'I suspect that we could not be that lucky,' Alarielle said. Tyrion did not doubt that she was correct in this.

They followed the path deeper into the woods and the taint of old, wild magic became even stronger and more obvious. Even Tyrion could sense it in the air. It went a long way towards explaining the feeling of closeness. He found that he had difficulty in breathing. When he listened closely he could hear a sound that was like the distant buzzing of a huge cloud of flies. Sometimes, he could have sworn that he was surrounded by them. He felt as if their tiny wings were tickling his face, but there were no flies or any other insects that he could see.

Alarielle looked as if the weight of the world was pressing down on her shoulders. There was something in the air that made her look as nauseated as Tyrion felt. He did not doubt that it was the aura of corrupt magic that surrounded them. If it could affect someone even as normally insensitive as he was, what must it be like for she who was a natural sorcerer?

He reached out and touched her shoulder and she flinched a little but did not draw away. 'What is wrong?'

'This part of the land is very sick,' she said. 'And it affects me.'

'Perhaps we should not have come here. Perhaps we should go back.'

'If we did that, we would merely be running into the arms of Malekith and his followers. There would be no escape for either of us then.' Tyrion knew that she was correct and that there was nothing he could say that she had not already thought about.

As they pushed on deep into the forest, the pain in his side intensified. It was as if something in the wound was drawing strength from the corruption of their surroundings. He mentioned his suspicions to Alarielle.

'It is possible,' she said. 'It is not mere poison that is in that wound. There is ancient dark magic. I curse the person that made that blade. What sort of smith would forge such a weapon?'

'A druchii one,' Tyrion said.

'It was a rhetorical question, Prince Tyrion,' Alarielle said.

'It deserved an answer. I have seen Naggaroth. I have fought against its people. I don't think they are sane as we measure sanity.'

'You're not the first to say this.'

'Nonetheless, it is the truth. Think about those witch elves that we met. They were mad.'

'They are the worst of their kind,' Alarielle said.

'Far from it. In them the madness is merely more obvious. In the others, it runs deep and strong.'

'Perhaps they shall find these woods more to their liking than I do,' she said. She meant it as a joke, but her glance flickered around nervously.

'We can't go back,' said Tyrion, glancing over his shoulder. Perhaps it was a trick of the shadows or his own feverishness, but he thought he saw someone moving there. 'We need to move on.'

'Yes,' she said. She raised the Moonstaff of Lileath. A faint aura of light played around it. 'I wish I could use this properly.'

'If I get to feeling much worse, I can use it to lean on.'

Something padded along softly in the shadows behind them.

⟨ CHAPTER EIGHTEEN ⟩

Slime oozed from the bark of the trees. In places it formed bubbles inside of which huge mutated woodlice twisted and fretted. Large, segmented, multi-legged creatures scuttled through the branches above them. The shape of their bodies flowed to conform to the surface they moved over. They were eyeless, with long twitching feelers. So far they had not attacked, but their presence made Tyrion feel uncomfortable. It was like turning over a huge log and having elf-sized monsters scuttle out.

Alarielle followed a path that was invisible to him. 'How do you know where we are going?' Tyrion asked.

'The rangers have left signs.' She pointed to a small mark chipped in the trees. 'These paths are safe, or at least they were when my people last passed this way.'

'That could have changed then?'

'Almost certainly. Not many people come here.'

Tyrion looked at what seemed like a huge spider web, draped between branches. Something large twitched inside a cocoon of silk. It was trapped up there. 'Why would anybody come here?'

'There are certain herbs that can be sold to Lothern merchants for great sums of money. I understand they have alchemical uses.'

'I can't imagine any medicine made from this stuff would have a beneficial effect.'

'I don't think they make medicine from it. I think it is used for sorcery and certain unclean rituals. The rangers try and stop people taking it. That is why they come here, and to hunt the monsters that emerge from the place.'

Tyrion glanced around again. 'That sounds exciting.'

'Perhaps too exciting for me,' she said. A growl sounded somewhere in the distance. It bore some resemblance to the sound made by the big cats Tyrion had heard in the jungles of Lustria.

'As I was saying,' she said. She stowed the staff on her back and took up her bow.

'It sounds like a jaguar,' Tyrion said.

'We never see those in Avelorn,' she said. 'If we are lucky it will be a ghost panther or a sabretooth. If we are not...'

'What?'

'Some mutant monster tainted by old magic.'

They advanced. The trees closed in overhead. The fungi grew taller than Tyrion's head and began to emit an eldritch, spectral glow like the ghostly lights that lead travellers astray in marshes.

'I always pictured Avelorn as a land of beauty and glory and brilliant sunshine,' Tyrion said. 'That's how the legends always portray it.'

'The legends usually miss out the darker parts,' she said. 'But they have always been here, for as long as I can remember, and those memories go very deep.'

The growling sound came again, but this time the note had changed. There was a yammering quality to it and what might even have been words chanted by a madman, as if some odd hybrid of maniac and predatory beast was giving vent to its hunger.

'I don't think that's a cat,' Tyrion said.

'We shall make a woods ranger out of you yet,' the Everqueen replied.

'It's following us,' Tyrion said.

'Yes,' Alarielle said. 'And it is not making any effort to cover up the fact.'

She was right. They could hear the massive creature passing through the woods behind them, grunting and grumbling and growling to itself. Occasionally when Tyrion turned, he could see a monstrous form pushing through the undergrowth. There were times when he thought he caught sight of a leonine head with human features and hair like a mane. Its eyes caught the light like those of a cat. It might have been a giant crawling very quickly, or a massive beast, or a creature that was some combination of both.

'What is it waiting for? If it is going to attack, why does it not do so?'

'I would imagine that our rangers have taught it to be wary of armed elves.'

'Not too wary. Otherwise it would not be on our trail.'

'Perhaps it is waiting for us to make camp, to fall asleep.'

'It would have been cleverer for it not to show itself then.'

'No one ever said manticores were very bright.'

'That is what you think it is then?' Tyrion said.

'Yes. With that body and that face I don't think it could be anything else.'

'Will it have poisoned spikes on its tail that it can fire like a mangonel?'

'It might. It's a mutant, a creature of Chaos. For all we know it might squirt intoxicating wine from its tail.'

'That seems a tad unlikely.'

'My basic point stands.'

'We shall soon know if it plans on attacking us when we make camp. It is getting dark.'

'Yes, and none of these trees look particularly homely.'

Tyrion looked at the twisted and mutated plants surrounding them. Slime coated many of them and dripped in webs from their branches. From some of them depended globes of mucus within which things wriggled. All of the undergrowth had a blotched unhealthy look.

'This looks like something you would expect to find in the Chaos Wastes,' Alarielle said.

'The Wastes are not so fertile.'

'You have been there?'

Tyrion nodded, distractedly. He was looking for a place to make camp that was not too close to the loathsome trees. He did not fancy sleeping anywhere near them.

'You have travelled far, Prince Tyrion.'

'My home is Lothern,' he said. 'From there fleets sail to every corner of the world.'

'I have never left Avelorn.'

'You are young. More so than I.'

'The Everqueen leaves Avelorn only under the most desperate of circumstances.'

'Is there any reason for that?'

'Her power is tied to the place. The farther from it she goes... I go... the less it becomes. And at the moment, the power is not too great anyway.'

'I did not know that.'

'It is not something that is made common knowledge. And anyway, when does the Everqueen ever need to leave Avelorn? Who would have thought a day like today would come?'

Alarielle had found a spot in a hollow. It was barren and dry and the plants looked less unwholesome than the others in the neighbourhood. There was even water gathered in puddles along the bottom.

'I would not drink any of that water,' she said. 'It is most likely tainted.'

'I think I might have worked that out for myself,' said Tyrion.

'We need a fire,' Alarielle said. She had already begun to gather wood. Tyrion stood guard, in case anything should come upon them suddenly. A pair of feelers poked over the edge of the small depression. One of the giant woodlouse creatures scuttled in. Tyrion drew Sunfang and advanced upon it. It turned and rippled away.

'I do not like those things,' he said, turning to see Alarielle confronted by the manticore. The great beast moved forwards. It seemed impossible that anything so large could move so quietly. Close up, Tyrion could see it was bigger than a mountain lion. Its body was the size of a horse although lower and much more cat-like. This one had a tail tipped with a scorpion-like sting. Vestigial wings, not large enough to let it fly or glide, emerged from its back. The face was humanoid but might have belonged to an idiot or a madman. The expression on it was one of slack-jawed lunacy, mingled with hunger. For all that, its inhuman eyes were not without a certain cunning.

It growled again and the air seemed to vibrate. Curved claws sharp as sickles emerged from its paws. The tail lashed the air.

Alarielle continued to move back towards Tyrion. The elven warrior swung his sword in a great figure of eight to get the manticore's attention. The passage of air made the flames on the blade roar and flicker. The great head jerked to one side, and it studied Tyrion as a cat might study a particularly foolish mouse.

Tyrion knew that on the best day of his life this creature would over-match him, and he was weakened now by his poisoned and infected wound. He needed an advantage. The only one he could think of was the power that he knew lay dormant within Sunfang. He pointed the blade tip at the manticore and willed it to blast the creature with fire. Nothing happened. He sensed something within the blade, but he could not bind it or make contact with it.

Desperately he tried to remember what had happened when he had blasted the Cold One riders. Perhaps if he could replicate that trick, he would know the sword's secret. He knew from his long talks with Teclis that part of the secret of magic was connected with mood and the manipulation of mental imagery. He never had possessed any talent for such things though. He was not a sorcerer.

Of course, the blade had been intended to be used by one who was not a sorcerer. Perhaps he was over-thinking what needed to be done. Perhaps it was all much simpler than he had imagined. He tried to imagine the flame blazing brighter in his mind.

Had it responded? Had the runes along the blade got ever so slightly brighter? The manticore growled. It carried its weight low to the earth and seemed almost to undulate as it slunk closer. Tyrion could see the great muscles gather in its haunches as it prepared to spring.

Tyrion imagined a ball of flame emerging from the tip of the blade and arcing towards the manticore, just as he had seen it do previously. Something happened. A faint blast of heat singed the hairs on the back of his hand as a small ball of light emerged from Sunfang and wobbled through the air towards the manticore. It exploded at the creature's feet. A smell of singed fur filled the air. The manticore let out a faint bleat and turned and sprang away over the edge of the crater. Its faintly acrid animal stink hung in the air along with the stench of sulphur.

Alarielle looked over at him. 'You surprise me, Prince Tyrion. I thought mastery of the blade was beyond you.'

'I have not mastered the blade. I think I have merely worked out how to make it work. It may be some time before I can harness its full power.'

'Nonetheless, I think you have done enough to save us from that Chaos creature.'

'Let us drink that toast after that particular tournament is won,' said Tyrion. He moved to the edge of the glade, but there was no manticore in sight. The beast's tracks ran to the edge of a deep thicket and then vanished from sight.

Tyrion felt Alarielle move up beside him. She had her bow in her hands now and an arrow nocked and ready to fly.

'Are you going to go hunting?' Tyrion asked.

'The thing is no good for meat,' she said.

'I thought you might like to try it for the sport.'

'Let's put your sword to good use and get a fire going. If nothing else it ought to help keep such monsters at bay.'

Tyrion was glad that Sunfang still possessed enough power to get the fire going. They settled down to a long night with nothing to eat but waybread, and nothing to drink but the last remains of their brackish water.

'What was that?' Alarielle asked. Tyrion stirred feverishly. He pushed himself upright. Four strangers were approaching the fire. Something about their manner and their garb marked them as druchii although these were not common soldiers.

'You have led us a merry chase,' said one of them, a tall, slender elf who carried a bow as if he knew how to use it. It was nocked and the arrow pointed directly at Tyrion's heart. 'It is over now.'

'We were sent to capture you, your serenity,' said a lovely female in a soft husky voice. 'I think there might be a bonus for us if we take your handsome friend back alive. Our ruler will be most anxious to meet the elf who has caused us so much trouble.'

'He does not look as if he will live that long,' said a huge brutish-looking elf who carried an axe with a blade at each end of its shaft. 'That wound has been infected by poison out of Har Ganeth, unless I miss my guess. I am surprised he is still alive. He should have died a long time ago.'

'Unless you have been keeping him alive with your magic, your serenity,' said the final elf, who bore no obvious weapons at all, which made Tyrion suspect he was most likely the most dangerous of them.

'Who are you?' Tyrion asked. He kept his tone polite and conversational even as he tried to work out a way of killing them.

'We are but humble servants of Malekith,' said the debauched-looking one, whom Tyrion suspected was a sorcerer. His twin had worn similar amulets under certain circumstances. 'I am Khalion. The winsome lady is Amara. The primitive with the bow is Vidor. The large and forceful-looking chap is Balial.'

'You talk too much, Khalion,' said Balial. His voice was deep and rumbling. He was scarred like a pit fighter. From the way he held the axe Tyrion could see he was enormously strong. The dislike in the voice was obvious. There was some rivalry between these four, that was obvious. Doubtless they would have to split any reward between them. If any of their companions were to suffer an accident it would be all the more for the survivors. It was something to bear in mind.

'At least I am capable of intelligent conversation,' said Khalion. 'And I am not an unmannerly boor, like some I could mention.'

'That is debatable,' said Vidor. He looked directly at Tyrion. 'I confess I am disappointed. I was expecting an epic battle when we found you. Your exploits have already made you quite famous. What is your name?'

'I am Prince Tyrion.' Vidor nodded.

'The reaver who assaulted the coast of Naggaroth. I remember seeing some of your handiwork then. You killed a lot of people, Prince Tyrion, and burned a lot of warehouses.'

'I regret to inform you I would do it again.'

'I doubt you will be given the chance. Our ruler's hospitality makes it hard for his guests to leave.'

'I will see that you are made comfortable,' said Amara, smiling. It was the sort of smile Tyrion was used to getting from women, and its sincerity just made him trust her less.

'Be careful of him,' said Khalion. 'He carries a powerful magic weapon.'

'I don't doubt it,' said Amara.

'That is interesting,' said Vidor.

'I found it first,' said Khalion.

'Of what possible use is a sword to you, mage?' asked Vidor.

'It can always be sold, if it does not prove useful for research.'

'The bounty belongs to our master,' said Balial. 'He shall decide who it belongs to.'

'Doubtless our good Balial hopes it will be awarded to the most faithful lapdog.'

'Once our mission is done, wizard, you and I will discuss manners.'

'I will be only too glad to give you a lesson in etiquette.'

'Take it,' said Tyrion, struggling feebly to unbuckle his sword belt. 'I would hate to be the cause of any falling out between such good friends.'

'Carefully, Prince Tyrion,' said Vidor, keeping the arrow sighted on him. At that moment a low growl sounded behind him. The manticore had returned. Tyrion whipped the blade from its scabbard. Vidor turned and put an arrow through the manticore's eye with an almost lazy ease. He turned back, already putting another arrow to the string.

Tyrion pointed the blade and invoked its power, putting all of his anger and desperation into the summons. If it harmed the trapped elemental, too bad. He could not risk Alarielle falling into the hands of these four.

A blazing fireball arced towards Vidor. He released his arrow but it passed through the flame en route to Tyrion and was partially deflected, becoming a burning comet disappearing into the trees. The fireball exploded next to Vidor and Khalion. The blast sent Vidor flying, his hair and clothes on fire. Khalion just stood there, limned by flame. Some sort of protective aura had kept the blast from affecting him. He smirked and pointed a finger. Forked lightning flashed towards the spot where Tyrion stood, but he was already in motion. The smell of ozone warred with the smell of flash-fried flesh.

Tyrion raced towards Khalion, ignoring the stabbing pain in his side from his wound. He knew he needed to finish this fight quickly. Khalion spoke a word of power and Tyrion's limbs became leaden. It was like running through deep mud. He threw Sunfang directly at the mage. It sparked when it hit his protective wards but the metal buried itself deep in his chest.

'Foolish, Prince Tyrion,' said Balial, stepping between them. The strange double-bladed axe whipped towards Tyrion with surprising speed. Balial was a lot faster than his size and musculature would seem to imply. Tyrion only just managed to spring backwards and away.

From the corner of his eye, he saw Amara running towards the Everqueen. Alarielle spoke a word and roots and the stalks of plants erupted from the ground, grasping Amara's legs. The assassin raised her hand and suddenly there was a dagger in it. She drew back her hand and threw it. The blade spun end over end towards the Everqueen, till the heavy-balled handle hit her on the forehead and sent her slumping stunned to the ground.

'Alarielle!' Tyrion shouted, turning towards her. Somehow the roots did not seem to grasp for him, the way they had done her enemies. He reached Amara, who slashed out viciously at him with another knife. He could see the blade of this one was poisoned. He sprang back out of her reach. Still immobilised by the grasping plants, she did what he hoped and threw the knife at him.

It came spinning through the air with eye-blurring speed. It seemed to take forever for the blade to reach him. He plucked it from the air by the handle. With a flick of his wrist he sent it back at her. There was a strange sucking sound as it embedded itself in the jelly of Amara's eye. She screamed and died as the poisoned blade pierced her brain.

A splintering sound nearby told Tyrion that Balial had chopped his way out from the imprisoning roots. He glanced around for a weapon. The only thing he could see was the Moonstaff of Lileath, which lay on the ground near Alarielle. He picked it up, turning just in time to block the sweep of the great axe with it. The wood of the staff caught the haft of the axe. Tyrion found himself breast to breast with the massive dark elf.

Balial pushed and Tyrion was sent tumbling backwards. He only just managed to roll clear as the axe blade chunked into the ground near him. His side felt as if he had been stabbed as he flipped himself to his feet. He gritted his teeth and forced himself to lash out with his staff held at full extension. There was a sound like wood hitting stone when he stuck the nerve cluster in Balial's leg, but the larger elf did not fall, he only grinned. The shock that passed up Tyrion's arm felt like he had just hit armour.

'I am glad you killed them,' said Balial. 'Now all the glory will be mine.'

'You will be joining them soon,' Tyrion said. His tone gave Balial pause.

'You are serious,' Balial said. 'You actually think you can win this. You are an arrogant pup.'

Tyrion lashed out with the tip of the staff again. Balial eluded him easily. His return stroke hit the staff. A normal weapon would have broken, but the Moonstaff was not even chipped. The force of the impact nearly tore it from Tyrion's hand.

Tyrion circled, trying to get to Khalion and Sunfang. The blade stood out of the wizard's chest, still burning. The smell of charred meat filled the air. Balial sprang. Tyrion blocked his blow. The pain in his side was so great he almost passed out. He knew he could not take many more impacts like that. He lashed out at Balial's stomach. The giant ignored the stroke. Again there was a sound like wood hitting rock.

'The Witch King's mages have protected me well,' Balial said. 'My skin is like stone.'

It could not be that way everywhere, Tyrion thought. Otherwise the giant would not be able to move. He eluded another stroke, crouched down, stepped forwards and, wheeling, struck Balial behind the knee. This time the giant fell. Tyrion brought the base of the Moonstaff down on his windpipe. It crunched but Balial did not stop moving. He rose. Still Tyrion thought it would take only minutes for him to suffocate through lack of breath. Lack of air would soon slow him.

Balial brought one blade of his axe slashing across his own throat. Air wheezed into his lungs through the bleeding wound.

Tyrion aimed a blow at his groin, figuring that would be a part of the body that no elf would want alchemically armoured. Balial parried the blow and lashed out with his booted foot. Tyrion twisted to avoid it, but the kick caught him on the side of his leg and sent him tumbling onto his back. Stars danced before his eyes. The world seemed to turn black. His breath came in gasps.

As if from a long way off, he saw the blade of the great axe come swinging down towards him with all the inevitable force of a meteor strike.

Move, he told himself. His body refused to respond. Pain surged through his side. Waves of nausea and dizziness passed through him. All he had to do was lie here for a few more moments and all that would end.

He began to roll to one side. It was like moving the biggest boulder that had ever existed. It was an exercise in futility. If he dodged this blow there would be another and he would just have to dodge that.

The blade crashed to the ground beside his head, shaving locks of his golden hair. Tyrion lashed out with his boot, catching Balial in the groin. The massive elf groaned and stood still for a moment, paralysed. Tyrion threw himself over to the corpse of Khalion, ripped Sunfang from his charred breast and reeled over to where Balial stood. He lashed out with the blade. Balial parried. Tyrion struck again, knowing he would be parried, but angling his blow so that his burning sword would come down next to Balial's fingers. A look of agony passed over the giant elf's face but he held on to his axe. Tyrion struck again with all his desperate fury.

His blow sheared right through the handle of the axe and hit Balial on the chest. His tunic caught fire but the magically hardened flesh resisted even the bite of Sunfang. Balial was left holding the two bits of the haft. It was as if he was holding two hand axes the wrong way. He tossed one into the air and caught it again so the blade was held outwards. He used the remnants of the other half to desperately block Tyrion's blows. The air wheezed through the great gap in his throat.

Tyrion drove him back, slashing out with desperate strength. Balial reeled back, trying to bring both axe heads into play. Tyrion herded him in the direction he wanted him to go. Balial's foot came down on the corpse of Khalion, sending him stumbling back off balance. Tyrion leaned into a long stroke, sending the point of Sunfang through the wound in Balial's throat and right through the other side, severing vertebrae and nerves. Balial flopped to the ground in his final death spasm.

He looked at Balial, then at Khalion. 'He killed you in the end,' Tyrion said, staggering over to where the Everqueen lay and slumping down beside her.

Vidor lay there dying. Agony ripped through his burned body. His flesh was blackened and cracked in many places. Pus wept through broken skin. He knew that soon he would join all of those he had killed in death's dark kingdom. There was something he needed to do before that happened. He needed to take revenge on the elf who had killed him. He had one last duty to perform in the service of his master.

He tried to move his blasted fingers. Burned flesh peeled away from the bone. He would have screamed if he could, but the only sound that came out was a whimper. He forced his hand to move despite the pain, and somehow managed to bring it up to the stone amulet hanging from his neck. It was warm from the blast of the fireball with which Tyrion had killed him. He touched it and felt strange magical life within. Some distant spark of the Witch King's magic which would serve his purpose now.

He murmured the words that would bring it to life, forcing them out of his cracked lips with his blackened tongue. He felt the stone move beneath his hand. It grew warmer and more pliant. Within heartbeats, it had become softer. He felt feathers beneath the broken remains of his hand. Even their faint touch sent needles of agony spiking into his flesh. He looked down and saw that where there had been a stone amulet there was now a black raven.

'Vidor. Alarielle. Tyrion. He killed us. Seek your master.' The bird looked at him with preternaturally intelligent eyes, squawked once and then flapped skywards faster than any normal bird should have been able to travel. Vidor lay flat on the ground. He was satisfied that he had done all that he could to take revenge. He would have swapped that and all the gold in the world for a drink of water.

Malekith studied the raven that strutted backwards and forth in front of him. The barbarian warlords he had brought to heel looked at him nervously. Enormous anger burned within him. He knew that his assassins had failed, that General Dorian had failed. He knew that one element of his great plan had failed.

The Everqueen was still alive and free. She had been saved by the elf called Tyrion. It was a name he was familiar with. It was a name that most elves of Naggaroth were familiar with. It was a name that

N'Kari was certainly familiar with. He sensed a rage even greater than his own burning within the daemon's breast. He knew that if he wanted to, he could put that anger to use. He turned and looked at the Chaos creature.

'Tyrion!' N'Kari said. The venom in his voice could have poisoned an army. Malekith knew that at that moment he and the daemon were totally of one accord.

'You think you could kill him?' Malekith asked.

'You jest. The last time I encountered him only the god Asuryan saved him.'

'He has grown more skilled since then.'

'No amount of skill can save him from my wrath.'

Malekith considered the risks and potential rewards of the situation. If he unleashed the daemon, he was certain that he could kill Tyrion and bring him the head of the Everqueen. On the other hand, if anything went wrong, he would lose the services of the one creature that provided the advantage of mobility to his armies. He would be stuck here on the plains of northern Saphery with only his mirrors to keep him in touch with his distant forces.

It was an enormous gamble.

It would take only a few days for the daemon to hunt down the troublesome elf prince and the ruler he guarded. Everything else was going so very well. His armies were triumphant everywhere. Nothing could stand against them. In the north, the remaining horde of Chaos barbarians was laying waste to an entire kingdom. Nothing could go wrong.

'Go, N'Kari. Use all your power. Slay Tyrion and return with the head of the Everqueen as soon as possible. I will place it on my standard and use it for my war-banner.'

'It will be my very great pleasure,' said N'Kari. For once, the daemon sounded entirely sincere. His shape altered and twisted, becoming once again the monstrous four-armed being that Malekith had first bound into his service. It let out a roar of rage and pleasure and snapped one massive claw together.

'I will take the head of the Everqueen with my own claw.' It turned and loped from his presence without another word. A gate opened in front of it and it vanished.

He was alone in a darkened land. The sky burned. Strange patterns of elemental fire underlit the clouds. Armies of daemons marched. The greatest flight of dragons ever assembled swept by overhead. Fleets full of mutated monsters ploughed through the dark and stormy seas. From the back of a huge dragon, he watched everything pass.

He was burning up. He walked closer to a flame. He had seen it before. It was the sacred fire within the Shrine of Asuryan. A horde of richly clad elves watched him and laughed. It was odd, he thought. You were supposed to burn when you passed through the flame, not when you reached it.

He was cold, so cold it burned. His teeth chattered. In the distance, the black fangs of a giant mountain range marked the edge of the sane world. Beyond that lay only the Realm of Chaos, a place where daemons walked and the flesh of mortals became warped beyond all recognition. He was marching towards it, a black blade burned on his hip while an army of elves followed. He did not want to turn and look back because he knew he would not like what he saw.

Tyrion sat bolt upright, eyes wide open. Above him the waning moon glared down through the branches of trees. Sweat dripped from his brow. His limbs felt weak. His breathing rasped from his chest.

'What is it?' Alarielle asked, looking over at him. A frown marred her brow. He could tell by the way she stared that she was both worried and frightened.

He tried to rise but his limbs felt weak. He almost collapsed so he let himself slump to the ground again. She moved over to where he lay and placed her hand on his forehead. It felt like it was made of flame.

'You are sick,' she said. 'You are burning up with fever. If you go on like this, it might well kill you. You have put too much stress on your body over the past few days. The last fight was too much. That and the march out of the tainted forest.'

He laughed at that thought. He could not die this way, of a fever in a forest far from the fighting. It did not make sense. Teclis was the sickly one, not him. He told her this.

'Lie quiet,' she said. 'We don't want you raving if the druchii come this way.'

'Maybe they will catch whatever I have and it will kill them,' he said. The thought was oddly amusing.

'Not fast enough,' she said.

'Don't you have any magic for this?' he asked.

'I have been trying to remember, but her memories won't come.'

'Her memories?' Tyrion said. 'Why not yours?'

'We are the same. Sometimes I can remember what she has seen and done. Often I cannot. It takes calm and clarity and time.'

'And you are not calm?' he said, trying to make a joke of it.

'I am alone in a forest surrounded by deadly enemies who want to hand me over to the most evil elf who ever lived. My only companion is sick and raving. Why would I not be calm?'

'Good,' said Tyrion. 'You had me worried for a moment there.'

'Be at peace, Prince Tyrion. I think there may be some herbs around here which will help ease your condition. I will see if I can find some.'

'I am supposed to be protecting you,' Tyrion said. 'That is the champion's duty.'

'So you have finally accepted that you are my champion then?'

'I don't see anyone else here,' Tyrion said. He fell back into hallucinatory dreams.

N'Kari moved along the trail away from the tournament grounds, head down, tracking by scent like a hound. It felt good to be wearing something like its normal battle-form again after weeks bound into the form of an elf-maid. The chains were still there, still binding it, but at least it was enjoying some variety. It chafed its protean nature to be confined to one shape for so long.

Of course, it was not as powerful as it should be. The chains bound it to this world but they inhibited its ability to draw on its full powers. It was far stronger than anything it was likely to meet in this pitiful plane, but it had only a fraction of the strength it normally possessed even here. Still, it should be more than enough for the mission it was supposed to perform.

It sniffed again. The trail was an easy one for it to follow. It knew the accursed scent it was following only too well. It was Tyrion, and judging by the faint taint of corruption in it, he had been wounded and poisoned.

Good, he deserved it. Of course, it would be a pity if he died before N'Kari could reach him and enact its vengeance.

There was another descendant of Aenarion with him, a female, one touched by an extraplanar being. This would be the Everqueen. N'Kari had to give Malekith credit for something – this was a task it was truly going to enjoy. It did not mind being bound to complete it in the slightest. The only thing that troubled it was the compulsion to complete the task and return as quickly as possible. This was something it wanted to savour, to derive the maximum possible pleasure from. Well, no doubt it would find a way to do that and still stay within the letter of the command that Malekith had laid down.

For the moment, it was enjoying being free to hunt and prowl. It made a pleasant change from being a mere ferryman for the druchii armies. That thought sent a ripple of fury through N'Kari. At some point, it would find a way to take its vengeance on the Witch King too. With that thought, it bowed down over the trail once more and, scuttling along on multiple limbs, began to follow a trail that might have baffled the most sensitive bloodhound.

'Better?' Alarielle asked. Tyrion nodded and drank more of the bitter tea. The fever had subsided. Strength was returning to his limbs. He felt strong enough to grasp a sword once again.

'You were right,' he said.

'Did you ever doubt it?'

'Yet again, I find myself feeling very foolish,' Tyrion said. Moonlight filtered down through the branches. It was the middle of the night but the drugs in the tea made him feel strangely restless.

'Why?' Alarielle asked.

Tyrion swallowed another bitter mouthful. 'I sometimes think I am very stupid.'

'I don't see it.'

'No? I spent my boyhood thinking I was very stupid,' Tyrion said.

'You?' Alarielle said. 'I find that hard to believe.'

'My father is a mage. My brother is a very powerful and very gifted one. My mother is dead. We lived alone in the mountains except for one old servant. I understood nothing my father and Teclis talked about, and it was so important to them. Nothing I was interested in was important to them.' He smiled a little sadly at the thought. 'I think I was very lonely. It was only when I went to Lothern that things were different. People preferred me to Teclis.'

'Women, you mean.'

'No. I mean people in general. It had never occurred to me that it might be the case. Then my grandfather started talking to me about politics. It was obvious he had ambitions for me. He was one of the Lothern cabal who helped put Finubar on the Phoenix Throne. He thought he could do the same for me. In many ways, he was an evil old elf, but he treated me as if I was someone who mattered.'

'Of course you matter.'

Tyrion looked at her and saw that she was sincere. 'I found out quite young what my real gift was for.'

'What was that?'

'Killing. I have always been good at it. No. I have always excelled at it. And I have always loved it. You were right about that too.'

She looked troubled. 'I was angry when I said that...'

'You were still right. I used to think I wanted to be a hero. I could not be a mage but I could be a mighty warrior. I told myself that many times. The truth was I simply liked killing things. There was a great anger in me, very well hidden. I liked proving I was better, stronger, faster than all the people I killed. It made me feel superior to them. There was no more conclusive proof, was there?'

'I don't know.'

'Believe me, if you stand on a battlefield and look down on the corpse of someone who has tried to kill you, you will be glad, and you will think you were stronger, tougher, or maybe just luckier. No matter. You will never feel more alive. It is certainly how I felt.'

'I think I can understand how you might.'

'And it was a game I was good at. Most of my life has been like that. It's been a game I knew I could win. It stopped being that when the dark elves attacked your court.'

'You have fought them before.'

'I fought them in their own land. I fought them at sea. I helped beat off an occasional raid. I never saw anything like this... I never even believed it was possible.'

'I don't think anyone did. Who would have thought it – druchii in the heart of Avelorn, the Everqueen their captive. Until it happened I would have said it was impossible.'

'I find myself wondering how he did it, how Malekith did it,' Tyrion said. 'He forged this invasion force in secret – he's done that before, it is part of his pattern. He is good at deception. But how is it possible that he managed to infiltrate an army into the heart of our realm without it being detected? I can only think of one instance of this happening before, and...'

The thought hit Tyrion with the force of a warhammer hitting a shield. He had seen something like this before. It had been part of his own life. The sickness and the chase had hidden it from him for a very long time.

'What is it?' Alarielle asked. 'Has the fever returned?'

'I am stupid. I should have seen it before now.'

'Seen what?'

'A daemon once moved regiments of warriors around Ulthuan. It was hunting me and my brother and others of the line of Aenarion. It laid siege to the Shrine of Asuryan.'

'N'Kari?' she whispered.

'N'Kari.'

Alarielle's face went pale. '*She* remembers N'Kari. The daemon commanded the Rape of Ulthuan in the Age of Aenarion. But surely it must hate Malekith as much as it hates us. He is Aenarion's son.'

Tyrion shrugged. 'I am not sorcerer enough to know what is possible. Perhaps Malekith bound it or made a pact with it. It almost killed me once... it will want to kill you.'

'These are very worrying things, Prince Tyrion.'

'We live in a very worrying world, your serenity.'

They both fell silent for a long time. Tyrion felt tired but could not sleep. Alarielle lay down beside him and closed her eyes. Absentmindedly he stroked her hair.

N'Kari studied the bodies intently. The corpses were old and they had been left to lie. A few had been bitten and chewed on by massive jaws that N'Kari guessed belonged to Cold Ones. The scent of Tyrion led to this place. It had taken it a little time to pick it up when it crossed the river, but it was using magic as much as its nostrils and it had found the scent again though a hound might not have. It was obvious that Tyrion had passed this way and had been joined again by the Everqueen nearby. It was curious though about what had happened here. It was curious whether the one it hated was even still alive. Fortunately, it knew a way to find out.

It extended a claw and inscribed the sign of Slaanesh in the mud around one of the corpses. It spoke the words of an ancient ritual and felt power flow from it into the body. A sigh emerged not from the mouth but from a gap in the cadaver's chest as the lungs wheezed rotten air. The corpse sat upright and its head swivelled until it looked at N'Kari with empty eye-sockets.

'What do you want with me? Why have you disturbed my soul's dissolution in the realm beyond?'

'I would ask you the three questions allowed by spell and ritual.'

'Ask away then and let me fly back to hell. It is too cold for me here now.'

'Who killed you?'

'An elf with a flaming sword. He stepped out of the night and slaughtered us as if we were children.'

'Why?'

'Because we were enemies, why else?'

'Is his soul with yours in hell now?'

'Not to my knowledge, and I would know for he was my killer.'

'Then go, you are dismissed.'

'I go.'

The corpse slumped and the witchfires died in its eyes. N'Kari laughed long and loud. Its prey was out there still. It was good to know. Now it was only a matter of finding it.

'I feel like I have just woken up, like all of my life I have been playing a game and things have only just now become serious.' Tyrion felt the sadness in his voice even as he spoke. He was so weak now he could barely even move. He knew he was dying. He had tried to get her to leave him, but she would not. All he could do now was talk.

'Why? Because you saw your friends killed?' She sounded as if she wanted to sneer or cry or perhaps both. He shook his head.

'I have seen friends die in battle before. I killed one in a duel once. But I have lived in a world where these things have had no real consequence, except to make me admired.'

'I don't follow you.'

'I have raided the coasts of Naggaroth. I have fought against the warriors of Chaos. I have defended our shores against the Norse, but there was never anything at stake before except my own life.'

'Surely that is enough.'

'You would think so, wouldn't you? But it's not.' He paused and stared into the fire for a moment, trying to find the words to say what he meant. They were not easy for him to uncover. 'If Malekith succeeds in what he is doing, our kingdom ends. Our world will be changed irrevocably and not for the better. And his capturing you or killing you makes this more likely to happen. You are the last link to one of our old gods, one of the things that makes us who we are and not druchii. That is why he must destroy you.'

'And why is this important to you?'

'I don't want him to win, and not just in the way I don't want someone to beat me at chess. I don't want him to win because I hate him and his people and what they stand for.'

'And what is that?'

'They are us, without you.'

'And you said you were not a poet. That is a very pretty phrase.'

She tilted her head to one side and looked at him thoughtfully. 'You are not quite what I expected you to be, Prince Tyrion.'

'No one ever is. That is the truth of things.' He started to cough. The world spun. The shadows lengthened, his sight became very dim. He felt as if he had only the slightest grip upon his life, as if the smallest breeze could separate his spirit from his body.

She reached down and stroked his brow. Her hand felt very cold. She pulled it away as if he burned. She seemed to have come to a decision. She closed her eyes and murmured what might have been a spell or a prayer. Her face twisted as if she were in agony or undergoing some great internal struggle.

Tyrion looked up at Alarielle.

She was not there. Someone else was. Someone much older and calmer and altogether more majestic. The spell that normally surrounded her was much stronger. He had the impression of other elf-women superimposed on her, many of them, all of whom resembled her but were not quite the same. When she moved, she moved differently as if a stranger were wearing her body.

'Who are you?' Tyrion asked.

'We are the Everqueen.' He did not need to ask why she used the plural.

'Where is Alarielle?'

'She is with us.'

Tyrion knew he was somehow looking at a composite of every personality of every elf woman who had ever been the Everqueen and upon something more, something tinged with divine power. Even as he watched they seemed to go in and out of focus. An expression of pain flickered across her face.

'What's wrong?'

'Our land is in pain. We feel it. It disrupts the flows of power. It makes it difficult to think. This vessel is unprepared to receive us.'

'Can you help us?' Tyrion asked, thinking that if Alarielle could tap into the power of the goddess for even a moment, she might be able to do something that would aid them greatly.

'The wound,' she said. 'Let us see it.'

She staggered like someone imperfectly in control of her body over to where he stood and reached out to touch the wound. Despite himself he flinched as her fingers found it, but he felt no pain. Her touch was cool and oddly soothing.

'Can you help us?'

'Our daughter is too young and too untrained to take the full brunt of our power. The Cold King has chosen his moment too well.'

'Can you help us?'

'Hush. This wound is a vile one filled with poison and powered by potent runes. The blade that did this was wound round with foul spells.'

The Everqueen closed her eyes. She murmured something. The coolness spread from her fingers. The wound pained him less although it would not close. It became less black. He felt as if he had some more energy.

'It is the best we can do. You must find help soon or you will die.'

The Everqueen slumped like a puppet with her strings cut. 'Alarielle!' Tyrion said. He did not have the strength to catch her as she fell to the ground.

N'Kari loomed over the dead bodies of the Witch King's chosen assassins. The stink of magic hung over the battlefield. It had been unleashed here and quite strongly by the standards of mortals. It was enough for N'Kari to recreate what had happened. Tyrion had been more than a match for Malekith's pet killers. The boy had improved over the last century. His wound had become worse though. He smelled as if he was rotting away inside. Fortunately, he was close now. It would not take long to overhaul him and the Everqueen.

Tireless as ever, N'Kari put its head down and followed the trail. It moved with the speed of the storm wind. Lust for revenge made its bounding stride all the faster.

Teclis froze. He suddenly felt the closeness of a being of terrifying daemonic power. He sensed its psychic spoor as it moved past him. In the distance he could hear the panicked shrieks of dark elf soldiers as they too felt its presence. He turned to Alanor and said, 'Run!'

The ranger looked at him, bewildered. 'Get away from me or you will die!' Teclis said. Something in his tone must have compelled belief because Alanor turned and ran. Teclis gathered his power to him and waited for N'Kari to arrive.

It would not take long. He cursed. They had finally made their way through the hordes of druchii. His brother was so close he could feel it. It was all going to be in vain unless he defeated the daemon.

N'Kari laughed aloud. It sensed the presence of the wizard who had banished it over a century before. Of course, he would be looking for his brother. Briefly N'Kari considered turning aside and swatting the troublesome mage, but it found the compulsion laid on it by the Witch King was strong. Not that it mattered. It was close to Tyrion now. All it had to do was wait for a few moments and Teclis would come upon his dead twin. Then N'Kari would take its revenge on him.

Teclis braced himself for an attack that never came. The daemon moved past him and on into the woods, its pace suddenly so slow that Teclis could almost keep up. Teclis understood what that meant. Tyrion and the Everqueen must be close. That was what N'Kari had been sent to find. It was the only thing that made sense.

Teclis limped on, pursuing the daemon as quickly as he could.

'Thank you,' Tyrion said. He felt better since the Everqueen had worked her magic on his wound. The pain had lessened and he could move again. It still felt as if his strength was slowly leeching away, but at least he had some.

'I did not do anything,' Alarielle said. 'She did.'

'I thought she was part of you.'

'I think I am part of her. At least that is what it feels like when she manifests.'

She looked a little frightened when she spoke of it. Perhaps because of the lessening of his pain, his mood had lightened. The woods looked bright and sunny. A bright red bird fluttered from branch to branch above them. The sun looked golden. War and death might as well have been a hundred leagues away.

'What is it like?' he asked, genuinely curious.

'Like drowning,' she said.

'That does not sound pleasant.'

'They say a drowning person relaxes and enjoys it towards the end, after they give up the struggle.'

'Is that what it's like?'

'The Everqueen is so big and I am so small. I don't think this was the way it was meant to be.'

'I don't understand.'

'Neither do I. There is a process of transition when the power moves from one Everqueen to the next. It can take years before it's complete.'

'We don't have years,' said Tyrion.

'I know, and it makes me feel so... useless.'

'Why does it take years?'

'I don't know. I don't think the elven mind was meant to encompass what the Everqueen is – a god, a composite being, an elemental power. They are all in there, you know...'

'Who?'

'All of the ones who went before me. My mother. I see her sometimes, in my dreams. Sometimes when I am awake and I feel the power bubbling up in me. I think I am going to go mad...'

She looked very pained now. Tyrion was sorry he had started the conversation. It was not at all what he had expected. He had never thought there would be such a price to pay to become what she was. 'You are not mad.'

'But I may go mad. There are rituals to be undergone when you become the Everqueen. Hundreds of them. They stretch out over a period of years.'

'And you have not undergone all of them.'

'Not even the tiniest fraction.'

'Does it matter so much?'

'Yes. My tutors explained it to me. They are intended to accustom me to being the Everqueen and the Everqueen to being me.'

'I always thought you were one and the same.'

She shook her head. '*She* is a living goddess, a spirit, a power that passes from one host to another. I am a vessel. She is the power that flows into me. When one vessel dies, another one must be found.'

'Or what?'

'We don't know. It has never happened. Not in all of elven history. The power has always passed from mother to daughter.'

'And all descended from the original Everqueen.'

She nodded again. 'I think I am the anchor. If I die, the power is lost. The spirit will have no way into the world.'

'The Shrine of Asuryan...' Tyrion said. 'You are like the Shrine of Asuryan.'

'What?'

'My brother and I were there once. He reached out and touched the god, or perhaps it touched him, I don't know. He told me that it was the only place in the world where such a thing could happen. That is why the Phoenix Kings have to be crowned there.'

'And you think that the daughters of the line of Astarielle are like the gateway that exists on the Blessed Island, a sort of mobile place of power?'

'I am no sorcerer. I don't know about these things. I am just guessing.'

'You are guessing very well. That is exactly the way it is supposed to work. It is a sacred mystery. You must become my champion now. You know this.' Her voice told him she was joking, but there was nothing here to joke about.

'Malekith knows this too.'

'You think he planned his attack now, knowing I would be weak?'

'If he wanted to ensure the elves had one less god, he is going about it the right way.'

'That is sacrilegious.'

'We are talking about an elf who took it upon himself to walk into the Flame of Asuryan without any protection, who once attempted to destroy all of Ulthuan. I don't think the idea would trouble him too much.'

'You speak as if you understand him.'

'I am trying to. I am trying to understand what is happening here.'

'It might not be the wisest of things, trying to think like the Witch King. He is almost seven thousand years old. I doubt that he is sane as we understand sanity.'

'A few minutes ago you were telling me that you doubted your own...'

'That is why you should listen to me,' she said, with a strange, sad smile. He thought about what it must be like to share your body with a god.

Something she said came back to him. 'Do you have their memories? All of them, all of the previous Everqueens?'

'*She* has them. I can sometimes remember them. Why?'

'That must be a heavy burden,' he said, not wanting to say what was really on his mind, not yet anyway.

'Prince Tyrion, you sound almost sympathetic.'

'I find you more sympathetic than I used to,' he said. 'And I am grateful to *her*.'

'Don't become like everyone else,' she said. 'I have enough worshippers.'

'What?'

'At least you don't give me *the look* – of adoration.'

'I would have thought you enjoyed it.'

'I did at first, but it gets odd and lonely after a time. I am not *her*. I am just the person *she* speaks through. She weaves her spell around me so that people will listen. For whatever reason, you at least can see *me*... and I am grateful for that.'

She reached out and took his hand. He looked up into her eyes. 'So am I,' he said. She leaned forwards. They were close enough to kiss.

Out of the corner of his eye, he caught sight of something. He pushed her to one side into the undergrowth beside the path.

'Quickly,' he said. 'Get out of sight.'

N'Kari could sense the presence of more of the blood of Aenarion. One of the scents belonged to Tyrion, the warrior who had done so much to help defeat it over a century ago. The other scent belonged to a female. It was a subtle scent and there was the suggestion of great power to it. Somewhere, deeply hidden, nearby there was a deity. It was not quite as warlike or as potent as Asuryan but it was, or it could be, very powerful.

This made N'Kari wary. It moved carefully closer, adjusting its shape to keep it camouflaged among the dense undergrowth. It padded softly closer, sniffing the air and readying itself for anything. Tyrion's scent was even more sickly and tainted. The warrior was very ill. Of course, it did not matter very much because his life was just about to come to an end.

N'Kari was pleased by the fact that it was not only going to be able to carry out its orders for Malekith but take revenge on its greatest enemies in this world at the same time. It could sense the presence of Teclis close behind it but somewhat muffled as if by powerful, deceptive magic. It seemed that fate or the dark gods had conspired to give it the perfect opportunity for vengeance.

It was close enough now to peer out from the bushes and see the pair as they sat by a fire. They looked comfortable, which was also a good thing. It would take great pleasure in tormenting them; these things always went better if the victims felt secure to begin with.

It listened to the conversation for a while. It was the usual mortal trivia, nothing very interesting to one of its age and predisposition. It knew that it could waste a great deal of time waiting for them to say something that piqued its interest.

Instead it moved farther away into the undergrowth, changed its shape again and went crashing through the bushes as loudly as it could, determined to get their attention and unsettle them before it finally took its vengeance. It wanted to draw this moment out, to savour it and feel the fear building in the minds of its prey. It laughed softly to itself. It had waited for this for a very long time.

'What was that?' Alarielle asked. Tyrion forced himself upright and his head spun, dizziness threatening to overwhelm him. He felt sick as he had never felt in his life. And he felt something else, something that was in its own way as bad as the sickness. He sensed the presence of something evil. A faint, sickly-sweet aroma that reminded him of perfume. It also brought to mind something else that he had scented a long time ago.

'I don't know, but I don't like it one little bit,' he said. He forced himself to his feet and stood there swaying. A worried expression fluttered across Alarielle's face. He knew that he was the cause of it, not whatever she had heard out there in the darkness.

That was wrong. There was something that they needed to be afraid of out there. It worried him that she had sensed that before he did. He leaned forwards and threw some more sticks on the fire although he already suspected that whatever was stalking them was not some beast that was going to be frightened of flame.

The twigs caught fire. The sap inside them sputtered. Sparks drifted upwards. He looked around, trying to penetrate the shadows with his vision. Something big was moving out there in the wood. It sounded as large as a bear and it was making so much noise now that it was almost as if it wanted to be detected. Tyrion turned his head to look at the point from which the sound came, and at that moment all of the noise ceased. Tyrion drew his sword, the flames blazing along its length sending shadows dancing away. It just seemed to make the night all the darker.

The poisoned wound pained him deeply. It was as if his whole side had been sprayed with acid.

'I think it's gone now,' said Alarielle. She sounded more hopeful than convinced. Tyrion shook his head. He suspected that whatever it was that was out there was creeping stealthily closer.

Perhaps though it was watching them and getting ready to spring. He turned around just so that he could be rid of the crawling sensation between his shoulder blades. There was nothing there that he could see. No sound came from the woods. Just the simple movement made him feel even dizzier. Alarielle rose now. She held the Moonstaff of Lileath in her hands, clutching it so tightly that her knuckles were white. She looked around as well in the opposite directions from the ones that Tyrion was looking in.

The sounds started again, receding into the distance, crashing away into the darkness. If he had been healthy, Tyrion would have investigated, but he knew that it would be folly to go out into the darkness and look for a creature the size of a bear in his present condition. He gestured for Alarielle to sit down again, looked around once more, sheathed Sunfang and forced himself to remain upright.

'What will you do once we reach our people?' Alarielle asked. There was an aura of false cheerfulness about her that Tyrion disliked. It was as if she believed that he was not going to live to reach their people and wanted to pretend otherwise. He supposed he could not really blame her for that. Her position was not a cheerful one under the circumstances.

'I think I will have a bath,' Tyrion said. It took all his willpower to stand upright and speak. 'It seems like a lifetime since I've had one. The closest thing I've had to a wash was when I fell in the river when we were swinging over it.'

It seemed like a very long time ago that he had done that. The memory of it made him laugh for some reason. She joined in although her laughter was soft and sad. 'That seems like a lifetime ago to me,' she said. 'I did not really know you then.'

He looked at her across the fire. 'Nor I, you. I thought you were a spoiled princess back then.'

'And you don't now?'

He shook his head. 'Find some noble knight to be your champion.'

'I am not sure a noble knight could have got me this far.'

'It was you who brought me this far,' Tyrion said. 'I would not be here now if it was not for you.'

'We did this together. And we will finish it together.' She leaned forwards and touched his hand. Her touch felt very cold, but that was perhaps only because he felt as if he was burning up.

She leaned closer to him until their faces were almost touching. Her lips were slightly parted. Again Tyrion felt the urge to kiss her.

'That you most assuredly will do,' said a voice from the darkness. 'I will see to it.'

A chill ran down Tyrion's spine. He had last heard that voice over a century before but he could never forget it. It haunted his darkest nightmares. He looked up. Emerging from the forest was a massive four-armed figure. One of those arms ended in a monstrous claw. A faint wave of musk hit him. He realised that it must have been there all the time, and it probably explained Alarielle's actions. He knew the powerful aphrodisiac effect it had on others.

'N'Kari,' he said, forcing himself to hold his blade level, even though he was so weak he could barely stand.

'I am glad you remember me,' said the daemon, beckoning in an awful parody of an exotic dancer trying to entice one of her audience. 'I certainly remember you, blood of Aenarion.'

Tyrion knew that his life was over. Even at his best, he would have been no match for this daemon. Now, as things stood, sick and weary, there was almost nothing he could do that would even slow N'Kari down. Without taking his eyes off the daemon, he said, 'Run!'

'Please do,' said N'Kari. 'I will enjoy it all the more. Once I have killed this one, it will give me great pleasure to hunt you down. I would be very grateful to you if you could prolong this for as long as possible.'

Tyrion drew his blade. The flame burned much brighter than it normally would, as if somehow it recognised N'Kari and what it stood for.

'You're somewhat better armed than the last time I met you,' N'Kari said. 'That should make this slightly more enjoyable as well.'

'I see you are wearing chains,' Tyrion said. 'You were your own master, the last time we met. Now it seems you're someone's slave.'

'I will have my revenge on the one who bound me, just as I will have my revenge upon you,' N'Kari said. 'My vengeance will be as terrible as it is inevitable.'

'What is it like being a servant? I have heard that the followers of Slaanesh enjoy submission. How do you find it?'

'If you're trying to convince me to initiate you into its pleasures, it will not work. I simply do not have the time. I must kill you and I must kill her and then I must return to plotting my revenge.'

'It seems to me that you spend more time talking about revenge than taking it.'

'And it seems to me that you're very keen to meet your death. Do you really suffer so much? Does your wound pain you so?'

'Run!' Tyrion said to Alarielle. 'I will hold it for as long as I can.'

'I am not going anywhere,' she said. 'I would not give this the pleasure of seeing me run. Nor will I leave you.'

'How touching,' N'Kari said. 'Don't you realise that your lover wishes to die? He cannot live with that wound and he wishes to leave this world heroically. I am almost tempted to let him live and watch him die in slow agony. It has certain advantages. He can witness what I do to you before he goes. Do not be afraid. There will be as much pleasure as there is pain in it for you, and you will come to enjoy both before the end.'

Tyrion sprang forwards. Sunfang flashed through a blazing arc. He put all his remaining strength and speed into the blow. N'Kari evaded it easily and laughed.

'It seems I have touched a nerve,' it said. Alarielle spread her hands and spoke a word. A wave of greenish energy flowed towards the daemon. N'Kari's hands made the gestures of a counterspell and neutralised it.

'Pitiful,' said N'Kari. 'An apprentice could do better.'

Tyrion moved in close and struck again while the daemon was distracted. Sunfang bit into its flesh. There was a sound of sizzling as the skin burned away. A faint sweet aroma filled the air. The daemon lashed out with its fist and batted Tyrion away like an elf tossing a small animal across a room. Tyrion fell badly. Blackness swept over him. He tried to force himself to rise but could not.

He knew that the end had come.

From the shadows of the undergrowth, Teclis resisted the urge to intervene. Striking before he was ready would merely result in all of their deaths. Instead he studied N'Kari. The daemon looked very much as he remembered it. Of course, there was no way that he would ever forget his encounter with the greater daemon of Slaanesh. There was something odd about the creature. It was bound not just by spells but by some ancient artefact grafted onto its wrist, a thing almost as potent as the daemon was.

It radiated an aura of awesome power. Teclis did not recognise the workmanship. He knew it was not made by an elf. Perhaps, judging by the runes upon it, it had been made by a Slann or perhaps even one of the creatures that had ruled the Slann back in ancient times.

All that he knew was that those chains had been made in a fashion that not even Caledor could duplicate. They were not only potent enough to bind a greater daemon indefinitely but they had other effects as well. They helped to maintain the presence of N'Kari in this plane of existence.

Normally, entities as powerful as greater daemons could not maintain a physical form for any great length of time except when the winds of magic blew much stronger than they normally did. Normally, only at times of great peril, such as when the northern warp gates were open, could they do so. The last time that had happened was during the reign of Aenarion.

No, there was something woven into those chains that bound the greater daemon. Perhaps he could use that to his advantage.

If he was going to do so, he was going to need to do it quickly. N'Kari was advancing upon Alarielle with something more than merely killing her on its mind. Tyrion, like the idiot he was, was trying to fight. Both of them were going to be killed very quickly unless Teclis intervened.

The daemon radiated an aura of awesome power, but not quite so much as it had the last time Teclis had encountered it. The wizard was sure that that was not simply his imagination or a bad memory. N'Kari was much weaker than it should have been. Teclis suspected that that too had something to do with those strange chains.

If you're going to bind a greater daemon, it made sense to bleed off some of its power. It would make the act of controlling it much easier. Such a creature would still be powerful enough to make a terrible servant or weapon, even if it was not quite so strong as it would normally have been.

There was something familiar about the spell on those chains. Something about it reminded him of the locking spell that had controlled the door back at the Slann city of Zultec, where Tyrion and he had found Sunfang. It would be easy enough to undo that spell and release the chains, although that seemed like madness. At that point N'Kari would be completely unbound and able to bring all of its power into focus. There would only be a few moments where the daemon would be vulnerable and perhaps Teclis could banish it.

Even at the best of times though, such a spell was not without risks. All Teclis knew was that it was theoretically possible. He had never summoned a greater daemon. He had never bound a greater daemon. He had never banished one either. He was familiar with the spells. He had studied them in the White Tower a long time ago, when he had first gone to study there. The masters had allowed him, for they had known as well as he did that one day he was going to have to face N'Kari again. Now that day had come. The question was – was he ready for it?

There was only one way to find out. N'Kari had almost reached Alarielle. It had stretched out its huge arms like a lover and was herding her towards a great tree. Tyrion lay on the ground and did not move.

Teclis spoke a word of power. A bolt of magical energy hurtled towards the daemon. It screeched. For a moment, it seemed to be outlined in the fire and lightning. It turned to face Teclis and roared.

'It seems I have got your attention,' Teclis said. 'Depart now and I will spare you.'

The daemon said, 'Little Teclis – my, how you have grown!'

'I see you have not lost your taste for melodramatic dialogue,' Teclis said. He made his voice sounded utterly bored even while he studied the locking spell on the chains. With his magesight he could see the intricate pattern woven into the structure.

'It seems your skill at magic has greatly improved,' N'Kari said. The daemon was coming closer, its movements reminiscent of the stalking step of a great predator. Teclis knew that if it got within springing distance he was dead. He did not have Tyrion's lightning reflexes. There was no way he could avoid the fatal strike of those great claws.

Teclis worked the spell of opening, using his powers to undo the intricate magical locking mechanism on the chains of binding. They fell away to the ground. N'Kari spread its claws wide and laughed. It seemed to expand with a new influx of power and evil.

'You have made a mistake, little Teclis.'

Teclis knew he had only one chance. He spoke the words of banishment. N'Kari's outline wavered. Without the chains to anchor it, it was prey to instability once more. Teclis manipulated the flows of magic around him, adding to the resistance of normal reality, aiding it in its attempts to expel N'Kari back to its natural home.

'No!' it cried, realising what was happening. It strode towards Tyrion, determined to take its revenge on one of the brothers.

Teclis invoked another offensive spell. An enormous blast of magical energy ravened through his body and washed over the daemon, limning it with witchfire.

N'Kari faded away, still screaming.

Malekith felt a sudden pain inside his head. What was happening, he wondered? Had death finally overtaken him in the moment of his greatest triumph? Had the Flame of Asuryan and the spells woven into his armour finally failed? Was this what death was like? He was surprisingly untroubled by it.

The faces of his followers turned towards him. He realised that he was swaying and that he had raised one massive, gauntleted fist to his forehead. He forced himself to stand upright and assume his usual, dominant posture. He was not dead.

It dawned on him what it was. The sense of linkage with the dae-mon N'Kari was gone. Something had happened. Had the daemon finally broken the spell that bound it? Or was this something else entirely?

He paused to consider these questions. He did not think that the daemon could possibly have broken the spell that bound it to this world. Even if it had, the chances were that instability would cause the daemon to vanish back into the Realm of Chaos.

If not, Malekith realised that he had a very big problem on his hands. An angry Keeper of Secrets was not something that anyone wanted to have hunting them. Which brought another terrifying thought to mind – if the daemon had not managed to break the spell binding it, someone had banished it from this world or sub-orned it to their own purposes. This spoke of magic of the highest level and the most frightening level of power.

He cursed the Everqueen and the land of Avelorn. It did not seem to matter what he attempted – it foundered among the forests of that dreadful place. Another thought filtered into his mind. Without N'Kari, his armies really were reduced to the same level of mobility as his enemies. He could no longer reinforce them using the dae-mon's transportation magic. He had taken a gamble by despatching the daemon to seek the Everqueen and it had failed – now he was going to have to pay the price. Swiftly he made a few calculations. The war was still winnable. His forces still enjoyed an overwhelm-ing advantage against a surprised and demoralised enemy.

He had contingency plans. He always did. It seemed like he was going to have to regroup and get ready. The war was going to take longer than he thought, but he could still win it. He was going to have to assemble his forces into one mighty sledgehammer and use it to smash the high elves once and for all. He had his own force. He had these tribes of barbarians. He would hunt down the Ever-queen himself.

'I am very grateful to see you, brother,' Tyrion said. 'And I'm sure that's not something you hear anyone say very often.'

He looked spent, Teclis thought, hovering on the very edge of death. It was a precipice he could fall over at any moment. It was unsurprising. That last blow from N'Kari would have killed a normal elf. The broken ribs he sensed were easy enough to repair. It was something else that troubled Teclis. A dark and evil magic was present within his twin.

'Hush,' Teclis said.

Alarielle hunkered down beside him. 'Thank you,' she said. Teclis looked at her. She was beautiful and her beauty was enhanced by a variety of subtle and complex magics. He sensed another presence within her. He fought to keep her glamour from swaying him.

Teclis spoke a spell of sleep, and Tyrion closed his eyes.

'How was he wounded?' Teclis asked.

'With a poisoned witch elf blade,' Alarielle said. 'He has borne that wound since we left the tournament grounds. I am surprised he is still alive.'

'Then you do not know my brother. He is too stubborn to die.'

'Yes, he is.' Teclis was not surprised by the emotion in her voice. Tyrion always had that effect on women. It appeared not even the Everqueen was immune. 'I tried to heal him, but my grasp of magic is not sure.'

'You might well have killed him.'

'I did not have much choice. He was going to die anyway.'

She was looking at him warily now, measuring him and judging him. It was something he was quite used to from other elves.

'Let's take a look at this wound,' he said, cutting away the area around the tunic with his athame and removing the improvised bandages. The stink of rotting flesh and something else hit him. He looked at the wound. At its centre it was the colour of raw liver, and it was black round the edges. The smell was enough to make him gag. 'I am surprised he is still able to walk. All most people would be able to do in his condition would be lie on the ground and moan.'

'Can you do anything?' Alarielle asked. A frown marked that perfect brow. Long-suppressed tears glittered at the corner of her eyes.

'Let's see, shall we,' said Teclis. He fumbled in his pack and found the small jar of diamond-glass crystal he was looking for. The contents writhed within it. They were maggots of a very special sort. Teclis took them from the jar and placed them on the wound. They inched their way out onto the poisoned flesh and with a horrible slurping sound began to devour it, turning from a sickly yellow to a rotted black as they did so. They ate their own weight in corrupted meat and grew larger and more bloated as they did so, growing from the size of a pared fingernail to the size of a finger in a matter of minutes. Tyrion groaned and stirred in his sleep, but Teclis's spell held him.

The surface of the wound was soon cleared and the edges eaten away until there was only pink natural flesh and seeping blood visible. One by one Teclis took the maggots away, impaled on the point of his athame. They crawled over the blade and tried to bite his hand with their lamprey-like mouths. He dropped them on the ground and incinerated them with magic on a small bonfire made from the stained bandages. A hideous stench arose that was even worse than the smell of the wound.

The wound looked clear. He invoked a forensic spell and studied his brother. The flow of life energy was weak and there were areas of taint and damage in his aura. Teclis wove magic that would cleanse those areas and start them repairing themselves. He spoke wave after wave of spells intended to neutralise poison and cleanse disease. For hours he worked, minutely, carefully, with total concentration and utter care. When he was certain he had done all he could, he spoke the spells that would cause the wounded flesh to knit and then put new bandages in place.

'The healers at my mother's court could have done no better,' Alarielle said.

'I became something of an expert on medical magic at an early age,' Teclis said. 'I have been my own worst patient.'

'Will he live?'

Teclis considered the matter as dispassionately as he could. His brother was very pale and looked more dead than alive. It was shocking to see someone who had always blazed with health looking so sick.

'I do not know,' Teclis said. 'All we can do is wait.'

Teclis sat looking over the fire at the Everqueen. She stared into the flames and then at Tyrion and then back at the flames again. Teclis brewed drugs and medicines that he thought might be needed in a small crucible before transferring them to alembics.

'It was only a few hours ago we were talking about what we would do when we got out of this,' she said. 'It seems like a lifetime ago now.'

'Life is like that,' Teclis said. 'Things that seemed permanent vanish in an instant.'

'Nothing has seemed permanent since the druchii attacked us. We have lived a heartbeat from death for a week.'

Teclis looked at Tyrion. 'I am sure he would have enjoyed that. He always loved danger.'

'Don't talk about him like that. As if he were already gone.'

Teclis simply stared at her. She was not used to being looked at that way, he could tell. 'You look like him,' she said at last.

'You are the first person ever to tell me that. All my life I have lived in the shadow of his good looks.'

Alarielle laughed softly. 'I meant you look at me like him. As if you see a person and not the Everqueen.'

Teclis cocked his head to one side. 'That is interesting. He never had any gift for seeing through magic. I can see the glamours that surround you. I doubt even one in ten mages could. They are fantastically subtle.'

'I don't think he saw any spells at all. He simply reacted against them. I think they made him dislike me, to begin with.'

'Tyrion never disliked anybody in his life. He was... he is very amiable.'

'I did not think so when I met him.'

'I am surprised. Women usually find him very charming.'

'Lots of women?' She sounded jealous and curious at once. Teclis nodded. He felt oddly touched and he was not sure why. He rose from beside the fire and went to check his wards. When he came back the Everqueen was sitting beside his brother, running her hand through his hair.

'What are we going to do?' she asked.

'We can't move him now,' Teclis said. 'We are just going to have to wait here.'

'What if the druchii come?'

'I will deal with them,' Teclis said.

'Can you deal with an army?' she asked.

'I guess we will find out,' he said.

'You don't lack confidence, do you?'

'It is a recent development. I find I have a talent for warfare. I used to assume he was the only one in the family who did.'

'I can see the power in you. Or the Everqueen can. It blazes like a forest on fire.'

'Let's hope I don't have to do that – set the forest on fire!'

'But you will if you have to, won't you?'

'Indubitably, yes.' Teclis wove spells of concealment around them, and they settled down to wait. 'If it would save you both.'

'I've felt better,' Tyrion said. His eyes were open. His voice sounded weak. He was, however, still alive, and these were the first words he had spoken in days.

'I am glad to hear that you are still capable of complaining,' Teclis said.

'It's odd. I thought N'Kari had appeared. It turned out to be you. Not much difference I suppose.'

'The daemon was here,' said Alarielle. 'Your brother banished it.'

'Not for the first time,' said Tyrion. 'It seems it's becoming a habit.'

'I arrived just as you were preparing to make a heroically foolish last stand.'

'You saved me a bit of effort, but I would have beaten him in the end,' Tyrion said. 'I feel fairly confident in saying that.'

'Illness has not increased your intelligence,' said Teclis.

'Nice hat,' Tyrion said. 'We interrupted you on your way to a fancy-dress party, I take it.'

'It is the War Crown of Saphery, worn by defenders of the wizards' realm since time immemorial,' said Teclis.

'It's the right size for your head, and it hides the point your skull comes to, so I suppose it has some benefits.'

'You don't seem surprised that I found you.'

'You have a habit of showing up when least expected.'

'How did you find us?' Alarielle asked.

'It wasn't easy,' Teclis said.

'Don't ask him,' Tyrion said. 'He's a wizard. He will just look mysterious and talk about divinations and the winds of magic.'

'I followed the trail of corpses you left across Avelorn, if truth be told,' Teclis said. Tyrion had fallen asleep again.

'At least I got the last word,' Teclis murmured. 'That happens little enough.'

'That really is the War Crown, isn't it?' Alarielle asked.

'I am surprised you recognised it. It has not been out of the tower for centuries. Most people think it's a legend.'

'*She* recognises it,' Alarielle said. '*She* has seen it many times. It was always worn by heroes.'

'Not this time, I am afraid,' said Teclis. 'They made the mistake of giving it to me.'

'I don't think they made a mistake.'

'That remains to be seen,' said Teclis, reddening. 'What is that staff you are carrying?'

'It is the Moonstaff of Lileath,' Alarielle said. 'I rescued it from the cache in the Winterwood Palace.'

'I wish I had had it when I was fighting N'Kari,' Teclis said. 'It is a powerful magical amplifier. Do you mind if I look at it?'

Alarielle handed the staff over. It fitted Teclis's hand as if it had been moulded for it. He studied the ancient workmanship and the runes inscribed in the shaft. Power flowed through it and around it and he instinctively knew how to use it. With great reluctance, he handed it back to the Everqueen.

'A wondrous thing,' he said.

'Yes,' she said. 'Although I have not been able to make it work.'

'It was intended for certain types of magic.'

'It carries the blessing of the moon goddess, so that is not surprising. She is a patron of spellworkers.'

Teclis said, 'I could tell.' He settled down again by the fire. He was starting to feel restless, stuck here in one place while all around armies of druchii were on the move. Alarielle watched him thoughtfully across the flames.

Teclis studied the chains that had once bound the Keeper of Secrets. They were a potent artefact indeed, ancient, powerful and wrought with complex, sinister magic. Power flowed through them still. There was a sense of presence to them, one not simply associated with the daemon.

He concentrated on them fully, extending his magesight to the point where he no longer looked upon the world of light and shadow, only the flows of magic. He saw the glittering souls of those near him, and the gigantic, deeply hidden power that worked through Alarielle. He saw the whirlpools of magic that vanished into the chains and flowed out again somewhere else. He reached out with a divinatory spell and touched them, and in a lightning-like flash made sharp, shocking contact.

Suddenly he was elsewhere, in a land of cold grey skies, of ice and fire, where glaciers flowed from the north, and lava pits spurted burning rock. Before him stood a massive armoured figure. It turned to look at him with cold, cruel eyes. Teclis knew at once who he faced. He had made a mistake. The chains were still connected with N'Kari's binder, the Witch King of Naggaroth.

Malekith looked at him. Teclis felt himself being judged by a being older than kingdoms, only little less than a god. Malekith had walked the world in the time of Aenarion. He was one of the oldest sentient beings on the planet, perhaps the mightiest. The Witch King's mere presence made Teclis acknowledge his own insignificance.

He forced himself to meet Malekith's gaze and smile.

The eyes surprised him. There was a sadness and a loneliness in them that shocked Teclis, mingled with an astonishing, rapacious lust to dominate was a sense of black wisdom. Most of all there was pride – the pride of one who had sought to emulate a living god and could not admit that he had failed, had been judged and found wanting. Malekith was a titan who had once defied the will of the gods and defied it still even though the struggle was hopeless.

Teclis had expected to feel hatred and fear. What he had not expected to feel was pity.

'You look like him,' Malekith said in a voice like a brazen gong being smote deep underground. There was power and assurance in that voice, a timbre acquired from aeons of chanting time-lost spells and bellowing commands across long-forgotten battlefields. It rang with malice and hatred and something else it took Teclis a moment to recognise – loneliness.

There was no need to ask who *he* was. Malekith could mean only one being, his father, Aenarion.

'You do not,' Teclis forced himself to say. It took an effort of will comparable to invoking the most recalcitrant elemental. He made it sound effortless. Nothing else would do.

Malekith laughed, and Teclis felt himself lashed by the Witch King's bitterness and scorn. 'I can see why Urian liked you, little cripple. You are somewhat alike.'

'Urian?'

'You know him by a different name, but no matter. He told me about you, Teclis.'

'I have banished your daemon,' Teclis said. 'You will no longer be able to move so freely around Ulthuan.' Teclis felt he had somehow caught the Witch King's interest. Malekith was not used to being challenged. His curiosity was piqued. He was like a great cat amusing itself with a small mouse before the kill.

'So you have learned that secret, have you?' Malekith said. 'And defeated the Keeper of Secrets again. Hell will be filled with its screams of frustration this day.'

Malekith sounded amused. Teclis was surprised to discover he had a sense of humour. He noticed something else in the air, a psychic scent he had encountered before; it came from Malekith. It was the faintest trace of the Flame of Asuryan. Of course, Teclis thought. It still burned within the flesh of the tyrant, must have done so since his attempt at apotheosis all those millennia ago. The merest beginning of an idea occurred to Teclis. Perhaps there was a way to defeat Malekith using magic, if only he could get close enough.

'Leave Ulthuan,' Teclis said. 'You can do yourself only harm here.'

'It is not for you to tell me what to do, little cripple.'

'If you do not, this little cripple will give you a lesson in using magic.'

Malekith laughed. Teclis did not flinch. He had endured a lifetime of mockery from his fellow elves. He had schooled himself to endure it.

'You do not lack for confidence, I will give you that,' Malekith said. 'There is power in you, youth, power such as I once saw in Caledor, but it takes more than power to make a wizard. It takes centuries of experience and a willingness to face the deepest, darkest secrets of the universe.'

That caught Teclis's attention, as any mention of magical secrets always did. He thrust his curiosity to one side. 'Perhaps, but to achieve victory, it only takes knowledge of one spell, if that spell is the correct one.'

'Do not let your triumphs over N'Kari make you overconfident. I am not some bound daemon.'

'Nonetheless, if you face me, you will know defeat.'

Malekith regarded him steadily, as if taking him seriously for the first time. He was looking at him, really looking at him. It was not the sort of attention that was calculated to make anyone comfortable. 'I have known defeat many times,' Malekith said, at last. 'But I doubt you are one to inflict it upon me.'

'Then face me if you dare.'

'That day will come soon enough,' said Malekith. 'When it dawns it will be your last.'

A wave of power erupted from him. The link with the chains that had bound N'Kari was broken. Teclis opened his eyes and looked upon Alarielle and his sleeping brother. It seemed as though his audience with the Witch King was over. It was just as well. Through the link he had sensed that Malekith was much closer than he had expected. It would not take the Witch King long to come find them.

Malekith brooded. The incursion of the young sorcerer Teclis into his very thoughts was unexpected.

The youth had shown a power that was awesome. It had taken Malekith millennia to become so strong. Teclis had been born into it. Now, Malekith regretted not instructing Urian to kill the mage when he was still a youth. In the course of a century he had become powerful enough to challenge Malekith himself. If he lived, he would become one of the great powers of this world.

It seemed that like his brother, Teclis was destined to be a thorn in Malekith's side, to spoil his plans at every turn. Tyrion had saved the Everqueen. Teclis had saved Tyrion from N'Kari. They were his own kin in a distant way, blood of Aenarion. He supposed that they had some claim to the throne of Ulthuan and Naggaroth too. It was another reason to wipe them from the face of the earth. He would brook no challengers to his mantle of power.

Malekith knew roughly where Teclis was now. The link had given him a sense of that. He lay along the path that Malekith had to take anyway, to find the Everqueen and crush all asur resistance in this part of the world.

When the time arose he would find this Teclis and destroy him. Yet there was something in the youth's confidence that troubled him. Could it be that Teclis knew something he did not? Was he about to endure another setback to his great plan?

No matter, he told himself. Whatever happened, he would endure and ultimately triumph. He summoned Urian and his generals to him. He knew now where Teclis was through the link the chains had given him. He knew he would find Tyrion and the Everqueen there too. It was time for the hunt to begin.

Caledor studied the gameboard. So much was happening now, so many pieces were in play, it was difficult to keep track of everything. At least part of his plan had worked, and for that he felt grateful. Tyrion and Teclis were reunited and between them they had saved the Everqueen. Two of his greatest enemies, two of the greatest challenges facing him had been removed from the board – Morathi and N'Kari were both out of play. All that remained now was Malekith, and he was sure to prove the most difficult of all.

A small part of his mind whispered that he could stop now, with the removal of Morathi and the Keeper of Secrets his great work was safe for the moment, but he knew this was a lie. If Malekith ruled Ulthuan, Morathi would find some way to undo his spell, or the secret masters of the Cult of Luxury would, or perhaps even Malekith himself would be tempted. The druchii still needed to be stopped and he still needed to do what was necessary.

All of Ulthuan was a great swirl of confusion. Armies were on the move. Forces from everywhere were being drawn into a great whirlpool of violence, moving through forests, along the coasts, across the Inner Sea. Caledor found his attention inevitably drawn to this great nexus of conflict. His vision settled on the vast flat expanse of Finuval Plain in Saphery. This was the place where the crisis would come, where this conflict would be resolved for good or ill. It was there that the small, embattled force of high elves would make their stand and the fate of the world would be decided.

Malekith was in Saphery, uniting a great force of barbarians with his army. One by one he was bringing their chieftains and warlords to heel. He knew now where Teclis was and Tyrion and the Everqueen, and they were still central to the struggle. Malekith had a huge army of humans and druchii with him, as well as his own not inconsiderable talents as a sorcerer. He could still triumph all too easily.

One by one, forces of high elves were converging together to oppose him, small warbands coming from all over the island continent, drawn by rumours of imminent conflict and the news that the Everqueen was still alive. They were drawn to her banner from every part of the island. Many of them had been pilgrims on their way to visit Avelorn when the invasion came. Some of them had survived the invasion itself. Wizards came from Saphery. Riders from the proud land of Ellyrion. Mountain-dwellers from Cothique and Chrace. At first they gathered together in their scores, then scores became hundreds and then hundreds became thousands. They went from fighting a guerrilla war to becoming an army, albeit one that was hugely outnumbered in its own homeland.

There was one last thing he could do. He reached out to a small pawn, travelling with a reforged suit of armour across the length of the plain. He nudged its thoughts and dreams in a certain direction. He needed what the figure carried to be in the right place at the right time.

Caledor was at the end of his strength. He knew now that there was very little more he could do to influence events. The fate of the elves was in other hands than his.

Dorian looked at the captain. The warrior looked tired. There were dark shadows underneath his eyes and his face was leaner. He did not look like part of the victorious army. He looked like many a soldier Dorian had seen before, one who had been fighting for too long without respite and with too little rest.

'You were attacked,' Dorian said. It was not a question. He could see from the way the elf's arm was bandaged and from the bruises on his face that he had been in a fight. The fact that half the captain's soldiers looked just as battered told the same story. The captain nodded.

'Yes, general.' Dorian realised that he had made another mistake. He smiled sourly. It was just the last of many in a stream that no doubt would put an end to his career once Malekith found out about them.

His army had ploughed through southern Avelorn, meeting no resistance. They had put the few elf villages that they had encountered to the sword or the torch when they had been inhabited. They had been abandoned by those who had lived there in the face of the oncoming dark elf army. He followed up all the reports of trails that might have led to the Everqueen and her mysterious defender.

Malekith's assassins had not returned, nor had the sorcerers Morathi had sent. Something told Dorian they never would.

He had kept his trackers out there looking for the Everqueen and hordes of warriors who could be trusted to find their way around in the deep woods. That had been a mistake.

Now at last the asur had begun to organise themselves. At first, the resistance had been almost pitiful. There had been a few ambushes committed by young and inexperienced elves. They had resulted in few casualties. Some of the attackers had been caught and made an example of by the druchii. They had learned though. They had gained in experience and they had been joined by others, silent, grim elves from the deep woods who knew how to track and avoid being tracked, who came and went like shadows in the night, leaving behind them sentries with slit throats and dead dark elves.

They had added hallucinogenic poisons to the food supplies, which left some of the druchii dying, screaming that they were being attacked by ghosts. He had been forced to regroup his forces into larger units, which made progress slower and following the trails harder. There had been more ambushes by larger groups of asur, and attacks that resulted in things that were almost as large as full-scale battles. His forces had taken more and more casualties. The offensive into Avelorn was being bogged down. Resistance was becoming stiffer. Morale was getting worse. The quest for the Everqueen still had not borne fruit.

Things might have become grim indeed had he not received reinforcements from a most unexpected quarter. Humans were starting to find their way into Avelorn in greater and greater numbers. He was not sure where they were coming from. It seemed like entire tribes and warbands had become detached from Morathi's offensive in the north and had somehow drifted south into Avelorn.

He sensed that there was more to this than a simple loss of cohesion in the great invasion force. These humans seemed to have their own agenda although they were not talking about what it was they wanted.

Now they too were stalking the woods and joining with the asur in battle. There were far more of them than there were druchii, it seemed like they were keeping more and more of the high elves busy. His troops were starting to come across battlegrounds where humans had fought with high elves. They had found the bodies of the tattooed invaders and their black-armoured leaders mingled with those of the denizens of Avelorn. Having spent a great deal of his career fighting against the servants of Chaos, Dorian felt a certain satisfaction. He was not looking upon the bodies of dead allies when he saw the worshippers of Chaos lying there. He was looking upon the corpses of potential enemies.

There were tales of some mighty wizard stalking the forest as well. A messenger had reached him from his starting point at the tournament grounds, telling him of a great massacre that had taken place there. It seemed impossible to believe that one magician, no matter how powerful, could have destroyed the holding force he had left behind to guard his evacuation route, but there had been no mistaking the truth in the messenger's words or the fear on his face when he described the massacre this wizard had perpetrated.

Not for the first time, he wished that Cassandra was still with him. She would have been able to advise him on how to deal with this wizard. She had not only been a very powerful sorceress but she had been very skilled in the tactics needed to overcome her fellow mages. He missed her more than he could find the words to say. It was just as well there was no one left for him to say them to.

It was clear that the captain before him was looking to him for orders and encouragement. Dorian could not find the words for that either. Instead he dismissed the captain with a gesture and said, 'Go, get some food and then some sleep. Tomorrow we shall set out and find these ambushers and teach them not to attack our forces.'

Horns sounded. A troop of riders rode up to his tent. One of them was Lord Telmar, a high noble from Malekith's entourage. Dorian was shocked. He knew this druchii should be hundreds of leagues away.

Telmar gave him an ironic salute that revealed the signet of Malekith. 'General Dorian, you are not an easy elf to find. Our king requests your presence, General Dorian, along with all your army. He has work for you out on Finuval Plain.'

Briefly Dorian considered refusing, but it was pointless. The alternative was to remain here until his command was slaughtered by the asur. 'He requests my presence personally?' Dorian asked.

'Oh yes, the Witch King is there himself. Malekith the Great is only a few days' march from here. He intends to do with his own hands what you could not – find and kill the Everqueen.'

Dorian shrugged and began to issue orders. It seemed that he would be facing Malekith sooner than he had expected.

So it was true, Tyrion thought. There was an elven army here. Coming over the rise, walking wearily with his brother limping on one side and the Everqueen on the other, he realised that they had done it. It had taken them long weeks of walking and hiding, of spreading the word that the Everqueen was still alive whenever they met a high elf, but it looked like finally they had reached a safe haven. Over the past few days, he had had his doubts whether they would. It seemed like a vast army of druchii was moving across the plains; they had come close to being captured more than once.

Ahead of them lay a small city of tents that looked far more makeshift than the great tournament grounds ever had. Among the tents were the banners of hundreds of elven noblemen. It seemed as if elves from all over Ulthuan had come to this place. It was as surprising as discovering a great festival in the middle of nowhere. But, at last, he told himself Alarielle was safe.

He felt better now – Teclis had proven what a master healer he was. The effects of the witch elves' poison were completely gone. His enormous vitality had reasserted itself. His side was healed and he was as fit as he ever had been.

It was strange. Over the past few weeks a distance had grown up between himself and the Everqueen. Teclis's mocking and sardonic presence had been part of the cause, but there were other reasons. Tyrion was sick and withdrawn most of the time and Alarielle distant as she communed with the power within her, seeking solutions for the problems of her people. They were no longer as close or as intimate as they had been during their long flight through the woods of Avelorn. Alarielle had withdrawn into herself, as if shrinking from him, becoming daily more silent and thoughtful.

They reached the edge of the great army camp. Elves looked at them with suspicious eyes. Of course, Tyrion thought, they were worried about spies. They were wondering who the strangers were. There was a simple answer for that. He gestured for the watchers to come closer and gather round. Once he had attracted a crowd, he shouted, 'Kneel! The Everqueen is among you.'

Alarielle removed her hood. The spell that compelled adoration radiated out from her. All of the elves present knelt and gave thanks for her delivery. Word of it rippled out through the camp. They were ushered into the presence of the army's leaders, hastily arranged in council to greet their queen.

A great cry went up, 'The Everqueen is saved!'

Tyrion looked around at the assembled group of nobles and warriors. He was astonished to see a number of familiar and unexpected

faces in the crowd. Korhien Ironglaive was there and so was Arhalien of Yvresse. Tyrion wondered if any others had survived the
surprise attack on the tournament grounds. There were clearly stories that he needed to hear as soon as possible, but for the moment
he needed to concentrate on the asur army and its leaders.

This was not an army in the traditional sense, he realised. It was a
gathering of desperate elves who had come together because there was
no place else to go. Now Alarielle was the focal point of their effort,
partially because they wanted to protect her but partially because they
needed protection themselves. They were huddling together like a herd
of wild cattle forming a circle to protect themselves from predators.

He had to admit Alarielle formed an admirable living banner for
them to rally to. The spell of the Everqueen kept all eyes focused
on her; he knew that there was not an elf present who would not
give his life to protect her, with the possible exception of Teclis. He
would do it himself, and not because he was compelled by ancient
magic. He would do it because...

Looking at those adoring faces, he wanted to punch them for
their stupidity. Could they not see she was worth protecting for
herself, not because of the spells around her? Was he the only one
who understood that?

He forced himself to unclench his fists, to relax. They were not
responsible for their actions here, any more than she was. In this, as
in so much else, they were the pawns of powers greater than themselves. Speeches were given welcoming the Everqueen. She spoke,
thanking Tyrion and Teclis for her deliverance. The brothers were
cheered to the high heavens when the tale was told, but business
pressed on. There was much to be discussed.

Scouts had brought word that a huge army under the Witch King
was approaching. It would be upon them in a few days, maybe less.
They were badly outnumbered. The thing to do was flee, a few of
the nobles claimed. Their words sounded sensible, but could they
not see they were making a huge error? Alarielle must have noticed
something written on his face for she said, 'Prince Tyrion, you obviously disagree with what Lord Marin said.'

All eyes shot to him. He stepped forwards, giving them a chance
to look at him. He weighed his words carefully, trying to put his
objections into words. 'If we flee, our army will fall to pieces. The
different components will all move at different speeds. The cavalry will outrun the infantry. The refugees who have joined us will
be left behind.'

A tall elf garbed like a lord of the riders of Ellyrion said, 'We will not leave our people to be captured by the Witch King.'

'Then you will be overhauled and destroyed. The druchii have a disciplined army. It can march leagues in a day if it has to and maintain its formations. We cannot. This is not a picked force dispatched on a mission by the Phoenix King. This is simply a ragged assembly of survivors.'

There was a hubbub of voices. Many disagreed with him. A few took his words as an insult. Many of those with military experience knew he was talking sense.

'What would you suggest we do?' Korhien Ironglaive asked. He held up a huge hand for silence. His tone was challenging, but Tyrion knew the White Lion was really giving him a chance to explain.

'Our position here is as strong as it's going to get. We have the advantage of high ground and a flank protected by the Everflow on one side and woods on the other. We can take our stand here. If the gods are with us, we can win. If not, a force of fast riders must be prepared to take the Everqueen away. It would be better if she departed at once and we can hold the ground until she escapes.'

Alarielle shook her head. 'I have run far enough. I will not leave this place unless I have to.'

'But we cannot face the Witch King and his champion, this Urian Poisonblade,' someone shouted. 'He has slaughtered everyone who has faced him.'

'Ah, but we can,' said a sardonic voice from the edge of the council. It took Tyrion a long moment to realise that it belonged to Teclis. His twin stepped up to his side.

'Malekith can be defeated,' he said.

'How?' a voice demanded.

'By magic,' Teclis responded. 'He has a weakness that can be exploited.'

'And what would this weakness be, that no one has been able to discover for six thousand years?'

'I will not say,' said Teclis, 'lest word of it reaches his ears and he takes measures to protect against it.'

'You are seriously claiming you can beat the Witch King?'

Teclis nodded. 'I dismissed his pet daemon. I walked unscathed through his armies. Trust me, I can do this.'

All eyes looked at him, some with disbelief, some with awe, some with hope.

A scout ran up and shouted, 'We have sighted the Witch King's army. It will be upon us by tomorrow evening at the latest.'

Alarielle looked at the council and said, 'What is it to be? Stand or run? For myself, I will stay, but anyone who wants to is free to go.'

There was silence for a long moment, then a roar of affirmation that the army would stay.

'I hope this magic of yours works, brother,' Tyrion said so quietly that no one else could hear him.

'So do I,' Teclis replied. 'Our lives depend on it.'

'More than just ours,' Tyrion replied, unable to take his eyes off the Everqueen.

'Tyrion!' He turned to find the source of that well-remembered roaring voice pushing through the crowd, and found himself whirled into the air by the massive, muscular arms of Korhien Ironglaive. 'It is good to see you again.'

'Korhien!' Tyrion shouted. 'I might have known I would find you where the action was thickest.'

Korhien gave a sour grimace. 'That is everywhere these days. It seems like our land is overrun by these pests from Naggaroth.'

He was speaking loudly so that his confident assertion could be overheard. He wanted his contempt for their enemy well known and spread about the camp. He was doing his bit to keep up asur morale.

'How did you get here?' Tyrion asked. 'I would have thought you would have been in Lothern. I hear there has been fighting there.'

'I was dispatched to carry the war torch to our armies, to summon our people to the defence of the land. I was dispatched to the White Tower with messages, and from there was taking the word to Prince Moranion. I fell in with your father. He carries a burden of great importance.'

'My father is here? I thought he would never leave his beloved armour.'

'He has brought it with him. He was plagued by prophetic dreams. It seems half the wizards of Ulthuan have been, and the other half have not been getting enough sleep to do so.'

'How did you get here?'

'Once we were on the road, we just got caught up in the war. I was not jesting when I said those maggots were everywhere. We were chased hither and yon about the plain until I found Lord Marin's force, then we turned and gave those druchii a mauling.'

'I am very glad to hear it and even more glad to see you.'

'We must have a drink to celebrate. Come to my tent and we shall have some wine and you can tell me lies about your great feats of heroism.' Something about Korhien's expression told Tyrion that he wanted to discuss matters that were not for public hearing. He followed his old teacher through the vast encampment with a growing sense of foreboding.

They took a seat inside an old tent and Korhien rummaged in his pack for a bottle of wine. He pulled out the cork with his teeth and passed it to Tyrion. 'No fine goblets here, I am afraid,' he said. 'Drink it down. You will need it.'

'Why do I have the feeling I am not going to like what you are going to tell me?'

'Because you know me too well.' Tyrion took a swig of the wine. It had been a long time since he had drunk any of the stuff. It went down well but it tasted sour.

Korhien grinned. 'It's useful for washing out wounds as well as giving you hangovers.'

Tyrion handed the bottle over and Korhien gulped it down. 'It does the job,' he said.

'What news of the war?' Tyrion asked.

'Bad as bad can be,' Korhien said. 'The druchii took us completely by surprise. Armies everywhere as if by magic. A dozen towns fell before anyone even knew it. Fortresses were besieged. A horde of barbarians have set fire to the north and are swarming through the rest of Ulthuan like maggots in a corpse.'

'Not a pretty image.'

'It's not a pretty time. The worst of it is not just that we were made to look like fools and half-beaten before the war even started. The worst of it was that we were betrayed.'

Tyrion looked up at the note of bitterness in his old friend's voice. He accepted the bottle and took another swig. 'Traitors? Who?'

'Iltharis for one.' Tyrion felt as if the bottom had just dropped out of his world.

'Prince Iltharis?'

'Do you know anyone else of that name?'

'I don't believe it.'

'I said the same thing, but he was seen giving instructions to a band of druchii sympathisers who tried to open the gates of Lothern to the dark elves.'

'He would not do that. There must be some mistake.'

'No mistake at all. He took a swipe at me en route to attempting to kill Finubar.'

'No.'

'Yes. Walked up to me, greeted me like a long-lost brother and then smacked me on the back of the head with the hilt of his sword. Knocked me out and left me with a bump the size of a peacock's egg. Fortunately my skull is so thick or I would not be here to tell you this tale of woe.'

'He could have slit your throat.'

'But he didn't. He'll pay for that mistake.'

'He did not kill you. Maybe he was being blackmailed or did it against his will.'

'He was changed, Tyrion. I am not sure how or what I can say to convince you, but I don't think he was reluctant about what he was doing. Mad, maybe, the way druchii are mad, but not reluctant.'

'He tried to kill Finubar?'

'He would have done it too, but while he was slaughtering a few White Lions, the Phoenix King escaped through the old secret tunnels in the palace. Iltharis followed him too, knew his way through what was supposedly a sacred, secret area. He must have been scouting out the place for decades.'

'How did Finubar get away?'

'Out into the harbour and onto a ship. Lady Malene was there and a bunch of house archers and enough troops to give even Iltharis pause. He vanished into the night, while the traitors were spreading panic. No one has seen him since.'

'I can't believe it,' said Tyrion, but he found he could. After the events of the past few months, nothing could surprise him.

'I couldn't either at first, but the crack in my skull was real.'

'Iltharis? A druchii spy? It's impossible. Who would have the patience to playact for all those years?'

'He did obviously.'

'Maybe it was magic, a spell.'

'Maybe.' It was obvious that Korhien had already discounted that possibility.

'This is not good news. I doubt a more dangerous elf ever lived than Iltharis – he knows all our secrets. He was part of the Phoenix King's council. He worked out what N'Kari was up to all those years ago.'

'He calls himself Urian now, according to those who have seen him. He leads warbands across the plain and kills all who oppose him. Some say he is invincible.'

'We shall have to put that to the test.'

'At least N'Kari no longer fights against us. Your brother sent it back to hell. He's become quite frightening himself, young Teclis, if the tales are to be believed.'

'They are.'

'What changed him?'

'I think he has discovered that he likes killing elves.'

'If anyone ever had a reason to, it was him. His life has not been an easy one.'

Suddenly Tyrion was annoyed with his old friend. Now that Teclis was a hero, people were beginning to sympathise with him and to understand his pain. They had never managed that before. He managed to keep the smile on his face. 'That is the truth.'

Korhien smiled. 'And you. You have become quite the hero too. Rescuing the Everqueen right out of the middle of a druchii army. It's like something from one of the old legends.'

Tyrion shrugged. 'I was in the right place at the right time.'

'You were also the right elf. That is important.'

'She saved herself really though, and she saved me a dozen times. I would not be here now if it was not for her.'

'Nor she if it was not for you. You've picked a bad time to become afflicted with false modesty, Tyrion. What this land needs now more than ever is heroes.'

'And I look like one, don't I?' said Tyrion sourly. He and Korhien looked at each other for a long moment. There was an odd hostility in the air, then Korhien grinned and said, 'You most certainly do. I suspect you will look more like one before this is over.'

Tyrion wondered what he meant.

'Teclis!' The wizard looked round to see Belthania waving at him. She was in the presence of a company of Sword Masters from Hoeth. More wizards accompanied her. He limped wearily over to where she stood.

'Hello,' he said, and she surprised him by kissing him on both cheeks.

'You did it,' she said. She was smiling. The Sword Masters were smiling too. 'You saved the Everqueen.'

'My brother did that. I just helped them escape.' He felt embarrassed. He did not like being the centre of attention, or the hero of the hour. He seemed to be recognised everywhere he went now. People pointed at him. He felt self-conscious. For some reason, he limped more.

'You banished a greater daemon. You spirited them out from among the armies of the Witch King. It's like something out of an old heroic tale.'

'I am not a hero,' he said.

'You are to most of us.'

'How times have changed,' he said sourly.

'You haven't,' she said. 'You are still a sour bastard.' She was smiling as she said it though.

'I like to be consistent,' he said. 'Is there any news from Hoeth?'

'The White Tower still stands. No one has attacked it so far though. There is other news...'

'What?'

'Malekith is here on the plain. He has come with his army, seeking the Everqueen no doubt.' Teclis felt cold fingers run up and down his spine. He had challenged the Witch King. Now it seemed he might actually have to face him. He hoped his idea about Malekith's weakness was correct.

Teclis felt a hand on his shoulder. He turned and much to his surprise saw Prince Arathion.

'Father,' he said, 'what are you doing here?'

'I came bringing the armour of Aenarion to where it was most needed.'

'Then you're in the right place.'

'I am not so sure about that.' Something in his father's tone alarmed Teclis much more than it should have done.

'So, Urian, what shall I do with this one?' Malekith asked. Urian looked at the elaborately dressed and yet shabby figure before him. It took a few moments to recognise his own half-brother. He had heard word that General Dorian and his force had just joined the great army of humans and druchii surging across Finuval Plain in pursuit of the Everqueen. He had not realised that the general might prove to be his brother.

Dorian had aged greatly for an elf. The last time Urian had seen him he had been relatively young. So this is what I used to look like, Urian thought. He did not doubt that there was a certain resemblance in his brother's features to the way he had once looked. Of course, the Witch King's magicians had changed all of that when they had transformed him into an assassin. His features no longer bore any resemblance to those worn by his family. This did not stop him from feeling a certain nostalgia. In fact, it virtually guaranteed it.

Dorian looked at him, confused. He was obviously wondering why this stranger was being addressed by his brother's name. Was it possible that he did not yet suspect the answer?

Malekith's iron gaze moved from one brother to the other and then to the huge crowd of druchii nobles and human warlords gathered around his throne. Urian knew that he was enjoying this. It appealed to his cruel sense of humour. 'This is a general who failed us. He had the Everqueen in his grasp and he lost her. He made no report to his ruler over many weeks while he sought to rectify his error, or so he claims. And he seems somewhat lacking in fraternal feeling – he has failed to greet his younger brother.'

Dorian's eyes widened. He studied Urian closely and then shook his head, as if he could see no resemblance. In some ways, Urian knew that what was happening here was in some ways a reward for his services. There had never been any love lost between him and his brother when they were younger, which was something of a tradition among druchii siblings.

He was expected to name a punishment for Dorian, the crueller the better. After all, it was what most druchii would do to their elder brother. There had been times when he had dreamed of doing so himself when he was young. He had hated Dorian for standing in his way, for being the heir, for being the eldest. He had disliked his older brother's self-confidence and the way he seemed to feel that he was born to command and that others were born to obey. There was a time when this would have been a reward indeed, and Urian knew that.

He did not feel that way now though. He felt almost nothing. He did not resent this cowed-looking stranger. He did not desire revenge. He did not even desire to be particularly cruel. He knew though that such an admission would be seen as a weakness. It was not something he could afford to let slip before his ruler. He did not want Malekith to know how much he had changed during his time among the high elves. He did not want anyone here to know that or even suspect it.

The prospect of ordering Dorian to be tortured did nothing for him. In fact, he found himself thinking back to the long-gone time when they had been young, and he discovered that there were some points of contact that he did not regret – there were moments of shared experience that he even had rather enjoyed.

He did not owe Dorian anything – no favours but not a cruel death either. He looked around at the faces of the courtiers. All of them were watching him closely, some of them licking their lips in anticipation. No doubt all of them were thinking about what they would do to their own kin in a similar situation.

Urian felt nothing but repulsion for those who surrounded him. He wished most devoutly that he was back among the high elves and fighting on their side. The intensity of that feeling surprised him. He had changed much more than he liked to think and not in a good way as far as his prospects of survival were concerned.

Dorian looked up at him baffled. No doubt he was thinking about what he would do in a similar situation. He was probably working his way through all of the inventive tortures that could be inflicted by the minions of the Witch King if they were so instructed. Clearly he anticipated nothing except a long-drawn-out and painful death.

Urian took another glance at all of those surrounding them and felt the pressure of compulsion upon him.

With one lightning-like move he drew his blade and slashed off Dorian's head, then he picked it up by the hair and presented it with a flourish to the Witch King.

'Failure deserves nothing but swift punishment,' Urian said as loudly as he could.

Malekith looked at him enigmatically. Urian wondered what he was thinking. There was a long moment of silence while the audience waited for the king's response. Malekith reached out and accepted the severed head and studied it for a moment before tossing it away.

'You're correct, Urian,' he said. 'Your efficiency surprises me and rather pleases me. It seems you have learned something during your stay among the asur.' Urian wondered whether anyone else detected the ambiguity in Malekith's words.

'Soon we shall encounter the ragtag army that has gathered to protect the Everqueen. I shall have a new duty for you then,' Malekith said. 'There are several people I want you to kill.'

'I look forward to it,' Urian lied.

The blood-red light of the setting sun blazed down on the chaos of the battlefield. The screams of the dying and the hellish clamour of blade on blade echoed in Tyrion's ears. Leaning forwards in the saddle, he rammed his sword into the heart of a howling dark elf foot soldier, smashing him down to be trampled under the hooves of his borrowed steed.

Glancing around quickly, he took in the battlefield.

What a terrible place this Finuval Plain would be to die, he thought: a horrible, empty, dreary moorland that few had ever heard of before today. His small cavalry force was badly outnumbered and surrounded by chanting dark elf infantry, part of the vanguard of the Witch King's approaching army. The dark elves fought with the mechanical discipline of automatons and a cold courage as impressive as it was daunting.

Tyrion turned in the saddle and lashed out with his blade, sending the head of his foe flying among his comrades, leaving an arcing trail of blood in its wake. He let his stroke continue and his blade crunched through ribs. Another dark elf flopped to the earth, his spine severed and his body writhing uncontrollably.

Tyrion raised his shield to deflect a blow he saw coming out of the corner of his eye. He felt the impact all the way up his armoured arm. He brought the edge of his shield down on his attacker's face, smashing nose and teeth, leaving another enemy to be trampled beneath the metal-shod hooves of his steed.

'For Alarielle, for the Everqueen!' Tyrion shouted. Just mentioning the name of his lady gave him new vigour and renewed his determination to fight and win. The tired high elves around him responded, hacking about them with more energy, smashing through their foes and into the clear plain beyond.

Tyrion raised his sword above his head and gestured for them to form up, turn around and charge once more into the foe. They responded like heroes. Their formation tightened, their ranks drawing together with the same precision they would have shown on a parade ground. The gaps in the ranks vanished as the unit's frontage collapsed.

As one the proud cavalry wheeled and trotted forwards, gaining thunderous momentum as they went. Amid the ranks of the dark elves, sergeants bellowed instructions, trying to ready their line to take the shock of impact.

Tyrion sensed there was something wrong here. He glanced around to see what it was and noticed that from the left, coming down from the nearby hills was a formation of dark elven cavalry. If Tyrion's force kept to the same course, the dark elves would take his warriors in the flank even as they buried their blades in the druchii infantry.

'Wheel right!' Tyrion bellowed, his voice carrying over the oceanic roar of battle. There was nothing else to be done. Charging upslope would put his knights at a disadvantage, but it was better than being taken in the flank or rear. Also they were heavier armoured and mounted on better steeds.

Lesser horse-soldiers would not have been able to respond to his command, but these elves adjusted their course instantly, and tensed as they saw what their leader had seen and the trap they had so narrowly avoided.

Metallic thunder raged as the two lines came together, the heavier high elf cavalry smashing through the lighter dark elves despite the other's advantage of slope and momentum. As the two lines came together, Tyrion was shocked to see a familiar face among the dark elf lines. Fear and hatred warred in his heart. He had been seeking a worthy foe and suddenly he had found one.

'Iltharis! Or Urian or whatever you call yourself! Face me, traitor, and die!' His bellow carried above the sounds of battle, as did the answering laugh.

'Prince Tyrion! This is a not-unexpected pleasure.' Somehow Iltharis's mocking voice carried over the ring of metal on metal. It sounded almost conversational. There was magic in that voice, although the dark elf gave no sign of being a mage. Iltharis carried a glowing runeblade in each hand and he used them to cut his way towards Tyrion, slashing through seasoned elf warriors as if they were no more than children. He guided his black steed easily with his knees, a war-rider with centuries of practice in his art.

Blade rang against blade as steed encountered steed. Tyrion's steed was heavier. He reared and lashed out with its fore-hooves and crushed the skull of Urian's mount. With the grace of a tumbler, the dark elf left his saddle, somersaulted and landed on the ground beside Tyrion. His blades rose and opened Tyrion's horse's belly, sending ropes of gut dripping to the ground. Less gracefully than his foe, Tyrion left the saddle and hit the ground. He tried to roll but the shield strapped to his arm prevented it, and he flopped gracelessly down.

Even as he rose, he felt a blade at his neck. It glowed with evil magic, far worse than anything on a witch elf's weapon. He knew that he was dead if his opponent wanted him to be. His luck had finally run out and he would never have the chance to look upon Alarielle's face again. Everything seemed to slow, as if they stood in the heart of some magical maelstrom, untouched by the battle raging around them.

'Shall I kill you, Prince Tyrion?' Iltharis whispered in his ear. 'Shall I do you that great favour?'

'Do what you wish, traitor,' Tyrion said. 'This is the sort of treacherous attack I am sure you would call a victory.'

Iltharis's laughter was mocking. 'You were unlucky, my prince. I would not claim this as any sort of victory. You are almost worthy of my blade now.'

'A traitor's blade, Iltharis.'

'Alas, though it pains me to contradict you, Blood of Aenarion, a traitor I am not. I have always been loyal to one master. And please call me Urian. It is my name, after all.'

Tyrion lashed out with his elbow, hoping to catch Urian off guard. The dark elf avoided the blow effortlessly.

'I would be doing you a favour killing you, you know,' he said.

'Really?'

'My master holds a grudge against you, you and your brother both. His vengeance will be as terrible as it is inevitable. Take my advice, kill yourself and your brother and your beloved queen. It would be better for all three of you than falling into his hands.'

Oddly enough Urian sounded sincere.

'Is that why you have not slit my throat? Because your master wants me alive?'

'Astute as ever, Prince Tyrion. I knew I could count on that razor-sharp wit of yours.'

'You will forgive me if I do not take your advice,' said Tyrion.

'I fear the day will dawn when you will have cause to regret that. Believe me or not, Prince Tyrion, I have always liked you and your brother, and I am not lying to you now. I never really have.'

'You have a funny definition of the truth.'

'All sentient beings have their own definition of the truth, and it is usually a funny one when you get down to it. Life is a black cosmic joke.'

Tyrion threw himself forwards, rolling, and came to his feet facing Urian. It seemed the dark elf was sincere about not killing him. He had not planted his blade in Tyrion's back although he was more than quick enough to have done so. Tyrion advanced, shield angled, blade ready. Urian stood waiting, blades held negligently in each hand, as if he faced a foe unworthy of real effort.

Tyrion struck. Urian parried. Tyrion unleashed the full fury of his sword arm. Urian parried, slowly at first and then faster and faster as Tyrion's strokes gained momentum. Tyrion had never fought so well. His every movement was eye-blurringly swift, his every blow was struck with a force that would have cut through his target if he had managed to land one.

He never did.

No matter how swiftly he struck, Urian always parried. No matter how cunningly he feinted, Urian always avoided the trap, and slowly, with the effortless grace of a big cat, he began to fight back, working ripostes into his swordplay that Tyrion was hard put to parry, gliding forwards easily, and with such cunning that without really knowing how it had happened Tyrion found himself on the defensive, backing away, taking blows on his shield that fell with all the force of a blacksmith's hammer on an anvil.

Urian grinned. 'You have been practising, prince. I don't believe you have ever fought better.'

Tyrion did not respond. He lashed out with a wild flailing cut that Urian ducked under. In return Urian stepped forwards and sent Tyrion reeling with a blow to the helm with the pommel of his sword.

'Given time, I believe you could almost be as good as I am. Maybe even better. So sad that your time is over.'

One of Tyrion's soldiers, seeing what had happened, let out a war-cry and charged towards them. As the rider bore down on him, Urian leapt, kicking him from the saddle and twisting himself to land on the horse's back. A moment later he raised his blade to Tyrion in a farewell salute.

'Goodbye, Prince Tyrion. We will meet again. Unfortunately for us both.'

He let out a loud whistle and his riders broke off the fight and followed him, not fleeing but retreating in good order, leaving in their wake Tyrion's confused company. The dark elf infantry had already begun a withdrawal, taking their dead with them. Tyrion signalled for his soldiers not to pursue. He was well aware it would lead only to their slaughter.

'What just happened here?' Tyrion's lieutenant asked.

'I just encountered someone I knew.'

'You know a dark elf?' There was horror and suspicion in his voice.

'He was not a dark elf when I knew him.'

'How can that be?'

Tyrion did not reply but stared into the distance, lost in thought. After a moment, he found himself a new steed from among the mounts of his dead riders and gave the signal to saddle up and ride back to camp.

Tyrion stared into the fire, watching the flames dance. From the night sky, the huge white eye of the greater moon gazed down on a vast camp. Banners from all across Ulthuan fluttered above the silken pavilions of elven princes. The clank of metal and the neighing of horses told him that more and more troops were arriving. He could hear words spoken in the accents and dialects of half a dozen elven lands. The sophisticated discussions of Sapherian wizards mingled with the terse banter of Ellyrion horse soldiers. A sad and lovely voice sang an old folk song from Tiranoc telling of a drowned land, a drowned city and a lost love. Tyrion listened to the last few fading notes and felt as if a dagger were piercing his heart.

Life was sweet and he did not want to die. His encounter with Urian had convinced him today that it was all too likely he would when the armies clashed on Finuval Plain.

Suddenly the shadows dancing near the fire warped and clotted. A tall figure stood there. Soldiers scrambled away, reaching for blades and spears. Tyrion looked up from where he sat but did not reach for his weapon.

'You need to work on your entrances, brother,' he said. 'I don't think that was quite dramatic enough. At least half of my warriors were not startled out of their wits.'

Teclis smiled sourly and once again Tyrion was struck by the changes time had wrought in his twin. Gone was all trace of weakness and lassitude. Teclis was still gaunt and pale for a high elf and he walked with a slight limp, but that was the only trace of the illnesses that had threatened his life for as long as Tyrion could remember. His features had taken on a gaunt handsomeness they had never had before.

It was not just Teclis's physical appearance that had changed. Perhaps a mage or someone more gifted with the Sight could have expressed it better, but all Tyrion could say was that his brother was cloaked in mystery and incandescent with power. It blazed within him, more than in any other living being Tyrion had ever encountered. Perhaps Alarielle possessed as much, but in the Everqueen it was hidden, like water bubbling up from an underground lake through a deep still well. Teclis was like a massive river in flood. He behaved now as if he had the power to sweep anything from his path.

It made Tyrion worried as well as proud. His brother was like a young warrior who had suddenly discovered he was strong and takes all sorts of crazed risks to test his own strength. He smiled sourly. That was something he certainly knew all about himself.

'You are troubled,' Teclis said.

'Yes,' said Tyrion, cursing his brother inwardly. Could he not see that this was not the time or the place to discuss his troubles, that these warriors looked to him for leadership, for strength not doubt? He rose from his place at the fireside and clasped his brother by the shoulder, the way he had done from childhood, and began to lead him away from the fire.

'Come, brother, walk with me,' he said. It was not lost on Tyrion the way Teclis shrugged his hand away. He needed to assert himself, to break out of the old pattern of their relationship. Tyrion felt a mixture of hurt and pride. It seemed that he was no longer going to get to play the protective elder brother.

'That was a mistake, wasn't it?' said Teclis when they were out of earshot of the fire. Tyrion looked around. They were still the centre of attention as they walked, which was understandable. They were the two heroes of the moment, who had saved the missing Everqueen from daemons and assassins, who had won most of the few small high elf victories there had been in this terrible war.

Tyrion kept his silence till they reached the edge of the camp, and Teclis had the sense to do the same. Tyrion considered his options. It was pointless explaining to Teclis that his soldiers were unsettled and his appearance in such a manner would only have spooked them more. It was not something that warriors needed on a night before battle. Teclis was clever enough to already have understood that. There was no need to batter the point home with a warhammer.

'How goes it?' Tyrion said at last. 'Are you ready for battle?'

'As ready as I will ever be,' said Teclis. 'I will almost be grateful when day breaks and this matter is settled.' Teclis sounded puzzled and looked at Tyrion circumspectly. This was not what he had come to discuss. It was not what Tyrion wanted to talk about either, but the words for that were not ready to come yet.

'Why do you ask?' Teclis asked eventually.

'Because this is a battle that will be decided by magic. We do not have the numbers to overcome the dark elves by strength of arms.'

'That is not what I hear the warriors say or the princes. They all talk of the certainty of victory.'

'What else can they do? They are whistling in the dark, but in their hearts they all know the same thing as I. We do not have the numbers, the advantage of initiative and morale lies with our opponents.'

'I will take your word for it. You are the expert on military matters.'

Now that he had started talking Tyrion felt the need to continue. 'If it had been a year ago, when our troops were more confident and we had not lost so many warriors, things might be different, but it has been a season of defeat – many of our best are in their graves. Others are scattered over Ulthuan, defending their homes. The Witch King has gathered his forces here and he intends to land a hammer blow that will shatter us.'

'You think we should not be fighting here?'

'We have no choice.'

Teclis nodded, and seemed more interested now than he had when Tyrion had mentioned troop numbers or morale. Then he said something of a perceptiveness Tyrion would not have expected from him at all.

'You love her, don't you?'

'More than I can find the words to say. If I am to die, I would prefer for it to be at her side.'

'You picked a fine time to fall in love, brother, as our world goes down in blood and fire.'

'I never had any choice in the matter. And whatever comes, I do not regret that it happened.'

'If I did not know better I would say that you were afraid,' said Teclis.

'I *am* afraid,' Tyrion said at last. The words hung in the air for a long moment.

Teclis's laughter was soft but there was no mockery in it.

'So the intrepid hero knows fear at last,' he said. 'I always thought nothing could scare you. Fear was my speciality.'

'I have been afraid before,' said Tyrion. 'Often. I have just chosen never to admit it to anyone. Not even to myself.'

'So why are you telling me this now?'

'Because I think I may die soon, and I feel the urge to confess it. I cannot tell it to the soldiers or to the Everqueen or to anyone else, so I am telling you.'

'What brought this on?'

'I met Urian, as Prince Iltharis now calls himself, while scouting the battlefield today.'

'And?'

'And he was better than me. He has always been better than me.'

'He has never been better than you.'

Tyrion laughed. 'I don't mean morally! I mean with a blade he is better than me.'

'Then don't fight him with a blade.'

'The weapons don't matter. If I fought him with a pig's bladder on a stick, he could still beat me.'

'You might want to keep your new choice of favoured weapon to yourself. I don't think it would hearten your troops. They think you are invincible.'

'I am very, very good,' said Tyrion without any false modesty. 'But it does not matter how good you are, there is always someone better.'

'You can't be certain Urian is better than you.' Teclis sounded shocked to be contemplating the fact.

'Believe me, brother, I can. Your gift is for magic. Mine has always been to be able to use weapons. And with any weapon Urian will beat me.'

'Then don't fight him with a weapon.'

'What should I use then? My cutting wit?'

'You have a brain, little as you choose to use it. Battles are fought as much with the mind as with weapons. I seem to recall someone standing not a thousand leagues from me now telling me that once.'

'Urian is too quick. The sort of fights you have with the likes of him happen at speeds too fast for thought. It is all down to reflex, training and experience – the last is the thing he has more of than me. He has had centuries to learn his trade.'

'I would submit to you, brother, that you are wrong. That the battle has already begun and it is being fought out in your mind now, and that you are losing it.'

'As ever, you are being over-subtle.'

'Think about it, Tyrion! Do you think it was an accident that you met Urian today? Do you think it just happened? That the fates threw you together?'

'If Urian wanted to kill me, he could have done so.'

'And he didn't. Because that was not his purpose. He did not want to kill you, not today at least.'

'Then what does he want?' Tyrion was aware that his brother might have caught something that he had missed. Teclis always made him feel slow.

'Think! Who is the current hero of the high elves? Who saved the Everqueen in her darkest hour?'

'You did.'

'No. You are the one who dragged her out of harm's way and kept her free when all seemed lost. Who is known to be the greatest warrior in the high elven host?'

'Korhien Ironglaive.'

'That is not what all the warriors are saying now. They are saying it is you. You have the Blood of Aenarion. You are the hero of this hour. You are the one who can lead us to victory.'

'Even if what you say is true, then why did Urian not kill me today when he had the chance.'

'Because it would not be public enough. Because he wishes to crush you in the dirt and to break the will of our army.'

'You think he means to fight a Contest of Champions?' Tyrion laughed out loud.

'Count on it.'

'There has not been such a duel fought since the time of Caledor the Conqueror. It is not the dark elf way.'

'It will be tomorrow. You could bet our family villa on it.' Tyrion turned the idea over in his head. In a strange way it made sense. If he was challenged and turned the challenge down, it would demoralise the whole high elf army to see their champion refuse battle. If he was defeated, it would have the same effect – it would clearly demonstrate the Witch King's warriors' superiority to the best the high elves could put forward.

Tyrion was enough of a soldier to know that battles were not always decided by strength of arms or force of magic or weight of

numbers; they were decided by the courage of warriors, their determination to conquer. Soldiers had won battles before by standing
firm when they should have run, by fighting long after the time had
come when everyone but them had known they were beaten. They
could be inspired to that by their belief in one elf, a general or a
hero. But not if that elf did not believe in himself.

'I knew you would see it… eventually,' said Teclis. 'You are not
entirely slow of mind.'

'Then why the meeting today?' Tyrion asked, although he already
knew what his brother would say.

'To sow the seeds of doubt in your mind. To soften you up. To
make you afraid. Fear slows a warrior down. You told me that too,
once upon a time.'

Tyrion shook his head. 'Maybe, in part, but I don't think that is
all of it.'

'What makes you say that?'

'Urian had a message for me, for you too. He said we should kill
ourselves.'

Teclis laughed. 'I hope you do not expect me to take his advice.'

'He seemed sincere.'

'I think he sincerely wants us both dead.'

'He says that Malekith's vengeance will be as terrible as it is inevitable. It would be better to die than suffer it.'

'I do not doubt that he is correct in that. But I am not planning
to allow myself to fall into the Witch King's hands.'

'We may not have a choice.'

'We always have a choice. The same choice as the Conqueror
had when he threw himself into the sea, but I for one will wait
until I am surrounded on a burning ship and about to fall into the
hands of my enemies before I make that choice. I suggest you do
the same, brother.'

They both glanced into the distance to the camp of the dark elves,
where an evil as old as elven civilisation waited, surrounded by its
implacable minions. They were both aware of it, Tyrion sensed.
They both felt its brooding power and its malevolence. They both
knew they were kin to it too, through the line of Aenarion for, like
them, Malekith was of his blood.

'How can we beat him?' Tyrion asked at last. 'He is the most powerful sorcerer in the world. He has the largest army assembled by
the elves since the time of Aenarion. He has been planning this
for centuries.'

'He could not have planned for you and me, brother. And as you said yourself, no matter how good you are, there is always someone better. The same applies to Malekith as it applies to you and me.'

Tyrion looked at his brother as if seeing him for the first time. 'You are planning on challenging him, are you?'

Teclis's cold smile gave him his answer.

'You are mad,' Tyrion said, but there was admiration as well as humour in his words.

'Maybe, but so was Aenarion at the end and he still defeated the hordes of hell.'

'Yes, but at what price?'

'Whatever the price is, we will have to pay it, brother. If our lands are to survive, if our people are to be free, if our world is to avoid destruction. Tomorrow, for better or worse, it will be our names that are written in the pages of the history books. If there is any-one left to write them.'

Tyrion looked at his brother, as if seeing him for the first time. 'You've come a very long way,' he said.

'We have both done that, brother,' said Teclis.

A Sword Master of Hoeth appeared out of the gloom, a massive greatsword on his back. He looked flustered and not a little anx-ious, which was unusual in one of the legendary guardians of the White Tower. 'Prince Teclis, I have been looking for you everywhere. Your father wishes to speak with you.'

'I will come with you,' Tyrion said.

The Sword Master looked embarrassed and said, 'I was told to bring Prince Teclis alone. It is wizard business.'

Bitterness burned in the pit of Tyrion's stomach. Even here as the world ended, their father could not bring himself to treat him as Teclis's equal.

Teclis shrugged. 'I must go. There are plans that must be set in motion. You were right about one thing, brother. This battle will be settled by magic, but for that to happen our armies will need to stand firm. You can make them do that. They believe in you. Remember that. Good luck on the morrow. May Isha smile on you.'

'May you live a thousand years.'

And in a moment, he was gone, although how he left, Tyrion was not sure. He stood for a moment on the edge of the vast armed camp, staring at the fires of the even larger one where the Witch King and his minions watched and waited. He felt small and lost, a tiny particle of life caught up in a whirlwind, buffeted by forces beyond his control, a pawn of destiny. He felt unsettled by his brother's words. A vast weight pressed down on him now, for he had sensed the truth in them. Somehow, the fate of everyone and everything they cared about rested on their shoulders tomorrow. They had both gone from despised outsiders of no consequence to standing at the very fulcrum of destiny.

How had it come to this, he wondered?

CHAPTER TWENTY-FOUR

His father was troubled, Teclis could see that. Of course, who would not be under the circumstances? The old elf had witnessed the greatest invasion of Ulthuan since the first Chaos incursion. He had doubtless seen people he knew killed and entire villages laid waste. Like every other elf who had lived through these dark times, he had reason to be unhappy. Somehow though, Teclis doubted that this was all that troubled his father.

'What is it, father?' He asked. His father simply looked at him. His gaze was bleak. He looked sadder than Teclis had ever seen him look in his life and that was quite a feat. His father shook his head and gestured for Teclis to step within his tent.

Inside was a large wooden box that resembled a coffin. Teclis immediately sensed powerful magic within although it was contained by potent runes inscribed in his father's unmistakable hand. His father went over to the box and unsealed it using a crowbar. As the seals were broken, a blast of powerful magic swept over Teclis like heat coming out of an open oven door. The magic was powerful almost beyond imagining and there was a dark taint to it that Teclis did not like in the least.

Lying within the wooden structure like a corpse within a coffin was the armour of Aenarion. It looked very different now from the ancient, dormant artefact that had lain within his father's laboratory for all those decades. It glittered now. It glowed with magical energy. It looked fresh and bright and newly made. It looked magnificent, a tribute to his father's skill as a wizard and to the skill of the ancient archmage who had made it. It blazed with power and Teclis could see that it would protect any warrior who wore it from harm better than any other armour ever made. Not only that, potent enchantments would enhance the strength, speed and skill of the wearer, making them powerful beyond belief.

It was not this that troubled Teclis. There was something else about the armour, a resonance, an imprint of someone's personality that was troubling. There was a sense of rage, a lust for death, that was almost overwhelming. Just looking at the armour made him want to grind his teeth and shout abuse at his father for the stupidity of what he had done. He was a wizard too and he recognised the magic for what it was. Swiftly, he threw a screen around himself and Prince Arathion. He was relieved to see the look of anger vanishing swiftly from his father's face as well.

'You see it?' his father asked. 'Can you see what I have done?'

'You have recreated the armour of Aenarion,' said Teclis. 'This might be the greatest feat of forensic magic in the history of the world.'

'I do not think it was meant to be this way. I have failed.'

Teclis examined the armour with his magesight. He could see that his father's work was flawless. The spells had been recreated perfectly, lovingly, by a mage who had known exactly what to do and have done it. His father had made no mistakes. This was something else.

'Your spellwork is perfect,' Teclis said. 'Whatever happened here is not your fault.'

'I do not think the armour was meant to be like this,' his father said. 'I have read every primary source in existence and there is no reference to something like this.'

'I think what we are seeing is the influence of Aenarion,' Teclis said. 'He was so full of power that he left his mark upon the armour. I suspect also that the Sword of Khaine may have left its mark as well. He carried that blade for a good deal of the time that he wore this armour. It may have affected Caledor's creation as well as Aenarion himself.'

'Such were my thoughts too, my son,' said Prince Arathion. 'The question is what effect will this have on the person who wears the armour.'

'You saw the effect that simply looking upon it had upon you and me. I would imagine that wearing the armour, being connected to it by the web of spells inherent in it, would be much worse. It might affect the personality of the wearer, twisting it and altering it unless that person was very strong-willed indeed.'

'You don't think there is any way that we could cleanse the armour?'

Teclis considered this for a moment. The imprinting was very strong and the effect was potent. He knew next to nothing about the Sword of Khaine's magic and he could not calculate the effects of it. He had made contact with the Flame of Asuryan himself and he could sense a great similarity between the resonance of the flame and the magic that was on this armour that had not been put there by Caledor. He suspected that that was the effect of the flame that had burned inside Aenarion after he had passed through the sacred fires in the shrine. Perhaps what they were seeing was the shadow of Aenarion cast by the flame onto the armour. It was hard to tell. He could not see any way of purifying the armour at this moment. Of course, that did not mean that there was not such a way. It just might take an age to find. He said as much to his father.

'I had feared that this was the case,' Arathion said. 'I am not reassured. It is a pity. I spent so much time recreating this armour and so much effort bringing it here, and now it might be useless.'

'The armour itself will perform all the functions it was intended to,' Teclis said. 'It is a mighty weapon, a great artefact, and these are desperate times. The fate of the elven people hangs in the balance and anything that gives us even the slightest of advantages is to be seized upon.'

'That is what the council of princes says. They say that the armour may be needed to give our champions a fighting chance on the field of battle. They say that the power of Malekith is overwhelming and that we need to grab every opportunity presented to us with both hands.'

'And they are correct,' said Teclis. 'If we do not win here, darkness may eclipse our people and Ulthuan may fall forever.'

'I agree with you,' said his father, 'and still my heart misgives me.'

'You're afraid to ask someone to wear this armour?'

'Wouldn't you be?'

'I would wear it myself if I thought it would help,' Teclis said.

'I know you would, but you are unlikely to be asked to wear it.'

Suddenly Teclis understood who was likely to be asked and he understood his father's misgivings. 'They want Tyrion to take this armour?'

His father nodded. 'The Everqueen is going to present it to him before the battle. They say it will hearten the troops and be very good for morale.'

'They are right and I suspect that the effect is carefully calculated. Tyrion looks like Aenarion, so everybody says, and to see him wearing this armour would be like having Aenarion fight on our side.'

'So you agree with the princes? You think that Tyrion should do this?'

'It does not matter what I think,' Teclis said. 'If he is asked, he will do it. That is the sort of fool he is.'

'Then what can we do?'

'We can try and see whether we can come up with some way to mitigate the effect of the armour's aura.'

'We don't have much time,' said his father.

'Then we'd better get started,' Teclis said.

Tyrion inspected the armour of Aenarion. It looked different. He had seen it almost every day during his childhood, and very often in the years of his adulthood. It had never looked then the way it did now, alive, malevolent and full of power. There was a shadow in it that he could sense and that shadow called out to something in him.

Suddenly a moment from his childhood came back to him. He remembered standing in the chill of the night in his father's alchemical laboratory inspecting the armour. His father and Korhien Ironglaive were somewhere in the house, talking about the old days. Lady Malene was in her chambers writing something. He was standing in his bare feet, looking at the armour and half-fearfully, half-hopefully waiting for something to happen, for some sign to be given, for the same supernatural power that had touched Aenarion to reach out and touch him. Of course, back then, nothing had happened and he had been glad of it.

But something had happened now. The armour was not the same. His father had succeeded in his long labour and finally repaired this ancient artefact. He finally had something to show for squandering the family fortunes, neglecting his family and letting his life fall into ruin. The armour was alive. That was the only thing that could be said about it. It was like a living thing, with a personality of its own.

No. That was not right. It held the echo of a personality, of the elf who had worn it so long ago, of Aenarion. Now, Tyrion had a sense of what his ancestor was like. He did not like what he was seeing. The armour gave off an air of malevolence, of rage, of an anger so great it might consume the world. Aenarion had left something of himself in it, and his father had succeeded in awakening it.

Do I want to be like this, Tyrion asked himself? Do I have a choice?

Someone is going to have to wear this, to inspire our troops, to give our warriors some hope. He knew that if he put on the armour, he would never be the same afterwards. All of his life he had wanted glory, to be a hero. He was surprised to discover that he did not want it so badly that he was prepared to subsume his own personality to another's, to sell his soul for it.

Or was he? He already knew the answer to the decision he had to make.

He sensed Alarielle's presence in the tent. He turned to look at her. She was beautiful in the lantern-light. It had been a while since he had seen her. She had been very busy, talking with princes and wizards.

'What are you thinking?' she asked.

'I was remembering looking at this armour when I was a boy,' he said. 'It always seemed so much larger than it was. As if the wearer was a giant, much bigger than me.'

'It looks as if it was made for you,' she said. 'And you for it.'

'Aenarion wore it. It seems somewhat presumptuous for me to.'

'Tomorrow will be the greatest battle the elves face since his time,' she said. She walked over to him and took him by his hand. 'Someone needs to wear it, to give our people hope.'

'And you think it should be me?' For a moment, something ancient, powerful and unforgiving looked out of her eyes. It was the pitiless presence of the Everqueen. She was here and Alarielle was not.

'I can think of no elf better suited to wear it.' She squeezed his hand gently.

'Aenarion,' Tyrion said.

'He is not here. You are.'

'It's always the way,' he said. 'Heroes are never around when you really need them.'

'You are here.'

'I am just an elf who likes to kill. I am not a hero.'

'You are the only person who thinks that.'

'Doesn't my opinion count?'

'I do not think you see yourself as we see you.'

'I see myself as I am.'

She shook her head. 'I had never thought you so modest, Prince Tyrion.'

'I am not modest. I am just not Aenarion.'

'Has it ever occurred to you that that might be a good thing? We do not need another Aenarion.'

Tyrion smiled. 'It seems most of my life people have been comparing me to him, because I look like him.'

'You do more than look like him. You have something of his power and his grace. Believe me, *I* remember Aenarion. He was not an elf you could forget.'

'That is a chilling thought.'

'You are not him though. I think you are someone better.'

Tyrion laughed.

'You do not have his cruelty. Or his despair. Or his titanic arrogance.'

'They made him what he was, the saviour of our people.'

'Caledor saved our people. Aenarion almost destroyed them. We do not need another Aenarion. We need you.'

'And yet you want me to take up his mantle, don his armour.' Suddenly the sense of ancient presence was gone.

'I want you to wear his armour because it is among the most powerful protective artefacts ever made. I want you to come back to me. Tomorrow there will be a battle. I want you to live through it.'

She looked as if she was going to cry. Tyrion reached out and stroked her cheek. 'We've come a very long way, you and I,' he said.

'Let us hope we have a long way further to travel.'

She reached out and took his face in both her hands. He leaned forwards and kissed her gently. The armour of Aenarion watched over them, brooding in the background.

From outside there came the sounds of an army preparing for war.

CHAPTER TWENTY-FIVE

The sun rose as if it was the last day of the world. Red light blazed down upon the two vast armed camps that sat on the edge of Finuval Plain. Tyrion stood upon the small rise and looked aghast at the size of the Witch King's army. It was plain that the high elves were hugely outnumbered. There were not only dark elves over there but a high proportion of humans, followers of Chaos, dedicated to the dark gods.

The assembled asur army looked at the Everqueen. They were drawn up as if ready for battle. In the distance, the horns of Malekith's army sounded but no one was distracted. All of the asur present looked upon their living goddess with reverence.

Alarielle smiled at them and Tyrion thought she had never looked lovelier. Something old and primal in her was responding to the presence and adoration of those present. She was the focus of every gaze, beloved in every eye, and suddenly he felt jealous in a way he never had before of anyone or about anyone.

He actively resented the way all of those elves looked at her, and he realised that for the rest of his life he was going to have to compete with that untiring, relentless torrent of adoration, and that there was no way he could. The sensation was a sour one, made all the more so because it was the last thing he had expected to experience at this moment.

He knew that he should be proud of her courage and her beauty and her gift for inspiring others around her, but instead he found a small, mean thing that wanted to hide her away and keep her for himself. She was revealing to him that he was smaller than he thought he was, and he resented her for that. He told himself it was unfair and unworthy, but unfortunately it was the way he felt.

She seemed unaware of it too, unaware of him. Her attention was focused on the crowd of elves whose attention was focused on her. It was like the relationship between an actor and his audience but multiplied a thousand times by the force of her magic. He was fooling himself if he thought he could compete with that. No living thing could. He might as well slink away now and leave her to her adoring worshippers.

Then she looked at him sidelong and with a small secretive smile. It was aimed at him alone, as if there was some shared joke or knowledge that lay between them and existed only for them – he saw the other side of what being the Everqueen meant. He was her friend, possibly the only one she was ever likely to have now, the only person to whom she was not the avatar of a living goddess but who saw her as a person.

It was a thing that would make a goddess lonely, he thought.

Good, he thought, the small, twisted jealous side of his nature responded. It would make her all the sorrier when he was gone. But he smiled himself now, understanding that what he was feeling was not the sum total of all his feelings for her, only part of them and not the better part either. It was something he was just going to have to get used to, much as he resented it.

'My friends, we are gathered in very dark times,' Alarielle said. Her voice was one of those magical ones that would have carried to the furthest corners of the assembled throng even if she was talking in a whisper. There was something in it that commanded respect and belief as well.

Teclis recognised the sorcery but it was so subtly done that even he had trouble identifying quite how. 'Our enemies are mighty and our allies few. We have suffered defeat after defeat and loss after loss. I would not blame any of you if you had lost all hope of eventual victory.'

She paused to give her listeners a chance to absorb what she had said. Teclis was no great expert on public speaking but he thought that perhaps her message was somewhat too downbeat for this audience.

'Nonetheless, you have not done so. You have not given up even in the face of a foe who delights in displaying his cruelty and power. You have not admitted defeat even in the face of overwhelming odds. You stand before me ready to fight and die for your homeland, and that makes me proud of each and every one of you.

'I would not have been here to tell you this if it had not been for two brothers. They saved me from the servants of the Witch King and they are here now to fight alongside you in battle tomorrow.

'I owe them my life and I wish to repay them. Teclis, step forwards.'

Teclis was surprised to be summoned, and embarrassed. He did not like limping forwards to be greeted by the Everqueen in front of the whole army. He would have remained where he was had not Tyrion pushed him forwards.

He limped up and was surprised to hear his name roared in acclamation by the assembled warriors. Alarielle gestured for silence. 'It has been said that you may turn out to be the greatest wizard since Caledor. I truly hope this is the case, for we have need of great wizards today. As a token of my respect and esteem, I give you this staff.'

She held aloft the Moonstaff of Lileath. It glowed in the moonlight, looking more than ever like an artefact of the ancients. Even those with the poorest magesight could see it radiated power. Teclis was stunned. He barely found the words to say, 'It is a queenly gift, your serenity.'

He accepted it from her, and it felt right in his hand, perfectly balanced, augmenting his power in a way that few things could. She leaned forwards to kiss him on the cheek. He was touched by that gesture and bowed to her, before backing away.

As he returned from the rise, he felt hands reach out to touch him and slap his back. He was unused to such gestures of affection or respect. He realised that many of those present were in awe of him. It was intoxicating and disturbing at the same time. He did not like being the centre of attention.

Alarielle continued to speak.

'If it was not for Teclis's brother, Tyrion, I truly would not be here today. He saved me from the midst of a druchii army when all hope seemed lost, and he stayed with me until I found safety among you, despite taking terrible wounds from the poisoned blades of the followers of Malekith.'

She gestured and heralds brought forward a covered wagon. 'Recently, the greatest artefact of our greatest hero has been restored to its full power by the father of these destiny-touched twins. He has spent a lifetime reforging the work of the master-mage Caledor...'

She paused to give her words time to sink in. A silence like that before the breaking of a storm settled upon the army. Teclis knew everyone present was wondering what she was going to say. It was more than magic that compelled their attention now, it was a genuine curiosity. She sprang onto the back of the wagon and stood beside an object covered by a tarpaulin. Teclis knew what was coming, but he still found himself holding his breath as she pulled the cover away.

In full view, on the great stand Teclis remembered so well, stood the armour of Aenarion. It looked new. It was burnished till it shone and it glowed with awesome power. His magesight allowed him to see deep into the intricate web of spells overlaid on it. Even he was awed by the power and complexity of them though he had added to them himself in an attempt to protect his brother from the armour's power.

There was something else about the armour that compelled attention, a sense of awesome, ominous presence, of a magic that dated back to an earlier, darker, more primitive age. It stood there like a god emerged from the red murk of that ancient era. No one who looked upon it could doubt what it was.

'This is the dragon armour of Aenarion,' Alarielle said. 'And I can think of no one more worthy to wear it than my champion, Tyrion, son of Arathion.'

Tyrion stepped forwards and raised his arm to receive the army's acclamation. He looked the part, Teclis thought, as if he had been born to wear the armour and lead this army to victory.

They cheered him as if he could do it, and it was then that it sank in to Teclis exactly how desperate they all were.

'Let's get this over with,' Tyrion said quietly. He knew that the army was waiting to see him in the armour.

His father and Teclis nodded. They looked more serious and more worried than he could ever remember them doing in his entire life.

'Cheer up. We're not dead yet,' he told them. No one else was close enough to hear his words.

'Only a matter of time,' said Teclis, ignoring the annoyed look his father shot him. Tyrion understood what his brother meant.

'It happens to everybody,' he said.

'To some sooner than others,' said his father. He looked lost and a little gloomy. Tyrion was reminded of the human explorer Leiber after they had found the treasure house of the lost city of Zultec. He would have expected his father to be more excited. Instead he seemed more than a little depressed, seemingly unaware that there was an entire army waiting expectantly.

'I did not expect to live forever,' Tyrion said.

'You always behaved as if you did,' said Teclis. Again Prince Arathion looked annoyed. He did not seem to be able to realise that Teclis had a different way of dealing with tension than he did.

'Are you sure you want to do this, my son?' he asked. There was genuine concern in his voice, and Tyrion was touched. The elf he remembered from his childhood would have been in a hurry to see him in the armour to make sure that it worked as he expected it to. Perhaps his father had changed.

'I am ready,' Tyrion said. He glanced from face to face and saw only concern there.

'I am the one who should be worried,' he said. 'All you have to do is get me into the suit.'

'It's the first time anyone has worn this armour in over six thousand years,' said his father. He glanced from Tyrion to the armour. A troubled expression flickered across his face. 'This is not without risks.'

'The time for worrying about those risks is long since passed,' Tyrion said. 'We will all die here if Malekith has his way. Some of us more painfully than others.'

Teclis nodded. His father sucked in his cheeks and made a clicking sound with his teeth. 'There is no need for this bravado, Tyrion. No one doubts your courage.'

'I am starting to. Please begin before I have second thoughts.'

His father nodded. He took the armour piece by piece from the stand and placed it reverently on the ground around Tyrion. He strapped the chestpiece into place. It was, for some reason, heavier than Tyrion expected it to be and colder, as if the metal had lain in snow for a long time. He rapped its surface with his knuckles. It rang. It was a strange thought that the last person who had done this was Aenarion, before setting out for the Island of the Dead. Tyrion wondered if he was going to his own death too. There were those who might see it as a fitting punishment for his presumption.

His father put on the armguards and the gauntlets while Teclis helped him into the greaves and leg-pieces. He stepped into the boots. At last, Teclis placed the helmet on his head. It shut down his field of vision and muffled his hearing. There was a certain finality to the act, like the closing of a door. Tyrion could feel the power in the armour. It was heavy and magic flowed through it; there was something else, a sense of anger and power and... resentment there, as if whatever was in it did not wish to see him wearing the armour.

'This is not the most pleasant sensation,' Tyrion said.

'It's about to become less pleasant,' said Teclis. His father nodded. Teclis raised the Moonstaff of Lileath and began to chant the words of an incantation. His father joined in, singing a counterpoint. As they did so, Teclis touched the runes on each section of the armour one at a time with the staff. Power seemed to flow out of him and into the armour.

Tyrion could feel it becoming lighter, or perhaps it was him becoming stronger. The sense of another person being there became more intense too.

He felt a great rage start to settle within him, a bloodthirsty desire to stride out of the tent and face his enemies, to slay them, to tear them apart with his bare hands. It was the sort of rage he had never felt before, but he knew that it had always been there, deep within him, part of his ancient bloodright.

Teclis touched his arms and he felt as if he could lift a horse. When the enchantments in the legs were activated, he felt as if he could run for miles. The activation of the helmet made his senses seem suddenly much clearer. He regained all the keenness of vision and hearing it had cost him, and more besides. He had a sense of *awareness* of what was going on all around him. It was not like anything he had experienced before. He felt those around him as a *pressure*. He knew that if Teclis stepped behind him he would know exactly where he was.

Teclis touched the centre of the breastplate and the armour blazed to full life. For a brief ecstatic moment, power and energy and a sense of something else flowed into Tyrion. He felt stronger and faster than he ever had before. He knew that great wards had slid into place around him, protecting him from magic and harm. He felt for one brief moment like a god.

Both his father and Teclis stepped back from him with looks of awe and something like fear written on their faces.

'It worked,' Tyrion said. His voice had a booming quality to it and he knew somehow that when he spoke on a battlefield his words would be heard and understood by his warriors no matter what the din of arms was like around him. 'I am ready.'

Teclis held up his hand in a gesture of warning. Prince Arathion walked around him, inspecting him, and then emerged into Tyrion's field of vision exactly when Tyrion expected him to.

'It is done,' his father said. 'The dragon armour of Aenarion has been re-made. The gods help us all.'

Tyrion did not feel like he was wearing heavy armour, more like a suit made from the lightest cloth. He felt as if he could run and jump and fight completely unencumbered, and fight was exactly what he wanted to do. The spirit in the armour demanded it of him.

Tyrion fought down the rising tide of bloodlust. He did not want to be anyone or anything's pawn. He was himself and he intended to remain that way, even if it meant whatever was present in the armour would not help him to the fullest of its abilities.

Slowly his rage subsided a little. He drew Sunfang. It blazed more brilliantly than it ever had before, as if the presence of the armour had lent it new strength. He took another deep breath and raised his burning sword. The watching army roared its approval at the sight of him.

'Prince Tyrion!' A group of strange elves walked towards him out of the crowd. They led the largest warhorse he had ever seen. It was armoured with heavy barding which it bore as if it were a saddle blanket.

He did not recognise any of them. They were garbed in thick leather armour and they had a peculiar, slightly bowlegged way of walking. Some of them still had spurs attached to their riding boots that clinked as they walked.

'I am Prince Paelus of Ellyrion,' said the leader of the newcomers. 'I wish to thank you on behalf of my people for all you have done. If it were not for you, we would be without a queen at the moment.'

Tyrion knew exactly what the hero of the hour was expected to say. 'I only did what any loyal elf would have done,' he said.

'I'm sure you did what any of us would have liked to do but which very few would have been capable of. You saved the Everqueen from the clutches of the druchii, and we would like to present you with a token of our appreciation.'

'That will not be necessary,' Tyrion said.

'Necessary or not, it would be ungracious of you to refuse us,' Prince Paelus said. 'This is Malhandir of the line of Korhandir, Father of Horses,' Prince Paelus said. 'We were bringing him to the great tournament to be the mount of the Everqueen's champion. Of course, we came too late and were caught up in the great war against the Witch King.'

Malhandir ambled towards Tyrion and nuzzled his shoulder. Prince Paelus laughed.

'It seems Malhandir has already made his choice,' he said. 'Once such a beast chooses a rider, he will never take another.'

Now that Malhandir was near, Tyrion sensed the strangeness in the horse. It was clear even to one as magically blind as he was that this was no normal beast. Malhandir radiated power, intelligence and a potent burning magic.

He was larger, more graceful and stronger than any horse Tyrion had ever seen and there was a wisdom in his eyes worthy of a scholar. Instinctively, he found himself reaching out to stroke the horse's muzzle.

He felt a great affection for the horse, such as he had never felt any moment before. There was a bond between them even after only a few heartbeats. The horse whinnied as if it was laughing at him and then shook its head and Tyrion found himself laughing too. His laughter echoed through the assembled ranks of the elven army.

Tyrion was glad. He truly wanted to be the rider of this steed. It was a warhorse that could carry him through any battle, he felt. Malhandir moved its head in a way that told Tyrion that it was time to mount up. Tyrion vaulted onto the great horse's back.

'Now I am ready to do battle,' he said. The army cheered. The set of Alarielle's face told him she was worried, but she kept the glorious confident smile on her face.

'So it begins,' Malekith said. His huge army was already in position. It looked ready to sweep forward and destroy the asur where they stood. Before that happened, there was something else that needed to be done.

'I am ready, sire,' Urian said. Malekith had reinforced the already potent magic in his armour with still more powerful spells. The magical blades blazed in his fist.

'First you will destroy their champions and then I will destroy their army – then I will have all of Ulthuan under my boot.'

Urian nodded. How many of those people down there faced their last day? How many would be dead before this day was out so that Malekith could realise his mad ambition? For a moment, he was tempted to take his sword and bury it in the Witch King's back. Only the knowledge that it was almost certainly not powerful enough to penetrate that almost-indestructible armour stopped him.

He told himself that today the Witch King would triumph and he stood at the Witch King's right hand. Somehow that knowledge did not make him as happy as it should have.

Tyrion reined Malhandir to a halt and watched the army move around him.

Even now in the face of that enormous and seemingly invincible enemy horde, it stirred his heart. He had always loved this time before the blood, the mud and the chaos of battle overwhelmed everything. The formations were drawn up. Everything was in order. There was this sense of being part of something much larger than himself.

Being part of this crowd was something that spoke to something deep within him. He could smell the oiled weapons, the leather and steel of the armour and the animal stink of the cavalry horses.

He felt like he was one very small part of a very large living thing. When he breathed, it breathed. When it spoke, he was part of its voice. Perhaps this was what it was like to be a god. Or perhaps part of a god.

He felt as if he was enormously strong, as if he could do anything, as if all he and all of the other soldiers round about him needed to do was will something to be done and it would occur. He was part of this vast hydra-headed entity that was far greater than the sum of its parts.

Of course, over there, on the other side of the battlefield, was another colossal entity, equally strong, if not stronger, that felt itself to be invincible. Soon these two huge monsters would come crashing together like stegadons in the jungle of Lustria. Then they would rend each other with their sword-like claws until great chunks were ripped bleeding from the flesh of the monsters and the army would lose all cohesion. In some ways, that would be a bit like dying, Tyrion thought.

All around him voices rumbled. The air vibrated as with the droning of a vast hive of bees. The earth shook beneath the tread of the marching army. He felt like a tiny particle being driven before a huge storm wind. It was as if somehow his life had taken on the momentum of the army and it had transferred some part of its vast purpose to him.

Looking at the faces of those around him, he could tell that they all felt the same way. They had a bemused, inebriated look written on them as if the owners of those faces were sodden with drink or under the influence of some potent drug that deadened their sense of individuality and made them less than individuals and yet greater.

He took a deep breath and allowed himself to luxuriate in the sense of being part of a greater entity, then he focused his concentration on his own body and became Tyrion once more, a small mote of life being driven before the vast hurricane of the army's purpose.

He urged Malhandir forwards to the place where the two armies would meet.

Teclis hated this. He hated the way the army marched together like one monstrous automaton. He felt more alone than at any time since he had begun his quest to find his brother. He could not be part of this. He could not join in.

He disliked the idea of being one mindless creature in a herd of mindless creatures. He disliked the way all of the faces around him showed one fixed purpose: unquestioning, obedient, willing to kill at the orders of someone else. He knew then exactly how different he was. It was simply part of his character that he could not be part of this huge, violent, unthinking community.

It was not that he was incapable of violence or indeed lack of thought – it was simply that he could not lay down his sense of self, subsume it to the will of the crowd.

He was not a leader but he was not a follower either. He was something different, alone, isolated, not part of this vast strange thing that was happening around him.

He was glad of that. Crowds were less than the sum of their parts. For some elves, there was a temptation in that. Perhaps it would be nice to stop thinking for himself for a moment, to suspend his judgement, to not look at the world through his own solitary eyes. He simply was not capable of doing that though. There was no temptation because there was nothing in him to be tempted.

He looked at the faces around him and he felt nothing but contempt at their slack-jawed acceptance of what was going on round about them. He was glad he was not like them.

He was not a sheep. He was an individual. His life had been a lonely one but it had prepared him for this moment, it had prepared him to stand apart and maintain his own critical faculties and be prepared to look with his own eyes upon what was going to happen.

Perhaps if all elves were capable of this, or all sentient beings, wars would not happen. Perhaps this loss of the sense of being an individual was a necessary precursor to mass violence. Perhaps one had to lose one's sense of self in order to become capable of killing.

He knew though that he was deceiving himself. He was certainly capable of killing. The question was whether he was normal, and he knew the answer to that already. He kept walking, carried along by the flow of the army.

Ahead of them a vaster force waited. He sensed the magical power summoned in its midst. Overhead dark clouds flowed, driven by cold winds. There was a storm coming. He could feel it.

The armies halted just out of bowshot of each other. They halted as if a signal had been given, and glared at each other.

A dark elf herald rode right up to the front of the asur force. He was accompanied by a few bodyguards, carrying the flags of truce.

He smiled mockingly, confidently, with contempt. He looked perfectly at ease, as if he had nothing to fear, which was nothing less than the case. No one was going to attack him while he bore that flag.

'Malekith the Great, king of all the elves, commands you to listen!' The herald's voice was clear and ringing, some trick of magic allowed his words to carry to the furthest edges of the high elf camp. 'If any of you have the courage to face his champion in single combat, present yourself on the plain between the two armies and allow yourself to be slaughtered. He doubts that any of you will dare do so. He believes that none of the children of Ulthuan have the courage of their ancestors.'

'I will fight!' Someone shouted. Tyrion recognised the voice as belonging to Arhalien of Yvresse. 'I will show you that we do not fear your pathetic master.'

The herald laughed outright. 'You shall pay for the disrespect you show. Still, present yourself! Your death shall be a swift one.'

Tyrion wondered if Arhalien was being wise. Doubtless, Malekith was confident that his champion would be victorious. There was no reason for calling this challenge otherwise. It was meant, as Teclis had claimed last night, simply to give him one more advantage in the coming battle. It was intended to drive another nail into the coffin of high elf morale. On the other hand, Tyrion was not sure it would have been wise to turn down that challenge. To do so would simply be to admit that there was no warrior in the high elf army willing or able to accept the challenge.

He could see that a number of eyes were on him. It was true that he was looked upon as a hero in this army. They had expected him to speak up. It was too late now. Arhalien had spoken. He must be allowed to fight.

Arhalien came riding over to the rise upon which Tyrion stood. The pavilion of the Everqueen was behind him. It was obvious that Arhalien felt himself to be the true champion of Alarielle and this was his way of proving it.

'I have come to ask for the Everqueen's blessing and her favour before I ride out on her behalf,' he said.

Tyrion winced. This truly was playing into Malekith's hands if Arhalien should be killed. That a warrior carrying both Alarielle's favour and blessing should be slain was the worst of all possible omens for the army that represented her.

Did Arhalien not realise this? Did he even care? Or was he so wrapped up in his own personal quest for glory that he was willing to have that happen? It did not matter, Tyrion thought. He had already done it.

Alarielle looked as radiantly beautiful as ever, the expression on the faces of all the watchers changed to reverence by her mere presence. Tyrion wondered if he would ever get used to it. Why was he incapable of feeling that level of reverence and respect? He cared about the woman, but nothing about the goddess touched him at all.

'My blessing you may have,' she said. 'But my favour is reserved for Tyrion, son of Arathion.'

Arhalien accepted her words with a graceful gesture. 'Your blessing is enough for me, your serenity,' he said. 'I accept your decision.'

He rode forth to the centre of Finuval Plain. The soldiers of the high elf army left their camp behind him, just as the dark elves were doing on the far side of the plain. It was a mistake, Tyrion could see that. It meant that if battle erupted after the single combat, the high elves would not be in a good formation. It mattered less to the dark elves that the same would apply to them. They had the advantage of numbers. Tyrion wondered if Malekith had planned it this way all along.

Leaders bellowed instructions trying to hold formations together. The princes sent messengers everywhere, telling them to hold their formation. It was like watching a rout in reverse. It was as if the army was losing all coherence in its quest to get close enough to watch the champions fight. Tyrion kept close to Alarielle. He noticed that those assigned to protect the Everqueen were doing the same. It was good. If Malekith planned any treacherous attack upon her, she would at least have bodyguards. Somehow, Teclis emerged from the crowd.

'I told you this would happen,' he said.

'As ever, brother, your gift for prophecy is impressive,' Tyrion said. 'I don't like this. I don't like it at all.'

'That's why I decided to join you. This might be cover for something else.'

'What frightens me is the idea that it might not be.'

'What do you mean?' Teclis asked.

'This might be exactly what it appears to be. Malekith may be so confident of victory that he merely wants to put on this little show to damage our morale. This might be the only point of this exercise, as you suggested last night.'

Teclis nodded. 'If any wicked magic is attempted, I will at least be here to counter it.'

'I find your presence oddly reassuring, brother,' Tyrion said.

'As I find yours,' Teclis replied. They moved closer to Alarielle. She reached out and squeezed Tyrion's hand.

'What is going on?' she asked.

'Apparently Malekith wants to be entertained by some gladiatorial combat before he puts the rest of us to the sword.'

'Do you think Arhalien has a chance?' Alarielle asked.

'I think we shall soon find out. Here comes Malekith's champion now.'

Urian Poisonblade moved exactly the same way as Prince Iltharis moved. He looked exactly as Prince Iltharis looked. It came to Tyrion that that was because he was Prince Iltharis in truth. There could be no mistake about that. He was garbed all in black armour, with two blades strapped to his side. He walked with a certain jaunty confidence that had always been Prince Iltharis's.

'I wish I had killed him back in Lothern,' Teclis said.

'You never had that chance,' Tyrion said. Teclis looked at him coldly.

'You might have it now,' Tyrion told him, 'but you were not capable of killing him in the past.'

Teclis shrugged. 'You might well be right, brother.'

Korhien Ironglaive walked up to the brothers. 'It is all so easy for him, isn't it?' he said, indicating Urian. There was admiration as well as cold hatred in his voice.

'He always was an overconfident bastard,' said Teclis.

It seemed that they were not the only ones who recognised Prince Iltharis. Loud booing emerged from the ranks of the high elves. Urian drew his blades and raised them in an ironic salute. He seemed not in the slightest daunted by the hatred that the massed army expressed towards him.

Tyrion admired his coolness. Prince Arhalien rode up towards Urian. He vaulted lithely from his saddle, looking every bit the poised and polished hero. Behind them, officers still called orders to the army, trying to restore some semblance of discipline and formation.

Tyrion noticed that the druchii were drawn up in ordered ranks. They were already in battle formation. The barbarians were not and they moved restlessly as if they were prepared to attack treacherously at any moment. It was entirely possible that they might – perhaps this was what Malekith was counting upon to give him an excuse to break the truce when he needed to. Equally though, Tyrion felt certain that the time was not upon them when the Witch King would do that. He wanted Urian to fight against Arhalien. He wanted his champion to demonstrate his superiority.

Having fought them both, Tyrion knew that Urian was almost certain to win. The only thing that was likely to save Arhalien would be some stroke of luck of the sort that could never be relied upon but sometimes happened in combat. It was not something Tyrion was counting on seeing. Fighters like Urian made their own luck.

Both of them turned and raised their weapons in salute to the respective armies. Arhalien raised his blade to Alarielle. For once, Tyrion did not look at her. He looked in the direction that Urian raised his blade. He looked upon Malekith, Witch King of Naggaroth, for the first time in his life as he emerged into full view on the cold hillside overlooking the field of combat.

Malekith was a fearsome figure, as terrifying in his own way as a greater daemon. He towered over those around him, a giant among elves. It was the armour, Tyrion told himself. That was what did it. It made him look bigger than he was. There was magic in it that did that and more.

He was not fooling himself. Malekith was bigger than any other elf. Tyrion had no idea why that should be. Perhaps it had something to do with having lived for millennia. Perhaps it had something to do with what had happened to him when he had passed through the sacred Flame of Asuryan and been rejected by the god. Or perhaps it was something else entirely.

All Tyrion knew was that Malekith looked like a giant. There was a sense of terrifying power and strength about the Witch King that was palpable. It radiated out from him. He seemed like a monster made of metal, indestructible, invincible and utterly confident of victory. He raised one gigantic armoured hand in response to Urian's salute.

The two warriors leapt together. Blades flashed too fast for the eye to follow. A flower of blood blossomed on Arhalien's chest and he fell to the ground dead. The high elf army groaned. No one seemed able to believe that the fight was over so quickly.

Tyrion could. He knew exactly how good Urian was.

'Perhaps I should challenge Urian myself,' Teclis said. 'I could probably blast him with a lightning bolt from here.'

'That's not very sporting.'

'What he did to Arhalien was not exactly fair either.'

'Arhalien knew what he was letting himself in for. He chose to do it anyway.'

Teclis looked hard at Tyrion. 'He is going to challenge you next. That is the point of this whole exercise.'

'This is not looking good,' Korhien said.

Tyrion looked at the older warrior. He understood at once. If the battle broke out now, the dark elves would be at a high in their morale. The armies were so close together and so disorganised that they would roll over each other.

Urian brandished his blade over his head. He moved like a showman playing to his audience, walking along the front of the druchii line, punching his fist triumphantly in the air, accepting their cheers like a pit fighter accepting the plaudits of the crowd.

'Is that the best you can do?' he shouted into a momentary silence. His words sounded clear after the oceanic roar of the druchii and the Chaos worshippers. He was staring directly at Tyrion. 'Pitiful! Do the asur have no better warriors than that?'

Tyrion was about to step forwards but Alarielle's hand on his arm restrained him for a crucial moment, and Korhien stepped forwards. 'I will fight you, traitor!' he shouted.

Urian looked off to one side for a moment, and Tyrion thought he saw something like a look of shame pass over his face. For whatever reason, the traitor did not seem all that keen to face his old friend. Korhien strode proudly towards the druchii force. He did not seem in the least afraid and such was his presence that they fell silent.

'A representative of the Phoenix King will be the next to fall before our champion,' the herald of Malekith spoke. Urian glared at him. The herald fell silent.

Korhien and Urian came face to face and exchanged words. Tyrion would have given a lot to know what they said. After a moment they stepped apart and Korhien unlimbered his axe. Urian raised his blade in salute.

Tyrion glanced along the front line of the asur force. The units were falling back into formation. It looked as if Korhien had bought them some time.

The horns sounded. Combat began. Axe and sword clashed, glittering in the sun. All was silence. Korhien lashed out. Urian sprang back and then forwards and his blade passed through the body of his old friend. Tyrion shrugged off Alarielle's hand and stepped forwards.

He was not striding towards a fight, he was rushing to see to his old friend.

'Wait, Tyrion,' said Alarielle. He ignored her cry.

Tyrion walked forwards through the ranks of the asur army. All eyes were upon him. Elves stepped back to get out of his way. Something of the power and the terror of the ancient armour was felt by all of the observers. One by one the soldiers began to chant his name, taking it up until it became an awesome, ominous, thunderous roar.

The armour felt as light as cloth now he was wearing it and he himself had never felt better. He felt strong. He felt ready for battle, in some ways too ready. He burned to get to grips with the foe, to lash out with his blade, to bury it in flesh. He felt a low simmering anger deep within his soul, which kept bubbling up and threatening to become stronger.

He tried telling himself that it was not his anger, it was something alien, external, part of the magic bound into the armour itself. He knew that this was not true. Something deep within him responded to the rage that the armour of Aenarion embodied. The magic called out to some deep-rooted part of his being, and that part responded.

He was angry with himself because of this. Some echo of the mighty personality of Aenarion sought to use him as a vessel for its wrath, to turn him into an engine of rage. Much as he wanted to give way to it, to revel in that awesome molten anger, he refused to do so.

He was himself. He was not the tool of some ancient godly ghost. He would, as he always had, make his own decisions, fight his own battles, remain himself, even if it meant he could never tap into the deeper powers of the armour. He did not want the magic so badly.

Even as that thought ran through his brain, he realised that in some ways the armour had already changed him. He sensed the presence of magic as he had never done before. He felt the presence of dozens of magical weapons all around him borne by asur and druchii. He sensed wizards weaving spells, and the simply potent presence of the mages themselves.

More than anything else, he felt the chill and awesome presence of Malekith, Witch King of Naggaroth, as he would have felt the presence of a cold wind blowing out of the north. He could have closed his eyes and pointed to Malekith as surely as if he could see.

He sensed another nearby presence, almost as potent, and far more familiar. It belonged to his twin. Teclis had grown strong indeed, he realised, rivalling the force of that ancient evil entity with a cold, brilliant power of his own. Beyond Teclis he sensed Alarielle and the ancient slow entity that worked through her.

The thought struck him – it could not be chance that brought so many powerful magical beings here today, or so many potent ancient artefacts. Something else was at work, destiny, fate, the will of the gods. It did not matter what you called it. He sensed that he and everyone else here was caught in some great web, woven by beings more powerful even than Malekith.

The last of the high elf army had parted before him now and he walked out onto the open field between the two great elven forces. Ahead of him stood Urian. He wore armour of a strange and alien design. For the first time in his life Tyrion could see the spells woven into it. In their way, they were as awesome and complex as the ones woven into his own. He sensed an evil presence there, a powerful dark magic that drew on the energies of Chaos, that was semi-sentient. There was a daemon bound into it, he realised, a slumbering evil being that powered it and gave it strength beyond any mortal.

In each hand, Urian held a greenishly glowing blade. They radiated a curdled, malevolent energy that seemed to suck the life out everything surrounding them. Black blood dripped smoking from channels in the metal and where it spattered the ground, the grass withered and died and the earth itself cracked as if unable to bear the touch of the poisonous fluid.

Urian wore a great helmet, moulded into the shape of the visage of some daemon prince. The visor was lifted to reveal his pale features. They were sunken and gaunt, and his eyes were tormented and strangely horror-filled. He raised his blades in mocking salute but Tyrion's gaze was drawn beyond him to the real enemy.

On a bleak low hillside overlooking the battleground, Malekith lounged on a great metal throne set atop a huge metal shield. A score of enormously muscular male slaves held that shield aloft. They must have been strong indeed to do so, for Malekith must have weighed far more than any mortal elf. He was more than a head taller than Tyrion and the armour encasing his body must have been inches thick. From within a helmet that might have encased the head of a giant, a cold gaze blazed.

An aura of immense, ageless strength radiated out from the Witch King. Tyrion felt the malevolence and power in it and something else as well, curiosity and... recognition. He gazed right at Malekith, meeting those ancient eyes, and was surprised to see something like shock in them.

It took him a moment to realise why.

Tyrion was wearing the armour of Malekith's father. Perhaps, at this moment, it appeared to the Witch King as if that potent ancient had returned from the grave to judge him. Tyrion certainly hoped that Malekith felt that way. He drew his own sword. It caught fire. He raised it in grudging salute in the direction of Urian and his master. This was a formal duel, the most important of his life, and the proprieties must be observed.

Then he looked at the one who lay on the ground at Urian's feet.

Korhien sprawled, blood pouring from his chest. He looked pale and it was obvious he was on the edge of death. 'Well, doorkeeper, it looks like this is farewell. Kill him for me.'

'I will,' said Tyrion.

Urian raised both blades above his head, acknowledging the applause and cheers of the dark elves who watched, while never taking his eyes off Tyrion.

'Prince Tyrion, it seems we are to duel again,' Urian said. His smile was friendly and mocking, if not for the presence of that huge army of dark elves and Chaos worshippers behind him, they might easily have been meeting in the old practice ground in the Emeraldsea mansion.

'For the last time,' Tyrion said. There was something about the armour of Aenarion that altered his voice, made it more resonant and powerful. At least that was the way it seemed to him. Perhaps it was merely his own hatred that lent his voice such power.

'Sadly, that is true,' Urian said. 'Of all the fights I have had in my life, this is the one I regret most.'

'I don't,' Tyrion said. 'I am going to kill you.'

'That remains to be seen,' Urian replied. 'You'll forgive me for saying that you have never had the skill to do that in the past.'

Tyrion let a cold smile touch his lips. 'I never had the will to do that in the past, or the need.'

'Neither will nor need count as much as skill.'

Tyrion spoke slowly and calmly. 'I am going to kill you.'

'Many have tried,' Urian said. His voice was casual, uninterested. 'They are all dead.'

'You do not understand me, Urian, Iltharis, whatever you call yourself now. I am going to kill you, if I have to throw myself on your blade and tear out your throat with my teeth. It is going to happen.'

The anger and hatred in his own voice were corrosive. The determination in it reflected exactly how he felt. In that moment, he knew he was capable of it too. For the first time he thought he saw something like fear in Urian's eyes.

He held the killer's gaze and it was Urian who looked away first. Urian took a step back, before realising the error of doing so. The watching dark elves murmured among themselves when they saw what was happening. Urian made another mocking salute and made it look as if the step backwards was simply part of that.

It was a nice recovery.

'I see you have acquired new armour,' he said. 'It seems somehow suitable for one of the blood of Aenarion to be wearing it. At least you will make a pretty corpse.'

'They will not be able to say the same about you,' Tyrion said. Once again, he was surprised by how flat and cold his voice came out. There was an eerie quality to it, as if the ghost of Aenarion was speaking through his lips.

'It pains me that we will not part as friends,' Urian said.

'If you had not betrayed our people, we would be fighting on the same side.'

'They were never our people. They were your people.'

'Are you sure about that?' Tyrion said. His instinct for going for the jugular told him that was the correct thing to say. Urian shrugged.

The sound of murmuring from the dark elf army was increasing. They were growing restless. They did not like to see the two champions speak. It was not what they expected. It was not what they had come here for. Tyrion and Urian looked at each other warily. It seemed to Tyrion that Urian was reluctant to start fighting. He felt as if there must be some way that he could turn this to his advantage.

The longer he drew things out here, the better it would be for his own side. It would give them more time to get back into formation and recover from the shock of seeing its two champions cut down.

Of course, all of that would mean nothing if Urian killed Tyrion here. Seeing three champions defeated in succession would most likely prove too much for high elf morale, particularly since Tyrion was wearing the dragon armour of Aenarion and carrying his sword. It was impossible to imagine a worse omen than Tyrion being defeated here as far as they were concerned. It came to Tyrion then that his threat to Urian had better prove true. He needed to kill Urian here no matter what it cost – that was the only way to restore the balance even if it cost his own life.

There had been a time when he could have made the decision to do that without a single regret. There had been a time when he was truly fearless. That time was in his past. He did not want to die now. He wanted to live and be with Alarielle.

Of course, that did not really mean anything. If the dark elves won here, they would have no future anyway. It was not that he was afraid to die, he realised, it was that he wanted to live with her. If that was not possible, then he did not have anything to live for. If by his death here he could save her life, he was prepared to do that too. Not because it would help the elven nation but because it would help her. He wished that he had taken the time to tell her this before it was too late, and it came to him now that he had missed the opportunity to do that, perhaps forever.

He looked across at Urian and wondered if the dark elf had similar regrets. Somehow, he doubted that. Anyone who could do what Urian had done must be completely without conscience.

'The audience is growing restless,' Urian said, pulling down the visor of his helmet and turning himself completely into a metal-faced daemon. 'Let us give them a show.'

'I will give them your death,' Tyrion said.

Urian advanced like a big cat. His strangely glowing green blades left odd afterimages on the retina.

Was it his imagination, Tyrion wondered, or was the dark elf champion advancing more slowly and cautiously than he normally would? The two sickly emerald blades slashed towards him almost tentatively. Tyrion took the impact of one on his shield and parried the other with Sunfang. He launched his own counter: savagely, swiftly, surely. The high elf army roared, seeing the speed of his response. Urian danced away, not even attempting a counter at this stage.

What was going on here, Tyrion wondered? He had never known his opponent to be so cautious previously. Perhaps it was all part of some new strategy that Urian was using to toy with him. Or perhaps it was something else – perhaps he really had worried his opponent with his threats. Knowing how fearless Urian was, Tyrion somehow doubted that.

It didn't matter – he was committed. He was going to kill Urian, no matter what it took. Sunfang blazed in his hand, almost dazzlingly bright. Its glow was stronger than Tyrion had ever seen it and it radiated heat.

Perhaps this was what had Urian worried. He had never faced Tyrion with this magical weapon before and perhaps he was cautious, not knowing its abilities. Tyrion could not blame him for feeling that way.

Sunfang was a legendary weapon. No one really knew what it was capable of except perhaps Malekith or Morathi. Tyrion wondered if he could summon the fire from within the blade that he had used to kill the four assassins back among the woods of Avelorn. It did not seem either honourable or sporting, but now was not the time for such considerations. All that really mattered now was victory.

Almost as if he sensed the thought, Urian came gliding back in. The two blades flickered towards Tyrion like the forked tongue of a serpent. This time they came in with Urian's accustomed speed and Tyrion was hard put to defend himself, back-pedalling away clumsily, taking blows on his shield and looking for an opening through which to drive Sunfang that never appeared.

For all their speed, Urian's blows were driven with enormous force. Tyrion felt as if his arm was becoming bruised with the force of the impact and he would not have been surprised to see the shield itself being dented and knocked out of shape. He did not have time to check. The dark elves were cheering now, certain that their champion was on his way to victory.

Why should they not be, Tyrion thought? Urian had easily dispatched the previous two high elf champions and they were among the greatest warriors in Ulthuan.

He felt as if, if he allowed this to continue, he would be ceding entirely the advantage to Urian. If he allowed that to happen, his threat would seem to be hollow. It was not the case. He sprang suddenly forwards, driving towards Urian, ignoring those deadly blades.

Driven by all his weight, he knocked Urian off-balance and slashed out with Sunfang. Lightning-quick, the druchii ducked beneath it and drove his sword forwards. Tyrion flinched as it struck home. He felt a surge of pain in his side and wondered if it was all over. He did not look down. He did not allow himself to be distracted.

Instead he brought Sunfang down in a mighty arc, hoping to split his opponent's head with a reflexive death strike.

Urian's blades crossed as he parried, catching Sunfang between them. Tyrion tried to press home but he was only using one arm and his opponent was using both. Urian slowly but surely managed to push himself upright. Tyrion struck at him with the edge of his shield, catching him among the ribs and sending him reeling backwards.

The two armies were silent now as the champions leapt apart. They stood glaring at each other like maddened wolves. All appearance of civilisation, of urbanity, had dropped from Urian now. He glared at Tyrion in fury, knowing that he was fighting for his life as he had never had to fight before.

'I see your armour is everything the legend said it was,' Urian said. His voice sounded level but there was an undercurrent of menace in it that had not been there before. This pleased Tyrion. It meant that he was getting to his foe, that Urian was worried. He wondered what Urian was talking about then he realised that he did not feel any blood flowing where his enemy had struck him. He felt some pain but no more so than from a normal bruise. Given how powerful those magical blades were, it was a testimony to the work of Caledor and Teclis and his father that he was still standing.

Tyrion sprang forwards, slashing with Sunfang. Urian jumped backwards. The two blades slashed into action once again. One of them cut high, aiming at Tyrion's head, the other was aimed at his leg, at the weakest point in the armour where it guarded the knee.

Tyrion stepped away from the low blow and parried the high blow. It was what Urian had been waiting for; he brought his left-hand blade upwards and slashed at Tyrion's throat. Tyrion raised his shield to block it, partially obscuring his own field of vision.

If it were not for the awareness of magic that his armour had given him, he would not have sensed Urian shifting his position to come in from the side. As it was, he was able to circle and face him, striking out once more and catching Urian on the side of his head.

Urian staggered backwards, taken off guard for once. The dark elf army groaned. Tyrion was surprised. His blow would have beheaded anyone else. He'd put all of his strength behind it. It seemed that the armour that Malekith had given his chosen champion was every bit as good as the armour Tyrion himself wore.

Tyrion felt something new. Cold magic flowed over him, slowing him down. He risked a glance at Malekith from the corner of his eye. He knew the Witch King had cast some sort of spell, invisible to others, that was affecting him even through the armour. His timing was off. He could not press home quickly enough to take advantage of Urian's weakness.

His heart sank. He was not fighting against just Urian now. Malekith himself had entered the fray on behalf of his champion. It seemed like the Witch King was taking no chances. He fully intended that Tyrion was going to be beaten.

Teclis saw Tyrion slow. He sensed the flow of spellwork coming from the Witch King. It was so subtle that he doubted that anyone else present could perceive it, let alone counter it. It was not a very powerful spell. It did not have to be. In a contest between two warriors so closely matched, even a spell that slowed a combatant just slightly would be enough to secure victory.

What was worse was that if Teclis tried any overt counterspell, it would look as if he was the one trying to influence the outcome by magic. It was a strategy of daemonic wickedness. Even if Tyrion won, the Witch King would have achieved his purpose. The only way the asur could be seen to win was by treachery.

Teclis closed his eyes and studied the near-invisible gossamer web that Malekith had woven. He would need to be as subtle as Malekith. He extended tendrils of his own magic, reinforcing some of the ancient protections of the armour, one by one unknotting the tendrils of Malekith's spell. He prayed that he would be quick enough.

Suddenly, the fit passed. The feeling of lassitude lifted. Tyrion felt his body respond with its accustomed speed. Mere heartbeats had passed but it had been enough for Urian to regain his balance.

Tyrion struck again, hoping to take advantage, but Urian countered with his left-hand blade and slid a blow over the top of Tyrion's shield. The poisoned blade glowed where it hit Aenarion's ancient armour and threatened to pierce it. Tyrion stepped away so that it glanced off. Urian landed another blow on Tyrion's shield. The clamour rang out across the field like a daemonic blacksmith striking an anvil in hell.

Malekith had risen to his feet now, apparently to get a better view of the battle. In reality his burning gaze contained potent magic. Something was countering it now. Tyrion suspected his twin was working counterspells. Nonetheless the Witch King's looming presence distracted Tyrion for a moment and Urian struck once more, his blade aiming for his throat. Tyrion parried. Sunfang blazed dimly against a background of infernal green.

'You have improved greatly, Prince Tyrion,' Urian said. His voice was so quiet that Tyrion knew only he could hear it.

'You have not.'

'It is impossible to improve on perfection.'

Time seemed to slow for Tyrion. Everything narrowed down to his awareness of his enemy, of his flashing blades, his constant attacks. He had no idea how long they fought, only that he existed in the middle of a storm of violence, parrying an endless series of subtle and deadly attacks, replying in kind with volcanic onslaughts of violence.

All around them, quiet deadly magic flowed as Teclis and Malekith strove to influence the battle. Tyrion's limbs ached. His breathing was laboured. Even the armour of Aenarion was starting to feel as if it was made of lead. Lifting Sunfang was like trying to lift a tree trunk.

Urian gave no sign of any slackening of his technique. He seemed to fight with the same polished precision as he had when they started, but Tyrion could see sweat rolling down his chin and noticed that he too was breathing hard.

He sensed that despite appearances, his foe must be as weary as he. If he were not, then things were going to end very badly. Tyrion started to limp a little, to slow his parries. Under normal circumstances such a stratagem would not have fooled Urian, but these were not normal circumstances. His enemy must be as tired as he was. Urian sent a sledgehammer blow smashing into Tyrion's guard. Tyrion did not have to fake the slip. His leg gave way and he fell to the ground. Urian raised his blade, going for the final, flashy finishing blow.

'Now you die,' said Tyrion. Leaving himself completely open, trusting to his armour and not caring whether he died as long as he killed Urian; he struck the most brutal, simple and direct stroke he could, aiming upwards for Urian's groin. Urian partially deflected it and struck home with his own blade, a stroke as simple and direct as Tyrion's own. The armour of Aenarion held although the force of the impact was brutal. Sunfang pierced the armour of Malekith and came out the other side. Urian's eyes widened in surprise.

'Well done,' he said, and slid to the ground. Tyrion rose, spat in the direction of the Witch King and then turned and raised his burning blade in salute to the Everqueen. For a moment there was a terrible silence, then from the ranks of the asur a great cheer rang out.

With a bellow of incoherent rage, Malekith signalled for his troops to attack. From the body of the asur forces Malhandir raced forwards, coming for its master. Tyrion vaulted into the saddle even as the steel tidal wave engulfed him.

◄ CHAPTER TWENTY-EIGHT ►

With a mighty roar the two armies came together. Tyrion rode through the vanguard of the conflict. Malhandir moved smoothly beneath him, sure-footed in the mud and blood. Sunfang blazed in his hand, cleaving through his foes. The armour fed him a terrible strength and a rage that drove him forwards like a drug.

He glowed with the joyous rage of his victory over Urian and the knowledge that he had given hope to an army so close to defeat. It would take more than hope now, he realised.

He fought like a mortal god, killing everything within reach with the sword that had been borne by his famous ancestor. Wherever he rode, his foes fled from him such was the terror inspired by his appearance. The humans would not face him at all, but turned tail as he came closer. He rode them down, and the cavalry that followed him broke them.

The weight of numbers was still on the side of the druchii and their allies, but at least it felt like the asur had a chance, that if nothing else they would make a last stand worth singing about.

Teclis felt the cold power of the Witch King grow. Malekith had begun to summon the winds of magic to him and sculpt them into a massive, cold storm front of power. Gone was all attempt to subtly shape things. Now he was building a spell to smite his foes down with all the force of a hammer wielded by a god. The skies turned black. Strange polychromatic lightning danced along the underside of the clouds. The fingers of the wind tore at Teclis's cloak.

The winds of magic spiralled in around Malekith, forming a cyclone of power. Teclis exerted his will to counter the spell, twisting the currents out of shape, making it ungovernable, poisoning the structure of the spell even as it was created so that it would become unstable. His hope was that Malekith would try and cast the spell and it would run out of control, but the Witch King understood too well the ways of sorcery.

He gave up all attempts at forming the massive attack spell and sent lines of force racing back along the currents of Teclis's own weaving. Teclis had only a few heartbeats to counter them before bolts of scarlet lightning impacted on the wards he had set. He ground his teeth together with the effort of parrying the bludgeoning stroke.

Sweat stood out on his brow. He cursed himself for over-confidence. Until this day he had not encountered a magician who was beyond his strength and skill to cope with.

He had never encountered anyone as powerful as Malekith. He had a real battle on his hands, and he felt certain that if he continued to fight at this range, Malekith would win. The spell that he had been counting on to smite the Witch King with could be used only at close range, and there was a massive army between him and the blasted hillside upon which the Witch King stood.

Tyrion smashed through the ranks of black-armoured Chaos warriors, Sunfang burning in his hands. He chopped through the pole holding the obscene banner of a Chaos champion, grasped what remained of it with his shield hand and drove the broken point through the chest of one of his enemies like a spear.

He took in the field of battle at a glance, understanding it in a way that few could. The play of forces was immediately obvious to him. It was like looking down on a chessboard from above. He saw the main lines of advance the druchii army were taking towards the Everqueen's tent. He saw where the forces of the asur were weak and faltering. He understood where they would stand true and hold firm.

Seeing a line of elven spearmen struggling to hold their ground in the face of a tight phalanx of dark elf warriors, he raced forwards on Malhandir, shouting his battle-cry. The mighty armoured steed smashed through the front line of the druchii soldiery. Sunfang arced downwards, splintering the helmet of the dark elf captain. Blades sleeted off the dragon armour of Aenarion and Malhandir's heavy barding. Seeing Tyrion in their midst, the asur took heart, rallying around him, smashing through the broken ranks of their enemies.

From the left, Tyrion saw a company of Cold Ones approaching. They were about to take his own force in the flank. He wheeled

Malhandir and charged towards them. For any other elf, it would have been a suicidal attack, but Tyrion was mounted on the greatest warhorse Ellyrion had produced in five thousand years, encased in the dragon armour of Aenarion and equipped with a blade forged by Caledor in the dawn ages of the world. He was among the Cold Ones in an instant, burning sword beheading the first. Malhandir rose on its hind legs and with a massive blow of hooves it crushed the head of a Cold One to pulp.

Unflinching, the remainder of the druchii cavalry closed in and Tyrion found himself surrounded by snapping jaws and hostile blades.

A mass of druchii infantry hurled itself at the rise on which Teclis stood. Crossbow bolts turned the air black around him, but so far his warding charms had held good. He wondered how well they would do when the druchii were upon him. He did not intend to find out.

He spoke the words of a powerful incantation, and a blast of lightning smote the dark elf ranks, overloading the warding spells around them, leaping from metal spearpoint to metal spearpoint, jumping from armoured form to armoured form. A score of druchii died in the first blast. More died with his second. Again and again he sent the lightning smashing into them, until it was more than even druchii flesh could bear and the surviving warriors turned and fled.

Teclis's heart leapt with momentary elation, then he shivered as he realised that the attack had distracted him from Malekith, and that the Witch King had prepared a new abomination. From the midst of the enemy ranks a bubbling, boiling cloud of poisonous, putrescent magic emerged. Teclis wracked his brain for a counter-spell to this ancient evil sorcery, but nothing came.

The asur screamed as tentacles of the poisonous cloud descended among them. Where it touched, skin sloughed from bone, flesh rotted in a moment, bone turned from yellow to white. In the distance he heard gigantic evil laughter as if the Witch King fed upon the death and could not contain his mirth. The cloud stretched out its monstrous arms, reaching for Tyrion.

Tyrion smashed his way through the riders surrounding him, and found himself confronted by powerful evil magic.

Tyrion saw the elven spearmen start to die as the evil magical cloud settled on them. The asur were not the only ones to die. The druchii infantry they engaged died just as harshly. Clearly the Witch

King did not care too much who got killed by his magic as long as his foes were smashed.

Tyrion realised at once that Malekith was concentrating on him. Perhaps this could be used to his advantage. He pulled Malhandir round and moved towards the cloud, veering at the last second to race ahead of the poisonous mist that reached out for him with ghostly tentacles.

The Cold Ones pursuing him were not so lucky. They raced through tattered streamers of mist and where it touched them, scales fell off to reveal the diseased flesh beneath. Where it touched riders' armour, metal corroded and flesh turned to a loathsome, stinking pus.

He only hoped he could outrace it.

Teclis summoned an enormous wind to him. He drew it down from the skies, shaped its cyclonic force and then sent the hurricane ravening out over the battlefield. It smashed into the monstrous poisonous cloud pursuing Tyrion and rent it asunder, driving small ribbons of mist back into the druchii ranks, where they killed as they went until the storm force of the wind dissipated them entirely.

Teclis knew that Malekith could keep this up all day and that it would only work to his advantage. His army had the greater numbers, could afford to take the greater casualties. It did not matter how brave the asur were, they would be defeated unless something was done. He needed to get across the battlefield now and get close enough to the Witch King to work the spell he had planned.

He cast his mind back to his first flight on Silver Wing's back, when he had tried to derive a spell of levitation from first principles. It was time to put that spell to the test. He summoned more power to him, and stepped upwards as if walking on an invisible stair.

One step at a time, he walked upwards into the sky above the battlefield and saw all of the carnage laid out beneath him. He saw the thin lines of the asur being overwhelmed. He saw Tyrion rally the high elves again and again, his blade a burning banner, the dragon armour of Aenarion terrible to his foes. He knew that given the weight of numbers, eventually even his twin would be pulled down.

If he was going to do something about that, he had better do it now. He kept walking across the face of the sky, towards the distant figure of Malekith.

* * *

Tyrion looked up at the sky, realising that victory or defeat did not lie in his hands any more but in the frail form of his brother, whose magic carried him overhead towards a confrontation with the greatest enemy of their people.

He offered up a prayer and returned to smiting his foes, determined if he could to carve a way to the throne of the Witch King himself.

As he stepped onto the ground before Malekith, Teclis was shocked by the sheer presence of the Witch King.

It was not just the magical energy which radiated from him like a blast furnace, Malekith possessed an aura of power that had nothing to do with his strength in magic. He gave out a sense of physical might that struck Teclis with the force of a blow from a mailed gauntlet. This massive metallic form was capable of breaking the mightiest of warriors with his bare hands.

Not for the first time, Teclis questioned the wisdom of the course of action he had chosen for himself. He pushed his doubts aside – the time for having them was long since passed. Now he had to concentrate all his faculties simply on completing the task at hand.

'You should go home, mighty prince,' Teclis said. 'You are not welcome here.'

'Welcome or not, I am home,' said Malekith. 'This is my land and I am its rightful king. Soon all will acknowledge that, or die.'

'You will be king of the dead then in a land of ruins, even if you succeed.'

'If that is how it must be, then so be it. Lands can be repopulated, ruins rebuilt.'

'Not if Caledor's ley lines are destroyed and the world unmade. That is what your mother plans if you are successful.'

'I will deal with my mother.'

'She might prove stronger than you.'

'Do you think you are stronger than me?' Malekith asked.

Teclis knew he was not. At best, he was Malekith's equal in power and he was far inferior in knowledge and skill. All the things Tyrion had said when comparing himself to Urian were just as true for him when he compared himself to the Witch King. More so. Malekith had had millennia in which to perfect his arts.

'You cannot survive this,' Malekith said. He sounded almost sorry.

'I do not need to survive it,' said Teclis, smiling brightly. 'I just need to make sure you do not survive as well.'

'I think that is beyond your skills, little cripple.'

'I must beg to differ,' said Teclis.

'Are you really willing to die?'

'Are you, mighty prince? That is the real question here. I have not found life so much to my taste. If I die here, they will say of me that I died slaying the greatest evil in elven history. If you die here, they will say *he was killed by a crippled boy*. Which of us comes out of that better?'

Teclis held his breath. He was close enough to Malekith to sense the fires of Asuryan that still burned within him. He had touched those fires in the past, had woven them to his will when he had faced N'Kari. The question was, would he have time to do so now?

'Do you really think you can hurt me?' Malekith asked.

'We both know the answer to that.'

'I suspect we do,' said Malekith. His fingers traced a pattern in the air. Teclis could not be certain what he was attempting, but he sensed immense force gathering in response to the Witch King's will.

Teclis invoked the power of Asuryan. He reached out with his will and called upon the flames that burned within the Witch King's body. They blazed up in response to his spell. The wards woven into Malekith's armour could not protect him against the attack from within.

'No!' Malekith's voice boomed across the battlefield. Teclis called upon the full power of the Moonstaff of Lileath, using it to sculpt all of his power into one massive bolt of ravening destruction, knowing the pain of the awakened flame within his body would keep Malekith from countering. Malekith however surprised him.

As the titanic bolt smashed home, he spoke a potent spell. The massive armoured form vanished, leaving an outline limned in fire and the web of energies collapsing around him. Teclis was not sure what had happened. Had the Witch King been destroyed? Had he managed to escape by using some sorcery of translocation or displacement? One thing was certain: his baleful presence was gone, and Teclis knew he was alone on the hilltop.

He was not the only one who knew that.

Beneath him the entire dark elven force let out a great roar of horror and despair. They had seen their king and their mightiest champion destroyed before their eyes – at this moment they did not share Teclis's doubts as to his fate. They only knew that they faced his vanquisher and that thought was not at all to their liking.

* * *

Teclis drew upon the winds of magic again. He leapt upwards into the sky above the army, his aura glowing around him like that of a god.

Teclis began to weave spells of destruction, drawing upon all the grim knowledge he had acquired in the library at Hoeth. He felt mad exultation build within him and knew that once more his soul was in danger. He did not let that stop him.

Great clouds swirled over the ranks of the Naggarothi, rains of green acid showering down on them, burning their flesh. Bolts of chromatic lightning stabbed down from the sky, searing flesh and cutting great swathes from their ranks. Thunder so loud it burst eardrums and caused blood to gush forth made them cringe in terror.

For long minutes an unleashed tide of destruction played over the battlefield such as few had ever witnessed or ever would again. There were times when Teclis thought it was all going to slip beyond his control and the powers he had so rashly thought to bind to his will were going to break free and destroy as much of his own side as they were destroying his enemies.

Somehow, by dint of desperate effort, and mighty exertion of skill and will, and through not a little luck, he wrestled the forces under control, and the great storm of unleashed energy passed, leaving him standing alone on the hillside: drained, elated and empty.

Slowly the magnitude of his triumph sank in. He had beaten the Witch King. He had routed the druchii army. Victory was his. Already the army of Malekith was in retreat and Tyrion and his warriors were riding them down.

Death tipped the piece representing the Witch King to one side, signalling his resignation. He raised his pale hand in ironic mocking salute.

'Well played,' he said, rising from his chair with an air of resignation. 'Perhaps next time I will win.'

Caledor felt strangely confused and oddly empty. He knew he was missing something. He knew he had forgotten something. He had a task to do but he could not remember what it was.

'Perhaps next time I will let you,' he said, so softly that he doubted Death could hear.

ABOUT THE AUTHOR

William King is the author of the Tyrion and Teclis saga and the Macharian Crusade trilogy, as well as the much-loved Gotrek & Felix series and the Space Wolf novels. His short stories have appeared in many magazines and compilations, including *White Dwarf* and *Inferno!*. Bill was born in Stranraer, Scotland, in 1959 and currently lives in Prague.

DEATH ON THE PITCH
by Various authors

Prepare for the brutal, bone-crunching action of the classic fantasy football game in an action-packed anthology of short stories from on and off the gore-soaked Blood Bowl pitch.

YOUR NEXT READ

WARRIORS OF THE CHAOS WASTES
by C L Werner

Many horrors stalk the blasted wastes at the summit of the world. Mortals and daemons alike wage war – and in this volume are three tales of such monstrous, god-touched warriors.